More books by Isabella League

I0563882

The Jongleur
Dragons' Pearls
Land of the Firebird
Murder Moon
Darkest Magic

The Scholar Gypsy

An Adult Fantasy Novel

Isabella League

HELENENTHAL BOOKS

This work is a creation of fiction. Names, characters, places and incidents are from the imagination of the author. Any resemblance to actual events, localities, or persons living or dead, is entirely coincidental.

For more information, write to us at: HELENENTHAL BOOKS, 4191 Bradfordville Road, Tallahassee, Florida 32309-6401.

Visit us at: http://galtman.books.officelive.com/default.aspx

The Author encourages her readers' comments and may be contacted at her website: www.isabellaleague.com

FIRST EDITION

10 9 8 7 6 5 4 3 2 1

ISBN: 1-888071-22-2
EAN 13: 978-1-888071-22-1

Credits: Neptune woodcut used in page 1 and all chapter openings. Plate 215 of *1800 woodcuts by Thomas Bewick and his school*, Blanche Cirker, Dover Publications, New York, 1962 edition.

Cover Artwork and book illustrations by *E..E. Coad*
Layout, Design, and photography by *Gregory S. Coad*

For Mr. Darcy...

the absolute ruler of our house and hearts.

Prologue

St Peter Port, Guernsey, the Channel Islands, Friday, 13th of May, 1803

"You will go at once! At once, do you hear me!" Sir David Dieudonné thumped his clenched fist on his shining desk top to emphasize his point.

The man sitting in the ornate chair in front of the Bailiff's desk merely smiled in a condescending fashion and steepled his long thin fingers. "My dear Sir David," he said in the smooth manner that Dieudonné found so irritating, "We have legitimate reason for remaining here on your pleasant little island."

"The Peace of Amiens was signed over a year ago, Bishop, and the French troops have all withdrawn from our islands! Only the Inquisition remains here and we are finding your excuses as to why you have not departed more than a little tedious." David picked up a sheaf of papers from his desk and looked through them angrily, tossing each down on his desk as he finished with it. "First of all it was to care for wounded men. I was not aware that the Inquisition was a nursing order! Then it was illness, lack of transport, and many other specious excuses!" He threw the papers down on the desk and they rose up into he air to fall on the floor, carried by a fresh, salt-tinged breeze from an open window, for the steep streets of St. Peter Port looked down on a deepwater harbor.

David paused, his chest rising and falling heavily, his fists clenched in futile anger, glaring at the Bishop of the Inquisition, *Monseigneur* Amaury de Ollivier.

Sir David, at nine and twenty, was very young to be the Bailiff of *Bailliage* or Bailiwick of Guernsey, consisting of the islands of Guernsey, Alderney Sark, Herm, Jethou and

Lithou, as well as assorted islets, but he had been one of the few government officials left after the French had occupied the Bailiwick in 1799. The magical population had fled the Inquisition and its weapons of Cold Iron and many of the remaining non-magical men had been conscripted into the armies of the French Republic.

He had been wounded in the early fighting and still used a cane or crutches and he would no doubt be crippled for life. He had been a *Douizaine,* which was a parish administrator and a junior one at that, of the small parish of Torteval, where the inhabitants were traditionally nicknamed *Âmes à pids d'ch'fa* or donkeys with horse's hooves, in the Norman language, *Guernésais,* spoken by much of the population.

David was tall for a man of the islands, his hair and dark eyes showing the Norman French blood of his heritage. However, in spite of the fact that most of the Island's business was conducted in French, David, like most of the Islanders, considered himself English and his allegiance was to the Crown and the King, George III, of the Six Nations of the British Isles, since the Channel Islands were a British Crown Protectorate.

"May I remind you, Bishop, yet again," David spoke between his teeth, "that the Catholic population here owes no allegiance to the Church of Rome. Our Pope sits in Dublin. The Irish Catholic Church and the Romish have been split nearly a millennia, since Arthur drove them from Britain. Perhaps you had authority here during the French Occupation, authority to torture and burn innocent citizens and put them to the Question."

"These Islands are a hot bed of heresy," the Bishop interrupted.

"Wizardry and Witchcraft are not heresies in the laws of the Irish Catholic Church!" Sir David shouted. "Our Pope himself is a Wizard! And a Druid!"

The Bishop smiled indulgently, as if Sir David was a small child who must be humored.

Never, thought David, realizing that he had lost his grip on his temper, had he seen a professed man of God who appeared so Satanic. Amaury de Ollivier was almost a parody of an illustration of Satan with his dark, deep-set eyes, a pointed beard and sleek close-clipped hair. Islanders he passed in the street often made the sign of the evil eye behind his back. All he needed to complete the illusion were horns, a forked tail, a pitchfork and a red costume. Sir David would not have been surprised to find that the Bishop, in his elegant Italian shoes, had cloven hooves.

He wore the purple and black robes of the Inquisition, with a huge cross of amethysts and pearls set in silver on a heavy silver chain about his neck. The Black Cross of the Inquisition was stitched on his left breast and a huge amethyst ring adorned one hand.

"You do not have access to the very latest news as do I, Sir David," said the Bishop consideringly.

"You know that we do not!" David snapped. "The Dragon Post has yet to be reinstated as the French so obligingly dug trenches in the fields of the Dragon Port! And thanks to the depredations of the French and of yourself, Bishop, we have no men, and no Wizards, to restore the Port. All men conscripted into the French army were to be returned home when the peace was signed, yet that has not happened! There are still French privateers in the Channel who like naught better than to shoot at passing dragons and hippogriffes and at flying horses!"

"They are but doing their duty to Mother Church who tells us that such creatures are minions of Satan and must be destroyed," said the Bishop smoothly.

"And are our packet ships Satanic as well?" asked David sarcastically.

"We are but searching for smugglers, Sir David," the Bishop returned. "There are many smugglers in these waters, taking French goods and those from the heretic country of Holland to the British Isles. It is forbidden for French goods to enter England."

"Forbidden without a stiff tax you mean!" David retorted. "How are we to get any news at all when you French stop and search every ship that makes port, seizing what you like?"

The Bishop smiled once more. "Every ship? I think not! Look out in to the harbor and you will see any number of pleasure yachts from England who have arrived here unmolested. Surely one of them will have a newspaper or two!" He laughed mockingly.

One of the things that David hated most about de Olivier

8

was that the man had an answer for everything.

"As you no doubt know," the Bishop said blandly, "I am in touch with Paris by use of courier pigeons. It is highly likely that the British Isles Ambassador will leave Paris today, for talks have broken down over the continuing concessions your country has arrogantly demanded regarding our possessions in Haiti and in the Batavian Republic. And our first Consul, Napoleon Bonaparte, can not tolerate the British Naval presence in Malta."

His smile broadened and to David, his eyes seemed to light with bale fire. "So you see, Sir David, it is more than likely that soon our countries will again be at war. If I were you I would not be so insistent on our departure, for we are but like to turn about and come straight back. I shall not rest until these islands are free of heretics and when Napoleon plants the *Tricoleur* in London, we shall rid all of the Isles of this pernicious evil of Wizardry and Witchcraft if we have to burn in a multitude of *auto de fés* every person of magical bloodline."

1
Star of
the Sea

The English Channel,
Thursday, 19th of May, 1803

Stellamaris pushed with her tail and shot out of the water, laughing delightedly as she did so, the blue green sea water cascading from her hair and upper body. She was ten years old and this was the first time she had been allowed to swim off from the pod on her own. Of course, her guardian seal was with her; all Merchildren had a seal that kept watch over them while they were small and Orva would not allow her to stray too far.

The pod was on its annual migration from the warm waters of the Greek Isles to their summer home near Sule Skerry, a rock in the Atlantic about fifty miles southeast of the Orkney Islands at the northern tip of Scotland. Here they dwelled beneath the sea while their friends the seals summered and bred on the rocks above. The seals of Sule Skerry were not just ordinary seals, but magical creatures, Selchies, that were men and women on the land and Seals in the sea. Orva was about fifty in human years, a 'settled' Selchie, who no longer thought of nothing but mating this time of year. Her own pups were long grown and gone.

Stellamaris had been following a human ship all the afternoon. It was a pretty thing of white sails like wings, and a white bow that sliced through the waves as a fresh wind pushed her along under a clear blue sky. The Merchild found humans interesting, although somewhat pitiable. Imagine not being able to breathe underwater!

But what charmed her most about this little ship (Orva said it was called a yacht) was that they shared the same name. Her name, Stellamaris, meant "star of the sea" and that was the name of the yacht. And the figurehead of the yacht was a small Mermaid, holding a Triton shell. Stella-maris was thrilled when she saw this as whoever had made it knew what Mermaids really looked like with a long greenish tail and flowing waist length locks of a faint green tinge. The figurehead was bare above the waist and wore a necklace of pearls and a starfish in her hair, just as Stellamaris herself did, but the wooden Mermaid's pearl necklace was far longer.

As she was but ten the Merchild only had ten pearls to her necklace. Every year her parents would give her a pearl to add to her necklace until she took a mate and then it would be his duty to provide her with a perfect pearl every year on the celebration of the day she was born.

The water beside her slid away smoothly and Orva's head emerged. She was a Gray Seal in appearance, silver gray, with a straight head profile and nostrils set wide apart. Her large dark eyes were warm and full of affection as she looked at the Merchild.

"Are you still following her?" the Selchie asked.

Stellamaris nodded. "Why do humans call a ship 'her', Orva?" she inquired. "Is it because of the figurehead?"

"Many ships do not have mermaids or even human women as figureheads or any figurehead at all," the seal pointed out. "There are males as well, and other creatures, not just of the sea but dragons and horses and hippogriffes. Most sailors are men and they say that a ship is like a woman."

The little Merchild thought this was ridiculous, a ship was wood and a woman, even a Mermaid, was flesh and blood, but she dismissed it as just another example of human foolishness.

Her agile mind leaped to another wonder. "I saw a land horse once," she said, "It was so strange looking with four legs instead of a proper tail! How does it swim?"

"Not all creatures can swim, child. That is why it is Neptune's Law that we must try and save any creature that falls into the water and get it to land. Unfortunately, there are not always Sea-folk near, such as ourselves, who can save those who cannot swim. Many drown."

Like Stellamaris, the Selchie watched the yacht skim-ming along the water ahead of them for a few moments and then said "Come child, we must join your parents. The pod will reach the waters near Brighton this evening," Orva knew all the human names for the land.

Stellamaris gave a wiggle of pleasure, causing her tail to flip and agitate the water at the thought of visiting the fashionable seaside resort for humans. "I love to watch the humans in the bathing machines!" she said "They are so odd looking and so afraid of the water! They are silly!"

"Remember what it is like to be stranded on land," admonished Orva, for it was her job to teach as well as to guard. "Do not forget the time you misjudged the tide and were trapped on that rock until the tide came back in. You could not move and you became dehydrated. You could have died. It is the same for humans who cannot swim. Remember how afraid you were and be not so quick to judge and make game."

Stellamaris was a good child and looked abashed at Orva's gentle remonstrance. "I'm sorry," she began but never finished, for ahead of them came a loud splash

Orva was instantly alert. "That sounds as if a human fell into the water!" she said. "Come, child! We may be needed!" She dived beneath the water and swam at high speed towards the sound, the Merchild following behind.

In but a few moments they came upon a body in the water. It was a human man, and his eyes were closed as if he were asleep or unconscious. Orva dove beneath him and pushed up rapidly until his head was above water. He wore only a pair of white cotton duck trousers and she could not grab him by the collar of his clothing as she usually would.

Stellamaris, well-drilled even at her age in rescue, had swum ahead at top speed, trying to catch the yacht and attract the attention of someone else on board. She had turned and come back at the same fast speed. "They're not stopping! I can see no one on deck at all!" she said breathlessly to Orva.

"Sometimes the humans sail alone, which is very foolish," said Orva. "Here, Stellamaris, if you will hold up his head — "

The Merchild slid into place and put the human's head on her shoulder, the water giving the body buoyancy so that it was no task for a Merchild to keep him afloat. Merchildren were far stronger than their human counterparts.

"What shall we do with him, Orva? Even if we were able

to catch up the ship –" Stellamaris asked worriedly.

Orva was looking at the position of the sun. "We shall have to get him to land," she said decidedly. "If there were other humans on board they would have come about by now, I should think. We cannot leave him on the ship by himself, even could we overtake it. We are closest to the island of Guernsey. We shall take him there where other humans may care for him."

Stellamaris looked at the head lolling on her shoulder. "Orva! He's bleeding!" she exclaimed as a trickle of red ran down from the water soaked dark hair.

"All the more reason to take him to Guernsey," Orva decided. "There may be doctors there if he needs one. He is a young human – and quite good looking," she added, studying the dark head and clear-cut face. "He would make a handsome seal," she said. "No doubt he will have friends who will be looking for him. The yacht tells me that he is a person of wealth and position, no doubt."

Stellamaris wondered if she would ever know as much as Orva did. Of course, Orva was a Selchie and she lived on land as well as in the sea and knew both worlds. This was one reason that the Merfolk preferred Selchies as the guardians of their young for the Merchildren could learn so much about humans from them.

"I also smell magic on this man," Orva added, as they began to turn and swim in a southerly direction. "He is probably a Wizard."

A Wizard! Stellamaris loved nothing better than Orva's tales of human Wizards and Witches. The Sea-Folk had their own magics, of course, but Stellamaris never tired of hearing about Wizards who flew on dragons and who had talking animals that they called familiars. She had always wished to meet a Wizard. It was too bad that this one was insensible.

"Faster," urged Orva, looking anxiously at the blood on the man's head. "I shall go below and help propel him."

As they had raced well away from the yacht *Star of the Sea* they failed to hear a second, smaller splash.

13

Earlier that morning, when the tide was low, a solitary figure searched the rocky shore for ormer, a corruption of *oreilles de mer*, ears of the sea, known elsewhere as abalone.

Ormers clung to rocks near their food source – kelp. If one was fortunate, ormers could be found only a few inches down, but many times the tidal pools were three feet deep or more, which required putting one's head beneath the water and holding one's breath while prying the shellfish from its rocky habitation.

There were others gathering ormer as well, but not many, and for once they were not driving her away. Everyone was far too worried over the threat of an new invasion by the French.

The girl gathering ormer did not know that confidential message had been delivered to the capital yesterday via a hippogriffe which had nearly been shot down by the French. Both the 'griffe' and its rider had been injured. The message they had risked their lives for had been grave indeed. The day before, on the 18th of May, a declaration of war against France had been laid before Parliament in London and in the Parliaments of every country in the Six Nations of the British Isles.

She cared little for the war or the French. Her concern at the moment was filling her stomach and that of the older woman for whom she was responsible, having taken her in when no one else would give her a place.

The little bay she was searching in held but a few boats. There were not many working fishing boats now as there were few men to man them. All the heads she could see on the boats from the stony beach were white. The French had taken most of the men between sixteen and sixty to serve as conscripts for Napoleon.

There was one exception. Since she had come here with her reed basket and large knife she had not been able to resist studying the one young man that could be seen

She knew little of boats but his was not a stolid fishing boat as were the others. It was a light, graceful craft with a carving on the front. Now at low tide, it was almost sitting in mud, for the spring tides were of great highs and lows.

He was very attractive, she thought. He had hair as fully dark as her own, and a supple strong body that made light of the chores he was doing on the little boat. He was barefoot and shirtless and had a nice white smile as well. Sound carried well over the water and she could hear him singing and whistling. At this distance she could not tell the colour of his eyes, even though her long distance vision was excellent.

His skin was darker, like her own, and she wondered if he might be of her people, the Romany, called Gypsies or Egyptians by the *Gajé* – non-Gypsies – hereabouts. But she doubted it for she had never heard of a Romany who traveled the Road on a boat. A *vardo ,a* wagon, like her own, was the preferred mode of transport. The *Gajé* some times became quite dark from the sun; that was more than likely why this man looked as if he might be one of her own people.

She bent to pry another ormer from a rock, luckily only in a few inches of water. Her bare feet were hard and well used to any surface. She clung easily to the rocks. Her ragged skirts were kilted up about her hips and her tangle of black hair, which curled wildly, was held away from her face by a brightly coloured kerchief. In spite of a slight chill of this spring morning she wore a white short sleeved blouse made with a drawstring neck. A wide belt of shiny sateen that had seen far better days cinched in her very small waist. She was thinner than she had been a year ago, for times had been very bad for her and her dependents.

Her name was Rosal Lovel and she was two and twenty years of age and already a widow. Obedient to her father's dictates she had jumped the broomstick at sixteen, with a man of her father's choice. He was far older than she, older even then her father. She had not loved him but at that time she was an obedient daughter and had done as she was told, according to the *leis prala*, the law of the Romanies.

It had been an unhappy marriage from the beginning. He was abusive and drank to excess. He was also an arrogant man of boastful temperament. Many times she had been tempted to run away, but he was her Rom, her man, and she stayed, for after two years, something very good had come of the marriage, her small daughter, Cinerella. She had loved the baby with all the passion of which she was capable, which was considerable. Everything the child did enchanted her.

But Sylvester, her husband, had been jealous of the

attention she lavished on the baby. And one day, when she had been forced to leave the child for just a while, to tell fortunes at a fair, Sylvester having drunk up their small store of coins the night before, he had let Cinerella become chilled. The baby had already had a cold and the chill was enough to send her into pneumonia. Even the *Gajo* doctor could not save her.

Rosal was never certain whether or not Sylvester had done it deliberately. She would not have put it past him, for he was of a ruthless and a selfish nature and had, in times past, before he had come to Guernsey, killed a man in a knife fight.

Things went from bad to worse after that. He wanted no children, he told her, ordering her to visit the *Daia*, the old crone who read the crystal and cast spells, for the herbs which would prevent a pregnancy. Sylvester had several strong, fine sons by his first woman. He wanted the young and lovely Rosal to warm his bed and cook his food, not to be giving her attention to a squalling brat! He thus doomed Rosal to never be treated as an adult by the other women in the *cumpania*, for a Romany woman without a child was forever treated as a child herself.

More than once Rosal was tempted to kill him. She came to hate him as passionately as she had loved Cinerella.

But fate,in the form of the French, had stepped in.

A French officer, among the first to arrive on the island, had accused Sylvester of stealing his horse, and without benefit of trial had shot Rosal's Rom dead. Later, it came out that the horse had wandered off on its own, but no one made apologies, made amends or was even punished. Sylvester was only Gypsy trash. One less Egyptian in the world was no doubt a good thing.

When it became apparent that the French were going to treat them worse than the natives of Guernsey always had, the Romanies left the island in the wake of the magical folk, who feared the Inquisition.

And Rosal had been left behind, for a simple act of kindness. Her father had renounced her, had told her that she was fortunate that he did not order her killed for what she had done. He never wanted to see her again and she was as dead to him and to all their tribe.

What she had done was taken into her *vardo* a woman of her own race whom she found in a dying condition on the road. This woman, Hagar Buckland, had been starving, ignored by all the Romany on the island, condemned to die for her crime.

Her crime had been to love a *gajo*, and sleep with him and have a child with him.

And he had eventually left her and taken their son, the *pos ratt* , half breed, with him.

Rosal understood what it meant to lose someone one well loved and her heart had gone out to Hagar.

But now she had two to feed and work for, for even after three years Hagar was still often weak and ill. They were dreadfully poor. Rosal had never been accustomed to having a great deal of money but times had never been so desperate as they were now.

How she wished she had a Rom! A young, strong man like the one she was watching on the boat. He would protect her from the French officers and fight for her if necessary. And he could give her another child. A young man would want sons and surely would not begrudge her another sweet little girl.

But no Romany would have her now. She was cast out from her own kind forever. And a *gajo* would want a mistress, not a woman who would give him children – half breed children he would be ashamed to own.

As she stood up, with another ormer in her hand, she saw that another young man had come up on the deck at the opposite end of the boat. She did not like his looks as well as the dark one's. He was a *gajo*, no doubt, for he had red hair and pale skin and reminded Rosal of a fox in a picture she had seen once. There were no foxes on Guernsey.

As she watched this new one cupped his hands around his mouth and shouted to the dark man "Felix! Are we to have breakfast any time soon? I'm famished!"

The other gave a grin and waved and headed towards the foxy man with a comment that Rosal did not hear as an altercation between two sea gulls broke out near her. Involuntarily, she turned to look at the birds and when she turned back, both young men were gone.

Enough dreaming, there were mouths to feed, hers and

Hagar's, the little black pony, Kälo, who pulled the *vardo* and her dog, Chavé, a black and white coally. Chavé meant child and Hagar had protested Rosal's naming the dog thus, but to Rosal it seemed as if the dog was the only child she would ever have now.

He had been another rescue. He was a wonderful dog, but had no talent as a sheep dog and had been driven away from a farm, unwanted. Rosal had wanted him the moment the great dark eyes looked up at her with love and trust.

All three of these were counting on her. There were few enough ways to make money, as the priests that had come with the French troops had forbidden *dukkering, or* fortune telling, even palm reading, the Tarot and the crystal. They also forbade love charms and such like. One could make a bare living from *dukkering* and love charms, but not if the threat of burning was over one's head.

When she had enough ormers for a stew that she, Hagar and Chavé could share, she left the shore, balancing her basket carefully on one hip.

She cast a last glance back at the white boat. He was still below. Remembering his strong young body and flashing grin, she sighed. Felix. It was a nice name but it could never mean anything to her.

2
Overboard!

He had been sleeping peacefully when rough hands seized him, grabbing at the loose skin around his neck, thus effectively immobilizing his front and back legs with their wicked claws that might have enabled him to defend himself.

No sooner that he had begun to scream "Help! Help!" than he was thrust into a canvas bag; it was tied shut; tossed by a powerful arm and sailed through the air to land with a splash in the water.

Water! He could drown! Frantically, he began clawing at the bag as it began to sink.

He was a strong and muscular cat and the bag shredded beneath his claws. In minutes he was out of it pushing away with his hind legs until his entire body and tail cleared what nearly had been his coffin.

But now he was in bad case. Although he could swim, an exercise he would usually avoid, he had no idea how far from land he might be.

His black fur, a bit longer than the fur of most English cats, was already sodden and all he could seem to smell was salt water at the moment. If he was close to land he might be able to sniff it out.

The sun was still high in the sky, he noticed as he treaded water, but had begun its western decline. That meant past noon time, no doubt. He had no idea how long he had napped, for the sun had been comfortable on the deck and he had fallen into a deep sleep. And already he could see no sign of the yacht he had been on. He was all alone in the middle of the ocean. How he wished he had paid more attention to the charts in the main cabin! All he knew was that they had departed from Guernsey, on the high tide early that afternoon on their way to the Isle of Wight in England.

What had happened? Why had he been thrown

overboard? He had a rather shrewd idea of who had done it, but he had no idea *why*. Why hadn't his Wizard prevented it from happening? This gave him a new worry; what had happened to his Wizard that stopped him from keeping his familiar safe? That was part of the bond between them, they looked out for and protected one another.

But all the conjecture had to wait for another time. Right now all his wits and strength must be bent towards survival. Once dry land was under his paws again he could try and find out what had happened to his Wizard, even going to the authorities if needs be.

Using the sun as a guide he began to swim south.

Two hours later he realized that he was not going to make it.

He was tired beyond belief. In spite of frequent stops where he would float and catch his breath, his limbs were beginning to fell leaden, and difficult to move. His lungs were laboring and more and more he wanted to close his eyes and just drift. There was still no land in sight.

Was this how he was to end? Without the proper rituals would he still go and stand before Bastet to account for this life before the Goddess of all cats sent him on the next of the appointed nine? He was a familiar, he was supposed to live the life span of his Wizard, not drown out here in the English Channel away from his Wizard!

"A cat out at sea," said an amused voice next to him. "Peculiar, to say the least."

Startled, he turned in the water towards the voice, so quickly that his head went below the water for a moment and he came up sputtering and coughing.

The owner of the voice was a seal, her head just above the water's surface. Her large dark eyes were filled with amusement. "I had no idea that cats were aquatic creatures!" She spoke in Animal Speech, the common tongue that all animals used in talking to one another.

"I'm glad that you are so amused," he said sarcastically. "I'm afraid I don't need an audience to watch me drown, thank you very much!"

"Where are you going?" she inquired.

"Guernsey. Do you know where that is?" he returned. She might not know the human name of the island and he had no idea what the seals might call it.

"I live nearby on the island of Sark," she said. "It's too far for you to swim. You'll never make it."

"No!" he exclaimed in mock disbelief. "Surely you are joking me!"

"However," she said, "it is not too far for me!"

With this she disappeared beneath the slight waves that were beginning to kick up.

For one terrible moment he thought that she had vanished and left him but then he was suddenly pushed from the water as a broad back came up underneath him.

"I'll give you a ride to Guernsey," she said, turning her head back to peer at him. "Just don't stick your claws into my back!"

"That would be rude," he said, very grateful to have something solid beneath his feet. "I thank you very much. I'm Pyewacket. May I know your name?"

"Pyewacket?" she repeated, again sounding amused. "You don't look to be almost one thousand years old! Aren't you Merlin's familiar?"

"I am named *after* Merlin's familiar," he said. "It is a tradition in the Six Nations that any pure black cat of familiar stock, with green eyes, no mark of white, and longish fur be called Pyewacket in honour of Merlin's familiar. But I am surprised that you know of our great Wizard. Do seals study human magics?"

"I'm not a seal," she said "I'm half Selchie. My mother was a Selchie and my father was a man of these islands. My childhood was spent largely on land, for being but half my seal nature did not mature until I reached adolescence. My father was a Wizard as well, a Weather Wizard, a prog-nosticator, so I know something of Merlin and Wizards. I am Grizel Sarchet."

"Very pleased to meet you," Pyewacket said, inclining his head. "And very grateful that you came along when you did. I was thrown overboard from my Wizard's yacht."

"Not by your Wizard, surely! My father and his familiar

were inseparable," Grizel said, sounding rather shocked. "His familiar was a hedgehog called Yves."

"No," said Pyewacket darkly. "He would never do that to me. I am almost positive I know who did it, but I shan't make any accusations until I have proof. And for the moment I am far more worried about my Wizard. What has happened to him that he let someone toss me out like so much rubbish? That is why I must needs get to Guernsey, and talk to the authorities if needs be."

"I am going to take you to my home on Sark first," said Grizel. "You will need to get the salt from your fur and have some food. And there is another difficulty – the French have landed on Guernsey."

"What!" Pyewacket cried. "Are we at war again?"

"It would seem so," said Grizel. "I doubt that you will be able to consult the authorities, for where the French troops go, there goes the Inquisition. Indeed, the Inquisition never left Guernsey or Alderney. Only Jersey, Sark, Herm, Jethou and the smaller islets are free of their polluting presence." She spoke rather bitterly, for Selchies, like Wizards, familiars, dragons and others of their ilk were on the Inquisition's list of those to kill by fire, without trial. They were considered demons, minions of the Devil, abominations in the eyes of God and more importantly, it seemed to Grizel, in the eyes of the Inquisition.

"Do you have reason to believe that you might find out what happened to your Wizard on Guernsey?" the Selchie asked.

"My Wizard is *Magus Magistra,*" the black cat said. "If he fought with the evil people on our yacht I have no doubt he defeated them. And he will not rest until he finds me. Logically, he would no doubt back track to Guernsey. We sailed from there this morning."

"From St. Peter Port?" Grizel inquired.

"No, a small harbor in the west," said Pyewacket. "It was called Gull Rocks and there were certainly a lot of gulls there."

"I know where that is," Grizel said. "I shall take you there after dark if at all possible. You will need to be extremely careful," she cautioned. "The Inquisition is always on the lookout for magical creatures to burn. Most of the magicians and their familiars left a long time ago. They are probably on the mainland, safe. Perhaps I should take you to England," she added thoughtfully.

"No!" Pyewacket said emphatically. "I know my Wizard. He will look for me here. I must be here when he comes."

"If he ever does," Grizel thought sadly. It sounded as if something had happened, something very ill indeed, to Pyewacket's Wizard.

Orva, leaving Stellamaris to tread water with the injured human, went ahead to Guernsey to find the best place for their unwitting charge. Her first thought was St. Peter Port, for a large place such as that would have other humans and a doctor.

But when she surfaced in the harbor there she was appalled to see French troop ships, flags of the *Tricoleur* snapping in the breeze. All was confusion as the soldiers disembarked, watched by a sullen and resentful populace.

Someone had taken the precaution of ordering rifles leveled on the townsfolk. They were not happy to see the French back.

Neither was Orva. She could not leave a Wizard on the beach where the Inquisition would be certain to find him. They would have a Witch- Sniffer with them perhaps.

She herself and Stellamaris would be in danger here as well. A Selchie and a Mermaid were fair game for the Inquisition.

Nor could she take him much further. Stellamaris said he was still bleeding weakly and showed no signs of waking any time soon. That was the head wound, no doubt. He had to be left where local people would find him and care for him, perhaps even hiding him from the French.

If this were Scotland she would simply take him up on shore, make the change to human form and take him to a town. The Scots thought nothing of a bare woman walking into a town for they would at once know her to be a Selchie who did not have a cache of clothing nearby. They would help her, not arrest her and condemn her to death. She had heard stories of what had happened to Selchies caught by the

Inquisition, particularly female Selchies. Multiple rape would be the least of her worries. If the French were not here...but they were and Orva could see little choice in what she much do. She had not only her own safety to consider, but that of Stellamaris. She could not desert her charge.

But the Wizard had to be helped as best they could manage. Therefore Orva swam back out to where the Merchild waited. They would take him to a small harbor that she knew of, where there were fishing boats and fishermen and people who walked the shore, looking for edibles. One of them would find him and see that he was cared for. The natives of these islands were good people.

Dusk was falling as the Selchie and the Merchild arrived in the small harbor. All the fishing boats were anchored, there seemed to be no one about.

The tide was running out and Stellamaris could not draw too near to the beach. Orva would have to take care of the man her own self.

Until she reached the shallows it was relatively easy, but she found it still easier to change when the water was knee deep and as a woman, draw the limp body up onto the beach, carefully pulling him well above the high water line. There were many stones – she could not help but damaging his exposed body a bit. She winced in sympathy. In addition to the head injury he was going to be somewhat battered. As a seal she was very strong, as a woman less so and she could not lift a full grown, well muscled man. Pushing him with her nose in seal form would cause even further damage to his body.

High tide would be near midnight. Orva hoped that he would be found before then. When the tide was all the way out there should be people coming for ormers, periwinkles and other shell-fish.

She lay him on his side, directly in front of a path that came down to the water. Anyone using the path would have to stumble over him.

Orva listened to his heart before she left him. It was

24

beating steadily. She also examined the head wound now that she had hands to do so. The bleeding had stopped, but it was a nasty wound. It might even need stitching.

Not too far away Orva heard the rattle of stones. Someone was coming! She ran into the water, her bare woman's body shimmering and changing to gray seal fur as the water deepened around her.

"There's a boat coming!" Stellamaris informed her as she joined the Merchild.

"Then we had better go. Your parents will be wondering where we are. It's a long swim and we shall have to go as fast as we can," Orva said.

"Will the Wizard be all right?" the Merchild asked anxiously.

"I left him where they will be able to find him easily," Orva replied, sounding more confident than she felt. "Now we must go, dear one."

Together, they dived deep, where the people in the coming boat could not see them.

Grizel Sarchet, in human form, stood in the open door of her little cottage on Sark. She wore a blue gown of faded cotton that had seen much washing. Her bronze coloured hair was tied back with a blue ribbon that was as frayed and worn as her dress. She was sipping a cup of herbal tea and from behind her she could hear the sounds of Pyewacket softly snoring as he slept on the hearth in front of a small driftwood fire.

The cat had been exhausted. After she had washed and dried his fur she had fed him, fish was something she always had in the house. It was easy to catch fish when one could go underwater and hunt it in its own territory. After he ate a plate of pollock drenched in cream, he yawned loudly and murmured something about closing his eyes just for a moment and soon was deeply asleep.

Grizel's cottage stood near the edge of the precipitous headland of stone rising from the sea that was known as the Hog's Back. It separated the two incredibly beautiful bays of

Derrible and Dixcart. To reach the hog's back from the island itself, one walked through Dixcart Valley, lately blooming with bluebells and wild garlic, and heavily wooded.

But up here it was stark and wind-torn, with little or no vegetation. Grizel had no near neighbors, which suited her. The only sign of human habitation was the remains of the defenses built against the Spanish Armada back in the days of Good Queen Bess, ruins of a tower and of an old cannon.

The way to her cottage, the way she had brought Pyewacket up, was a series of hand and footholds on the cliff face. She had no fear of heights and neither had Pyewacket. He had not minded being slung over her bare shoulder as she had climbed and had kept his claws to himself.

Taking another sip of her tea Grizel thought that she would not be taking the cat over to Guernsey this evening. Bad weather was coming. She still had all of her late father's weather instruments and knew how to use them, although she lacked his prognostic skills. She had to rely more upon her observations of the natural world and the weather sense that most animals had.

The wind was now backing, blowing east to northeast. If she checked the barometer she was certain that she would find it was high and falling fast. This probably meant severe wind and rain and high seas. The day before yesterday there had been a sky full of mare's tails, which usually meant bad weather in a day or so, and today had been blindingly clear. As she had stood here and watched she had seen scores of sea birds flying inland. They knew what was coming. She could not carry Pyewacket on her back to Guernsey in a high sea, even though it was not that far. Better to wait out the storm.

She had heard the gulls talking about the many French ships arriving and the good pickings from the garbage thrown overboard.

Grizel smiled to herself as she finished the last of her tea. If those ships did not make port before the storm broke there would be many French sailors and soldiers sick with *mal de mer*. It served them right.

3
A Gift from the Sea

From the rocky shore to the location of the camp in the woods was a short walk for Rosal, even with her basket to carry. She had gathered enough ormers to make a stew that would feed herself, Hagar and Chavé. The pony could graze, which she supplemented by cutting grass for him from other locations.

Summer was coming and life would be easier. There was no longer the problem of keeping warm, for although the island climate was mild and snow and severe frost quite rare, winter days could be wet, windy and raw. And most important, food was more readily obtainable in summer weather.

And the weather had definitely improved. The woods resounded with birdsong and everything had burst into flower. She could put the *vardo* in a permanent location and perhaps raise some vegetables.

The present location was a good one; it was private, quiet and well off any main roads. The wood belonged to Marie Brehaut, a local woman who had a farm where Rosal sometimes worked. She had permission to camp here.

From here Rosal could walk to the shore for shell-fish and sea weed or to the little town of St. Cécile for supplies, if she had money to spend. There were also a few farms in the area where she was sometimes hired to pick stones or do weeding. Now that so many men had been stolen away by the French, hired help ws at a premium and those who would have scorned to hire her before 1799 now sought her services. She did not now hear so much of the comment she had heard all of her life – "dirty, thieving gypsies."

Rosal did not steal unless it was absolutely necessary. She would have to be starving to do so. Stealing was stupid for if caught, she would hang and Guernsey was a small place, only 24 square miles, they would know where to look if too many things went missing. And she was not dirty, she kept herself and the *vardo* and her animals as clean as she could. That was another advantage of summertime. There was a pool in the woods where she could bathe, fully immersed, not washing piecemeal from a pan of hot water in the *vardo* as in the cold weather.

She could have earned more money, now that fortune telling was forbidden, by dancing at one of the little *cafés* that the French had taken over in the larger towns such as St. Peter Port or St. Sampson.

But she did not want to dance for the French. She did not like their crude comments or their assumption that she was any man's for the taking. They thought she was loose of morals because she was Romany. They could not have been more wrong. She had been virginal when she had married Sylvester as was expected and had kept to herself since she had been widowed.

As she approached the *vardo* through the woods she could smell the fire and a few moments later Chavé came streaking towards her.

He was a quiet dog, not given to much vocalization. He was black and white in colour, with a ruffled white chest and legs and a narrow white stripe from muzzle to forehead, with four white paws and a plumy tail. His ears, sometimes quite erect in his breed of Border coally, drooped a little.

His tail was wagging furiously as he ran towards Rosal. He had a keen and intelligent expression in his dark brown eyes. Indeed, Rosal found him so intelligent that she could not imagine why he had been unable to learn to herd livestock as the farmer had claimed. She could not understand it at all until she talked to a neighbor of the man's, who had said dryly that to train a dog one must be more intelligent than the animal and Chavé's former owner had not met this requirement.

Rosal put down her basket and bent to the important task of greeting Chavé. He was quite enthusiastic, for although he was gentle and friendly with Hagar, his most passionate love was saved for Rosal.

"Good dog, good dog!" she said, running her hands over his silky head and body, and drawing his ears gently through

28

her hands, which he loved. "You have protected Hagar and the *vardo*, have you? I found some good food for our meal and you shall have your share."

He looked up at her as if he understood every word she said and trotted along happily by her side as she hefted the basket up and walked on towards the camp.

She found Hagar seated by the fire. Even on these warm spring days the older woman seemed to feel the cold. Since Rosal had found her she had been often ill. Rosal thought that this was as much as a lack of will to live as it was to the privations she had suffered. Hagar kept living because there was nothing else to do. She missed both the *gajo* who had kept her as his mistress and the son she had borne him. Rosal thought she was well rid of the man who treated her so ill and the adolescent boy who had rejected his Gypsy mother.

Hagar looked up as Rosal approached. Although she was not yet forty, she looked older, with streaks of gray in her dark hair and a tired look on her features. She had once been very beautiful, and like Rosal, she had long dark eyes, high cheekbones, dark hair and bore herself with a supple grace. Many people on the island thought them mother and daughter. And like Rosal she wore a bright skirt, much mended, with a heavy blouse belted over it and a kerchief over her hair, from which peeped golden earrings. She also huddled into a shawl, pulling it tight around her now rather bony shoulders.

"Were you in luck?" she queried as Rosal set the basket down by the fire.

"Enough for one good mea, and there's winkles to be had, and seaweed after that storm. I'll take Kälo and go back tonight and get as many winkles as I can," said Rosal, dropping down on the piece of log that served them as a seat.

Hagar was looking at the ormer shells. "I can make buttons from those to sell," she suggested. The ormer shells shone like pearl inside and many people made buttons and jewelry from them.

Rosal looked at her in surprise. Hagar had never offered to do anything to supplement their income, and Rosal had never pressed her to do so.

"You don't have to –" Rosal began but Hagar interrupted her.

"Yes, it is time and gone long past when I should be earning my keep! You are too tender hearted, Rosal! Only look what you have burdened yourself with: a useless old woman, a dog that no one wants and a pony that any horse coper would sell for dogsmeat. I can make buttons and weave baskets to sell to the *Giorgios* at the market place, now that they will not let us tell fortunes."

Hagar was an English Romanichal and she always referred to white people as *Giorgios,* while Rosal's people had been originally Spanish, driven from that country by the Inquisition, and she used the Spanish term of *gajo.* When they were together like this they spoke in a blend of Romany, English and Island French.

Hagar would brook no argument and taking a knife out from her belt, began to pry open the ormers. "There's just enough of the winter vegetables left," she said "to make a stew."

Rosal went to the wagon, the *vardo,* and put one bare foot on the step plate that hung down beside the smaller front wheel and swung lightly inside up over the driver's seat.

She was immensely proud of the *vardo.* Few of the Romany had one, instead existing in tents, with their goods in a rickety cart. Of course, the *vardo* had been Sylvester's and by right it should have been burned after his death but Rosal had seen little reason to follow this custom. She needed a home and it was the least he owed her after the neglect that killed her child.

In Sylvester's time it had been a gaudy red and gold but Rosal had painted it apple green with a band of flowers around the bottom of the narrow body and another band of four leaf clovers, in gold on a darker green, at the bottom of the canvas top. Her fancy, and her love of bright wildflowers, had led her to paint all the panels of the doors and sides with pictures of flowers, with the paint she had purchased from a peddler.

Each side had two windows of frosted glass that could be lowered into the body when she wished to roll up the apple green canvas sides, as the windows, etched in a floral pattern, were mounted in a sash. The paneled doors that could be opened from the drivers' seat into the vardo had panes of red and green glass that Rosal had salvaged from a trash heap, from an old house that had been demolished. She loved the rich light they gave to the interior when the sun streamed though.

At the rear, inside, was a platform with a brass rail, made up as a bed, with deep storage underneath. Over this bed were three windows with more coloured glass. Along each side was a bench, narrow, but wide enough to sleep upon, with more storage underneath. On one side a table, supported with brass chains, could be swung down from the wall. A large brass lamp swung from the ceiling. This had come from the wreckage of a ship and was the pride of Rosal's heart. Everything was neat, scrupulously clean and compact. With a brazier in the winter and the canvas walls doubled it could be very cozy. There was nothing of Sylvester Lovel left in it. Also gone was the small cradle that had been occupied by Cinerella. Rosal had not been able to bear looking at it after the baby's death and by custom, it, too, had to be burned.

Now she searched under the bench and pulled out a handy bin which at the beginning of the autumn had been full of root vegetables. It now contained a few withered potatoes, one onion and a handful of wizened carrots. Enough for today, but there would soon be early vegetables, spring peas and early potatoes and other greens that made her mouth water just thinking of them. For now she would supplement the meal by making some dumplings that would cook on top of the stew.

Hagar had the ormers cleaned and ready by the time she came back outside and Rosal left the vegetables with her. Calling Chavé, Rosal took a bucket from a hook underneath the vardo and went to the nearby spring, for water for the stew. She would check on Kälo on the way.

The pony was where she had tethered him that morning, in a small grassy meadow in the woods. Kälo meant 'black' in Romany and his dark hide shone with health and brushing in the dappled sun coming through the new leaves.

Kälo was another of Rosal's rescues. He was a good-sized Dartmoor pony, about 12 hands at the withers, with an elegant small head and alert ears, and a well set-up tail. He was very strong for his size and had no trouble pulling the large *vardo*. He was solid black with no trace of white and was a fine looking animal except for the blemish of broken knees. He had been ridden too hard by the son of a prosperous farmer and had fallen on the road and cut his knees. When it was seem that he was to be scarred the young boy wanted no more of him. Rosal had found him at a horse fair and taken him in trade for the heavy draught horse that Sylvester had owned to pull the *vardo*. This animal was too expensive for Rosal to feed. Kälo was an easy keeper; he thrived on a handful of grain and grass.

He put up his head and nickered as he saw her. He was a friendly little soul and, like Chavé, was exceptionally fond of Rosal.

"Would you like to go to the shore, later, Kälo?" she asked, rubbing his velvet soft nose. "I'm going gathering."

He nodded his head vigorously as if he understood her and she laughed delightedly. Chavé wagged his tail, looking from the pony to the Gypsy girl, and gave a lone bark. "Yes, you shall go too, Chavé!" Rosal promised. "This evening, when the tide turns."

"There's going to a storm later," Hagar warned Rosal as the girl set out for the shore again, "Try to be back before dark."

Rosal nodded. She had seen the weather signs too. It looked as if it was going to be severe. There had been a storm two nights ago as well, but it had been of short duration and not too violent. but this one promised to be a bad one.

But they needed the winkles and the seaweed for meals and if this storm lasted into tomorrow they'd have next to nothing to eat if she did not go to the shore tonight.

She walked down to the rocky beach, leading Kälo, who bore panniers on his back that she would fill with winkles, seaweed, and hopefully some driftwood. Chavé frisked around them, wanting to play and Rosal obligingly threw rocks or sticks for him, laughing at his antics.

The path through the woods led to a roughly crescent shaped bay into which a rocky headland jutted. Since the tide would not be high until nearly midnight, Rosal led the pony carefully over the rocks around the headland. She would work her way back, prying periwinkles off rocks and looking for the best seaweed and pieces of wood tossed up on the shore. She loved to burn the driftwood, as the salt-soaked wood made such beautiful colours as it burned.

Rosal worked steadily as the sun began to decline. She saw no one else out at all. It was curiously still, which was strange. Even at low tide, when the boats were not going out, there was usually someone at work about the little harbor. No one else was out gathering shellfish and that was strange as well. Rosal could not know that the return of the French to the island was occupying everyone's thoughts to the exclusion of all else.

As she worked her way back she hummed to herself, every once in a while finding something to throw for Chavé. The tide began to come in; she heard splashing in the water. She stood up abruptly, a hand to the small of her aching back, just in time to see a French frigate sail by.

It was definitely French – the *Tricoleur* snapped in the rising wind and even in the lessening light she could see the uniforms of the men on deck. She too well knew what a French uniform looked like. They could probably not make her out, here on the shore, for which she was thankful.

What were *they* doing back? Her heart began beating more rapidly. Even as far away from civilization as she was, she had prayed daily for the French, and, in particular, for the Inquisition, to leave Guernsey.

Dusk was now falling and the wind was rising, tugging at her hair and skirt. She could smell the coming rain and the sun, a poor, pale yellow, was disappearing beneath a mass of low, dull, leaden clouds. Time to get back for she had gathered quite a bit of wood, weed and winkles.

Chavé raced ahead of her at top speed. He did this continuously, running ahead and making a circle back again, as if he found the progress of Rosal and the pony too slow.

They were almost to where the path led into the woods when Chavé did not come back, but instead, began barking in an agitated fashion.

This was so unlike the coally that Rosal grew concerned, and dropping Kälo's reins to ground tether him, picked up her skirts and ran ahead, nimbly leaping over rocks in her way.

"Chavé, Chavé!" she called "Where are you?"

In the fast gathering dusk, made darker by the heavy

cloud cover she saw him, nosing at something on the ground and lifting his head to bark sharply, as if calling her.

"What is it?" she gasped as she ran up to him.

"Oh!" she exclaimed as she saw what Chavé had found and she fell to her knees beside his find.

It was a man, a young man, clad only in cotton duck trousers and completely unconscious.

He was lying on his side and she turned him over to lay upon his back. He was much bruised and as she turned him, blood sluggishly trickled down his face.

A quick examination showed a head wound, a deep gash in the back of his head that ran almost all the way to the front.

"How did this happen?" she wondered out loud. Had he fallen from a boat, perhaps? The tides were strong hereabouts and it was rocky. If he had fallen from a fishing boat he would have been tossed in the surf and battered by the rocks.

Chavé, with little whines, began to lick the man's face. This was unusual behavior for him as he was standoffish and did not take to many other people, particularly men.

Suddenly the man groaned, startling both Rosal and the coally. He moved his head from side to side on the rocks as if trying to escape the pain she could see in the lines on his face. He opened his eyes, to look right up at her. He stared at her a long moment, looking confused and at last said "Do I know you?"

It was an English voice, with no trace of the Guernésais accent. "Oh, God! My head!" he swore and put a hand up to his forehead. "What happened to me?"

"You hurt your head – don't move, just lie still," she began and started to get up, thinking vaguely of running to the closest farm house to fetch help.

As she began to get to her feet his hand shot out and grabbed her wrist in a surprisingly strong grasp. "Tell em who you are!" he demanded, his voice rough. "And, oh, God, tell me who I am, for I cannot seem to remember at all!" His voice was full of anguish.

It was then, as Rosal remembered where she had seen him before, that her great idea was born.

4
The Great Lie

Rosa looked down at the man who stared back at her with such confusion and pain in his eyes. They were a deep brown, she noticed, much like her own.

It was this last that decided her and told her that this had been meant to happen. Had Hagar not seen exciting changes and a young man in the Tarot for her?

Now she said quickly, "What a bump on the head you've had! You're my man, my Rom, how can you not be remembering that?"

"Your what?" He put a shaky hand to his head and winced as his fingers touched the scalp wound.

"My Rom, my husband!" she said. Oh, this was a marvelous idea! Ever since she had seen him on the boat that morning she had thought about him – a young, strong Rom... And if he could not remember who he was, and since he was an Englishman, the French would put him in prison, surely, where he would die of neglect. She would actually be saving his life.

"What is my name?" he asked, closing his eyes briefly as his injury sent a wave of pain over his head.

She remembered the name she had heard that morning when she had first seen him. "Felix – Felix Lovel and I'm Rosal. This is our dog, Chavé."

Chavé seemed to have taken a fancy to the stranger, for as the man looked at him, the dog's tail wagged and he thrust his head forward with a sharp 'woof!', acting as if he had known this man all of his days.

"What happened to me?" the stranger asked hesitantly.

"You fell off a rock," Rosal said promptly. "We've been out gathering winkles for our supper. You hit your head when you fell."

"I feel so sick..." he said, closing his eyes again. "None of

35

what you tell me seems the least bit familiar."

"You'll remember after a bit," she lied. "I've got to be getting you back to our *vardo*. There's a storm coming, a bad one. I'll go and fetch Kälo. Chavé, guard your master!" she ordered the dog.

When she ran off he attempted to sit up but his senses swam so sickeningly that he soon gave this up. His head was a mass of pain and when he tried to remember anything it was as if there was a huge blank where his memory should be and almost unbearable pain lanced through his brain. Could this happen from a blow on the head?

That woman stirred no chord of recognition. Yet she said she was his wife! And the dog, who now lay regarding him with head on his paws seemed to know him. He stretched out a feeble hand to the dog, who promptly licked it. "Good dog," he said weakly.

The dog wagged its plumy tail again.

Another wave of pain swept over him and this time, it led back down into darkness.

"Rosal!" said Hagar in horror. "Have you gone mad? You cannot do this!"

The older woman had been surprised when Rosal had arrived, just before the storm broke, with an injured man draped over the pony's back. She had not been unwilling to help tend someone who was injured for they could not leave him on the shore to die, but as soon as the storm passed they should take him into the town where he could be cared for by his own kind.

At Rosal's urging Hagar had bathed his head wound and put some of her healing herbs upon it, holding these in place with a clean bandage. Then Rosal had put the man in her own bed and covered him up with the bright quilts, and watched as Hagar gave him a draught of distilled poppy syrup. Sleep was a good healer.

And then she had told Hagar what she had done.

Hagar was completely appalled. "Rosal, what will he do to you when he remembers who he is? How could you have done such a foolish thing?"

"He may never remember," said Rosal. She was sitting

upon the edge of the bed, having lowered the brass rail, wiping the man's brow with a cold cloth. As Hagar had thought it would, a fever was rising in him. "In Spain there was an old man on a farm that fell from a hay mow and hit his head. He never remembered his past, only what people told him. My father told me about him. My father heard of him from his grandfather."

"So you would steal his life from him, to give yourself a Rom?" queried Hagar scornfully.

"He was a servant on that boat I saw," Rosal said. "He was working and a man with a face like a fox called him in to make breakfast for him. Is it not better, Hagar, for him to live free as my Rom than to be a servant?"

"And what if when he wakes up and remembers everything, Rosal? What about that?" Hagar demanded.

Rosal shrugged. "Than I tell him that he dreamed it all and he thanks us for tending to him and maybe pays us."

"With what?" Hagar said. "There's not a penny in his clothes, what there were of them!"

"His master on the boat will pay us. He is a good, hard-working servant, the kind the *Gajé* don't want to lose."

Hagar threw up her hands. The girl had an answer for each of her objections. "I shall tell him myself –" she began, but Rosal turned on her so fierce a look that Hagar shrank back, frightened by the glare in her young friend's eyes. It was a look she had never seen before.

"You will not!" the girl stated. "I do not wish to put you back upon the road, Hagar, but I will do it if you tell him! We need a man to protect us and help us. And he can give me another child," she added, almost to herself.

Hagar's heart sank when she heard this. Rosal was obsessive about having another child. She would never give up on an opportunity to further this aim. She was cut off from her own kind now. No Romany man would want her, banished as she had been. This *Giorgio* cast up from the sea must seem a golden chance to her.

Hagar could only hope that the man would wake with his senses intact.

It was indeed a bad storm. Wind and rain swooped down upon the Channel Islands, battering them with heavy surf and a shrieking gale.

In Grizel Sarchet's stone cottage on Sark, Pyewacket stared miserably out at the violence of the storm, safe in her snug parlor where a fire of driftwood burned in a small hearth.

"Come away from the window," Grizel suggested. "Staring at the weather will not make it go away. According to my father's instruments, we are in for a two day blow."

"I must get to Guernsey!" Pyewacket said in distress. "What if he is waiting for me?"

"Unless he is a fool, he has sought a safe harbor and will ride out the storm there," said Grizel. "Has he much experience sailing?"

"All his life," said Pyewacket, turning from the window ledge on which he sat to look at her. "He grew up on the water. Ever since I have been with him he has had one type of sail craft or another. We spend every spare moment out on the water. This new yacht - this was her maiden voyage - was made for my Wizard in America." The cat paused and then said in a thickened voice "It's a cat boat. I thought that would be lucky, a good sign."

Grizel said nothing. She had all the instincts of her Selchie breed and this entire situation was making them jangle. She ws very much afraid that the cat would never be reunited with his Wizard. She was still willing to take him to Guernsey when the storm blew itself out but she thought he ws putting himself into unnecessary danger. If the French caught him he would be burned in an *auto de fé* for the Inquisition reserved a special enmity for black cats, which they saw as Satan's own.

Better he stay here with her - she would like the companionship, for she missed both her father and his familiar, who had died not long after her father. The bond between them was very close and the hedgehog had lost all will to live without his Wizard.

She was much afraid that Pyewacket, too, would not last very long if he found that his Wizard had departed the earth.

"Complete to a shade!" the fox-featured man lifted a glass of a very fine brandy to his companion and drank down a good gulp.

His companion, a man in an English style clothing but with a turban upon his head, inclined his head graciously. "I told you that you worried unnecessarily," he said in English that was only faintly tinged with his Persian origin. "My plans do not fail," he added complacently.

"You ain't cutting me a wheedle about this potion? It's the prime article?" the first man asked.

"My dear Reynard," said the Persian smoothly. "in my country this potion has been used for thousands of years to rid ourselves of inconvenient persons! Even should he survive the sea, he will never remember who he is or where he came from! You did not need to hit him so hard."

"Liked flooring him," said Reynard, downing the last of the brandy and pouring himself another glass. "Been compared to him since we was schoolboys, m'grandfather actin' as if I was some sort of scapegallows! And he was going to get the lot of it," he added savagely. "the money, the house and lands, the title! Well, he ain't getting it now !"

"Yes, one can see why you might resent him," the Persian agreed. He was not drinking brandy as his religion forbade it.

"If they find him and there's a knock on the pate they'll be sure it ain't a take-in and he was hit by the boom and there wasn't any havey-cavey business," Reynard said. "There won't be nay trace?" he asked, suddenly anxious.

"None," the Persian replied. "In Persia, we have given the potion to many men and destroyed their memories. They are then released out in the desert where they wander until they die. When the bodies have been found before the vultures pick the bones clean there is no trace of it left. It is a well disguised method of murder."

Reynard shuddered and put down his glass. "Don't like that word."

These English were so squeamish! "Nonetheless, that is what we have done, my friend, murder, all for gain, both yours and mine. You must not forget what you owe me when you are confirmed as the heir. And remember, if you have a mind to cheat me, my powers far outstrip yours and I shall protect myself quite easily from anything you choose to try," the Persian said, with a look in his eyes and on his bearded face that gave emphasis to the threat — for that was what it was.

Reynard's bulky cravat felt suddenly tight, and he felt as if he was suddenly far away form this elegant hotel suite in the Isle of Wight — someplace dark and dangerous, from the look in the Persian's hooded eyes.

Reynard turned away from that look. He suddenly wished that he had been able to do this on his own, that he had never had to become involved with Ali Amir Bahram, the Persian sorcerer. Nervously, he said "I' am a gentleman, ain't I? A gentleman don't cheat his friends!"

"*Perhaps not*" thought Bahram cynically, "*but they feel no scruples in murdering their relatives.*"

"Had time to send off a 'griffe express before the storm broke," Reynard said, attempting to pour himself another glass and discovering the bottle to be empty. "Not all that far from Devon — the old man will more than likely have the message tonight. Storm passes, he'll be here starightaway, I'll lay odds on it! Only a matter of a few days now and I'll be rolling in the soft! Stand me another bottle of brandy? My pockets are quite to let," he added hopefully.

"You have had quite enough intoxicating drink," said Bahram firmly. "You must have all your wits about you when you face this— what is his title again?"

"Earl, the Earl of Belmaray," Reynard answered. "My grandfather, and my cousin's too." A crafty, self satisfied look that made him look more vulpine than ever came over his face. "I want the heir's title. I like being called my lord and addressed as Viscount Hightor." He laughed suddenly. " Even do I pay you I'll have more than enough of the ready to cut a dash in Town. I'll have a handsome allowance and punt on Tick if needs be, for the old man will cut up to several hundred thousand in the Funds and I don't know how much else in lands and other holdings," he said in no little satisfaction. The future was good. Trying to live as a gentleman ought on a curst inadequate allowance was in the past.

The Persian sorcerer smiled to himself. He had no

intention of accepting but one payment from this pigeon, no matter what he had promised, not when he could be bled indefinitely. Reynard would find that Bahram's long fingers would be plucking from his very deep pockets with increasing frequency. Reynard was a young man and would serve as a source of easily obtainable funds for a very long time.

He had a headache. This in itself was a miracle of deductive reasoning, for his thoughts were so incoherent, so chaotic that managing to think this out had made his head pound and his stomach roll.

Opening his eyes proved difficult. Pain shot through his head as he attempted it, for a bright light struck his sight and instinctively he winced away from it.

Moving his head proved to be a mistake. Involuntarily, he let out a moan and found at once that a cool, small hand was laid on his brow. "I think that the light bothers him," he heard a female voice say.

There was a noise in the background and then she said, "There now, we have dimmed the lamp. You can open your eyes now!"

Behind her voice was a terrible shrieking noise and the entire place in which he lay seemed to be buffeted by some force that caused it to creak and sway. Was he on a boat? he wondered confusedly, clinging to the thought of a boat as the one rational thought in his brain. There was something almost comforting in the thought of a boat.

He tried opening his eyes again and found it easier this time. But moving his head was definitely not an action he was eager to repeat.

Her face was right above his vision. It was a young, rather lovely face with golden skin, dark eyes, a wide, generous red mouth and a mass of curling dark hair that hung down past her shoulders. She had gold hoops in her ears and a white blouse fell off one shoulder.

He searched her features for some knowledge of who she was. But hadn't he seen her before, on the shore when he first woke? "Pray excuse me," he said, his voice a harsh croak in his own ears, " But I don't remember your name."

"You don't remember me yet?" she said, her face lighting in pity. "Oh, poor Felix! I'm your wife, Rosal. And we're here in our *vardo*. You're in our bed."

Felix — was that his name? He had to remember that. "Are we at sea?" he asked her.

She laughed. Her laugh was low and soft and very attractive. "No, there's a big storm outside and the walls on our *vardo,* our caravan, are made of canvas."

"Here, he sounds as if he needs this," A hand, holding a cup, thrust itself into his view. He was suddenly conscious of extreme thirst and said "Water..."

"I'll help you," the girl said and with gentle hands helped him raise his head slightly. Even this little motion hurt so much that he almost cried out. But his need for water was too great and he gulped at it. However he was glad to have her return his head to the pillow.

She looked down at him. "Try to go back to sleep," she said. "Every time you wake up you'll feel better. Hagar is doctoring you. She has green fingers and knows the ways of herbs."

He was more than glad to close his eyes again and slip back into the comfortable darkness, away from the pain. But first he had to know one thing. "When I wake up again, shall I remember?"

"More than likely," she said soothingly.

With that he had to be content and let go his tenuous hold on consciousness.

In Devon, on the English mainland, near Torquay, in an old mansion overlooking the sea, an elderly gentleman sat in a deep wing chair in front of a coal fire.

His chair was in a handsome old library, oak paneled and hung with coaching prints in the little space left where there were not bookcases, tier upon tier of them. The walls, two stories high, were full of books, their worn spines attesting to the fact that these volumes were well-read and well-loved. A narrow balcony, complete with sliding library ladders, offered easy access to the multitude of volumes.

Stained glass windows faced the sea, whose roar on this stormy evening could be heard as if it was a great beast attacking the manor house.

But the old man was unconscious of the noise of the sea, of the lash of the rain on the windows or the ticking of the tall case clock in a corner. In his hand he clutched a message, one that had been read again and again. Now he stared blindly at the fire, his face haggard and suddenly much older than his years.

On the arm of the chair crouched a gray tabby cat, a neat appearing creature with a white bib and paws and mackerel striped. He said nothing to his Wizard, merely laid a paw on his arm in silent sympathy. A terrible tragedy had come to the house of Belmaray. And the cat had no idea how they were to survive this loss.

5
Witch Weather

Witch weather, the country folk called it. A storm in the Channel at this time of year was rare. It made them repeat the old stories, stories of how the Witches and Wizards of the British Isles had raised a Cone of Power and repelled the Spanish Armada in the days of Good Queen Bess and the Wizard Sir Francis Drake by calling up a terrible storm, known to the Spanish as "The Wind of God."

Gaffer Silas Cobblley, in the tap room of the Green Man in the hamlet of Belmaray near the manor, insisted that the Witches were causing the weather now to keep the French away. Had he not seen them at it himself one night when he was coming home, out at the stones on the heath?

"We was but doin' our Rites, Gaffer," said the bar-maid, Suzy Chafee, who was a Witch and a member of the local Coven. "Dancing sky- clad and drawin' down the goodness of the moon for the fields. 'Tis no secret. Mayhap you had a bit too much cider at the King's Arms," she added slyly. The Green Man and the King's Arms had long been rivals for the quality and potency of their Devon cider and the habitués of the Green Man thought the other cider miserable stuff that would make one muzzy-headed in no time flat.

The listening men roared with laughter at this, as she intended, and when she invited Silas to come and watch the dancing the talk turned to teasing her about how her buxom figure would look completely bare beneath the moon. She traded jests with the men as she served up more ale and cider, grateful that no one seemed inclined to pursue the topic of repelling the French invaders with Witchcraft. What the Witches might or might not be doing was their secret to keep.

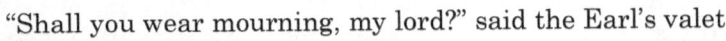

"Shall you wear mourning, my lord?" said the Earl's valet respectfully and sadly.

Richard Jourdaine, the Earl of Belmaray, looked into his valet's face. Pearson had been with him since the Earl was a young man and now they were growing old together. Pearson's hair was as white as his own and since the news had come two days ago the valet had aged as rapidly as had he.

The Earl was a tall, well set up man nearing seventy. His thick white hair, once dark, which had only receded a little from his high forehead, was worn in the new short classical style that was becoming the mode. Long, full side-whiskers, as white as his hair, met in a mustache over his firm lips. His eyes were very blue in his tanned, rather angular face Unlike many of his contemporaries, who clung to the powdered wigs and full-skirted coats of their youth, the Earl prided himself on being modern and wearing the fashionable pantaloons, tail coat and Hessian boots worn by younger men. These were a great deal like riding dress, which he had always found more comfortable as he spent far more time upon his estate than he did in Town.

"No," he now said firmly. "The blue coat, Pearson and the white sarcenet striped waistcoat. There will be no going into mourning as yet. I am not certain in my mind that he is dead."

"But Mr. Reginald's express said that Mr. Felix was knocked overboard and they were unable to find any trace of him," protested Pearson.

"He might have been picked up by a fishing boat, or rescued by one of the Sea-Folk," said the Earl. "When I reach the Isle of Wight I shall use the Triton horn and ask my friend Madoc if any of his people have seen Felix. Madoc is acquainted with many of the Selchies as well. Any of them might have rescued him as it is their duty to do so."

Pearson, a slight man whose white hair was rapidly thinning, exchanged a helpless look with the gray tabby sitting upon the Earl's dressing table beside a pile of unused muslin cravats.

"You seemed convinced the day before yesterday, Richard, that he was gone," said the cat carefully.

"I lay awake most of the night last night thinking about it and realized that Reginald, the lazy dog, had, more than like as not, *not* pursued every avenue he ought. When has Reginald ever done any more than he had to? And he would get no cooperation from the Sea-Folk as they have never liked him," said the Earl, shrugging into the blue coat Pearson held up for him and then putting a well-filled purse in a pocket. A single fob, with the seal of Belmaray, hung from his waistcoat and he slipped a chased hunter watch into his other pocket.

"Pascoe is all saddled and ready," said Greymalkin, jumping down from the dressing table to trot behind his Wizard. "I saw to it myself. He's waiting for us in the drive."

"Thank you, Grey," said the Earl gratefully. "My flying suit, Pearson?"

"Brushed and ready, my lord," the valet answered.

The cat and the valet followed their master from the paneled bed room, done in red brocade in a style not seen since the reign of Charles II — for tradition had it that the Merry Monarch had once slept there, and on into the long hall and down the broad staircase that curved ever so slightly and ended in a black and white tiled hall under a domed ceiling mural of ships tossed in a rough sea as Neptune, trident in hand, looked on.

Here stood at rigid attention, the Belmaray butler, Horrocks, and two footmen, one of whom held a leather flying suit over his arm.

"Good day, my lord," said the butler with a bow. "The dragon stands ready." He gestured to the footman who gave the flying suit into Pearson's keeping. The valet then helped his master into the suit which was a garment of leather, well lined, that closed snugly. There were gloves and a close fitting cap as well. A well-made flying suit slid on over a gentleman's clothing and protected it from the exigencies of flying and the rider from the cold, high in the air.

"Shall I order the hatchments, my lord?" asked the butler. He had wanted to put up the, proper, respectful signs of mourning as soon as they had the news, but his lordship had forbidden it.

"No," said the Earl again. "Pray, do nothing towards that

end. I shall let you know when and if it is required. And if any of the county calls, tell them that we are not yet certain that it is true. After today I shall have a better idea. I shall no doubt remain on the Isle of Wight for a day or so while I check into matters."

"Very good, my lord," said Horrocks. He was very correct, and the notion of not putting up the hatchments, placing a mourning wreath on the door, covering all of the mirrors with black bombazine, as well as giving all of the servants a black mourning band to wear about their upper arms shocked him. But his lordship's wish was law.

He sprang forward to open the door his own self as the Earl took his gloves and cap from the other footman and opened the door upon the graveled drive.

In front of the double railed crab-pincer staircase that led down in two directions to the drive stood a copper-coloured dragon, with a small saddle for carrying only one passenger with a traveling basket secured on behind. This basket was for the convenience of Greymalkin. In the dragon's breast harness, a mesh bag, was a small corded trunk of the Earl's travel necessities.

This was Pascoe. He was a Cornish Copper, about thirty feet long and only fifteen years younger than the Earl. He had been employed at Belmaray since he was but five and had become over the years a great friend to both the Jourdaines who lived at the Manor. His scales were a tarnished copper colour but the edges and the striations of his horns gleamed as brightly as Cook's cherished copper pans in the kitchen of the great house. His underbody was a very pale yellow and his wings a transparent copper.

His eyes, like most British dragons, were a colour between yellow and amber. He now turned these with concern upon his rider, but said nothing about the recent loss of the Earl's heir.

Squatting down, he offered up a foreleg for the Earl to mount. "The grooms checked the safety harness," he said in his deep voice. "I had them do so to save time. I knew you would like to get into the air as soon as possible. It's a beautiful day for flying."

It was indeed. After two days the storm had blown itself out and left behind it a clear, sparkling, nearly perfect spring day. Later it would be warm but high up, it would still be chill.

After thanking the dragon for his thoughtfulness, the Earl climbed up to the saddle and put his familiar in the traveling basket, securing it tightly. He then strapped himself in and the dragon, after making certain that his two passengers were both comfortable and safe, sprang into the sky, heading towards the Isle of Wight, off the southern coast.

Sir David Dieudonné's thoughts were black indeed as he gazed at the scene below him. He had ridden out that morning, feeling a need to escape and the aching of his leg and hip told him he had ridden too far and too fast. The doctor had told him that he must give up riding and go about in a chaise like an old woman. David would be damned if he would follow that advice.

There were times when a man needed to get on a horse and cover the ground at a gallop, to feel the wind in his face and try and leave his cares behind, even if it did make his leg hurt like the Devil.

He had ridden quite a ways for a man with a bad leg, down past Fermain Bay and back again. Now he stood on the edge of the cliff at the bay and looked out over a sandy cove with blue sea, the waves still high.

Before his injury he had thought nothing of scrambling down the steep cliff path between the heavily wooded slopes. Now, even if he could make it down he knew he would never make it up again.

Behind him, his horse's bit jingled as the animal grazed on new grass.

David's thoughts were bleak. The French had returned. That morning he had been roused from his bed in the small white-washed cottage he shared with his mother Majorlaine, by a French corporal, who had demanded that Sir David accompany him at once to meet with *M. le Colonel* Arnaud Fournier, the new commander of the French troops in the area.

David had disliked Colonel Fournier on sight. There was

an air if cruelty about the man. It showed in his heavy-lidded eyes and narrow mouth beneath a pencil thin mustache and straight dark hair slicked back with Circassian hair oil. He was brisk and slim and efficient and was full of new regulations for the island. He did not approve of the way things had been done in the past. He did not intend to work with David, but only to give out rules: unjust, strict, confining rules, that would make the Islanders' lives a misery to them.

Every week, there were to be two assemblies in every parish. All parishioners were to be present and accounted for, with no exceptions. Babies, invalids, the elderly: everyone would assemble and be counted. French troops were to be quartered in every parish, not only St Peter's as had been previously. Every house would be visited to judge which were suitable for quartering officers. The owners of the property would have no choice but to accept their 'guests'.

All weapons were to be turned into the French. No one would be allowed a gun, a sword, or even historic weapons, not even for hunting to feed their families. All houses, barns, wagons, shops would be searched. Colonel Fournier informed David that anyone on the Island, high or low, would be subject to search and seizure at any time deemed necessary.

"In short, we are to live beneath martial law!" David had said angrily.

"If you chose to look at it that way," said the Colonel. "This is a conquered land, *M'sieur*, and I mean to make certain that it remains so. I shall cut out the cancer of resistance before it begins."

"There was no trouble during the previous occupation," said David. "Captain Dubois and I—"

"You will find me far different than Captain Dubois," the Colonel interrupted. "And as for you, *M'sieur*, you will be but a figurehead. It is I who will rule this island and you will do well not to forget it. You will not so much as order new quills for your desk without my permission. Is this understood?" His eyes were cold and heard as his voice. "You will sign what I tell you to sign and give the speeches that I may write for you, or else I shall seize your property and throw you and your entire family into prison."

He turned away and gestured at a large map that hung on the wall (they were in David's office) and said "We shall be building fortifications and prisons here. To save our French Republic our hard-won monies we shall be levying taxes upon the Island —"

"And by taking away all of our men you have condemned most of us to poverty for the last five years!" David protested. "We are an agricultural, fishing society here. There is little industry and there are not enough men left to work the land or to man the fishing fleet! Many people are going hungry even now and are in serious financial distress! How can they pay a new tax?"

Fournier smiled. "That is not my concern, *M'sieur*. One more thing I shall tell you. The Inquisition will be given full powers here, not the minor role it has heretofore played. All heresy will be completely stamped out. And all will be expected to attend the *auto de fés*. Rewards will be paid to those who alert the Church to suspected heretics. There are more Inquisitors and a Senior Witch-Sniffer coming from Rome."

David now thought of this conversation with utter despair. The previous occupation had been bad enough but Dubois had interfered very little with the day-to-day workings of the island. The Inquisition had been busy searching for Witches and Wizards, few of whom it had found, as most of them had fled ahead of the French advance. They had paid little attention to the Church of England worshippers, Presbyterians, Methodists, Jewish and Gypsy people upon the Island.

But the full Inquisition, with a Senior Witch-Sniffer, would mean practically everyone would be suspect of heresy. The Roman Catholic church did not recognize the Irish Catholic church as 'true' Catholicism. David had read enough about the Inquisition and its methods to think that they would have any mercy, or any compassion. *Why don't they just take us all out and shoot us one by one?* he thought as he stared at the surf. *It would be far kinder than to die under the Question or in the fires or even of starvation!*

And what was he to do, personally? How could perhaps he share an office with the Colonel, put his name to documents he abhorred, and give speeches to the people that would stick in his throat? Perhaps he should resign...suddenly he wished that he had been killed back in '99, instead of being left a useless cripple who could do naught to help his people or himself. Better to be dead than see what would happen to his beloved home when the French and the Inquisition had done with it.

It was while his thoughts were the blackest that he suddenly saw such a strange sight that it completely turned his thoughts.

Down below in the surf was a gray seal, which was not an uncommon sight. But this seal was a most uncommon sight indeed. For upon the seal's back was a sack tied to its body and riding on the sack was a black cat.

As David watched the seal beached itself and the cat jumped off onto the sand. The cat tugged at the sack and it fell to the beach.

The seal pulled itself all the way out of the water, for like most seals it was awkward on land, and then to David's amazement, its outline shimmered and within a few moments, where there had been a gray seal was a naked young woman.

David caught his breath. He had read of Selchies, of course, had even heard tales and songs of them. But he had never seen one before.

And she was one of the most beautiful women he had ever seen, with a glorious figure and rippling, wavy, bronze-coloured hair that fell well past her waist. She squeezed her hair dry and tossed her hair back over her shoulders and bent to the sack. From it she drew a blue dress and shrugged it over her head, to David's regret, covering her lovely form. A ribbon from the sack bound her hair and she picked up the empty sack.

She bent down, as if consulting the cat and then they both set off up the beach, heading, David realized, for the path that led up to the top of the cliff, where he was standing.

"There's someone at the top of the cliff," said Pyewacket

as they began the climb upwards.

"I know, I saw him when we were still in the water. He's not a French soldier but far too well-dressed to be a fisherman," Grizel answered.

Cats had excellent vision for distance but this was beyond even his sight. She must have magical eyesight, Pyewacket decided.

"Perhaps we should wait until he leaves," the familiar suggested.

Grizel disagreed. "I am willing to wager that he is an Islander. They are used to magical folk. Perhaps he may even be able to help us. At least he will know where the French are stationed so that you can inquire well away from them. Now, save your breath for the climb. It's not an easy one."

David was waiting for them at the top of the cliff path.

By now he was wishing that he had a place to sit down from which he had a hope of rising. He was leaning heavily on his cane and despised the fact that he had to appear as a wretched cripple in front of this woman.

He had not been conscious of what he must look like to a woman since the death of his fiancée, Ghislaine Renouf, five years earlier when the first French invasion had taken place and the Islanders had fought back. She had been killed at the same time he had been wounded, in a skirmish between the Islanders and the invaders. He had not been able to make her stay safely at home. She could shoot as well as could he and she had insisted that every gun had been needed.

Now, at night, when he could not sleep, he could not help but think that if it were not for this war and the French occupation they would have been married by now, perhaps with several children, living happily on the old farm in Torteval parish.

The cat appeared first and sat down in front of David, staring up at the man with large green eyes.

The woman followed. David noted that she must be in superb physical condition, for the long climb had scarcely winded her. And she was barefooted as well

She was as tall as he was and he stood a shade over six feet which was unusual for a native of Guernsey, who were usually shorter, which was said to be because of Faerie blood, although few of them had magic. Close up, she was even more striking, with the largest, most heavily lashed dark eyes he had ever seen.

"I've seen you before," she said slowly. "Here on Guernsey. You're the Bailiff of the Bailiwick, are you not?"

"Yes, I'm David Dieudonné," he admitted. "The French prefer to call me the Lieutenant Governor, but the *Guernaise* title is Bailiff."

Grizel made a face when he said 'the French'. "I'm Grizel Sarchet and this is Pyewacket."

David looked at the cat briefly and then said "Sarchet? From Sark? Was your father Hugues Sarchet, the Weather Augur? My father knew him well. We were sorry to hear of his death. We had the news just before my own father passed away."

"This is all very social and charming," Pyewacket interrupted, "but it is not helping me find my Wizard!"

David looked at him in surprise. "You're not from the Island! That accent is English. Was your Wizard here then? All the magicals are long gone."

Grizel had been looking at David closely and noticed the greyish pallor under the tan, the sweat starting on his forehead and the tight clutch on the cane. "Here," she said kindly, "let's sit down and Pyewacket can tell you the entire story."

"If I sit down I doubt I can get on my feet again," David said wryly.

"I'm as strong as a seal .I'll help you!" said Grizel with a grin.

She knew he had seen her change, he thought. And she was not blushing and shy that he had seen her without her clothes. She was frank and forthright and what is more, sprang forward to help him sit, without pity or looking away in disgust and distress as some of the more refined females here did when he met them in the street.

Pyewacket's tale was soon told and his fears that his Wizard, too, had gone over the side, and David shook his head. "If someone had been washed ashore near here a report

53

of it would have come across my desk," he said. "But it is conceivable that in one of the more rural districts some fisher folk or a farm family might have taken him in. With the French coming, if they determined he was English, they would have more than likely tried to hide him."

He looked beyond them for a moment, as if he saw something unpleasant, sighed and said "If he is being sheltered by our Islanders, he will be shortly found and imprisoned by the Inquisition since he is a Wizard. Every house on the island is to be searched for heretics and weapons. And I have no doubt that they will be spreading out to Sark and the other islands as well," he added, looking at Grizel. "You are both in terrible danger from the Inquisition! They are bringing in a Witch-Sniffer from Rome, a Senior Witch Sniffer! Familiars and Selchies will be high upon their lists as fuel for the fires. You cannot stay here or even on Sark."

"I cannot leave here," insisted Pyewacket, "without at least trying to find out what happened to Felix!" Determination was in every line of his black body. "Nothing you tell me can sway me on this!"

"Very well, then," David said. "I shall take you home with me and try to protect you as best I can. I shall try and convince the French that you are a pet. Do you think you can act like a pet cat?"

"I *am* a cat," said Pyewacket dryly.

"And as for you, *Mam'selle* Sarchet," David continued, turning to Grizel "you'd best stay out to sea, or on the rocks with the other seals."

"I will protect myself, don't you worry," Grizel tossed her hair back from where a westerly breeze had blown it into her face. "Now it is time I was leaving. The tide will turn soon."

She helped David to his feet and insisted he lean on her until they reached his horse.

Mounting was an undignified process but she was so matter of fact about it that for once David felt neither shame nor anger. Her strength, which was indeed considerable, for all that she looked like a fragile young maiden, made the act of mounting less painful as well.

"Will I see you again?" he blurted out impulsively as she handed Pyewacket up to him.

A slow smile crossed her face. "I do have something I wish to talk to you about," she said. "I shall come to Le Bouet in Belle Grève Bay tomorrow evening at the ebb of the tide. Can you be there?"

"I will be," he promised recklessly. He would let nothing stand in his way, not even the French.

"Then go with God until we meet again, both of you," she said, and watched until David turned his horse and rode off, Pyewacket tucked inside his jacket.

6
Powder & Shot

If Majorlaine Dieudonné was worried by the fact that David had brought home a familiar and expected to conceal its presence from the French, she did not voice her fears. She accepted Pyewacket, warned him that he would have to learn to communicate his wants with a 'meow', especially when there were strangers about, and chose a new name for him. Pyewacket as a name was definitely too magical and it would be suspect to the Inquisition, who studied such things. She would call him 'Suie' which meant 'soot'.

Of far more concern to Majorlaine was something in David's attitude. That morning he had ridden away from the cottage, against her wishes, in the blackest of moods. She had worried over what he meant to do. Between the death of his fiancée and that of his father shortly after, as well as the heavy responsibility that had fallen upon him in the governance of the island and trying to cope with the French invasion, she had seldom seen him smile or laugh or act care-free as of late. And she had never seen him in such a dark frame of mind as he had been in this morning after returning from St. Peter Port and his meeting with the new commander.

She had hoped that he would find another young woman to love. There was no lack of eligible young ladies on the island but he seemed to think that his injuries had made normal social intercourse impossible for him. Only very rarely would he give into her wishes and accompany her to a dinner or a tea. Some women had reacted badly to his wounds Majorlaine admitted. They were such ninnyhamers, looking away from him or being cloyingly sympathetic. Her son had been wounded attempting to save their home from foreign invaders! He was a hero!

Majorlaine, unlike many women who did not wish to lose their son to another female, wanted a daughter-in-law badly.

Not only did she want grandchildren, but she had always longed for a daughter, someone she could share the work of the house with, as well as female interests. Their farm in Torteval parish was rather remote and she grew tried of masculine talk of farming, horses and politics and wanted someone who would be amenable to speaking of needlework, gardening and cooking and would notice that she had rearranged the parlor or put up a new paper in the upstairs hall. David and his father Nazaire were wonderful men but they were just that: men, with all the faults of their sex.

After Ghislaine's death, it had seemed as if David would never look at another woman. Of course, he had been ill and there was all the trouble with the French, but social life, even restricted as it was, had gone on and gone on without David. Majorlaine worried that he was in a fair way to becoming a hermit, a recluse, for he had spoken more than once of resigning his office and going home to the farm.

Majorlaine paused in her task. She was rubbing butter into sieved flour and salt on the white scrubbed kitchen table to make David's favorite, Guernsey *Gâche,* a light bread made with sultanas and mixed peel and little sugar. This last was fortunate, for sugar was becoming difficult to come by. The sultanas came from their own grapes

David sat in front of the fire with the cat in his lap. They had been conversing in low tones about what they might do to try and find Pyewacket's Wizard but had now fallen silent. David was almost automatically petting the cat, who had a singularly loud, contented purr.

What struck Majorlaine was a subtle difference about her son. As exhausted as he looked (and she could tell that he was in some pain from his hip and leg as well) he had a little half-smile on his face, as if he was thinking of something quite pleasant and even looking forward to something. Every once in a while he would look into the leaping flames on the hearth and his smile would broaden.

Majorlaine's heart beat a little quicker in hope and her dark eyes filled with tears. Oh, she had prayed each night to *le bon Dieu* that David wake from his lethargy and begin to live again! And something, she had no idea what, had made him smile! Somehow she did not think that it was the cat.

Colonel Fournier was quite satisfied with himself. He had been hand picked by the First Consul, Napoleon Bonaparte himself, to implement this new plan and everything that he was to do here on Guernsey was to that one end. A similar force was to occupy the larger island, Jersey, and the smaller Alderney. But he was to be supreme commander. The others would report to him. If he did well here he would be a General with a place on Bonaparte's staff.

He now studied the map on the wall above what had once been David's desk. Already his engineers had scouted likely locations for the fortifications which were to be built. Prisoners of war, most of them English, would be brought from France and made to work upon the forts and prisons. Many guns would be aimed at the Channel in hopes of blasting the British Channel Fleet from the water. Once the Channel was cleared of the English Naval presence they could begin the real business, the reason why they had returned to these islands: the invasion of England.

It had always been Bonaparte's intention to invade from Boulogne, the closest French port to England, just across the Strait of Dover, a space of only about twenty-one miles. But this had proved impossible, for all too often the weather was poor, the seas rough and the Strait heavily guarded by British ships-of-the-line.

Guernsey was further away; 30 miles west of the Normandy coast and 75 miles south of Weymouth, England. But it was ideally situated for both the new French fleet that even now was being built and commissioned in Brest, as secretly as was possible. Building was going on in Boulogne as well, invasion barges that the Channel fleet could spy upon. And Guernsey was an even better location for the new secret weapon that would bring the English to their knees.

Colonel Fournier anticipated no trouble from the *Guernaise*. They were a cowed and beaten people. Most of the men were gone, leaving an island of women, children, the elderly and cripples such as the so-called Lieutenant Governor. The residents of this island would find that he ruled with an iron hand, and the supplementing of the small

Inquisitorial order would keep them too busy trying to avoid being burned for heresy to offer him any trouble.

The Inquisition was a very useful tool. People became very afraid wherever it was established and many times betrayed one another to it as well, for the order paid lavish rewards for information about heresy and paid another reward when the heretic was condemned to burn. And if one turned in one's neighbor as a heretic perhaps one would then not be branded a heretic himself. The Colonel actually cared very little about heresy for his God was the same as that of his master and that was *la gloire* or glory. The name of Arnaud Fournier would go down in history. He saw himself in a very short time awarded with a Marshal's baton, for this plan would not, could not, fail. And Arnaud Fournier would live in fame forever as the man who conquered England.

"How well can you swim?" Grizel asked, looking at David speculatively.

"Far better than I can walk," David answered, with a rueful smile.

It was a fair night, lit by the faint light of a new moon. Belle Grève Bay was a good-sized bay, taking a large bite out of the east side of the island, to the north of St. Peter Port. Its beach was sand and rocks, with many tidal pools. And at this time of night it was deserted. Out to sea, in the stretch of water called the Little Russel between Guernsey and Herm could be seen the lights of French frigates, swinging at anchor. They were too far away to see two people on the beach, both dressed in dark clothing.

"What happned to your leg?" Grizel asked frankly.

"When the French first invaded we tried to defend ourselves and I was shot in my left hip and leg. There were still Wizard Healers on the island then, otherwise I would have lost it to amputation. I should have had more treatments but there was no one left here to do them."

Why was it so easy to speak of this to her, he wondered. He did not like to talk about his disability, even to his mother.

"I should also ask you how well you can hold your breath underwater," said Grizel.

"Quite long, actually," David said. "What is this all about, *Mam'selle* Sarchet?"

"Call me Grizel. Yes, I know that is not an island name," she said when he started to speak, "but I was named for my Scots grandmother as my mother was a Scots Selchie," she said and then bent her head as if gathering her thoughts. It was a moment before she spoke. "When you told me that there was a Witch-Sniffer coming here I was suddenly afraid. The Inquisition has done terrible things to my people. In the Mediterranean Sea. They set nets for us and for the Merfolk too. And what they do to us when we are caught does not bear thinking on. That is why we must fight back."

David blinked in surprise. "But how?" he said. "Today the French began gathering up everything that could be used as a weapon, even metal pitchforks! We are all having to go back to wooden farm implements. They are going house to house, and besides, there's no one left to fight the French. There are only the young and the old and females, and of course, useless cripples such as I."

"And Selchies and Merfolk," she corrected him. "This is our home too. And why can women not fight as well as a man?"

"But what can we fight them with?" he repeated.

"I may have the answer to that," she said. "Come, swim with me." She pulled her gown over head, revealing nothing underneath.

She was even more beautiful up close and he noticed, somewhat surprised, that she had no body hair at all.

Trying not to stare at her (she was totally unself-conscious or coy) he stripped down to his linen drawers and followed her into the water.

The water in the Channel was not truly warm this time of year and David felt the cold immediately. It was hard walking through the rocks without his cane, which he had left on shore with his clothes, but Grizel slipped a hand under his elbow, again, somehow managing not to make him feel like a cripple.

"I am going to swim rather fast once I change," she said, "so hold onto my flipper, David, and when I tell you, take a

60

deep breath. I'll try to keep you underwater as short a time as possible."

With this her outline shimmered and the lovely young woman shape-shifted into a gray seal.

They were now knee-deep in water and without hesitation David took the flipper she held out to him and fell forward into the ocean.

He was pulled through the water faster than he had ever gone, even riding a horse at full gallop. When they were a considerable distance from the shore she said "Breathe now!" and he obeyed her, drawing air into his lungs. As soon as she felt this, she took him below the surface, plunging deep.

It was dark and cold and he could see nothing. She was still swimming at top speed, her seal body designed for the maximum efficiency in the sea. David could scarcely see anything, so swift was the passage of the water. He closed his eyes and decided to be good passenger and give her as much help as he could by kicking his feet.

His lungs were ready to burst by the time they broke the surface again.

Taking deep, welcome breaths he looked about him with interest.

They were in a sea cave, the entrance to which was entirely underwater. That was all he could make out in the dark.

He still retained his hold upon Grizel and she drew him forward until he found rocks under his feet. He heard her slide from the water and then she said "Wait there. I have a lantern."

A moment later a light lit the darkness and David could see that they were in a very large cavern. The water lapped at a rock shelf on which Grizel was now standing, again in human form.

David climbed from the water and looked around. "What is this place?" The light from the lantern cast light ripples on the roof of the cave, making shadows jump and adding to the mysterious atmosphere.

"We are beneath a tiny islet," she said. "I discovered this a long time ago. It is my special place, where I come when I want to be alone. But there are things here that you will be very interested in." She took his hand and led him to a back wall where a natural door opened into yet another cave.

This one was even larger than the first. It was high and dry and as Grizel lifted the lantern David saw crates, boxes and barrels stacked up in orderly fashion.

All had the Royal seal branded upon their wooden sides.

He went forward to look more closely and saw the initials ER intertwined beneath the seal. "ER?" he questioned.

"Elizabeth Regina," Grizel answered. "This has been here since the days of Queen Elizabeth."

"What is it?" he asked, puzzled.

"Gunpowder, old fashioned muzzle loaders and shot. There are even cannon balls. There are your weapons, David! They've been here since the days of the Spanish Armada!"

"But after all of this age —" he protested. "Grizel, that is nearly three hundred years ago! Surely the damp air alone has corroded the metal and dampened the gunpowder so that it is useless!"

"My father was a Wizard, you must know," she said "and when I first found these things I brought him out here. He told me that they are under a preservation spell and they are all still as viable as they were in the days of good Queen Bess! We can use these to fight the French, don't you see? And we Sea-Folk will help all we can. I spent most of the day talking to everyone in the area, the dolphins, the Merfolk, the other Selchies. No more than you do, do we want this island and the British Isles to be conquered by the French and the Inquisition. We shall do whatever we can to help you repel them!"

Hagar was an herb mistress. She had what the country folk called 'green fingers', a natural talent for healing. Her mother had been the *drabarni*, the herb woman, of their tribe and had Hagar not ruined herself with a *Giorgio* lover, she would have more than likely inherited her mother's position.

Felix received care almost as good as that of a Wizard Healer and better than that of many a quack apothecary. Like many Romany, Hagar had a small amount of natural magics, mostly in her healing touch. Her fingers could soothe away the frequent head pain and caused the injury to heal faster than might have been expected. She gave him catnip tea for his headaches as well and lined under the mattress with gorse to keep away fever. She used chive oil on his head wound to prevent infection and saw it begin to heal neatly, cleanly and quickly.

At Rosal's insistence the very first day they found him, she gave him a gold earring and healed the resulting hole in his earlobe quickly with the talent in her fingers. No Rom would go about without a gold earring! Just as it was unlucky for a Romany woman to give birth to a child without having had her ears pierced, a Rom needed at least one earring as well. An earring would convince him that he was indeed a Romany.

Hagar still did not like this entire scheme of Rosal's. She was afraid that it would only bring ill luck upon them. Listening to this stranger talk convinced her that he was gentry, not a servant as Rosal seemed to think, or what was more likely, had talked herself into believing.

Gentry nearly always had family or friends, important people who would clap the Romany women into prison or they would be at the very least, transported. They might even end dancing in the air on the Nubbing Cheat. Hagar could almost feel the rope tightening around her neck.

But nothing could convince Rosal of her folly. Hagar had never known the girl to be so stubborn, so set on a path. She was taken with the notion of a young man of her own and especially of another child and no argument put forth by Hagar (and she had many) could convince Rosal that what she was doing was both foolish and dangerous.

One thing that Rosal said was true. Even as he began to recover, in the next few days Felix's memory was not returning. He relied on Rosal to tell him about their life and she was spinning such a fantastic blend of lies and truth, so skillfully woven, that Hagar remarked Rosal had ought to have become a storyteller, going about the countryside with a tambourine in which to collect monies from credulous *Giorgios*.

Hagar could only hope that when he was fully recovered he would remember and be forgiving of the deception. They *had* tended him and saved his life, after all.

But nothing in her experience with *Giorgios* or men had

led her to believe that anything good would come of this. Even when men professed to love a woman, they were still cruel and tore her heart out as well as bruising her body.

7
On the Isle
of Wight

It was a short flight from Devon to the Isle of Wight and as the day was proving warm, Pascoe was able to take advantage of rising thermal cells and glide over Lyme Bay, past Weymouth and Bournemouth and towards the Isle.

On the west side of the Isle of Wight stood the Needles, tall pillars of stone thrusting up into the sky, a popular sunning spot for the dragons who were employed as messengers for the Channel Fleet. No dragon could fly very far out to sea, but the Channel, so close to land and a source of firestone so necessary to dragon flight, was heavy in dragon traffic.

As Pascoe was gliding noiselessly above the sparkling blue green waters he turned his head towards the Earl and said "When I've left you and Grey in Bembridge, Richard, I shall come back here and find out what these courier dragons know. They are a gossipy lot, and they've many acquaintances amongst the Sea-Folk"

The Earl agreed to this at once for any source might yield some important information.

Pascoe followed the coast, flying up the Solent, the seaway which separated the Isle from the bulk of England and then turned south to where Bembridge lay at the estuary at the mouth of the Yar River on the east side of the Isle.

Brading Harbor was full of Naval traffic, fishing boats and small yachts. It was here that the Fleet often sheltered from the strong westerlies of the Channel and could refit as well, for boat-building and sail-making were important parts of the Isle's economy and ship's chandleries abounded.

Outside the town lay a small Dragon Port. After landing and letting his passengers disembark and the Earl's small trunk be unloaded, Pasco took off again immediately, heading back towards the Needles.

There were always hackneys available to take passengers into the town and the Earl and Greymalkin boarded one of these, directing the jarvey to take them to the Ship's Wheel, an inn much frequented by yachtsmen. Richard arranged for his trunk to be sent to the inn, as the hack was a small one.

It was still a beautiful, clear day and his lordship thought with a sudden pang of intense grief that it was not right that his grandson was not here to enjoy it. It was not natural that one outlive one's children and grandchildren. Felix's parents were both gone. Cedric, Richard's eldest son and his wife Nydia, who the Earl had loved as a daughter, had died tragically when Felix was a small boy. Reginald's father, too, was gone. Cedric's half brother, Alfred, had drunk his way into an early grave, leaving behind a mountain of debt and a wife and son, neither of whom the Earl had much use for. He considered Reginald both sly and dishonest and looked to be following in his father's footsteps as far as drink, debauchery and debt were concerned. And Reginald's mother, Devora, was a crying, clinging female who could not hold household and was taken advantage of by the servants. She lived in London, fortunately, but every week brought some tear-stained missive about a debt she could not pay or a complaint about how she had not been well-treated by persons who did not seem to know who she was. Each letter began the same way: *"You would not wish your son's widow to be treated in such fashion"*. Richard was tempted at times to ignore her letters. She was a most tiresome female, but family pride kept him from doing so and he sent draughts to cover her debts and tried to write back soothingly which was not an easy task when he would prefer to lecture her on standing on her own feet and grow some backbone.

But Reginald was another matter. He was not a middle-aged female but a young man in his prime. He showed no signs of settling to a profession, which, as he was not the heir, he needed to pursue. Since he was a Wizard, although had only barely managed to make *Magus Majori*, the Army and the Navy were out of the question. Since a Wizard had to take an oath to do no harm, military professions were largely closed to him. The military only employed Wind Wizards and Augurs and Reginald had talent for neither of these callings.

But there was still the law, the Church, the diplomatic service, or even such a mundane career as a Dust Sprinkler on the roads or employment at a retail establishment manning the scry bowls for customer orders. These last two professions were not considered gentlemanlike, but Richard felt as if he would be glad if Reginald did anything with his life other than run into debt and play the fool with expensive barques of frailty. Reginald had his own estate, a snug little property the Earl had settled upon Alfred at his son's coming-of-age, but Reginald did little with it besides run it into the ground, squeezing every groat from the land and his tenants and hosting there parties from London with a set of rackety young men and doxies, which scandalized the neighborhood. And again, family pride had prevented Richard from ceasing to pay Reginald's extensive debts. He could not bear the odium of having his own flesh and blood taken up for debt and ending in Fleet prison.

And now this unworthy young excrescence was to be heir to the ancient Earldom of Belmaray! It did not bear thinking on. Richard could have gone to his grave knowing that the heritage of Belmaray would be safe in Felix's hands, for his eldest grandson was a far cry from his cousin. Felix was a scholar, and a gentleman in the finest sense of the word. He was an accomplished Wizard as well.

Most telling of all, in the Earl's view, was that Reginald had never been chosen by a familiar. This was always a very bad sign. When Reginald was a boy he had been introduced to any number of familiars: cats, hedge hogs, ferrets, owls, and not one had chosen him. This was usually accepted to mean that the unchosen Witch or Wizard had a strong leaning towards black magic, for it was said that familiar animals could read a person's heart and soul. But Richard had been unable to discover any black sorcery or even interest in it on Reginald's part. He was a barely competent *Magus Majori* and those who embraced the Dark were generally powerful and clever *before* they were subverted by the Dark. Powerful and clever were the last two words that Richard would ever use in describing Reginald.

The Ship's Wheel was a tidy little place and from the looks of it, not inexpensive.

"I'll lay odds you will have to pay Reginald's shot, Richard," said Grey as they climbed from the hackney. "I daresay the dibs are not in tune as is usual," he added, using the cant term for being in a poor financial state. "No doubt he's told the landlord that you will cover his debts. Let's hope he as not as yet drunk the cellar dry." Greymalkin did not like Reginald in the least.

The landlord had spied the hackney cab disgorge a most important looking guest and was at the door to throw it open for Richard. With a low bow he welcomed the party of two to the Ship's Wheel, introducing himself as Josiah Small. His face fell when he saw no manservant or any luggage, but a smile crossed his features again when Richard booked a room and told him that a trunk would be arriving from the Dragon Port shortly.

"My grandson is staying here, I understand. Mr. Reginald Jourdaine?" Richard said, handing one of his visiting cards to Mr. Small.

After a quick perusal of the pasteboard a strange look crossed the landlord's face and he said "Yes, the young gentleman and his friend are here, my lord." His tone seemed to imply *"And I wish they were not!"*

"I shall be good for any bills he has run up," Richard said on a sigh. Even during a bereavement Reginald could not resist drink.

"Thank you for that, my lord, but I am not as concerned about that as I am about the incident with one of the maids. She's only sixteen, my lord, and a good girl. My maids are not available for gentlemen to meddle with. Their mothers would have my head on a pike if I allowed such goings on. The foreign gentleman seemed to think that Betsy was a slave and must do his bidding, which was that she undress and get into his bed. He became rough with her when she refused and she screamed fit to bring the house down. And it just so happened that I had an Admiral, two Captains and several Lieutenants dining in one of the private parlors and they all dashed to her rescue. It was quite a turn-up and it took the parish beadle, the Vicar, who was passing by, and the Sheriff to restore order! The damage was considerable, my lord."

"Put it on my account, landlord," said Richard resignedly. "Where is my grandson?"

"I shall show you to his private parlor, my lord," Mr. Small gave a low bow. Here was a gentleman, even if certain members of his family were not.

Reginald, known to his intimates as Reynard from an early age as his resemblance to the vulpine was pronounced, waited nervously in the private parlor, pacing up and down in an agitated fashion and running his hands through his red hair. He had to make certain that he could tell this story in a coherent fashion without tripping himself up. It had seemed so easy at first, but the longer they waited for the Earl to arrive the more Reginald remembered the stern looks his grandfather could give, looks that made him feel guilty even if he had not done anything.

Ali Amir Bahram sat by the fire, puffing on a water pipe. He felt no agitation whatever — if anything he was angry. He had wanted a woman last night and that is what female servants were for. In his own country she would have obeyed him instantly and done what he had directed her to do. Reginald informed him that here unless a female was willing, that they had the right to refuse a man's advances and he also must pay for his pleasure. Pay a woman, an inferior being, to lay down for him? The very idea was ridiculous! There were many things about England that he did not care for in the least, but since he could not go home at the moment he was here for better or worse. At least he had a plump pigeon, ripe for the plucking in Reginald. He hoped that the young fool's elderly relative would arrive shortly and loosen his purse strings. Bahram's fortunes were at low tide as well.

A knock came at the door and Mr. Small poked in his head and announced "His lordship, the Earl of Belmaray."

At last! Reginald tugged at his rather florid waistcoat, gave his ill-tied cravat a twitch and tried to summon up a suitably lugubrious expression.

The Earl entered the room, closely followed by Greymalkin.

Bahram was surprised. The Earl was not the doddering old wreck with one foot in the grave that Reginald had led him to expect. This was a strong, vigorous man with all of his wits about him. And to Bahram's eye, he glowed with magic.

After the Earl trotted a cat. Bahram did not like cats in the least. He did not like the way they looked at him, as if he was dirt beneath their paws.

This one, a gray tabby cat with white bib and paws, was no exception. He seemed to wear a sneer on his furry face.

"Grandpapa," said Reginald, bowing deeply to Richard. "I would give anything not to be the bearer of such ill news!" He remembered to speak properly, as he knew Richard despised the abbreviated speech and cant affected by the young men of Reginald's set.

"How long did you search, Reginald?" Richard demanded.

"Until we were forced to stop, sir. There was a bad blow coming and we were in danger of being swamped. The rigging of the boat was not one I am familiar with and my friend Bahram here is not used to small craft at all. Oh, I should have introduced you! Grandpapa, may I present my friend Ali Amir Bahram of Persia. Ali, my grandfather, Richard Jourdaine, Earl of Belmaray." He waved a hand towards the cat. "And his familiar Greymalkin."

Both the Earl and the cat inclined their heads and Bahram made a eastern obeisance, waving a hand from his forehead gracefully.

"Pray be seated, sir, and I shall tell you what happened," said Reginald a little nervously. "I'll ring for some sherry, shall I? Won't you make yourself comfortable and take off your flying suit?"

Greymalkin jumped to a convenient table top and said, a little sarcastically "More on Richard's bill, Reginald? From the looks of it you've been imbibing pretty freely already and I doubt it is grief that is keeping you bosky!"

Reginald flushed. Greymalkin had always been able to disconcert him. How he wished his grandfather had left the wretched beast at home! The only thing that could have been worse was if Pascoe had come along. Those draconic eyes could see deeply into one's soul.

Greymalkin looked about the room as if expecting to see someone that was not there. "Where is Pyewacket?" he asked sharply.

"He seems to have gone overboard as well," said Reginald.

Richard had shed his flying suit and draped it over the back of a chair. He sat down as the door opened and a waiter bustled in. Reginald gave the order for a tray of sherry and biscuits and coffee for Bahram. Greymalkin ordered a bowl of cream and then returned to the subject at hand. "Are you trying to tell me that Pyewacket jumped in after Felix? No familiar would have done anything so stupid! He would have raised an alarm!" he said scornfully.

"Mr. Felix Jourdaine was sitting on the deck holding the cat when we went below to seek our beds," put in Bahram smoothly. "Perhaps he was still holding the animal when he was knocked into the water."

Reginald nodded eagerly. "No doubt that was what happened, sir! We both went below to bed and left Felix and his familiar up on deck. When we awoke the boom was swinging loose and there was no sign of either of them. We had drifted off course. We really have no idea when the accident happened or where and we can only assume that he was hit by the boom. Neither one of us was on the deck when it happened. We were both sound asleep."

"In the middle of the day?" the Earl queried, a frown knitting his brow.

Reginald flushed again. "We were up late the night before and I had a little too much to drink – "

"Three sheets to the wind, no doubt," muttered Grey.

"Ali and I sat up very late talking. He is very interested in English magic and had a great many questions for me," Reginald continued.

"Then one would have assumed if he had wanted good information he would have asked Felix!" the Earl retorted. "Felix is *Magus Magistra,* after all and far more know-ledgeable than you. What I do not understand is why you were out with your cousin in the first place! When have you ever cared for one another's company or even cared that much

71

for sailing?" Reginald was a competent sailor as the entire Jourdaine family had been yachting enthusiasts for generations, but he had not possessed the passion or the skill that Felix had for the sport.

"Ali and I went out to Guernsey with a party of friends and there was a quarrel between the yacht's owner and his mistress. It was dashed uncomfortable. In a fit of temper, he abandoned us. We were stranded there. You may imagine my relief when Felix arrived," said Reginald. "what with the French coming and all. He was obliging enough to offer to take us home. Else we might have ended in a French prison!" Reginald declared.

Richard frowned again. The French retaking the Channel Islands was a complication. If Felix had indeed been picked up by another boat, perhaps a fishing boat from Jersey or Guernsey, he might even now be a prisoner of the French. Even the Merfolk or the Selchies might have taken him to one of the islands where he might have been captured.

"I am going to go out to St Catherine's Point and blow the Triton horn for Madoc," the Earl said abruptly. "If Felix was rescued by one of his folk, Madoc shall be able to tell me where they took him."

Reginald blanched. The Sea-Folk knew Felix well. "There's not much possibility of that, is there?" he asked.

"There is always that chance," said the Earl firmly as the waiter entered with the refreshments. "Neptune has commanded that his folk be on the lookout for those who go over the side of a ship and save them if at all possible. I shall not consider Felix gone until I have instituted a search amongst the Sea-Folk and questioned everyone that I can possibly talk to."

"Even the terns and the gulls may have information," said Greymalkin, after a few laps at his cream." I shall be talking to them. Pascoe is sounding out the messenger dragons."

Within a few moments Richard had downed his sherry and was gone back to the Dragon Port where he had arranged to meet Pascoe, then to fly out to the southern end of the Isle, near Niton.

"What is this about the Sea-Folk? What are they?" Bahram demanded when he was again alone with Reginald.

72

"Mermen and mermaids and the seals, the Selchies. Magical creatures, seals in the sea but on dry land they're like us," Reginald explained.

"Persia is far from the sea and we have no such creatures there," said Bahram. He picked up the elaborately decorated mouthpiece to his water pipe again. "I do not think, my dear Reynard, that your grandsire will meekly accept your cousin's death and confirm you as his heir as easily as you seemed to think. Nor is he as ancient and feeble as you led me to believe. There is a man who could very well live to be one hundred or older. And I am not a patient man. I was promised a goodly sum of money for disposing of your cousin and I cannot and will not wait forever. There is only one thing to do if we are both to prosper." He took a few long slow puffs on the water pipe and expelled the smoke in a series of perfect circles.

"What can we do?" Reginald asked in some irritation. The entire scenario had not gone as he had envisioned it. He had pictured the old man so broken by grief that he allowed him, Reginald, to orchestrate the confirmation of a new heir right away. He had not even imagined that the Earl would prove obstinate and refuse to accept his cousin's death. The inquiries of which he was speaking could take months, even years!

Bahram took another long draught of smoke that was laced with hashish. His features took on what Reginald privately termed his 'devilish' look.

"Why, we shall have to kill the Earl as well," he said as if it were the most reasonable thing in the world.

8

The Prince of the Sea

Pascoe was waiting for them at the Dragon Port, enjoying a dragon-sized cup of tea and several enormous sweet rolls.

The courier dragons had heard nothing, he reported. Due to the severity of the two-day storm which had just ended late last night, they had not been out and about. There had been severe lightning which had driven them to the shelters. Lightning was the thing a dragon feared most. A strike meant a dragon could explode in a ball of flame from the ignition of the gasses in his or her flight cavities.

But, he added, the couriers had promised to keep their ears and eyes open.

"The French have taken the Channel Islands again," said Pascoe gloomily as Richard and Greymalkin waited for him to finish his snack. "It is all that the couriers talked about. Do you think that Felix could have been picked up by the French, Richard?"

"I hope not," said the Earl shortly. As a Wizard Felix would be turned over to the Inquisition, subdued by Cold Iron and die a horrible fiery death, most likely after torture. Richard would prefer his grandson's death by drowning, a far kinder death than at the hands of the Inquisition.

"They didn't waste any time, did they?" said Greymalkin sarcastically, his tail lashing. "Why did we not send troops to the Islands, to prevent such a thing and to support the local militia? The whole business is very ill-managed, if you ask me! I wonder that the Channel Islands don't give up on the British Isles since we treated them so ill. They were virtually left to themselves with few defenses."

"And the French were back in the Islands in no time flat," said Pascoe. "Our Ambassador left Paris on the 13th, war was declared on the 18th in all Six Parliaments and here it is the 22nd and the French are already back in possession. That argues that this was planned long before talks broke down."

"Perfidious!" snarled Greymalkin.

Richard always found it rather amusing that his dragon and his familiar were better read and more knowing of political matters than some of his neighbors in Devon. They both were avid readers. Richard always shared the *Wizards' Times* with Grey and gladly paid extra for a special dragon-sized version of the news-sheet.

Pascoe finished his meal and was ready to fly. He would not need to chew more firestone until they left for Devon. He told Richard that one of the courier dragons had offered him a sleeping place at the Courier's large dragon pen, where there were both shelters and sand for basking. Greymalkin, of course, would share Richard's room and bed. With everyone thus properly disposed of, they were ready to lift off.

St. Catherine's Point was at the bottom of the Isle, its southernmost point, and jutted out into the Channel. On St. Catherine's Hill stood an ancient light house, built in 1323, called St. Catherine's Oratory, locally known as 'the Pepper-pot'. It was the second oldest lighthouse in Britain; only the Roman-built light at Dover was older. The Point was very often very foggy, so it was perhaps not the best location for a lighthouse, but today the sky and sea were as blue as lapis-lazuli and sparkling clear, as it was so often after a violent storm.

The lighthouse stood on the hill atop the chalk down, also called St. Catherine's Down. Greymalkin grumbled to himself that the residents might have shown a little more originality and imagination in naming the geographic locations hereabouts.

The Down measured 778 feet at its highest elevation, between the towns of Niton and Chale, and fell in chalky cliffs to the sea, where there was a beach of sand and rocks, narrow at high tide.

Pascoe was able to land on the beach and waded out into

the water a little ways to save Richard having to go out into the cold water. Only at extreme high tide could a Merman like Madoc approach the shore, and as they needed to converse, Richard could do so more comfortably from dragon-back.

Dragons could swim and even float if they had enough dragon gas built up, but many of them were not overly fond of water; it depended on the breed. Pascoe's breed, the Cornish Copper, happened to be one of those quite at ease in the water, although for long immersion even he liked to have a dragon float, which was a flotation device made of inflated sheep hides upon which a dragon could rest his bulk and be buoyant.

The Earl had taken the immense conch shell that served as a Triton horn from a pocket on the saddle. As soon as Pascoe had settled firmly in the water, he raised it to his lips and blew a long, rather haunting call sounding much like a fog horn. He waited a few moments and blew a short blast and then another long one.

This was the signal by which he had always called his old friend, Madoc, the Prince of the Channel, who ruled here with Neptune as his overlord.

Richard, or so it seemed, had always known Madoc. When the Earl was but a boy he had met the then young Merman, much his same age, stranded in a shallow tidal pool by a rogue wave. It was due to Richard that the Merman had not dehydrated and died. Richard had used his cloak to drag Madoc back to the sea and thereby saved his life. They had been fast friends ever since.

A few moments passed and then from the ocean, with a huge arc of sea water a tall form burst from the sea.

If Madoc had been a man and walked upon two legs, he would have been almost seven feet tall. He had a broad, bare chest and a head of now white hair, tinged with green and a full beard, neatly trimmed. His eyes were sea-green and his head and profile were like a fine Roman coin. About his neck was a golden scallop shell edged with pearls which was the sign of his office, while a narrow gold diadem sat above his brow. A gold armlet circled each of his well-developed biceps and in his left hand he bore a trident. His vertical tail was of green scales, ending in an immense fan shape, with another fin on his posterior and two additional, small fins on each side of his lower body. Since he was of royal blood, gold lined the edge of each scale.

The Merman grinned with pleasure when he saw who had summoned him. "Well met, Richard, old friend!" he said in a deep booming voice. "And Pascoe too! And is Greymalkin in that basket as well?"

"I'll stay in here where I am in no danger of falling into the sea, thank you, Madoc," came the familiar's voice from the closed basket. Greymalkin disliked water even more than most cats.

"What brings you here to my domain?" the Merman said, with a chuckle at the familiar.

The Earl saw no reason to not give the truth with no bark on it. "Felix has gone overboard," he said shortly. "I need to know if any of your people, the Selchies or the dolphins have seen aught of him."

Madoc was shocked. "Felix gone overboard? A fine sailor such as he and an excellent swimmer also, has gone over the side of his boat? Richard, does he not bespell himself to breathe underwater each time he is out upon the waves?"

"He's always had enough sense to do that," agreed Richard. "But my nephew, Reginald, who was on the yacht with him, seems to think he was struck by a boom and might have been unconscious."

"In which case," said Madoc thoughtfully, "being bespelled he might not have drowned, but he could have been carried a long ways away by the tide. It is very strong here in the Channel, particularly at this time of year. When did this happen, in human terms?"

"On the 19th."

"Just before the storm," The Merman shook his head. "My own court has seen naught of him, Richard. We all know him. He would have been brought to my palace where, with his breathing spell, he would have been safe until the storm passed."

The Earl's face fell but Madoc held up a hand. "There is a good possibility that someone else, not of my court, picked him up. It is the time of the annual migration, you know, and the Channel is full of Sea-Folk moving between their winter and summer homes. Many of them are on their way to the Orkneys, Sule Skerry, Shetland and the Hebrides, to Ireland

and the Western Isles. Since a bad storm was coming they might have decided to take him along with them. Or they might have put him on a friendly shore if he was injured. Since many of my people pay little attention to human affairs, if he was swept to France they might have put him ashore there, not knowing that your nations are at war. I shall send out inquiries at once, but it will take some time, especially as many of the Sea-Folk are still in transit."

Merpeople used dolphins or sea-horses, the large half horse, half fish creatures so common near the Isle of Man, as couriers between their various courts, for each section of the ocean was ruled by a Prince who had sworn fealty to King Neptune. The King spent half the year in the Atlantic and the winter in the Pacific. These sea kingdoms were roughly divided in much the same geographical designations given them by man. There were five kingdoms about the British Isles: the Channel, the North Sea, the Celtic Sea off Wales and Cornwall, the Irish Sea and the Norwegian Sea to the extreme north. The difference was that no human could pronounce the names the Sea-Folk had given these regions.

"I am most afraid of the Inquisition, Madoc," said Richard in worried tones. "If he were left on a French shore or taken from the sea by a French frigate ..."

Madoc's face darkened to a scowl. "The Inquisition!" he said and shook his trident angrily. "No one is safe from them! My people have been suffering terribly from them in the Mediterranean. The Princes of the various regions of the Mediterranean, those of the Aldoran Sea, the Balearic Sea, the Adriatic, the Tyrrhenian, the Ionian Sea, the Sea of Crete, the Aegean and even the Bay of Biscay had a Congress to which I was also invited as Europe intrudes upon my kingdom. What I heard there was horrible!" His frown grew deeper. "They are setting nets for us now, not content just to torture and torment their own kind any longer! They have declared our kind and the Selchies, the sea-horses, the Tritons, the sea-nymphs and the nereids and all of the sea-folk an abomination in the eyes of God! Who do they think created us?"

"The Inquisition grows even stronger," said Pascoe sadly. "We first thought, when the Revolution took place in France and religion was banished, that it might die out or at least lose some of its power. But the First Consul of France has invited them back in. He courts the favor of the Roman Pope, who is a supporter of the Inquisition."

"And now it is a danger to everyone, not merely to the magical human kind!" said Madoc harshly. "That is why I have made a significant decision and the other Princes support me in this. Even Neptune has given his permission. We are going to help rid the Channel Islands of the French."

Richard looked surprised. Other than saving the drowning, or guiding a ship of any nationality in peril to safety perhaps the Sea-Folk had always made it a point to remain out of human affairs.

Particularly around the British Isles and in the Aegean where the Greeks had no Inquisition or ban on magic, they were quite friendly to man and it was not unusual for human children on the coasts of the Six Nations of the British Isles to have Merchildren, Selchies and other Sea-Folk as playmates and form friendships, as Richard had, that lasted into adulthood. But most Sea-Folk cared little for human wars and politics. They stayed away from Naval battles, invasion forces or other conflicts. That was land business, not that of the sea. Indeed, many Sea-Folk would prefer that man remain on land to fight his wars.

"What shall you do?" Richard asked.

"There is a Selchie from Sark who came to us with this idea," said Madoc. "She has access to weaponry and is in touch with the humans of the Islands. There is a meeting in two days time for both Sea-Folk and humans to decide what we shall do and how and when to do it. She has information that a Senior Witch-Sniffer is coming from the Papal Court in Rome. This is the worst possible news for it is the Witch-Sniffers who have turned their attention to us, Richard. She is quite correct; we *have* to fight back. If we can at least return them to the Continent where they belong! They are far too close to the British Isles! If the French conquer the Six Nations we shall be forced to abandon our homes here. We have lived here and been happy since out remote ancestors first became sentient, at about the same time as did humans. Nor do we want to see our many human friends enslaved or put in the fires."

Richard was deeply moved that the Sea-Folk would give

up their long neutrality and help in this war. "Thank you!" he said to his friend and leaned down from the saddle to shake Madoc's hand with his. "Call upon me for any help that you need."

"And Richard, I shall not forget about Felix. I am more than fond of him, as you know. He is like one of our own. The minute I return to my palace I shall send out messengers, you may be assured of that. Even if he is drowned we shall find his body and return it to you for your burial rites. One way or the other, I promise you that you shall know his fate," Madoc assured his human friend. A promise from one of the Sea-Folk was as good as an oath.

With this he bade them goodbye and disappeared beneath the waves.

Romany law required that a dead person's bed linens, eating utensils, clothing and other personal possessions be burned upon his death, even the *vardo* or tent.

Save for the *vardo*, Rosal had obeyed this law. Her *cumpania*, her clan, would have been horrified to know that she had not burned the *vardo*, for this would tie Sylvester's spirit to the earth. Rosal had seen no sign of his spirit. But most of her *cumpania* had left the island before Sylvester had met his fate. Only her father had remained behind, for as headman of the *cumpania* it was up to him to see that everyone got away safely. The very next day after Sylvester's death, Rosal had taken in Hagar and her father had broken with her, leaving her behind, but expecting her to follow custom, after sitting with the body of her husband for the requisite time, and burn the *vardo*. Defiantly, she was glad that she had not done so. If Sylvester's spirit was still tied to the earth he deserved it.

But of course this meant that she had no dishes or pots to cook her new Rom's food in, as a man's food had to be cooked separately from a woman's, just as his laundry had to be done separately. It was the *lies prala,* the law. And when her Rom was able to rise from his bed he would need clothing and his own dishes. Right now he had but the trousers she had found him in. And she had sacrificed some of her own dishes for him, which was in actuality breaking the law.

Hidden in the floor of the *vardo* was a secret stash of coins. These too had been Sylvester's and Rosal had discovered them by accident. There was a small amount of them, both English coins and the Island currency as well, both of which were legal tender here.

Three days after she had brought Felix to the *vardo* Rosal took several coins from the hidden cache while he was asleep and Hagar was outside at the fire. She had already dipped into them to buy him a razor and shaving soap and his own towel.

She put them in the deep pocket of her skirt taking a last look at Felix. He was sleeping peacefully, without the frown between his eyebrows that told of pain. The more he slept, the better, Hagar had explained. Sleep would speed the healing.

Rosal wanted him well. She was afraid that the French had returned after seeing that ship on the night of the storm and she wanted a protector. But even more than that she wanted him in her bed, to give her another child. Her arms ached for a child again. For a Romany woman there were every few things worse than being childless and Sylvester had denied her this right, again, against the law. It was bad enough that she had been so old (sixteen!) when she had married, for most girls married at thirteen and had a child within a year. Other women in her *cumpania* had looked down on her for being such an elderly *boria,* a bride, and taking two years to conceive a child and become a *daj,* when it was well known that Sylvester was a lusty man who had filled his first wife's womb with no less than four sons in six years. It was just bad luck that the first wife had died in birthing the last one, who also had not lived and that one of the boys had died in early infancy.

So for now there were only two in Rosal's entire *cumpania.* But it warmed her heart to think that there would now be three and perhaps more.

She went outside into a warm, beautiful spring day. Hagar, as usual, huddled over the fire, shawl tight about her shoulders.

"He is sleeping," Rosal announced. "I am going to walk to the farm and see if the lady has any work for me. If she cannot pay me in coin perhaps she will pay me in eggs or milk."

"Take the eggs and milk," said Hagar. "He could use the strength," she added a little sourly.

"Don't you like him, Hagar?" Rosal inquired. "You must learn to call him by name, else he will find it strange."

Hagar gave a short, mirthless laugh. "That is not all he will find strange!" she said. "Rosal, it is obvious to me that you have not thought this out properly! He is a *Giorgio!* He will not know our customs or our tongue. How can you explain that away?"

"That he was one of the ones whom the *Gajé* stole away when his parents died to put in their church schools, of course! But he wanted to be a true Romany and so ran away!" said Rosal triumphantly.

Hagar threw up her hands. The girl had thought of everything!

Calling Chavé to her, Rosal left for the farm which lay a mile or so away. The distance was nothing to her as she had walked much further many a time.

The farm was called *Les Huit Lapins* and was farmed, now, by only *Madame* Marie Brehaut and her young daughter Joisaine. Before the French had stolen all the men away Madame's husband, Eudes, and their three sons, Evrard, Gautier and Gilles, had all worked there, as well as several hired men.

Madame seemed always willing to hire Rosal for nearly any task and when short of coin to pay her, was generous with food in lieu of money. She also, every autumn, allowed Rosal and Hagar to glean what they could from the fields after the harvest. Rosal had been paid, in the past, with bacon, grain, honey, apples, and fruit and vegetables as well as dairy goods.

But there was little or no work over the winter. Every year that the men were gone the island's economy suffered and coin became scarcer.

Why the farm was called 'The Eight Rabbits' no one knew any more. It had been called so forever. The oldest part of the house, a two story, plastered and white-washed affair covered in flowering vines, dated, the parish priest, (a very learned man) had said, back to the time when the Islands were part of the Duchy of Normandy, hundreds of years ago.

Mullioned windows stood open to the fine day and the door into the kitchen, a half door, had the top standing open. From inside came the aroma of baking bread and another delicious scent. In appreciation, Rosal took a deep breath of the wonderful smell.

The *Gajé* liked their privacy and as she had been taught, Rosal knocked on the door frame.

"See who it is, Joisaine!" came *Madame's* voice.

A few moments later the girl Joisaine came to the door and greeted Rosal. "*Maman* and I were wondering when you would come, Rosal," she said. "There is much work to be done and we need your help."

She spoke in the Guernsey dialect which was a form of Norman French. Since Rosal's people had been here since her grandparents' time, she had grown up speaking it, in addition to English and Romani.

Joisaine was now nearly eleven and she had begun to get tall. She had the dark hair and eyes so typical of her Norman background and her brown curls were worn cut quite short. Since the men had been taken away she had worked on the land and found wearing her hair this way and working in her youngest brother's cast-off clothing of linen trousers and a smock frock far easier than in skirts.

"*Maman*, it is Rosal!" she called back over her shoulder, opening the bottom door for the Gypsy girl. She bent to greet Chavé, who had always liked the girl and now licked her enthusiastically, making Joisaine laugh.

Madame, a small, round, busy women in a blue dress covered in a spotless white apron and a crisp cap on brown braids wound around her head, bustled forward. "Rosal!" she said, sounding pleased. "I am glad you have come! We have weeding to do, plants to get in, and sowing and digging. We can truly use you! But I shall have to pay you largely in produce as coin is increasingly scarce these days."

Rosal genuinely liked these *Gajé*. They never made her feel inferior. They invited her to sit at their table and eat with them and they worked as hard as they expected her to. When *Madame* paid her with a basket of food it was always good quality and generous.

"I will be glad to have the food, *Madame*," said Rosal.

Madame Brehaut looked at her critically. "Yes, you look as if you need it. It was a hard winter, *non?* Come, I've just taken a loaf from the oven and there is hot soup. You shall tell us what you did this winter while we eat and then we shall talk about what needs to be done."

Before she had become outcast, and *mahrime*, unclean, Rosal would have never eaten food prepared by the Gajé or sat at table with them. Such was against the law. But such mattered no longer and besides, she was hungry.

Rosal sat down to a large bowl of thick and rich beef soup with potatoes, carrots, and leeks. *Madame* had several cold frames in her kitchen garden where these root vegetables grew all winter. The bread, made with honey from the hives of *Les Huit Lapins,* was sweet and crusty.

"I married again, *Madame,*" Rosal said when the first pangs of hunger were satisfied. "My new Rom is young and strong and he will be ready to work for you too. But he had a fall on the shore and is recovering now." She took care to speak properly, as her mother had taught her. The *Gajé* treated you better when you spoke nicely and politely and kept a beggarly whine from out of your voice.

"*Félicitation,*" said *Madame* sincerely. "You are too young to be without a husband, particularly with these French around again!" she added bitterly. Earlier today they had been visited by a French troop who had taken the two guns of the household which were elderly pieces used by her husband and sons for hunting birds and vermin. They had also taken the metal pitchforks, the small plow and the metal harrow. "Work will be harder this year, Rosal, for we shall have to use the old wooden implements," *Madame* Brehaut said, explaining what the French had taken.

"*Maman,*" Joisaine interrupted "if Rosal's new husband is young will the French not take him for the Army?"

"The army does not want us Romany," said Rosal and *Madame* nodded in agreement. Gypsies reacted badly to army discipline and usually ended in deserting, fading from sight so efficiently that they were never found. They were far more trouble than they were worth, for, as well, many of the other men would not accept serving with a Gypsy.

"As soon as your Rom is recovered, bring him around. There is more than enough work for everyone," said *Madame.*

That was another thing Rosal liked about *Madame*. She tried to use the proper terms when talking about the Romany.

Rosal finished her soup and said "*Madame,* my Rom needs some clothing. He has little. Do you know of a place that I can get second-hand things and some pots and pans as well perhaps even some plates and cups? Perhaps in the town?"

"How big is he?" *Madame* wanted to know.

Rosal indicated with her hands how tall and wide he was. She had studied him minutely to make certain that she knew.

Madame and Joisaine exchanged glances. "About the size that my Gilles was when he left," Marie said. "I have things that you may have, Rosal, for they will no longer fit Gilles when he returns." Unsaid was the thought that she perhaps had ought to have said "*If* he returns". Nothing had been heard from any of the Brehaut men since they had been taken away.

All the Brehaut men were very large and Gilles would be no exception. Madame was certain that he would never again have any use for the clothes he wore when he was but seventeen.

"I also have old things, kitchen things, I was planning to dispose of. If they are not too worn and they are what you can use, you can have those as well," said *Madame* Brehaut.

"Oh, thank you, *Madame!*" said Rosal in gratitude. She would have to spend none of her stash. What good friends these *Gajé* were! And this good fortune only confirmed what she firmly believed: finding the man was *meant* by fate. He was *meant* to be hers and to give her a child.

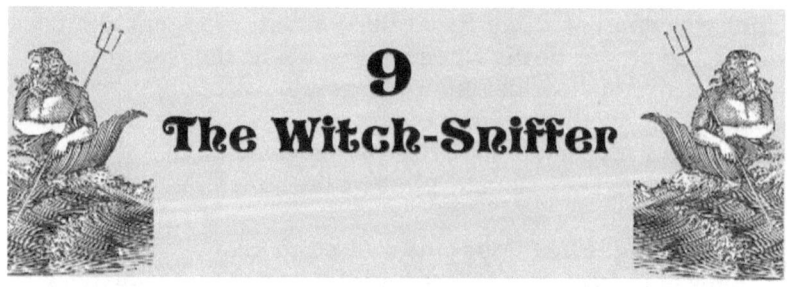

9
The Witch-Sniffer

Running before a brisk wind, a French frigate headed towards St. Peter Port from the south. She was a floating fortress with three decks of guns and carronades on the deck. From her mizzenmast flew the *Tricoleur* and below it, the flag of the Inquisition: white, bordered with purple and a large black cross on a background of leaping flames.

She was the man o' war *Acadie*, upon a very special mission. At Citavecchia, port of Rome in Italy she had taken on her main passenger, a Senior Witch-Sniffer, and had boarded him, his assistant, the torturer, and their complement of several Junior Witch-Sniffers and instruments of heretical persuasion stowed below in the hold.

At the bow, on the Marine deck some thirty feet above the waterline stood the Senior Witch-Sniffer, gazing toward their destination. The Captain had sought him out and kindly informed him that Guernsey should be sighted quite soon. It had been a safe voyage; they had met no English ships, slipping past Gibraltar and through the Bay of Biscay without incident.

But like most people, the Captain had shown little inclination to linger in the company of Father Guenaël Maël, the Witch-Sniffer.

Maël was a man of medium height, rather stocky as to frame and giving the impression of a coiled serpent, ready to strike. He was completely bald, the only hair on his head a small beard that circled his down-turned mouth. A small gold cross, a gift from the Pope, hung in his left ear. His deep blue eyes glowed the light of fanaticism under heavy brows.

He stood now with his legs braced wide against the movement of the ship and his arms crossed over his chest. He wore a simple black cassock, with a heavy silver cross about his neck. A collar ornament of a small enameled flame indicated his status in the hierarchy of the Inquisition.

A Witch-Sniffer was a good deal more that the name indicated. True, they were persons who had the ability to sniff out magic, a major heresy, but they dealt with all sorts of heresies as well from people fallen away from the true beliefs, who dared such pernicious things as reading the Bible in their native language, or not attending enough of the *auto de fés,* to wrangling with evil creatures such as black cats and dragons.

Maël was looking forward to this assignment with keen anticipation. He had read all of Amaury de Ollivier's reports and thought that the man had not done nearly enough to suppress the heresy that was so rife in these islands.

In an audience with the Pope, Puis VII, the Holy Father had exhorted Maël to do his best to not only rid the Islands of any and all magical persons and creatures, but to bring the islanders back into the embrace of the Roman church. Irish Catholicism was not true Catholicism. These people had been led far astray. Now that they were to be a part of France again they must be given every opportunity to repent and recant their misbegotten faith. If they did not, Maël knew what to do.

In his youth (Maël was a Breton, born and bred) he had fallen under the influence of a Dominican priest in his small village. This priest, Father Pierrepont, had tirelessly hunted heretics, particularly those of a magical nature. Brittany, considered a Celtic country, was one of the former hotbeds of magic and there were still those who practiced this heresy in the shadows, in great secrecy. Stone menhirs dotted the land and resisted all attempts of the Church to pull them down. It was well known that Witches still danced in these stone circles, doing their unhallowed rites and indulging in naked orgies of sensuality. Somewhere off the coast on a mythic island was thought to be a haven of Druids. All efforts to find this island and scour it of Satanic influences had failed.

Had Maël not lost his father, a wise and tolerant man, at a very early age, he might not have come so deeply to be swayed by Father Pierrepont and his life might have taken a different turn altogether. But the young Maël was just what Father Pierrepont wanted in a disciple. By the time he was sixteen Maël had already committed his life to the Dominican order and soon after, was noticed by the officials of the Inquisition and offered a minor post.

Mael had proved to the Inquisition that he was both dedicated and ruthless for he had tuned his own mother over to the Inquisition.

One evening he had seen her leave the house. Following her, he had seen her dance naked beneath the moon, with other village woman, other Witches. The very next morning, he had denounced her and had seen her, and the others who had danced with her, burn.

He felt no guilt over this at all, only shame that his mother had been a Witch. He could only expiate this sin and shame by hunting down and burning as many of these magicals as was possible.

Maël had been instrumental in pushing the Inquisition towards its present persecution of magical creatures in the sea. Once, on a ledge overlooking the Adriatic Sea, he had watched with deep disgust while a family of Merfolk had frolicked in the sea below. The bare-breasted females, the lusty males, and above all, the half-beast aspect of a human's body ending in a fish's tail had offended him deeply. Surely these were creatures of Satan, unnatural and perverse! He had read old books telling how the Mermaids lured sailors to their doom. Had he but known it the books were mistaken, written out of ignorance. There had been things in the sea that had preyed upon sailors, the Kraken amongst others, but they had been long controlled by Neptune.

But Maël now saw himself as being upon a Holy Crusade to make the waters safe, removing the scourge of these minions of the Devil which included the Selchies, the Nereids, the Tritons, everything that lived in the sea that parodied mankind.

He firmly believed in the purpose of the penalties and punishments of the Inquisition as published in 1578, laid out for Inquisitors: *"Quoniam punitio non referur primo & per se in correctionem & bonum eius qui punitur, sed in bonum publicum ut alij terreantur & malis committendis avocentur...."* *"...for punishment does not take place primarily, per se, for the correction and good of the person punished, but for the public good in order that others may become terrified and weaned away from the evils they would commit..."*

The person being punished was usually beyond all hope of redemption. For instance, a magician could not be saved. Their very being was so intertwined with the Lord of Darkness that there was no hope of extricating it from the evil one's toils. Only the fires could bring purification. Mages were tortured to give up the names of others who shared their sin.

With Maël traveled his chief torturer, Narcisse Roux. They had worked together for many years now and very few were as skilled as Roux in obtaining a confession from heretics. Some said he enjoyed his work too much but Maël dismissed this charge for the foolishness it was. A torturer had to be immune to feelings of sympathy or compassion. After a particularly taking female was put to the question she was often passed man to man, but as she was by then condemned to burn, it seemed fair enough, for her sin of fornication was about to be punished as well as for her other sins. Maël had found that letting the men have a woman kept them well in line. They all crowded into the room to watch her being tortured, which was done while she was naked, of course, as it was his job to search her for Witch Marks, perhaps an extra teat where imps could suckle, not always found on the breast, or a mark that indicated that the Devil had branded her as his own. It was necessary that the entire body be rigorously searched and there must be witnesses to this process, hence the Junior Witch-Sniffers and lately, the presence of French troops, at a questioning.

Neither Roux nor two of the three Junior Witch-Sniffers were priests. They were employed by the Church but had never taken vows. In the Inquisition's twisted logic, it was therefore acceptable, even desirable, for such good Christians to fornicate with a Witch as it was part of her punishment.

Yes, he looked forward to this assignment. It could not help but add luster to his career. He anticipated the fires that would burn so brightly, the smell of roasting flesh, the screaming of the condemned as they burned alive...and this was nothing as to the fires that would inundate the land when they conquered the British Isles, perfidious Albion, with its plethora of Witches, Wizards and Druids and magical creatures of all descriptions, all of which would be purged.

For the first time since he had been injured, Felix awoke felling slightly better. The headache was a dull throbbing in his skull, not the overwhelming pain it had been and he became aware that he was actually hungry.

He seemed to be quite alone in the *vardo*. By the way the sun came in through the stained glass over his bed he assumed it to be late afternoon.

The incongruity of this suddenly struck him. How could he know that the slant of the sun meant late in the day but not know his own name, nor have any memory of his wife and their life together?

For no memory had come back at all. The huge blank wall was still there. Any attempt to cast his mind back ended in terrible, searing pain in his head.

On the few occasions that he had been awake he had listened eagerly to Rosal, trying to make some sense out of what she had told him. Sometimes it had been difficult even to retain a hold upon what she had said. But each time he woke he had remembered more, but only of what she had informed him.

She had told him that they had married in the early winter in a Romany ceremony, jumping the broom. They were very happy, she had said. She admitted that she had been married before. She had been a widow and there had been a child that had died. She was hoping for a new baby. There had been some trouble with a group she called her *campania* and now they were a *campania* of three: himself, herself and Hagar. And when the babies began to come ...

Surely he would feel more towards her if they were as deep in love as she claimed? He thought she was very pretty but he felt no stirring of passion, but perhaps that was because he was so ill. He was very grateful to her and to Hagar, for their care of him. Rosal cheerfully and readily performed all the most personal tasks for him with no embarrassment. That argued long intimacy.

He was not precisely certain what relationship Hagar was to either of them. Rosal addressed the older woman by name, not calling her mother or grandmother or aunt.

Perhaps Hagar was his mother?

He was still trying to puzzle this out, and fingering the earring that adorned his left ear. Every time he had turned his head he had been aware of the strange feeling of it.

The door to the *vardo* opened and Hagar entered. She carried a steaming pot in her hand and said rather brusquely "Good, you're awake. It's time for your catnip tea. I'll help you sit up but it's about time you started feeding yourself."

This operation was not as excruciating as it had been and it was almost comfortable, propped against the pillows with the light coming in. Hagar bent over the end of the bed and flung open one of the stained glass panels. A fresh breeze smelling of damp earth and growing things wafted in and Felix could now see the branches of trees, covered in greenery and swaying in the light wind.

"Let me see that head of yours," Hagar ordered and he obediently bent his head so that she could unwrap the bandages and look at the head wound. Even this process was not as painful as it had been.

"The hair near the wound has gone white," she said, pulling a pot from her pocket and unscrewing the lid. This was the herbal potion that she treated the wound with three times a day.

"Am I that old?" he said in surprise.

She almost smiled. "No. I've seen it happen before when there is a shock .You'll have a white streak from front to back."

"Like a skunk," he said without thinking.

Hagar stared at him. "A what?"

"A skunk- " he repeated.

She shook her head."I don't know what you mean."

Suddenly, in almost a panic he realized that he did not know either. The wall had gone up again and whatever he meant by 'skunk' it was now gone. "Oh God, I can't remember what I mean!" he said, and put his face in his hands.

"You'll remember in time," Hagar said. "Drink your tea." Her voice was matter of fact. "Come on now, drink the tea before it is cold."

Felix looked up, putting his hands down on the quilt that covered him. "Are you my mother?" he asked abruptly.

Hagar nearly spilled the tea. Suddenly, painfully, she

91

remembered her son, the one who had so easily shed her, ashamed of the ignorant old Egyptian, as he had called her. Her son, Charles, the *Giorgio* name given him by his father. Charles would now be eighteen, a little younger than this one. But Felix did not look at her in contempt and coldness, but in anxiety that spoke of a hope that it might be so.

For the first time since Rosal had brought him to the *vardo* her heart was touched. She saw him as a person, not a problem and her face softened as she said, "No, I am kin to no one. Rosal took me in when no one else would, when I was dying out on the road for breaking the law and my *cumpania* would not take me back. That was three years ago." She handed him the tea as she spoke.

"Before Rosal and I were married?" He sipped at the catnip brew.

"Yes," she said shortly. She could have very easily claimed him as her son, just as Rosal had claimed him as her Rom, but a deep core of honesty within her would not let her do this. He was being fed enough untruths.

"Why would your people not take you in?" he asked then.

Briefly, she explained how great a crime it was for a Romany woman to sleep with a *Giorgio* and have a half-breed child with him. It seemed rather ironic that this, her great crime, was now what Rosal proposed to repeat without even the excuse of overwhelming passion.

He frowned as he listened. She used Romany words as she talked and he had to ask her to translate. He was not stupid; she could see that he was wondering why, if he was Romany as they told him, why did he not understand Romany words.

This question was trembling on his lips as the door flew open and Rosal, with Chavé at her heels, staggered in with a huge basket from which good smells were coming. Hagar felt her mouth water. They had grown tired of seaweed soup and by the sudden eager look on Felix's face Hagar could see that he was hungry as well.

Rosal put the basket on the table. "I worked all day and *Madame* paid me with good things!" she said, delving into the basket. "Beef soup, a cooked chicken, eggs and milk and cheese and fresh bread, even some new peas and some potatoes from her root cellar! There is an apple pastry too, made from dried apples! When she heard that you were ill, Felix, she insisted that you needed good food." She reached into the bottom of the basket and pulled out some seeds in twists of paper. "Look, Hagar! we can start our own garden! She has promised me some onion and potato sets as well!" she added in elation.

"You worked for this?" Felix said in an odd voice. "Where?"

"At the farm," Rosal answered. "I picked stones and weeded and we set out vegetables ..."

"You were doing hard physical labor?" he said, horrified. "And I am lying here like a fine lady, letting my wife go out and ruin her hands and health – "

"But you are sick!" she said and picked up a piece of bread, tearing into it with her sharp little teeth.

"I am much better. I shall be the one who goes out and works. I shall get up tomorrow and look for work," he said determinedly.

"There's enough work at the farm for both of us," said Rosal. She could not understand why he was upset, but he clearly was. Sylvester had been glad to live off her earnings.

"There is no need for you to work at all," he said rather stiffly. "I can support both of you."

Both of the women stared at him. "But Romany women always do the work. Our Roms are busy with other things," said Hagar. Her *Giorgio* lover, too, had not worked at all for he was a gentleman.

"I am not the sort of parasite who would live off the labors of a female!" he said in outrage. "Every feeling revolts!"

"Well," said Rosal reasonably, "We'll both go to work for *Madame*. There is plenty of work and we'll make twice as much in wages!"

He continued to frown though, even as they ate a good supper of soup, bread and cheese. As Rosal fed some of the chicken to Chavé she was wondering what was bothering him, why was he so upset.

And Felix, even though he was hungry, found his appetite fading as he began to wonder about himself. Was he the sort of despicable man who would let a frail young wife go out to earn his keep?

Their reaction seemed to indicate that this was what they were used to. The thought sickened him however. If he *had* been that sort it was about to change.

10
The Don

Aurelius Bretton looked at his beloved books, scattered all over the floor, wantonly and unnecessarily desecrated by alien hands, hands that did not appreciate the accumulated knowledge of centuries within those calfskin bindings.

The French had arrived this morning, looking for weapons. They had torn the house apart, even to pulling out all the books and searching behind them and all without offering to clean up after themselves. Of course they had found nothing. Aurelius had no weapons of any sort.

Aurelius had hoped that his little house, *Trois Chiminées,* Three Chimneys, was far enough out of the way to be disregarded by the French. He had had no contact with the conquerors when Captain Dubois had been in charge. They were not interested in an elderly man in a Bath chair who had only an equally elderly manservant.

This new commandant, Colonel Fournier, was a different sort all together. Life, which had been difficult enough under the previous occupation forces, was going to be even more so.

On the desk in front of him was a copy of the new rules and regulations for the inhabitants of the island, given to Aurelius that morning by a supercilious young corporal. According to this document, the French had the right of search and seizure at ant time, for any reason. Twice weekly assemblies, on Tuesdays and Thursdays, to which everyone must go, would be held in front of the parish church of Castel and all persons accounted for. This would be a great hardship for Aurelius. Arthritis made him house-bound and struggling in and out of the pony cart from his chair was going to be nearly impossible.

All fishing boats were to be moved to St. Peter Port and their comings and goings would be strictly regulated. There were to be no gatherings of more than three persons unless permission was granted by the newly appointed parish commanders. French officers would be garrisoned in homes deemed suitable and the homeowner would bear the expense of having the troops quartered there.

At least they would be spared that, Aurelius thought, grateful for the one small favor. His humble little cottage had no extra room at all. There were but two rooms above stairs and both were small, under a sloping roof with a tiny window each, amid the tiled roof. Below stairs was a large drawing room that also served as a dining room, and opened into the kitchen, which, save for his library, was the largest room in the house.

He himself slept in an alcove off the library. His manservant, John Grant, slept in a tiny box room off the kitchen for the steep stairs to the attic rooms were beyond both of them now.

A gasp interrupted his musings and he turned, not without difficulty, in his invalid chair and saw *Madame* Brehaut, whom they had to hire as a housekeeper when John's back became so painful. She could only come two mornings a week, however, as she had the farm to run. But she needed the coin that he paid every week.

"*Mon Dieu, M'sieur* Bretton, what has happened here?" *Madame* exclaimed, looking in horror at the pile and piles of books upon the floor underneath now empty shelves.

"Colonel Fournier is convinced that I have weapons hidden behind my books," he said dryly.

Madame Brehaut's face darkened. "They have visited my farm as well and taken all of my metal tools and Eudes' fowling pieces and all the powder and shot. We will have to work with wooden tools. It is fortunate that most of the ploughing has been finished! They are not happy that I can scarcely work the farm with my husband and sons gone and now they steal my tools as well! But I shall not have to bear having an officer in my house as *Les Huit Lapins* is too small and old fashioned and too out of the way, I was told."

"But what are we to do about this, *M'sieur?*" She waved her hand at the books. "I have not the time to help you. In fact, I was coming to tell you that I can only give you two hours this morning. I must get back to the farm. There is so much work!"

"John's back is very bad this morning," he said sadly. "And I am tied to this chair. We're a pair of old crocks, John and I."

Madame looked sympathetic, but then said slowly, "I have an idea, *M'sieur*. I have hired two Gypsies to help out upon the farm and the young man is recovering from a bad fall. He is not quite up to farm work as yet but he could, with direction, pick up your books and put them away."

"A Gypsy?" said Aurelius uncertainly. Illiterate and dirty was his first thought.

"These two are quite superior," said *Madame*. "Clean and respectful and hard-working, both of them. Let me send him to you and see if he will be helpful to you. You may tell him what to do as he is intelligent enough, I think, to follow your instructions."

Aurelius had his doubts. What little he knew of Gypsies was not encouraging but he knew that there were very few options. Everyone was occupied with the business of the farms. There were no young men or even old ones any more and even the smallest islanders and all the females were otherwise busy on the land. John had tried to hire a man to dig the garden and do some much needed maintenance only last week and had come up empty handed.

"Send him along as soon as you might, *Madame*," he said at last, thinking that he had little choice in the matter. The books could not remain on the floor. But he had little hope that a Gypsy would be of much use in sorting books. What he really needed was one of his former students from Cambridge.

Rising from his bed had been a test of endurance for Felix. Sitting up without the support of the pillows had made the interior of the *vardo* go topsy-turvey around him. If it had not been for Rosal he would have fallen when he attempted to stand. She was there to offer a supporting shoulder and she was far stronger than she looked.

But he gritted his teeth and pushed himself, managing to stand and get dressed by sheer willpower alone. His head hurt, there was no doubt about that, and even these past few days in a bed had weakened him. But he was determined to rise and stop being dependent on Rosal's working to support him. That was wrong.

She and Hagar both worked hard here. He had seen, even in the past few days, how difficult was this existence. Water had to be hauled from a stream, firewood gathered, and before Rosal had gone to the farm, food was difficult to come by. The two women had baking and laundry and cooking over an open fire as well as the care of the pony and the *vardo,* many of the things that he should be attending to, as well as bringing in much needed money.

Rosal had to help him dress, and the clothes, like everything else seemed unfamiliar: linen trousers that were a little loose, a full-sleeved shirt, made soft by much washing, and a leather vest, with a bright kerchief to tie around his neck. There were no shoes, but his feet seemed quite used to that as he found when somewhat shakily he ventured outside. But he was glad to sit down by the fire.

Rosal wished that the clothes she had been given were of brighter colours. Sylvester and her father, indeed, most of the men in the *cumpania,* had favored brilliant reds and yellows and blues but the island men seemed to favor dull colours, particularly in their work clothes. At least she had possessed that piece of bright material (she had been saving it for a head scarf) to give him to tie about his neck. She was surprised at how much he truly looked like a Gypsy Rom, with a scarf and earring. His skin was deeply tanned and he had dark hair, as black as hers and eyes of a very deep brown. Once again, the way he looked only enforced her belief that this was *meant.* Everything pointed towards that! She wondered that Hagar could not see it.

And if he kept recovering so well, she could soon invite him to her bed and become with child. She had already begun drinking various herbal concoctions for fertility. Perhaps by next winter, if she became pregnant right away, she might have another baby! It was a thought that filled her with happiness.

Felix insisted on going to the farm with Rosal the very next day. He was quite set on earning his keep, and what is more, providing for the two women.

But nothing would sway Rosal from going to work as well. Why should she not work, she asked in answer to his protests. She was strong, she had always worked and if she worked too they would make twice as much. Besides, she enjoyed the farm; she liked being busy and out of doors.

Even as they were walking up to the farm he attempted once more to change her mind, but soon had to give up. It was difficult to argue with a person who would not argue back. His disapproval left her entirely unmoved. She would go her own way no matter what he said.

"Rosal," he said, changing the subject abruptly as he realized that there was no hope of swaying, "how is it that I cannot understand Romany?"

"Because you have only begun to learn it," she said. "When your parents died the *Gajé* came and put you in a school where they made you speak only English and trained you to be a servant to some fine *Gajé*. But you ran away because a Romany has to be free and live beneath the sky. And then you found us and we married and I am teaching you to be a proper Rom."

This seemed plausible as somehow he did not think that he would have enjoyed being a servant to anyone.

He did not notice that she avoided looking at him as she spun this web. It was becoming more difficult to lie to him. When he had been ill and had depended so heavily upon her he did not seem a real person to her, only the means to an end. But now, like Hagar, to her he was suddenly different, walking along here with her, Chavé following behind or ranging up ahead.

She stole a glance at him as they walked along. How fortunate she was to have been given a young and very good-looking man! Sylvester had been old, and heavy in the belly from incessant drinking and eating. His breath had been rank as well and his hands ungentle when touching her.

Would Felix want children? Most men wanted a son. She was willing to have as many children as he wanted. The more children a Romany woman had, the higher her status. And they had a *cumpania* to build.

She was proud when she introduced him to *Madame*, who was very surprised at how handsome her Rom was, and what good French he spoke. Rosal was a little surprised that he spoke French for she had not even thought to ask, for of course *Madame* and Joisaine spoke English as easily as their native tongue.

"Have I always been able to speak French?" he asked her as they headed towards the stables. *Madame* had told Felix that the animals needed to be groomed and turned out and Rosal at once offered to help.

Rosal shrugged. "As far as I know," she said.

Felix frowned again. When *Madame* had begin speaking he had understood her easily, although her accent seemed strange, and why this was he did not know. He had replied in the same language, his tongue seeming to operate independently of his brain. Again, when he tried to think about *why* he knew French, it was as if a gate slammed shut in his mind and it could not be opened again. He was finding that it was best not to question. If he spoke and did things without inquiry he was able to go on very well. Thinking about it, however, produced only pain and confusion.

Therefore as he cared for the animals, a task he seemed to be familiar with, he tried not to think, but to just let his hands and body do their work. Together, he and Rosal, joined by Joisaine, cared for the two plough oxen, the driving and riding horses, and the small herd of dairy cows.

On through the day of thinning the parsnip field, spreading two inches of straw for a mulch and picking early peas, Felix continued to work automatically, without thinking. In this way he saved himself a worse headache, but the mere action of working hard after rising so quickly from a sick bed was taxing and more than once he caught Rosal looking at him, as if wondering when or if he would give up.

He managed to last the whole day, although when they returned to the *vardo*, he was glad to crawl into his bed once again, after eating but a small supper, for the next day would be the same. Only on Sundays, when the Brehauts went to church, was there no work on the farm, save feeding the animals, the milking and egg gathering.

The third day on the farm as he was hoeing between rows of young plants in preparation to fertilizing them with the favorite local fertilizer, *vraic,* or seaweed, which created a very rich soil, *Madame* approached him. She said "You are a very hard worker, but I think perhaps you have taken on too much too soon after your illness. I have perhaps something that will be a trifle easier until you are healthier."

Felix straightened up and said "I have not complained, *Madame.*"

"No, of course not," she agreed, "but I have eyes in my head! Let me tell you what I have to suggest. Two mornings a week I keep the house of *M'sieur* Bretton, who is old and confined to a chair. His manservant is as old as his master and they have no other help. Before the French came and took the men away he had a groom and a gardener and even a man in the kitchen. *M'sieur* Bretton was *le professur* at an English university and he has many, many books. Today the French came and searched his house for weapons and threw all of his books upon the floor. He needs someone who can pick them up and put them away. Do not worry; he will not expect you to read anything. He will tell you what to do," she added kindly, thinking that it was doubtful that this young Gypsy could read at all. "And he is willing to pay you in coin as well."

It was this last offer that decided Felix. *Madame* had paid them daily, but mostly with food. However, they needed things that food could not buy. Kälo needed new shoes, Felix had noticed that morning when grooming the pony. A crack was forming in one of the wheels of the *vardo* and that meant a wheelwright. Rosal and Hagar were both looking ragged. They needed new skirts, at the very least and he wanted to get them each a small present for taking such good care of him as an expression of gratitude. Even one's family should be properly thanked when they worked so hard for one's comfort. They had had to do all of his work while he was laid up as well, all without complaint.

He listened carefully to *Madame's* directions as to how to find the house of this *professur. M'sieur* Bretton wanted his books taken care of without delay.

"Of course," said Felix unthinkingly, "the spines or pages could be damaged and that would be a tragedy."

Madame looked somewhat surprised at this statement but she sent him on his way, telling him that she would tell Rosal where he had gone.

It was a clear, warm day and the woods between the farm and the tiny house of *Trois Chiminées* on the edge of the equally small village were full of flowering trees, birdsong and sunlight dappling the path that led between thickly growing woodland.

This island was certainly a beautiful place but it awoke no chord of memory in Felix's mind. His brain supplied, when he did not struggle to remember, the names of birds and flowers and trees. Again he wondered, how could he know all of this and not know his own name or remember the people in his life? It seemed perverse.

He felt too as if something were missing. He found himself looking down on the ground at his side as if something should be there. Did Chavé usually accompany him everywhere? Was that what he was looking for? But Chavé, although he was friendly and even affectionate with Felix, as he was with Hagar, seemed to give his deepest love to Rosal, and stayed with her most of the time. And looking around the *vardo* he missed something there as well, but again, he did not know what it was. Rosal, when questioned, had said that they had the same things they had always had. Nothing was missing.

But all the same, Felix felt the lack of something, but what it was he could not begin to guess.

John Grant smarted under the injustice of it all and then almost groaned aloud as his back gave a particularly painful twinge as he stood in front of the kitchen table.

First of all there were those damned Froggies, coming here in a stupid and useless search for weapons! Weapons! Even a blind man could see that his master, confined to a chair, had no need of weapons! John had wanted to plant that corporal a facer.

And then there had been the look on the Professor's face when he saw his books cast all over the floor. It had made John angry all over again. The Professor, a Cambridge Fellow, a Don, had neither chick nor child and those books were to him what a child would be to another man. They were precious.

He could do little to help his master, either. That morning he had managed to pick up some of the books but his back had soon betrayed him and he had to give it up. The Professor was sorting them. He had them in a special order so that he could find things when they were wanted, even though he, John, was the one who had to slowly climb the library ladder and fetch down the desired volume. John could not help sort either for most of the Professor's books were in long-dead foreign languages, since he had taught Classics at Cambridge. All John could read was English, and that not very well.

John sometimes wished that they had never come to Guernsey. When the Professor had at first developed arthritis the doctors had suggested a warmer climate. With the continent closed to English visitors this meant Egypt or the Levant, all too bloody foreign, John thought.

Too far from the great English seats of learning, the Professor thought. He wanted a place where his friends could visit with ease and he could be *au courant* with the latest scholarly news.

When a long forgotten relative had died and left this property to the Professor it seemed the answer to a prayer. Winters were mild here and instead of laying out capital on a property the Professor was able to save his money and do what he most enjoyed instead, which was to buy more books.

But that had been a number of years ago, before the French had come for the first time, before they had both grown so crippled. The Professor had been able to walk and putter in the garden when they first came here and John had not as yet hurt his back. And even once they were both less able to get about they had been other menservants to take the burden. But now they were all alone, and they reduced to having a Gypsy in the house to do tasks that John should have still have been able to do.

He had protested vociferously when the Professor had

told him what *Madame* had proposed. Gypsy trash in this house! A Gypsy would steal them blind as well as being dirty and lazy! The Master would get no work out of an Egyptian and he'd regret that such a plan had even been suggested.

But the Professor would not listen. The books had to be re-shelved and there was no harm in trying out this Gypsy lad. *Madame* had vouched for him.

But that cut no ice with John since *Madame* was a woman and what is more, a Frenchwoman, even if she called herself English. To John, the *Guernaise* ought to decide for once and all whether they were English or French and, if English, stop using French at all. He had a difficult time doing the marketing and errands for his master, for he had barely a word of French and stubbornly refused to learn more.

He had just put a mustard poultice on his aching back and was buttoning up his waistcoat when a knock came at the rear door. With a grimace, he went to answer it. This was probably the Gypsy.

One of the first things Rosal and Hagar had told Felix before he began working at the farm was that many *Gajé* treated Gypsies with contempt and derision. In order to get along with them (and take their money) he could not let them see that anything they said or did insulted or offended him. They were just *Gajé* and they didn't know any better.

He was not then, unprepared for the hostility he saw in the manservant's face when the door abruptly opened.

Felix saw a tall old man, with a bald head and a beak of a nose, slightly stooped, with large hands and feet. He wore a scowl, with a deep vertical line between very heavy brows. Other than a pair of handsome bushy side whickers, he was clean shaven and the side whiskers, like what remained of his hair in a fringe around his bald crown, was grizzled gray. His eyes were the deep gray of a stormy sea and filled with disdain as he looked up and down the unwelcome intruder.

"I'm –" Felix began but John sniffed audibly in a rather nose-in-the-air fashion and said "I've no need for names. You're here to work temporary-like, not joining staff! If I want you I'll call you Gypsy. And you may be certain of one thing. I'll be checking your pockets when you leave. There'll be none of your light-fingered nonsense in this house! I know your kind and you'll not put anything over on me."

104

He pointed at a soapstone sink with a pump. "Go over there and wash up well. My Master won't wish dirty hands touching his books. Use the soap, it won't kill you."

Felix was taken aback and hot words sprang to his lips. He did not steal and he was not dirty! But he remembered Rosal's advice and pressed his lips together, hard, to keep from speaking. He turned away from John and went to the sink to do as he was told.

When he was done John, tight-lipped and rigid with disapproval, took him along a very short corridor and through a drawing room into an immense room, lined with shelves, all of which were empty.

And lying upon the floor, in crumpled condition, were hundreds, if not thousands of books. Everything in Felix cried aloud in protest at seeing books treated so.

"Here's the Gypsy, Professor," John announced in a voice full of protest.

"Thank you for coming, young man," said a clear, cultured voice and Felix, his attention drawn from the books, turned to face the owner of the voice, who sat in a Bath chair behind a massive desk, the top of which had stacks and stacks of books.

Aurelius Bretton was about seventy or so, with a full head of white hair, a little longer than fashion dictated, for it curled under his collar slightly. Pain was etched into his face, which must have been very good looking in his youth. He had blue eyes, somewhat faded now, but still sharp and full of intelligence. His expression wore none of the hostility of his manservant's. He wore a silk brocade dressing gown and a knitted robe was thrown across his legs.

"You may leave us, John," said the Professor. "I can explain to him what I need done. I have no need for you to stand there overseeing. Go and rest your back," he added dryly.

"John, I am afraid is in an ill-humor. He is angry at himself that his back will not allow him to clean up this mess," the Professor said, as John stamped away down the corridor.

"He is more afraid that I shall steal something," said Felix, with a slight bitterness in his tone.

One of the Professor's brows shot up. The accent, the

diction: it was not what one expected. Someone had taught him to speak properly. It might be interesting to find out how and where, but not until these books were taken care of.

He put his hand on one of the stacks on the desk. "I have begun to sort these in their proper order. It is important that they be shelved correctly so that I might find them when needed. John was able to pick up most of the Greek works and I have them in order here. I should like you to begin by putting these away and then perhaps pick up the volumes upon the floor and stack them neatly so that they are all closed properly. I am very afraid that the precipitous manner in which they were knocked from the shelves may have damaged more than a few of them. Indeed, I cannot conceive how there would not be significant damage. Pray start with this stack of Greek tragedies. They will go to that top shelf on the far end." He pointed. "And there is the ladder. He indicated the library ladder, the top of which slid along a brass rod that ran all around the edge of the ceiling. "Perhaps you might shelve half a stack at a time as you would not wish to fall from carrying too much at one time."

Something in Felix warmed to the old gentleman at once, something that had not warmed to his manservant. The Professor handed him a stack of books. There were five of them, and Felix glanced at the spines.

"Excuse me, sir," he said abruptly "but did you not say that these were to be all Greek tragedies? Here is Aristophanes' *The Clouds* in company with Sophocles' *Antigone* and *Oedipus Rex* and Euripides' *Alcestis* and *Medea*."

The Professor stared at him and at last said, bemused, "Those titles are in Greek! Can you indeed read ancient Greek? And how did you know that "The Clouds" is a comedy?"

Felix could not tell him and he felt the familiar headache closing in and the now habitual feeling of despair washing over him for he just did not know *how*.

11
Resistance

Late on the evening of the 24th of May David rather nervously dressed for a most important meeting. He was to meet Grizel, near midnight, at the beach at Bell Grève Bay. Once again, Grizel was to take him to the sea cave where the gunpowder was stored. There they would meet the Sea-Folk in safety and privacy.

David, in the last two days, had begun sounding out various groups of trustworthy people: the few men left upon the island, most of them elderly, or halt and lame as he was himself. He was in despair as to being able to mount any sort of resistance. What could such elderly men manage?

However, David's frequent trips had not gone unnoticed by Colonel Fournier. Within a day of his travels beginning David was called to the Colonel's office and asked why he felt himself obliged to leave his office so frequently and be jolted about rough roads in a cabriolet.

"For it seems to do your leg no good, *M'sieur*," said Fournier, with an oily smile and false compassion in his voice. He sat perched on the edge of David's former desk, and toyed with a leather riding crop, slapping it into a gloved hand. He had made certain that David was at a disadvantage in a low, uncomfortable chair.

"Many of the persons I am visiting, Colonel, are elderly and have protested to me about your new orders," said David stiffly. How he disliked this man! "I felt that I should go to them personally, as their Bailiff, and convince them to be reasonable and obey your new rules, that it would be to their advantage to do so. They will listen to me, for they held my father in high esteem. And for some of these people, travel is even more difficult for them than it is for me. Nor do I have room in my new office to make older persons or ladies comfortable," David added. The new office he had been allotted was small, windowless and exceedingly cramped. Rather than a desk, he had a rickety table and a chair that seemed as if it had formerly been used as an instrument of torture by the Inquisition. The light was also inadequate and the atmosphere was suffocating, all designed, he knew, to show him his very low place in the new scheme of things.

Fournier stared at him for a few moments and then said, "And have you had much success, *M'sieur* Dieudonné, with your persuasions?"

"Some," said David. "Their chief objections are to the disrespect that your soldiers showed when searching their homes for weapons. Many things were damaged or broken. Farmers will find it extremely hard to work their farms with but ancient wooden tools. And the old and lame find the twice weekly assemblies difficult, particularly those who do not keep a carriage and shall be obliged to walk some distance."

Fournier laughed unpleasantly. "First of all, my soldiers are not obliged to show any respect to a conquered people and you *Guernaise* would do well to remember that. It is necessary that we purge this island of any thought at all of fighting back. And if people are too old and lame to come to the assemblies in a timely fashion, then perhaps they had best begin the trip the evening before. No one will be excused; no one! As stated in my directive, the first assembly will be upon the 26th, two days from now, on Thursday. Everyone must be present and a list shall be taken of names, occupations and habitation. In this way, *M'sieur,* I can make certain that everyone is where he or she should be at all times."

It was only with extreme difficulty that David remained in his chair. He wanted to rise and strike that smug look from the Colonel's face, the look that said "you are helpless as a new born infant."

"On that day, also, will be appointed the commandant of each parish, who will make himself known to the people," Fournier continued. "I am rather amused, Dieudonné, that already I have received requests for some ten groups to meet. Do they think I am a fool, to allow this ?" He reached behind him and pulled out a sheaf of papers."*La Société du Gran'mère du Chamquière?*" he said in derision. "What is that?"

"It is an organization of women, Colonel. They knit, sew

and make baskets for the poor. It is also a social organization. My mother is a member and looks forward to the meetings to see her friends and gossip and exchange receipts. There is a chapter in each parish," David answered. "They are neither dangerous or subversive. It is named for the ancient statue of a woman found in the cemetery of St. Martin de la Belieuse."

Colonel Fournier scowled. "I have seen this statue and the Holy Fathers of the Inquisition are agreed that it is a pagan thing and must be destroyed. It represents the old religion. To call such a piece of crude carving the Great Mother of the Churchyard is sacrilegious and heretical. Should these women expect to meet to sew and gossip with my permission they must call their society by a more acceptable name. And you may tell them so." He stood abruptly, signifying that the interview was at an end.

David stood with some difficulty, and began to limp towards the door when Fournier's voice stopped him.

"From now on, *M'sieur*, you will obtain permission for all your forays into the countryside from me. You take too much upon yourself. Remember, you are but a figurehead."

Furious, David could not trust himself to speak, but merely bowed, a short, jerky bow, and turned as fast as he could and quit the office, Fournier's mocking laughter following him.

Now, remembering this interview and what a poor light it cast upon him, he was ashamed to meet Grizel's eyes when she came up out of the surf and changed from a seal into a woman. She wore a sack tied to her back which contained her gown and had room for David's clothing as well.

"What is wrong?" she asked abruptly when they had exchanged greetings.

For some reason he found himself easily telling her all that had happened and his own feelings of shame and inadequacy when dealing with Fournier, how angrily helpless he felt. There was something about her that encouraged confidence. Perhaps it was the clarity of her gaze as she listened intently, without interruption. Her eyes, so dark and deep, were like a pool one could gladly drown in. But there was no pity in those eyes, nor any contempt.

"Well," she said in extreme practicality "that is why we meet tonight, to discuss how we may rid ourselves of these pests. And what good would it have done, David, to throttle the Colonel? You would be taken prisoner and hung at once. Our resistance will have need of you. Indeed, you are vital to our success! There are none of us that can penetrate the Colonel's office and perhaps learn of his plans. You must stay safe and pretend to go along with him." She came closer and lay a hand on his arm. In the moonlight he could see the fine webs between her fingers. She was still wet and her body shimmered even in the low light, sleek as the seal she so often was. "It is very difficult, I know, to have to swallow both pride and your knowledge of what is right. But it must be done," Her voice was warm and low. "Indeed, there is nothing else you can do and I am quite certain that everyone understands. Even if they do not, when the enemy troops have quit this place, everyone will know what part you played and you will be honored. I shall see to it myself."

Her voice was sincere and earnest. He was very conscious of her nearness, the fact that she was still unclothed and of her hand on his arm, warm, rather than cold from a creature of the sea. He liked her candid look, the way she met his eyes squarely. He could see the truth of her soul. He did not find the webbing on her hands or toes, or the fact that she was half a seal at all offensive as some men might, particularly the occupying French. He realized that he was extremely attracted to her and not just because she was naked most of the time they were together.

"Thank you," he now said. "That you think so means a great deal to me. I have been despising myself for ages, for not doing enough..."

She put a finger to his lips. "Do not think that way. And tonight we begin to fight back!" She looked up at the sky quickly. " It grows late. We had better go. Put your things in this sack with mine and lean on me when we go into the sea."

Once again it was a breathless ride under the sea until

they reached the cave. This time, however, Grizel had some dry burlap sacks waiting and they used these as towels and dressed themselves in the clothes from Grizel's watertight bag, magiced by her late father.

They were the first to arrive. As she had before, Grizel lit the lantern while David waited in the water. She seemed to see in the dark very well.

There had been some changes in the cave since David had last been there. A flat rock that could serve as a table now occupied the ledge, with boulders for seats drawn up near it. A half circle of rocks, half in and half out of the water, faced the ledge. Those were seats for the Sea-Folk, Grizel explained. She and some of her Selchie friends had done all of this work.

Upon a natural wall, facing the water, hung a most unusual map. It was of Guernsey, but all about the island were marked what David assumed to be the contours of the bottom of the sea. Grizel confirmed this when he inquired. He was interested to see that there were marked on the map were the locations of many shipwrecks. "There may be things in those ships that we may perhaps use," she said.

Behind them a sudden loud splash sounded and David turned awkwardly to see the first Merman he had ever seen up close emerging from the water.

He had seen the Mer from a distance for there were not many on Guernsey who had not, but since the French had first taken the island back in '99 it had become rare to see them at all. Their island friends had been mostly amongst the magical populace, the Witches and Wizards who had fled the Inquisition.

"Ah, Prince Madoc! Welcome!" said Grizel, dipping a curtsey. David bowed and was introduced. He was much impressed by the size and strength of the bearded Sea-Prince. Grizel explained that he was the Prince of the Channel, answerable only to Neptune and without his help and cooperation they could do little.

"Then we *Guernaise* are very grateful indeed to you, sire," said David, with another bow.

This struck precisely the right note with Madoc, who inclined his greenish head graciously.

Other creatures began to arrive; first, a bevy of Nereids

riding sea-horses. These Nereids were beautiful, golden-haired maidens, looking like naked adolescent girls. They did not have fish tails like the Mer, but had legs, although almost transparent fins, long and sweeping, were in several places upon their limbs and, like Grizel, their finger and toes were webbed. David was to find that Nereids always traveled in groups of at least three and it was highly unusual to see a lone Nereid. They could be mischievous and very playful. They could also be malevolent if offended.

The horses they rode were half-fish half-horses, white in colour like sea-foam, more properly called hippo-campi. Madoc greeted the Nereids as Doto, Galatea and Thetis and explained to David that they were three of the chief ladies-in-waiting to the sea-Queen, Neptune's wife, Amphitrite, who was a Nereid herself.

"We are very angry that one of our favorite playgrounds has been taken over by our enemies. We have long loved to frolic in the surf here on Lesia," announced Thetis in a very musical voice. "We are more than willing to help rid our sea of the French." She smiled and showed teeth that suddenly seemed very sharp and pointed. "And the Inquisition must go!"

Lesia, David knew, for his father had been somewhat of an antiquarian, was the ancient Roman name for Guernsey. Had these creatures been here this long?

The Nereids perched close together on one rock, sending their restive steeds away until such time as they were needed.

Next arrived a pair of Selchies, friends of Grizel's who were introduced as Hamish and Elspeth. Selchies had originated in Scotland millennia ago and most clung to Scots names no matter where they had spread throughout the waters of the world. Elspeth heaved herself up upon one of the rocks and shape shifted into a young woman but Hamish stayed a seal in the water.

More sea-folk began to arrive: sea-nymphs, Tritons, dolphins, and others David did not even recognize. Soon all the rocks were full and even the water had little space left.

A very calm and self-possessed Grizel stood up and addressed the group. "We all know why we are here. Guernsey and the other isles here in what the humans call the English Channel or *La Manche* are now threatened by both the conquering French and, what is even worse, the Inquisition. We all are aware of what has been going on in the regions of the Mediterranean, where our people are being persecuted and killed by the vile agents of the Inquisition. Many of you may say that what goes on in the human world, on the land, is none of our affair. But I tell you that if the British Isles fall to the French we shall be in worse danger than we have ever been. We were all raised with tales of what the Inquisition did to the dragons, the magic folk and the Faerie creatures of the continent, of the killings and burnings and how even the Faerie Host was forced to flee from Cold Iron. At one time our kind was all throughout the land across the Channel and we were welcomed. If we let the conquerors win this battle we will be banished from our homes here as well. Do you wish to have to go far across the sea where the sea bottom is strange and we may not be welcomed by those already living there? This is my home and I am willing to fight for it!"

A ragged cheer went up, some of the sea-folk still looked dubious. Prince Madoc spoke next, telling of the capture of the Sea-Folk in the Mediterranean and the appalling treatment they had received from the French. "I will not make you ill with tales of the tortures. They have even enslaved some of our people to draw their ships through the water as they enslave other humans. This Bonaparte, their First Consul as they call him, is a ruthless man and seeks to dominate the entire world and the Inquisition is at his side. I propose to help these humans who have long been our friends and in doing so help ourselves. The Inquisition must not be allowed to gain purchase in these islands or in our waters!"

This speech generated a larger cheer, the dolphins leaping out of the water and flipping over in mid-air.

Grizel then introduced David, explaining who he was and how he would be able to help.

Somewhat nervously David addressed the company. "A Senior Witch-Sniffer has arrived from Rome and from what I have overheard he intends to fully rid the islands not only of heretics, which by French definition seems to be nearly everyone on the island, but also of, as he told Colonel Fournier, "the pernicious influence of Satan that manifests itself in the sea", meaning all of you."

There was an outcry against this until Madoc bade them all be quiet.

"At this moment there is a French frigate sitting in St. Peter Port harbor, laden with the tools of the Inquisition: machinery of torture, nets of strong metal to catch your people, harpoons to spear you and who knows what else," David continued. "Grizel and I thought that if somehow the ship could be destroyed before Father Maël has a chance to find a suitable place for them, it would be a good thing. He is considering Castle Cornet at the head of the harbor at the moment, thinking that it would be convenient for putting both humans and Sea-Folk to the question." Grizel stood beside the map and pointed out the places that he had mentioned, for some of the Sea-Folk did not know the human names for the places on and off the island and she repeated them as well in the speech of the sea.

They all began to talk at once, each with a plan until Grizel gave a shrill whistle and all faces turned towards her, startled.

"We have here, in the back of the cave, gunpowder and shot from the time of the Armada, which time no doubt many of you remember. The easiest method would be to make a bomb and destroy the ship from beneath. I have a waterproof case magiced by my father that could be attached to the hull of the ship and a fuse lit to blow it up. We would need someone who was both stealthy and fast. David has also learned that the ship has a magazine that holds both ammunition, arms and gunpowder. We might be able to convince the French that their own carelessness destroyed the ship!"

There were no lack of volunteers. In the end it was decided that Hamish, with one of the dolphins, would carry the homemade bomb to the *Acadie* and attach it to the most vulnerable part of her hull, just above the waterline. The dolphin, Nim, would provide a diversion by leaping about and making a display in at the bow of the ship. Sailors considered dolphins good luck and would watch their antics eagerly. Once the bomb, in its waterproof case was attached, Hamish would light the fuse with flint and steel, in his human form. Then he would shape-shift and the two would swim as fast as they could to get away.

In the midst of a discussion of how to fasten the bomb most effectively to the high waterline of the ship and how long the fuse needed to be and how to keep it dry, an eerie phosphorescent glow of shimmering green began to fill the cave. One by one they all fell silent as a large ball began to gather itself above the table, solidifying into a smaller ball and they watched in consternation as it began to glow and change, filling the air with a sweet humming and pulsing brightly, sending reflected fingers of green light over the waters and touching the faces of all, who watched it in fear or awe. Some of the creatures dived beneath the water, sliding from the rocks to get away from what they did not know. Others, like Madoc, were braver. Even Grizel shrank back a little against David, who put an arm about her. David had no idea what was happening and he could see that no one else did either. But somehow he sensed no evil from the green mass of light. They would know what it was shortly, for even as all of them stared at it, the smaller light in the center began to take shape in the semblance of something or someones.

12
Mr. Lovel

Careful not to look Aurelius in the face, Felix said "I was taken from my people when my parents died and educated by the *Gajé*."

"*Gajé?*" Aurelius queried.

"Non-Romany," Felix explained, repeating what Rosal had told him. Somehow he did not want to admit that he knew nothing about himself save what she had told him. His memory loss was not only a source of anger and frustration but he was also beginning to find it shameful that he knew none of his personal history. Why did he know some things and not others? He seemed to have some very odd knowledge, being able to read ancient Greek, for one, and other things that he should know, such as the Romany tongue and customs, were a perfect blank.

Aurelius was very well used to dealing with young men who were reluctant to disperse information as he had begun his teaching career in a boys' school as a house-master and he recognized in the posture of this young man: face turned away, shoulders hunched defensively and in the tone of his voice, that something was wrong. Wisely, he did not pursue it, but instead said, "Do you know, John did not introduce us properly? I am Aurelius Bretton, late of King's College, Cambridge."

Felix turned around, grateful that he was not asked questions he could not answer. "Felix Lovel, late of the *vardo* in *Madame* Brehaut's woods," he said with a smile. "A *vardo* is a wagon, or a caravan," he added, for Aurelius clearly did not understand the reference.

Aurelius extended his hand and they shook solemnly, each man feeling an instinctive liking for the other.

"Your man said it was not necessary to know my name as I was not joining staff," Felix said.

"There are several thousand books to sort and shelve," said Aurelius dryly. "If you can bear it. I think that you shall be staff for a good while."

"If I can bear it!" Felix echoed. To be near books – ! He suddenly realized what he had been missing at the *vardo:* books. There was not a single book in sight there.

"Perhaps you could see if John missed any other volumes in Greek," Aurelius suggested. He still burned with curiosity about his new employee, (curiosity, he sometimes thought, was his besetting sin) but he also had patience in abundance. It was indeed odd that a Gypsy (and the young man certainly looked like a Gypsy, with his dark looks, gold earring and bare feet) read Greek. It was a true mystery and it intrigued Aurelius as nothing had for a long while.

He was to find out that the Gypsy read, with equal ease, Latin, Medieval French and Old English. Encouraged by Aurelius, who knew how to get the best from a reluctant pupil, Felix made comments on many of the books he picked up and stacked. There was an all too high pile of books that would have to be mended but to Aurelius's joy, his helper was able to sort the books as well as he could himself.

And even more enjoyable was the conversation. It had been years, since the French had first come and visits from England had ceased, that Aurelius had been able to enjoy a conversation with another scholar. He felt more alive than he had in a long time, his mind stimulated and rejoicing in scholarly debate and the give and take of ideas. Lately, he had felt a lethargy creep over him and some days it seemed too much effort to get out of bed. John, of course, would not let him loll about. But today the time went by so quickly and so happily that when John came in with a tray of tea and biscuits Aurelius was surprised to see that it was after eleven.

They were deep in the midst of a conversation about the folklore of medieval Normandy and Brittany as written in the *Roman de la Rose* and in the translations of Breton *Lais* by poetess Marie de France of the Court of the Plantagenet Henry III.

Folklore had long been a hobby with Aurelius. At one time he had spent the Long Vacations tramping about on walking tours, collecting tales from anyone willing to tell them. He was especially interested in Faerie lore and when he had first come to Guernsey, he had begun to collect stories of Faerie sightings. But confinement to the house and to his chair soon put paid to that.

The Gypsy's breath of knowledge on the subject was exhilarating. How he would have liked to have a student such as this! Aurelius thought. The young man was a true lover of books. It was in his voice and in the way he tenderly handled the volumes, as distressed as Aurelius himself at the rough treatment they had been given.

On Felix's part, he found that if he did not try to remember *how* he knew the contents of all these books, he could easily talk about what lay between the covers. And he found the talk exciting as well. Sometime, someplace, he was certain that he had participated in such debate. The slightest attempt to recall when or where or with who, sent pain racing through his head and again he confronted that blank wall beyond which he could not penetrate. He gave up trying and gave himself up to the pleasure of the moment.

John stamped in with the tea tray jingling and a frown on his face, just in time to hear Felix quote Marie de France: *"Mut unt este noble Barun / Cil de Bretaine li Bretun."* and Aurelius cap it with Chaucer: *"Thise oldé gentil Bretons in hir dayes / Of diverse àventurès maden layes."*

They smiled at one another with such accord that John, suddenly alarmed, thumped the tray down in front of Aurelius unnecessarily hard to gain his master's attention and take it away from that Gypsy.

"Is it that time already?" said Aurelius in surprise and looked at the tray, which contained a teapot, a cup, a sugar bowl and creamer and a plate of water biscuits. He looked up at John "I do believe you have forgotten, John, to bring a cup for Mr. Lovel. And have we any of those little savories *Madame* was so obliging as to make for us? I find myself unaccountably hungry this morning. I hope *Madame* left one of her *pot au feus* for our nuncheon."

John could not believe his ears. A cup for the Gypsy? John had not even intended to give him a mid-morning repast in the kitchen as he would have if Aurelius had hired a local to do the work. And calling him "Mr. Lovel" as if he was a Christian and not one of a dirty, thieving band of tinkers!

Muttering to himself, John went back to the kitchen and

118

fetched another cup (imagine letting a Gypsy use the good Lowestoft!) and tossing the remaining savories carelessly on a plate. These he deposited with an ill-grace on Aurelius's desk. He was affronted to see that Aurelius had already invited the Gypsy to draw up a chair and join him.

And even more annoying was the fact that the books had all been sorted into neat stacks and were no longer laying higgledy-piggledy upon the floor. The Gypsy had to have done all of that work as the Professor could not have managed it. This was completely contrary to what John had expected. He had thought he would be able by now to say "I told you so."

"Shall I pour, sir?" John grated, with a glare of pure dislike at the Gypsy. Although the arthritis in Aurelius' hands was not as severe as that in his legs he still found lifting objects as heavy as a full tea pot difficult.

"Thank you," said the cheeky Gypsy, dismissal in his voice "but I shall pour out."

John ground his teeth in rage. Aping his betters, the bastard, trying to sound and act like a gentleman when he was no such thing! How could the master be so taken in? John retreated to the hall, not quite into the kitchen where he could see and hear but not be observed.

He writhed when he heard the Professor address that trash as "my dear boy" and heard the Gypsy address the Professor as if they were equals. John could not understand much of what they then talked about over the teacups as a lot of it was in some foreign tongue. Poseidonios' work on the Celts of Gaul was the current topic of discussion if he had but known it. John could also not bear the pleased and interested look on his master's face, a look he himself had been unable to raise no matter how he had tried. And the Professor was eating heartily, something else he had not done recently. Soon John was in a jealous rage. That this animation and appetite was due to an Egyptian — due to road rubbish! — it was nearly unbearable.

And there was born that day John's intense dislike, verging on hatred, of Felix, which emotion when acted upon very nearly ended in tragedy for almost all concerned.

Pyewacket had settled into his new home as easily as he could, heartsick though he was. Every day when David returned home the cat questioned his host closely as to what he had learned that day, for David had not neglected to set inquiries into motion, letting the other parishes know that he was interested in any and all rescues from the sea.

The west coast of the island, from which they had set sail, was low lying, with a number of rocky headlands and only a very few small bays sheltered enough for a yacht. Many reefs and rocks abounded near the shore. The prevailing wind was westerly and this area had been and still was the scene of many shipwrecks and loss of life.

Since Pyewacket was unsure as to his location when he had been tossed into the sea, and he had swum a fair distance when Grizel had come upon him, he could not even begin to guess where Felix might have ended, particularly if he had gone over the side too, as Pyewacket was beginning to suspect. It had to have been something like that else wise Felix would have protected his familiar. The only question was how it had been done.

The island waters were relatively shallow and the tides strong, changing direction many times daily. And the tidal range was actually one of the largest in the world. It was an area of hazardous navigation and great peril to ships, for reefs and rocks lay everywhere and the charts in existence were none too reliable.

And as David told his feline guest, he himself was no sailor. He was a farmer by training and inclination, only having accidentally become a politician. On Guernsey there seemed to be two sorts of men: the farmer and the sailor, and the sailors did not only fish, but sailed the oceans of the world in trade, as well as in in a privateer fleet that had been chased off by the French. Many a Guernsey man served in the Royal Navy as well, including the island's most famous son, Admiral de Saumarez, who had been Nelson's second-in-command at the Battle of the Nile in '98.

David had been forced to confess that he could tell Pyewacket little of the probable drift of tide as he lacked the ability to read a nautical chart. Again Pyewacket wished that he had paid more attention when Felix had tried to teach him. Navigation was not part of the duties of a familiar and

Pyewacket had found the entire subject a trifle dull.

Guernsey was not large but there seemed to be countless places his Wizard could have come ashore. And what if he had gone to another of the islands, Jersey or Alderney for instance? Pyewacket was certain that he was not on Lihou, Sark, Herm or Jethou which were the four closest to Guernsey, for Grizel had been keeping him informed. All of those isles were quite small and she visited them regularly. She had promised to visit Jersey and Alderney, as well as the many other small islets, the Minquiers, Ecréhous, Les Dirouilles, Les Pierres de Lecq (the Paternosters), Burhou, the Casquets and the French Channel Islands, Les Îles Chaussey. There were a bewildering number of them and Pyewacket could not decide where Felix might have ended. And, too, there might have been a rescue by one of the Sea-Folk. Perhaps he even managed to get back to the yacht and was even now sailing around, looking for his familiar.

Every evening Pyewacket faced east and prayed to the cat Goddess, Bastet, that Felix was still alive and that they might be reunited. He felt half-alive without his Wizard. They had been together since Felix was eight and he himself was but a kitten and had chosen Felix as his own. He had never regretted his choice and been extremely happy, even though Felix insisted on sailing as much as possible when Pyewacket's own inclination was to stay on land. There was a special bond between Wizard and familiar that was like no other and as time went by Pyewacket refused to give up and clung to the hope that somewhere Felix was alive and they would be together once more as they were meant to be.

And worrisome indeed was the presence of the French and of the Inquisition. When the French had come to the cottage to search for weapons, Majorlaine had hidden Pyewacket beneath the floor in what she called a smuggler's hole. It was very cleverly hidden. A sliding panel that had to be pressed a certain way and one would have to know where it was to even see it. She was very afraid that a black cat would be taken by the Inquisition. The Order did not care for cats in the first place, much less black ones. Many times, just the keeping of a number of cats, or so Pyewacket had read, was enough to bring the attention of the Inquisition down on some poor and lonely old woman.

Pyewacket often lay awake wondering if the French had Felix. David doubted this for Amaury de Ollivier, he was certain, would have made public announcement if he actually had a Wizard in his clutches and all of the other commanders of the islands were obliged to report to Colonel Fournier and the Senior Witch-Sniffer, Maël. And the capture of an English Wizard would be puffed off by any one of these commanders, all eager to curry favor with Fournier.

All too often, Pyewacket played 'what if' in his mind: what if they had not come here? What if Felix had not taken his cousin and that horrible friend of his on board the *Star of the Sea*? Pyewacket had disliked Bahram from the minute he had met him — he had involuntarily let out a hiss. And he had never much use for Reginald as a Wizard without a familiar! Why hadn't he insisted to Felix that Bahram was dangerous when he knew in his heart that no good could come from having him on the yacht?

Each day that passed, he fretted and grew thin, and became more and more quiet, until he seemed but the house cat he was pretending to be.

Bahram much disliked walking any distance at all, but for what he had to do this day neither a cab nor a horse was practical. He wanted no one to see what he planned to do and horses might be frightened by it. He would not even share this with Reginald.

The Earl had remained but two days in the Isle of Wight and then had returned home. His Merman friend would contact him there in his own sea cove. And, as Bahram had predicted, he had not confirmed Reynard as his new heir, nor had he advanced the young man any more than what Reynard termed a 'pony', £25, not the thousands the idiot had confidently boasted would be his. That pathetic amount, the Earl had said grimly when bestowing the banknotes on his grandson, would have to last him until the next quarter day, June 24th, and the paying of his allowance. Belmaray had paid Reginald's shot at the inn until the end of the current week and then they must vacate or pay it themselves.

Reginald's plan to live on the yacht was forestalled by the Earl's arranging to have it sailed to his own dock at Belmaray in Devon. The old man had not even informed Reginald of the fact until the *Star of the Sea* had already left port with a hired crew of two. The Earl, it seemed, was awake on every suit.

All the more reason that he must die, for both Reginald and Bahram were very badly in need of money and must have it soon.

Bahram chose to leave the inn when Reginald had taken a 'bit too much' and was sleeping it off. It was not yet evening and Bahram had looked at his erstwhile friend in contempt as Reginald snored in a drunken stupor on the settle in their private parlor. The hashish Bahrain smoked granted him visions and wisdom but the drink this tosspot slopped down his throat only made him muddled, unable to make plans or carry them through.

That was why Bahram, with a small satchel, was walking to St. Catherine's Point.

Yesterday afternoon he had a most interesting conversation with the bar-man, who had told him all about the lighthouse that had been begun in 1785 to replace St. Catherine's Light, also known as the Pepperpot. This new light was called the "Salt Pot", but was now deserted, as it had never been completed. This would seem to be perfect for his use.

As Bahram walked, the air became noticeably cooler and a fog began to roll in from the sea. This was even better!

By the time he reached the Salt Pot the fog was thick and everything was quiet, muffled in the soft cotton of the fog. Not a soul was about; not a sound broke the stillness.

Bahram found a room in the bottom of the light house that seemed to have been designed for his use. It was large enough, but private, and he quickly set up.

First he drew, with a piece of chalk from his satchel, mystical symbols on the floor in a large Circle, very few of which would have been recognized by an English mage. Carefully, he stayed inside this Circle, closing it with a last flourish of the chalk. Then he passed his hand over it and muttered in Persian. The white chalk symbols began to glow with red light.

From the satchel at his feet Bahram drew an object

wrapped in three heavy layers of silk. One by one these fell away to reveal a lamp of beaten gold. It was a lovely thing, etched in a delicate Moorish floral design, on a pedestal, with a long spout and a lid that was fastened with a strong lock. It had no wick, however, protruding from its spout.

Lovingly, Bahram began to rub it, and said "By virtue of my necromancy, become thou my slave, O Djinn of the lamp!"

With a great noise as of rushing wind a vast cloud of blue smoke gushed forth from the lamp spout, filling in inside of the Circle, but halted therein by the magical energies.

The blue smoke turned from pale blue to a darker shade, thickened and coalesced into a shape that in a few moments was that of am immense male form, head touching the ceiling, blue of skin and dress. He wore a blue turban, a silvery blue earring in his right ear. A blue vest, trimmed in silver, was open over a broad chest. Armlets of blue were on each arm, as large around as an elephant's leg. Blue pantaloons ended not in feet, but trailing wisps of blue smoke.

Upon the blue face was an expression of thunderous rage. "Who disturbs my rest?" he demanded, his booming voice causing a few stones to fall from the wall of the unfinished light house.

"I, Ali Amir Bahram, your new Master," said the Persian calmly. "You will do my bidding, Djinn, by the names of the Seven Maleficent Spirits here inscribed. This Circle gives me power over them and over you, for I know their true names and yours as well." He pointed to the flowing Persian opposite his feet.

The blue Djinn writhed, for this was so. He could neither leave the Circle nor return to the lamp. He was bound to obey.

He folded his arms over his chest and said in resignation, "I hear and obey," and hesitated only a moment before he said "O my Master."

"This is what I wish you to do," said Bahram. "There is a man I wish to die, a magician. I shall tell you who he is and how to find him. When you have killed him you may return to your rest."

The Djinn made a low salaam. "I am yours to command, Master."

"Now listen closely," said Bahram.

124

13
Le Faeu Boulanger

The phosphorescence solidified and became a human-like form, some three feet tall. It became a handsome little fellow, with golden hair and a merry eye, dressed in the shade known as Lincoln green in a style that brought to mind Robin Hood. He wore a green cap with a pheasant feather perched rather rakishly on his fair curls and a golden sword hung at his side. He was obviously of Faerie, for he had ears as pointed as the toes of his ankle high shoes and the narrow features with soaring brows seen in pictures of the Elfin Court. At each side of this apparition hung two glowing balls of light.

As they watched, the green clad figure grew rapidly until he was the size of a well grown lad of seventeen or thereabouts. Indeed he seemed little older than that, but being a Faerie creature he was more than likely far, far older.

He took off his cap and swept a most elegant leg. Jumping off the table top he said "Greetings! I am Robin Goodfellow, sent by my father Oberon, the High King of Faerie, to offer any assistance the Selighe Court may render. We have as little desire as you do to be forced to flee these blessed isles of Britain where we have been so happy for near one thousand years. These are Will O' the Wisps," he added, waving a hand towards the balls of light.

"*Le Faeu Boulanger!*" said David involuntarily. This name, which could be translated as 'rolling fire' was what the *Guernaise* called these lights, more commonly known elsewhere as *ignis fatuus*, or foolish fire, although they had many names in the British Isles alone.

Robin smiled at him, a smile that deepened when he saw Grizel at David's side. Robin much appreciated a handsome woman, whether Faerie or mortal.

One of the balls of light spoke in the *Guernaise patois*. "We are coerced by Oberon to help you humans! We are not usually helpful!" This was an understatement, for their usual function and their delight was mischief, if not outright malice, using their lights to lead weary travelers to disaster and doom in a ditch or swamp until they were thoroughly lost or even dead.

"My father has charged you, as he has me," said Robin sternly to the Wisps "that there will be no trickery or mischief, save with the French. They are our enemies, particularly the minions of the Inquisition. Faerie folk have long memories and we well remember how they drove us from our homes in France and elsewhere in Europe. The High King is determined that they will not come here."

He turned again to face the company. "In spite of our mischief, good people, we are of the Selighe Court, the Bright Court, and our nature is for good. We cannot kill our enemies as you can, but we can make them very miserable indeed with torments and enchantments enough to make them wish that they had never come here. My father wishes to offer his apologies that we did not help when first the enemy came to these isles. We thought that the peace would resolve the conflict, but recent events have shown that we can no longer remain neutral. This Bonaparte seems a madman determined to conquer the world. He is encroaching everywhere and we are determined that we will not be driven away from these shores. I heard your plan. It is a good one. And to that we will cry havoc against the French." His smile changed and became almost sinister. "They will wish that they had never come here," he repeated

"Thank you, my lord," David said with a bow.

"I am but Robin to you. My father is the High King but my mother, alas, bears no noble blood," Robin corrected. "And now I bid you farewell. You would do well to spread the word amongst the people to look for strange and diverse happenings. But no *Guernaise* will be imposed upon. We save all of our malice for the enemy." He looked at Grizel. "Even we Faerie folk may have use of your gunpowder." And with this, and a last admiring look at Grizel, he and the *Faeu Boulanger* vanished as if they had never been.

His departure caused an outbreak of conversation and some of the Sea-Folk who had been frightened by Robin's appearance surfaced from where they had remained in safety beneath the waters.

Madoc was very pleased. "We can do naught upon the land," he said to David, "And your people can do little that will not be smoked out by the French and punished. But Faerie help now, that is a very good thing! But I know little of this Robin Goodfellow. Who is he? Is he to be relied upon?"

"I know very little either, sir," said David, exchanging glances with Grizel. "But there is a man I know, an old acquaintance of my father's, whom I might consult. He would certainly know about this Robin."

"Very well," said Madoc. "I shall be in touch again before we implement the plan and would hear what you learn of this Goodfellow. Miss Sarchet is a frequent visitor to my palace and she will be our messenger." He slid from his rocky seat and plunged beneath the water.

This seemed to be a signal for a general exodus and in twos and threes the others disappeared as well. leaving only Grizel and David in the cave. Without the Sea-Folk it seemed vast and empty.

"It went very well," said Grizel in satisfaction.

"At last we are doing something," David agreed. still slightly bemused by the appearance of the Faerie.

Grizel grew suddenly sober. "David, before we return to Belle Grève I must warn you that I sensed someone watching us at the bay. I do not think that whoever it was saw me shape-shift, but he saw us together."

"That damned Fournier has probably set someone to spy upon me!" said David bitterly. "What if they find out who you are, Grizel? You will be in danger from the Inquisition if Fournier and that terrible Father Maël find out that you are a Selchie!"

She smiled at the concern in his voice. "I have thought about that and you must say if questioned that I am your mistress, and you are meeting me for a romantic tryst. There is a sea cave along the coast that is very popular with lovers and the only practical way to get to it is to swim. You must give him the impression that I am a married woman who is entertaining a lover and take refuge in the fact that a gentleman does not reveal the names of his amorous *liaisons*."

"But your reputation!" he stammered. "You're an unmarried lady—! "

"I am half a seal and no stranger to male attentions, although it is generally with male seals, not human men. In fact ..." she paused and suddenly removed her gown, pulling it off over her head in one rapid movement. "I have been attracted to you since I met you," she said in her candid fashion. "And I think that I am not wrong to assume that you want me as much as I want you." She took his hand in hers. "Come, David, before we must return. I have made us a soft bed in the next cave. Come and love me. Then you need not lie that I am your lover, for we will be that in truth."

He followed her willingly, with no protest, heart beating fast.

The next morning when David arrived at Government House before he had even time to go to his office, the very young and earnest Lieutenant Girard, recently appointed *aide de camp* to Colonel Fournier, waylaid him with a message that the island commander required his presence urgently.

David felt a momentary spurt of sheer anger and rebellion. Why must he answer for his every movement to this obnoxious man? When Dubois was here the islanders had been largely left alone to do their business. Dubois had even turned a blind eye to the smuggling, as long as he was paid with a fine bottle of brandy regularly, appearing like magic upon his desk. But Fournier's edicts had halted the smuggling and nearly brought the fishing to a halt as well, for what few superannuated men there were left to ply the trade, that is.

David managed to contain his anger and limped after Girard, who deliberately set a fast pace that David could not hope to emulate.

"*Vite, vite, M'sieur*," Girard called out impatiently. "The Colonel is a busy man and cannot wait for you all of the day."

David gritted his teeth and walked as fast as he could. Did Fournier lay awake at night thinking up ways to torment him?

Once again, Fournier was sitting on the edge of his desk, which gave him an advantage over anyone sitting in the low basket chair where he carefully placed his visitors.

Without waiting for Girard to shut the door Fournier, with a heavy frown on his brow said "I thought that we were agreed, Dieudonné, that all your little journeys were to be approved by me. Yet I am told that you went out to Bell Grève bay yester eve for a *rendez-vous* at a late hour."

David felt himself flushing, for the Colonel's words had brought back a tantalizing memory of the hours spent with Grizel in the sea cave. He had come home in an almost euphoric state, not even noticing how much his leg and hip hurt.

"What I did last evening was my own personal affair, Colonel, and I scarcely felt that I had to have your permission to meet my mistress," he said stiffly.

"Are there not more comfortable places to conduct a love affair than on a rocky beach? " the Colonel said mockingly.

"The lady is married," David managed to get out. "And I live with my mother who would hardly approve. An inn is too public. This is a small island, Colonel and gossip travels fast. The sea caves have long been popular with lovers and the easiest, least visible way to get to them is to swim. Most islanders, even the females, swim well."

"Who is this swimming female who does not scruple to appear on a beach completely unclothed? I should like to make her acquaintance," said Fournier.

"I am a gentleman, sir. You cannot expect me to tell you that," David stated. "Such behavior would be dishonorable in the extreme. The lady trusts me to protect her name." He wanted to rise and strike Fournier. Someone was indeed spying upon him if the Colonel knew that Grizel had been naked when they met. The spy had probably not seen her shape-shift if he had not been following David too closely.

And he did not like the leer upon the Colonel's face.

Fournier studied David for a moment longer. "Still waters run deep, Dieudonné, do they not? I had the impression that you were a straight-laced Mama's boy, but here you have been conducting a torrid love affair beneath our noses! The lady must be desperate indeed for a lover if she takes a cripple to her bed!"

David's hands clenched into fists.

Fournier laughed when he saw this and began to speak

when Girard, without knocking, thrust his head inside the door and said "Father Maël is here, *mon colonel.*"

"Thank you, Girard, Send him in, *s'il vous plait.*" Fournier stood up.

"You may keep your *poule* for now, Dieudonné," he said abruptly. "But if she is even half as attractive as I have been informed, know that I shall soon be the one meeting her on the beach. For I shall find out who she is, you may rest assured and I shall lose no time in pointing out to her how great the advantage to herself in taking me as her lover."

David looked quickly at the floor so that Fournier would not see the hatred in his eyes. He wanted to leave the room and this disgusting man behind. But there was something important that he must ask first, although it went sorely against the grain to crawl to this petty tyrant.

David, to immense self-disgust, heard a tremor in his own voice, for it was all he could do to control his anger when he said "I need to make a visit to an elderly friend of my father's out in Castel parish. He is infirm and my mother has made him a basket of comforts — "

"Yes, yes," said Fournier, waving a negligent hand as the door opened again and Father Maël entered. "Go upon your errand of mercy."

The cold eyes of Father Maël raked over David as the priest of the Inquisition entered the room. His gaze seemed to say that David was of no account to him, but an insect to be swatted away if it should be troublesome.

Neither man offered David a hand when he struggled with difficulty from the basket chair. David was so angry that it made him clumsier than usual. He fancied he heard Fournier snicker when at last he managed to get from the chair.

Once the door to Fournier's office (*his* former office!) had shut behind him David changed his mind. He would not go and see what awaited him on his desk. He would go home, collect the basket Majorlaine had made up, and tool his cabriolet out to St. Cécile in Castel parish and pay a call upon Aurelius Bretton who, if anyone, would be the one man on the island who could answer his questions about Robin Goodfellow.

Aurelius had awakened that morning with a feeling of pleasurable anticipation that he could not account for. He lay still for a moment before ringing the bell for John and wondered why. Then he remembered. The young Gypsy was coming again today and there would be more stimulating conversation and exchange of ideas. It would be as if he were back at Cambridge and having a discussion with a colleague.

When John came with the morning's first cup of good China tea, strong and hot as he liked it, Aurelius said "I shall get dressed this morning, John. I've lain about too long in my dressing gown."

"Are you certain you're up to that?" John blurted out, setting the tea cup down on the bedside table. He looked rather dismayed.

"Yes, indeed I am! If it is as beautiful today as it was yesterday, in fact I think you may serve a luncheon to Mr. Lovel and myself out on the terrace."

John stiffened. "That Gypsy isn't coming here again, is he?" he demanded, his heavy brows beetling over his nose.

"Of course he is! The books are far from done, John!" Aurelius looked at his manservant, rather surprised. "In fact, I shall talk to him this morning about digging the garden when he is done with the books. I much dislike seeing my garden so shabby and overgrown and now is the time to rectify that before the fullness of summer makes it entirely impossible to tame."

"You can't have an Egyptian in this house!" John burst out. "He's just waiting for an opportunity to steal us blind! I made him turn out his pockets last night –"

"You did what?" Aurelius said in disbelief. "John, have you run mad? How could you insult him so?"

Insult a Gypsy? John stared at his master, completely flummoxed. "He's put one of those Gypsy spells on you!"

"Nonsense! From what I know Gypsies have little magic; it is not as if they are Wizards! Now help me get dressed, John, and stop this foolishness. Mr. Lovel is a very pleasant young man and very well-read and most gentlemanlike indeed. You would like him if you would but let go of this stubborn prejudice of yours. It is most unbecoming in you. I do not want to hear of you embarrassing him, and me, by treating him as if he had come to rob the house. Is that clear?" Aurelius's voice was quite stern. It had not been often that he had to lay down the law to this old retainer and friend but he would not have someone he liked treated in this fashion. What young Lovel thought he could only imagine.

As Aurelius had requested, Felix had come to him early that morning. First, he had walked with Rosal to the farm and had asked her "Why don't we have any books, Rosal?"

She stared at him as if he had two heads. "What do we need with books?" she said "We none of us can read them. Those things are for the *Gajé!*" The Romany had little use for reading or writing. In fact there were no words for 'read' and 'write' in the Romish language. If a Romany had to refer to these skills they would borrow from other languages or would use euphemisms: *chin,* which meant to cut as in carving, was used for 'write', while *gin,* to count, was used to mean 'read'.

"I can read," he said. "I found that out yesterday. I can read several languages in fact."

"Oh, you probably learned in that *Gajé* school," she said carelessly.

"Did I never talk about what I had learned in that school?" Felix asked as Chavé frisked up to them, tail wagging furiously with a stick in his mouth, wanting to play. Absentmindedly Felix took the stick from him and threw it.

"No, why would you? You were glad to get away from the *Gajé.*" Rosal tried to keep her tone light but her heart was beating fast. Surely he was not remembering! Last night he had come back to the farm and walked back to the *vardo* with her and Chavé, in a quiet mood and had remained quiet all evening. All through the meal, after what had become a nightly altercation about them serving him first and then not sitting with him to eat as was Romany custom, he had worn a slight frown. She assumed he had a headache and even Hagar had said "You got from bed too soon!"

His next question made her uneasier still.

"Do you know the name of the school and where it was located?"

"No, you never told me," she answered.

"Were you not curious as to where I obtained my education or what I did before I met you?" he said in disbelief.

"Why should I care?" she shrugged. "We met, we loved and we married and soon we will start a family. We have food and money coming in. What else matters?"

A great many other things mattered, for instance, what lay between the covers of all of those books of Professor Bretton's. That mattered a great deal. Felix could not reconcile his knowledge of books with the other facts of his existence. He had decided that in the past he must have been a farm laborer as the tasks at *Madame's* seemed so familiar to him and he had not had to be taught how to plant the parsnips or tend the animals. The tools in his hands seemed right somehow.

But so did the books. And why would a farm laborer need Latin or Greek and where would he learn it?

John soothed his lacerated feelings by banging about in the kitchen a great deal and muttering to himself. The Gypsy had shown up promptly, sparkling clean save for slightly dusty bare feet which he wiped carefully on the mat. There was nothing John could criticize.

The Master welcomed the Gypsy as if he were a long lost son and even now John could hear them talking a way, nine to the dozen and even laughing!

It was with relief that John heard a knock on the front door a little after ten. Perhaps this was some decent Christian person who would take the Master's mind from the Gypsy.

Indeed it was and John greeted the visitor with pleasure, taking a basket laden with good things from him. John put the basket in the kitchen and then led the visitor to the library.

"Sir David Dieudonné has come calling, Professor!" he announced, thinking that a real gentleman like Sir David would show up that Gypsy and make the Professor see the difference, as plain as the nose on his face.

Aurelius looked up from an inspection of an elderly volume of Herodotus' "History of the Persian Wars". The spine was sadly cracked and the leaves badly mussed. "David, my dear boy, how good to see you! It has been too long!"

"Indeed it has, sir, and I apologize for my shameful neglect," David said, shaking the elder man's outstretched hand. "My mother sends her regards and I just gave John a basket of her jellies and some baked goods as well as some stockings she knit for you."

"It is not as if you have not been busy with other things, such as governing this island! Pray thank your mother for me. I miss her company and that of your father more than I can say. We had such fascinating talks about antiquities," said Aurelius. "But sit you down and tell me all your news. As for my news, well, as you can see, I was visited by the French." he nodded towards Felix. "This is Mr. Lovel. He's helping me put the books back in place and sorting them. He is a scholar, David. He has learned Latin, Greek, old English, Medieval French and, as we found out this morning, Spanish, Italian and who knows how many other modern tongues. He is a modest fellow, though, and won't tell me the sum of his knowledge no matter how I tease him."

David had not much interest in the young man. He looked at him briefly and murmured a greeting, which Felix returned and then bent over his task again, which was sorting into chronological order the old English works. This visitor, he supposed, would put an end to any interesting conversation for the while.

After a brief catching-up, David came to the point of his visit. "I need some information, Professor, and I think perhaps you are the only one that can provide it."

"I'm always glad to help you, David," Aurelius replied.

"I need to know all you can tell me about Robin Goodfellow and the Selighe Court. It's rather urgent," David said quickly.

14
Death from the Sky

"Robin Goodfellow?" Aurelius asked in surprise. "I had not thought you interested in Faerie lore, David. Your father was the antiquarian and folklorist."

"I know, I was never interested in much save agriculture," David admitted. "But I have a particular reason for my interest now, sir, and can only tell you that it is rather important. And I was certain that you would know, better than anyone else."

"You flatter me," said Aurelius. "Of course, I shall tell you all that I know." He gathered his thoughts for a moment and then said, "Robin Goodfellow is the son of Oberon and a country girl and therefore only half a Faerie, but nonetheless at least near four or five hundred years of age. Some authorities equate him with Puck; indeed Shakespeare does so in "A Midsummer's Night Dream", when the wandering Faerie speaks to Puck, beginning by addressing him as Robin Goodfellow. She obviously thinks that he prefers being called Puck, for she says *Those Hobgoblin call you and Sweet Puck, you do their work and they shall have good luck.*" Robin is considered a Hobgoblin, which are friendly spirits of the Brownie type, helpful, good-natured but some think over fond of practical jests and japes. They also enjoy tormenting and annoying the mean, the clutch-purse and the ill-natured of humankind. You are no doubt familiar with Brownies? "

"Is that the same as the Lob for whom my mother puts out a bowl of cream each evening?" David asked. "She said that they came here from England long ago and finished up the tasks left undone in the house and on the farm."

Aurelius nodded. "They are known by many names and found all over the British Isles. They are known as Hobs, Lobs, Brownies, Bwcas in Wales, Bodachs in the Highlands of Scotland, the Fendoree on Man, and in the West country

Pixies sometimes perform the function of a Brownie. Anyone with any sense leaves a bowl of cream and perhaps an oatcake for the Brownie. I know John does so. But we were speaking of Robin Goodfellow."

"He seems to have been a precocious child, for at the age of but six he ran away from his mother's care and while he was wandering about, fell in to a deep sleep and had a vision of Faerie. When he awoke, a golden scroll lay at his side. It was from Oberon, and in it he conferred certain Faerie powers upon Robin: the power to obtain whatever he wished and the ability to shape-shift. Oberon indicated that these powers were to be used in aid of good people and to torment the bad, which of course is a hobgoblin's primary function. In return for using these powers wisely Robin was to be granted entrance into Faerie. But like many of his kind, he enjoys playing practical jokes. He is also associated with the will o' the wisps and indeed, some books claim that he is often a wisp himself. There is a chapbook of 1628 and if my books were not in such disorder I might show it to you, entitled "Robin Goodfellow : His Mad Pranks and Merry Jests". He likes to laugh – a hearty 'Ho! Ho!. Ho!' Many English country folk say 'To laugh like Robin Goodfellow' of a person who has a hearty laugh."

David nodded. All this seemed to support what he had seen of Robin and would indeed seem to indicate that the Faerie was what he had claimed. He said carefully "Are Faerie promises generally kept, sir? Is it considered a good thing to have Faerie help?"

Aurelius smiled a little wryly. "It depends upon the Faerie."

"Say, for instance, Oberon?" David said.

"Oberon is actually an Elf, even though he is High King of Faerie and has dominion over all Faerie. Elves of the Bright Court, the Selighe court, are kindly disposed towards humans, particularly Wizards and Witches, and Oberon never breaks his word. The Unselighe Court is another matter altogether. They are evil and devoted to our destruction but Merlin bound them beneath the earth for all time, with Oberon's cooperation, it is thought. The only creature left that makes life miserable for man is the bogle and in the Six Nations there are Wizards called Repressors who do naught but hunt and destroy bogles. Unfortunately, bogles breed like rabbits and where you destroy one there are ten more the next day." He smiled. "Forgive me, David, but I am telling you far more than you wished to know. Once I begin talking about my hobby I begin to lecture, which is habit, I daresay." Aurelius was extremely curious as to why his old friend's son, who had never evinced any interest in the subject before, should suddenly and urgently want to know about the Faeries.

"What about *Le Faeu Boulanger,* what you call Will o' the Wisps? Are they disposed towards good? They have a reputation here on Guernsey for leading tired travelers astray," David queried.

"There are two types of Wisps. One is the Selighe Wisp, which delight in misleading people. Sometimes, though, what is supposed to be a prank has turned to tragedy. The Unselighe Wisp, more often known as the Corpse-Candle, is regarded as a death omen. Many times it is thought that these Corpse-Candles caused the deaths they foretold. But they are now sealed away with the Redcaps, the Gwyllions, the Nixies, the Leanan-Sidhe and the others that seek to kill humans as their food," Aurelius answered. "The Selighe Wisps, of course, are under Oberon's governance and must obey him."

Felix, while still busily stacking an sorting books, listened to this conversation with absorption. It seemed some how familiar, as if he had heard it or something similar sometime before. He attempted to follow the memory but again was rewarded with a pain in his head so severe that he was forced to put his head in his hands, almost as if this act could keep his brain from exploding. David and Aurelius, deep in their conversation, did not notice.

After a few moments, in which he tried gamely to think of nothing at all (not an easy task) Felix was able to raise his head again and go back to his work, but still feeling weak and shaken. It was perhaps fortunate he was already seated on a low stool.

Rosal kept assuring him that he would remember but every attempt that he made to peer through the fog that obscured his past rewarded him with nothing but pain. And the pain, he had observed, was growing more acute, not lessening. Thanks to Hagar's magical touch the head wound was mostly healed and the pain of the wound gone. But the agony in his mind, both mental and physical, was at its worst when he attempted to recall anything personal, not just his name and his life before and with Rosal, but when he sought to recollect where he might have learned about books, or on what farm he had been taught to work the earth and tend animals. It was all gone and he became panicked when he thought that it might never come back. Rosal and Hagar were of little help for it seemed that he had known them for such a short while and appeared to have told them almost nothing about himself. They did not even know where he had lived before coming to Guernsey. He could not imagine why he and Rosal had married if she had discovered so small an amount about him. Surely one wished to know all about the beloved? Perhaps that was the way it was amongst the Romany; he had no way of knowing. Many of the Romany customs he found very strange.

A short while later David took his leave, after thanking Aurelius for his help. He would not stay for tea, he explained; he had not as yet been to his office at Government House and could not neglect his duties there.

Aurelius stared after him for a moment and murmured to himself "Another mystery. The area is becoming rife with them." Something in David's manner had prevented questioning. With a sigh, he turned towards Felix and said "What are you working on at the moment?"

"I have just begun to sort the Faerie lore. Many of the books are badly damaged," Felix answered. "Michael Drayton's *Nymphidia* will have to be completely rebound and Simon Steward's *A Description of the King and Queene of Fayries* is in like case."

"Yes, the French seemed to have a particular malevolence towards anything of Faerie," said Aurelius on a sigh. "Both of those volumes are nearly two hundred years old. One would think that their age alone would engender some respect ...but come, do you ring the bell for John and we shall have our mid-morning tea. I find myself sharp-set this morning."

Felix did as he was bid and then joined Aurelius at the desk, moving several stacks of books to make room for the tray that John would bring.

"The worst part of growing old," said Aurelius, "is losing friends. David's father was a man whose company I much enjoyed. Before I was confined to this chair we spent much time exploring the many dolmens hereabouts. Years ago it was thought that the mounds of grass and granite were Druidical temples from the time of Julius Caesar. But David's father, Nazaire, was among the first to discover that they are barrows, grave sites of a people no doubt much earlier than the Romans. When we are done with this project I shall show you the collection of bronze and copper and iron artifacts I have amassed. I am thankful that they are locked away in a hidden place else the French would have no doubt relieved me of the spear heads and arrow tips, thinking they could be used as weapons. Ah, here is John with the tea things. He must have been expecting a summons, although it is a trifle early."

When Aurelius said 'Druid' a fleeting pain stabbed through Felix's head, red hot, come and gone so quickly that it showed only briefly on his face. As Aurelius had been looking up at John as he spoke the Professor did not notice.

But John did and misread it. He thought that the grimace, so quickly suppressed, was one of triumph, for Aurelius was planning to show that thieving tinker where the household treasure lay. John had often heard both Sir Nazaire and his Master talk about the probable worth of those bits of old metal. John though it just a lot of rubbishy old junk, scarcely worth the work it took of grubbing about in those nasty old graves. But there were other precious things locked up with that old stuff; silver and snuffboxes and miniatures set in gold frames...things the Gypsy would love to get his dirty paws upon. Thumping the tray down upon the desk John gave the Gypsy a sharp look. He was not going to get away with anything in this house, not while John Grant was on guard! And somehow, he was going to get rid of the Gypsy altogether, John resolved.

After a strenuous morning working out in the fields with his laborers, Richard walked down to the dock, with Greymalkin at his heels.

Richard had always liked the feel and smell of the earth. He was keenly interested in agricultural improvement and corresponded with other leading agriculturists all over the country. He had attended gatherings of eminent farmers, including in Norfolk, where he had been welcomed to Holkam by Thomas Coke himself. Indeed, he and Felix had been invited to Holkam for the sheep shearing, coming up in the next month. His grandson was as interested in agriculture and the productivity of the estate and the welfare of the tenants as was Richard himself and knew as much about planting and husbandry as did his grandsire, most of his knowledge gained by practical experience on the land and in the great barns.

Thinking of Holkam and how much the two of them had enjoyed the trips there, Richard said abruptly "Grey, I sometimes wonder if I love Felix so well and Reginald so little because Felix is much more like me. We shared so many passions. I could l see myself in him, in his love of the land, of learning, of magic, art and music for we shared all of that. Reginald seems but to love gaming, drinking an playing the fool with women, all things I find abhorrent. Perhaps if I had loved him more he might have turned out better. I am afraid, looking back, that I might have let him see my disdain, perhaps compared him to Felix or to Felix's father too often. It may be laid in my dish that I ruined him through neglect."

"Oh, rot!" said Greymalkin feelingly. "When Reginald arrived here at the age of ten, after Alfred's death, he had already been expelled from Eton for lying and dishonorable behavior and persistent lying at that. He cheated on an exam and lied about it and his house master was certain that he had stolen money from other boys. And don't forget he then proceeded to get himself sent down from Winchester as well *and* Oxford! It seems to me he was rusticated at least every other term. Once, I remember, for having a doxy in his rooms! No, Richard, his character was formed for ill long before he came here. I doubt if there was anything you could have done. All the love and care in the world would not have affected his natural bent. Look at the care you took with Alfred for he was much the same. What's bred in the bone comes out in the flesh and they both took after Matilda."

Richard's face darkened. Matilda, Alfred's mother and

Reginald's grandmother had been his second wife. Cedric's mother, the love of Richard's life, a beautiful, loving, laughing Welsh Witch called Olwen, had died at Cedric's birth. And Richard, uncaring, certain that he would never love again, had allowed his father, who was still living at the time, to arrange a 'good' second marriage to give the baby Cedric a mother. In the end Richard had almost ended in hating Matilda, for she was whining, selfish and cold-natured, as well as shallow and a bad mother. It was from her family that came the tendency to drink and the love of gaming. He had seen nothing of himself in Alfred and felt the same about Reginald.

Grey was right. But how he now wished Reginald was otherwise! if Felix were truly gone, the estate would be Reginald's and a careless master he would be! The only thing that Richard could do would be to tie everything up, legally, so that Reginald could not bring it to wrack and to ruin and pray that Reginald made a good marriage and espoused a young woman of sense. He needed to make an appointment with his solicitor in Torquay immediately.

The estate of Belmaray was an old one. It had been awarded to the first Jourdaine, Sir Philippe, who was in the train of William the Conqueror in 1066. The name, Belmaray, it was thought, was a corruption of the name of Sir Philippe's wife, known to all as *la belle* Marie, a beautiful and accomplished Breton noblewoman, and accomplished in Witchcraft as well as needlework and music.

The old house, originally a Norman keep, but added onto by each succeeding generation, stood high on a hill or tor as it was called here in Devon, commanding a view of both the narrow combe in which lay the village, also called Belmaray, and of the sea. Devon was famous for rugged coastline as well as its verdant beauty. The way down to the dock on the Earl's cove was steep and many years ago a stair had been built to make it easier to get up and down. The stair was as steep as the narrow streets in the village, which seemed to the visitor unaccustomed to Devon, almost vertical. Cobbed, thatched buildings seemed more like steps for a giant. The Earl loved every inch of it and Felix had also. But Reginald? Did Reginald love anything save his own pleasure?

Richard and Greymalkin had nearly reached the dock

where they were going to inspect the *Star of the Sea* when suddenly the trumpet of an enraged dragon filled the air and Richard, grabbing the railing of the steps whirled in time to see Pascoe, flaming, rising from behind the thick bands of trees that hid the house from the dock and beach. Instinctively, he reached for his wand in the breast pocket of his jacket.

Greymalkin hissed, his fur on end and his ears flat against his skull. "Richard! Look out!" he shrieked.

Above them was a huge blue mass in the sky, approaching them rapidly. As it came nearer, Richard could see that it was in the shape of a man, but blue of skin and enormous in size. Pascoe, thirty feet long, was nearly dwarfed by it. This apparition crackled with energy and hostility.

He spied Richard below and with a malevolent leer he gathered a ball of energy and threw it at the Earl.

Richard pointed his wand upwards and threw up a shield. The blue energies broke upon it and scattered.

"It looks like something from the Arabian Nights!" Richard shouted to Grey, who crouched at his feet.

"I don't care what it looks like! Get rid of it!" the familiar shouted back. "It seems to want to kill us!"

Above them Pascoe let out a long stream of flame, which appeared to hurt the blue creature, for it shrieked and turned on the dragon, throwing another ball of energy at him.

"Oh, no you don't!" said Richard and quickly threw a wall up between Pascoe and what he was beginning to be certain was a genie of some sort. Where had a genie come from? And what was more, why was it attacking them?

Wizards were trained not to kill unless absolutely necessary. But self-defense was allowed and to kill black magicians was a duty. Even at this distance Richard could sense the evil intent of the genie.

The energies that the genie had thrown slammed into Richard's defensive wall and rebounded back on him, causing him to scream with rage and pain. He whipped around in the sky, his legless body trailing blue vapor like a cloud. His face was distorted in rage and he raised a hand as a huge as a giant ham once more and tossed another blue ball at Richard and Greymalkin.

Violet light flared from the   tip of Richard's wand, through the fire opal that was his focus stone and spread out to catch and destroy the blue ball. The sound as the two met was louder than most thunderclaps, the light brighter than lightning.

"Get behind him!" Richard shouted to Pascoe. "When I let loose my leveler, flame him for all you are worth!"

The copper dragon dipped his wings to show that he had understood and flew a little ways away while Richard distracted the genie with a series of fast and furious violet bolts that exploded all around him.

Then Pascoe turned, fast, and came at the back of the genie, who was occupied in fending off Richard's barrage.

The very minute that Pascoe was at the precisely correct distance Richard yelled "NOW!" and completely   opening himself to the ley lines, drew all the power he could, which was considerable, and compelled it to go through his wand. Pascoe opened his maw to its widest and let out a monstrous wall of flame, white-hot and billowing.

The genie was caught in the middle of a mingled conflagration of violet energy and red and orange flame. Blended, it was horrifyingly strong, almost as if hot lava from an active volcano had caught the blue giant in its unstoppable path. He began to yell in pain and fear, causing Greymalkin to drop to the boards of the steps and cover his sensitive feline ears with his paws.

The fire and smoke seemed to fill the entire sky as, twisting and turning, the genie tried to escape his fate. But he could not. Still burning, he fell into the sea, where an immense cloud of steam at once billowed up as the fire was somewhat doused.

But dragon fire would burn for a while, even beneath the waves, until all that remained of the enemy would be consumed.

With a thump, Pascoe landed on the dock at the foot of the steps.

"Good work, old friend!" said Richard gratefully, putting his wand away.

"What was that thing?" Pascoe asked."I was in the dragon pen, dozing, and I looked up to check the clouds when I saw it coming. I knew at once that it was evil from the look on its face! Thank the Dragon Lord I ate a good amount of firestone this morning!"

"And thanks be to Bastet that you trumpeted and warned us!" said Greymalkin, sitting up with a shudder. "It gave Richard a chance to get out his wand and for me to start praying!"

"I think it was a genie, or Djinn," Richard said in answer to Pascoe's question. "They are found in Arabia, Persia, and the Levant."

"Arabia?" Pascoe repeated, shocked. "Then what is it doing in Devon? And why was it trying to kill us?"

Those were questions that Richard would also like very much to be answered. Where did it come from and who had sent it? And why did someone want him and his friends dead?

15
Faerie
Impediments

It had been a long day for Didier Durand. He had never realized that becoming a corporal would involve so much more responsibility. His sergeant had impressed upon him the value of hard work and the example he must set for the men.

But now, finishing up a long day, he could only think of his supper, a glass of wine, and then bed. But instead he was out on patrol, riding around the parish of St. Martin on the eastern side of the Island. Tomorrow would be the first assemblies of the civilians and Durand had already been informed that it would be his duty to collect the names and addresses and other necessary information from all of the inhabitants.

But tonight, the new commander of St. Martin's parish, Lieutenant Duval, had ordered Didier to go out and make certain that all the people, on this long summer's eve, were not out and about, but in their homes and not meeting in groups that might be conspiring against the new government.

Didier thought this singularly stupid. Since they had been here in St. Martin he had seen no one who looked capable of a conspiracy of any kind. There were but women and children and old men, most of the latter quite infirm. It would be all one of those superannuated men could do to walk across a room, never mind mount a resistance. And to think females could fight against them – it was ludicrous! And had not everything that could be used as a weapon been taken from them?

But here he was, riding uselessly about the parish when he had far rather be in his bed.

Guernsey was a beautiful place, Didier supposed, if one cared for that sort of thing. The tree-edged lanes were canopied with ivy and the scent of honeysuckle hung heavy in the warm air, intoxicating the senses. Flowers bloomed in the hedge-rows and he had seen apple orchards, set inside embankments covered in furze. Far too rural for Didier's taste. The cider produced here was very good, though.

He had ridden by lovely Moulin Huet bay, with its wonderful chain of rocks, partially hemming in the bay. One of the rocks was called 'Andrelot' by the country people hereabouts. This strange, figure-like rock was considered the guardian spirit of the bay, called *le petit bonhomme* and every boat that went by dipped its ensign in Andrelot's honour and a small oblation was cast over the side, "just for luck", as the local fishermen sailed past.

Didier thought of this and of other superstitions with amused contempt. He was a Parisian and held such things in abhorrence as the simplistic beliefs of rustics who did not understand the difference between enlightened thought and myth. All this nonsense about Faeries and Goblins and the powers of Witchcraft – it was foolishness!

Colonel Fournier and the Inquisition would soon bring rational thought to these islands. They were to pull down the primitive statue of a woman that was found here on the church grounds in St. Martin, the one known as *La Gran'mère du Chimquière*. The dolmens, the other primitive statues, the menhirs; all were to be destroyed and the granite used to make the new fortifications.

It was his horse who first noticed the noises. They had been proceeding at a sedate walk through the lanes, and Didier was certain that Marron was thinking of his stable as much as he, Didier, was thinking of his bed.

Marron, who had been named for his chestnut coat, suddenly stopped short and flung up his head, snorting. The bit jingled and at first Didier did not hear anything. A hand laid on Marron's neck reassured and quieted him and then Didier heard the first sweet notes of a harp.

It was quite the most ravishing music he had ever heard and called to him, both enticing and commanding. It drew him onwards and, as he emerged from the trees, he could suddenly see lights ahead.

As he drew closer to the site (it was near one of the menhirs) he heard singing begin and he found tears pouring down his face as it continued. Never had he heard its like, not even at the Paris Opera. It was piercingly, unbearably lovely, haunting in its strangeness, in a language he could almost, but not quite, understand.

He should not have been able to see as clearly as he did. The moon was between the new and the first quarter, not at the full and its light was somewhat obscured by the thin veiling of high clouds. But quite near inside the circle of the menhir stones, he saw figures dancing, lit as brightly as if it were the full light of day.

He stopped his horse and dismounted, forgetting to tie Marron to a nearby bush. As silently as possible Didier crept towards the dancing and singing company, compelled by he did not know what. It drew him as nothing else had ever done.

The dancers were all female and the loveliest creatures Didier had ever seen. They were tall and slim with either dark or golden hair that came well past their waists and floated about them like a seductive cloud as they moved in impossibly graceful patterns. Their gowns were of diaphanous green, clinging to beautiful bodies, easily seen through the gauzy fabric and their feet were bare.

He got as near as he dared, staring with longing at them as the dance continued. He had never seen such lovely women.

One them caught sight of him suddenly and stopped the dance, and whispered to her friends, who laughed at what she said, a sound that was more like silver chimes than laughter.

Lightly, she then ran towards Didier and put out her hand. "Come! Dance with us!" she demanded.

He stood up, eagerly, from where he had been partially concealed by a rock, everything forgotten: his horse, his duty, his patrol, as he looked into her strange, slightly slanted eyes under brows that went up towards her hairline. So bemused was he that he did not notice her pointed ears or her narrow, alien face. He only saw her beauty and felt overwhelming desire for her.

When they found him in the morning he could only babble and was quite unable to tell them what had happened to him. He had to be sent back to France, to the care of his family, and was of little use to anyone for several months.

Madame had told Rosal of the new edict demanding that all persons in the parish assemble each Tuesday and Thursday and was insistent that the Gypsy girl and her family attend, for the penalties for not doing so were severe. She even gave Rosal a paper, which stated, although Rosal could not read it, that the *vardo* was in the Brehaut woods with *Madame's* permission, and that Rosal was gainfully employed at the farm. She told Rosal to have her Rom ask Aurelius Bretton to do the same for him.

Aurelius, faced with the daunting task of getting in and out of the pony cart, requested that Felix come early on the day of the assembly and help him. John could no longer do it. John's back was so bad that outdoor tasks were getting beyond him. Even with *Madame* Brehaut coming two mornings a week he could just about keep up the inside work, but caring for the grounds or the pony and the garden were now really an impossibility. They had been obliged to hire Joisaine to take care of the pony. That was all the girl had time for, as she was needed on the farm too badly.

Aurelius had quite made up his mind to offer young Mr. Lovel a permanent position. There was enough work as the pony needed care, the gardens, both the kitchen garden and the flowers, would soon be bursting with new life and need constant tending. There were repairs to be done about the house, for it was now five years since the French had stolen the men away to be forcibly conscripted into the army and Aurelius had been able to have additional servants.

And Aurelius much enjoyed talking to the young man, although he was no closer to solving the mystery of a Gypsy well-versed in the classics than he had been the first day. Perhaps as he gained Lovel's trust the young man would become more confiding. But the Gypsy had a fine mind and being with someone who shared his taste in books had made Aurelius feel alive again. He had so missed intellectual stimulation! He looked forward to each day now and in a haze of new-found happiness and satisfaction, chose not to notice John's black looks.

The recent spate of foul weather seemed to have vanished on that Thursday morning which promised to be both fair and warm. It seemed as if everything had sprung into bloom all at once. The apple trees were a riot of pink and white blossom and every other flowering thing had made good on its promise of beauty to come overnight.

Aurelius had not enjoyed getting into the relatively low two-wheeled chaise. It had been a struggle, even with young Lovel's strong arm. He cursed silently the necessity of these weekly assemblies. All winter he had not even been to church as it had proved to be too much effort, and the pony was getting fat and lazy.

He was an Exmoor pony, tough and hardy, a bay with no white markings, and had been christened Diogenes by Aurelius for no other reason than it seemed to fit him. As Aurelius settled into the seat behind the pony he noticed that Diogene's bay coat shone from currying and brushing and the chaise, unused most of the winter save when John went to St. Cécile for the marketing, had been cleaned as well.

Aurelius was correct in assuming that Felix had come even earlier than requested and had done these tasks. That should show John that the Gypsy was not dirty or lazy and that he seemed to know the way things needed to be done in a gentleman's house.

With difficulty, for he refused any help from the Gypsy, John climbed into the chaise beside his Master and took up the reins.

John, however, was far from pleased at this evidence of industry, and done on his own initiative as well, on the part of Felix. He grumbled to himself and brusquely told Felix that there was no room when Aurelius suggested that they could squeeze up and make room for him.

"I shall walk, sir," Felix said "Grant is quite correct. You would be made uncomfortable if I were to climb in to the carriage as well. I doubt Diogenes can walk much faster than I can."

John fumed. The Gypsy had the gall to call him "Grant" as if he were John's equal, or even, by his tone, his superior! The Gypsy must be gotten rid of! Perhaps the French, when

149

they saw him, would take him away as cannon fodder for the army. That was all that he was good for, in John's view.

The assembly point for all the inhabitants of the parish was to be the parish church, which in the case of Castel, was the church of St. Marie du Castro. This church was clear across the parish, on the border of St. Andrew parish and a considerable distance for the old and infirm to travel, even on a warm and bright morning in May. They were to all be there by nine A.M. and the new parish commander, Captain Gaspard Martel, awaited their coming impatiently.

Captain Martel, no taller than the First Consul Bonaparte and much heavier, bitterly resented being assigned to this backwater, away from the fighting on the continent. Four days ago, according to the latest courier pigeon, a force under General Mortier had invaded Hanover and that was now the place to be if one wanted to achieve military greatness.

But if he had to be anywhere on this cursed island, why not at St. Peter Port, where the main command was to be? Not out here in this rural fastness with a lot of peasants! And on top of this annoying assembly of people beneath the Captain's notice, the man sent out on one of Colonel Fournier's new patrols had disappeared last night. He had never reported in and his horse had been found wandering this morning. There was no sign of his rider, nor any sign of violence. The soldier had just disappeared into thin air, or so it seemed.

And other soldiers, who had gone to a public house last evening had reported seeing strange lights far off on their way back to their barracks and hearing voices on the wind. One, walking in the woods, was certain that he was being followed. He claimed to have heard mocking laughter and when he passed beneath a tree his hat had been snatched from his head.

Captain Martel, of course, dismissed these as the ravings of men who had imbibed too freely. The missing soldier was probably lying at the bottom of a quarry with a broken neck or in a ditch, dead drunk. All the same, it had to go into his daily written report to Colonel Fournier and a detail would have to be dispatched to search for the missing solider. It was just another annoyance.

The church here had another of those crudely carved statues of a woman, this one even less finished than the one in St. Martin and somehow much more sinister. It was to pulled down from its place beside the west door of the church. It had actually been discovered in the church itself, a fact which Captain Martel, a devout man, found disturbing. And why had they not disposed of such a pagan object, instead of enshrining it near a church? These islands were too full of pagan superstitions and heretical leanings. The sooner the fires started burning heretics, the better.

By nine nearly fifty persons had assembled, a number that the Captain found agreed with his preliminary figures. And a rag-tag, motley crew they were too. Children, many of them in outgrown, outworn clothing (for cloth, like so many other things, had become difficult to come by), their mothers and grandmothers, some young unmarried women, many old people and even a trio of Gypsies.

Corporal Robert and Sergeant Lavasseur questioned each person as to their name, habitation and occupation. The Gypsies, Martel was glad to learn, were gainfully employed and allowed to live in a wood attached to a farm but nonetheless the Sergeant warned the two women against any kind of fortune-telling, promising that they would burn if they plied this trade so despised by the Inquisition and told the man that horse or chicken stealing would be punished by hanging.

Each person was then given a number and told that they must utter the number from now on when the role was called at each assembly. When the Corporal and the Sergeant were finished with this part, it was Martel's turn. He had new, more stringent rules to announce.

Unless permission had been given, for an innocuous meeting such as the women's meetings to knit and sew, all persons were to be in their homes by nine at night and all lights were to be extinguished by ten. Church attendance would be compulsory, in a Roman Catholic Church, not the Presbyterianism that had shocked the priests who had come here with the occupying forces. It seemed heretical to them that a French-speaking people should be Presbyterian, of all things!

A placard was given out that would be attached to their house, near the main door, and beneath it would be listed he number of people who occupied the home. There would be unannounced visits, to ascertain that everyone was where they belonged and permission must be obtained and a written pass issued to go anywhere at all outside one's village, save for these twice weekly assemblies.

Captain Martel reiterated yet again that the attendance at these was compulsory. If one of the islanders was ill, he or she must see the army doctor, who would write an official excuse, if he thought the illness were serious enough to warrant remaining in bed.

And beginning on the very next day, the Inquisition would be going from house to house, looking for evidence of heresy. Non-attendance at church would be counted as proof of heresy, as would non-compliance with any of these commands. Any *auto de fés* in the parish would be attended by all with no exceptions. Even children must come to learn the fate of heretics, to keep their feet upon the right path. To stay away was another mark of a heretic. It would be the islanders' duty to turn in any of their neighbors that might be heretics, particularly of the magical sort. The Captain read out a list of the amount of reward that could be expected for becoming a Judas, and paused as if he expected someone to come forward at that moment to point an accusatory finger at someone else.

But no one stirred. The faces gazing back at him were singularly blank.

Captain Martel was disappointed for he, too, would be granted a monetary reward for each heretic that was found in his parish, with a double sum if the heretic was magical.

"You are dismissed," he said brusquely. "Remember, Tuesday next, here, at nine! Make certain everyone is here and promptly! There will be fines for those who are late in reporting. Constant tardiness will mean time in gaol or a flogging and neither age nor the sex of the offender will matter for punishment *will* be administered."

The crowd, who had been almost completely silent

except for several sobbing children, quickly hushed by their mothers at Captain Martel's glare, began to disperse, still quietly.

Aurelius was glad to be escorted by John back to the chaise. Standing that length of time had been difficult for him and he realized ruefully that he would have to resort to a cane for these assemblies, or perhaps even a pair of crutches, as the soldiers had not allowed him to lean upon young Lovel as he had wished to do. The Gypsies were made to stand together, apart from the other parishioners.

Aurelius had wondered who the females might be. Perhaps his sister and his mother? They had been standing too far away for him to hear their answers to the questions the soldiers had put to them.

Felix came quickly when he saw Aurelius making his slow painful way to the chaise. John, too, was in pain. His back injury was such that he could walk quite a long way but standing in one position any length of time was excruciating.

Rosal came after Felix, walking behind him as was proper for a Romany woman. She was curious to see this man who was hiring her Rom.

"Let me help you, sir," said Felix and gave Aurelius the support of his arm as he made the painful climb into the chaise.

"Thank you," said Aurelius gratefully. As he settled into the seat he smiled at his young friend. "And this young lady is –?"

"This my wife, Rosal. Rosal, this is Professor Bretton," Felix performed the introductions.

Aurelius was surprised. "Your wife? But are you not over young to be married?"

John, once again refusing help, had crawled in to the seat on the opposite side of the carriage and grimaced at this revelation. A wife! Just what was *not* needed! Gypsies breeding!

"We Romany marry young," said Rosal, and took Felix's arm in a proprietary manner. She felt some sort of threat from this old man, as if he might steal her new Rom from her and wished to establish her rights. "We hope to start our family very soon."

Aurelius began to speak but just as he began a roar like

thunder magnified ten times split the sky and echoed back, sending roll after roll of sound inundating the island.

There was screaming and the babies began to cry in earnest. All was confusion, everyone looking about wildly.

"Gather them up again!" Captain Martel was shouting. "Let no one go anywhere! That was not thunder! Something has exploded and they shall all have to be questioned!"

And even as the soldiers, with leveled bayonets, began herding the people into a group once more, bells began to wildly peal from the east from the direction of St. Peter Port.

16
Repercussions

"Once again, Dieudonné," said Colonel Fournier angrily, "you have exceeded your authority! I did not give my permission for this flotilla of carriages!"

"Colonel, I but organized transportation for the sick and infirm to enable them get to your assemblies!" said David, equally angry. "How, pray, is someone like *Madame* Michel of this parish, who is above eighty years of age, very lame and nearly blind, to get to the assemblies? She is too poor to keep a carriage and her neighbor, *Madame* Bertrand, who looks after her since *Madame* Michel's son is now in the army, does not keep a carriage either. And *Madame* Bertrand has small children who cannot walk the entire distance. She cannot carry all three of them! I intend to make the same arrangements in all of the parishes by Tuesday next so that no one is forced to suffer unduly. I fail to see this as a criminal act, nor one that needs permission. You yourself have said that the people must attend the assemblies. I am but making it easier for them to do so!"

"It might be said, Colonel, that Sir David has but obeyed your edict and is bowing to your commands. Perhaps without the carriages many of these persons would not arrive at the assemblies in time," suggested a smooth, resonant voice from near the window.

Colonel Fournier turned to face Father Maël, who stood, arms crossed over his chest, in front of the window that looked out over the harbor. It was a peaceful view of blue water, ships riding at anchor, gulls and terns flying overhead. It was a picture of pure tranquility.

Fournier much resented the priest's comments, but no one protested the Inquisition's interference in any matter, whether civil or ecclesiastical, particularly not a Senior Witch-Sniffer who wore the mark of Papal favor. One might find oneself on the rack being put to the question. Nevertheless Fournier was aggrieved that Father Maël had presumed to chide him in front of his inferiors.

"Some provision must be made for the halt and the sick, Colonel!" David continued. "This is a small island, but a walk of even one mile for an elderly or crippled person can seem insurmountable. And a small child cannot be expected to walk four or five miles. They are simply not up to it."

"Very well," Fournier acquiesced with ill grace. "I shall allow it, but if you again take so much upon yourself, Dieudonné, I shall have your hide. Is that clear?"

"Very clear," answered David.

"Colonel Fournier has had some interesting reports come across his desk this morning, Sir David," said Father Maël. Unlike the Colonel he always addressed David properly. "Missing soldiers, strange lights, voices and music in every parish. What can you tell us about this strangeness?"

David looked blank. "Strange lights? Music?" he repeated. "I cannot imagine what that might be, Father. If there were still magical folk on the Island I might think that they were celebrating one of their rituals but, they are all gone and it is the wrong time of the month at any rate."

"And how do you know what time of the month these 'rituals' were held?" demanded the priest quickly.

"Why, everyone knew, magical or not!" said David in surprise "The times and the meeting places were published in our news-sheet, the *Gazette de L' Île de Guernsey*. And it was common knowledge that they conducted the dances and gatherings during the full moon. The moon is not even at the quarter as yet. Perhaps your men saw *Le Faeu Boulanger*, the *ignis fatuus* lights. They are quite common here. We islanders have learned to disregard them. I cannot imagine what else they might have seen or heard. I have asked everyone that I have come in contact with to remain in their homes after dusk and they all agreed to do so."

"Then either they have lied to you, Dieudonné, or you are lying to us", Fournier began angrily, "for there is something going on here! The commanders of each parish were my personal choices. All are sober, well-trained men who do not have fancies! And yet this morning all ten daily reports speak of such things! How do you account for that, pray?"

A thunderous boom shook the room, shattering the glass in the windows and showering Father Maël in broken glass.

Colonel Fournier jumped to his feet, swearing, while David rose painfully from the low chair. "What was that?" he exclaimed.. He had of course, knowledge of what it probably was, but the plan had been for Hamish and Nim to blow up the *Acadie* at a time of their choosing so that no one would have to play-act astonishment. And he *was truly* astonished at the strength of the explosion.

Calmly, Father Maël shook the broken glass from his black cassock and then leaned out the window. "Something has blown up in the harbor but there is too much smoke. Fournier, have you a spy glass?"

Fournier ripped open a desk drawer and took out a brass-bound spy glass and crossed the room quickly to stand by the priest who took the glass from him, putting it to his eye and leveling it at the harbor.

Outside, the air was full of screaming, smoke and the crackle of flames. Bells began to ring out and there was the clatter of many feet in the streets and shouting from many throats.

Father Maël lowered the spyglass, his face darkening. "It looks as if the *Acadie* has been destroyed," he announced, the only sign of his anger a frown line between his brows.

"What!" Fournier snatched the spy glass from the priest and adjusted it. From what he could see through the drifting smoke, where the *Acadie* had been moored that morning was a flaming wreck, sinking even as he watched. Small boats were already heading towards what little remained of the frigate, picking up bodies and survivors from the water.

Running feet were heard outside and the door to Fournier's office crashed open, revealing a horrified and breathless Lieutenant Girard. "Sir! The *Acadie* has blown up!" he gasped.

"I know that, fool!" snapped the Colonel. "Go at once and order that all of the people in this entire parish are to be rounded up for questioning!"

"But, sir, they are all here ,at the assembly! Captain Parmentier has not as yet dismissed them! And Dieudonné is here with you and the Holy Father. Everyone is accounted for!" stammered Girard.

"Then the culprit will be someone from some other parish!" Fournier almost shrieked. "Messengers are to go out at once. Everyone is to be questioned! Everyone, until someone confesses!" He watched until Girard saluted and ran off again and then turned on David. "I will get to the bottom of this, Dieudonné! You will not get away with this!"

Maël interrupted him, his lips tight pressed together. "Do not be more of a fool than you can help, Fournier! What do you think? That Sir David is able to be in two places at once? And he is crippled as well. He has made very effort to cooperate with us."

"And that is exactly why I suspect him! One of these islanders, under his direction, has no doubt done this!" Fournier said.

"And how are we to effect an explosion, Colonel?" David protested hotly. "We have neither gunpowder, or ammunition of any kind, not even pitchforks left!"

Fournier stared at him angrily and then said abruptly "Get out of my sight. Go to your office and stay there. Someone will be along to question you shortly."

David limped to the door, and with a short bow, left without a word.

"You *are* a fool, Fournier," said the priest shortly.

"He defies me at every turn," Fournier muttered.

"Because he makes arrangements for other cripples and the elderly to have a method of getting to your assemblies? You see conspiracy underneath each rock! No, it was probably one of these English Wizards that destroyed the *Acadie*. We are not really certain of what those foul creatures of Satan are capable. From what I have read and studied a Wizard would not need powder with which to destroy a wooden ship. Satan grants them the power of calling down the lightning. They no doubt chose the *Acadie* as she was full of our Holy instruments of persuasion," stated the priest. "It would not surprise me to learn that a Wizard is in hiding somewhere on this isle of heretics, that they are even perhaps protecting him. But we will find him, and he will burn, for I know a Wizard's weakness."

Captain Martel harshly questioned each and every person at the Castel assembly as to what they knew about the explosion. While he was conducting his investigation, messages arrived from Colonel Fournier. Captain Martel was happy to find that he had already anticipated the Colonel's orders: all persons were to be detained and thoroughly interrogated as to what they knew about the destruction of the *Acadie*. Martel was shocked beyond measure that a frigate, one that had borne the Holy Inquisitors from Rome, had been destroyed in a peaceful harbor. This was resistance on a very high level indeed.

But the interviews with the people were frustrating for most of them said "What do you mean?" when he ordered them to tell him all they knew of the affair of the *Acadie*. Most of them claimed never even to have heard of the ship at all.

Aurelius when questioned, said "Captain, these people are simple farmers and most of them are women or as old as I. The ladies have enough to do with caring for their farms and their children and we have no news here. Yes, it is a small island, but the news-sheet has been suspended and travel between parishes discouraged and now is forbidden without permission. How, pray, are we to get news of even what happens in St. Peter Port?" This was said reasonably but Martel gave Aurelius a look of deep dislike. He was not in a mood to listen to logic.

Not one person seemed suspicious or seemed to be feigning surprise at what had happened. There were no evasive looks, no triumphant glances. Captain Martel could not think of an excuse to take any of them into custody, not even the Gypsies as the young ones had been at their places of employment all day yesterday and had eaten their supper at the farm.The Captain could not conceive of a woman doing such a thing at any rate. A woman would not have the nerve and daring, nor the skill with munitions that was needed. Captain Martel had a poor opinion of female capabilities.

And the inescapable fact was that at the time of the destruction of the Acadie, everyone in this parish had been right here, under the very noses of the French Force of Occupation.

At long last, near three in the afternoon, a day without

meals and with only water from the nearby Holy well to drink, the Captain was forced to dismiss the Castel parishioners, everyone having been questioned forward and backwards and nothing at all illuminating had emerged from any of his inquiries. Not intimidation, nor threats nor accusation produced any result except reiterated statements of "I do not know!"

Curfew, he announced grimly before he allowed them to disperse, would begin this very evening with everyone to be in their place of habitation and locked in by sundown. His men would be conducting random checks. Lights were to be off early tonight, by nine.

Rosal returned with *Madame* Brehaut and Joisaine, for there had been little time that morning to do else than milk the cows and feed the animals. The stables still needed work and there would be the evening milking as well.

Felix walked back with Aurelius and John. Both older men were in much pain, as they had been kept standing about most of the day. John could scarcely crawl into the pony cart and had to grudgingly accept Felix's help out of the cart.

When Aurelius and John were led carefully into the library Felix stood for a moment looking at them both. "Sir," he said to Aurelius, "perhaps I had best stay the night. You are in no fit case —"

"We don't need your help, Gypsy!" said John harshly. "Once I've rested a moment —"

"Don't be ridiculous, John," said Aurelius tiredly. "The only thing that will help you is a mustard plaster and your bed, in that order. We both need food and are incapable of getting it for ourselves. if Mr. Lovel will indeed stay the night with us and help us out I shall be very grateful to him." He smiled in an exhausted fashion at Felix.

"I shall make you some tea and take care of the pony and then I shall go to the farm and let Rosal know what I plan to do. I shall be back as soon as I may," Felix promised.

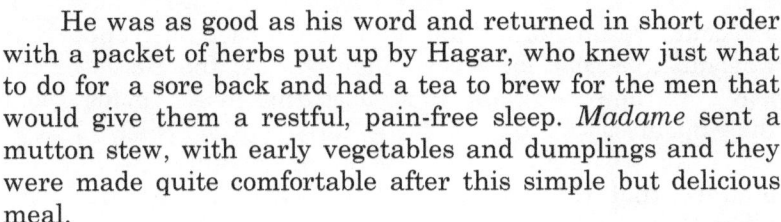

He was as good as his word and returned in short order with a packet of herbs put up by Hagar, who knew just what to do for a sore back and had a tea to brew for the men that would give them a restful, pain-free sleep. *Madame* sent a mutton stew, with early vegetables and dumplings and they were made quite comfortable after this simple but delicious meal.

In spite of the fact that the poultice Felix made up for John and put on his aching back relieved the pain far better and smelled better than any remedy he had as yet used, the manservant was resentful of the Gypsy being in the house at all. He was most ungracious and downright snappish as Felix took care of him.

Felix paid this no heed. Somehow he knew that pain made some persons irritable and he paid it little heed. From what he had seen of John the man was always grumpy.

Aurelius was grateful for the care. Hagar had sent some thing that could be applied to aching legs and Aurelius almost fell asleep as Felix rubbed it into his limbs.

Young Lovel's hands were soothing and warm. After he drank the herbal tea, before he drifted off to sleep, Aurelius decided definitely that he would ask the young man to join the household. Today had proven that he and John need help, young help, on a daily basis.

In the Brehaut woods, at the *vardo*, Rosal had taken a pillow and blanket out of doors and made a bed near the fire. Hagar, who had been sleeping under the wagon since Felix had been added to the household, was sleeping inside tonight. Rosal had invited her to do so when Felix had said he would not be returning with them but would stay at *Trois Chiminées*.

Rosal felt an urge to be outside, out under the stars and she sat in front of a dying fire, blanket draped over her shoulders, with Chavé leaning against her, sighing in bliss as she pulled gently on his silky ears. Through the canopy of trees over head she could see the brightness of the heavens above. Out here the stars were very big and close, almost as if she could reach out and touch one if she tried hard enough. It was quiet, except for a few night birds, the rustle of the leaves in the breeze, and some nocturnal insects going about their business.

Rosal was suffering from acute disappointment. She had planned that this would be their first night together, the night that might result in a child in her womb. All the signs pointed to it.

Last night she had seen a falling star, which meant a birth. Today the farm wagon, on its way to the church assembly, had passed a pasture and there had been a white horse there, looking over the gate and he had looked right at her. That was good luck indeed, and Rosal had taken all these signs as pointing to the conclusion that she would soon be pregnant.

But it would not happen if she did not sleep with Felix. She had little doubt that she could tempt him to her bed, for all men wanted a woman on a regular basis and he had been without one for quite a while now, longer than Sylvester would have ever been. Only being so drunk that he could not walk or when she was suffering her monthly courses, during which she had to sleep apart from him as she was *mahrime*, unclean, kept Sylvester from her bed every night. She was not fond of the sex act, indeed, she could barely tolerate it, but it resulted in a child and that was worth the pain and indignity.

She had been right, she now thought, to worry about that old man stealing her Rom from her. She now remembered the look he had given her, incredulous and shocked, that she was Felix's wife. And now he was keeping her Rom overnight at his house on this night, a beautiful, warm night, just made for the activity that resulted in a baby! They could lay out here under the stars and conceive a very special little girl indeed.

The moment she knew that she was pregnant she would go to a glade she knew near here where red and white roses were growing together. There, beneath a full moon, she would spin moon-wise or counter-clockwise, eleven times with her eyes closed. Without opening her eyes she would then pick a flower. If it were white she would have her little girl; red, a boy. A double-headed flower was especially fortunate, for it meant an easy birth and perhaps twins. And if the first child was a boy they would have to try again as soon as possible. She would keep drinking the fertility charms.

But nothing would happen if Felix started spending every night with the old man! Something would have to be done about that and soon. Rosal wanted so badly to feel the quickening in her womb, to watch her belly swell, knowing the child was growing within her and most of all to hold her daughter in her arms. Nothing else mattered. Nothing at all.

17
Monsieur Blériot

For the next few days the islanders were continually harassed by the French. Everyone was questioned again and again about the destruction of the *Acadie*. People never knew when a patrol might appear at their door. Invalids were pulled from their beds, many persons followed about as they did their work and all were intimidated in every way that Fournier could imagine. Some were dragged off and tortured, mostly the old men, one of whom died under the treatment.

And every evening, without fail, there were strange lights and voices but, when a augmented patrol, as no more soldiers would be allowed to go out singly, investigated, they found nothing. They would hear the sounds of music or revelry ahead and would never come upon the scene of such activities. Always, always, it seemed just over another rise, or in the next wood. Every morning reports would cross Fournier's desk of lights, music, odd noises and voices and, here and there, a soldier disappeared and no sign was ever found of him. Nerves were becoming taut.

And nearly every day something was blown up. The new fortifications were leveled on a daily basis and explosions became commonplace. The new construction was making no headway, save at the heavily guarded old Dragon Port. No trace of anyone being where he or she shouldn't be was ever found. Everyone had alibis.

Fournier was beside himself. Why could this not be resolved and the people responsible caught? He was convinced that David knew what was going on and, indeed, directed it. He stationed a guard outside David's office and at his home at night, even assigning two troopers to escort him back and forth from his home to his office at Government House. Every day, Fournier spent at least an hour questioning David, who said the same thing every day; that he had no idea what was going on or what had happened to the *Acadie*.

For some reason it was easy to lie to Fournier. David had but to think of Grizel and the memories gave him strength. Of course, being so closely guarded now he was unable to see her at all and this was proving an extreme hardship. Sometimes he could not stop thinking about that night in the sea-cave....

The close watch by the French also proved difficult for Pyewacket. Rather than keeping him hidden at all times, for the French were constantly in and out of their house, Majorlaine resorted to dye, a dye she had purchased from a Witch who specialized in such things. Pyewacket became a black cat with a white bib, stomach and paws. He actually had to chase mice but he never really killed one and he apologized profusely to the mice for the subterfuge. However, they threw themselves into the spirit of the thing and let him catch them while the French were near, squeaking in terror realistically, in performances of death and dying that would not have disgraced human actors at Drury Lane in London.

Everyone was questioned repeatedly, even Aurelius, John and Felix, who was now officially a member of the *Trois Chiminées* household staff, much to John's disgust.

And to Rosal's consternation, her Rom had spent more than one night at the home of his new employer, for John had come down with a heavy cold and dragging himself from his bed on a rainy Tuesday at the end of May to attend the assembly had not helped his health. Aurelius needed help getting in and out of bed as well as meals and personal care. Felix even spoke of moving the *vardo* nearer the cottage if the Professor needed him at night. Rosal did not care for this idea in the least.

So matters stood when, on the first day of June, which happened to be a Wednesday, another ship arrived from France.

This was not a rare occurrence. Foodstuffs for the army, also sold to the islanders at grossly inflated prices, arrived almost daily both from Normandy and Brittany.

But today's ship bore a special passenger and a precious cargo.

Colonel Fournier dispatched his *aide-de-camp* Girard to await the ship in the harbor, along with a contingent of soldiers who were to keep a weather eye upon the populace to prevent any further 'incidents' such as the *Acadie*. A courier pigeon from Boulogne had warned the Colonel that the 'special cargo' would arrive on the tide this day and he would take no chances.

Fournier's frustration level was high. He had not been able to halt any of the goings-on at night as he was not even certain what they were. An investigation of the *Acadie* matter had proved fruitless. There were a few survivors, but none of them had seen or heard anything. The ship had just suddenly blown up, as near as could be determined, near the waterline on the same side as the powder magazine. There was not enough left of the *Acadie* to tell if she had exploded from the inside or out.

Father Maël preached patience. He was certain that everything that had happened was the work of sorcery and that sooner or later someone would crack under torture, or would betray someone for money. Enchantments were the only explanations for the music, voices and lights for they were unholy, matters of the Prince of Darkness.

Maël thought himself well versed in Wizardry. But all of the books he had studied so assiduously were full of misinformation, written by earlier Witch-Sniffers and others who had confused rumors and hearsay and delusions with facts. Wizardry was represented as a Dark craft, and under the aegis of the Evil One. Such books as Heinrich Kramer and Jacob Sprenger's *"Malleus Maleficarum"*, considered one of the Witch-Sniffer's Bibles, along with Jean Bodin's *"De la demonanie de sorciers"* were filled with arcane 'facts' that had caused many a Witch or Wizard of any magical nation, to go into fits of hysterical laughter.

But Maël did know one true fact. Witches and Wizards could be subdued by what they called Cold Iron. Exposure to this metal caused them to become ill, even unto death if the exposure were long enough.

And sooner or later, he would catch the magical person

that was playing all these tricks. He dismissed Fournier's belief that it was David Dieudonné that was responsible. Sir David had not so much as a whiff of magical talent about him. No, it was someone else, someone in hiding, someone clever and wily, protected by these foolish islanders.

But he, Maël, could be clever and wily as well. And if he bided his time, he would catch the magus, for after all, God was on the side of the Inquisition.

Lieutenant Girard had no idea what to expect when he went to meet the ship that was even now settling into her berth in the harbor. He had been told that he was to meet a *M'sieur* Benoit Blériot. It seemed strange that a visitor so eagerly anticipated by Colonel Fournier was only a *M'sieur*, not a high-ranking army officer. Girard had been ordered to do whatever *M.* Blériot desired and to accommodate his every wish.

That *M'sieur* Blériot was going to be a major headache was apparent to the Lieutenant from the very beginning. The civilian was rowed on shore, clutching a large traveling case to his rather sunken chest. He was a small man, painfully thin, with a shock of brown hair that, if combed properly, would have reached to his collar. Instead, it stood out in a wild nimbus all around his head. He was clean shaven, with a very thin, intense face and hostile dark gray eyes behind a pair of wire-rimmed spectacles. He radiated nervous energy and suspicion.

Lieutenant Girard, trying to be helpful, attempted to relieve *M'sieur* Blériot of his case and had the case rudely jerked away from his grasp and the civilian declared, "Remove your filthy paws from my case! No one touches it! No one, do you hear me?" he shouted shrilly.

"The entire quay can hear you, *M'sieur*," said Girard stiffly. "I was only attempting to give you a hand."

"Well, keep your hands to yourself!" retorted Blériot, hugging the case tighter against himself. "I have four large crates that must be unloaded from the boat immediately. And they must be handled with care. Are any of these fellows —"

he looked scornfully at the soldiers "intelligent and careful enough to undertake this delicate task? I cannot trust those sailors. They are a stupid lot!"

"You, Patrique," said Girard, nodding at the sergeant "take Mercier, Depardieu and Pelletier with you and bring *M'sieur's* crates. Mind you take care," he added hastily when Blériot glared at him.

The four crates proved to be heavy, enormous mountains of wood that caused the men unloading them to puff and pant. It took four trips from the ship, the *Égalité,* for even one crate made the small boat carrying them to the quay sink low in the water. The task was not made easier by Blériot's constant impatient and angry instructions. He literally jumped up an down in agitation, putting down the case he had clutched so tightly at his feet so that he could pull at his hair as he screamed. Girard could now understand why his hair looked as it did. What he could not understand was why no one had as yet murdered Blériot.

Girard was forced to requisition two wagons to take the cases to Government House, for Blériot would not hear of them being brought up later. They had to go NOW and he, Blériot, would not be parted from them.

He sat up on the wagon seat, still clutching his case, beside Girard, constantly turning and twisting to keep an eye on the wagon following them from the quay.

When Government House was at last reached, he refused to go in. "Bring Colonel Fournier out here to see me!" he shrilled. "He promised me that my materials would have a safe and a good home, all prepared for them! I wish to go there immediately! I hope that my instructions as to what I wanted were followed precisely, but military persons are very slow-witted!"

Grinding his teeth in an effort not to give in to his impulses and strangle Blériot, Girard was forced to go in and ask for the Colonel's presence out in the street.

To his surprise, the Colonel was agreeable, merely taking up his hat which hung upon a convenient hook, and asking Girard to request of his orderly that his horse be brought around.

"Excuse me, sir, but this *M'sieur* Blériot is most unpleasant!" Girard cautioned his commander.

"So I have heard," said Fournier. To Girard's amazement the Colonel seemed in a better mood than he had since the *Acadie* had exploded so mysteriously. "He may be a most unpleasant man, Girard, but he is a genius and has invented something that will conquer England. He can be as unpleasant as he likes if he delivers the British isles to France."

Girard thought that even the conquest of England might not be worth having to spend much time in Blériot's company. Therefore, he was much relieved when the Colonel left him in charge of the office, while Fournier rode out to the building project that had been occupying everyone for the last two weeks. No one had known what this facility, erected at the site of the old Dragon Port, was going to be used for. It seemed now that they would find out.

Bahram eagerly awaited the Djinn's return.

But time went by and the blue giant did not come back. Every morning which was the time that he had told the creature to make an appearance, Bahram went to the Salt Pot and waited for him, carefully tracing the calling symbols in the dust on the floor of the uncompleted lighthouse. But nothing happened. There was no stirring in the magical firmament, no sign of an occupant in the lamp.

What could have gone wrong? The Djinn was invincible. No one had ever defeated him! Bahram had not been impressed so far by English Wizards and he doubted an old man like the Earl could defeat a creature of pure magic like the Djinn. Bahram began to wonder if the Djinn had run away, but how could he do that? He was tied to the lamp.

In the meantime he and Reynard were sinking deeper into financial trouble. Reynard would not or could not stop drinking and gaming. They had moved to a far from salubrious part of town one which seemed to cater to common seamen, for grog shops and cheap whores abounded. Something had to change and soon. The situation was intolerable.

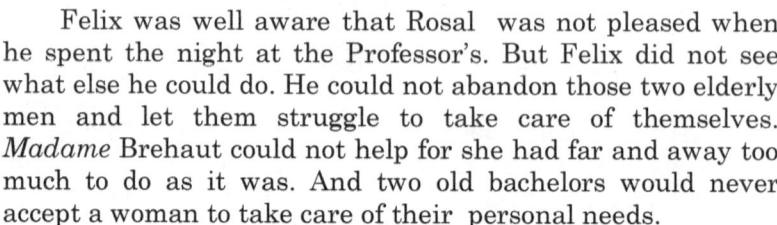

Felix was well aware that Rosal was not pleased when he spent the night at the Professor's. But Felix did not see what else he could do. He could not abandon those two elderly men and let them struggle to take care of themselves. *Madame* Brehaut could not help for she had far and away too much to do as it was. And two old bachelors would never accept a woman to take care of their personal needs.

And the instinctive liking he had felt for Aurelius had grown deeper. Felix felt more comfortable with the Professor than he did with anyone else he had come in contact with since the loss of his memory. They could talk for ages, easy talk, good talk, on a wide range of subjects. He felt on a secure footing with Aurelius. For hours at a time he could forget that his memories of who and what he was were non-existent. If he just *talked,* without trying to justify how and why he knew things, it was wonderful. Aurelius never asked him questions but accepted him as he was.

Aurelius, however, was as curious as ever about his new young friend. The mystery of him deepened daily. Not only was he well educated, with the vocabulary of a scholar and the diction of a gentleman, but his manners were those of the very well-bred: manners learned in the nursery so young that they were instinctive. Young Lovel never held a knife or a fork incorrectly, nor used his serviette improperly or sipped from a cup in an ill-bred way. He never failed to offer a needed arm politely, without making Aurelius feel like a useless hulk, and he bore John's continued ill humor with good grace.

But Aurelius had decided that he was not going to be a Paul Pry. Every day seemed to deepen their intimacy. It was a great deal like having a well-loved son or nephew in the house, and he was confident that one day he would hear the full story.

Rosal was growing increasingly impatient and asked Hagar to make her a love potion to give to Felix.

"He has not lain with me yet," she complained as she and Hagar made the meal over the fire one evening. They were waiting for Felix to return from *Trois Chiminées*. "It will be next summer before I am child again at this rate! What is wrong with him? I am pretty! One of the Frenchmen who came to the farm today tried to flirt with me and suggested that we go into the woods together and go behind the hedge." This phrase was a Romany euphemism for illicit sex.

"Telling a man that he is your Rom does not make him love or desire you, Rosal," said Hagar, stirring a pot of rabbit stew. *Madame* had given them permission to snare rabbits as these pests were over running the vegetable gardens.

"But you'll brew me a potion, won't you?" Rosal insisted, looking up from the flat bread she was cooking on a rock.

Hagar hesitated as Rosal stared at her impatiently.

"If in a week you have not managed to get him into your bed I will see what I can do," she said at last. She looked up at the sun. "It will be another hour before he comes. Take that nice smelling soap *Madame* gave you and bathe in the pool until you are fresh and sweet. Then rub yourself with sweet grass and comb out your hair. Put on fresh clothes and tempt him. Touch him as much as possible. Lightly brush your hand across his and lean over his shoulder. Let your blouse fall from your shoulder."

"I never had to do any of that with Sylvester," said Rosal. "He always wanted me, several times a night and even during the day."

"All men are not like Sylvester and that is why I am telling you these things," said Hagar patiently. "And yes, I know Sylvester was very like your father who could also not keep his hands from a woman but I think that this one, your new Rom," she said sarcastically, "is not like that at all. He will require different behavior from you. Just being available is not enough."

"I *have* been touching him and letting him see that I am eager for him," Rosal said in protest.

"You have been too quiet about it," said Hagar. The girl had no idea how to flirt and seduce a man. Sylvester had been so eager for her that she had to do nothing to attract him.

Her mother and father had kept her away from young men until she was given in marriage. As the lord of the *cumpania* her Father had an inflated opinion of his own worth and that of his family. His sons would marry well; his daughters would be given to men who had property, such as a good string of horses or money. She had never been allowed to be amongst young men who knew how to flirt and tease a pretty girl.

"Perhaps you should dance for him," Hagar said. In the dance Rosal was a different person. She was seductive and sensual. She forgot herself when dancing. "After we eat I shall play upon the *cembalo* and you shall dance with your tambourine. That will enflame him, I have no doubt."

Rosal eagerly agreed to this idea. For days now, she had a bed ready in the woods near the pool where she bathed, made soft with bracken and sweet smelling with the petals of dog roses. Of what use was this bed if there were not two bodies in it, making a baby?

Happily, she went off to the pool with fresh clothing over her arm.

Hagar remained at the fire, watching the stew glumly. She still thought that no good would come of this ill-judged scheme.

Last night, when Rosal lay sleeping and Felix had been at the Professor's cottage, she had read the Tarot again and again. The Tower had shown up each time, signifying a shocking change, a moment of truth. Hagar very much feared that it meant that Rosal's little scheme would collapse about her and that they would both end in prison for having tried to steal the *Giorgio's* life from him when he remembered and realized what they had done to him. And she was as guilty as Rosal. She could have stopped it but she had not.

18
The Dragon Port

On the afternoon of the first of June the two wagons, escorted by Fournier and a small company of soldiers, had headed south from St. Peter Port. They were heading for the now unused Dragon Port, that lay near Le Bourg, between Icart Point and Pleinmont on the southern end of the island.

During the first French occupation, trenches, for some obscure reason, had been dug in the leveled area that was the Dragon Port and some of the buildings in which the mail had been sorted, packages and goods received, and dragons and riders accommodated, had been torn down.

But since arriving in Guernsey, Colonel Fournier had a crew of good strong men out here, filling in the trenches and smoothing the grounds and had the engineers, using much of the discarded materials from the demolition, to build to *M'sieur* Blériot's specifications.

The entire site had been surrounded with a fence of palings held together with stout wire which had been brought from France. Every few feet a large sign read *"Entrée interdite"*, No Entry, in bright red letters. Guards stood at the single gate. They leveled their muskets at the approaching party until they identified Colonel Fournier, and sprang instead to open the wide gate, saluting their Colonel as he rode by.

Blériot seemed unimpressed by what he saw. He stared straight ahead, still gripping his case tightly. Only when he saw the central structure which was a wide, high building, did he say to Fournier "The roof slides open, just as I wanted?"

"Indeed, *M'sieur*," said Fournier reassuringly."We have tested it and the mechanism works perfectly. I think you will find that all of your specifications have been met."

"And my workers?" Blériot said sharply.

"Prisoners, as you desired. They arrive tomorrow. And I have chosen some young officers, hand-picked, to help you in the tests."

"It is too early for that!" said Blériot sharply. "I and I alone will conduct the first tests and the effectiveness of this method. I shall not share my secrets with anyone until I judge the time is correct. That is why the workers will labor apart from one another so that none shall know what the others do. You have made arrangements to house the groups separately, I assume."

"Indeed," Fournier said again. "Everything that you required has been accomplished, and all in good time as well."

If the Colonel expected a compliment or any gratitude from Blériot, he was doomed to disappointment, for the little man merely looked about him further. "What was this place?" he asked abruptly.

"They called it a Dragon Port, where mail and goods were delivered, carried by dragons," Fournier answered as the wagons pulled up in front of a long, low building.

"A Dragon Port!" Blériot crowed in delight. "This is a rich joke! Dragons will cower before me when I am done with my work!"

It would be enough, Fournier thought, if the British cowered before them. The Colonel expected to easily conquer these Isles of perfidious Albion with Blériot's brilliant invention. Dragons, he had learned, were not used in war and neither were Wizards. He found this stupid beyond belief. Here the British had incredible weapons at their disposal and made no use of them! If France but had dragons and magicians! What could not be accomplished! The world would belong to France.

"Have your men carefully remove the crates," Blériot directed. These two," he gestured behind him, "will go in the largest building" he pointed out the buildings he meant "and the other two shall go in the manufactory. More materials will be arriving from France in the next few days. If all goes as planned, Colonel, and the prisoners do their work properly, we shall be ready to invade England in a month."

Fournier could almost feel the Marshal's baton in his hand.

Late in the afternoon of the day of Blériot's arrival on the island David was at work at the ramshackle table that he used as a desk. It was stifling in the windowless little office and he had removed his jacket and loosened his cravat. Once again, he thought longingly of his office above stairs, with the wide windows opening onto the harbor and the ocean breezes that came in through the window.

Yesterday afternoon Fournier had dropped a load of work upon him. David was to check the new occupation records of inhabitants against the parish census and tax rolls to make certain that all people were who they said they were and were living in the correct place. Fournier also wanted updated records of what men had gone to serve in the French Army. He wished as well to learn the evaluation of each property and what each householder had paid in taxes these past five years. There were to be several new taxes, he had said vaguely when David had questioned him as to the need of this. He had become quite ugly when David pressed him and tersely ordered David to do his work and mind his own business.

David's thoughts were black once gain as he worked. It was close work and the heat and the poor light in the room where one lamp hung on the wall at an inconvenient angle far from the desk, were giving him a headache.

Everything seemed to be going badly today. He and Majorlaine had been surprised at breakfast by a French patrol who had helped themselves to all of the fresh *Gâche*, which David had been looking forward to eating. In that bread had been the last of their sugar and sultanas.

Pyewacket too, had been in a morose mood, missing his Wizard and fretting about it. The French had come on them so suddenly that they had almost caught him talking. Fortunately the soldiers had been too focused upon the smell of the fresh-baked bread.

David was distressed over the close guard Fournier was keeping on him. At least here in Government House he was left alone and there was no guard on the door. But the moment he poked his nose outside, there was a guard. It was more than irksome.

And this task that Fournier had given him! He could have easily used four clerks to help him. The parish records for the past few years had been haphazardly kept, for the men who usually did this task had been stolen away and the old men and the women, all of them overworked, had tried to keep up with it, sometimes not too successfully. And Fournier wanted it done immediately.

The only comfort that David had was that the *Acadie* and her cargo of instruments of torture had been destroyed. Of course, it was not as if the French could still not torture anyone. Old Bernard Pommier had died under the lash, being questioned. Pommier had been very elderly and mostly senile. Why anyone would think that such a man had any useful information David could not imagine. David's attempt to plead clemency had been unsuccessful. Fournier had threatened to whip Majorlaine if the Bailiff made one more protest. Now David felt as if he himself had been responsible for Pommier's death.

"Such a long face!" said a little whisper close to his face.

Startled, he threw up his head and beheld the most extraordinary little creature he had ever seen.

She was no bigger than his thumb and she hung in the air on almost invisible wings of gossamer gold, like a dragonfly's. She was rose-coloured and speckled with more gold, even to her hair. He could see this easily, for she was naked, a delicate, yet feminine form with a cloud of fine-spun hair. Her eyes too, were golden.

"You are wanted," she said. "Come with me."

"Who are you?" he said, not quite believing his eyes.

"I am a Faerie of the flower you call the Guernsey Lily," she said. "You may call me Amaryllis, for that is what mortals who study flowers have named my flower: *Amaryllis sariensis.*"

A closer look revealed that she was indeed, coloured and patterned exactly like a Guernsey Lily, a plant that, legend had it, was given to Guernsey by a Faerie man as a memento when he stole an island girl for his bride. Some did not care for the Lily as it had no scent.The scent was the soul of a flower and therefore the Lily had no soul. But David had always found the Lily beautiful and grew them in their

176

gardens both in Torteval and here in St. Peter Port.

"I cannot leave here. I am watched." he told her regretfully. He wanted very badly to go with this Faerie.

Amaryllis smiled. "But you go to where time is different that what you are used to," she said. "No one will notice that you are gone. Come!" she said and held out a tiny hand. "Take my hand."

This statement about time was some what ambiguous, but David stood up and somewhat gingerly extended one finger to her.

Her touch was lighter than anything imaginable. David could only compare it to thistledown. He had once trained a black-capped Great Tit to eat seeds from his hand and he had marveled at the fact that all he could feel of its weight was its tiny feet clutching his finger. But this was even lighter.

She lead him to the back wall of his little office and to his amazement, the wall dissolved and faded away. When he had his wits about him again he realized that he was in a wood, a very old wood.

And there, beneath a huge beech whose branches curved down to meet the ground, waited Grizel in her familiar, well-worn blue dress.

She held out her arms and he went into them gladly. "Robin wishes to meet with us," she said, "but first, the moss beneath this tree will make us a comfortable bed."

"But we haven't the time..." he began.

The Faerie laughed, a sound like tiny bells. "You are in Faerie now," she said. "You have all the time that you will need, all the time you want!"

Later, after what seemed like hours and hours to David, they left the shelter of the beech and followed a path through the woods.

Since the path was very narrow though the dense woodland, Grizel walked a little ways ahead of him. Watching her graceful body and the beautiful bronze hair rippling down her back Davis realized that he was falling in love with her. Not only because their physical union had exceeded his wildest dreams but because he also wanted to talk to her, to hear what she had to say, to exchange ideas and dreams with her. He was already imagining marrying her.

But would a Selchie, even a half Selchie, be content as the wife of a farmer? Could she forsake the sea for his sake and would she want to? He had heard all the old tales of how the seal women were passionate creatures and eager for a male embrace, even marrying a mortal man and giving him children. But all the tales ended in the same way. The seal woman sickened for the sea and the freedom she knew as a seal. In the end, she either ran away back to the sea or was taken back by her loving spouse and set free to be a seal once more.

These thoughts were banished as they reached a small clearing where Robin Goodfellow lounged at his ease on a giant toadstool, waiting for them.

"Moss makes a pleasant bed, does it not?" he said, his green eyes twinkling. This was said in such a merry, companionable manner that David could not take offense.

Robin pointed out a fallen tree to the couple, where they sat side by side.

"What do the French think of us?" he asked David.

"They think it is us, the *Guernaise*, playing tricks. Colonel Fournier thinks it is me! The Witch-Sniffer thinks that it is being done by a Wizard whom we are hiding somewhere on the island. Not a few of the soldiers have asked for transfers and some have disappeared altogether," David answered.

"They are now in France, save one who refused to leave us. He has an Elfin mistress and declares that France can conquer the world without him!" Robin informed them happily.

David did not ask how the soldiers had been returned to France. He had a feeling that he would understand it as about as well as he understood how the wall had dissolved and they were suddenly in Faerie.

"We have many more excitements planned for them," said Robin cheerfully. "This is only the beginning! Your people have made a good start as well. That ship was well and truly destroyed. I have heard from Prince Madoc that the machines of torture were taken well out to sea and dumped into a deep trench. Unfortunately we could not do that as they are all of Cold Iron."

The smile left his face and he said "There are Faeries living in the garden underneath the Colonel's windows and I instructed them to keep their ears open. They understand little of what they hear but they are very good at remembering what they do hear. And perhaps you can confirm for me, David, that what they have heard means ill for Guernsey."

David nodded. Grizel's hand had crept into his and he felt her give his hand a squeeze.

"The Colonel and the Inquisitor spoke of a new tax. It will be a heavy one, if the Faeries are correct," said Robin, frowning slightly. "They also spoke of a new weapon that will subdue England by the end of the summer."

David and Grizel exchanged glances. "A new weapon?" David repeated. "I have heard nothing of this. Of course, I am hardly in the Colonel's confidence. He doesn't trust me at all. Indeed, I am under almost constant guard. When they find me missing this afternoon there will be the devil to pay."

"They will not find you missing," Robin reassured him. "Time is different here. In the World Above you have not left your desk, even though you have spent hours of bliss with your lady and here the sun is setting."

"But we need to find out what this weapon might be. If it is not of Cold Iron perhaps we can eliminate it. If it is of Death Metal we can do naught," the hobgoblin added.

"I shall do my best to find out for you," David promised. "And I cannot tell you how much we appreciate your efforts. Fournier is frustrated. It is almost worth my close watch, just to see the expression on his face when he reads the reports each morning! He is coming to realize that everything cannot be explained away by a charge of drunkenness."

Robin sat up on the toadstool and folded his legs tailor fashion "But what about this new tax? Shall your people be able to pay it?"

David felt a tightness in his chest. "No, he said heavily. "Coin is in short supply on the island. For five years now under the precious French Occupation we have done little trading or selling of our produce, knit goods or fish to the British Isles. I do not know where we will find the money to

179

pay a new tax. Already I am receiving letters from people who cannot pay their current taxes. Many are on the verge of abject poverty. I have been dipping into my own pocket to help some of them but I am not a rich man; my resources are limited and I have my own taxes to pay as well."

"Then this will help you all!" Robin waved his hand and a brass bound trunk appeared at David's feet.

"Go ahead. Open it!" the Hobgoblin directed.

Letting go Grizel's hand, David bent down and opened the lid and threw it back.

Beside him he heard Grizel gasp.

The trunk was full to the brim in gold coins, mostly British, but also some of the *Guernaise* coin. It looked new minted.

"Once we distribute it, it will begin to look old and will be worn and tarnished as if hoarded in a cellar hole or in a mattress," said Robin. "Pay the French with this! And the joke will be on them, David, for this is Faerie Gold and it will not last! When they attempt to remove it from the island it will disappear like dew before the summer sun. But everyone's taxes will be paid!"

19
The Prisoners

After a disastrous run at Faro, where Reginald, plunging deep, succeeded in losing what little he had gained by day after day of gaming, Bahram took charge. He pawned Reginald's watch and tie-pin and, after inquiring at a coaching inn, booked both of them on a stage coach for Devon, the price for which included a ferry from the Isle of Wight to Portsmouth and from there on the coach to Torbay in Devon.

Since their funds were at low ebb, they could only afford an outside seat on the coach, perched high above the ground in the open air.

Reginald, ape-dunk as usual, soon became sick from the motion of the coach and began to moan about how he had never had to lower himself to ride in, or rather, *on* a coach. As a gentleman he had always traveled post, or more often, ridden a dragon.

Exhausting this subject when the coachman and the guard threatened to throw him from the roof if he did not shut up about it, he then whined about the fact that his grandfather was swimming in lard and how the old man would never have missed a roll of flimsies for his only surviving grandson, yet was too much of a nip-farthing to loosen his purse strings.

Bahram was becoming well-used to Reynard's constant use of cant and correctly translated this to mean that the Earl was rich, but was too cheap to give his grandson a large wad of paper currency.

Reginald finally ran out of complaints and, bleary-eyed, looked at Bahram. "Tell me again, why are we going to Devon?" he inquired. "Nothing to do there! No lady-birds, no gaming. Place is a dead bore!"

"We are going there to live on your grandfather's bounty," said Bahram. "I am as purse-pinched as are you and

181

we must rusticate, as you call it, until our pockets are not to let." He had paid attention to Reginald's mode of speech and had learned it well.

"Oh," said Reginald, looking green to the gills. "Wouldn't have a flask of Blue Ruin about you?" he asked the guard hopefully.

The guard was insulted. "It'd be as much as my job is worth if Mr, Jorkins was catchin' me wi' a bottle o' gin!" he said in outrage. "Fine jobbernoll I'd be to go riskin' my position!"

"Next, 'e'll be wanting to take the ribbons. All alike, these swells," said the coachman in disgust.

Reginald disclaimed any desire to tool the coach. To his present eyesight there seemed to be four wheelers and four leaders in the team of coach horses although one pair of each was a trifle transparent.

"You're lookin' as queer as Dick's hat band," the guard said. "If'n you're goin' to cast up your accounts, lean out over the back and don't be hitting the boot and spatterin' the baggage!"

This was enough to send Reginald scrambling to the rear of the coach where a few moments later he did part company with the contents of his stomach.

Bahram watched him cynically. Idiot! He would be fatally easy to milk of any amount of lucre once his grandfather was dead and he had come into full possession of the estates and their bounty. But first his grandfather had to die.

The Persian wanted to go to Devon for another reason. The Djinn had still not returned, despite Bahram's call every morning. The slave was bound to the lamp. He was compelled to return to it once a given task had been completed. Bahram had to find out if the Earl had met his end. But surely they would have been notified by now! He could not conceive of the Djinn having failed. Something was wrong and it must be investigated. And Devon was the place to find that out.

Rosal was feeling put upon. Despite her best efforts she had been unable to share a bed with her Rom as yet. The evening she had taken Hagar's advice had been interrupted by a French patrol, who tore the *vardo* apart. Fortunately they did not find the hidden floor board where the small cache of coins reposed, but they had thrown everything out of the caravan, searching for weapons, or so they said. The three Romany had been forced to stand there, under guard by soldiers with leveled bayonets as the French handled their few belongings with contempt and many crude and derogatory comments.

It had taken until well after midnight for them to restore order. Most of their clothing would need washing or mending, as the French had trampled it underfoot. They had no supper, for the patrol had tipped their stew into the fire. Even Rosal did not feel as if she wanted to take Felix to the bed in the woods after that.

"At least they did not burn the *vardo*," said Hagar when the French left. "I heard, when I went to the village with my buttons, that a farm in the next parish was burned because one of the family did not go to the French gathering."

"We will go every week without fail!" said Rosal. "No one is going to burn my *vardo*!"

Felix was seething with rage. What right had these people to treat them so horribly? Why were Hagar and Rosal so accepting of this? Their attitude seemed to be that it could have been worse. His attitude was that it should not have happened at all.

When he voiced this thought Hagar shrugged. "That is the way that we Romany are always treated. We are driven off, forbidden to use the shops, or send our children to school, or even go into the churches. If something is stolen in a neighborhood we are the first to be blamed. The *Giorgios* think us all horse thieves and cut-purses. It could have been worse," she repeated. "They could have burned the *vardo* and the French could have taken us behind the hedge and hung you," she said to Felix. "Such has happened and will happen again as long as there are *Giorgios* and Romany. It is the way things are."

"It isn't right!" he said stubbornly.

Hagar thought him foolish. Just because something was

183

not 'right' did not mean that it did not happen every day. Such was the way of the world.

Felix's resentment of the treatment from the French kept him from noticing that Rosal was far from happy that evening and still unhappy the next morning as they walked to the farm where they would then separate as he would continue the walk to *Trois Chiminée* .

"You be certain and come back to the *vardo* tonight," Rosal insisted as they parted, deciding that only forceful action was going to result in a baby. She reached up and pulled his head down for a kiss, which unlike most of the embraces she had given him was not quick, but lingering and even suggestive. "You are well enough now to come to my bed," she said. "Would you not rather lay with me than be with that old man?"

He was not quite certain how to answer this. He was not in love with her; he felt no overwhelming passion for her, no urgency to bed her, but she was very attractive and the kiss was stirring. She had been seductive lately. A seemingly careless touch on his shoulder or hand, brushing against him, looking up at him from under those long dark lashes and he would have been made of stone if he had not responded. And he was certainly not made of stone! Perhaps in her embrace memories would return and he could rekindle the passion he must have felt for her. "Yes, of course I would!" he answered at last and it was his turn to deepen the kiss.

They parted to go their separate ways, both now determined that they would be together that night. Rosal was certain that in another month she would be with child from this night's work. The potions she had been drinking practically guaranteed it. And Felix was hoping for the return of memories. If he remembered one thing such as loving her perhaps the other memories would come back as well.

David would have rather been anywhere else at the moment rather than on the quay at Fournier's side.

Another ship had arrived from France this morning, ironically called the *Liberté*. Ironically, because a ship called the *Liberty* held a cargo of slaves, prisoners of war who were now to be put to use at the new facility at the old Dragon Port.

Fournier had assigned David to inspect the list of prisoners and ascertain which were fit for work. At David's protest that surely a doctor would be better suited for this duty, Fournier had angrily ordered him to be quiet and do as he was told. Only the thought that he might get to see what was at the Dragon Port kept a heated retort from David's lips.

They were a mixed lot of German and Austrian prisoners, mostly men from the ranks, from the First Consul's campaigns in the Piedmont of Italy, where he had success-fully overturned the Austrian held government and from campaigns in Germany and Austria. Some of these men had been captives since the battles of Marengo in Italy and Hohenlinden in Bavaria some three years earlier.

The only interpreter was a young Austrian officer named Johann von Weber, haggard and ill in his ragged uniform and iron fetters. He spoke slow French with a heavy accent and had to stop frequently to search for words. David bore with this patiently as von Weber told him briefly about each man on the list, which were healthy and which were not, but Fournier grew increasingly impatient. "Is there not someone else in this benighted island who can speak German?" he fumed.

"Perhaps one of the priests?" David suggested. wishing he dared offer the exhausted and probably hungry von Weber a seat and something to eat and drink.

The young officer, a Lieutenant of cavalry, could not be much above three and twenty. Under normal conditions he would have been a good-looking young man, with thick blonde hair and the lean frame of the cavalry-man, but sickness and long confinement had robbed his complexion of its healthy tan, sunk his blue eyes deep in his head and made him painfully thin as well. Like all the prisoners, he was blinking in the sunlight reflecting off the water in the harbor, with watery eyes. They had not seen the sun in a long while.

Von Weber looked confused at the rapid French of the Colonel, and listened with a painful intensity. Since he had been stationed in the Piedmont, he had learned Italian, not

185

French. It now appeared that he would have been better had to learn French, as it seemed they were going to conquer the entire world.

At this moment he had little real idea where they were. He assumed it was some where in France. They had been told nothing, of course, only that they were to be moved and the men were counting upon him to learn as much as he could in order to pass the information onto them. This civilian seemed sympathetic but the Colonel was impatient and arrogant.

Fournier barked an order at one of the soldiers who stood at rigid attention, ready to level their rifles at any of the prisoners who looked to be threatening insurrection. The Corporal saluted and took off at a run. "There are enough priests around here," Fournier said almost to himself, "Let them earn their keep."

"These men ought to be given a drink and some food, Colonel," David ventured. "They will be of little use if they are not fed and allowed to drink and rest. And perhaps they could sit as well. Many of them can scarcely stand."

This was said in slow French, so that von Weber could understand. The Austrian looked pleased at this kind attention and glanced hopefully at Fournier.

After glaring at David, Fournier grudgingly said "Let them sit. Water will be brought, but there will be no food until they are taken out to the Dragon Port."

Von Weber had understood one or two words in this reply among them 'dragonne", dragon, and he felt a sudden terror that they were to be fed to dragons. "No, please!" he begged in his slow French. "Do not give us to the dragons to eat!" He clutched at David's arm, with terror in his eyes.

It took David a few minutes to soothe him, informing him that there were no dragons on the island at the moment and at any rate they did not ever eat people. He also told him that the men could sit and would be given water.

Almost immediately women began to arrive with pails of water and dippers. They had obviously been close by, listening. Many of them brought bread with them and other baked goods, which the starving prisoners fell upon with eagerness.

Fournier was incensed again. "What is this?" he shouted. "Have you no control over your people, Dieudonné? I gave no permission for this!"

"We are a hospitable people, Colonel, and the women are only doing what they would hope would be done for their men in another country, were they in a like situation," said David shortly. He was growing increasingly sick of Fournier.

He was to be even more disgusted with the Colonel when the Corporal arrived back breathlessly and gasped out that none of the priests were familiar with German.

"Then it is up to you, Dieudonné," said the Colonel rather maliciously. "Find me some one who can speak German or learn to speak it yourself! This is insupportable. *M'sieur* Blériot will not tolerate it. And I know for a fact that he cannot speak German, as he told me to be certain and obtain a translator."

"None of your men – " David began.

"Most of my men are Parisians or from the south of France. They had no reason to learn a barbaric language such as German," said Fournier unpleasantly. "At any rate, they have other duties. Blériot will soon be stealing a number of my officers and I cannot spare any more people, not with this island in a ferment of revolt!"

"A ferment of revolt?" David echoed. "What are you talking about?"

Fournier laughed nastily." Oh, very good, Dieudonné! That wide-eyed look of innocence is almost convincing! As if you did not know what I was talking about!" He put his face close to David's and hissed in a low voice, "I shall find out who is behind all of these tricks: the lights, the voices and things disappearing, and all of the explosions, and when I catch whoever is playing tricks I am certain that he will lead me straight back to you! Now, find me a translator or it will go badly with you!" In the Colonel's mind was the displeasure of *M'sieur* Blériot should he be unable to convey his requirements to the workers.

David could not think of anyone left on the island now that was a linguist, only Professor Bretton and he was a linguist of dead languages. But something clicked in his brain. Had not the Professor said the man assisting him to put his books in order was a linguist of modern languages?

"There may be someone," he said shortly as Fournier glared at him. "If I might go to Castel parish tomorrow?"

"Have Girard write you out a pass," Fournier said. "Now let us finish here. I want these men on wagons by the end of the day."

Madame Elvire Pommier of St Andrew's parish was now a widow, living all by herself in her tiny little house on the edge of the farm they had made over to her son Jules.

Elvire had not understood why the French had taken Jules and his eldest son Michel to serve in the French army, for in spite of their French names, the *Guernaise* were British and both Jules and Michel had been in the Militia, loyal to King George.

Even less had she understood why the Inquisition had come and taken Bernard. All of their lives they had been good Catholics. They had been married in the Church, and all of their children had been properly christened. They went to church each Sunday and observed all of the Holy days and festivals. They had also lived in harmony with their neighbors, even those who belonged to the Presbyterian church and those who were Wizards and Witches.

According to the Inquisition, though, this was heresy and Bernard, amongst others, had been put to the question. But Bernard, at eighty nine on his last birthday, and wandering in his wits, had died.

And the small pension that had been paid out to Bernard from his former employer whose dairyman he had been for years, had died with him. They had been struggling to get by on it. Jules had left them as much as he could spare after providing for his wife and children, but it had been long gone and they had been barely existing on the pension since then.

Elvire did not know what to do. Her daughter-in-law, a Witch, had fled with the children to England and she had been right to go. Elvire had not wanted to take Bernard and go with Amy and the grandchildren, for Guernsey was their home and she was afraid that Bernard would never adjust to living away from here in a place where most persons spoke only English, in unfamiliar surroundings.

But now she was panic-stricken. The new tax bill had arrived this morning, delivered by a troop of French soldiers, and she had nearly fainted when she read the amount she was expected to pay and the very short time in which she had to pay it. It stated that unless the taxes were paid in full and on time, all her portable property or anything of value at all would be confiscated and sold.

Where would she go and what would she do if this happened? What if they took her house? Her priest, a man she knew and trusted, had been taken away and there was no one to apply to for Parish relief.

Elvire spent several hours crying hopelessly before she thought of Sir David Dieudonné. She had seen the nice young Bailiff recently for he had come personally to see her to tell her about Bernard and had been so sympathetic. When he left she found he had tucked £25 beneath the sugar bowl on the table where she had served him some herbal tea. She had been touched by that. He was looking both tired and a little shabby and she was certain that the money had come from his own pocket. Perhaps she would write to him and see if he knew what she could do.

She was so exhausted by the crying and the endless refrain of "what shall I do?" that repeated itself endlessly in her brain, that for once she did not finish her household tasks. She felt much older than her years, which numbered eighty-two, and she left plates and glasses in the soapstone sink and did not brush out the hearth or sweep the floor one more time. It was just too much for her.

Several years ago they had given up their cow and drank mostly cider. A neighbor brought them the little milk and cheese they needed, as well as eggs. And usually, some of the cream went to the Hobgoblin.

There was no cream left today, so she set out a mug of cider and a plate of fresh bread on the hearth. Elvire had always known that there was a house spirit, a Hobgoblin, in the kitchen who did unfinished tasks at night when she was in her bed, although she had never seen him.

But every morning the bowl of cream or the small *gateau* was always gone and the bowl put neatly in the sink. Usually the Hob had but little to do as Elvire was a meticulous housekeeper. But tonight she just could not manage.

Elvire slept the sleep of utter exhaustion and arose much later than usual the next morning. As a farmer's wife she was used to being up with the sun, a habit that had not changed even when they no longer had a farm to tend.

She came down to a kitchen so sparkling clean that she rubbed her eyes before she looked at it again.

It was true! It was as clean as if she had been in her prime and had just completed the spring cleaning. Even the plate and mug had been washed and put away, the floor swept and the hearth brushed out, with the fire brasses gleaming.

But wait, there was something left on the hearth. It was a little green bag that gave a metallic clunk when she bent and picked it up. A scrap of paper, a brownish parchment, had been fastened on it with a pin. In brown ink, in a spidery script, had been written in French '*For your taxes*' and when she opened it, gold, a great deal of it, winked up at her.

Elvire fell to her knees, sobbing once more, with the little bag clutched to her breast. But this time they were tears of joy and relief.

20
The Translator

David had gone back to his hot and stuffy office once the soldiers began to put the manacled men onto the wagons for the trip out to the Dragon Port. There was still an obscene amount of paperwork to be done.

He had scarce had time to remove his coat and sling it across the back of his chair before a young Corporal, breathless with running, burst into his office. He bore a paper in one tightly clenched fist.

"Here!" he panted, thrusting the paper at David. "You're to go at once to Castel and fetch the person who can speak German. This is a pass for you and whoever it is."

"But I thought I was not to go until tomorrow! Why this haste?" David protested.

"The Austrian fainted and we haven't been able to revive him. The doctor is on his way," the Corporal answered at top speed. "Quickly, quickly, *M'sieur*! We shall both be in trouble if you do not obey the Colonel!"

Less than fifteen minutes later David found himself on his horse Thierry, a dapple gray gelding. Trotting on a line in back of him was one of the army horses, saddled and bridled. David was to go to Castel, find the German speaker and meet Fournier on the road to the Dragon Port. The pass Fournier had given him would allow him access to the facility. David was astonished that he was being allowed to go on his own but the Corporal explained that the Colonel needed all the men to guard the prisoners. But *M. le Colonel* would be taking note of how long it took the Bailiff to accomplish his task, so

191

that he mustn't tarry on the way.

Things could not have worked out more fortuitously. He was going to get a view of the Dragon Port and perhaps even what was going on there, David thought in excitement as he headed out towards Castel.

He had to remain upon the roads, however, rather than riding cross country, for at the boundary of each parish he would have to present his pass to the guards whose business it was to make certain that no one was moving unlawfully between parishes. This had the effect of lengthening his trip.

At long last, after having to bear with over officious guards at parish crossings as he had to cross the boundaries of St Peter Port, St Andrew's and Castel, David was able to alight, painfully, from Thierry's back outside Aurelius Bretton's cottage. He tied the horses to the fence of white palings that showed signs of recent painting, leaving them tethered loosely so that they could graze.

John admitted him at once and took him to see Aurelius, who, as usual, was in the library.

The Professor looked far better than the last time David had seen him. He was dressed and alert and was busily writing at something, books and papers strewn over his desk.

"Good day, David!" he said. "This is a pleasant surprise! John, bring us some sherry and some of those little sweet biscuits. "

"No, thank you, sir. I cannot stay," David said with regret.

John, looking disgruntled, stamped off.

"I have been sent by Colonel Fournier to inquire if perhaps the man you hired to help you with your books speaks German You said he knew many modern languages?" David inquired.

"Indeed he does," Aurelius answered, looking puzzled. "I have yet to find a language Mr. Lovel cannot understand. There is something almost magical about his talent for languages. He was able to translate Goethe's "*Iphigenie Auf Tauris*", which is of course, based on the work of Euripides. I am presently writing a comparison of the two works which is something I have long wanted to do, ever since the Goethe came into my hands, but without a translation table –"

"A translation table?" David asked. He had never heard

of such a thing.

"All Universities and great libraries have one. It is magiced and if one were to put a book in it in a language one does not understand the magic will enable the reader to see the pages in his own language so that it may be read easily. It is a remarkable thing," he said rather wistfully. "I wish that a small, inexpensive version were available for scholars such as myself. I had been used to sending to Cambridge for translations as needed when we had our regular Dragon Post. They were most obliging at University and translated many things for me. But now I have young Lovel, who is equally obliging and writes a fine hand as well."

"Does Lovel live nearby?" David inquired, a little anxiously.

"He is here," Aurelius answered. "I have hired him to come daily. In addition to being a fine scholar he knows his way around a garden and is bringing mine back to life. John and I grow increasingly incapacitated and need a strong young arm here. I would have liked for him to live in, but it turns out that he is married and since they are Gypsies, I imagine that his family will not leave their caravan."

"A Gypsy scholar?" David said in surprise. "I thought most of them to be illiterate!"

"It is a bit of a mystery," Aurelius admitted, "and young Lovel is quite close-mouthed about himself. But I am hoping to solve the conundrum one day soon." He reached for the bell pull as he spoke and gave it a tug.

John appeared a few moment. "Changed your minds, have you? You'll be wanting a tray after all?"

"No, John, we have not changed our minds. Would you be so good as to step into the garden and ask Mr. Lovel to come in here? Sir David needs to speak to him," answered Aurelius.

John glared at them, and then, muttering under his breath, stomped out to the garden through the open French doors. These led onto a stone terrace and John traversed this and went down a short flight of steps that led into the garden. They heard him call "Here, you Gypsy! You're wanted! Stir your stumps!"

"John is having trouble adjusting to the fact that he now needs help and I think he resents Lovel, as he sees it, for taking his place," said Aurelius apologetically. A sudden thought struck him. "You won't be taking him from me, David? We really cannot do without him."

"I am hoping this will be but temporary," David answered. "The Colonel needs some interpretation work done since a cargo of Austrian prisoners just arrived and most of them speak but little French and no one seems to have a knowledge of German." That was all he dared to say.

"And we cannot refuse Colonel Fournier anything," said Aurelius dryly, "even should it be to our complete inconvenience and to our detriment."

John came back into the house grumbling audibly. "He's coming," he said to Aurelius. "Said he's got to wash up a little at the garden tap."

"Thank you, John, that will be all," said Aurelius. He could see the curiosity writ large upon John's face but David had not bothered to explain to the manservant why he wanted to see young Lovel. Therefore Aurelius reasoned that it was perhaps information not to be readily shared.

John, his booted feet louder than ever, went back to the kitchen, saying audibly, "A fine day it is when gentleman consort with Gypsy trash!" and slammed the door to the kitchen behind him.

A few moments later Felix entered the room, wiping his hands on a bit of rag. "Do you need me, sir?" he inquired. "I was rather a mess. I've been wrestling with a particularly nasty Bishop weed and I did not like to come to you in all my dirt."

"It is Sir David Dieudonné who has need of you," replied Aurelius. "You remember Sir David from the other day, perhaps?"

"Yes, indeed," said Felix, with a slight bow that would not have disgraced a ball at Government House. "How do you do, sir?"

David inclined his head. This young man was not what he expected of a Gypsy. Although he looked the part, he was not in the least to what David was accustomed The others he had met on the island were rather furtive in manner, and attempted to be ingratiating when directly applied to.

"Professor Bretton tells me that you are familiar with the German language," David said. "Are you familiar enough to serve as a translator for some Austrian prisoners of the French?"

"I think so," said Felix slowly. He had only the example of his fluent French to go by, for, of course, there was no one here to whom he might speak German. But he had read it easily and had seemed to understand the pronunciation as well. And he could not tell these two men that he did not know if he could speak as well as read German. He had no desire to explain his memory loss.

David's relief was immense. In a few moments Lovel had agreed to go with him and they both went outside to where the horses waited.

"I have no notion how long we will be gone," David said as they mounted up. He also had no idea how Fournier would greet the sight of a Gypsy as the expected translator.

"Are you mad, Dieudonné?" said the Colonel angrily, when, over an hour later they met him on the road to the Dragon Port. "A *Gitan*? They can't speak understandable French! " He looked with contempt at Lovel, speaking about him as if he were deaf and impervious to insult.

"Mr. Lovel is quite accomplished in languages, both modern and dead," said David, trying to maintain a hold upon his temper. Lovel was angry too. David could see that in his tight hold upon the reins and in he set of his shoulders. David suddenly thought that it must be terrible, all of one's life, to be treated as an inferior being, and allowed to exist only upon sufferance, He himself had but to put up with it since Fournier had arrived upon the island and was finding the attitude unendurable. "I know of no one else, Colonel, who can speak German. Most people here have no need of anything but English and French."

"And most of you barely speak decent French!" muttered the Colonel.

He looked Felix up and down, noting his bare feet in the stirrups and his loose shirt, open at the throat. "Blériot will never accept this," he said to himself. He thought for a moment and said to David. "There is a second-hand garment shop in Le Bourg," he said abruptly. "Take him there and find him the clothes of a gentleman, particularly something to put upon his feet! It is too much to expect that he ends in actually looking like a person of Quality! Then bring him to the Dragon Port and be quick about it!" he wheeled his horse and galloped away, closely followed by his small troop.

"What does he think I am," said Felix bitterly "a parcel?"

"He speaks to everyone like that, I am afraid," said David apologetically. "We'd best hurry, for he can be most unpleasant and quick with the whip when crossed. I don't know what we shall be able to get with two pounds ten, for I came out with very little money."

"Professor Bretton gave me my wages this morning," said Felix. "I have more than enough, I should imagine, for he has been quite generous."

David was surprised at what they were able to obtain at the shop. There was quite a bit of choice for coin money. The proprietor of the shop explained that when so many people had left the island in a hurry they had sold up any extra things, needing the money, even the slim amount paid for used goods, more than an extensive wardrobe.

He was even more surprised when Lovel, with no coaching from either himself or the proprietor, chose a tasteful, well-matched outfit of a blue coat, biscuit-coloured pantaloons and a double-breasted pale yellow marecella waistcoat. They even found a pair of not too battered Hessian boots. They were a bit large, but better than too small, said the owner, seeing that the young man was unused to wearing shoes.

To David's further astonishment, the Gypsy stood in front of the small cracked mirror in the back of the shop and tied a perfect "Mathematical" neck cloth with the air of someone who had tied a muslin neck-cloth many times before. David had thought that he would have to do this for Lovel as tying a neck cloth properly was a tricky business. And with the earring removed, David was surprised how much the Gypsy looked the gentleman. Even Fournier would approve. In fact, David rather maliciously looked forward to

196

seeing the Colonel's face.

Felix was surprised how familiar the clothing felt to him. The fit was not precisely right as whoever who owned them before had been a trifle larger, but it was not too bad. He was not uncomfortable, nor did he feel restricted; even the muslin cravat seemed to be something he was accustomed to wear. Had he dressed like this before? And if so, why? Why would a farm laborer who was also Romany need to don the clothing of a gentleman? The more things he discovered about himself the less sense it made. It was a mass of contradictions. And there was no one who could help sort them out, not even his own wife.

When they at last joined Fournier, David was hugely entertained to see first a hastily repressed spasm of fury upon the Colonels' face and then how he schooled his features in to a semblance of approval. The Colonel hated having his misconceptions corrected and he could not comprehend the transformation of Gypsy into gentleman. David could hardly wait to share this with Grizel.

Fournier wasted no time in taking them to the office Blériot had set up for himself. In the short time he had been there Blériot had already left his untidy mark upon it. Plans, papers and parts of unidentifiable objects lay all over the desk top and the floor. Bookcases were crammed full of books haphazardly thrust into the shelves.

Blériot was in his usual mood which was that of belligerence. "Half of those prisoners are ill, Fournier," he snarled as the Colonel ushered David and Felix into the office, "And none of them speak French!"

"You wanted foreigners, *M'sieur*, so that they could not communicate your secrets," Fournier reminded him, through gritted teeth.

"But how am I to convey to them what they are to do?" Blériot shrieked and then, his suspicious eyes lighting upon David, said to him "Who are you? Have you come to steal my ideas? I am a genius, you must know! I doubt you can understand them!"

"I am the Bailiff of Guernsey, *M'sieur,* the nominal head

of the government at the moment," David said.

"He answers to me, Blériot," put in Fournier. "He has brought you a translator until the Austrian von Weber grows fit."

"This is Mr. Lovel," said David, drawing Felix forward. "He has kindly consented to –"

"Consented!" shrieked Blériot. "He should be *honored* that I am allowing him the opportunity to see part of the inner workings of my genius!"

"And it is charming to meet you as well," said Felix rather sarcastically, and added under his breath in English, so that only David, standing next to him heard "Mutton-brained clunch!"

Fournier shot Felix a nasty glance and said "Indeed, *M'sieur* Blériot. Lovel is only a *Gitan* who chances to be able to speak a foreign tongue..." The minute the words left this mouth he realized that he should have not allowed his temper to get the best of him. Blériot would no doubt be incensed that he had brought a Gypsy to do this work.

But Blériot was delighted. "A *Gitan*?" he said in delight. "Then his education will be too lacking or he will not have the wits to understand what I am making here! He can repeat the instructions like a parrot! Oh, this is good, Colonel! If you had brought me an educated man I might have been worried!"

Only David saw Lovel's hands clench into tight fists.

"Now, fellow!" said Blériot to Felix in a most condescending tone. "Today I shall want to divide the prisoners into groups. We shall need four groups," he went on, holding up four fingers as if he suspected that Felix needed the reinforcement to correctly understand the concept of four. "I shall also wish to know which of these prisoners are mechanically inclined and which have experience with needle and thread and find out those who have a skill in basket making. Do you understand me?" he added, as if he were speaking to a very small child or an idiot.

"You have made yourself perfectly clear, *M'sieur*," said Felix, sounding as if he had been grinding his teeth.

"Let us go, then," Blériot said. When Fournier began to follow them Blériot said "I don't need you, Fournier. Remain in the next room with this other one." He flipped a careless hand at David. "The *Gitan* is all that is necessary. After all, neither of you speaks German! Now leave my office so that I may lock it against prying eyes."

Two and a half hours later, after David had to endure watching Fournier fuss and fume for all of that time, Felix and Blériot returned to the room where David and Fournier waited. Blériot then escorted all of them to the locked office. The little man had a smirk upon his face as he turned the key in the lock.

"It went far better than I thought! A great many of those men are engineers and will be of much help. They did beg for food, Fournier, and I told them that you would see to it that they had the best of everything. They cannot work on empty stomachs. The brain does not work without fuel!"

"You exceed your authority, *M'sieur!*" Fournier said threateningly. How dare this little upstart make promises in his name?

"No, I don't!" Blériot corrected him. "The First Consul said that I was to have everything the way I want it and I want my workers well fed. Of what use are they to me if they are sick and fainting when they should be working? Do you doubt this, Fournier? Do I need to show you the orders I have, with the First Consul's signature, giving me full authority over this entire project? Everything shall be done as I say it will!" He gave a short unpleasant laugh at the look on Fournier's face.

"Bring the *Gitan* back tomorrow. He has already told the men that after the food is delivered tonight they are to finish unpacking the cases. I myself began the work as I was anxious to see that everything has survived the trip," Blériot continued.

He walked away and seated himself behind the mound of papers on his desk, deaf to Fournier's gobbling in rage.

When Blériot paid him no heed, Fournier turned on David. "I am making you responsible for this *Gitan*, Dieudonné!" he said harshly. "If he makes one slip-up it will be on your head!"

David bowed. He could not trust himself to speak.

In silence he and Lovel went outside to the horses.

After a long ride and then standing about a nearly empty room for all that time for Fournier had taken the only chair, David's leg was stiff and sore and mounting proved nearly impossible The soldier guarding the front door merely stared at David impassively when he saw the Bailiff struggling to mount. Just as David was wondering how he was going to get upon Thierry's back, for there was no sign of a mounting block, he heard Lovel say "Here, I shall give you a leg up," and David was tossed lightly into the saddle. Lovel mounted and they rode off, stopping only to present their papers yet again at the gate, which seemed foolish as they were leaving, not entering, the facility.

When they had left the palings well behind Lovel spoke. "So you are to be my nursemaid?"

"It certainly looks that way," David agreed.

"What are they doing here?" was his companion's next question.

"I wish I knew," said David on a sigh. "Whatever it is does not bode well for England. There are rumors of a secret weapon of some sort."

"I saw crates of machinery but it was impossible to tell what it was," said Lovel, " There were piles of willow canes, and vast rolls of silk."

"Silk?" David repeated, puzzled. What sort of a weapon would use silk? He had thought that Blériot's weapon was prove to be some sort of rocket or perhaps a long range gun.

Lovel spoke nest as if to himself. "I kept thinking of one word: Lunardi,"

"Lunardi?" David repeated. "That sounds Italian! What does it mean?"

"I can't remember," was the answer.

David, of course, thought the Gypsy was but having the ordinary memory lapse that everyone suffered on occasion. It was a wonder that he remembered anything at all, considering how angry he must have been at being treated so shabbily by both Fournier and Blériot, who seemed to think that he was some sort of performing animal and found it amazing that he could speak coherently.

"No doubt it will come to you," David said cheerfully. "I usually wake up in the middle of the night with what I could not remember earlier suddenly in my brain-box! The mind works curiously."

But Felix was quite certain that he would not suddenly remember for the harder he tried the further away the memory seemed and he was beginning to feel a headache coming on. Resolutely, he put the word Lunardi to the back of his mind. He wanted this evening with Rosal in the soft bed of bracken she had mentioned. After enduring Blériot's company he needed an interlude of peace and pleasure. He would rather dig up every garden on the island with his bare hands than return here tomorrow, but he was certain of one thing: Fournier would not allow him to refuse this duty. Nor did he wish to make trouble for David Dieudonné, whom he was beginning to like for his unspoken sympathy and the way he spoke, as if Felix were not just a Gypsy, one of a despised race. And Sir David, too, was caught in a trap not of his own making.

21
Discoveries

When David and Felix arrived back at *Trois Chiminées* Aurelius was waiting on the tiny porch in his Bath chair and insisted that they both come in for a cup of tea and some sandwiches.

David realized that the Professor was burning with curiosity. Since his leg was now throbbing, David was not eager to ride back to St. Peter Port without a rest. It had been a long time since he had spent this much time on horseback and standing so long had not helped either.

Felix, too, felt that he wanted some respite before going back to Rosal. He was angry over the way Blériot had spoken to him and he still had the headache that trying to remember what 'Lunardi' might mean had caused. Tea would be most welcome.

The only one not pleased was John. He was appalled when that Gypsy showed up on their doorstep, dressed like a gentleman. And to add insult to injury the Egyptian LOOKED like a gentleman! John muttered darkly to himself as he made the tea, slamming things about in the kitchen to relieve his feelings. He had to get rid of that Gypsy somehow! All of their peace had been cut-up since his arrival. They had gone on just fine without him! Every day the Gypsy was inveigling himself more and more into the Professor's good graces. By the winter he'd be living him with them, no doubt, him and that rag-tag woman of his and perhaps a squalling brat as well, eating at table with the Professor as if they were Quality! He would be damned if he would suffer any insolence from a pack of Egyptians and have to bear the humiliation of taking orders from them! Giving themselves airs!

John seethed as he took the tea tray into the Professor and dumped it on the desk with ill grace, making the cups rattle and slopping the milk onto the tray-cloth. He noted with disgust that even Sir David seemed to be taken in by the Gypsy and was speaking to him as he would an equal. What was wrong with the Professor and Sir David? Could they not see what was right in front of their noses?

John went back to the kitchen, again slamming the door behind him.

David looked up at the sound. "John seems in a very bad skin lately," he remarked.

"He is in a lot of pain. It is his back, you must know," said Aurelius apologetically. "And he will not give up his duties and rest as the doctor has directed."

"I suggested to him that he let Hagar, my wife's aunt, treat his back," said Felix, "but he will have none of it. She is an herb woman and has the Healer's touch." *Madame* Brehaut had thought it best that the French think Hagar was related to them and not just a 'stray' and they had taken this advice to heart.

"Her remedies have much improved my legs and I am sleeping better," said Aurelius as Felix poured out the tea. "But tell me more of the changes at the Dragon Port. Do they give any hint of what might be going on there?"

"The Receiving Office has been torn down as well as the dragon shelter and pens," David answered. "There are four smaller buildings. Did you manage to get a look at those?" he asked Felix.

"They are to be used as barracks and work-rooms for the prisoners," he answered, handing a full cup of tea, just as the Professor liked it, to him. "The odd thing is that the four groups of prisoners are not going to be allowed to mix with one another. Tomorrow I am to give instructions to each group as to what they will be doing. Blériot thinks that I am far and away too stupid to understand and put together the sum of his genius," he replied somewhat bitterly. That 'parrot' remark still stung.

David made a sudden decision and put down his cup, leaning forward and gazing earnestly at Felix. "You could be of much help to us," he said. "There is a resistance movement and our goal is to rid these islands of the French presence entirely. Any information you can gather, any educated guesses could help immensely."

"You do not feel that as a Gypsy I owe my allegiance but to what might most be to my advantage?" Felix asked with a wry twist to his mouth.

David shook his head. "The Professor trusts you and so do I," he said. His instincts were generally good and they were telling him that Lovel was honorable and trustworthy.

"I may be a Gypsy, but I am also an Englishman and I would give much to be rid of the French," said Felix. "Anything that I can do I shall."

"Thank you," David extended his hand and the two young men shook hands, sealing the bargain.

Aurelius was pleased that they seemed to take to one another. Now if only John could be brought around! He was quite aware of John's resentment and wished that his old servant were not so stubborn. But he had learned over the long years they had been together that the more he tried to change John's mind, the more John dug in his heels.

David picked up his cup again. "The building that intrigues me, however, is the tall, narrow one in the middle of the field. What can be the purpose of such a building?"

"Blériot took me and several of the prisoners inside," said Felix. "I had to instruct the men how to open the roof."

"Open the roof?" said David, frowning. "Is it a gun tower, then?"

Felix shook his head. "There is no platform for a gun, nor any windows or gun ports. It must be three or four storeys in height. It is largely empty."

"Whatever could it be?" David queried, puzzled. "We have heard talk of a secret weapon. Fournier could not resist boasting about it in front of me when he has been talking to the Inquisitors and his senior staff, but he has not let slip what the nature of the weapon might be. He claims that they will be able to conquer the British isles with whatever it is, since neither Wizards nor dragons will fight."

Felix gave a short laugh. "The man is a dolt! Both Wizards and dragons will fight if their lives and homes are threatened!" How he knew this, he could not explain, but he was as certain of it as if it was in a book in front of him.

Neither Aurelius nor David had much experience with dragons and knew but a limited amount of Wizards. There was a College of Magic at Cambridge, that of Dee, named after John Dee, the Wizard, astrologer and alchemist who had served Queen Elizabeth. Alchemy, of course, since the seventeenth century, been a banned science in the Six Nations, but Dee had made many valuable contributions to the field of magic.

Aurelius had known but few of the Dons in the College of Dee and unlike some of the Fellows, had never kept a dragon. David's history with dragons had been limited to those he had seen in the sky and at the Dragon Port on the occasions he had business there.

"Then Fournier will be in for a surprise," said David, with no little satisfaction. "I think that he expects Britain to lay down and roll over for him, as if we British were pet dogs!"

"Sir," said Felix to the Professor "when I was looking at the materials Blériot has gathered a word came to mind , but I cannot place it. Perhaps you might know it?"

"I have little knowledge of warfare and the materials of war, unless it were those of ancient Greece and Rome," Aurelius said. "but I shall be glad to try and help in any manner."

"The word is 'lunardi'," said Felix.

"Lunardi!" exclaimed Aurelius. "He is never building hot air balloons! But that is idiocy! A friend of mine at Cambridge was much interested in them and even dragged me along to see some balloon ascensions. Duckworth, my friend, claimed that they had no practical application, for they are at the mercy of the winds. However could they be used in war, except perhaps as an observation platform? They could never be used as an invasion force!"

"What is lunardi?" David asked, exchanging a glance with Felix.

"Not what, but whom," Aurelius corrected. "Lunardi, his Christian name was Vincenzo if I remember correctly was an Italian. He was a balloonist or aeronaut as they called them. He had escaped the Inquisition and emigrated to England. I saw him make an ascent, at Duckworth's behest, from Moorsfield to Ware back in, I think '84. If you saw that flight, my dear boy, you must have still been in short coats! Perhaps that is why you did not fully remember. Lunardi continued to give exhibitions throughout the '80s until his last ascent ended in disaster. He nearly perished in the North Sea. I remember Duckworth telling me about it." Aurelius shook his head. "If these Frenchmen think that hot air balloons are the answer to subduing England they are sadly mistaken."

"The prevailing winds here are westerly," said David. "They would be swept back to France! It's probably too much to hope for that Fournier would go aloft and disappear over Normandy!"

"That," said Aurelius "would be the answer to a prayer." He thought a moment and then said, "I think I might still have a copy of Lunardi's book here. Duckworth sent me a copy; he thought my interest in the subject far greater than it was."

"Yes!" exclaimed Felix "I remember seeing it!" He jumped up from the table and went to the now refilled, neatly positioned bookshelves. A few moments later he pulled out a volume and read the title aloud, *"An Account of Five Aerial Voyages in Scotland". "* He began to leaf through the pages.

"Perhaps you'd best study it," David suggested. "The more you know about balloons the more you will be able to tell us what they are doing."

"By all means take the book home with you," said Aurelius. "It will be my contribution to the resistance." He smiled sadly. He wished that he could be of more use. But resistance to this tyranny was for the young.

"We must keep this private between us," David cautioned. "We must give the French no chance to find out that we have guessed their game."

This was agreed upon and the party broke up. It was getting late and David would be expected back in St. Peter Port, while Rosal would be looking for Felix.

Felix, with Aurelius' blessing, left his gentleman's garments at *Trois Chiminées*. They would be needed the next day when he returned to the Dragon Port. It was agreed that David would call for Felix at the cottage early in the morning, as Fournier had appointed David bear-leader.

Aurelius hoped that this translator position would not last for a long while. Already that afternoon he had missed young Lovel's company and the hours, as they had before the Gypsy had arrived, had gone by on leaden feet. Even the paper he was writing had lost its savor. It was foolish, he knew, to tie his happiness to the presence of another person but he had been without an intellectual equal for so long. He had best enjoy it while he could.

Felix did not think that Rosal would like to see him in *Gajé* clothing. She seemed to have a good amount of scorn for non-Romany, save those she considered 'friends' such as *Madame* Brehaut and her daughter. He almost forgot to replace the earring, remembering only at the last minute. It still seemed an alien thing but Rosal had assured him that all male Romany wore them.

Rosal was waiting for him at the gate of *Les Huit Lapins,* the usual basket of foodstuffs on her arm. She was outlined in light by the declining sun and she looked very pretty indeed. Her black hair shone with bluish highlights and her lips and cheeks were red and inviting.

Giving into an impulse, he took the basket from her and placed it on the ground. He pulled her into his arms and kissed her deeply. She was as aroused as was he by this he thought, for he could hear her ragged breathing and feel her heart beating as she wore nothing beneath the simple drawstring blouse.

"After we eat I shall show you the bed I have made for us in the wood," she said in a husky whisper and wound her lifted arms tighter about his neck. "Tonight we will make a baby, I know it!"

Felix was not concerned with making a baby but he had become increasingly conscious of her. While outdoors this morning, working in the garden allowed much room for thought, and he had been able to think of little else than of being alone with her and making love to her. He still did not feel 'in love' with her but he certainly desired her. He wished he could remember how it had been between them. If her response now was any indication, it would be good.

While Rosal and Hagar made their supper, Felix went to

the pool in the woods and bathed. When he returned he took over Rosal's duties and insisted that she go and enjoy the pool.

Hagar still grumbled when he persisted in doing unsuitable work, such as tonight, frying the new potatoes and tiny onions while she poached chicken and herbs. That was woman's work, not suitable for a Rom. He was to lounge at his ease while they worked. But he would not hear of this, any more than he would sit and watch them drag water from the river for washing and cooking. He did not like to be waited upon and would not allow them to stand behind him while he ate his meal before they ate theirs. He insisted upon them eating with him. At Hagar's protest that this was not the Romany way he said calmly, "Then I care not a reed for the Romany way."

When Rosal returned from the pool, fresh and sweet, they ate. The food was good and plentiful Both Hagar and Rosal had gained some much needed weight in the past weeks.

Hagar watched the other two as they enjoyed the chicken and potatoes. The glances between them made her smile, a trifle sourly, to herself. She did not think that the love potion would now be needed. When they went off together she would take out the cards again. Every night she had read the cards the Tower showed itself. It still made her uneasy.

But Felix had shown no signs of remembering anything. He had come to her several times for a headache cure. Even this evening he had complained of a headache and had drunk her special remedy. He spoke no more of the memory loss and had seemed to accept his life as a Romany. Taking Rosal to his bed and perhaps giving her his child would seem to be the final stage in his acceptance of his new life.

The end of the meal and the setting of the sun could not come too soon for Rosal. All day long she had been longing for this moment, when she would lead him into the woods and there they would create a new life together. In not quite a year she would have a babe at her breast once more.

When she looked at Felix, she did not see a man she was in love with, nor did she desire him for anything but his ability to sire a child. She had responded to his kiss because that was what men liked and expected. She had learned that lesson from Sylvester. He had liked to think that he 'excited' her with his kisses, although once they were in bed he had not expected anything of her but that she lay there and let him do what he wanted. True, Felix's kisses were far more pleasant than Sylvester's had been.

That things were not going to be quite the same was readily apparent when they went into the woods and she drew him towards the bed of bracken. She had taken care to make it soft and inviting with grasses and flower petals.

Starlight shone down upon them, and to her joy she saw a falling star as she wiggled first out of an embrace he attempted and then out of her clothing.

"Come on, what are you waiting for?" she said impatiently as he did not follow suit. She lay down on her back on the ground and looked up at him. "Don't you want me?" she demanded.

"I rather thought that there might be some pre-liminaries," he said in an odd voice "I wanted to undress you myself and kiss and caress you first."

"Why?" she said "Kissing doesn't make babies!" She put herself in the position Sylvester had always demanded and said, screwing her eyes tightly shut, with her arms stiff at her sides. "I'm ready! Get on with it!"

"Rosal —" he began and seemed unable to go on. He was quiet for so long that she opened her eyes and looked up at him. Even in the faint starlight he wore what she thought of as a 'funny' look.

"What's wrong?" she asked "Why don't you love me?"

"Because this is not love," he said in a low voice. "You are acting as if you cannot wait for it to be over. I thought you wanted this as much as I did. Was it always like this between us?"

She blinked. What other way was there? This was for a man's pleasure and a woman's reward for enduring it was a child. "Of course it was," she said.

"And you put up with this–this– sanctioned rape?" he said. "My God, what sort of monster was I? First of all you tell me I let you go out to work to support me and that I let you do tasks beyond your strength and now this! I don't like what I am hearing about myself! I don't like it at all!"

He turned and walking rapidly, disappeared into the woods.

Rosal sat up, staring after him in the darkness. What was wrong? Why had he left her? With a wail of frustration she turned over on the bed of bracken and beat her fists against the ground. Sylvester had never acted so! He would have been on top of her the minute she lay down! How was she ever to have a baby if her Rom would not lay with her? She burst into sobs of vexation and rage.

22
The Light In the Air

Something had gone wrong last night. As Hagar had expected, neither Rosal nor Felix had returned to the *vardo*, but this morning Felix returned by himself. He had eaten breakfast silently, feeding bits of bacon to the dog, as if he was thinking deep and not too happy thoughts. He had shaved and dressed in a clean shirt and trousers and left for the Professor's, all without asking after Rosal or telling Hagar where she might be and uttering no more than his thank-yous for the breakfast of eggs and bacon Hagar made him.

Moments after he left the area of the *vardo* Rosal emerged from the woods as if she had been waiting for him to leave before she showed herself. Her face was set in unhappy lines, with traces of tears. Absently, she greeted Chavé, who, last night, had been tethered to the wheel of the *vardo* so that his master and mistress might have their privacy.

"I need that love potion!" Rosal finally broke out.

"I take it nothing happened?" said Hagar dryly. "What did you do, Rosal?"

"What did I do?" the girl cried. "More like what he didn't do!"

"Tell me what happned," said Hagar. "Here, have some food." She filled a plate with eggs and bacon from the frying pan she had made her and Rosal's breakfast in, separate from the one Felix's meal had used.

Rosal ate half-heartedly while she told Hagar what had passed between her and Felix on the evening. Before she had finished Hagar was shaking her head.

"I told you that this one was different from Sylvester!" she said. "How could you be so foolish, Rosal? Why did you not let him do as he wished? Just because Sylvester was so like your father does not mean that every man is like that! Some of them do not want a woman who does not want them, particularly *Giorgios* who have been raised to be gentlemen."

"But how am I to get a baby if he does not take me to bed?" Rosal protested.

"Not by acting as if you cannot wait for his embraces to be done with," said Hagar. "Perhaps I should give *you* the love potion!"

"I can't pretend, Hagar. I don't like to do it," Rosal said stubbornly. "I just want a baby!"

Hagar was thinking rapidly. "Perhaps making a potion for you is not such a bad idea," she said slowly. "A potion to make you feel passion and desire so that you will long for his embrace. A Rom does not like to hear that he is valued but for his ability as a baby-maker. A man such as your new Rom, unlike Sylvester, wants to think that his woman is eager for him. And that, I think, is what you must be to get this one in your bed. I will think on this. The potion must be subtle yet strong. Perhaps a little for both of you..."

Rosal looked at her eagerly, her eyes shining again. She put down her plate and counted on her fingers. "If you do it right away I could l still have a child by early spring!" she said happily.

Hagar shook her head. "Rosal, you must stop talking and thinking about a baby! That is a good way to curse your marriage bed and remain barren. And it is no way to bring a man to your bed. Remember what I said! He must feel that you are eager for *him,* not only his seed. It will take time to brew a potion such as is needed. You must be patient."

In this case patience was something Rosal almost completely lacked. Her longing was so acute, her need so great that it consumed her. By now she was completely convinced that her only happiness lay in a child. Without a child she was *nothing*. She was cursed, and outcast, *mahrime,* unclean, and without a child would remain alone all her days with only another outcast for company. She desperately needed something beside a dog and a pony to love. She remembered how little Cinerella had held up her arms to be taken up and had snuggled against her breast, how holding the child had made the baby quiet and happy and peaceful, the very feelings that had flooded Rosal when she had the baby in her arms, or even looked down on her when Cinerella slumbered in the cradle. Rosal wanted to feel all of that again. Only then would she feel alive once more. And she was willing to do anything that would make that possible.

Felix's thoughts as he walked alone towards *Trois Chiminées* were black indeed. He had not slept for a long while and then had made a bed beneath a tree for the balance of the night, rising at first light unrefreshed.

He had found it appalling that Rosal expected him to just fall upon her and use her as if she was some tavern trull. She was his wife, and presumably, even though he could not remember it, they had loved each other. Had he actually always used her like that? Everything in him wanted to rise up in denial of the picture of himself he had obtained from the way Rosal, and Hagar too, acted and from what they had told him of himself. It was a picture of a monster of selfishness, a bone-idle layabout who was content to live off females and take his pleasure where he wanted it with no thought for his wife's wants and needs.

But there was no logic behind this line of reasoning. Surely a blow upon the head and a memory loss could not change one's personality so much that what was normal behavior before had now become a source of shame, and complete anathema?

He was far out of his depth and wished desperately that there were someone, such as a doctor, that he might discuss this with. Unbidden, came the thought that a Wizard Healer might be able to help. Where had that thought come from? He knew nothing of Wizards or Wizard Healers. Professor Bretton had, at any rate, told him that there were no magical persons left upon the island since the French came.

The day echoed his mood. The sun had fled and a dark mass of cloud pressed down upon the island, a vast bulk of sullen, heavy clouds that promised rain and perhaps thunderstorms later in the day. It made the walk between the trees gloomy, with heavy, stagnant air bereft of any refreshing breeze. Up in the air, above the clouds it would be cooler.

Up in the air? How did he know that? Had he perhaps been up in a balloon? Was that why he knew the name Lunardi?

With a groan Felix stopped in his tracks and leaned his arm against the trunk of a tree, pillowing his head against it the friendly bark. His head was beginning to throb once more. With every question he asked himself the pain became more acute. All he had were tantalizing glimpses, as if a curtain had been lifted for one moment and then dropped, heavily, again. He could not even discern if what he was seeing was real memory or something he had read or been told.

Only with the books in the Professor's library was he on firm ground. Only there could he look at a title and *know* with certainty what lay with in the covers, only with those volumes of knowledge was his footing a surety.

The tree he had leaned against was an apple, an elderly one, but it still bloomed, like an ancient bride, with beauteous blossoms. Perhaps, ages earlier, there had been a farm here, or an apple core had been dropped and a seed taken root. With no conscious thought or intention he found himself murmuring " *'Old apple tree, we wassail thee/ And happily thou wilt bear./ For the Lord knows where we shall be / Till apple's another year..'* "

"Halloo, Wizard!" said a silvery little voice. "I thought you were all gone from here! Do you mean to come and wassail our tree?"

Startled, Felix backed away from the tree and looked upwards. Amongst the apple blossoms was a tiny winged female creature, as pink and white as the apple blossoms. She glowed with a silvery sheen and her face was pointed and puckish, with a friendly smile. "No one has wassailed our tree in many a year and wassailing is needed for apples to grow well, you know!"

He could not comprehend what she was talking about and his mind fastened on the only thing that made any sense. "Our tree? Are there more of you then?"

"Oh I am the Faerie of the apple blossoms and later I shall be the guardian of the apples and direct the bees in their work," she said. "When I say we, I mean the Dryad of this tree and I. She lives in the trunk and is rather shy, but I am certain that she will come out to greet a Wizard who will properly wassail our tree! Come out, Daphne, do!" she said coaxingly. "Here is a Wizard who knows the old ways!"

"But I am not a Wiz —" Felix began but then could not continue, as to his wonder, the bark in front of him blurred and shifted and he saw clearly the face and shoulders of a beautiful young girl. Her hair, the colour of the apple bark, was bound about with vines, holding it up high on her head and a green gown draped from one shoulder. A bare foot peeked out at the roots of the tree. She smiled, very shyly, and said in a soft voice, "We thought that all of the magical folk hereabouts had forgotten us. I have heard from the other Dryads when their voices are borne on the wind and on the sighs of the leaves that few know the old ways any more and do not honor the trees and their gifts properly. We, Flowerlet and I, are honored to meet a *magus* well versed in the Celtic way." She curtseyed deeply to him, bending forward from the protecting tree.

He bowed in return as he could not think what else to do. "I am not a Wizard," he said "and I do not know the Celtic way."

The Dryad and the Faerie laughed, kindly, indulgent laughs. "But you reek of magic!" the Faerie Flowerlet stated. "Certainly you are a Wizard. Why, it would be obvious to a blind person!"

"And you know the wassail ritual! The poem you repeated, that is spoken before the cup is poured at my roots," said the Dryad. "And look, Flowerlet!" she pointed at Felix's forehead. "See the gold star on his brow! He is a Faerie friend!"

Felix felt as if he had stumbled into the sort of dream that quickly became a nightmare in which everyone save the dreamer knew what was going on. Star on his brow? He had studied his face in Rosal's tiny mirror many a time, hoping that his own features would remind him of who he was. He had never seen a star of any sort. And why did they persist in telling him he was a Wizard? Surely this was some sort of dream and he would awake to find himself back in the *vardo*?

Suddenly, close by, bridles jingled and hooves, softened by leaf debris, sounded. So quickly that Felix could not really make it out, the Dryad faded back into the tree. The Faerie leaned down from the blossom she sat in and said "Count on us if you ever need us, Wizard. Come to this tree and whisper our names, Flowerlet and Daphne, three times and we shall do whatever we may to help you! Remember now!" And then she too was gone, the apple blossom closing up around her.

He was still staring up into the apple blossoms when the French soldiers rode up, a small patrol of four privates and their Corporal.

"What do you do here, Gypsy?" the Corporal demanded with a frown, taking in Felix's appearance. "It is forbidden for *Guernaise* to wander."

"I am on my way to my place of employment," Felix said quickly. "I merely stopped to admire the apple blossoms."

The Corporal demanded to know where he was employed and when Felix answered with no hesitation, the Corporal said brusquely, "Be on your way then. This is no time to be standing and staring. This is not where you should be at this hour."

Felix wanted to retort that there was always time to look at the beauties of nature as it was what nurtured the soul. To do so, however, would be injudicious. Fournier wanted travel time kept to a minimum. One was no longer to stop and gossip with neighbors, enjoy the loveliness of the day or saunter in a leisurely fashion. One was to leave one's home for only absolute necessities and hurry wherever one was going and then back again. As he walked away towards the Professor's cottage, Felix felt the Corporal's eyes upon him, as if he suspected that Felix would go elsewhere.

This was no way to live. The burden of the French occupation was growing intolerable. Yesterday, Rosal had told him on the way back to the *vardo*, that the French had come and taken most of *Madame's* cheeses, making a mess of her cheese room as they did so. They had also taken all the day's eggs, most of the fresh milk and new churned butter. Scarcely a day went by when some farm or house was not raided, at any time of the day or night. Protests earned a visit from the Inquisition. And it was not as if the French needed what they took. Everyone knew that supply ships came regularly from France. The French were eating far better than were the *Guernaise*. Felix resolved again that he would do anything that he could to help David rid the island of their French foes.

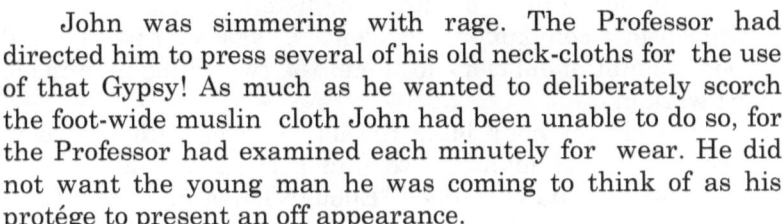

John was simmering with rage. The Professor had directed him to press several of his old neck-cloths for the use of that Gypsy! As much as he wanted to deliberately scorch the foot-wide muslin cloth John had been unable to do so, for the Professor had examined each minutely for wear. He did not want the young man he was coming to think of as his protége to present an off appearance.

Felix had scarcely changed his clothing when David arrived, not on horseback, but in his cabriolet, pulled by Thierry, who was both saddle and shaft broke.

"Colonel Fournier has directed me to provide your transport," David explained to Felix "And I am very much afraid that we are in for some heavy rain today. The cabriolet has a folding hood and a large apron that will somewhat protect us from the rain." He could have added that he was in significant pain from his leg as well and simply was not up to another long ride. Yesterday's journey and now the change in the weather was causing it to ache abominably. In the cabriolet too, wrapped in oil cloth, was a bundle of tax records that he intended to work upon while waiting for Lovel to accomplish his translations. David also had asked Majorlaine to pack a nuncheon for two, as even his limited acquaintance with Blériot did not lead him to believe that Blériot would think of anyone's needs save his own.

David was proved correct. Blériot made everyone work until *he* was hungry, and then he darted off to his office to eat beef sandwiches and drink wine, without any regard for anyone else. As far as he was concerned, only his workers were important and that only because hungry men could not work well. The *Gitan* and his *Guernaise* transport were not his responsibility. He did not even inquire if they had food, instead locking himself into his office, after announcing that

217

everyone had better be ready to resume work in an hour as there was still a lot to be done today!

As much as he longed to ask Lovel what he had seen and been able to figure out that morning, David did not dare. There was no telling who might be listening. They ate their nuncheon in a companionable silence. Majorlaine had packed a good amount of delicious food and the two young men made short work of it.

Precisely an hour later Blériot bounced into the room where David had managed to find a chair and a table he might work on and exclaimed "Enough lounging about! Back to work! I have some complicated instructions for the next group of men and it will require all your attention, *Gitan!*"

It was not until well after six in the evening that Blériot released Lovel from his service. "Be back all the earlier tomorrow!" he said in his shrill voice. "I wish to begin production immediately and either the men are slow and stupid or you do not speak German as well as you claimed, for they did not seem to comprehend as quickly as I expected."

David had been hoping for the last hour that they could soon be on their way. There was only a small window in the room he had been confined to where a soldier had stood on duty outside the door all day to prevent him from wandering about, and the sky had steadily grown more ominous, with blacker clouds boiling up over the horizon. He hoped that they could at least return to Castel before the full fury of the coming storm was upon them.

Lovel helped him gather up his mountain of papers. Even a day's steady application had not made much of a dent in it. And the Gypsy insisted upon carrying it, for when David stood, his leg almost buckled under him.

"Thank you," David said gratefully. "A day sitting in a poor excuse for a chair such as this is perhaps not the best idea."

He leaned heavily on his cane as they began to walk out to where the cabriolet had been brought up by one of the soldiers. The guard followed them closely, as if he was afraid they would steal something on the way out.

David could see that his companion was not in the best of humors. He was tight-lipped and he seemed tense and angry. David could not blame him. Fifteen minutes or so of Blériot was unbearable. He could not imagine spending an entire day in the man's company. It would make anyone feel homicidal.

Thunder rumbled in the distance as they mounted into the carriage. David was grateful for Lovel's help and even more grateful when the Gypsy offered to drive. All David wanted to do was lean back, stretch out his leg in as much room as the carriage offered and try not to think about the day he had passed.

"What is all that paper?" Lovel asked him as he skillfully tuned the carriage and set Thierry towards the gate at a brisk trot.

"Tax records," said David on a sigh. "Fournier has given me the task of ascertaining the amount of taxes paid by each householder for the past five years and the most recent evaluation of their property, in order that he may send out a new, much higher tax bill."

"Does he want to completely ruin us?" Felix said. "The French are like locusts! They seem intent on destroying everything!"

With an abrupt change of subject he said "I am reasonably certain that they *are* building hot air balloons. Today I was told how to instruct the men to cut the silk and sew it. The shape is correct for the balloons as I saw in the book. And I also told another group how to make the baskets. but they are very odd baskets, unlike any I saw in the illustrations. They will be making a large cavity in one side, a squared shape, that is to be lined with some material that has not as yet arrived from France."

"What could that be?" David said. "A holding place for some weapon? I still can not imagine how they think a balloon can be of much use in a war, particularly after listening to the opinions of the Professor's friend."

"Travel by balloon would seem to be a chancy thing at best. And there is the added problem that the higher one goes in the sky the colder it is," said Felix thoughtfully.

"Is it?" David queried with interest. He had never given

219

much thought to what it was like up in the sky, above the clouds.

"The temperature falls about four degrees Fahrenheit for every one thousand feet up into the atmosphere, generally speaking," said Felix, with the air of one who knew what he was talking about.

David wanted to ask him where and how he had learned this, but they were approaching the gate and had to stop and present their papers yet again, an action that seemed curiously redundant as they were already within the fence. Their identities could not have changed in this time. Like most of Fournier's dictums, this seemed to be designed but to harass and annoy.

Once out of the gate there was no time for any more talk, for with a huge crash the sky split open and rain burst from the clouds, accompanied by thunder, lightning and a strong wind. It was all Lovel could do to keep Thierry on the road that soon turned into a quagmire. The gelding was frightened and wanted nothing more than to bolt for his stable. David was forced to hold onto the ribbing of the leather carriage hood to prevent it blowing away.

It was a nightmarish journey to Castel. In spite of the violence of the weather they were obliged to stop at the parish crossings of Forest / St. Saviour and St. Saviour / Castel and present their papers and the pass signed by Colonel Fournier allowing them to travel from Castel to Forest parish where the Dragon Port was located. At each check point the soldiers seemed to delight in delaying them as long as possible, with endless, repetitious questions and close scrutiny of their papers.

When at last they reached *Trois Chiminées*, they were soaked through, for the slant of the rain had come straight under the hood, which by now was ripped half off.

As they drew near the Professor's cottage in the gathering darkness a small, rain cape clad figure darted out from the porch, holding a lantern aloft.

It was Joisaine. "Quickly, *Messieurs*! get yourselves

inside and dry! I will tend the horse. *M'sieur le Profeseur* says you are to spend the night here as the weather grows worse."

"But you, *Mam'selle?*" Felix asked in concern.

She shrugged. "I have my rain cape and it is but a dash through the woods," she said. "I have baited the pony and made him all ready for the night, as well." The lantern was swinging wildly in her hand from the wind and as she spoke an immense crack of thunder sounded, closely followed by a extreme flash of white lightning, arcing across the sky from cloud to cloud, splitting into myriad streaks of fire.

Felix thanked her and then took up the package of tax records and offered his arm to David, whose leg was reacting rather badly to the weather.

Traversing the garden path to the font door was difficult for it was ankle deep in water. It seemed a long time before the safety of the porch was reached and they nearly fell into the house when John, prompted by Aurelius, swiftly opened the door.

"Not a word, not a word!" Aurelius cried as the two wet and bedraggled young men came to stand before his Bath chair, dripping with wet. "Change from those wet clothes immediately! John has laid out dry things for you and there is tea on the hob and hot soup. We can't take a chance on a feverish cold! There is little worse than a summer cold."

Half an hour later they were relatively dry and sipping tea in front of a roaring fire. Outside, it was far darker than it would be for this time on a summer's evening nearing the longest day of the year. Rain still poured and the lightning often lit the room. The thunder was not as loud, indicating that the storm might actually be moving away.

The candles in the room flared and danced as the wind continued to assault the house. The old house was full of draughts and even the fire would suddenly depress or roar up into the stone chimney, one of the three that had given the cottage its name.

They had discussed, while eating soup, a thick rich barley and vegetable stock, what Felix had seen that day and Blériot's impatience with both the translations and the men's understanding. They had all tried to guess what the compartment in the basket might contain and why there was so much secrecy.

Aurelius had found some old letters from his friend Duckworth with detailed drawings of several hot air balloons and they had been studying these to see if any of them might contain a compartment such as the one in Blériot's basket design.

A sudden, incredibly strong gust of wind shrieked out of doors slamming into the house with stunning force and all of the candles on the table near the group at the fireplace went out, and the fire, just as suddenly, sank down to nearly embers.

"Do not move," said Aurelius in the darkness. "I have tapers here somewhere." The noise of a drawer opening was heard and he began to fumble within it, searching blindly for the tapers.

A white light, bright and steady winked on above them and shone down, lighting up every nook and cranny as it grew in brilliance.

"A mage light!" gasped Aurelius, for he knew all too well what it was as very little else was used at Cambridge.

John, coming in with a tray to collect the tea things, paused in the doorway to the kitchen and felt an almost overwhelming surge of triumph.

There was little doubt who had been responsible for that magical light hanging in the air. It was over the Gypsy's head, just above his fingertips from a hand stretched into the air.

"I have him now!" John exulted. The Inquisition would want to know about this!

23
Good News
and Bad

To his disgust, Reginald and his friend had ended in being housed in the Dower House, rather than in the manor itself.

The Earl had greeted them with scant welcome and no more money had been forth coming, even when Reginald admitted he was rolled-up. The Earl had stared at him, with a black look and told him he had better rusticate for a while and as his own house was available, a snug little property in Somerset, near Shepton Mallet, so he had best go there until his allowance would be paid on the next quarter day.

Reginald was forced to admit that he could not go there as he had rented it to raise the wind for a gambling spree and it would be occupied by tenants until Michaelmas.

With obvious reluctance his grandfather told him that he could stay in the Dower House, but at the first hint of any of his rackety friends from London visiting, or behavior that would scandalize the neighborhood, he would be sent packing. That meant no gambling, or taking advantage of the maids. However, Reginald was welcome to the contents of the cellar. Richard admitted that Reginald was incapable of not indulging at least one of his vices.

Horrocks' nephew, Swann, who had been an under-butler in Warwickshire, was hired as butler, and told to keep an stern eye upon Reginald.

Swann might have done well to keep an eye upon the guest they all termed "the foreign gentleman". Bahram was quite content to remain at the Dower House. The food and service were excellent, there was a good library of arcane knowledge, for most of the Dowagers inhabiting the Dower House had been Witches, and what was more he had the Earl right under his eye and was able to observe his habits.

There was also a room at the very top of the house that

made a fine, private workroom. Years ago, it had been used as an Observatory and a telescope still stood in it. A feigned interest in astronomy and an actual bent for astrology provided an excuse for much late night activity and a jamming curse locked the door each day so that Bahram did not have to ask for a key, which might have caused questions to be raised.

All in all, he went out of his way to be as quiet and as innocuous as possible. Remembering the lesson about English servants learned in the Inn on the Isle of Wight, he was respectful and courteous and the servants soon had a better opinion of him than they did of Reginald. They thought him pleasant and so fascinated by the minutiae of English life for he asked many questions about the estate and its people of everyone he met in his many long, strolling walks, listening with great attentiveness to each answer.

He soon heard the story of the great blue man that had appeared in the sky and how the Earl and his dragon had defeated it. This was told and told again by the locals, each time growing in the telling until the blue Djinn was a colossus and had threatened the entire coast line from Dartmouth to Exmouth and points in between, out into Tor Bay and Babbacombe Bay.

So that was what had happened to the Djinn! It was no doubt in hiding or being held someplace, for if it was truly dead, as the locals hereabouts seemed to think, the lamp would have changed to dust. The lamp and its occupants were firmly bound to one another. A Djinn could be killed by destroying its vessel and the receptacle would dissipate when the Djinn was vanquished.

But the lamp was still in one piece, although it had lost some of its lustre. Somehow, Bahram would find out where the Djinn was and perhaps even heal it with the aid of a particularly nasty demon called Az, she who was the result of evil thoughts and deeds and a very powerful demon indeed.

Bahram realized that English dragons were far more dangerous that he had understood. They seemed so benign, carrying the Royal mail, giving rides to children and used as all sorts of transport. They seemed to lack the fierceness of the ancient beasts who had once inhabited his homeland. There were a fair amount of books in the library on dragons, some of them in very archaic English that Bahram had to struggle to understand. But he learned enough to begin to put together a most cunning plan.

Richard had fallen into the habit of spending a fair amount of time on the cat boat, the *Star of the Sea*. Somehow, it made him feel closer to his missing grandson, for in the cabin were many of Felix's favorite things: much-loved books, his guitar, his journal and the log book of the cat boat, which he had kept meticulously. Richard was touched to see miniatures of himself and Greymalkin, Pascoe, and Felix's late parents when he open the hinged front of the tiny desk. There were magiced spring flowers in a planter in the main cabin. Reginald and Bahram had not been the neatest of housekeepers, but underneath their surface mess was a neatness and an order of which Richard approved. He took care of their untidiness his own self and restored the boat to what Felix would have liked.

He could still not accept the fact that Felix was gone. When he had finished setting the cabin to rights it was as if the cat boat was waiting for her owner to reappear at any moment.

Soon it would be a month since Felix's disappearance, Richard thought one afternoon in June as once again he found himself in the cabin of the *Star*. He had heard nothing yet from Madoc, who had promised to let his friend know one way or the other, even if it was to report his grandson's body had been found. Every day he lived in hope that the sea-prince would report to him and that it would be good news.

A sudden splashing sounded outside and Richard, who had been looking again at the log of the *Star*, raised his head sharply.

"Richard!" Greymalkin called excitedly from the deck where he had been sleeping in the sun, "Madoc is here!"

It was but a step up to the deck and Richard took it in a bound.

The Merman was riding on the crests of the gentle waves of the incoming tide. The look on his face caused Richard to catch his breath and almost stagger, for Madoc wore not an expression of sorrow but a broad smile.

"It took a good while, old friend !" he said, " But we found a Selchie and a Merchild who conveyed a man they thought to be a Wizard to land. The description that was given answers to that of Felix."

Richard felt the world reel around him. He was obliged to suddenly sit down on the edge of the cockpit, experiencing a relief so overwhelming he thought for a moment he might faint. He put his hand over his eyes and he said "Was he badly injured? Is that why we have heard naught?"

"Yes, there seemed to be a blow to the head," said Madoc. "The bad news, Richard, is that he was put ashore in Guernsey, hours after the French occupied the island. The Selchie felt that he should get out of the water as he was still losing blood from a head wound. She put him on a beach well away from where the French were landing in a an area frequented by fishermen and those who gather food from the sea's edge. Someone will have found him."

Richard raised his head and looked at his old friend. "Madoc, the Inquisition is in Guernsey! If he was turned over to them –" he stopped suddenly. He could not even think of such a horror. Greymalkin jumped up in his lap and patted his face with a sympathetic paw, meowing in distress.

"I am in touch with many folk on Guernsey at the moment Richard, and there are no tales of a Wizard being taken. And the Inquisition would brag of such a thing as they are always proud to have caught a magus. There has not been even a rumor anything like that happening," Madoc assured him. "And now that we know that he is on Guernsey I shall have my contacts on the island look for him. But it is my guess that whoever found him is hiding him from the French. That may make it difficult."

Richard stood up, putting his familiar gently down on the deck. "I would like to go to Guernsey myself," he muttered, beginning to stride up and down the deck.

"That is what you must not do!" cried Madoc. "You would be arrested and put to the Question by the Inquisition!"

Greymalkin added his protests to this. "What Pascoe would say to such an idea I am sure I don't know!" the cat said fervently. "We will not let you undertake such a foolhardy journey! Then two of you would be in mortal peril!"

In the end Richard was convinced. It was difficult, if not impossible to not to want to rush to the aid of his grandson and bring him home where he could be looked after properly. Richard had to be content with the great joy that Felix was alive and hopefully, one day soon would be coming home. He looked forward to telling Reginald and cutting up all that young man's hopes to become the heir to the Earldom.

The storm had blown out in the course of the night leaving a sparkling clear sky on the next day.

Rosal went early to *Les Huit Lapins* farm, hoping that she might meet Felix returning to the *vardo*. She wanted to explain to him why she had acted the way she had. She had come up with a plausible story to explain it, she thought, although Hagar had looked at her askance when she had proposed it earlier. Again she said that Rosal should be a teller of tales, what the *Giorgios* called Faerie tales.

But she saw no sign of him. She guessed that the storm had kept him with the old man last night. She herself had barely reached the *vardo* before it broke overhead.

She went onto the farm. The lane was cluttered with debris from the storm, fallen branches and leaves and petals from the blooming trees.

Madame was glad to see Rosal arriving early. There was so much work to do this morning! The crops had to be checked for damage and there had been a leak in the roof of the henhouse. There was much mending and cleaning to do in the aftermath of so much wind and rain, so unseasonable and so violent.

They were in the muddy field of parsnips, assessing and trying to correct the damage when *Madame*, standing up for a moment to ease her back, saw a strange procession coming across the field towards them.

It consisted of two priests and two soldiers, all picking up their feet gingerly from the mud, the two priests holding the hems of their vestments up from the ground as a woman might hold up her skirts.

Rosal, glancing up, saw *Madame* staring and she straightened as well, saying "Joisaine, look!"

"What do they want here?" Joisaine's voice was sharp with worry. They had all heard how the Inquisition was snatching people at random and taking them to Castle Cornet, the new headquarters of the Inquisition, to be questioned. Father Maël had not let the loss of his instruments of torture deter him. A well applied whip could yield fine results. At each twice weekly assembly, there were people missing, who might or might not show up again and those who came back were often in pitiful case after the far from gentle 'persuasions' of the Inquisition.

The three woman waited until the priests drew close. The older of the two, a balding, thin, worried looking man called Father Meurice said "I seek a woman calling herself Rosal Lovel."

"She has done nothing wrong!" said *Madame* sharply.

"According to the laws of the church, my daughter," said the second priest, a round little man, Father Xavier by name, "she is indeed engaged in wrong-doing. She is living in sin."

One of the soldiers cleared his throat. "Our assembly records show that you claim to be married to one Felix Lovel. But there are no records of any marriage taking place."

"We're Romany," said Rosal. "We jumped the broomstick. It is how we marry."

"But that is a pagan belief, my child. You are not married in the eyes of the Church," said Father Meurice, shocked. "That could be construed as heresy. Unless you marry properly and ask forgiveness for your carnal sins I have no choice but to turn you and your lover over to the Inquisition. For the fires of the Inquisition are less than the everlasting fire you will suffer in hell for having known each other outside the bonds of Holy Matrimony!"

Rosal began to speak, but *Madame* forestalled her with a quick gesture. "What must they do?" she asked.

"Marry at once," said Father Meurice "They must make confession, coming to me or to my colleague, and be publicly married in the blessed sacraments. And they may not cohabit until after the wedding. Your illicit lover must remove himself from your bed and from your house until you are legally married," he said to Rosal.

"He can stay with the Professor or here with us," said *Madame*.

Father Xavier cleared his throat. "And there is another matter. All Christian women will be decently clothed here, by order of the Inquisition. Those garments you wear," he said to Rosal, "show your limbs in a shocking fashion and the bodice is immodest in the extreme. You must obtain garments suitable for a pious female. All married women must cover their hair with a cap. Short skirts and a bodice that droops from the shoulder serve to entice lust in the male and should be avoided at all costs. You cannot wish, *madame*, for your young son here," he looked at Joisaine, "to begin a career of venery at such a youthful age, which will be the unfortunate result if he is allowed to gaze upon such indecency daily."

"I'm a girl!" said Joisaine indignantly.

The two priests were so shocked that they could not speak for a moment.

"Where are your skirts?" thundered Father Meurice. "To dress as the other sex is heresy! Go into the house at once and change into the proper garments!"

"But I don't have any skirts!" Joisaine began angrily. "I cannot work the land in a gown!"

This outburst only served to enrage the priests further. "Such disrespect!" Father Xavier exclaimed. "Escort this erring child to her home at once!" he ordered the soldiers. "She is not to appear in public until she is properly and modestly clothed!" He turned to the two women as the soldiers took a protesting Joisaine towards the farmhouse. "I shall expect to see all of you at confession. What with the impiety of carnal sin and the blatant immodesty of allowing a young girl to appear in men's garments your penances will be heavy indeed! There may be a fine as well. You will be fortunate if Father Maël does not demand that you answer to the Inquisition!"

"We will be at confession, Father, you may count upon that!" said *Madame* hastily. She had quickly grabbed Rosal's hand behind their skirts as they stood together, and gave it a warning squeeze. Rosal was angry, she could tell.

"And you, Gypsy girl, you have not been coming regularly to church," said the priest Meurice. "We expect to see you, your *fiancé* and your aunt there this Sunday and on all Holy days of obligation hereafter. You will be married on Saturday next when you have completed your confessions. Remember, only true confession, penance and marriage will save you from the Inquisition. And come to church modestly dressed with your head covered and hair properly bound!"

He looked up. The two soldiers were coming back across the fields from having escorted Joisaine to the farmhouse. Without a word of farewell, the priests tuned and left. Their voices drifted back as they left, telling the soldiers that they were to go next to the home of a known Protestant who had not attended church the past Sunday.

Rosal began to speak but *Madame* Brehaut put a finger to her lips and waited until she heard the noise of a carriage rolling away. The mud had not allowed them to drive into the field, for which Madame was grateful. There might have been damage to the crops.

When they were well and truly gone Rosal burst out in anger. "What right do they have to order me about and tell me when I may marry and what I can wear? The priests and the reverends of the English church never bothered the Romany!"

Madame looked at her sadly. "Our church is not their church, Rosal. When Father Séamus was here the church was tolerant and open but that is the Irish Catholic church, in which I was raised. This Roman church is bigoted and small-minded and thinks it has the right to interfere in every part of our lives. And our fear of the Inquisition is too great to defy it. I shall have to see about making Joisaine some gowns and begin wearing caps regularly. And I advise you to do the same, for your family. You will have to be married in the Church, whether you like it or not, unless you want to be arrested and tortured as a heretic. All of you must come to church on Sunday." She sighed heavily and added, "Come, I have fabrics at the house and pattern books and some old clothes I have put away. We shall see what we can contrive for clothing for Joisaine and you and your aunt as well "

The Romany generally assimilated the religion of where they lived and Rosal's people, when still in Spain many years earlier had been Catholics. But their church attendance had been sporadic here, indeed, she could not remember the last time she had been in church since Cinerella had been christened at her mother's insistence, for Rosal's parent was still alive then.

Rosal generally looked on Sunday as a day of freedom after working hard six days a week. Now she had to attend church, in *Gajé* clothing no less! And she was not certain what some of the things the priest had said meant. What was a Holy day of Obligation? And what and why did she have to confess in order to be married? In her mind, jumping the broom was a legal and binding marriage. Of course, she had not actually done this with Felix but she had married Sylvester by this method, and even her mother, who had been the most religious person in their *cumpania,* had seen nothing wrong with this and considered her daughter a proper wife after the ceremony of jumping the broom.

She had no idea what religion, if any, Felix had. And would he be willing to marry her in the church with what had gone between them? Perhaps he wanted no more of her, never mind binding himself more firmly to her.

She was suddenly close to tears as she followed *Madame* up to the farmhouse. All she wanted was a baby, not all of these complications.

24
The Arrest

"Put that light out at once!" Aurelius's voice was sharp with fear. "Do you wish to bring the Inquisition down on us?"

"I–" Felix began but Aurelius made a gesture of dismissal and glared as he might have done at a hapless under-graduate.

A few moments later the light winked out and Aurelius's fingers closed about the tapers he had been looking for in the drawer. He handed one to David, who stood painfully, bent to the fire and lit the taper. Then he lit the candles so that once again the room was illuminated.

None of them noticed John, still standing in the shadows of the hall leading from the kitchen.

"Where did that come from?" Aurelius demanded. "How dare you jeopardize your safety, our safety, by performing magic? You cannot be unaware that such is proscribed by the Inquisition! Why have you not told me that you have magic?" His voice was rough with worry. His first emotion was fear that this young man, of whom he had grown so very fond, might end in the hands of the Inquisition.

"I didn't think that Gypsies had much magic!" said David, resuming his seat and staring very hard at Felix. "I had a friend, a non-magical, who was interested in the subject of why some people have magic and others don't and he said other than some small magics such as being able to read the future in a limited fashion and spells of concealment, the Gypsies are not magicians."

Felix could barely meet their eyes. He did not know where that light had come from. It had been instinctive. He had only been able to put it out by not thinking about it, again relying upon instinct.

He did not know how to answer their questions. To him, these two who had been so friendly now seemed accusatory and once again he felt an alien, which was something he felt only with Rosal and Hagar, not here in the Professor's library.

And he wanted that camaraderie and friendship back, not this critical blame.

His mind was a blank. He could think of no reasonable explanation. And they were waiting, giving him a chance to explain himself, wanting to know a good justification for having done such a thing. If this had not been a night of wind and rain when sensible persons, including French patrols, were staying inside, snug before a fire, someone might have burst in on them and seen the light, a light forbidden by the island's conquerors.

"Well?" said Aurelius in a voice that had put fear into many a student at Cambridge.

Felix swallowed hard. He had not wanted to tell them about his memory loss. Somehow it seemed to make him less of a person, a poor pitiful thing that did not even know his own name, a stupid creature who had to rely on very inadequate information from his wife, who knew little more than he did.

But he saw that he had little choice. He was going to have to tell them.

He took a deep breath and said "I don't remember how I learned to do that," he said in a rush, eager to get it over with and out in the open now that the moment had come for confession. "I don't remember anything at all about myself."

John had not waited to hear this confession. Making as little noise as possible he went into the kitchen and, going to a drawer in the dark oak Welsh dresser, pulled out paper and a stubby pencil. This was what he used to make his grocery lists before going to the market in St. Cécile.

He sat at the table and put the paper in front of him. Sucking thoughtfully on the pencil, he pondered how to do this. Although he knew there was a reward for denouncing mages, he wanted none of it. He did not want the Professor to know that he, John, had been responsible for turning the Gypsy over to the Inquisition. It would be reward enough when the Egyptian was gone and they could return to the way it had been before he came.

He had to write this letter to the Inquisition so that no one would know the identity of the writer. It was going to be difficult, for writing did not come easily to John. He had not written above two or three letters in his entire life. His handwriting was deplorable.

He decided to write it in big block letters. Slowly, he put the pencil to the paper and began to write.

Before Felix was halfway through his recital Aurelius had motioned to David to pour them all a glass of sherry, a decanter of which, with glasses, stood on a table near his desk.

Felix was grateful for the drink for this telling was proving far more difficult than he had ever imagined and it steadied his nerves for what was certain to be a barrage of questions.

He finished with "I know that you have been curious, sir, about where I obtained my education but I have been reticent because I simply do not know. It seems I have never discussed the matter with Rosal, for she has no idea either. But she did tell me that I am not a native of this island."

"But she told you that you lost your parents at an early age and were schooled to become a servant?" Aurelius said. His whole attitude had changed. He was eager to solve this mystery, and a fine mystery it was!

"Yes, but I cannot conceive why I learned Latin and Greek and all the other things I seem to know," said Felix, spreading his hands.

David had been listening quietly, sipping at his sherry, Now he said "I would think, rather, that you were trained to become a schoolmaster."

"I had thought, because of my familiarity with the farm that I was a farm laborer," Felix said. "And my hands are not those of a gentleman. I have done rough work." He looked down at those members, which were indeed work-roughened.

"I have heard of schools where the pupils, charity pupils for the most part, are expected to work a farm and do other tasks which teach them a trade and provides for the school's needs at the same time," said Aurelius thoughtfully. "I think that David has the right of it for why would a farm laborer need Latin and Greek? But it stands to reason that a schoolmaster would need such things. Perhaps, my dear boy, when your preceptors at whatever school you attended, realized your intelligence, they decided, quite rightly, that not to educate you for a higher calling would be a criminal waste."

Felix relaxed when he heard the 'my dear boy'. He was back in the Professor's good graces once more.

"But where and why and how would I have learned magic?" he asked. "If Gypsies are not magical –"

"Perhaps one of your parents was magical," David suggested. "There are people here or rather there *were* people here who had one parent magical and the other non-magical. Perhaps one of your parents was not even a Gypsy."

"Is making a light considered a difficult part of magic?" Felix wondered.

"That I can answer," said Aurelius, "for the University was lighted almost completely by mage lights and I was always told that it is the very first thing a Wizard is taught, in addition to something called grounding and shielding. I have no idea what those latter items are," he added, when he saw a question in Felix's face.

David was frowning slightly. "Your wife should have taken you to a physician," he said. "Perhaps something could have been done."

"My dear David, there aren't any left! In this whole parish there is but Mr. Smithers, the apothecary, a man who likes to use large, completely mispronounced words to cover his ignorance!" Aurelius protested. He turned back to Felix "What happens when you try to remember, really concentrating upon it?"

"Pain," said Felix simply. "The most appalling headache. Even discussing this is beginning to make my head throb."

"I shall have John bring you a headache powder," said Aurelius absently. This was the most intriguing conundrum! "Damn the French!" he suddenly said. "If it were not for them we could get to the bottom of this! But we have no access to records in the Six Nations now! David, are there records kept of persons arriving on the ferries? Perhaps if we found out the time that he actually came to Guernsey?"

David shook his head. "No, there never have been records

235

kept. At certain times of the year many farmers hire seasonal workers from off island and they come in on the ferries and leave the same way, quite anonymously. Since we are British we have never required a passport or any such thing from anyone from the Six Nations. Citizens are free to relocate here as long as they do not become a charge on the parishes. We never take names until they do become permanent residents and I don't think that this was ever done with the Gypsies in the first place. There is no booking required for the ferries beyond having enough money to pay for one's ticket. When the Peace was signed back in March of '02 the ferries began running that May and only ceased gain recently. Of course Fournier put a stop to that as he especially does not want anyone leaving here."

Felix's face fell. He had begun to look a little hopeful.

"Don't worry, my boy," Aurelius leaned forward in his chair and patted Felix's hand reassuringly. They had drawn their chairs close together both for privacy and ease in hearing over the wind which was still howling about the house. "We shall find out who you are. I am quite certain that if you but learn the facts of your education and home your memory will come back to you" he grinned suddenly "like magic! But until then, pray resist any impulse to conjure anything, even if it is done to be helpful!" His face grew suddenly sober. "I could not bear it if the Inquisition were to take you."

In the kitchen, John listened to the wind and the rain lashing the house. It would be tomorrow before he could post the letter. But the mail was quick on this small island and it would be in St. Peter Port tomorrow afternoon or even the late morning.

The writing of the letter was proving a difficult task. He had started three times now. But at last he thought he had some thing which would do the trick. By the next evening the Gypsy would probably be in custody, never to bother them again.

Father Maël, of course, did not open his own mail. Narcisse Roux served as his secretary at the present as there was little else for the man to do. His instruments of torture lay at the bottom of the harbor. There had been singularly few heretics who need torture so far, no Wizards amongst the old men, no Witches amongst the women, most of them good, Church-going Catholics; although attending an Irish Catholic church was in itself, a heresy. However, until the French occupation there had been no Roman church on these Channel Islands. At least they *were* Catholics. The people of French heritage who had become Protestants Maël found especially horrifying. To know the right path and to turn from it! It was inconceivable! Before he was done everyone in this archipelago would have his or her feet firmly on the right path. Today, several of the subordinate priests were out searching out persons who did not conform to the code of conduct that Maël was formulating. When Guernsey was in conformity and all heretics were routed out then he would be free to go on to the other islands and make them into proper Roman Catholic populations belonging to France.

For French these islands were to be from now on. The First Consul had no intention of ever letting England have them again. They were to be called, as they had long, long ago, the Isles of the Sleeve or *Îles d'la Manche* in Norman French, for 'the sleeve' was what the French called the English Channel.

The room he had chosen in Castle Cornet for his office had a beautiful view of the harbor, with the sun gleaming in the bright air after yesterday's storm, and the sea beyond it, but Maël did not notice it.

The mischief each night had grown worse. Now there were not only lights and music, men seeming to fall under a spell and strange explosions, but things disappeared and showed up again in odd places or were gone for good. Last night someone had broken into the barracks kitchens and eaten a feast, emptying much of the contents of the pantry and dirtying every pot and dish in the process.

But then the pantry contents and been found stacked, in precise neatness, out on the parade ground.

All of the horses in the stable had been discovered to be sweat-streaked, exhausted and in a nervous condition, their manes and tails tied in a multitude of knots. It was as if they had been ridden hard, all night, in exceedingly rough country.

Several soldiers had reported seeing a huge black dog with clanking chains draping its body, roaming the streets here in St. Peter Port. When it saw them it sat on its haunches and howled, a sound that the soldiers, who swore that they were completely sober, said came straight from Hell.

Only magic could explain these occurrences. There was a mage or mages on this island somewhere and sooner or later one of the random people brought in for questioning would crack and reveal his whereabouts.

The door to his office burst open without so much as a warning knock. Narcisse Roux, his round face gloating, waved a paper in the air. "We have him now, Father!" he said excitedly.

Roux was a short, rather portly man with a balding pate and the looks of a jovial publican. Nothing about him, except a certain look in the eyes, suggested the torturer. He gloried in his work, though, always finding new and better methods for inflicting pain. He had been angered beyond anything Maël had ever seen when the *Acadie* had blown up and he had lost his torturer's equipment before he had even had a chance to use it. He had laid the whip on the backs and shoulders of the *Guernaise* particularly heavily as a punishment.

"What is it?" Maël demanded, holding out his hand for the paper.

"Read that, Father! I think that we have our magus at last!" Roux said triumphantly.

The paper had been folded into an envelope and sealed with a wafer. The direction was in a most ill-formed hand and the interior was just as bad. The block printing ran uphill and was obviously written by a person of little education. Since all Inquisitors were required to learn English so that they could read the pernicious books about Wizardry published in England, Maël had little trouble making sense of it.

"To the Inkwsiton", it ran:

"Go to the house called three chimneys in Saint Saseal parish and you will find a magikian. I do not want the rewarred. I hate magic and want to be rid of it - 'tis evil."

It was unsigned.

"It arrived from St Cécile this morning," said Roux in satisfaction. "I took the liberty of drawing up a warrant, Father."

Maël stared at the letter, reading it again. He had learned that these 'tips' were often reliable. Some were the results of imagined slights or jealousies, but very often contained a kernel of truth to them. Each and every one must be investigated.

"We shall bring the warrant along, just in case," he said slowly. "Call the carriage, Roux. I shall want an escort of soldiers, and you will accompany me of course."

"Of course!" said the chubby little torturer, almost wriggling in delight.

"There will be a file on the inhabitants of that house. Pull it and bring it with us," Maël ordered.

John had a difficult time of it that morning, containing his glee. He had slipped out when Aurelius and his two guests still lay a-bed. It was possible to leave a letter and the small sum that paid for mailing it under the door at the tiny receiving office. John had addressed it to *The Guvermint, Cassel Cornett, Saint Peter Port,* rather than to the Inquisition. Spelling was not John's strong suit but he could not ask Aurelius for help as he would have, had the letter concerned any other subject.

As he served breakfast to the Professor and his overnight guests (he had curtly refused the help of the Gypsy) he wanted to tell the Gypsy that he had ought to enjoy himself while he could, playing at being a gentleman, as his days were numbered, that he would soon be kicking his heels in a cell in Castle Cornet, accused of Wizadry. And when they were all called upon to testify against him John would have to tell the truth under oath, that he had seen the Gypsy cast a mage light and he had bewitched the Professor too, into treating him as if he was Quality instead of trash.

By this evening it would be all over. The Gypsy was going off again today with Sir David, but John had heard them talking about the old Dragon Port. He could not imagine what mischief the Gypsy was up to there nor how he had inveigled Sir David into treating him as if he were someone important, but John would know where to send the soldiers when they came.

He was putting a bowl of *Madame's* beef and barley soup, nice and hot, on a tray for the Professor when the thundering came at the door. He smiled to himself in satisfaction as he put the tray a on the table and went to answer the summons. Earlier, he had had to listen to a bag of moonshine about how much the Professor missed that damned Gypsy. it was all codswallop as far as John was concerned. He would send the soldiers out to the Dragon Port and they could take the Gypsy into custody there.

From the beginning it was not as he had imagined it. John scarcely opened the door when four soldiers with leveled rifles pushed past him, followed by a priest in the purple and black of the Inquisition and a man all in black with a hood hanging down his broad back.

"Who is it, John?" Aurelius called from the library.

It was a short distance from the front hall to the library where Aurelius sat and the priest and the man in black went on into the room, ignoring John's "Here, now! here now!" protests at such cavalier treatment.

John's back chose this inopportune moment to go into a painful spasm and with a groan, and stooping over with a hand to the small of his back, he could only walk with a painful shuffle.

He hobbled into the room just in time to hear the priest say, in heavily accented English, reading from an unfurled scroll, "Aurelius Bretton, I hereby arrest you for the crimes of Heresy and Wizardry. You will be conveyed to Castle Cornet and there await trial." He then began to repeat this in French.

"NO!" John screamed.

25
The Wrong Prisoner

"No!" John yelled again "You've made a mistake! Leave him alone! 'Tis the Gypsy you want!"

Two of the soldiers were hauling Aurelius from his Bath chair. John grabbed at one of them, trying to stop them, for they were hurting his master cruelly. But the pain in his back limited his movement.

One of the other soldiers struck at John with his rifle butt, sending him crashing to the floor where he lay dazed, wave after wave of pain from his back washing over him, mingled with other agony from where he had been hit.

"Don't try and help me, John!" Aurelius shouted in English. "Get Sir David!" They were manhandling him with scant regard for his age or infirmities and he was in almost as much pain as was John.

The soldier holding his arms, a big, burly fellow shook Aurelius and ordered "Be quiet, prisoner!" in French. None of them had much understanding of English.

"Listen to me!" John shouted desperately, levering himself up on his elbow. "You've got the wrong man I tell you! 'Tis the Gypsy you want!"

He was so distraught that he did not notice the look of horror that came over Aurelius' face as he comprehended what John was shouting and what it must mean.

"Silence him," said Maël. Although Maël could read English reasonably well and even spoke it slowly, someone speaking quickly and shouting as John was just so much gibberish to him. All he knew was that the heretic's manservant was protesting them taking his master no doubt. Maël had expected some resistance as Wizards bound their unwilling servants to them with dark and evil spells. The stupid manservant should realize that he would be free of his servitude once the magician was destroyed.

242

A booted foot swung at John's head and he fell backwards, heavily, unconscious. He was not awake to see the soldiers drag Aurelius out to the waiting carriage.

Pyewacket had grown increasingly anxious. Each day he asked David if anything had been heard about his Wizard and each day the answer was the same, in the negative.

David had told him that inquiries had to be surreptitious as the Inquisition must not get wind of them. He could ask only the most trustworthy people for news of a Wizard. It was not as if they could put an advertisement in the newspaper, even if a newspaper were still being published. They had to be very careful that they did not bring the Inquisition down on Pyewacket's Wizard or on themselves.

Pyewacket understood the need for such caution. He had heard Majorlaine and David discuss the Inquisition and what it was doing to the island and its inhabitants. The cat had heard of the death of Bernard Pommier and the disappearances of other *Guernaise*.

But still the familiar chafed under the restraints of his position. He felt as if he ought to be doing something. Perhaps Felix was somewhere, lying ill, needing his familiar while Pyewacket sat here in the Dieudonnés' comfortable kitchen, playacting with a bunch of mice! They were nice enough mice. They had even instituted their own inquiries for him amongst the mice of the island and he was grateful. But no one had heard of any Wizard being found. One thing he had been relieved to hear was that there was no Wizard imprisoned by the Inquisition. Most of the prisoners currently in Castle Cornet were completely and utterly non-magical and seemed to be held for the information they might impart.

Pyewacket had grown quite friendly with the leader of the mice, Maurice. Maurice was one of the keenest actors for the benefit of the French and thought it a great joke. Maurice seemed to know everyone on the island or at least those whose houses and barns were infested with mice.

On the morning after the storm Pyewacket and Maurice were sitting outside on the back steps that overlooked the kitchen garden. The violence of the night's storm had done considerable damage to the new vegetables and Majorlaine had been up early to tend these.

David had not come home at all the night before but he had warned Majorlaine that he might not be able to do so since the weather seemed as if it would be very bad later. He had been right.

Still Majorlaine could not help but worry and for once Pyewacket had felt as if he was doing something useful, for he jumped up onto Majorlaine's bed and soothed her with his purr, sending her into a deep restful sleep in spite of the noise of the bad weather.

But now he was once again restless and unhappy. He should be doing something!

"Strange things are going on out at the Dragon Port," Maurice said suddenly in the common speech of animals. "We had a report yesterday of new buildings going up, many men working and more men arriving, prisoners, from the look of it. There are also many strange crates and bales of silk. One of the mice out there who well understands French thinks that they are building something with which to fight the English."

Pyewacket looked down at him. "A weapon? A big gun perhaps?" he said.

Maurice shook his head, setting his whiskers quivering. "My informants say that there is no gunpowder at the moment. It has a distinctive smell, as you know."

"They might bring it in later, after the gun is built," Pyewacket suggested. He had little real interest in what the French might be doing or building. He wanted only to find his Wizard.

"But what is the silk for?" Maurice persisted.

Pyewacket shook his head as he yawned. The sun felt good on his fur and he could easily slip into a cat nap.

"What's that?" Maurice was suddenly alert.

Pyewacket heard it too: hooves on the road, the jingle of harness and the creak of leather, and what was more he could smell the men and the horses. "It is the French, yet again," he said to Maurice. "Hide yourself! I shall be a cat sunning himself."

With a squeak, Maurice ran off to scurry into a mouse hole in the foundation. Pyewacket settled himself more

244

comfortably, trying to efface himself as much as possible.

His sensitive ears herd the banging at the front door,and heard Majorlaine, who had been scrubbing vegetables for a stew at the kitchen sink, put down her knife and answer the door.

Quite clearly, the cat heard Colonel Fournier's voice. "Where is your son, *Madame*? Did he come back here last night?"

"Surely you know that better than I, Colonel," Majorlaine replied with calm dignity in spite of the threat in the Colonels' voice. "He was out upon your business yesterday and warned me he might have to take shelter away from home yester eve should the storm be bad, as it was."

"And where did he take shelter?" the Colonel demanded.

That Majorlaine was puzzled by this line of questioning was apparent in her voice. "Why, with Professor Bretton I would imagine, since the young man who is working with David also works for the Professor and, by your order, it was up to David to provide his transportation" she added a little sarcastically.

Satisfaction was in the Colonel's voice as he said "It may interest you to learn, *Madame,* that this very day Bretton is being arrested for Wizardry and Heresy! And I and the Inquisition are very interested in learning why you son has been consorting with a magician and a heretic! Why did he not, as is his duty, inform the Inquisition of this mage in our midst?"

"You have all made a mistake, Colonel," said Majorlaine quietly. "Aurelius Bretton is no Wizard. Under the standards of the Inquisition he may be a heretic, but then so are we all, for we are not *Roman* Catholic and many of us are Presbyterians. Professor Bretton is no more magical than am I."

"You may not be magical, *Madame*, but you and your entire family have been consorting with a magician and moreover, concealing the fact! You are in serious trouble and will no doubt be wanted for questioning by the Inquisition," said the Colonel.

Pyewacket was intent upon this conversation, his ears to the front. Too late he heard someone sneak up behind him and a hand, once again, grabbed him by the loose skin around

245

his neck. He let out a snarl of indignation and brandished his claws, but to no avail. The person grasping him knew how to restrain a cat

And once gain he was stuffed into a sack. This one, however was of thick, stiff leather that he could not scratch his way out of. But he still hissed and spat and shrieked, clawing vigorously at the side of the sack, yowling as if he were a banshee.

Majorlaine heard the racket and came running. "What are you doing with Suie?" she screamed, and ran down the steps to try and pull away the sack from the soldier who held it. "Leave my cat alone!"

Fournier followed her more slowly. "You own a black cat, *Madame*. All such animals have been proscribed by the Inquisition."

Majorlaine turned to face him. "And since when has this been in effect, Colonel?" she demanded angrily. "Your soldiers have been here more times than I can count, helping themselves to our food and goods and they have all seen Suie many times! And he is a black and white cat, not all black!"

"It is a new ruling as of this morning. That cat is more than likely a Witch's familiar," said Fournier.

"Then why is he here with me?" Majorlaine retorted. "I am no Witch!"

"That has yet to be proved, *Madame*," said Fournier, with such evil intent that a chill ran down Majorlaine's spine. She suddenly wanted David with her, very badly, just to hold his hand or feel his arm about her.

Pyewacket kept up his scratching and howling as a non-familiar cat would, allowing his voice to get angrier and angrier and frightened as well. The last was not difficult to feign. He was in truth extremely frightened. He had read of what the Inquisition did to black cats. He felt the bag being swung up over a shoulder and he was in motion, leaving Majorlaine's protests behind.

Whoever was carrying him mounted his horse and the sack was tied to the saddle. He heard Fournier come back and order the troop to ride out. Soon he was jolting against the horse's side. He fell silent as the precariousness of his position overcame him. And there was no Felix to save him. Felix did not even know where he was.

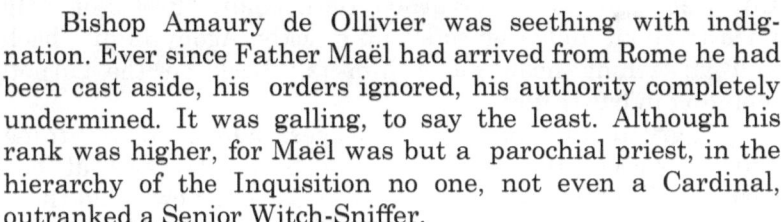

Bishop Amaury de Ollivier was seething with indignation. Ever since Father Maël had arrived from Rome he had been cast aside, his orders ignored, his authority completely undermined. It was galling, to say the least. Although his rank was higher, for Maël was but a parochial priest, in the hierarchy of the Inquisition no one, not even a Cardinal, outranked a Senior Witch-Sniffer.

His first meeting with the Witch-Sniffer had gone very ill. Maël had not been impressed with the amount of heretics prosecuted and burned under the Bishop's rule, or what he saw as the lax manner in which the Bishop had enforced the tenets of the Church. Presbyterians were still being allowed to practice their heresies, and there were even a few Irish Catholic priests left, promoting their heresies as well. All of these people should have been placed in gaol, tried and more than likely burned or at least fined heavily and punished with burdensome penances to perform. Maël considered that de Ollivier and Dubois, the former commander of the island's Occupation forces, had been lazy, more intent on a comfortable posting than doing their duty. And he did not hesitate to tell de Ollivier his opinion.

Maël had listened to none of de Ollivier's protests, dismissing him as if he were a small, recalcitrant child, not a Bishop of the Holy Mother Church, and Maël's senior in years as well.

And now de Ollivier resented him for it. He must do something to either put the usurper in his place or somehow get in his good graces, whichever proved the most advantageous.

When John at last awoke, with the taste of blood in his mouth and an aching head as well as a most painful back, the clock was striking five and the front door stood open, admitting a long bar of afternoon sun. It was this warmth and light shining on his face that had brought him back to consciousness.

With a groan he turned his head and the first thing he saw was Aurelius's overturned Bath chair. "Professor!" He tried to shout and tried to sit up quickly. Agony in his back and an aching head made him fall back on the carpet, moaning in frustration.

Angry tears came into his eyes. Why had everything gone so wrong? It was supposed to be the Gypsy that was carried off to the dungeons of Castle Cornet! How could those Frenchies be stupid enough to think that the Professor was a Wizard? What had they done to him?

All at once John heard voices and footsteps on the gravel of the path that led to the door.

"I wonder why the front door is open?" he heard Sir David's voice say. "I daresay is it is such a nice day that the Professor wanted as much light and air as possible. It really turned out warm."

"Sir David!" John croaked, his throat tight. Very little sound emerged.

A few moments later the footsteps had reached the doorway and then there were exclamations of "My God! What has happened here?" and both Sir David and the Gypsy were kneeling beside him, horror and concern on their faces.

"John!" cried Sir David "What has happened? Who did this to you? Where is Professor Bretton?" He had thrown himself down beside the manservant, disregarding the pain in his leg and hip and now helped John sit up. The Gypsy slipped a cushion from the sopha behind him, then went into the kitchen and returned quickly with a bowl containing water and a soft cloth. He knelt again beside John and began dabbing gently at his face with a wet cloth. Blood caked one side of the old man's face and his right cheek and eye socket was swollen.

"They took him, Sir David, those Frenchies from the damned Inquisition!" John gasped out. He glared at the Gypsy and lifted a hand as if to push him away.

"The Inquisition?" David repeated blankly. "But why?"

"They said he was a Wizard!" John ground out. A sob was welling up in his throat. He turned and shoved at that damned Gypsy. "This is all your fault!" he said viciously, making no attempt at all to disguise his hatred.

Felix fell backwards, pushed off balance by John's surprisingly strong push. The bowl fell from his hold, splashing water all over the floor. He looked at John, shocked. "My fault –" he began.

"Don't come off the innocent! You're' the one what has magic in this household! They'd have never come here if it hadn't been for you! " John suddenly began to cry, awkwardly at first, for he was not one to give into his emotions, but he was not only in pain but terrified for the Professor. "Damn it, it was supposed to have been you! Why didn't they take you like they was supposed to!" He crossed his arms across his chest and began to rock back and forth repeating "It should have been you! It should have been you!"

A horrible suspicion began to grow in David's mind and as he exchanged a look with Lovel. He could see the same terrible thought had occurred to the other man.

26
Exercise In Futility

"John," said David, "you did not call down the Inquisition! Tell me that you did not do such a thing!" he said pleadingly.

John, tears still running down his face and sobs choking his throat, could not meet David's eyes. His guilt was plain to see.

David was aghast. "Why did you do such a thing, John? Surely you realize that the Professor would be the first to be suspected, with his known interest in Faerie lore and the esoteric nature of his library? Many of the books he has here are probably on the Inquisition's banned list! I don't understand why you would do such a thing!"

Felix had picked himself up off the carpet and stood looking down at John. "He hates me that much," he said sounding shocked.

John glared up at him and suddenly shouted "Yes, yes, I hate you! It's all your fault we've come to this! Me and the Professor was going along nicely until you came and upset everything! Damned dirty Gypsy! Coming in here to sneak and steal from us!" Then followed a string of obscenities so vile and all directed at Lovel that David was rocked back on his heels. He looked helplessly at Felix and said "I think perhaps –"

"Yes, I'd best go," Felix returned. "If I stay on the main road will I get to St. Peter Port? Might I use the pass we used today to cross the parish boundaries?"

David stared at him in consternation, feeling confused. "St. Peter Port?" He put out his hand and Felix helped him to his feet, which was not easy as David would now pay for having thrown himself on the floor beside John. "Are you going to get a doctor for John? He'll be fine, I think."

Felix shook his head as John, too, finally was able to get

to his feet. Felix could feel John's enmity as if it were a blow.

"No, I am going to turn myself in to the Inquisition and tell them that they have the wrong man," he said simply. "Then perhaps the Professor will be released and will be home by nightfall."

"You can't do that!" said David in horror. "They'll torture you and you'll end up in the fire!"

"Serves him right!" said John in venomous tones.

David turned on him so fast that his leg almost buckled. "Be quiet!" he thundered. "And pray that God can forgive you, John, for what you have done, because I cannot. And I doubt that the Professor will be able to either! How could you wish someone to die in agony merely because you don't like him?"

"He's a stinking Gypsy, Sir David! Road trash aping his betters! Gypsies are the scum of the earth! They're all filthy whoremongers; they don't even marry properly! That little piece he calls his wife is just a slut! She probably lays with men and then robs them as they sleep; aye, and slits their throats too, for they're all murderers as well. All they do is take what isn't theirs and rob honest, hard-working people!" John declared vehemently, as if amazed that David could not see this.

"Gypsies are human beings, John, and not even a rat should be tortured and burned!" David said, appalled at John's fallacious reasoning. "What madness is in you that you can nurture such hatred, such unreasonable spite?" David had never seen such a depth of intolerance. He had been raised in a home that embraced liberal principles. His parents had taught him to judge each person by his or her actions, not by origins, religion, or place in society. He could honestly not understand such bigotry, such loathing. But from John's words he also discerned that there was not only blind prejudice but jealousy as well for Lovel seemed to be taking John's place.

"I know all about those thieving Egyptians!" John said angrily, swaying a little and pressing a hand to his head. "Where I was raised, in Essex, we had lots of trouble with them stealing everyone blind, taking chickens and piglets and anything that wasn't nailed down. They was even stealing children!" He took a deep breath and his eyes filled with tears again. "They stole my little brother, our Teddy. My Ma sent him on an errand and he never come back. And there was Egyptians passing through that day. They'd been warned off by the beadle and my father thought they took Teddy because they had no chance to steal from us! It broke my mother's heart!"

"But, John," David said, in a rational tone "just because there were Gypsies passing through does not mean that they took your brother! There might have been an accident, he might have wandered off and become lost, even run away or he might have been stolen by a sweep! That was quite common at one time."

"It was them Egyptians!" John insisted stubbornly. "Promised my old Dad that I'd do whatever I could to put a spoke in any Egyptian's wheel I come across! To see *him*, coming in here, play-acting the gentleman and calling me 'Grant' as if I was beneath him – it sticks in my craw! And to see the master taken in by him and making much of him as if he was a God-fearing Christian or one of the young gentlemen who was the Master's students fair made me sick! I couldn't bear it! He was just pushing himself in here to find out where we keeps the good things worth stealing! Probably take everything and murder us in our beds! The Professor was all set to show him the safe too! You know that's why you come here in the first place!" he shouted in accusation and turned to glare at Felix.

But there was no one there. While David and John were intent on their argument, he had slipped from the house and gone outside to where the horses were tied.

David heard the sound of hoof beats and started forward, determined to stop Lovel from throwing his life away. There were still attorneys upon the island, elderly and retired, but still good men, and he would get one for the Professor. Wizardry was a ludicrous charge again Aurelius Bretton!

But David's leg, already strained from the ride back and forth to the Dragon Port and then his quick descent to John's side buckled beneath him as he tried to run after Lovel. He found himself stretched full length on the floor. "Help me up, John! I must stop him!"

"Let him go, Sir David! Do you think he's actually going to go to the Castle?" said John scornfully. "He's running to save his scoundrelly hide! But they'll catch him, they will. There's no place to run to! He's the one who should have been in the dungeons in the first place!" he added in malicious satisfaction.

Shock had held Aurelius' tongue as he was bundled into the carriage. Surely he was mistaken! Surely what John had screamed out did not mean that he had meant to turn young Lovel over to the Inquisition! He could not, would not believe it of John! Aurelius had realized that John was a little jealous of the younger man, but he had not realized that John disliked him so.

No, dislike was too mild a word if it were true. To do such a thing, to condemn someone to the flames, spoke of a degree of hatred that Aurelius had not thought John capable of possessing. Aurelius was profoundly disquieted. He and John had been together since they were young men and he had thought that he knew John as well as he knew anyone. But this was a John which he had not even guessed existed.

He was taken from his black thoughts by Father Maël leaning forward across the seat and snapping a pair of iron cuffs, with a short length of chain between them, upon his wrists. "I shall not need you now," he said to the soldiers standing in the still open doorway. "Cold Iron is anathema to Wizards. He can not escape us."

"That would be true were I a Wizard," said Aurelius gently, "but as I am not, it is no better than any other metal as a restraint. I shall not escape because I cannot walk unaided, not because I am tethered by Cold Iron."

Maël looked at him with contempt. "We shall see how certain you are of that after a night spent in a room lined with Cold Iron, then put to the question," he said coldly.

Roux looked disappointed. He had anticipated being allowed to torture this prisoner as soon as they reached Castle Cornet. True, the prisoner was an old man, not a beautiful young woman, but to Roux the screaming and pain he could administer was almost as enjoyable as the fondling of and intercourse with a handsome Witch. He had enjoyed singularly few episodes of inflicting suffering and torment on this island and there had not been one suspected Witch with a tender young body just begging to be used by Roux.

No one spoke again until Castle Cornet was reached. When the carriage stopped soldiers appeared again and dragged Aurelius roughly from his seat and, at Maël's instructions, took him to the newly refurbished dungeons below the Castle. He was taken to an especially designed room, designed to cause the maximum pain and discomfort to mages.

The door was of iron and on the walls and floor were laid strips of this metal as well. The bedstead, too, was of iron, with but a thin horsehair mattress and a rather ragged blanket. There was no pillow.

Above the bed hung an iron ring and to this, with the addition of another chain, Aurelius was shackled. The chain had just enough play so that a prisoner could lie down and reach the chamber pot underneath the bed.

It was Maël's contention that Wizards and Witches ought to be made to suffer the poisonous effects of Cold Iron for at least twelve hours before they were questioned. This would weaken even the strongest magus and he or she would be more susceptible to the pain of the questioning. He had seen the effect of Cold Iron on a mage: the skin blackened as if burned, crippling pain took place in their joints and limbs and they became quite weak. Add to that the pain of the lash or other torture methods such as the rack or the *bastinado,* and a confession (and what was even more important, names of other mages) were forthcoming. He had little doubt that this method would work well on this old man who was already weak and crippled.

The old man would burn, but Maël first wanted to know the names of his confederates. One old man could not have done all that had been inflicted upon this island but Maël was confident that they would find them all out, for after all, he now had their master.

Aurelius was locked in securely, the door closing with a hollow sound after the soldiers had made certain that he was well secured.

The cell was largely dark. A faint light was coming from a small, barred window very high up, level with the ground outside. When the sun declined it would be as dark as the Pit.

It was damp and cold. The wall, when Aurelius touched it experimentally, was moist. He wrapped the blanket around himself as best he could but found that it was woefully inadequate. He was thankful that he had dressed that day and had not been in but nightgown and dressing gown. He also thought that any food given in this place would be poor and of insufficient quantity as everything seemed designed to weaken and intimidate.

Would John fetch Sir David? Perhaps John was dead. The soldier had kicked him viciously in the head, perhaps hard enough to kill. Would anyone realize where Aurelius had been taken?

All this conjecture was fruitless. Aurelius willed himself to relax by thinking of the poetry of Ovid, something he had thought to discuss with young Lovel one day soon. But thinking about that young man just led to more grief and worry. And that led back to John and how he could have done such a terrible thing, if indeed he had.

He at last fell into an uneasy sleep, waking himself with the clanking of chains every time he moved in the bed.

It was growing darker, but whether from the sun's setting or it declining, perhaps on the other side of the building was not readily apparent. The door opened abruptly and a soldier entered. Aurelius could not see him all that well, as he was followed by another soldier with a lantern, causing the first solider cast a large shadow against the wall.

"Here, mage!" said the first soldier. "You've probably been looking for this!" He tossed a large leather sack right on top of Aurelius. A furious squall arose from it.

From a hidden slot high in the door, only big enough for a pair of eyes, Maël watched. "Now we shall see them interact," he said to Roux, who stood behind him, eager for a turn at the spy hole. "It is Fournier's contention that the accused mage placed this animal, his familiar, with *Madame* Dieudonné to throw us off his scent."

Roux licked his lips. He liked torturing animals as well.

Felix had kept his tired horse at the gallop all the way to

St. Peter Port. He apologized to the animal, only hoping that he could get there in time before they tortured or hurt the Professor.

He was afraid, very afraid, of what they would do to him once he confessed that *he* was the mage, not the Professor. But he could not let the elderly man take the blame for what had been his own mistake, not after the many kindnesses and even affection the Professor had shown him. And it was not right to let someone else bear his punishment, no matter how painful or even fatal that punishment might be. He only wished that it would not be so painful as he knew it would be and that he would acquit himself well under the torture and in the fires. His mind shied away from the reality of what he would suffer. He hoped that Sir David would tell Rosal what had happened. She was going to be a widow again very soon.

The pass issued that morning by Colonel Fournier proved viable, since he had to cross from Castel to St. Andrew parish and from there into St. Peter Port. He had never been to St. Peter Port, not that he could remember, but a man on the street pointed him towards the waterfront, where the castle stood on a spit of land.

Felix was soon forced to abandon his horse, for the streets were thronged with French soldiers and the hillside the town was built on was steep. Tier upon tier of white houses with red tiled roofs led down to the quiet pool of the harbor. The town was traversed by a succession of long stairways. These were sectioned by cross lanes meeting at the 'carretours' which led to narrower and steps and dark, arched alleys. It had a decidedly un-English look to it. A sudden vision came to Felix, of a steep hillside crowned with houses like this, but so different in looks. A blinding pain followed this vision or memory, so bad that he staggered and found himself leaning against the side of a house while an elderly woman inquired if he were quite well.

"A headache," he said, thanking her for her solicitude. "The sun –"

"That is what happens, *mon fils,*" she said, "when one goes abroad in the hot sun without a hat! You would do well to return to your home and fetch a hat!"

"Thank you, *me mère,*" he said "I shall do that as soon as I complete my business at the castle."

"See that you do! The young are very foolish, but one does not find old heads on young shoulders," she said severely. She herself wore a large bonnet that screened her face.

It was quite unlikely, once he had completed his business, that he would ever need a hat again.

Castel Cornet was a somber, forbidding building, made more so by the many flags and banners of the Inquisition that adorned it. It was being rebuilt to the specifications of the Inquisition and was the scene of much activity.

It was easy enough to enter the Castle as people were constantly going in and out on various business, but Felix suffered his first set-back when he asked to see Father Maël.

The priest was not available, a rather bored clerk told him. When Felix said that his business was urgent the clerk yawned and said "Isn't everybody's?"

When he asked after Aurelius, the clerk told him that there were no visitors, not even family, attorneys or clergy. The accused was a magus and they were never, under any circumstances allowed visitors.

"But perhaps the Bailiff of Guernsey might visit?" Felix asked, feeling desperate, thinking that certainly they would let Sir David in.

"Not the First Consul himself," said the clerk.

"But you've got the wrong man!" Felix blurted out. "I am the mage, not the Professor!"

"Not another one!" the clerk rolled his eyes.

"Another one?" Felix faltered.

The clerk curled his lip. "Oh, yes, every time we make an arrest some member of the family or a friend. or even droves of them, come in and swears to it that they are the mage, not dear Grandpapa or Mother or whoever. Our arrests are made very carefully. The Inquisition does not make mistakes."

"It just did!" said Felix angrily. "I demand that you listen to me!"

The clerk yawned in his face.

"Listen to me, you officious little –" Felix began hotly but

257

a smooth, cultured voice like heavy cream said " What goes on here, Moreau?"

"Another confessor, Bishop," answered the clerk. "He swears that the prisoner brought in this morning is not the mage, that he is. He wants to see Father Maël but the Father left orders that he was not to be disturbed."

Bishop Amaury de Ollivier was well aware of that as he himself had been turned away from the priest's office door. This rankled.

He studied Felix and said "I shall see this young man, and save Father Maël the trouble, Moreau. Come with me, young man."

In de Ollivier's mind was the thought that he might put Maël under an obligation to him. Only yesterday Maël had complained about the 'confessors" and how much trouble it was to sort them out and get rid of them. Perhaps helping Maël out with this annoying problem would make the priest treat him as more of an equal.

De Ollivier's office was a short way down the hall and as he ushered Felix into it he said in a pleasant voice, "So you claim to be the mage rather than the man who was brought in this morning, one – ah – what was his name?"

"Aurelius Bretton," Felix supplied. "And that is correct. I am the mage. He is completely innocent."

De Ollivier looked at his desk, where a recently copied report of the arrest lay. He had only just finished reading it before being refused admittance to Maël's office. "It seems perfectly clear that this man is a dangerous mage and a heretic as well. He has many proscribed books and is a Protestant, a bad combination. What is your name? What relationship is he to you?"

"I am Felix Lovel and I am his manservant," Felix answered.

The Bishop smiled. "Ah, the *Gitan*! How extraordinary that a member of a race more known for lying, and stealing and preserving their own filthy hides should attempt to confess to being a mage to save a member of a race that they usually regard but as dupes to be robbed! I happen to know, *Gitan*, that your people have little magic. Most of it is in the females, in their devilish fortune conjuring. If you had come in here to confess to horse whispering and doctoring I should be more inclined to believe you. This borders on the comical!"

"But it's the truth, I tell you!" Felix insisted, feeling desperate.

The Bishop smiled slowly. "If that is so, show me some magic. We do not have the protections in place as yet here, so you can conjure up something to convince me. Go ahead," he said as Felix stood there uncertainly "show me some magic!"

27
A Cat in Gaol

The shackles upon his wrists allowed Aurelius just enough leeway to open the leather sack. Whatever was inside, and it sounded like a cat, was anxious to get out.

No sooner than he had pulled open the sack than a large, rather long-haired, mostly black cat jumped out, spitting and hissing with its fur standing up and ears laid flat against its head. It sprang for his face, but he quickly put his hands up before him and the cat fell back immediately. Aurelius thought he heard someone say "Cold Iron!"

The cat sat down on the narrow edge of the cot and looked at him with great green eyes, the pupils fully extended. His eyes seemed enormous but his fur had returned to its normal appearance and his ears now were perked up and leaning towards Aurelius. It was if the cat had decided in mid-leap that his fellow prisoner was not the one he had ought to be attacking.

Why had they thrust a cat into the cell with him? Aurelius wondered. What were they expecting?

Aurelius had never kept a pet, either cat or dog. He had always had a vague liking for cats especially. But he was in his rooms at Cambridge but little and it seemed hardly fair to any animal to expect it to exist on its own while he was teaching or in the library or even traveling. So he knew little of the behavior of cats.

Even to his inexperienced eyes this one certainly seemed to be behaving in a peculiar manner. It had recovered from its anger incredibly fast and now was regarding him as if it expected something.

"Nice kitty," he said experimentally and held out a hand to it, the miserable chain clanking as he did so.

The cat began purring and pushed at his hand with its head, signifying it wanted to be petted. Aurelius was not quite certain whether to pat it or stoke it, but the way the cat rubbed its head along his hand seemed to indicate that it would prefer stroking. He did this for a few minutes which the cat seemed to find more than acceptable, as the purring increased in volume and it began to knead its front claws on the thin blanket.

Then the cat crawled up onto Aurelius' chest, purring loudly and began rubbing its face against his cheek.

Aurelius was touched. The cat seemed to be very enthusiastic about claiming an acquaintance and he admitted to himself that it would be nice to have something else alive in this cell other than the rats he strongly suspected would be resident here. He had heard distinct scuttling in the walls. The cat would keep the rats away.

"Well," he said aloud, " I am glad you have come. I cannot conceive why they have chosen to give me a companion but it is an improvement in my condition." He continued to stroke the cat who was now purring so loudly that it seemed as if the entire Castle would be able to hear it.

The cat settled down on his chest and appeared to go to sleep, its purrs gradually dying back. Aurelius too, fell back into sleep, soothed by the purring and the stroking. The furry body, small as it was, radiated heat as well, taking away some of the chill that was caused by the dank walls of the cell. Comforted and warmer, Aurelius fell into a deeper, more restful sleep as the light in the cell gradually faded away, leaving it in complete darkness, as black as the cat's fur.

"I am waiting, *Gitan*," said the Bishop. "Only a little bit of magic. Make a light or move something from one side of the room from the other. You Wizards are supposed to be full of tricks! Prove to me that you are indeed a mage." Arms crossed across his chest, Amaury de Ollivier wore a mocking smile on his lips.

Felix clenched his fists to hide their trembling. He had no idea how he could perform a magic trick for the Bishop. Yesterday, the mage light had just come, unbidden.

He tried to relax, to just let it take over as it must have

yesterday, but his agitation was too great, his worry over the Professor too profound. His mind kept running into that gate, a huge, barred gate, that slammed shut in his mind. And for some strange reason he was beginning to feel weak and his joints were aching, as if he was coming down with the influenza.

He tried so hard that he broke into a cold sweat, his head beginning its relentless throb, and his senses swimming.

"Well?" he heard de Ollivier say as if from a long way off, "I am still waiting, *Gitan*! You are wasting my time."

Felix looked at him. The Bishop seemed misty to his gaze, with that cold sneer upon his face.

Felix made one last, concentrated, immense effort, willing himself to find the magic but a there came a wave of pain so bad that he crumpled to the floor as it swept over his head.

He did not quite lose consciousness. He heard the door open and Fournier's voice said angrily, "Bishop, this *Gitan* is my translator! I need his services at the Dragon Port facility, for that damned Austrian needs another week in bed, according to the doctor! You can have the *Gitan* to torture *after* he finishes his work with *M'sieur* Blériot! It is far too important!"

"Are you under the impression, Colonel, that I have been torturing him?" asked the Bishop sardonically. "What you see here was self-inflicted, I assure you. He was trying to perform magic."

"*Gitanos* have no magic," said Fournier in an irritated fashion. "What are you playing at, Bishop?"

"Your translator here has declared that the mage we brought in this morning is not a mage at all and that he himself is the mage," the Bishop informed him.

Fournier gave a low growl of annoyance. He walked over to Felix and drawing back a booted foot, kicked him in the ribs. "Get up you stupid *Gitan!*" he yelled. "How dare you come in here and take up the Bishop's valuable time! Who let you in here in the first place? Damned *Gitanos* don't know their place! One treats them with a little kindness and all they do is take is advantage of one's good nature! Get up and take yourself off!" His foot swung again. He watched with a heavy frown, as Felix, still sick and shaken and now in pain from his damaged ribs as well, struggled up.

"Perhaps it is just as well that my new directive will be announced and implemented at the next assembly," said de Ollivier. "All non-Catholic, non-French persons will be obliged to wear an identifying mark on their clothing. The *Gitanos* will wear a "G", the Jews a "J" and all the Protestants a "P" and so on until all ethnic types and proscribed religious are identified. Those are the ones that will bear watching."

Fournier agreed. "That will make it easier for my men to pick them out. Look at this one," he said as Felix staggered and brought himself up against the wall of de Ollivier's office. "Almost he could pass as a gentleman!"

"He ought to be clad suitably for his station," said de Ollivier.

"Which in my view would be as a prisoner. All these *Gitanos* belong in a cell or better yet, deported to the colonies, as the First Consul has suggested, where they can be put to hard labor," said Fournier. Raising his voice he said "Go, *Gitan*! Are you too stupid to realize that you are where you are not welcome? Go or I shall have you flogged just enough to teach you a lesson! I do not wish to see your face until the morrow!" He strode across the room and, taking Felix by the arm, thrust him out into the corridor and slammed the door after him.

Afterwards, Felix could never remember how he got away from Castle Cornet and returned to Castel parish There were people who helped him, he was aware, persons who had little love for the French occupation and had sympathy for anyone mistreated by the Inquisition. He was passed one from the other until, after a nightmarish journey on horseback, he was left outside the Professor's cottage which was now ablaze with lights.

David had been forced to remain at the cottage. After

what he had been through that day he was incapable of mounting a horse again and he had been detained by a French patrol, commanded by Lieutenant Girard who questioned both him and John rigorously and had once again searched the cottage, looking for evidence of magical practices and heresy.

All they found was books. But the mute evidence of both books on Faerie lore and a Protestant Bible was enough. David tried, in vain, to insist to Girard that in England these things were neither proof of heresy nor of Wizardry. Practically everyone who was a communicant of the Anglican church possessed a Bible and a prayer-book (Girard regarded this last as suspicious as well, for it was not a proper Catholic missal) and Faerie lore was actually taught at University. Why even Elizabeth College, here on Guernsey, taught Faerie lore.

"This is a French country now, *M'sieur*, and in France we do not study heresy and lies," said Girard contemptuously. "The filthy root of this evil must be torn out. A special patrol, with a priest in attendance, will come and burn these volumes of iniquity. And soon the owner of these pernicious books will burn as well, once he has told us of his confederates. And do you protest too much more, I shall think you a heretic as well and will take you and every member of your family to a cell in Castle Cornet to answer to the Inquisition."

"Please, Sir David!" John begged, Since his French was so rudimentary he had not followed all of the conversation between the Bailiff and the Lieutenant, but Girard's tone of threat was plain enough. John wanted Sir David safe for he pinned all his hopes on the Bailiff's influence to bring his Master home. He did not believe for one minute that the Gypsy had gone to turn himself in. He was certain that the cowardly Gypsy had fled, to save his own skin. Even now the Gypsy wagon would be on the road, trying to find a safe place to hide. But they would catch cold at that. On an island, particularly a small island such as this, there was little place to go where they would not be found.

David subsided, but his eyes were bitter as he watched Girard and his troops ride off. Were they never to be free of these French? What if Guernsey were to become a permanent part of France? Were they to live the rest of their lives like this, in fear?

"How are we going to get the Master back, Sir David?" John asked anxiously as the French troops rode off in to the now deepening twilight.

"I don't know," said David curtly. He was having a hard time even speaking to John. All of this was John's fault. Lovel had not returned. Even if they had accepted his confession, after Girard's visit David was all too aware that it had probably been in the minds of the French all along to arrest Aurelius eventually. The Professor was dangerous. He was an educated man who spoke his mind against injustice and tyranny.

But for John, Aurelius' arrest might have been delayed, perhaps even avoided all together.

"I hope that you are pleased with this day's work, John," David said at last. "I have no idea how we are to get your Master from out of gaol and soon they are coming to burn all of his books."

Jon blanched. "Burn his books!" he echoed in dismay. "That will kill him, that will! He sets such store by his books!" He looked towards the bookcases as he spoke and then said "Good God, what's that?" his eyes almost starting from his head.

David painfully turned to look.

In front of the bookcases a green light was growing and in a few moments shaped itself into the green-clad form of Robin Goodfellow. His face did not wear its usual good-natured grin but instead bore a sober frown.

He swept an elegant leg to David. "Good morrow I give you, Sir David! I was warned of what has happened here by the Faerie who lives in the bottom of this garden. We are sorrowed indeed to hear what has happened to such a distinguished scholar of our people. These French grow daily ever stupider and therefore more dangerous"

"Can you free him?" David begged, ignoring John, who was staring at Robin unbelievingly.

Robin shook his head. "Alas, no, for your Castle Cornet is hedged about with Cold Iron and the Death Metal is even more hurtful to us than it is to Wizards or Witches. But perhaps we can provide help."

"'Tis Witchcraft, Sir David," said John, finding his voice

at last. "Pay no heed to him! He'll be a devil for certain!"

Robin looked sternly at him. "Have you not the wits to recognize a Hobgoblin, you fool? An you an Essex man! You have caused enough havoc for one day! Be so good as to hold you tongue while wiser heads prevail!"

"The first help I shall provide is this –" Robin waved his hand and behind him the bookcases slid backwards. They shimmered and all of the volumes disappeared, leaving empty bookcases standing in a grove of ancient trees. The empty shelves then slid forwards, walling the room again, and there was no sign that the books had ever been there. "We will take care of them until such time as they are needed again," said Robin. "The Bright Court well loves books whether penned by our own Faerie denizens or by human kind. To burn books is an abhorrence to us. My father was outraged when I told him of it. He begs that you will assure the Professor that these volumes will be returned to him when it is safe to do so. Our artisans will mend those that have been damaged."

"The second help will be anything that we might provide, save storming the castle: weapons, artifice, whatever you may conceive of, it is yours. And the third shall be this: the rescued Professor is welcome to take his ease and live in peace in Faerie until such time as this island is rid of the French. There he may dwell in safety, in no danger of being found out and returned to durance vile and death in the fires of the Inquisition."

"Thank you, Robin; this is generosity indeed!" said David gratefully, but thinking ruefully that they now had but to figure out how they might rescue the Professor, which, at the moment seemed an impossibility.

A small yellow ball of light, a dandelion Faerie, burst into their midst. "Robin!" she said urgently. "There is a man outside on a horse who is injured! He bears the mark of Faerie favor on his brow!"

At first Aurelius thought he was dreaming. The cat was talking to him.

"Try not to react. Waken slowly. They may be watching. They were doing so earlier. I could feel their eyes upon us," said the feline voice. it sounded nothing like what Aurelius might have imagined a cat would sound like if one could speak. The voice was rich and mellifluous, not squalling or raspy.

Without opening his eyes Aurelius said, "You must be a familiar if you can speak. Are they watching us now?"

"No," said the cat, "for by my calculations it is close on three in the morning. You are not a Wizard, though, are you? Elsewise you would be in severe pain from the Cold Iron."

Aurelius opened his eyes and could still see nothing, for the dark was intense. He was aware of the cat still sitting upon his chest, his head close to Aurelius' own, so that they could speak quite privately, just in case there were ears to overhear.

"No, I am not a Wizard," Aurelius agreed. "But the French think that I am."

"They are idiots!" the cat said in a low, angry voice, his tail swishing back and forth angrily.

"Why have you been put in here with me?" Aurelius inquired.

"Because they think I am your familiar and that we will betray each other," the cat returned.

"Then we shall not speak during the day, only in the way a man would speak to an ordinary cat." said Aurelius.

The cat agreed. He was bursting with the need to talk but it was going to be difficult. They would be closely watched. Now his sensitive ears caught a noise outside the door and he said "Hsstt! We must be quiet. Someone is coming!"

A few moments later the steps stopped at the door and a panel up at the top was slid open with a grating sound.

A lifted lantern cast light into the cell and spread a long, flickering beam.

A French Corporal, yawning, stood up on his toes to peer in. He saw the prisoner, asleep on his side, snoring gently, with the black and white cat curled up beside him. The cat, too, was deep in slumber.

The Corporal shook his head. He was supposed to be looking for anything unusual but all he saw was an elderly man sleeping with a cat. As if he had not seen his own grandfather sleeping thusly many times! Some times he thought that his superiors looked too hard for heretics and magicians, seeing them under every bush. This old man seemed about as dangerous as did his grandfather. The panel slid shut once more and the Corporals' footsteps went into the distance.

Pyewacket found that his cell companion had drifted into slumber once more.

But Pyewacket could not sleep. He was too busy thinking and planning.

28
The Offer

Rosal had waited impatiently for Felix at the end of the lane that led to *Les Huit Lapins* farm. She had so much to tell him, both her explanation for her behavior at the bed in the woods, and the news that they must make confession and marry, and even that he could no longer stay with her at night.

Yesterday's storm had understandably kept him at the Professor's cottage. Joisaine had told her this morning of seeing him, 'drowned as a rat' arrive there last night. But this evening was calm and bright and there was no reason why he should not come.

But she waited in vain as time went by with no sign of him. At last she was forced to give up and take her basket of produce to Hagar so that supper could be put on the fire. He would be along later. Perhaps he was not yet back from wherever it was he was going these days. He had only told Rosal and Hagar, as he had been instructed by Fournier, that he was working in the south.

The evening wore on and the sun began to decline. Rosal and Hagar had their supper, for Hagar declared that she was hungry and did not wish to wait any longer. But still he did not come.

As twilight began to deepen and the first stars began to gleam in the deep purple of the sky Rosal had had enough.

"I'm going to that cottage and make him come back!" she declared to Hagar, standing up from her seat by the fire. She was wearing a cast-off gown of *Madame's,* obedient to the priest's wishes. *Madame* Brehaut had also helped Rosal brush out her hair and try to tame it in two long braids, wrapping them around her head to form a coronet. She still had no shoes, but going barefoot was quite common amongst the poorer citizens of the island.

Rosal had brought Hagar a bundle from *Madame* as well. The older woman was far more used to *Gajé* clothing and ways as her lover had preferred that she dress in this style, and did not demur when Rosal told her the new rules of the French.

"You have little time, Rosal, before the time comes set by the French for us to be here at the *vardo*," warned Hagar.

"I have plenty of time," said Rosal. "He is at the old man's house too long, Hagar! I shall never have him in my bed if this does not stop!" She picked up a shawl from the bundle *Madame* had given her and threw it about her shoulders.

She was feeling decidedly ill-tempered, and ran from the campsite, brusquely ordering Chavé to stay. It was probably against the French rules to have a dog at one's heels.

Rosal hated the *Gajé* clothing. The narrow skirt impeded the movement of her limbs and the longer length (for her normal skirt came to mid-calf) made her trip. Her clothes normally consisted of a drawstring blouse, worn over bare skin, tied loosely at the low neckline. A skirt and one petticoat, made of a circle of fabric tying at the waist, covered her lower body, cinched with a belt. Underwear was unknown.

And now she had a thing called a *zona* that confined her breasts in a tight wrap and a shift over that, and a petticoat with linen drawers about her loins. It was uncomfortable and constructing and completely in the way. She felt stifled by all the fabric.

She hated the hairstyle as well. The pins holding it up hurt her head and the mass of hair piled up was heavy. And when she married she would have to begin wearing a cap!

Her thoughts were angry as she hurried along the lanes in deepening darkness, hoping that at any moment she would find Felix coming towards her. He would not stay the night with the old man again! He had a wife and he owed a duty to her, she thought, highly irritated, completely disregarding the fact that they were not husband and wife at all. She had come to regard him as her own property

But Rosal met no one in the murky woods, and heard only the sound of a slight breeze in the trees and the night sounds of birds and animals that she was well used to.

It was not until she had reached the outskirts of the

cottage of *Trois Chiminées* that she was aware of anything being wrong.

There were people with lanterns moving about outside and a horse stamped his hooves restlessly and nickered. There were also odd lights floating about, lights of different colours, yellow, blue, pink, green, all the colours of the rainbow.

As she drew closer her gaze sharpened and she saw a tall, impossibly handsome youth in green, helping someone in poor condition from off the back of the horse. And that someone was her Rom, looking as ill as he had the night the sea had given him to her.

"What have you done to him!" she shouted, and, picking up the restricting skirts, she ran forward.

"We'd best get him inside," a gentleman, by his dress, was saying as Rosal ran up. "It's almost time for the French patrol and they had best not see all of the Faeries, either, or then we shall be in the basket, for certain."

He broke off and looked up as Rosal shouted and ran towards them.

Felix, supported by the man in the odd-looking green clothing, had an arm pressed around his ribs and his head hung down. She recognized all too well that look on his face, however. He had one of his headaches.

A fierce wave of protectiveness rose up inside her. They should have known better! The *Gajé* always mistreated the Romany! Her Rom looked as if he had taken a beating.

"What did you do to him?" she said shrilly and inserted herself next to Felix, glaring at the man in green and trying to push him away so that she could take Felix's weight on her own self. "Let him go! He is my Rom and I will take care of him! You *Gajé* leave him be! You've done enough to him!"

"*Madame*, I assure you –" David began, but Robin ignored Rosal and swung Felix up into his arms, as easily as if he were a child and weighed no more than thistledown. Felix gave a gasp and closed his eyes, looking as if he might faint.

Robin strode towards the door of the cottage, open to the night air, where John stood with a lit lantern. David followed, limping heavily and leaning on his cane while Rosal scrambled after them. They in turn were accompanied by a trail of lights.

Robin lay Felix on the sopha and said to the little lights "Some one of you must return at once and fetch Galen the Healer. We have two, perhaps three, here who are in need of his skills." He glanced at David as he spoke, for the Bailiff was looking ill and in some pain. John, too, looked battered, his face swollen and moving stiffly.

Rosal cast herself down by the couch and put a hand to Felix's cheek. He opened his eyes briefly and said on the thread of a voice "Rosal..."

"Who did this to you?" she demanded fiercely. "Was it them?" She looked up furiously at David and Robin, and John beyond them. She was so concentrated on Felix that she did not notice that Robin had a distinctly inhuman appearance and the the little lights were actually diminutive winged people.

"It was the French..." Felix managed.

"Don't try to talk," said David quickly. From the way Lovel looked and the way he was laying so stiffly, David thought that there were some broken ribs or at least badly bruised. Robin spoke of a Healer. There would be time enough for questions and answers after the Healer's ministrations.

"They wouldn't believe me," Felix said, trying to sit up against Rosal's restraining hand. He was forced to fall back with a gasp as pain from his ribs swept over him once more. "I tried to show them magic and I could not do it! I could not even think how!" He closed his eyes and said in tones of anguish "They would not listen to reason. They are convinced that he is a mage. They hold his books and the fact that he is a Protestant against him! They will burn him!"

Rosal listened to this with a frown between her black brows. She did not understand what he was talking about, nor even who all of these people were. "What is going on?" she said sharply. "Where is the old man and why did the French beat my Rom? Just because he is Romany?" she added, her lip curling.

"Who is this woman?" Robin said. "And this man, Sir David, who are they? He bears the mark of Faerie favor on his brow, but she does not." He pointed at Felix and very briefly, they all saw a brilliant gold star flare into sight in the middle of Felix's forehead.

272

Rosal's eyes widened and she looked swiftly up at Robin, noting for the first time his pointed ears and non-human beauty. She crossed herself which something she had not done in years. Looking straight at him she said *"Beng!"* which in the Romany tongue meant 'devil'.

Robin laughed heartily. "I'm not a devil, Romany *chal*! I am one of the good folk of the Faerie court."

He understood Romany? she thought in wonder.

"She's the Egyptian's woman. More Gypsy trash," said John harshly. "No better than she should be by my accounts."

"Be quiet, John!" said David quickly. "You are Mrs. Lovel?" he said politely to Rosal. He introduced himself and Robin and told her briefly what had happened that day.

She frowned. She did not understand why Felix had gone to St. Peter Port. And what did this strange being mean by a Faerie friend? Where had that gold mark come from? She felt quite out of her depth and more than a little frightened and she did not like the feeling. She had always prided herself on being in control in any situation.

John suddenly said "Not again!" and most of them turned to look at him and what he was looking at.

He was staring at the empty bookcase, where a mysterious green light was growing and began to change into a human-like shape.

Rosal gave a little squeak and for the first time in her life, fainted dead away.

When she awoke she was leaning against Felix's shoulder and his arm was around her. Everyone seemed to be speaking and their voices were loud in her ears.

"If you are indeed a mage," someone was saying "You have no more immunity to Cold Iron than do the Fair Folk! I may not know a great deal about Wizards and magicians but of that I am certain! All too often I have heard Father Maël talk of the cell he was building, designed to weaken any mage put into it, weaken them to near death!"

"But there are ways we can lend aid to a Wizard, for although we suffer the same malady, a mage has more natural resistance than do we of Faerie. Cold Iron is death to us, but with our protections a Wizard can stand it for a while and a while is all we need, do you get us the plans of that dungeon, Sir David."

"If the Egyptian is a Wizard as you all say he can just magic his way into that castle and take my Master out by force! After all, 'tis his fault the master's in that awful place! 'Tis the least he can do!"

"It's your fault, John, that the Professor is in the custody of the Inquisition!" David Dieudonné snapped. "And as I have been telling you, Mr. Lovel has been ill and has no real control of his magic."

"And magic works erratically in the presence of over much Cold Iron," came the voice of the Faerie being. "We need a plan that does not depend entirely on magic, but on stealth and surprise."

Rosal stirred and completely opened her eyes. She was sitting on the sopha with her Rom. He looked so much better. The pain was gone from his face and he held her tightly against him. "You're well?" she asked, feeling as if she had missed some vital part of what was going on.

"Yes. I've seen an Elfin Healer. That was him arriving, the green light that made you faint," Felix answered.

"I fainted?" Rosal was amazed. "I never faint!"

"Here, ma'am," David, looking and moving easier, gave her a glass of sherry. "This will help make you feel better."

John sniffed audibly. He too, had benefited from the attentions of the Elfin Healer. His bruises and swelling were gone and his head had stopped its ringing. But he hated having the Egyptians here in the house.

Rosal took the glass suspiciously. She had little experience with wine. At Felix's urging she took a sip and found that it was rather nice, and sent a pleasant warmth through her veins.

"You look so different," Felix said in a low voice. "Not like my Gypsy girl! Your dress and you hair – ."

"The French say that I have to dress this way," she said. Her heart leaped as he said "my Gypsy girl". Had he forgiven her for that night? His arm was tight and possessive about her. She liked the feel of it and she moved closer.

"What is this?" David demanded, frowning. "The French

are now laying down fashion rules for our womenfolk?"

Rosal explained, telling them what the two priests had said and done, leaving out only the part about the enforced confession and marriage. She wanted to be alone with Felix when she told him about that.

David sat back in his chair and cursed the French under his breath. "They are interfering in everything!" he said in disgust.

John muttered inaudibly to no one in particular. The French would give the little trollop anything she wanted. All she had to do was lift her skirts for them as she probably already had.

"Then the sooner we get rid of them the better," said Robin. "But our first order of business is to rescue the Professor. And we need those plans of the Castle, Sir David, so that we may plan our assault. Have you any hope of getting them?"

David frowned. "I know where they are kept in Government House," he said "I even have an excuse for going into the room as the tax records are also kept in there. But I am always watched. I would need a diversion of some kind, something that would draw the guard's attention out into the hall and away from me so that I could get them from the cabinet in which they are kept. I also need some way to hide them as I imagine they are not small enough to fit in beneath my jacket."

Robin shook his head. "I can supply you with a purse that will take and hold any sized object as if it were as small as a golden guinea. That is the least of our worries. But a diversion, one which would command the interest of the soldiers..."

All of them fell silent, looks of concentration and consternation on their faces, wondering what might be done. Rosal looked back and forth between each one of them, noting the concern and fear in their eyes.

And to her surprise, Rosal heard herself say "I'll do it! I'll make the soldiers pay attention to me! I can dance for them. They always wanted to see me dance!"

"Rosal! You would do that to help the Professor?" Felix said.

To her joy there was not censure on his face but pride

and she was thrilled to the tips of her toes at that look.

David said, "But, Mrs. Lovel, if you are sincere in your offer, we could use you indeed. No doubt the soldiers would pay a great deal more attention to a female, as I often overhear complaints that they are starved for female companionship."

"Hagar can play her cembalo for me to dance by." Rosal said.

"And some Bright Court musicians could add their sweet viols to the dance! With enough silver to wear they could stand the Cold Iron for long enough to accomplish our goal," said Robin enthusiastically. "The music of the Romanies is beguiling and compelling and add to that the music of the Elves and no one will be able to resist going to watch and listen! That should give you enough time, Sir David, to do what is needful!"

"But we must needs be quick about this," added the hobgoblin, growing suddenly sober. "I have much studied this Inquisition and it moves from Question to mock trial to condemnation very quickly. We have to act immediately. This plan had best be implemented tomorrow and the rescue made tomorrow night."

29
An Ill Wind

Reginald lifted his heavy head from the table and looked about the room, bleary-eyed.

He had begun drinking the night before, when his grandfather had told him of the news that his cousin was alive and well. All his schemes for naught! His damned cousin had not drowned as they had planned. Those thrice-be-damned Sea-Folk had interfered and rescued him! And even though Felix was now on French occupied Guernsey there was little doubt in Reginald's mind that the old man would somehow contrive to fetch him off that island. Bahram had insisted that his cousin would still have no memory of who he was, or as to what had happened to him, but to Reginald that mattered little. It was over. He was not to be the heir and he would continue to lead the pathetic existence of a hanger-on, forced to toady to both his grandfather and to his cousin to obtain anything but the bare subsistence of his pitiful allowance.

Reginald had attempted, yester eve, to turn his grandfather up sweet and secure an increase in his allowance.

The Earl had refused. Reginald was already getting some £2,000 yearly, £500 the quarter, and many, said the Earl severely, had to exist on far less.

"But Felix has twice over that amount!" Reginald had argued indignantly. "He has all of the money from his mother's estate!"

"And you should have twice that amount as well, did you see to your land and stop wasting the ready on gaming and drink!" stated the Earl. He had refused to be moved by Reginald's pleas that did he not obtain more funds he would end in the Fleet.

"Perhaps a stretch in debtor's prison would do you some good, mayhap teach you the sharp lesson that I have not been able to impart!" said his grandfather.

This was so heartless and uncaring that once they had parted company Reginald had started drinking, feeling desperately sorry for himself.

Now as he awoke, with the morning light showing a litter of empty bottles on the top of the dining room table, the events of the evening came rushing back to him.

He sat up with a groan. He had fallen asleep at the table and his neck and back were now protesting. No one seemed to have thought to put him to bed.

And he had the devil of a headache. What he needed was a little hair of the dog.

Before him, amidst the bottles, stood the silver bell that summoned the servants. He reached for this and rang it sharply, wincing as the clear tones jarred his pounding skull.

Swann appeared moments later. "Yes, sir?" he said impassively. Reginald disgusted him for he was not Swann's notion of a gentleman, always in his cups, quite morose when drunk and apt to paw at the maids. But a good butler never let his employer see that his butler had any opinion of him at all. At least his wages were secure as they came from his lordship the Earl. The one thing that Swann could say in Mr, Reginald's favor was that he was most obliging in emptying bottles and wasting wax candles. It was the butler's prerequisite to sell candle ends and empty bottles and Swann had already garnered a tidy little sum in taking advantage of Mr. Reginald's wastrel habits.

"More port," ordered Reginald brusquely.

Swann cleared his throat politely. "I am sorry to say, sir, that you drank the last bottle last evening."

Reginald glared at him. "Then I'll have gin!"

"The Geneva is gone as well, sir," said Swann.

"Madeira, then!" snarled Reginald.

"I am afraid that the Madeira shares the fate of the port and the Geneva," Swann said.

Reginald slapped his hand down on the table, making the bottles and glasses rattle loudly. He flinched at the sound. "Good God, man, what sort of a poor excuse for a butler are you! It's part of your duty to keep the cellar stocked!" he snarled.

Swann was unmoved by this condemnation of the

execution of his duties. "I have orders from Mr. Horrocks up at the great house, sir, that all expenditures for wine and spirits are to be authorized by his lordship. And so far his lordship has not granted this authorization."

With a curse Reginald picked up a nearby empty port bottle and flung it at Swann. The butler dodged it nimbly. Reginald's aim was poor, even when he was not suffering from an excess of drink.

The bottle shattered on the door just as it opened to admit Bahram, who in contrast to Reginald, not only looked sober, but well-rested.

The Persian took in the situation at one glance and said to Swann, "Black coffee and a great deal of it, if you please."

The butler bowed in acknowledgement of this order and silently left.

"Is this the best use you can make of your time?" Bahram asked Reginald, surveying the room and the jumble of glassware upon the table.

Reginald looked daggers at him from red-rimmed eyes. "You were there yester eve!" he growled. "My cousin is found and the old man, damned nip-farthing that he is, has refused to extend my allowance. It's all over, Bahram. I'm all rolled up, at low tide! We failed!"

Bahram looked at him coldly. "We have not failed. I have not as yet exhausted all avenues. You had best remain sober, for things are going to happen that will require a steady head and resolution on your part. Hitherto I have done but little. In order to accomplish all our objectives, and my objective, my dear Reynard, is the same as yours, to line my pockets well and live a life of ease. I intend to call upon some allies who can do what is needful."

"What do you mean?" Reginald demanded.

Bahram shook his head as he heard the rattle of a tray in the hall outside the dining room. "You shall soon see," he said mysteriously. "Now, drink your coffee and pray attempt to remain sober if that is at all possible."

Shortly after a cold collation of meats, cheese and fresh-baked bread, the very sight of which made him nauseous, Reginald followed Bahram up to the room at the top of the house. He was somewhat steadier on his feet for Bahram had ruthlessly plied him with cup after cup of black coffee until Reginald was sickened by the very sight of it. Then the Persian had forced him into the plunge bath, where he had been sluiced with cold water until he was shivering and sputtering, nearly blue in colour.

But this Turkish treatment had worked. He was far more sober than he had been in many a day. Already, though, he was craving drink.

But there would be none to be had in Bahram's workroom. Perhaps, Reginald thought as they toiled up the stairs, he had ought to try some of that weed the Persian was always smoking in his water pipe. Bahram claimed it was far better than drink.

When they reached the closed door at the top of the stairs Bahram opened it with a flash of scarlet light and ushered Reginald inside.

Reginald looked around with interest. He had always wondered what Bahram was up to, here in the attics.

If he had expected some thing esoteric and highly magical he was disappointed. There were not even the accoutrements that he could see in any Wizard's Tower in the British Isles. A deep pile of cushions lay upon the floor, and a sizable telescope stood beneath a skylight. There was a small bench with some jars on it, but no astrolabe, no armillary, no celestial globes or cauldron or mass of grimoires, no mortar and pestle and row upon row of herbs all neatly labeled in Wizard's Latin.

"Sit down," Bahram gestured towards the pile of cushions. "Tell me, Reynard, have you had a woman lately?"

"You know I haven't," said Reginald crossly. "The old man told me to keep away from the maids. And at any rate, the maids in this house are too old and ugly for a bit of sport! Fubsy-faced and butter-toothed, the lot of them!"

"Before this afternoon is ended I can promise you a naked *houri* of surpassing beauty who will be all eagerness to couple with you," said Bahram. In a large open space on the floor he was busily inscribing a Circle with chalk. Inside this he drew a Triangle. About the Circle he wrote names in the flowing script of Persia. He pronounced each one aloud and as he said the name it lit with a red flame. "Astwihad, the demon of death; Az, the demon of greed; Spozgar, demon of thunderstorms, Xeshm, demon of wrath; Nasa, demon of putrefaction; Tishn, demon of thirst; Bushasp, demon of sloth."

Inside the Triangle he wrote and repeated aloud "Druj, the lie, he whose name I now invoke: Ahriman!"

The atmosphere in the room changed abruptly from merely warm and stuffy to one of intense heat. A wind sprang up, a hot, dry wind, a desert wind, although the window and skylight were firmly shut.

In the midst of the Triangle a cloud appeared and boiled angrily, blackened and rolling. Lightning flickered in its depths.

"Who calls me?" a huge, angry voice came from the midst of the storm clouds which were lit with the lurid flames of the glowing scarlet names inscribed upon the floor.

Reginald shrank back on the pillows, terrified. Inside the Circle he could see other THINGS moving, things with grotesque forms and malevolent grins on evil faces, not wholly seen, but vanishing and reappearing in the vaporous foot of the cloud and clothed in red light.

Bahram showed no fear of the rolling mass of cloud. "I call you, Ahriman, by your true name, to do my bidding." He then pronounced a long, rolling Persian phrase, which Reginald supposed to be an incantation of some sort.

"What is it you desire?" the cloud said.

"First of all, for my friend here, a most exquisite bedmate, a *houri* of surpassing beauty and endless carnal appetite," said Bahram.

"It is done," said the cloud creature.

To Reginald's amazement, a column of smoke appeared in front of him, growing from a small point on the floor to a pillar almost as tall as was he himself. As he watched, it solidified, and turned into a human shape. A few more moments and he was gazing upon the most beautiful female he had ever seen.

She had dark hair that fell down over her slender shoulders, and equally dark, slightly slanted heavily lashed eyes gleaming with lust. Her lips were red and full, made for

281

kissing, provocative and slightly open over perfect teeth

Her golden-skinned body was exactly what he appreciated most with lush, full breasts, a small waist, rounded hips and long legs, all of which he could see very well for she was completely naked, save for some bracelets and anklets of gold.

She swayed seductively as she came towards him, and plastered herself against him, drawing his head down to hers for a deep, passionate kiss. She laughed. a husky sound deep in her throat as he returned the kiss eagerly and began dragging his clothing off. Before she pushed him backwards on to the cushions Reginald looked at Bahram gratefully, unable to believe his great good fortune. He eagerly helped the *houri* remove the rest of his clothing and in no time at all was on top of her.

"Enjoy yourself," said Bahram. "Unlike a human woman she will never tire of coupling." He watched the besotted Reginald for a moment, smiling in a rather condescending manner and then turned back to Ahriman. "Now that he is occupied, we may conduct our business." he said in Persian.

"And what payment do you offer me?" the lie asked.

"Death, destruction and a human soul," said the sorcerer.

It was a fine day for flying. Richard had flown to Portsmouth, to consult with an old friend in the Navy, who was now an Admiral of the White. Richard wanted to know the Navy's position on the Channel Islands. Did they think to try and retake them? Remembering how long the government had let the Channel Islands remain in French hands before the Peace of Amiens, Richard was worried that the Islands and his grandson would remain in the grasp of the French.

His old friend was encouraging. The situation had changed, for the government now realized that Bonaparte would not be content to remain upon friendly or even neutral terms with the British Isles and the time for diplomacy had passed. Conquest was the First Consul's aim and letting the French remain in the Channel Islands was as if the British were inviting him in. It was all too easy to launch an invasion force from the Islands. Plans were underway, Richard was assured, to take back the Islands. But more than that could not be said.

Richard was glad to hear this. He realized of course, that even an old and trusted friend could not tell him, for reasons of security, when and where they might strike. Aggressive action was the only step to take now since diplomacy had failed in the years that the French had occupied the islands.

Still, he worried about the Inquisition. He still wanted to go to Guernsey his own self, but both Pascoe and Greymalkin had been horrified at the thought. They thought it best to let Madoc try and search out Felix with the aid of his contacts on Guernsey.

As Pascoe flew back to Devon under a cloudless summer sky Richard still tried to think of ways he might secure Felix's safety. Not knowing was worse than anything and he was all impatience to see his grandson again. The relief of knowing he was still alive was immense, but Richard would be even happier when Felix was home, safe, where he belonged.

It happened suddenly, startling Richard from his reverie. Pascoe bellowed, banked sharply to the left and shouted to Richard "Crouch low and hang on!"

Richard automatically obeyed as his dragon would never give him bad advice, and so was not swept from the saddle by a swirling vortex of wind that, in spite of his evasive tactics, caught the copper dragon and spun him head over heels, then round and around.

They were losing altitude rapidly as Pascoe fought to regain control of the air and his wings.

Daring to open his eyes Richard saw to his horror that they were caught in a wall of air spinning about in a circle. "We're in a water spout!" he thought. He knew of no spell that could overcome the fury of the intense rotation of a tornado-like waterspout.

He heard Pascoe shriek in pain as the fury of the wind snapped one of his phalanges, a wing bone, and realized that they were coming near to the surface of the water as salt spray began to splash his face and hands.

Silently, quickly, Richard repeated the spell for breathing underwater. He was glad that Greymalkin had chosen to stay home that day. He need only worry about himself and

Pascoe. A dragon could breathe underwater for quite some time although they were not fond of SS the experience, being creatures of air, not water.

Richard braced himself as the surface of the sea came up fast, far too fast. Hitting the water at this speed might be stunning. At the very least it would be painful and Pascoe was already injured.

With a huge splash Pascoe hit the water, sending enormous waves up on either side of himself, and plunged deep into the salty ocean.

30
Plans and Rules

Felix had been touched by Rosal's spirited response to his having been hurt. For the first time in their relationship he felt as if there were some real concern, some real caring on her part. Always, in spite of the fact that she had said they loved one another, he had not sensed that she particularly cared about him, especially when she dwelt on becoming with child, as if nothing else mattered.

And when she had offered to help free the Professor he had felt proud of her. She barely knew Professor Bretton, but she was volunteering to do a difficult and a dangerous thing.

Perhaps they could now begin again and the mistakes he had made with her could be, if not eradicated, at least banished to the past. Seeing her in a faint, frightened by the magical presence of Robin Goodfellow, had brought out a feeling of protectiveness in him, wanting to shield her from hurt. For the first time he saw her as vulnerable. When she moved closer to him as they sat upon the sopha, he was not certain whether it was from fear or that she actually was enjoying his arm about her. But, after making her offer, when she turned her head and looked at him from under her lashes, hesitant, as if seeking his approval, he was confident that she was there because she liked being there.

Rosal was not positive what had changed. She had felt such a rush of anger and horror when she saw, as she thought, Felix being manhandled by the *Gajé* that it had surprised her. She realized that she would do anything to protect him and not just because he could give her a child. No, he himself was beginning to matter to her, very much indeed. And the thought that he might not want to marry her in church and would realize that he could leave her had made her sick with fear.

But the arm about her reassured her somewhat, that,

and the pride in his eyes when she suggested how she might help the old man. She had yet to tell him of the demands of the priests and she was still nervous about his reaction.

It was nearly half after eight before they finished talking over their plan. They were still discussing logistics; they had all forgotten that the next day was Sunday. All of them, save Robin, would be required to attend church.

"From what the priests told me," Rosal offered, "they will be carefully watching who goes to church. We must go or be given to the Inquisition." She sounded a little fearful.

Felix hugged her reassuringly, "Then we shall go to church," he said.

"That more than likely means," said David thoughtfully, "that the Inquisition will not, as we thought, put the Professor to the question tomorrow. They will do naught that might be even remotely described as work on a Sunday. I overheard Fournier telling Blériot that the men cannot be worked on Sunday. Priests will be sent to the Dragon Port so that even the prisoners will be at Holy worship."

Felix gave a rather mirthless laugh. "I'll wager Blériot was none too pleased with that!" Blériot seemed to have no God save his 'genius'.

"Then it must be Monday that we implement our plan," said Robin.

"And early in the morning," agreed David " before Lovel and I must go to the Dragon Port. Perhaps a good time would be during the changing of the guard when all is confusion."

John had been sitting a little ways from the others, listening, and now he interrupted them. "I want to go as well!" he said belligerently.

"John," said David patiently, "you have no reason to be in St. Peter Port. I have no way of obtaining a pass for you. The soldiers will be coming Monday to burn the Professor's books. In spite of what Girard threatened I doubt that the Inquisition will arrive tomorrow to destroy the books. It will be Monday before they come and someone, someone they expect to be here, must be here to explain to them what we decided. That while you were at church the books were removed and that you assumed a patrol had taken them away to be burned. Girard gave me permission to remain here tonight as you were injured and my leg was in no fit case to travel any further, but I will be expected to be in my own parish church tomorrow morning—"

"Why can't *he* stay here and talk to the Froggies?" John, a scowl on his face, gestured at Felix.

"Because Mr. Lovel shall have to be out at the Dragon Port," David tried to explain patiently. "The plan counts quite heavily on all of us behaving as usual. We cannot allow the French to become suspicious of any of us." And in this, David was certain, John might prove to be more of a liability than an asset.

"We shall meet here again tomorrow afternoon," said Robin. "I intend to take Mrs, Lovel to my realm, where she may practice her dance with some of our musicians." He smiled at Rosal." As the lady of a Faerie friend she is always welcome. And I shall make certain that your lady, too," he added to David, "is present." He disappeared in a flash of green. Rosal gave a little jump and burrowed closer to her Rom, who did not seem to be startled by this strange method of traveling.

Felix hoped to have a word with Robin about this 'Faerie friend' business. He hoped that one of the Fair Folk might recognize him and could tell him more about himself.

Robin's vanishing was the signal for the meeting to adjourn. David, walking much easier now thanks to the Elfin Healer Galen, accompanied Felix and Rosal to the garden gate.

"We cannot thank you enough for giving us your services, Mrs. Lovel," he said earnestly to Rosal. "You will be saving the life of an innocent man."

"We Romany hate the Inquisition as much as do you *Gajé*," she said. "I shall dance so that no one will be able to take their eyes from me."

David bowed low to them, and bade them good night.

Felix watched him go back into the house and then said to Rosal "We'd best hurry. It is nearly nine and close on curfew. The patrols will be coming. Shall we sleep beneath the stars, Rosal, or in the *vardo?* As he said 'sleep beneath the stars' he gave her hand, resting on his arm, a slight squeeze.

Now was the time to tell him of the French priest's decrees. She was reluctant to tell him for that look, the tone of

287

his voice and that pressure on her hand told her that he was willing to come to her bed again. Tonight could be the night that her womb quickened.

But she dared not do it. One never knew when the French would arrive with one of their patrols, shoving their long noses into everything. She had been commanded to remain apart from him until the wedding or suffer the Inquisition.

"I cannot be with you!" she blurted out. "The priests say that we are not properly married and are living in sin because we jumped the broomstick and were not married in the Church. Until we are properly married you can not stay with us at the *vardo*. They tell me that it is wrong." Felix stopped in mid-stride and said feelingly, "Damn them for interfering bastards!" He had hoped that she would agree to bedding down with him beneath the stars and this time things would be different. He would insist that she let him love her properly.

He could sense her anxiety. Her hand clutched at his arm and her breath had quickened. Did she expect him to refuse to wed her? Once again he was filled with a surge of tender protectiveness towards her.

"There's nothing for it, then," he said lightly. "We shall be married in proper style in the church and have a proper wedding night as well. We shall speak to the priest tomorrow. I shall ask *Madame* Brehaut for a bed for tonight."

Everything in her relaxed all at once and her heart lifted. He wanted to marry her!

It was difficult to go onto the *vardo* alone. There had been but one light lit in the kitchen at *Les Huit Lapins,* and *Madame* had answered the door cautiously, Joisaine's face peeing over her mother's shoulder.

Madame Brehaut agreed at once to Felix staying with them. He could have the boys' room and they would fetch the remainder of his things in the morning. She was horrified to hear what had happened to the Professor and stigmatized the Inquisition as the stupidest people upon the face of the earth.

She would not let Rosal stay, but insisted that she run along to the *vardo* before the parish bells rang out curfew. "For they will be watching you and they will come to see that you are living separate from your man. You must be very careful to follow all of their rules! You will see each other again tomorrow. Come to breakfast and we will all go to church together in the farm wagon. Be here by seven, for it is a fair drive to the church."

She turned her back and pulled away an interested Joisaine, so that Felix and Rosal could bid each other good night.

Felix took her in his arms and kissed her, very tenderly at first, but it rapidly deepened into something more, so much so that Rosal felt hot, then cold and totally confused. A kiss had never made her feel that way before!

"I must go; I will be late!" she said breathlessly. She pulled free from his arms and took to her heels, fleeing as if the devil himself were pursuing her. She was running through the darkened woods not only to reach the *vardo* on time but from her conflicting emotions. She was astounded at herself. She actually wanted him to bed her! And not just for a child for she had a sudden longing to be as close to him as she could be. Every nerve in her body seemed on fire. Whatever was wrong with her?

She found Hagar dousing the fire outside the *vardo*. A new rule of the French forbade fires after curfew, and Hagar was cursing them under her breath, for this rule made it impossible to bank the fire for the night and would mean making a new fire in the morning.

Chavé gave a delighted bark of welcome and bounded forward to greet Rosal. She knelt and buried her face in his fur, knowing that her cheeks were flushed.

"So, where is he?" Hagar said, finishing her task so that the fire was killed completely, the only light coming from a lantern hanging on the side of the *vardo*.

"*Madame* has given him a bed at the farm," Rosal said , and went on to explain what had happened to the Professor.

Hagar grunted. She would have agreed with *Madame* Brehaut's assessment of the lack of intelligence of the Inquisition. "Tell me, Rosal, how did he greet the news that you must be married in the Church? "

"He wants to marry me!" Rosal said. "He said that he will speak to the priest tomorrow."

"That is good," said Hagar.

"I have other things to tell you, Hagar," Rosal began but Hagar raised a hand and said "Listen!"

Horses were coming. That could only be one thing: a patrol.

"Into the *vardo,* quickly," said Hagar as the parish bell began to toll curfew. She grabbed the lantern from the nail it hung upon and used it to light their way

They had only made it inside, followed by Chavé, when the French patrol halted outside. "Come out!" yelled a French voice.

Rosal and Hagar went out through the folding doors at the front of the carriage, over the driver's seat and down the step plates to the ground.

The French officer motioned a private forward, who held a lantern. The officer then read from a list he carried. "Two *Gitan* women. Hagar Buckland, widow, and her niece, Rosal Brazil, widowed but betrothed. I am to make certain that you are not sharing a bed with your betrothed, one Felix Lovel. Is he here?"

"No, sir," said Rosal. It was strange to hear herself called by her maiden name again. "He stays at the farm *Les Huit Lapins* until we wed."

"We shall see if that is true. The priests of the Inquisition charge me to see that you act as a decent, moral Christian woman, not indulging in fornication until you are wed." Something in his glance as he looked up at them from the paper he was reading told Rosal that he would be more than willing to indulge in fornication outside marriage, given the slightest encouragement. But instead of making her the object of unwanted attention as she feared he said "You are both improperly dressed. Widows are obliged to wear caps."

He turned to the patrol and spoke to the Sergeant. "Give these women a copy of the dress regulations for females. You must find someone who may read it to you," he added condescendingly to Hagar and Rosal. "Illiteracy will not excuse your disobedience."

The Sergeant brought his horse close and, leaning down from the saddle, gave several pages of printed material to

Hagar. "The badges as well, Sergeant," directed the officer.

The Sergeant handed to Hagar two triangles of cotton, on which had been printed a large 'G'. "You are to wear this symbol on your left breast at all times. There are two of them there," he continued , as if Hagar and Rosal were incapable of counting, "one for each of you. These must be in use by Monday. You may copy the badge so that it is permanently affixed to all of your garments. Make certain it is shaped as this one is and is easy to read. Do you understand?"

Rosal was burning with anger, but she nodded and Hagar agreed as well.

They were then forced to stand outside while the French searched the *vardo* and the woods around the perimeter. Rosal had to collar Chavé and order the coally to be quiet. She was quite afraid that they would harm her dog. She imagined that they were searching for Felix, to make certain he was not indulging his lust. Of course, they told her naught.

Hagar said nothing, her face closed and secretive. Her crystal ball, her Tarot cards, even her herbs, all were well hidden in one of the secret compartments of the *vardo*, along with their small store of coins.

The French finally left, after changing the number of occupants on the card that was now nailed to the front of the *vardo* from three to two.

"Until you are properly married, *madame*," said the officer to Rosal as he swung up on his restive horse," that is all the persons that are allowed to live here in this wagon. And you, old woman, will see that she and her betrothed are properly chaperoned at all times. The priests will be watching for any sign of carnal knowledge."

"All those *Gitanos*," they heard him say to the Sergeant as they rode off "are like rabbits in heat! Not that I would mind bedding that tasty little trollop! The church is mistaken if they think they can force any of those beggars to morality! One might as well teach a whore to become a nun!"

Rosal opened her mouth to shout an angry retort after the patrol, who were roaring with laughter at their officer's wit.

Hagar grabbed her arm. "Be still!" she hissed. "They meant us to hear that! He only wants an excuse to take you behind the hedge! He could claim he was punishing you. He'd let the whole troop have you and then deny it if you went to the authorities. And who would they believe, a French officer or a Romany whore?"

Chavé whined and pawed at Rosal's skirts. She dropped to her knees and hid her face again in the dog's silky coat, this time to hide tears of rage. Felix was correct. It wasn't right that they could be insulted and treated so badly.

Half an hour later, much the same scene was played out at the farm of *Madame* Brehaut. The officer demanded to see that Joisaine had now proper female garments, changed the placard of the number of occupants from two to three. Temporarily, he assured *Madame,* until the *Gitan* married his mistress properly, and gave *Madame* the list of clothing regulations for females.

To Felix, he gave a triangular 'G' with the same instructions he had given Rosal and Hagar. "To be worn at all times," he said " so that the soldiers of the Great French Republic will know you for what you are."

In case there was some doubt in Felix's mind as to what he was, the officer very kindly informed him that he was a *Gitan,* a Gypsy, and the word began with a 'G'.

When they finally left, after taking the week's bread which she had spent most of the day baking, Marie Brehaut swore roundly, stamping up and down her kitchen.

"*Maman!*" exclaimed Joisaine, shocked that her mother knew such words.

"If I do not let my anger spill out, Joisaine, I shall burst!" her mother declared. "First they steal my husband and sons, then all my tools, now they dare to come into my house and steal my bread and insult us and our guest! At least, thanks to our unknown friend, we can pay our enormous taxes!" For the Brehauts, as had nearly everyone else on the island, had found a sack of gold on their hearth that would more than cover the tax bill. And like the rest of the *Guernaise, Madame* had not questioned where it had come from. But the offering she put out each night for the hobgoblin was of rich cream, flaky pastries and freshly-churned butter.

Felix stood looking down at the 'G' in his hand, not really seeing it. Instead he saw Rosal's face as he had seen it in the light from the doorway as they had parted. She looked a little frightened and also surprised, whether at him or at herself he was not sure.

One thing he was sure of: their relationship had changed, and for the better. When he went up to bed it took him a long time to sleep, for he could not stop thinking about her, about her soft lips and how she felt in his arms and of the brief glimpse he had of her slim, yet very feminine body that night in the woods. *Damn the French and their odious rules and meddling*! he thought viciously, pounding his recalcitrant pillow into submission, pretending that it was Fournier.

31
Land Ho!

Richard closed his eyes tightly as they hit the water and protected his face as best he could against Pascoe's neck. Dropping from a great height into water at this speed could cause damage to the eyes and even blindness. And being forced to so abruptly enter the water, even with a underwater breathing spell intact, was a shock to the system.

It was painful. Richard could feel the hurt of the plunge all through his dragon's body as well as his own. He was luckier than Pascoe. Crouched low over Pascoe's neck and back he was smaller, less vulnerable to the force of the water. Poor Pascoe was in the worst situation. He had been unable to fold his wings against his sides due to the power of the waterspout and he struck the water with them wide-spread, something no dragon would ever deliberately do, for the thin membrane of the wings could be torn by the impact of the water.

Once they were completely beneath the surface it was better. Richard's breathing automatically adjusted and he was able to open his eyes.

Pascoe had gone quite deep, but above them, ahead of them now, Richard could see the bottom of the waterspout as it ruffled the surface of the water. Long study by both dragons and Weather Wizards had taught them that waterspouts did not draw up water from the sea or lake below it. Apart from a small amount of spray at the base of the spout any actual water in the spout was the result of low pressure within the rapidly rotating air mass.

Richard wished he could talk to Pascoe but that was impossible underwater. With the Sea-Folk there was a form of mental communication but it was not possible with human /dragon relationships.

Pascoe was swimming reasonably well, but lopsided, with

294

one wing now folding, gradually, as he had adjusted to the water pressure, but the injured, still open, wing trailed alongside of him, making him lean over at an angle to the left, which side had the broken wing.

Even trying to turn and look Richard could not make out which of the phalanges was broken. Pascoe would be in considerable pain, for dragon wings were sensitive and considering the work they had to do to keep a dragon aloft, quite delicate. Richard often though that they were more like the wings of a dragon-fly, or a butterfly, for the membrane was thin, translucent and normally iridescent in colour and just as fragile. The bone would have to be set as soon as they found some land.

Richard had no idea where they might be. He, of course, was unfamiliar with the bottom of the ocean.He kept hoping to see one of the Sea-Folk, but there seemed a curious absence of life where they were at the moment, not even many fish.

It was a very rocky area and as they continued to glide past, Richard saw the barnacle and seaweed encrusted remains of many ships. That argued a reef, perhaps near a coastline. Unfortunately Pascoe would have no idea where they were either as a wind spout of any kind was the only thing that could destroy a dragon's sense of direction and place. As did a human, they became completely turned around in such a situation.

Pascoe began to swim upwards, toward the surface. Richard could not see the water spout anywhere above them now, and the floor of the ocean was sloping upwards.They had reached land.

It was too much to hope for that they had been swept towards Devon and home, and as Pascoe emerged cautiously from the sea Richard saw that his supposition was correct. Before him lay a strange, rocky coast. There was a promontory ahead of them and to the right a small island veiled in sea mist. The tide was high but apart from some sea birds sailing high above them, there was no one about, with no sign of habitation. The wind was strong and the sea, in long combers, was dashing itself against the jagged rocks.

It was a windswept landscape, with wind-twisted oaks. Richard felt hopeful when he saw that many of the oaks bore mistletoe. That might mean Druids who would gladly help a fellow Druid and his dragon.

"There is little beach at this time of the tide," said Pascoe, turning back to Richard. The dragon's eyes were filled with pain and already his bright scales were dull. "I see a path up from the tidemark. Perhaps there is a house."

"Perhaps a cave. I would hazard a guess that this is Druid territory and these cliffs look as if they would be full of caves. As soon as we find a place to rest, old friend, I shall tend to that wing of yours. I am glad I always carry that emergency kit with us."

Pascoe nodded, too tired to say anything else.

The copper dragon rode one of the waves into the beach, his long talons grabbing at the rocks as soon as the water was shallow enough, to avoid being dashed against the stones. The tidal water was strong but Pascoe was stronger. With in a few minutes he had reached what little beach there was and stood there, his long tail still in the water, with head hanging and gulping air.

Richard undid the safety harness and slid from the saddle. Even in pain, Pascoe remembered to put up his foreleg for his rider so that Richard did not have to jump a long ways on to the rocks below.

He went first to the breast harness and pulled out the medical kit, which ws carried in a pouch magiced to keep dry. This had several lengths of wood that could be used as splints, bandages, potions and salves of various types, calcium tablets and remedies for upset draconic stomachs and a sharp scalpel for what Richard would have to do in order to set the broken bone.

The phalanges, sometimes called 'the fingers" were the bones that supported the membranes, or 'sails' of the wings, much like a bat's. These were jointed in three places, and on a Cornish Copper there were four sections of 'sail, the longest at the outer edge being the primary, then the secondary, the tertiary and the quadri-sail, the smallest sail which attached to the dragon's back.

Pascoe had broken the secondary phalange bone, which supported the inner edge of the first sail and the outer edge of the second sail. This would be an awkward place to doctor.

"This is going to hurt," the Earl said to Pascoe in sympathy. "I wish I had a large tub of dragon beer to give you so that you could get bosky and not feel it as much. I've only the numbing salve."

Pascoe sighed. "You'd better get on with it, Richard. At least that seems to be the only damage. I was afraid that my sails would be torn to pieces by the water but I looked and they seem to be fine."

"Once this is over, I shall give them a good going over, top and bottom," Richard promised.

Pascoe squatted down as far as he could to get close to the ground, the broken wing still trailing out awkwardly.

The best way to fix a wing was from beneath it. A human weight on top of a sail could rip it from the bones. Veterinarians at the larger draconic hospitals used staging to get at wing repairs, but out in the field that was impossible.

Casting a small but intense mage light, Richard followed it underneath the outstretched, drooping wing with the medical kit in one hand.

With the aid of the light he could see the break clearly. It looked like a nice clean break, thank goodness. He touched it and felt Pascoe flinch slightly.

"It's not a bad break," Richard called encouragingly. "I'm spreading the salve now. I'll try to be careful but this may hurt."

The salve was basically comfrey, also called knit-bone, which had been magiced by a Wizard veterinarian. Not only would it help knit the bone but the numbing spell would ease pain, but not entirely get rid of it.

Richard waited a few moments before proceeding. Pascoe was hissing a little, steam escaping through his nostrils and mouth and Richard knew this meant he was feeling the pain.

When the dragon's breathing eased Richard went on with his delicate task.

In order to splint the bone Richard had to cut four holes in the sails, two on each side of the bone, tiny holes through which he could inset the splints and lay them along the bone to tie the splint around it. This he did very carefully as he did not want to make a large hole that might split and run the length of the sail. Pascoe tried to be as still as possible for this part. He knew how easily something could go wrong but he trusted Richard. A Draconic veterinarian knew regeneration spells, spells that only those born with Healer's magic could

297

use.

The holes, cut with the scalpel, were just big enough to slide through the thin strips of rowan wood, which had an especial affinity for dragons. With magic, Richard held them to the side of the bone as with a combination of magic and his fingers, he carefully pushed the bone into place. It gave a 'click' when the two ends aligned. Thin, tough ropes were then sent magically though the holes and tied them selves about the strips of rowan. Richard then put a paste of lamb's ears, also known as the herb *Stachys Byzantina* around each hole.This was a sovereign remedy for wounds.

Dragon bones were mostly hollow and so healed faster than did human bones. Richard was grateful that he had a good supply of calcium tablets. Pascoe's intake would have to be increased for a while and as soon as he could locate a source of fresh water, or a farm where he might buy milk, he would give the dragon calcium tablets dissolved in liquid.

Pascoe sighed in relief as Richard came out from under his damaged wing. "Thank you, that is much better." But he was frowning.

"Richard, there should not have been a waterspout there — there was something unnatural about it," he said at last.

"What do you mean?" Richard asked.

"There are two types of waterspouts — the tornadic and non-tornadic. Tornadic waterspouts are very rare," the dragon said thoughtfully."They are most often associated with *congestus* clouds, and the sky was clear." Only this year, the clouds had been classified by an Englishman named Luke Howard and his dragon. Pascoe had been fascinated by this, as most dragons were keenly interested in weather, since they spent much of their time in the air, and he had studied the classifications avidly.

"A waterspout like that one is formed by a rotation near the surface of the water and some sort of updraft. I would have been aware of an updraft. I am always aware of them," Pascoe said.

Dragons had superb weather sense. Pascoe had explained to Richard that an updraft was any movement of air away from the ground. This was usually associated with thunderstorms and since thunderstorms were a dragon's greatest fear every dragon was constantly watching for signs of one approaching.

Pascoe also told his friend about *congestus* clouds.These were clouds that were taller than they were wide, with a flat, sometimes dark base and a sharp outline in the sky and could grow to 20,000 feet high. These clouds produced moderate turbulence in the air at cloud level. They could develop into thunderstorms if conditions were right.

"There was something unnatural about that waterspout It came out of nowhere. One minute it wasn't there and the next minute it was," Pascoe continued. "And it came straight at us. When I banked so sharply, it should not have acted as if it was chasing us, but it did! Someone deliberately set that waterspout on us!"

"Who?" Richard said."The only one who has a grudge against me is Reginald and he is incapable of that sort of sorcery, even were weather magic a branch of the science that we in the Six Nations have learned."

"Perhaps that foreign friend of his?" said Pascoe darkly.

"No, no, old friend, this descends into the realm of a novel from the horrid press!" laughed Richard, shaking his head. "Next you'll be telling me about dreadful specters and clanking chains! Why would Reginald want to harm me? That would cut off his allowance! No, Reginald is many things, but I acquit him of murder. He is far and away too indolent for the exertion and he has to know it will do him little good! He must be by now well aware that I visited my solicitor, for I made certain to tell my valet about the reason behind my trip into Torbay. He'll have shared it with the servant's hall, and Reginald's man will have told him. You know the servant's grapevine! Reginald will know by now that I have tied everything up all right and tight. And at any rate, Felix is alive! Reginald is no longer the heir presumptive, thank God! There must be some other explanation for that waterspout."

"What about that genie?" Pascoe said.

Richard paused for a moment. That *had* been odd. "We'll probably never know. Perhaps someone brought back an enchanted bottle from their tour of the Levant and the genie escaped," he said finally. I shall ask about it at the Wizard's Club the next time I go up to London. Now, let me see beneath that other wing. I've plenty of the lamb's wool paste if there are any injuries."

Pascoe unfolded his uninjured wing so that Richard could go beneath.

As Richard pout salve on an assortment of scrapes and small tears Pascoe brooded about the waterspout. He knew thta Richard did not want to believe Reginald capable of true evil. It was too horrible, no doubt to think such ill of one's own flesh and blood.

But Pascoe had no trouble believing it. He had caught a certain look in Reginald's eye now and again and he did not care for that Persian friend of his. What did they know about Persian magicians anyway and of what they were capable of doing? The man freely admitted he was a mage and interested in learning more about English magic. Greymalkin frankly despised the Persian,and Reginald,and thought the Persian a proper Paul Pry, poking his nose in where it didn't belong!

The copper dragon was going to have a long talk with Greymalkin when they returned to Devon, and with Pearson, the Earl's valet. They would protect Richard in spite of himself.

When Pascoe was resting comfortably Richard shrugged out of his wet flying suit and found his clothes beneath to be wet as well. Flying suits were not made for submersion. That would have to be dealt with later. Pascoe's needs came first.

He took a canvas water bag from the breast harness and began trudging up the path that wound up and over the hill to look for fresh water. There was a little water in the travel bottle but not enough for a dragon.

With him he took his spy glass, magically altered to see further than any non-magical one. He was hoping to obtain a good view from the top of this tall outcropping of rock.

It was rather rugged country, wild, rocky and windblown, with little sign of life. But it was spectacularly beautiful. And since a seascape was always Richard's favorite, he approved of it wholeheartedly.

A trickle of noise alerted him to a small spring halfway up the rocky face and he decided to fill the pail on the way back down, but a short drink now would not go amiss. He noted with approval that a tiny statue of the Horned God, Cernunnos, was at the back of the spring, with a cup of carved horn hidden amongst the bracken for a chance traveler to refresh himself. He took a deep draught of icy water and then poured out a libation to the God.

He climbed higher, confident now that he would find a Druid or maybe a Wizard to help him and Pascoe. It might be weeks before the dragon could fly unless there was a Draconic veterinarian in this area. All the signs of a Celtic people who probably embraced Wizardry and Druidry were here. He just wished that he knew where 'here' might be!

At long last he reached the top. It was hot in the sun.It must be well after noon by now and very bright, with the sun shining sparkling diamonds on the sea, as clear and as blue as the heavens above. Not even a gull or a tern cried. It was as if all of the world were asleep in the hot sun of a summer's afternoon.

Facing south first, he saw, far away across a crescent bay, a town. Out to sea lay a tiny island, drowsing on the waves.

But to the north lay a fort and from the flagstaff on the highest point, streaming in the fresh wind, flew the *Tricoleur* of France.

301

32
Le Creux ès Faies

The moment he saw the *Tricoleur* flag Richard dropped to the ground and lay flat. He was exposed and vulnerable to detection on this high rock And as a Wizard, he could not fall into French hands as for both him and Pascoe it would mean death.

A French flag! Wherever had they ended up? He had expected to be somewhere along the southern coast of England, for they had been halfway back to Devon when the waterspout had overtaken them. How far had that thing carried them?

Very cautiously, laying on his stomach, he raised the spyglass to his eye and took another look at the French fort

It did not seem to be heavily armed, nor did there seem to be an excess of personnel. A sentry, two of them actually, walked the ramparts. The area was largely empty. Daring to sweep the spyglass around in a 360 degree arc Richard saw some farms, but they appeared to be deserted, but not so old that they had been abandoned long since.

Carefully, for he was not able to discern if the sentries might have spy glasses to use or not, Richard descended the rock to the spring, where he filled the bucket for Pascoe. He now looked more disreputable than ever, for dust, grass and bits of rock now covered his still damp clothing.

The first order of business had to be to find a place to hide. And the best idea was a cave. A rocky coast line such as this would be riddled with sea caves. Richard wished he had the Triton horn. He could blow it for Madoc and not only find out from the Sea-Folk where they were but the location of any suitable caves. And Madoc could keep them supplied with food from the sea as well. Food was going to be another problem. Food for himself and a hurt dragon was not going to be easy to obtain. Dragons could eat fish; they could even dive like an osprey and catch fish in the ocean. But they prefered beef, pork or mutton, well-cooked, with wine and spices, but they would eat sea food, although it would still have to be cooked. Richard would prefer his fish cooked as well. But how could he catch enough fish to sustain both of them for any length of time?

Richard's mind was busy with all he would have to do as he went back down to the beach, larger now that the time between tides, the slack tide, had passed and the tide was beginning to go out.

Pascoe was drowsing uneasily in the sun, his head drooping and the injured wing stretched out on his left side. It might be as much as four weeks before he could fly even a short distance. Dragon bones knit fast, compared to human bones, but a break in the bones supporting the sails was one of the most serious for so much depended on the wings.

Richard hated to wake him.Pascoe was obviously in pain, for leaving a wing outstretched was something a dragon only did when sunning himself on sand in a safe and roomy situation such as in a dragon pen.

But Pascoe stirred at the sound of Richard's footsteps on the pebbly shingle, and he looked up, his eyes a little dull. "Did you find out where we are?" he asked.

"In a bad situation," Ricardo said grimly. "Where ever we are it is French territory,"

Pascoe's eyes widened. "French territory!" he repeated, sounding shocked. "Richard, we've never blown all the way to France? A waterspout usually moves along a curved path and only lasts about fifteen minutes! We were halfway home! I think it pushed us easterly but I cannot be certain," he added apologetically. "I thought that we would end up near Bournemouth! But this obviously isn't Bournemouth!"

Richard put down the pail of water and put a hand on Pascoe's muzzle. "Of course you cannot be certain. I was completely befuddled as well.This will teach me to come out without a compass!" he said consolingly. He stroked Pascoe's muzzle and eye ridges for a moment.

The copper dragon sighed and said "Do I smell water?"

"There's a spring dedicated to the Horned God up on that hill," Richard said and picked up the pail.

Gratefully, Pascoe sank his snout in the canvas pail and

drank deeply. "Oh, that's good!" he said. "Water from a spring of Cernunnos is always sweet and pure," He raised his dripping muzzle and said suddenly "Richard! do you know what this means; a spring dedicated to the Horned God! there was a statue and a cup?"

"Yes, of course," Richard repeated, puzzled.

"We cannot be in France.The Inquisition would have eliminated such things long ago!" the copper dragon said excitedly. "I have read how they have scourged the countryside on the Continent, effacing each of what they consider pagan shrines. And they've done that for nearly the last one thousand years. We have to be in the Channel Islands! But how could we have blown so far in a water-spout?" he added and shook his head. "That waterspout was not natural! I think it carried us here on purpose!" he reiterated.

Richard thought it was pain and rising fever that made Pascoe insist that a waterspout seemed to be a thinking entity that had chosen to deposit them in the Channel Islands. But he did agree with one thing: the dragon's opinion of where they had ended up, for, as Pascoe had pointed out, any pagan shrine would have been removed many years earlier were this actually France or one of the Channel Islands which had always belonged to France. This had to be one of the English Islands that had only a few years earlier had a large population of Wizards, Witches and even Druids. The only question was which one?

When Madoc had told Richard that Felix was on Guernsey the Earl had at once gone to his extensive library and looked for information on the Channel Islands. He had never chanced to go to any of the islands and his actual knowledge was minimal. He had also scryed the Bodelian library at Oxford.

He had learned that there were seven good-sized islands, although some were very small indeed, and many more, perhaps ten, were but uninhabited 'flyspecks'. In general the smaller islands such as Lithou and Jethou had the – *hou* suffix and the larger ones, such as Guernsey and Jersey had the – *ey,* which was believed to be from the old Norse *holmr* and *ey* respectively. The islands were Crown Dependencies, but not part of the Six Nations and were largely self-governing.

Richard had been very interested to read about the many passage graves as well as caves that covered the islands. Perhaps he could locate a barrow that he and Pascoe might shelter in. First, though, he would give Pascoe a pain draught and cast an illusion about him so that no one would notice the dragon.

In the medical kit was a vial of highly concentrated syrup of poppies. Richard carefully measured several drops in the little water Pascoe had left in the canvas bucket, mixed it well with his hand, and gave it to the dragon to drink.

"Ugh!" Pascoe exclaimed when he had drunk this down. "I cannot believe that people deliberately drink that stuff and even become addicted to it! It's nasty!"

"It will ease your pain, old friend," said Richard. He took out his wand from the breast pocket of his jacket. "And now I am going to make it so that if anyone looks at you for the next two hours all they will see is a rock. Do you think that if I find a cave or a barrow you will be able to move to it?"

Pascoe said ruefully, "I shall have to, shan't I? An illusion can only be maintained for so long and then someone will see us. I am probably the only dragon here now. It's not as if I can blend in with the crowd!"

Once he was satisfied that Pascoe was comfortable and that the illusion he cast was in place properly, Richard began to look for a likely spot for them to escape the attentions of the French.

Richard's speciality was geomancy, the magic of the earth. It was what gave him such an affinity for the land and growing things. Now it stood him in good stead as he used his wand as a dowsing stick, not to locate water, but to find a passage grave or cave.

He fervently hoped that there was no Witch-Sniffer locally, for one of them might feel a stirring of magic. He was using the *praetermittere* or ignore spell, what was popularly known as ' don't look at me', but from what he had read of Witch-Sniffers, a spell like that one would not fool a Witch-

Sniffer for very long.

The land went uphill steadily from the shore and soon Richard found himself on a rough road, that showed signs of long, perhaps ancient, use, but no recent traffic.

The road branched off towards a wooded knoll and Richard climbed again through knee-high grass, shrubs and stunted trees, following the pull of his wand, which he held out in front of him. The pull was steady and strong. Up here, the silence of the shore was left behind and he was aware of both songbirds and insects. There were thistles and wild flowers scattered throughout the grass and he saw bees and butterflies intent on their business. In the drowsy, baking heat of the sun grasshoppers sang. Up here, every blade of grass, every limb of trees and shrubs stood out with startling clarity against the intense blue of the sky. Richard stopped and removed his jacket and loosened his cravat. Away from the shore the heat was more apparent.

But Richard saw no people or any sign that there had been people here recently. The French fort and the menace it offered seemed far, far away.

Midway up, Richard passed an oak tree, twisted by Channel gales, crowned with mistletoe. Here was a good sign. Druids had been in this area, for at some time in the not too recent past this tree had been carefully tended; the signs of neglect of the sacred tree were quite recent.

Each step to the top of the knoll was steeper until at last, wand quivering like a wild thing in his hand, Richard stood in a clearing at the top of the knoll.

A crudely lettered, weather-worn sign said *"Le Creux ès Faies". The Faerie's Hollow,* Richard translated to himself.

There was a shallow cave which the wand urged Richard to investigate. Once inside the cave he came up against a grayish-green rock face.

To most people it would have seemed but a depression in the rock, hardly big enough to shelter a small group of persons from the rain but Richard knew better,as did his wand. Almost of its own will it drew an arch in the air in front of the rock face, leaving a trail of violet light behind so that an inscribed arch hung in the air.

Within a few moments the wall in front of Richard began to glow with a greenish light and then the rock split and cracked open.

Richard stepped through, sighing in satisfaction. An entrance to Faerie! It would be a most satisfactory hiding place.

He lit the tip of his wand with a mage light and looked about.

It was a big, round room, but, contrary to what he had expected, there were no signs of Faerie occupants. Once the cave walls had been vivid with Faerie murals. These were now so dull that the subjects could scarcely be made out. There was no sign of furnishings, and an air of desolation hung over it as if no Faerie foot had tread there for many weary years. Dead leaves, mostly oak, littered the floor of the cave.

But it was warm and dry and what was more, it was safe from the French. Even though this cave was no longer used by the Faeries, all of their guards were in place and only a Wizard and a Faerie friend such as Richard could enter without harm to himself.

And there should be water somewher near as no self respecting Faerie would have an entrance to their world where they entertained human and inhuman friends would fail to provide water both for the Elfin-steeds, or with which to brew their potent wines and meads.

In a dark corner made by a jumble of rocks jutting out from the wall, Richard found a small pool into which a sluggish trickle came from a crack in the wall. He sniffed at it and tasted it with a finger dipped in. It was cold and pure. He could enlarge the crack with magic and make a larger basin for it where Pascoe could drink at his ease.

He looked about him, well pleased. Grasses and leaves could be brought in to provide bedding for himself and the dragon. Water was at hand. The only necessity was food. Once he had Pascoe settled in he would see if there were any way to contact the former occupants of Faerie who were always hospitable to Wizards, particularly those who bore the mark of Faerie favor.

It was a very hot Sunday afternoon in St. Peter Port and the town on the hillside drowsed in a Sabbath torpor.

His duties at the church finished until evening mass, Father Maël stood in the window of his office at Castle Cornet, staring unseeingly, as he did so often, at the harbor. He never saw its beauty at all.

St. Peter Port now acknowledged a proper Sabbath decorum, due to the Inquisition's rules. Children no longer played and shouted noisily in the street. No one was fishing from the quay. All shops, even the baker's and the pie shop, were closed and shuttered. No street musicians played while giddy young girls danced, dreaming of the day that the young men would return to Guernsey. No groups of women and old men gossiped. And best of all, everyone had attended church – everyone! – for they had been counted and tallied. And all would return for the evening mass today as well.

Father Meurice in Castel was to perform several marriages this afternoon. Not only had they found no record of the two *Gitanos* being properly married but an elderly couple was living in sin as well, having never married. Father Maël, with the authority of the Inquisition, almost equal to that of the Pope, had granted a dispensation to allow the marriages to take place at once, rather than waiting another week or so as had been planned. Sin must be stopped in its tracks.

Perhaps it was heresy to even think so but Father Maël had to admit that he was disappointed that it was the Lord's day, as he had looked forward to torturing the accused mage. His capture had not stopped the infuriating assaults, noises. explosions and lights at night. The mage had confederates and to put him to the torture was the only way of finding out their names unless someone, in urgent need of funds or suffering from a guilty conscience, turned them in to the Inquisition.

Things were going well and would go better now that the mage causing all of this fuss was caught. Without his leadership the nightly outrages would soon end. The populace of this island were bowing to the rules of the Inquisition.

There were new plans afoot as well.The Protestants who paid but lip service to the church would soon find themselves on work crews building the new fortifications, while their wives and daughters, if attractive, would be going to staff a brothel the army was building. Father Maël decried the necessity of a brothel at all. The men should all live celibate unless decently married, but the army thought otherwise. Morale was important and soldiers without women were unruly malcontents. At least the women in the brothel would be heretics and some might think serving the needs of the French army was their punishment.

And come September, all of the inferior races, the *Gitanos*, the Jews, the persons of mixed blood, on order of the First Consul, were to be deported to the Americas. Yes, things were going well. By the end of the week, when the mage would no doubt burn, Father Maël confidently expected the evening tricksters to have been caught or else quit, at a loss without leadership.

Father Maël became conscious of a strange tingling in his fingers and a sudden rush of adrenaline. He knew all too well the feelings and drew in a sharp breath.

Somewhere, somewhere close, someone was using magic, and powerful magic at that.

33
On a Sunday
in June

That morning, all over the Island, everyone, as required, had attended church.

Father Maël had sent out all of the priests to contact those who had not appeared the Sunday before or who had been lax in their attendance since the beginning of the second occupation. Many people had sustained a visit such as Rosal's and *Madame's* and told, on pain of the Inquisition, to mend their ways.

In order that all would attend, a special Sacrament of Penance was held before Sunday's first Mass. From now on, it was announced, all would be expected to attend weekly confession on Saturday evenings.

Confession was an interesting, and aggravating experience for Felix, and afterwards, he was reasonably certain that he had not been a Roman Catholic. None of the forms, nor the concept of penance, seemed in the least familiar to him, not as other things had been.

Father Meurice was shocked at his ignorance, and when Felix, in the privacy of the confessional, said he did not know exactly when he had last confessed, he was told that he must be more precise and enumerate the exact amount of times that he had committed a particular sin as saying 'several times' or 'quite often' was unacceptable.

In the end, Felix had to make up sins, for he could not think of any he had committed, in spite of the fact that Father Meurice had gone on and on about 'knowing' Rosal outside the bounds of Holy Matrimony. If he had indeed 'known' her, he did not remember it. Obviously, the priest thought if there had been sin in this area, there had to be sin in others.

And making up sins was lying, which in itself was a sin. Felix thought the whole thing idiotic, for if God saw everything why did one have to confess to a priest? The thought that every Saturday evening had to be spent in probably making up yet more sins was rather daunting. Felix wondered if it would not drive people to commit sins, in order to have something to confess.

They were all surprised during the service when the priest announced that this very afternoon, by special permission, before the evening mass, four sinning fornicators would be properly wed in the sacraments of the Church. "The *Gitanos* Felix Lovel and Rosal Brazil of this parish and Aubert Marrett and Esmée Luce of the same have been living in sin and will be lawfully united today, with all of their neighbors as witness," said Father Meurice severely before the Ordinary of the Mass began.

Of course, everyone stared, either surreptitiously or blatantly at the 'fornicators'. The elderly couple had actually married in Scotland, many years earlier, in an elopement to Gretna Green but as this was not a church marriage, since they were married 'over the anvil', the Church did not recognize their union.

Felix stole a glance at Rosal, who seemed almost a stranger in what she called *Gajé* dress, her face partly concealed beneath a large bonnet. This wedding had come up far earlier than they had expected. He wondered what she thought of it.

For himself he was determined to marry her. He must have loved her before else wise he did not think he would have jumped the broom with her. He wished that he could remember how he had felt. He certainly found her extremely attractive and within the last few days had spent a great deal of time thinking about being alone with her and what they might do together; which was probably enough to qualify for the "impure thoughts' that Father Meurice had gone on about.

When the Mass ended, the entire party of Felix, Rosal, Hagar and the two Brehauts went back to the farm, where *Madame* had put a *pot au feu,* rich with chicken, spring vegetables and barley, on the back of the stove where it had simmered all morning.

"Well, it seems as if we are to have a wedding this afternoon!" *Madame* said as she put plates on the table. There were soft rolls, the few of which had been left by the French, from Saturday's baking to eat with the *pot au feu.* "We shall have to find you something a little special to wear" she said to Rosal. "Since you are a widow it would not be proper for you to wear white."

Hagar, who had been very quiet, said, "And if one listens to the priest, she ought to be wearing the *Giorgio* colour of scarlet!"

"Why is it always the woman's fault if there is a sin of that sort?" asked Joisaine. "Surely the man is just as guilty?"

"It is the way of the world," said Hagar sourly.

"The priest called me a fornicator as well," said Felix "but I own, I did not care for the way he did it. It was rather embarrassing."

"Especially for the Marretts," said *Madame*, "To say that they are living in sin when everyone knows that they were married in Scotland over forty years ago! I felt so badly for poor Esmée. That terrible priest was acting as if she was a woman of loose morals! And you two were wed according to the custom of your people! What will be next, all of the Protestants will have to be remarried as well?" Viciously, she slammed silverware down up on the table.

"*Maman*, shall we have a wedding feast?" Joisaine asked eagerly. "There is the Madeira cake I made. It but needs to be iced and there is a ham and asparagus and new potatoes..."

Her mother approved this idea and said "When we have finished eating I shall rummage in my trunk for some finery and I shall look out an old ring that you may use as well, for the priest will expect that. I have one that has not fit my finger since I was a bride, but your hands are as slender as mine were then," she added, looking at Rosal's slim fingers.

Even Aurelius Bretton was offered the services of a priest.

After an inadequate breakfast of poorly made coffee, greasy eggs and a hard roll, Aurelius sat up, with Pyewacket in his lap, wondering how John and young Lovel were doing. He had not really been surprised that he had heard nothing from the outside world as he was quite certain that persons in his position were not allowed visitors.

It was extraordinary what a comfort the cat was. The familiar whispered to Aurelius when he was aware that they were being watched so that they could act naturally. Otherwise the cat spent much time in the Professor's lap, being petted, a process Pyewacket enjoyed as much as did Aurelius. Petting was soothing to both of them.

Sometime later a private had come and cleared away the breakfast things of a tin plate and a cup. Aurelius had shared the eggs with the cat. A few moments later a priest entered the cell. Aurelius recognized him as Amaury de Ollivier.

" I have come to hear your confession," the Bishop said.

"My dear fellow," said Aurelius, his hands still stroking Pyewacket, " I have nothing to confess. A man as old as I, and in my physical condition, has very little opportunity for sin! I have never doubted or denied my religion; I have not taken God's name in vain as I consider swearing an ungentle-manlike habit; I have remembered the Sabbath and kept it holy, even on the days I could not attend church. And by that I mean my own church, the Anglican church, due to physical infirmity; I have not neglected my parents, for they have been dead these many years and I respect and revere their memory; I have not been inordinately angry, nor offered violence to anyone, not have I drunk to excess; I have not had unlawful carnal knowledge of a woman.It has been a great many years since I have even thought about a woman; nor have I killed, borne false witness against my neighbor, nor stolen anything, not even an idea, nor coveted anything of my neighbor's. I have always been content with my own accomplishes and possessions. Therefore, what or why have I to confess? God knows all and sees all. And if He does not cavil at my actions, I quite fail to see why should you."

"You deny that you are a practitioner of Wizardly, that you have made a pact with Satan?" the Bishop demanded.

"Of course I deny it," said Aurelius reasonably. "How any sane person could imagine that I practice Wizardry? The imagination boggles at such a charge! The merest babe in the Six Nations understands that the practice of magic helps keep one strong and fit and slows aging. I look every one of my almost seventy years and then some. And only a blind man would call me strong and fit! Wizards do not make pacts with Satan. They serve the Light, not the Dark. Everyone knows

313

that." *Everyone save you,* his tone seemed to imply.

"And," he added,"there is the unalterable fact that all of this Cold Iron with which you have adorned this cell has had no effect upon me whatsoever. Even I, who know but little of Wizardry, know that a Wizard or Witch is unduly affected by Cold Iron, as are all creatures of Faerie."

"And how would you know that unless you practiced Wizardry?" said the Bishop triumphantly. "You library is full of proscribed, forbidden books!"

Aurelius sighed. "I was born and raised in England, not France. Although I taught classics at Cambridge for many years I have always been an amateur folklorist. In England, as in all of the Six Nations, it is not forbidden to read or collect books of Faerie Lore. Indeed, the subject is taught at University level. Owning such books as these was not illegal when I came to Guernsey. Only the most twisted logic would punish someone for such a crime."

"The Holy Mother Church forbids –" the Bishop began.

Aurelius sighed again, this time in exasperation. "I will tell you again, Bishop. I am not a Catholic, so it matters not a whit to me what the Church forbids. I am Church of England and shall all my days adhere to the beliefs I was raised in, beliefs which do not include persecution of individuals for magic or what you define as heresy. Nothing you can do or say will change that. Now I should be obliged to you if you will go away. I wish to take a nap after that magnificent breakfast." He leaned his head back and closed his eyes.

On his lap Pyewacket increased the volume of his purr to hide a chuckle. Oh, but he liked the Professor! The priest looked like an enraged turkey gobbler, red-faced and sputtering.

He remained in the cell for a few more minutes, shouting both accusations and questions which the Professor did not answer.

Stymied, de Ollivier at last shouted for the guard and left, uttering threats about what would happen to such a reluctant confessor on the morrow.

Pyewacket could feel Aurelius's worry about what was to happen tomorrow. The Professor's fingers tightened almost imperceptibly on his fur and his breathing quickened slightly.

The familiar increased the volume of his purr and let it

slide into 'sleep', a 'magic' given to all familiars to soothe ill or agitated Wizards and Witches and allow their human friends to rest naturally and quietly, with time for healing or repose.

Soon Aurelius was dozing peacefully and Pyewacket let his purr slow and die away. Time for him to think of a way to get out of this prison. So far, he had had to eliminate or reject every plan he had formulated for one reason or another.

He was not allowed to think for long for he heard a small, rather squeaky voice. "Hsst!! Hsstt!"

He looked down at the floor and saw a good-sized rat, crouched in the shadows, looking up at him.

"What do you want?" Pyewacket asked in Animal Speech.

"You're a familiar, aren't you?" said the rat. "Is that your Wizard?"

"Yes, I'm a familiar but this man is not my Wizard.He's not even a Wizard at all." Pyewacket answered.

"Then what is he doing in this cell? They made this cell especially for Wizards, did they not?" asked the rat.

"They've accused him of being a Wizard because of the books he owns," Pyewacket explained, wondering why he was bothering to expound upon this situation for a rat, a species he had always considered lacking in intelligence. He had always thought that, of the rodents, mice were the smarter.

The rat rolled his eyes. "Even I can see that he has no magic!" he said."I thought you were probably a familiar when you did not immediately come and sniff at our hole in the wall and then I heard you talking last night to the man and I was certain."

"So?" Pyewacket remarked, wondering where all of this as going.

"So, I'm Rainier, by the way, we, the other rats and I, want to help you both escape!" the rat finished in a hurry, as if afraid of rejection, or what might be worse, laughter.

But Pyewacket did not laugh. "I'm Pyewacket," he said and leaned towards Rainier. "Tell me how you think you can help us."

It was done: they were man and wife in the eyes of the

church.

Madame had found, in a trunk upstairs, an old fashioned gown from about ten years earlier, when the waistline was not as high as it was at present and a snow white fichu around the neck was still worn. Over Rosal's re-braided hair, dressed high, had gone Joisaine's old bonnet, refurbished hurriedly with a blue ribbon and a white veil made from a curtain. Rosal carried a bouquet from the front garden.

It had all seemed so strange to her, being nothing like a Gypsy wedding. She had been married to Sylvester in a bright red dress, ruffled and flounced and tight down to the knees, one that she danced in, with no bonnet or veil or bouquet in her hands. At that wedding her hair had streamed down her back and she wore a scarf fringed with gold coins about her head. Large earrings hung with coins adorned her ears and coined bracelets marched up and down each wrist, representing all the wealth she had earned, for she had been dancing and *dukkering* with cards and crystal since she was ten years old. A white handkerchief, flying as a flag from a wand-like branch announced to the entire *cumpania* that she was a *mozita,* a virgin.

Spanish fashion, her father, the leader of their *cumpania,* had nicked both of their wrists with a knife and when the blood flowed, he bound their wrists together with a red silk cord, making them one as their blood mingled. And then they had jumped over a length of broom together.

The rest of the night had been devoted to dancing, music and drinking. After many rather coarse jests and joking, Sylvester took her away into the woods where a bed of bracken had been prepared. There he quickly and brutally took her maidenhead. She had known what to expect but all the same it had been a painful experience and one which had not grown much easier with time.

This wedding today had been indoors, in front of the altar of the church and they had knelt before the priest. Much of the service had been in a language she did not understand, but Felix seemed to understand it quite well. She had been obliged to make a great many promises, in French, including one that said "So long as ye both shall live" and "till death do ye part". A ring had gone on her left hand, a tiny pretty thing, made in the forms of forget-me-nots, with tiny blue stones forming each flower. It felt strange there and she kept twisting it about on her finger with two fingers of her right hand.

The entire parish had been at the weddings and afterwards they had heard evening mass. When they left the church, handful of rice and flower petals had been thrown at the two couples and a laughing, Esmée Marrett had thrown her bouquet to a waiting crowd of girls and young women, one of whom had caught it. The others cheered and congratulated her.

Rosal did not understand why this was done, but she nonetheless threw hers as she had seen Esmée do and it was caught by Joisaine.

Everyone, or so it seemed, came up to congratulate the two couples, one young and one old. Rosal felt rather shy. She knew very few of these people or they were among those who had once called her a dirty Gypsy, but her new husband was smiling and accepted their good wishes gracefully. He seemed to know just what to say.

No one made any crude jokes, especially not Felix. Sylvester had boasted of his process in bed, but Felix never mentioned such a thing, confining his remarks to how fortunate he was to win such a wife.

Nor did he hurry her away from the feast in *Madame's* kitchen. Until nearly curfew there were people from all over the parish in and out of the kitchen, for the neighbors had arrived in force with foodstuffs when *Madame* had issued a blanket invitation and both couples were toasted and fêted.

Still, Rosal was nervous. Hagar had told her that the love potion was not quite ready (in another week it would have been perfect) but tonight was their wedding night, not next week.

And last night Rosal had woken up at midnight, with her heart pounding, for a horrible dream had ruined her sleep. What if he were already married? What if he had a wife and children somewhere? He would hate her if he remembered and it proved true. And Hagar had told her that the *Gajé* frowned on a man having two wives. A man could go to prison for such a thing. And what would they do to the woman who had married such a man? Why had she not thought of this before?

But she resolutely pushed these and all other negative thoughts to the back of her mind. He would *not* remember. He hadn't yet. They would marry and be happy and there would be a child, perhaps even more than one. Why should they not be happy?

All the same, when they finally left the celebration, which only the coming curfew was ending, she was quiet and nervous. She had to explain to him why she had acted the way she had on that horrible night.

"I want to talk about that night." she said in a low voice as they began to walk towards the woods. She could not imagine spending a summer night in the *vardo* as that was for sleeping only in cold or inclement weather or for the old or sick. Their bridal bed would be beneath the stars, in true Romany fashion.

Felix stopped in his tracks and put his hands on her shoulders, swinging her around to face him. "Rosal," he said very seriously, "I want you to forget all that ever happened between us. Tonight is our wedding night. Let us pretend that it is our first night and let me love you as I want to with no preconceptions or bad memories, just starting off brand new."

She nodded, grateful and thankful that she did not have to lie to him yet again.

He took her hand in his and led her down the dark path between the trees. Moonlight made patches of silver on the ground.

"It is almost like Faerie," he said. "I think that the Faeries enjoyed your dancing this afternoon." As Robin had suggested, they had gone to his kingdom to practice with the Elfin musicians before having to go to church again. "Were those Spanish dances?"

"Yes. The women in my family have always danced," she said "Even long ago when my family lived in Spain."

"You looked very beautiful and graceful," he said "*And desirable*," he could have added, for the dances were sensual, fiery and her slim body was very supple.

She had been awe-struck at first by the splendor of Faerie, but when the musicians, a guitar and a violin struck up she had been unable to keep from dancing For the music was compelling and so much like the Spanish music played by the older musician in her *cumpania* when she was a girl that she had felt all her fright and shyness evaporate.

"No one in St. Peter Port will be able to resist watching you," Felix said, drawing her a closer against him and putting his arms about her.

Her heart was beating very fast as she lifted her lips for his kiss. The very last thing she was thinking was that a baby might come from this night's work. As he swung her off his feet and up into his arms and allowed her head, now *sans* bonnet, to fall onto her shoulder, she thought that she might not need that potion of Hagar's after all.

34
Lovers' Bliss

When Rainier had outlined his plan Pyewacket nodded. It could very well work. He had only one problem with it. The rats were far more clever than he had given them credit for.

But first he had to understand one thing. "Why do you rats want to help us?" he asked curiously.

"Because we hate the French too," said Rainier. "When this island was populated with Witches and Wizards we rats were left pretty well unmolested. Familiars didn't hunt us down and kill us and magical people left us alone. They seemed to have no objection to letting us have a share of the grains and vegetables harvested. Many people even put out food for us in their barns. And because of this, we rats stayed out of homes and food stores. Now we are back to scrounging in dustbins and the French set traps and poisons for us. It is no way to live!"

"Magical persons with familiars think too much of their animals to want to hurt and kill other animals. Many of the magicals are even vegetarians," said Pyewacket. He could understand why the rats would object to the new regime.

"So," Rainier continued, "we decided that if any Wizards or Witches or Familiars were put into this prison we would help them escape and thwart the French. We hope the magicals will return soon. And we *can* help, for who knows the ends and outs of this Castle better than us? Our ancestors have lived here for many years and the *Guernaise* fed us properly. And there seem to be a lot more of us to feed now, for some reason." he added, puzzled.

Pyewacket knew the reason for this. There would have been contraceptive spells put upon the food left out for the rats, not rigorous enough to completely impede their breeding but enough to keep down the rat population to a manageable level so that the food sharing would not become a burden.

Without those spells, however, the rats had been breeding the last few years at what must seem to them a fantastic rate.

He decided that it was not up to him to inform the rats that their fertility had been manipulated by humans. They might take it amiss.

"When shall we do this?" he asked Rainier.

"As soon as is possible," the rat answered. "This morning one of my scouts who understand much of human speech was in the wall behind that terrible priest's office and they intend to start torturing your friend tomorrow morning!"

Pyewacket looked at Aurelius quickly. He was an old, frail human and already suffered much pain. He would not stand up long under the Question.

The familiar shuddered. How humans could do such things to one another! And all because their religions were different. It made no sense to an animal. Every animal had a different name for the deity they worshipped but animals also recognized that these were manifestations of the same spirit, put in terms each particular animal could understand. Pyewacket would never torture a hedgehog because it believed that the Supreme Being was a hedgehog rather than the cat Goddess Bastet. That was completely and utterly wrong. But humans were willing to kill, torture and burn each other over religion and even go to war. Yes, animals did kill one another in nature, but that was why man was supposedly superior; man should know better. They had other sources for food rather than killing one another.

Pyewacket sighed. Sometimes he felt that his understanding of humans was deficient, even after living with them for so long. He and Felix, particularly when out on the boat, sunning on the deck, had enjoyed many long and fascinating conversations about nature, philosophy and morality in both men and animals. How he missed that! Escaping from here also meant that he could once again search for Felix. He was still convinced that his Wizard was alive.

"We've carefully watched and the guards don't check on the prisoners as much between midnight and sunrise," said Rainier, interrupting the familiar's thoughts. "That would be the ideal time for your escape."

"I just don't know where I can take him to be safe once we leave here," Pyewacket began, thinking rapidly. "I cannot return him to his own place for that's the first place they will look." He also rejected taking Aurelius to Sir David. They could not get David and his mother in trouble with the French. "Do you know any of the Sea-Folk, the Selchies?" he asked, suddenly thinking of Grizel Sarchet. She had a house on another island.

"The seal folk?" Rainier said. "I don't know any of them personally but there are always seals in the harbor and sunning on the rocks near the Castle here. Some of them may be Selchies but I don't know which ones."

"Even the seals would help us if I ask politely. They are friendly creatures and usually like humans," Pyewacket was thinking out loud. "I daresay the main thing is to get him out of here and myself as well. This damned Inquisition throws black cats into the flames as well as Wizards."

Rainier shuddered. Traps and poisons were more easily evaded. The rats had watched, from hiding, as the Inquisition had tortured people and they had even tortured some trapped rats that Rainier and his compatriots had been unable to rescue in time. Rainier would never forget the looks upon the faces of the torturers. They *enjoyed* causing pain, suffering and death. They *laughed.*

"Tell your human what he must do and be ready after midnight," said Rainier. "I will post guards to let us know what the French are doing each moment and will come back here myself when it is time. Be ready!"

"One question, said Pyewacket, putting out a restraining paw. "He is chained to the wall. How do we get around that?"

"Oh, didn't I tell you?" said Rainier. "We have a key! We stole it!"

With this he sniffed the air and then looked about, scurrying off to a hole in the wall, whisking himself inside, his long tail disappearing behind him.

Pyewacket decided to let Aurelius sleep as long as possible. He need the strength that sleep would give. He wished that the Professor were not so frail, but even Felix, if he had been exposed to all of this Cold Iron, would be weak and nearly helpless. Rainier did not seem to think that the Professor's condition would be a problem, that the rats had everything under control.

Pyewacket hoped the rat was right. The plan was risky

and daring, but he had come up with no better alternative. The familiar was under no illusions. Both he and the Professor would die if they remained incarcerated. The Professor would probably die under the Question, and if he did survive the torture he would be subject to a farce of a trial and then consigned to the fires and he, Pyewacket, would be burned with him. Even this fantastic plan would be better than that.

David and Grizel lay together on the bed of moss underneath the enormous beech tree in Faerie. The branches, almost touching the ground and in full leaf, made a quiet, private bower for the two of them. A soft breeze, smelling of something sweetly floral, touched them lightly. It was a place out of time, and as they lay at their ease in the drowsiness after lovemaking, David felt himself relaxing from the stresses of yesterday and this morning, when he had arrived home to find that the Inquisition had taken Pyewacket and threatened his mother. Majorlaine had been almost hysterical when he had not returned the night before, fearing the worst. Girard had assured him that a message would be taken to her, but this had not been done.

And this morning had been difficult as well as all of the old and the lame and the young had to be delivered to church on time and many of the St. Peter Port parishioners were Presbyterians and it had taken all of David's powers of persuasion to convince then to go to church.

"There, is that not better?" came Grizel's voice. Her head lay on his shoulder and she cuddled up underneath his arm, her supple length pressed close to him. "You were as taut as a bowstring when we came here and now you are much more at ease," she continued. "A few more times and you will be completely relaxed!"

"Grizel!" he protested with a short laugh. "You are shameless!"

Seriously, she said " I love being here with you like this, making love. I cannot think of a better way to spend the afternoon. Why should I not let you know that? And there is nothing more relaxing, after all. All the while we were

323

watching the Gypsy woman dance I could see that your thoughts were elsewhere. You had a frown" she reached up and touched him lightly between the brows "right here. When I saw that I knew just what you needed and determined to make certain that you had it."

"When I am with you troubles seem to have a way of melting away like soap bubbles," he said. "I can forget, momentarily, that we have a difficult and dangerous task ahead of us. For now we have to rescue Pyewacket as well as the Professor. And the French show little sign of leaving in spite of all that Robin and the Fair Folk are doing to them. We have the problem of Blériot's balloons as well."

"You'll just have to spend more time with me, here, like this," she said. "Once a day, at least!"

He laughed happily. She was a delight; eager, responsive and never once had an expression of distaste crossed her face when she had seen the terrible scarring left behind by his wounds. He could not believe his good fortune, for he had thought that no woman could see those marks without turning away, revolted. But then Grizel was not a human female. She was half seal, and amongst bull seals, scars were marks of honor, records of battles won.

"Tonight I am going to reconnoiter about Castle Cornet," she said. "I have heard from the other Selchies that there were once secret entrances to the Castle that led into the sea, entrances that might not be on those plans you are going to steal."

"Grizel, I wish you would not!" said David worriedly. "If the Inquisition catches you —"

"I shall go when it is full dark and high tide," Grizel promised. "No one will see me and even if they do, they will think me only a seal. I shall take care not to change while I am anywhere near St. Peter Port." She laughed in her husky voice. "The Inquisition is so stupid! They have been trapping seals and ordering them to change by thrusting a crucifix in their faces! Even if they had been so fortunate as to catch a true Selchie that would not work on us! We have to be caught in the midst of changing from human to seal or the opposite. Many years ago Selchies had to don a sealskin over our human form to change but that is no longer true. We could then be captured by someone stealing our skins. But we have

324

evolved beyond that. Shape-shifting is much easier and less dangerous." As she spoke she had begun stroking his chest with her webbed fingers.

"Have they bothered you much on Sark?" he asked.

"Very little," she said. "I believe that they consider Sark unimportant. But I went to church this morning like an obedient citizen and wore my lace mitts so that no one could see the webs between my fingers. No one has visited my cottage. I think that they are not willing to make the climb to the headlands!" She laughed again and said "But come, David, enough talk about the French and our friends. This time and this mossy bed is for us and our pleasure. We have hours in which to love each other as yet."

David wanted to speak of his love to her, not just of pleasure in bed. But something held him back. They had known each other such a short time in the real world. Somehow he did not think that Grizel was feeling what he was. She was wild and untamed and right now he could not imagine her becoming a wife, concerned with the day's dinner and the mundane goings-on of housekeeping. That she adored their current activity was readily apparent, but if it was not with him, she probably would have chosen another man, or a Selchie, or even from what she had said, a male seal. Meeting her here like this was wonderful but he wanted something more, something he thought that she would never desire. Perhaps he had best school himself to be happy with what had been offered and cease crying after the moon, although his feelings for her grew every day.

In the Brehaut woods beneath the stars Felix and Rosal lay, intertwined much as David and Grizel.

Rosal had followed Hagar's instructions and let him do as he wished with her and what had followed had been tender, gentle and loving and she found herself responding as it escalated to passion. What had passed between them bore little resemblance to what she had borne from Sylvester. She felt as if she and Felix had actually shared something in which she was no longer a passive, unwilling subject but a partner. It was a revelation and suddenly she could understand why a woman such as Hagar would give up her *cumpania* and her people for love of a *Gajo*. She had never understood this before and had been a bit contemptuous of Hagar. She could have had a child with a Romany. Now she knew.

Felix had not given much thought to the hope he had once had, that in loving her he might remember, for he had been too eager to love her.

But no memory had stirred. The only thing of which he was certain was that he had loved a woman before for he seemed to know just how best to please Rosal and she had responded in a way that was everything he had wished for.

They both forgot that danger lay ahead of them tomorrow, particularly for Rosal. The two Elfin musicians would be in danger as well from all of the Cold Iron in St. Peter Port. They would be wearing silk against their skin, with shields of Elfin silver beneath their outer garments, but it would drain them, as it had Felix himself.

Robin had explained to him that as a Wizard, Cold Iron would hurt him as well and that was one reason that he was so sick after attempting to perform magic in St. Peter Port. The French, afraid of Witchcraft and Wizardry, had brought much Cold Iron to the capital.

Felix wished that he could remember being a Wizard, if indeed he was one, and could remember the spells. Perhaps with those he might save the Professor in an easier fashion than their plans permitted.

This night, their wedding night, seemed a night stolen from the terrors of every day, from being on guard and worried about what the French and the Inquisition might say or do.

Rosal gave a sigh and cuddled closer to him. Sylvester had never cuddled and she found that she liked it very much. Sylvester had always turned over and gone to sleep afterwards, snoring so loudly that she was deprived of sleep.

"What are you thinking?" he asked her, lifting his hand to stroke her now unbound hair. It was smooth and silky under his fingers and like her, it smelled of flowers.

"How much I like this," she offered a little shyly. "I was also thinking that one day soon I will dance the *farruca* for you. My mother taught it to me long ago, as her mother taught her and her mother taught her, all the way back to when our *cumpania* lived in Spain. She said it is the dance of the act of love and one day I would dance it for my lover and" her voice dropped to a whisper, "dance naked. I never danced like that for Sylvester."

"I would be honored," he said, and pulled her closer against him. Between what had been said about her first husband by Rosal herself and Hagar, and the revelations of tonight's marriage bed, Felix had gained a very low opinion of Sylvester. He seemed a monster of selfishness.

She relaxed as he said he would be honored and did not respond with a coarse jest. Sylvester had wanted her to dance the *farruca* for the *Gajé* as they would pay much to see the three-part dance which portrayed desire, seduction and delight. But she would not do such a dance in front of strangers, particularly the *Gajé,* although as Sylvester had pointed out, other Romany women did so, many of them naked to the waist, for amongst the Romany breasts were not considered sexual. They were for feeding babies. These other women had made very good money for their Roms. But even when he beat her for her obstinacy she would not dance this most intimate of dances. Now she *wanted* to dance it, for Felix.

How fortunate she was to have been given this man by the sea!

"Rosal," he said quietly. "if there was anything but this joy between us, as I said, let us forget it. I apologize for any other way I may have treated you. It will be different from now on, I promise."

She almost told him then. With the feelings that were building inside her the lie seemed worse than ever. She no longer saw him as a means to an end, to a baby, but someone she was beginning to love very much, someone she valued for his own sake and someone she wanted to be with, even in this most intimate of situations, where she had never expected to find happiness.

But she could not do it. She was afraid that he would turn from her, that the loving feelings she saw on his face and heard in his voice would turn to hatred when he found out how she had tricked him. And she was now terrified of losing

327

him. Pray God and the Virgin Mary he *never* remembered his past! He did not *need* to remember! She would make him so happy that he would no longer *want* to remember. She would be the best wife, the best mother and make him not only love her but also be proud of her and would never, ever wish to leave her.

35
The Brave Rats

Midnight, on a night of full moon. The moon had risen nearly an hour and a half ago and was sending a pattern of ripples across the sea, looking like a magic pathway to Faerie.

A French soldier had come at 11:30, slid back the window on the door and looked at them. Pyewacket could see him although Aurelius, wide awake and only pretending to sleep, saw little other than the silhouette of a head, outlined by the light of an lantern he held up.

The guard was bored and sleepy. Since it was Sunday, the Inquisition did not allow card playing or even anything but religious reading. Even talking about women was a forbidden subject. The guard had been in church twice that day, a requirement whether one wanted to go or not and had sat through two boring sermons on concupiscence, which once he understood what the priest was talking about, the private found very amusing – a celibate giving lectures on the evils of sex! Howe would a priest know what sex was like? And it wasn't evil, that was for certain. Like most of the soldiers, the private was looking forward to the brothels that were being built. He decided to catch forty winks before he had to check upon the old man again which was a waste of time, and dream about women, if he could not talk about them with his fellows until the morrow. He slid the little door shut and walked away down the hall.

"He's gone," said Pyewacket quietly. "We'd better get ready. Rainier will be here soon."

"My dear fellow, I am not certain that I can manage any of this," said Aurelius, worried.

"You don't have to do anything save lie down, I told you that," said Pyewacket. "We'll take care of all the rest. Just trust us. You told me you can swim."

"Not for a far too long length of time," said Aurelius

ruefully. "In my youth I was a great swimmer and oarsman as well. I rowed for Cambridge. But now I can barely walk!"

"You don't have to walk to swim," said Pyewacket. "At any rate, I shall be looking about for one of the Sea-Folk to help us."

When Aurelius still looked worried Pyewacket put a paw on his leg and said "Is it because you do not feel you can depend on the rats? I think we can trust them. I have a good feeling about them. Rainier has been very open and honest with me."

"I never conceived of the idea of trusting my life to a group of rats," said Aurelius. "It still seems a fantastic plan."

"It's the only plan we've got.It's either this or stay here to be tortured by the Inquisition tomorrow morning. I'd rather take my chances with the rats!" said the familiar. "Now, let me have the blanket." He took the blanket between his teeth and drew it to the floor. Then tugging it with tooth and claw, he smoothed it out on the floor as if spreading it on a bed. "Ready," he announced.

Earlier, Rainier had come with another young rat, who, he said, was clever with his paws. With them they brought the promised key. Between them the three animals had, with some trouble, unlocked one of the shackles and the chain and with a then free hand, Aurelius had been able to unlock the other. They had left the shackles looking as if they were still locked. No one ever checked them.

As far as Aurelius was concerned this next part might be the hardest. He had to get off the cot and somehow get to the blanket. He could not walk there. He would have to crawl.

He took his hands from the shackles and then painfully, he slid off the cot onto his aching knees, and, guided by Pyewacket's voice in the blackness of the cell, made his way on his hands and knees to the blanket.

It seemed to take forever to crawl but a few feet and he was trembling in every limb and dripping with sweat when the blanket was reached and he could lay down. Even to lay on the hard floor was a relief after the ordeal.

"Excellent!" said Pyewacket bracingly. "Just rest for a moment, Professor, I think I hear the rats arriving."

Aurelius wished he could see as well as the cat in the dark. That was another difficult part about this entire affair;

being so nearly blind and helpless, dependent on a group of animals, particularly rats, which he had always been taught to abhor.

Still as the cat said, the alternative was far worse. In spite of his brave words to the Bishop that morning Aurelius was terrified of what might happen to him on Monday. He did not think that he would last very long under the lash or any of the more esoteric tortures employed by the Inquisition. Before the rat had come up with this fantastic plan Aurelius's only prayer had been that he acquit himself well under the maltreatment he was sure to suffer, as an English gentleman ought. He was afraid that he might tell them about Lovel, a young man who had his whole life in front of him, and one moreover who had a young wife.

Pyewacket could smell the fear and the pain the Professor was suffering. He knew how difficult it was for a non-magus to put all of his trust in a group of animals, especially since so much counted on his doing so.

A sound on the exterior wall of the cell brought his head around sharply and he came to his feet.

Pyewacket could see very well in the dark, even better than most cats and now he saw in amazement a section of the wall slide out It was about a foot high, perhaps a little more, and three feet wide. Rainier, at the head of a large group of rats, came out from behind it and said, "Is he ready?"

"Yes," said Pyewacket, walking forward to the rats. "What is this, Rainier?" A strong smell of the sea came from the hole and Pyewacket sniffed it appreciatively. The air in the cell was far from fresh.

"Very long time ago this cell was part of a kitchen and this was the way they disposed of their rubbish. No one's used it in a long while. My great great great grandfather heard from his great great great grandfather who had it from his –"

"Yes, a very long time ago, I understand," the familiar interrupted.

"They swept the rubbish into this hole and pushed it down to the sea with a long-handled pole. After a few feet it slants downwards, which is going to make this easier. And the tide is very nearly high.You'll both slide into the water easily," said Rainier.

"How did you rats move this huge block of stone?"

Pyewacket said in amazement, looking at it.

"It's hollow!" piped up another rat beside Rainier. "Probably to make it easier for the people who had to move it every day. All of us pushed and pushed! We're going to put it back if we can so the French don't know how you and your friend escaped!"

"That's clever!" said Pyewacket in admiration.

"We'd better get going," Rainier interrupted. "We don't know how long this is going to take. Bring the rope!" he called.

Several enormous rats came forward, dragging a coil of rope.

Pyewacket went back to Aurelius. "Can you get yourself up on your elbows?" he asked. "We've the rope here. I'll take it under your back and bring it up over your chest."

"And when you tell me, I shall tie it about myself," said Aurelius. He levered himself up, not without difficulty and felt the cat pass behind him. Moments later Pyewacket said "Lay down, Professor and I shall give you the ends of the ropes to tie together."

This was accomplished. Aurelius found his hands were shaking slightly. He hoped this worked. He was not even certain where they were going once they were in the water. The cat had mentioned a friend who might be able to help.

He felt Pyewacket's paw pulling the blanket up over him. "I think it best that you keep your head turned to one side and the blanket up over your face as well," the cat said. "There seems to be enough clearance but I am not certain." Obediently, Aurelius pulled the edge of the blanket up over his face.

"It's the same height and width all the way to the sea," said a big rat who obviously understood human speech "We checked carefully. Your human will not get stuck halfway. You can tell him that."

Pyewacket conveyed this to Aurelius, who relaxed a bit at this news. He had been afraid of getting caught in this chimney-like tunnel.

"Close your eyes and let us do the work," Pyewacket said soothingly to the Professor.

Aurelius heard a barrage of rat squeaking and then suddenly the rope, which was now under his back and head grew taut. He could not see it, but at a signal from Rainier, hundreds of rats sank their teeth into the rope. Pyewacket, near Aurelius's head, sank his front claws into it as well. He would guide it, with his superiorly strength, so that Aurelius would be pulled straight through and not twisted or stuck.

"Heave!" Rainier called out and, with a lurch, the journey began.

They were unable to exert a steady pull. They dragged him a few inches and then stooped, took another grip on the rope and pulled again. It seemed to take an agonizingly slow time and Aurelius was afraid that the guard would come at any minute. It was also a most uncomfortable way to travel as the ground was not only hard but rough. The blanket protected him somewhat but his body felt every bump and crack he was dragged over.

The smell of the sea grew steadily stronger and suddenly moving was easier as the floor began to slope downwards. Behind them, Aurelius heard a dull 'clunk' as other rats inside the castle had managed to move the stone back in place. And the further they went the lighter it became as Aurelius saw when he dared to open his eyes once or twice.

He never knew how long the journey took but it seemed like hours until suddenly his head was out into fresh night air and he could see in the moonlight and hear the lap of waves against rocks only a little ways below.

"We've done it!" said Pyewacket in satisfaction.

"You can tie the rope here," said Rainier. "There's a ring where they tied up a boat once upon a time and you can lower yourselves to the sea. We'll get rid of the rope so no one will even suspect."

Aurelius of course, could not understand Animal but he could hear Pyewacket speaking to the rats and he said "Pray thank them for me. I can never repay the debt I owe them!" He sat up and leaned against the wall, fumbling with the rope. "I shall never think of rats in the same way again," he added.

Pyewacket conveyed thanks for both of them to Rainier and said "I shall make certain that all of the mages know what you have done. You will be honored amongst them."

"We were glad to help," said Rainier. "We live for the day that the French go back where they belong and this island is the place it was once more. If you ever need any more help, please call on us."

"I will," said the familiar and continued "Your help was brilliant, inspired and invaluable! I shall always hold rats in the highest admiration after this. Thank you again, Rainier, and all of your people. We owe you our lives."

Rainier bowed and turning swiftly, ran back through the opening, followed by all of the others There were rat-sized tunnels all throughout it.

"Now we have to get down into the sea," he said to Aurelius.

"Which might be more difficult than that trip through the tunnel," the Professor said ruefully. "I have never had much practice in rope climbing."

"Pyewacket? Is that you?" came a female voice from below them.

"Grizel?" cried the familiar joyfully. "Grizel, you are just the person I was hoping to see! It's Grizel Sarchet. She's a Selchie, a seal-woman," he explained to the Professor.

"I'm coming up," Grizel called and moments later had scaled the rock face and joined them.

If Aurelius was surprised at being joined by a completely naked young woman glistening with salt water, it did not show on his face. He had read of Selchies, but had never thought to meet one.

"You must be Professor Bretton," she said, sitting down beside him. "I went to a meeting this afternoon with many of your friends on how to rescue you, and Pyewacket," she said with a look at the cat. "But I see you managed to rescue yourselves!"

"Grizel, can we take the Professor to your house on Sark?" Pyewacket said eagerly.

"I have a far better idea.The Professor has an invitation from some new friends of ours and I think that is the best place for him, where the French will never be able to look," said Grizel, tucking a long strand of her hair behind an ear. "I shall lower you into the water, Professor and then I shall take you to Belle Grève bay and there perhaps we can contact our friends. You can ride upon my back, Pyewacket; you'd best go stay in Faerie as well."

"Faerie!" said Aurelius, astonished. "Are you joking me,

my dear young woman?"

"Not at all, Professor, you are invited by Robin Goodfellow on behalf of his father, Oberon, to reside in Faerie indefinitely until such time as the French are gone from these islands and it is safe for you to go back to your home," said Grizel. "Now we'd best leave here in case a sentry sees us."

Grizel was lithe and strong and made little of lowering Aurelius into the water. She put Pyewacket on a rock at the edge of the sea and then climbed back up and untied the rope, placing it as far back in the rubbish chute as she could manage, for the rats to find.

Reentering the water, she changed into a seal, and went close to Pyewacket's perch and allowed the cat to climb onto her back. She told Aurelius to float on his back and hold onto her flipper and she would tow him through the water. She then headed for Belle Grève Bay. At this time of night there were bound to be some Faeries somewhere near the bay, making mischief for the French.

"David! Wake up!" came a familiar voice in his ear. "Wake up! I've something important to tell you!"

David came up out of a deep sleep and saw Grizel leaning over him.

"Grizel, what are you doing her in my bedroom, naked?" he said, sitting up abruptly and reaching for a candle and flint "If my mother sees you – !"

She made an impatient gesture and sat down on the edge of his bed. "I came here from Faerie and to there from swimming behind Castle Cornet. I didn't have my gown with me. And it isn't as if you haven't seen me like this again and again!"

He lit a candle and said "No, but my mother has not. I would be hard put to explain to her why and how I have a naked woman in my room at," he looked at the bedside clock "two o'clock in the morning. Not that I do not like having *this* naked woman in my bedroom at two o'clock in the morning."

"And under other circumstances I should like being here," she said. "But I come only to tell you the news. The

Professor and Pyewacket have escaped! Even now they are both safe in Faerie!"

"What!" he exclaimed, sitting bolt upright. "But how?"

Succinctly, she explained. "So you see, there is no need for our carefully conceived plot. You needn't put yourself in danger! And I am very happy about that!" She bent forward and kissed him on the lips and put her arms around his neck, pressing her cheek against his.

"It was so touching. He nearly cried when he saw that all of his books had been saved from the flames! Robin had Galen see to him and he is now sleeping peacefully, as is Pyewacket. Robin says that they can stay there as long as is needful," Grizel said.

"Grizel," David said hoarsely. Her closeness and the fact that she wore nothing at all was having its inevitable affect on him. He hardly heard what she said.

"Come with me to Faerie, right now, David!" she said, her arms tightening. "You can be there when the Professor awakes and in the meantime our lovely mossy bed is waiting for us!"

God help him, he wanted her again! He allowed her to persuade him but as the wall faded away and they stepped into the beech wood he wished that he had the right to have her in his bed, in his bedroom, and most particularly in the old bed in the farmhouse at Torteval, as man and wife.

"Mage! Mage!" said a tiny voice in Felix's ear, as insistent as a mosquito.

He awoke abruptly and found himself in the woods, on a bed of bracken with Rosal in his arms. She was deeply asleep, head pillowed on his chest. Last night had not been a dream then.They had married and had a wonderful wedding night.

"Mage!" repeated the little voice and he looked up to see a Faerie suspended in the air by the rapid blur of her wings. She was the same as the others he had seen, her bare body and hair the colour of a flower, in this case a deep blue. He wondered what flower she guarded.

"I am a Bluebell Faerie," she explained as if reading his

mind. "Since my flower has gone past I returned to court and Robin Goodfellow has asked me to give you a message. It is this: the Professor sleeps in peace in Faerie as does the cat. There is no need for the lady to dance for the French. Robin bids you and your lady to dine with him upon the morrow and see the Professor."

"But how –?" Felix began.

She shook her little head. "I do not know how. You will find that out tomorrow evening. But he is safe and you must not worry any more!"

With this she winked out and was gone.

"Is somebody here?" said Rosal sleepily.

"It was a messenger. The Professor is safe and in Faerie," Felix answered.

"Then I don't have to dance?" Rosal sat up, this news bringing her wide awake. She was not certain whether she was happy or disappointed.

"I'm just as glad," he said. "I never like d the idea of all of those Frenchmen staring at you. But I would like to see you dance again. You were so beautiful yesterday," he said.

"You really think I'm beautiful?" Rosal was touched. Only to his male cronies had she ever heard Sylvester call her 'pretty'. He had never once paid her a compliment.

"Very beautiful. So much so that I want to –" He drew her down and kissed her and whispered in her ear.

She laughed and returned his kiss eagerly. She felt so happy. She would not have to dance for the French and he would not have to put himself in danger. Life was good.

But in St. Peter Port the guard had just discovered the empty cell and had raised the alarm. Already Fournier's troops were saddling their horses.

36
Elspeth

Richard spent the next several hours, after getting Pascoe up to the cave, in making it more comfortable for them.

Getting Pascoe to their hiding place had proved difficult for both of them. Pascoe was slow and in pain, and a little dazed from the syrup of poppy. He could not fold his damaged wing up against his side, so to prevent further damage, Richard levitated it. He was a little worried about the amount of magic he had expended on a French-held island where there might be a Witch-Sniffer. From what he knew of Witch-Sniffers, a talented one could 'sniff' the magic and perhaps even locate them. That was why it was crucial to get into the cave and stay there as much as they could. Once inside no one save another Wizard who knew how, or a Faerie could find them.

It took an hour to get Pascoe up from the beach and into the cave. The opening, of course, accommodated itself to their needs and opened wide for Pascoe and closed firmly behind them.

Once inside Richard removed Pascoe's saddle and made the dragon lie down on the grass he had brought inside before fetching the dragon in. Richard pushed a rock under the outstretched wing to keep it level, a process which Pascoe much appreciated as the weight of the rest of the wing was dragging on the broken bone.

Pascoe fell into a light doze after apologizing for being such a burden, which Richard told him was complete and utter nonsense.

Richard took off his jacket and cravat which had been damaged by the plunge into the sea. He could just imagine what Pearson would have to say when the valet saw the condition of his master's garments. They would never be the same and his Hessian boots were sodden and scratched; they would need the services of a leprechaun were they ever to look well again.

Since his clothing was damp and uncomfortable Richard stripped down to his linen drawers and shirt and spread everything else out to dry. He wondered if there were drying spells for clothing. Such spells would be the province of a valet who also happened to be a minor level Wizard. Perhaps his education had been sadly neglected, Richard thought, to not know such practical, useful things.

Inside the cave he did not have to worry about using magic. He could use as much as he liked and no Witch-Sniffer would ever know, for they were in the province of Faerie.

First Richard put up four permanent mage lights on each side of the cave. These would glow all of the time unless he dimmed them or put them out deliberately.

Then he enlarged the pool into which the water flowed and made another, lower pool beneath it that would serve as a latrine and could be magiced clean daily. When the pools were ready he enlarged the crack that water trickled through and turned the flow into a steady stream and watched them fill.

He tested the water again. It was pure and clear and icy cold. After all of this magical exertion he was obliged to rest and took a deep draught of the water, using his hands as a cup.

Richard was becoming conscious that he and his dragon would need food soon. He could not keep doing magic on a stomach that was telling him that his nuncheon had been quite a while ago and tea-time had been completely missed. One of the cardinal rules of magic was that magic needed fuel and any intelligent mage ate a good meal before doing any rigorous magic. Making mage lights and enlarging a hole in the ground, however, was not at all rigorous, being the most basic of magics.

Pascoe would need food as well, for dragons, unlike humans, required more food when they had a fever, and Pascoe's glazed eyes and dulling scales told Richard that his friend was running a temperature. This would require more magical use, for even with a fever a sick dragon lost body temperature. Their normal temperature was 130° and

Richard would have to throw a magical invisible blanket over Pascoe to keep his body temperature up, which he did immediately. Fortunately the emergency medical kit included a dragon thermometer.

But how were they to obtain food? While Pascoe slept Richard built a fire with some driftwood he had brought up from the beach to help keep Pascoe warm. Making a fire was one of the first things a young Wizard learned and long practice enabled Richard to roll the flames off his fingertips. The smokeless fire would not need a vent.

Then he set about trying to summon any Faeries who might still be in the environs.

Two hours later, exhausted, he had to admit defeat. No one had come.

"I think it is a long, long time since any Faerie was near here, Richard," said Pascoe. He had been awake for a little while and had been quietly watching Richard's efforts. "They probably stopped coming when it became too well-known that this was a Faerie place. They don't like it when too many humans know too much of their comings and goings."

Richard sighed and went and sat down near Pascoe. "I suspected as much when I saw that sign outside," he admitted, "No Faerie would ever label an entrance to Faerie in that fashion. And while you were asleep I tried to open the door into Faerie that once was here, with all the commands I know. The door has been long sealed."

He looked into his dragon's eyes and said "We've the problem of how to obtain food, old friend. Since we were not planning a long trip I did not pack anything edible. If I had only thought of it I would have included some Elfin way-bread! That could have kept both of us for a long time. I dare not use magic outside this cave for fear of Witch-Sniffers, otherwise I could magic up some fish for us. But that is impossible."

"What about a fishhook?" Pascoe asked.

"I don't have a fish hook, either," said Richard. "We came out ill prepared to be marooned on a French-held island, Pascoe."

"I think I can provide a hook," said Pascoe thoughtfully. "The old sheath on this talon is about ready to drop off. I was going to ask you to get out my sharpening stone when we got home again." He held up his right front leg and spread his talons. "Is my file in the bag?"

Like cats, dragons' talons were regularly shed, but unlike a cat a dragon scratched and sharpened his talons on a large block of very hard stone, such as granite. Part of a rider's duty towards his dragon was the care of his talons. Talons needed clipping on a regular basis and sometimes filing as well.

Richard, like any good dragon rider, always carried a bag of draconic needs: calcium tablets, oil, brushes and cloths for oiling the dragon's hide, which could itch, cloths for buffing and talon clippers and a file.

He rose and went to the area where he had stowed the saddle and breast harness. The saddle was resting on the pommel and leaning against the wall, so as to not spread the skirts of it and crack the saddle-tree that was the heart of any saddle. The tack would need attention too, when they returned home. Since it was magiced against damp it had fared better than had Richard's clothing, but it would still need a good bout with saddle soap and neatsfoot oil. The web mesh of the breast harness was in poor condition as well, curling from the damp.

But Pascoe's supplies were in a water-proofed by magic oil-cloth bag.

Richard took this back to Pascoe and sat down on a rock in front of the copper dragon. Pascoe extended his leg and Richard began the task of filling off a sheath.

The new talon beneath it was some what soft but the air would harden it almost immediately. The sheath, when Richard had freed it, would make a good-sized hook. "I'll use my cravat as a line," he said, thinking out loud. "As soon as it is dark I'll try my luck fishing for our supper."

"In the meantime," said Pascoe a little wistfully. "could I have an oil bath? The salt water made me itchy!"

"Certainly," said Richard. "It's time you had some calcium in water as well, and I'll give your scales a quick rinse with some warmed water first, to get all the salt off."

By the time this was completed both of them were tired and hungry and, according to Richard's pocket watch, which was magiced to be water-proof and to never need winding, it was almost nine and therefore, even this close to mid-summer's day, dark by now.

He dressed again.The clothes which he had put near the fire, were dry but the boots were still damp inside. His boots had been made in London, by Hoby, and like all good boots had been water-proofed by a staff Wizard, but they were never meant to be submerged completely. But he left his jacket off, only putting the waistcoat over on over his shirt. His cravat of course, was now in strips tied to the improvised fish hook.

When he emerged from the cave it was to a cool night with brilliant stars. The moon had not risen as yet and Richard lit a small mage light to see his way over the rocky path and beach. He hoped anyone seeing it from a distance would think it a local out with a lantern in search of food or wood.

He estimated that it was still some two hours to high tide. The tides here seemed to go in and out with great ferocity and the high water mark was at a greater distance up the beach than he would have imagined possible.

What kind of fish could he hope to attract in shallow water and with no bait? Did he dare cast an illusion of some sort of bait? What fish would be found here? At home, when out on their boats, Felix had caught bream, cod, whiting and plaice, amongst others. A good-sized cod of to 25 pounds or over would make a small start on a meal for Pascoe.

He walked to the edge of the water and threw the line out as far as he could, giving it a little magical push.

And to his surprise there was a tug upon it almost at once. And what was even more surprising, instead of pulling steadily away from him, the fish felt as if it was coming towards him. "I never heard of suicidal fish before," Richard muttered to himself as the fish or whatever it was continued to advance at him, now at tremendous speed.

Moment's later a seal's head broke the water and rode a wave into the beach, landing almost at Richard's feet. The makeshift muslin fishing line was in its mouth.

It was a Gray seal, and it stared up at Richard with a look of inquiry. It then shimmered and shape-shifted into a tall, sleek and naked young woman with a voluptuous figure. She had long dark hair and large dark eyes.

"That's the strangest fishing hook I ever saw," she said. "It's a dragon talon, isn't it?"

"Yes," Richard admitted.

"And you must be a Wizard!" she said and then laughed. "You must be, for if you were not you'd have your hands all over my tits by now and be trying to push me down on the rocks for a good mating! Wizards are the only men who don't stare and lunge at us when we shape-shift into our human forms. Why is that?"

"Between watching the Witches' sky-clad rituals and traveling, as I have, in Faerie, where clothing is optional, one grows accustomed," he said. Richard had never met a Selchie who was not completely unselfconscious about nudity or quite frank about his or her animal sexuality. He had learned early on not to stare and just accept their natural state.

"Is your dragon here?" she said 'I'd like o see him!" she said. "I would also like to know what you are doing here on Guernsey. I thought all the mages had left long ago!"

"I'm on Guernsey?" Richard said in astonishment. Guernsey, where Felix was!

"You don't know where you are?" She cocked her head and looked at him. Her long wet hair fell to one side and absentmindedly she wrung it out.

Briefly, he told her what had happened to them.

"And your dragon is hurt!" she said in distress. "Oh, that's too bad! What were you doing with this talon?"

"Trying to catch something for our supper," he said. "We've no food."

"Well, you'll not catch anything here right now," she said frankly. "Not with the tide running so strong. Perhaps at the slack tide, but that won't be for a while. I'll tell you what, if you'll show me your dragon and share the catch with me I'll go out and get all the fish you need."

"It's a bargain," he said and shook hands with her.

Moments later she threw herself in the water, changing before she touched the surface. And not too long after that a pile of mixed types of fish was growing at Richard's feet.

The Selchie came out of the water again and changed back into human form. "Is that enough for your dragon?" she called as she walked up the beach.

"More than enough!" he said. He had begun to string the fish for easier carrying on the lengths of his cravat and she helped him finish this task.

"By the way, I'm Elspeth Campbell.That's my human name. Even a Wizard couldn't pronounce my seal name!" she said as they began to walk up the beach towards the cave, each with a good string of fish under Richard's small mage light.

"Campbell, then you're Scots?" he inquired.

"Yes, my family comes from the Isle of Mull, but I am living here this year because the male I'm mating with is a native of this place," she answered. She laughed again. "Actually there are three of them I'm mating with. I met two other males too attractive to pass by! But tonight they all will have to do without me. I've got a chance to see a real live dragon and I won't give that up!"

As Richard introduced himself he thought of how all the Sea-Folk and many non-magical creatures of the wild seemed to be fascinated by dragons and wanted to be near them.

She watched with interest as he drew the magical arch and the gray-green wall split open to admit them.

Pascoe was asleep again and Elspeth noticed this. She was very quiet as she gave her fish string to Richard. She went and looked at Pascoe and at last whispered "He's very beautiful. What kind is he?"

"A Cornish Copper," Richard answered.

"And he's bigger than I thought. I've only seen dragons high up, passing over in the sky," she admitted. "If he wakes up, can I talk to him?"

"He'll wake when I start cooking the fish," Richard said.

"I'll clean it for you," she said. "I'll filet it and we can put it on some of those branches to cook it. I'll tell you what. Tomorrow I'll bring you some pots and things from a shipwreck. Do you mind if I sleep here tonight?"

"Not at all," Richard answered. He gave her the knife from his kit and watched in fascination as she cleaned gutted and filleted the fish at incredible speed.

She put aside the guts "I'll eat those later, when I'm a seal again. When I'm a human I like my fish cooked but when I'm a seal I want it raw."

She watched as Richard pushed a generous sized filet onto one of the slender pieces of wood he had gathered for the fire.

"That smells good. I'm hungry. I was mating all afternoon and it always makes me sharp-set. I'll tell you what," she said suddenly. "I'll mate with you if you like. You've been so nice. I've never mated with a human before. It should be interesting. One of my friends mates with a human all of the time; she likes it. But it must be strange to mate with someone who stays the same shape all during mating. We Selchies switch back and forth."

"Thank you, my dear, that is a very nice offer, but I prefer to be a little bit better acquainted with the females I take to bed and you are young enough to be my grand-daughter." Richard was amused by her candid sexuality. Quite the last thing he had expected this afternoon was to be propositioned by a Selchie.

She looked a bit surprised as no one had ever turned her down before. "I suppose I'd have to remain a human all during our mating, though," she said thoughtfully. "My friend does when she mates with her human. She says he wouldn't like to be suddenly mating with a seal."

"I would prefer that, yes," said Richard dryly.

She thought about this for a moment and then said "I still think it would be interesting. If you change your mind I would be glad to mate with you. I really like mating, quite a lot!"

"Thank you. I'll let you know if I change my mind," said Richard. She was so earnest and eager. There was not a shy bone in Elspeth' Campbell's body, whether in seal or human form.

"Do I smell fish?" came Pascoe's voice hopefully.

"He's awake!" Elspeth said joyfully. "All the other Selchies in Guernsey are going to hate me when I tell them I've met and talked to a real live dragon!"

"Guernsey!" Pascoe exclaimed. "Are we in Guernsey? Oh, Richard, perhaps we can find Felix! And perhaps this young lady knows Prince Madoc as well!"

"Certainly I do," said Elspeth. "All the Sea-Folk know the Prince! Tomorrow I shall go to his palace and tell him about my new friends."

Richard rose from wher he had been bending over the fire and took a nicely done filet to Pascoe."I'm sorry we've no seasonings to spice it up, old friend," he said. Pascoe was a bit of a *gourmet.*

Pascoe disposed of the generous filet in one gulp. "Oh, it's delicious!" he said, his forked tongue licking his gums. "Is there more?"

"I'm cooking it right now," Elspeth said, crouching near the fire with more fish on a stick.

"Thank you!" Pascoe called. He then lowered his voice and said "Richard, I heard what she said to you. If you want to sleep with her I shall close my eyes and try very hard not to listen."

Richard chuckled and put a hand on Pascoe's snout. "Thank you, old friend, but romantic dalliance is the last thing on my mind. And at any rate, as I told her, she is a little young for my taste. I doubt she is more than eighteen or so and it would be far too much like robbing the cradle."

Pascoe nodded. Over the years they had been together Richard's *amours* had been with females of his own years.

"Could anything have been more fortunate?" Pascoe then said "To end in Guernsey where we may search for Felix our own selves! And now we shall be able to contact Madoc as well!"

Richard hoped it *would* be fortunate. Guernsey, he had been told by his friend the Admiral, had been the first port of call for a Senior Witch- Sniffer from Rome.

37
Retribution

Aurelius awoke from a deep, peaceful sleep, the best he'd had in years. Usually he awoke in pain, his legs, in particular, aching before the day had begun. Most evenings he was grateful to be able to stretch out in bed but, after several hours, laying in bed was more like torture.

As he fully woke, though, he was conscious that he was not in his own bed, nor in any place he recognized.

It was a room lit by a soft diffused light, with the sheerest of white curtains all around. In fact, there appeared to be no walls at all, just the curtains and a ceiling overhead the looked more like tree branches in full leaf. A sweet smelling, soft breeze was stirring the curtains and the leaves overhead enough so that a gentle rustle filled the air. From somewhere far away there was a noise of tiny bells of some kind and even further away there was singing: beautiful, piercingly sweet singing of many voices blended. Try as he might, Aurelius could not make out the words.

He sat up experimentally and still felt no pain.

"Good morning. I hope you're feeling well," said a voice courteously.

Aurelius looked at the foot of the bed. There, with his tail curled around him, sat the cat. However all traces of white had disappeared from his fur.

"Where are we?" Aurelius asked, stretching cautiously. He really did feel most extraordinarily well! It had been a long time since a good stretch had not resulted in pain or creaking joints.

"We're in Faerie," said the cat. "Many friends have already come to visit you, Professor."

"Are they still here?" asked Aurelius hopefully. He wondered what had been going on while he was locked away.

"Galen, the Healer here, thought it best to let you sleep

as long as possible. Sir David was here and he stayed as long as he could but he had to leave to take a Mr. Lovel out to the Dragon Port and he said to tell you that they are all doing well, even John."

Aurelius's face clouded as he thought about John and his despicable act.

"Robin, that's Robin Goodfellow, who shall come and see you a little later," Pyewacket continued, "has invited all to a feast this evening and Grizel Sarchet, she's the Selchie who helped us yester eve, will be by as well. She went to see Prince Madoc."

"Prince Madoc?" Aurelius queried. He was bursting with questions and wanted to be up and dressed and exploring. Would they have such a thing as a Bath chair in Faerie?

Pyewacket told the Professor all about Madoc, why he himself was on Guernsey and what he had learned of the Faerie resistance against the French. While the cat talked an Elfin girl came into the room with a laden breakfast tray for the Professor.

She was beautiful, with slightly slanted eyes and brows, and pointed ears, soft-voiced and kind, and helped Aurelius arrange the pillows so that he could sit up and eat easily.

"The food here is quite different from the food in prison," said Pyewacket when she left and Aurelius, slightly bemused, took in the array of fruit, breads, and eggs on his tray, as well as several unidentifiable things which, however, smelt wonderful.

Aurelius had to agree. After one taste he said in wonder "As a classical scholar I have read all of my life about ambrosia, the food of the Gods. Surely I am now actually eating it!"

"I'm also to tell you," said Pyewacket, "that you are to stay in bed until Galen comes to see you again. He is reasonably certain that if you put yourself in his hands he can reverse your arthritis and get you out of your invalid chair."

Aurelius could not believe it. Only yesterday he had been expecting the ending of his life, to be abused by the French, perhaps to the point of death, locked away in a cold, black cell and instead he was in this marvelous place, being told he might regain the use of his limbs! And when he remembered that last night he had been told his books had been saved from the Inquisition and he would soon see his young friends again and be able to assure himself of their safety, his happiness was almost too great to be borne.

Fournier's anger, when he discovered the prisoner had fled, knew no bounds. He ordered the guard, Private Pascal Mercier, flogged within an inch of his life for dereliction of his duty. When Mercier's sergeant had pleaded for mercy, for who could expect a crippled old man, chained to the wall, to be able to escape, Fournier had snarled "He's fortunate I did not have him shot!"

Fournier wanted to punish someone as he himself had endured a tongue-lashing from Father Maël and another from Bishop de Ollivier that had made him feel as if he was a very stupid and raw recruit.

Father Maël, his eyes cold, had told Fournier, "I want every inch of this island searched until you find him! He cannot have gone far. Unless he was feigning he can scarcely walk! There will be fellow conspirators as well, perhaps even another mage. Find them, find them all! Bring them back here in chains! Do anything that is necessary to find them! Take Garceau, the Junior Witch-Sniffer, with you. He'll ferret out any magic."

Father Maël himself intended to track down the source of that warning he had felt yesterday when someone had been using magic. After a night's reflection and the escape of the mage Bretton he was certain that there was another mage on Guernsey, a very powerful one indeed who had no doubt aided and abetted the escape of the prisoner.

When Richard awoke the next morning he found Elspeth, in seal form, breakfasting on the fish guts left from the night before. Pascoe was still sleeping.

As she felt her eyes upon him she gulped down the last of

the guts and then shimmered and changed back into a young woman.

"Good morning!" she said cheerfully. "I slept very well indeed, even without mating even though it's very relaxing to mate just before sleep! The fire kept me comfortable. But I'll tell you what. I'm going to go out to the shipwrecks this morning and find some useful things for you, pots and plates and so forth. And I know that anything I find must not be of Cold Iron. We know all about that in Scotland! Then I'll get some more fish for you. But after that I really must find Hamish and the other males. I've gone far too long without mating and I'm beginning to feel the need of it, unless you've changed your mind and want to mate with me?" she ended hopefully.

Richard smiled at her. "Thank you, my dear, but no. As charming and lovely as you undoubtedly are I am far too old for you. But perhaps you might answer a question for me. You said that one of your friends is mating with a human man? Do you know his name?"

During the night Richard had suddenly awakened, wondering if Elspeth's Selchie friend was perhaps sheltering Felix. And with the easy sexuality of a Selchie she would naturally expect to sleep with him. The beautiful, sleek and naked and very willing Selchie female would be difficult for any young man of four and twenty to resist, particularly one like Felix, who was not currently enjoying the company of a mistress. The Elf maid he had been sleeping with had recently given her leaf to another and they had parted amiably.

Elspeth thought a moment. "I met him once. He's called David something, a French name I think. I do remember he's the Bailiff of Guernsey," she said at last.

Not Felix then, Richard thought in regret. That would have been an easy solution and Felix would have been safe (although perhaps exhausted by her attentions) with a Selchie, who knew all of the secret caves in the ocean in which to hide him and might have even presented him at Madoc's court. Many of the Selchies could be normally solitary creatures, but not at this time of the year, when, like Elspeth, all they could think of was mating. Even all this mating would not result in many pups, for Selchies, like many other Faerie creatures, suffered from a low birth rate.

Elspeth was gone shortly, promising to return with necessities.

Pascoe awoke but a few moments after she left. Richard had some more fish ready for him and a calcium tablet dissolved in water, to drink. The extra calcium would help the bone knit.

Richard took the dragon's temperature first and was pleased to see that it was not as high as he had feared it would be.

"Is Elspeth gone?" the dragon asked with interest.

"She'll be back," Richard answered. "She knows where she can obtain some kettles and cutlery and more fish as well."

"I like fish," said Pascoe on a sigh, "but I think that by the time we return home I shall be heartily sick of it. Fish is good enough in its way but it is not the same as a baron of beef or a nice shoulder of mutton!" He sounded rather wistful. "Richard, I had a thought last night. What if the human mating with Elspeth's friend is Felix?"

"I had the same thought," said Richard, "and I asked her. It is another man altogether." He offered Pascoe another filet on a stick. The dragon pulled it from the makeshift skewer gently and chewed it. "It would have been an easy solution to his disappearance."

"At least he would have been safe, although perhaps worn to the bone," said Pascoe. "Some of those Selchies, from what I hear, can wear a man out. They are so eager for mating; too eager if you ask me. It's all they think of and talk about!" He chewed on his fish and added. "Reginald resented that, you know."

"What?" Richard asked.

"That Felix was welcome into Selchie and Elfin beds and he was not. I heard him talking to that Persian one day when they were out near the dragon pen. He imagined that Felix was indulging in one long orgy, rather than having had a relationship with the same Elf maid, Oriana, for years, and that with her alone. He thought it was grossly unfair of you to censure him for his mistresses, when Felix was free to play the goat in Faerie," the dragon explained. "He was also angry about not being welcome in Faerie."

351

Richard sighed in exasperation. "Reginald should know by now, for I have told him so many times, that I censure him because he not only spends money he doesn't have on high flyers with extremely expensive tastes, but he poaches on other gentlemen's turf, importunes respectable females of the merchant class and even tried to force a young maid of Queen Mab's court, which is why he is no longer welcome in Faerie! It was all that I could do to save his life. The Queen was so outraged." The Faerie Hame of the West Country was ruled by Mab, who swore fealty to the High King Oberon. "Reginald is incapable of being faithful to one female, as Felix has been for years. There can be no comparison!" Richard finished.

Pascoe was quiet for a moment and then said "Perhaps Elspeth will contact Madoc for you?"

"She has said that she will," Richard answered.

"And perhaps he'll have news of Felix," said Pascoe hopefully. "I would not mind a bit more fish," he added.

By dawn most of St. Peter Port had been ruthlessly searched. If a householder was not quick enough answering the door, the French battered it down. Fournier's men gave the *Guernaise* little chance to save valued possessions or clothing, for closets were emptied and stripped, walls tapped for secret panels and the house was over-turned from attic to cellar as were all outbuildings, all places of business and even the churches. Everything was left in complete disarray.

All copses, all ditches, all woods were searched inch by inch by men on horses with drawn swords, beating each bush and patches of furze and gorse. These mounted men were followed by men on foot who looked in hollow trees and logs and even up in trees.

The troops spread out in to the countryside, stopping all vehicles and ordering the occupants out while the vehicle was covered inch by inch by the troops and two of the three Junior Witch-Sniffers.

Fournier rode out with Lieutenant Girard's troop to Castel and the cottage of *Trois Chiminées*. Fournier wanted to question the manservant his own self and have the distinct pleasure of burning those heretical books. With them rode Father Garceau, the only one of the Junior Witch-Sniffers who was a priest. He would also denounce the pernicious works of Satan as they burned.

John had spent most of the night wide awake. He did not know what to do. Sir David had been very upset with him. Indeed, John had never seen the young Bailiff so angry.

And what Sir David had said about the Professor never forgiving him had torn at John's heart. All he had tried to do was rid the cottage of that damned Gypsy, so things could go back to what they had been! But now his hands seemed tied. He didn't dare try the same plan again. And still the Professor was in the hands of the Inquisition and more than likely would feed the fires.

John had no idea that the Professor had been rescued and was safe. David had thought it best not to tell him. John, especially now, seemed to have lost all capacity for hiding his emotions and it was critical, when the Inquisition arrived to burn the books, that John knew nothing he could let slip.

It was a little after seven when Fournier's troops arrived at the cottage. John, without much appetite, had been eating his breakfast. The mere act of making a baked egg had reminded him of his master and he wondered bleakly if he would ever bake an egg for him again. The Professor had been the best of employers, hardly a harsh word or a reprimand since they had been together, since they were both young men. Only since that Gypsy had come into their lives, John thought savagely as he scraped the remains of the egg and some toast in to the dustbin, had the Professor upbraided him.

The rear door, which had not been locked, suddenly burst open and there were about a dozen French troopers, with a priest in tow.

"Get the books!" Fournier snapped and four soldiers took off at a run. "Search the house! Girard," he added, turning to the Lieutenant, "You speak English. Ask this manservant where his master might be!" His face was flushed with anger, his colour high and his eyes dark. So far there had been no sign at all of the escaped prisoner. It was as if the earth had opened up and swallowed him.

"Where is your master, *couchon?*" Girard shouted at John. He too was in a rage as Fournier had been screaming at him since three in the morning.

"You had ought to know that better than me," John growled. "You was the ones took him off to gaol!"

A young soldier, looking frightened, came pelting back into the room. "Sir!" he stammered. "Sir! The books are all gone. There's nothing in any of the bookcases! Even the desk is empty of papers!"

"What!" Fournier screamed. "Bring him!" He flung out a hand towards John and strode from the room in the direction of the library.

When he saw the bare shelves he cursed fluently and at some length. The priest, coming up behind him from the kitchen had a look of shock of his cherubic face.

"Where are they?" Fournier turned on John, who had been dragged into the kitchen between two soldiers. "Where are those damned books?" Girard translated this into English as languages were not Fournier's *forte* particularly when he lost control of his temper.

As he had been instructed by Sir David John said, "When I came back from church yesterday they was all gone. I thought some of you had come and taken them."

Fournier was almost incoherent with the rage when this was translated for him. Girard had never seen him so angry. The Lieutenant thought that in a few moments his superior would begin frothing at the mouth like a mad dog.

"Take him outside and give him twenty lashes for his insolence!" Fournier barked as the priest, who had been looking about stepped up to him. The two soldiers dragged John off, the manservant protesting volubly to being manhandled.

"Colonel," said Father Garceau quietly. "there has been magic done here, as recently as yesterday evening. It is of a strange sort, one I am unaccustomed to and is no doubt the work of a foul fiend from Hell itself. Only fire will purge its baleful influence."

From out of doors Fournier could hear his soldiers, well-disciplined as they were, promptly obeying his orders. The whip cracked as he said "Then we shall burn this nest of Satan's vipers to the ground, Father." Raising his voice, he called to a young private. "Bring the fire-starter!"

If he could not burn the books he would burn the mage's abhorrent den, no doubt the scene of many a vile sabbat and rituals dedicated to Satan. It would make a fine fire and a lesson to others who would flout the authority of the Church and also that of Fournier himself.

38
Fire!

It was with extreme reluctance that Felix left Rosal on Monday morning. It had been a night of sheer bliss and, after lovemaking, of sound, restful sleep.

Just after dawn they were awakened by Chavé, who, released from night-long bondage by Hagar, raced joyfully through the woods and playfully tugged the blanket off his still sleeping people.

Cool morning air on bare skin awake them at once.

When they sat up, Chavé began barking and frisking about. He wanted to lick Rosal's face as he had scarcely been able to bear being forcibly kept away from her all night long.

Rosal was worried. How would Felix react to Chavé bothering them so early? Sylvester would have kicked him, with many curses, as would her father. Then she might have been beaten for allowing the animal to interrupt them. Neither man had much use for "worthless animals" as they would have termed Chavé. He was a pet, pure and simple. He did not work for his food and demanded attention all the time.

But Felix laughed and tousled Chavé's head and ears. "You're better than a rooster!" he said to the dog. "If you can't stand being away from Rosal at night, we'll just have to train you to lie quietly when we are otherwise occupied. I can understand your not wishing to be away from Rosal at night.I don't want to be away from her either!" he said, with a merry look at Rosal, inviting her to share the joke.

Everything in Rosal relaxed all at once and she returned his smile. He seemed to actually like her dog. "You don't mind him? That I love him?" she ventured.

"Mind?" he said, still petting the dog who was now trying to lick his face as well. "Did you think I would be *jealous* of your dog? I should hope I am not so petty!"

The look on her face told him that this was important to

her. "Rosal," he said gently, "people can love more than one other, in many different ways. Why should you not have love to share with Chavé, the pony, Hagar, me and our children when they come along? I hope we *will* have a family, including a little girl who looks just like her mother."

Rosal was filled with happiness and impetuously threw her arms around his neck. "Perhaps we made a baby last night," she whispered.

"Perhaps we did," he agreed. "Rosal, it's very early as yet and we really need to see if Chavé will behave himself while I am making love to you."

She agreed and let him draw her back down on the bed of bracken.

Chavé watched with his head cocked to one side and with an occasional bark of approval, but otherwise did not interrupt them.

Hagar could see at once that this night had been far different than the previous attempt when at last they emerged from the woods with the dog frisking about them. Felix had an arm about her and Rosal had a glow about her that Hagar had never seen on the girl before. Her eyes lingered on her new husband and she seemed reluctant to be away from him.

Hagar had breakfast waiting for them: pan-fried potatoes, sausage from *Madame's* farm, eggs and bread. As usual she had cooked two separate pans full, one for Felix and one for herself and Rosal. Felix thought this a singularly foolish custom for it made twice as much work. The two women also washed his laundry separately from theirs and garments for the lower limbs were segregated from those for the upper body. All it did was increase the labor the women had to do. But it was the *leis prala,* the law, Hagar insisted stubbornly when Felix remonstrated with her about what he saw as unnecessary hardship. All the years she had lived with her *Giorgio* lover she had not abided by the law and that was why, she was convinced, that he and her son had left her. She was being punished.

The only custom she had given in on was eating with

357

him, instead if standing behind him while he ate. He was not going to eat alone, he had insisted and had talked Hagar around by the simple expedient of refusing to eat unless they joined him.

"I had to let the dog go," she said, filling plates. "He whined and cried all night. I got very little sleep."

"He can go with us from now on," said Felix. "He behaved very well this morning. He's a very good dog." He poured out herbal tea for all of them over Hagar's protests. Neither coffee nor tea could be found on the island any more, save for exorbitantly priced, small amounts in the French supplied grocery shop. It was far out of their reach, as it was for most *Guernaise*.

And as well there would be no sweetener for the tea until what "tame' bees remained had built their first wax comb and filled it with honey. *Madame's* husband had been a Bee Master, but the hives were now empty, as his expertise had gone with him to France. The farm now had few cows, and no pigs for the French had taken all of them. Only the oxen and the goats remained with the cows. The French occupation was making everything increasingly difficult. Actual privation was becoming common and it would only get worse.

Hagar, like Rosal, was surprised at his tolerance of the dog, but she made no comment. She merely said, "I've heated water for your razor and you must give me that jacket. Today is the day that patch must appear on all of our clothes. I shall sew it on while you eat. Rosal, last night I sewed a patch on your other gown and made you a cap as well."

She drew aside her shawl and showed them the "G" upon her breast, and took a wisp of cotton from her pocket and set it on her own head. She was determined not to give the Inquisition any excuse to drag them off to prison. All three of them would obey every order. "Later," she said told Felix, taking the jacket from him, "perhaps you can read their directions to us so we will know what we have to do."

Rosal looked rebellious. "I do not see why we must wear these things! We are Romany, not *Gajé*, who tie themselves up in these silly clothes that make me feel like a prisoner!"

"You would rather really be a prisoner?" said Hagar sarcastically, threading her needle.

"Please, Rosal," said Felix swiftly. "The Inquisition will

torture you if you do not do as they say. and what is more, as you are so very pretty, they would let the Witch-Sniffers use your body. I have read that they examine pretty young women naked, and search for Witch-Marks with their hands as well as instruments of torture. For all our sakes, just do as we are told. Perhaps one day soon we shall rid ourselves of the French and we can go back to the way it was used to be." He could not remember where he had read of the Inquisition's methods but he felt that he was well acquainted with them somehow.

He did not care to wear the humiliating badge either, but it was that or suffer a fearsome punishment.

Rosal's spurt of rebellion died when she saw the concern on his face. She wanted to please him and she took the gown with the "G' stitched on the bodice from where Hagar had laid it. "I'll wear this and the cap too." she promised. "But what does it mean, this mark?" She ran her fingers over the "G".

"It's the letter G.It stands for what we are, Gypsies. Gypsy or *Gitan* as the French call us, begins with a G," Felix explained. This served to remind him that she, and Hagar too, were illiterate. Perhaps he could teach them to read. He could not imagine not being able to read. So much of what was good in life could be found between the pages of a book: knowledge, humor, life itself expressed by the most brilliant minds of the ages.

"You had better shave before the water grows cold," Hagar reminded him. "The sun climbs in the sky."

It was now after four and Felix had to met David by five for Blériot had been so incensed at losing Sunday as a work day that he demanded they be out at the Dragon Port by half after six. Felix hoped that this week would see the last of his duties out there, as the army doctor had said that von Weber should be back on his feet soon. Then, it was already agreed, he would go back to work at *Les Huit Lapins,* since the Professor could not return to his cottage.

He parted with Rosal unwillingly, after washing and shaving. It would have been nice to have a honeymoon but they both had their work to attend.

And Rosal, for her part, was disinclined to part with him. She wanted to return to the bed in the forest where he had made her so happy. The hours would go by slowly today, she was certain, until they could go back there tonight.

It gave Felix a pang to see the cottage and know that the Professor was no longer there. But at least he and his beloved books were safe and where the French could never find them.

David was waiting with the cabriolet in the road, talking to John who stood in the front yard. Felix could hear what they were saying and it was obvious that John had not been informed of the rescue.

"How can you go out there today, Sir David, knowing what my Master must be bearing?" he said in astonishment. "Why aren't you trying to get him out of there? I thought it was today that you was going to divert them Frenchies and start helping him!"

"We have a new plan, John," said David soothingly.

"What is it?" John demanded.

David shook his head. "It's best you do not know, John, for you must sustain a visit from the Inquisition this morning and it will be difficult enough for you to stick to your story about the books disappearing. The less you know the safer you are."

Felix felt that this was a warning for him as well, and he did not mention that the Professor was safe when he came up to the others and bade them good morning.

John, of course, sniffed in a derogatory manner and turned away, refusing to even look at Felix. He was heard to mutter under his breath, "Damned stinking Gypsy!"

Felix decided to ignore this, and greeted David who said, "Good morning, Lovel! Are you ready for another day of *M'sieur* Blériot's fussing and tantrums?" Then he looked closer at Felix and said "What the devil is that?" He held a driving whip in his hand and leveled it at Felix's chest.

"A new rule of the Inquisition. All undesirables such as Gypsies, Jews and Protestants are to wear an identifying mark at all time," Felix answered lightly, trying to make little of it.

"And a good idea that is," said John, *sotto voce*, "So that honest Christian folk will know who they are!" He turned and glared at Felix.

"John, as a Protestant you will be obliged to wear such a mark as well," said David dryly. "No doubt a large 'P'."

The look he then gave Felix was distressed and full of sympathy. "I'm so sorry. It must be humiliating to be branded," he said. "Since I am both French and a Catholic I will probably be exempt from such ill-treatment. It isn't right."

Felix warmed to him again. He had come to like David very much. Like the Professor he had never once made Felix feel an inferior being, as the French, particularly Fournier and Blériot, made him feel.

"We'd best leave," David said. "Considering the times we must stop at the parish crossings we will be fortunate if we reach the Dragon Port on time."

Felix jumped up in to the cabriolet and David snapped his whip at Thierry, telling the gelding to step out.

The last thing Felix saw as they set off was John, standing at the cottage gate, glaring after them as if ill-wishing them.

Rosal and Hagar began early with the laundry, since Rosal did not have to be at the farm until just after seven. There was always laundry and water had to be hauled from the stream and dumped into four small kettles on the fire for each type of laundry, male and female and top and bottom.

Felix had insisted upon hauling some of the water for them and had spoken of getting a large barrel for water to be stored so that they would not need to make so many trips to the stream.

Hagar sprinkled a handful of bran into lukewarm water, with a pail of cold water for rinsing standing by. The coloured cottons of their gowns would be washed first in this fashion, and then hung inside-out in the shade so that the colour would fade as little as possible.

"He's a good man, that Rom of yours," she said abruptly as she stirred the bran into the water with her hand. "He has some strange ideas and makes light of the *leis prala*, but his heart is good for all that."

Rosal, shaving soap into a kettle of hot water for their white things, said "Hagar, I never thought – the way he made me feel –!"

Hagar chuckled,the first time she had laughed in genuine amusement since she could not remember when. "So the marriage bed is not just for the making of babies now!" She suddenly had a sweet memory of what it was like with the man she had loved and envied Rosal.

Rosal flushed, not only from the heat of the kettle she stood over. "He says he wants children, a little girl that looks like me! He said nothing about a son at all!"

"And I think that making that child will not be at all painful to you," said Hagar slyly.

Chavé, who had been laying quietly under the *vardo,* sat up and barked sharply, sniffing the air. He whined and sniffed again.

Then Hagar and Rosal smelled it as well: smoke, thick and acrid, coming from the direction of the village, borne on a breeze.

The wind carried something besides the smell of smoke: voices. They were shouting in French *"Au secours! Au secours! Au feu! Au feu!"*

("Help! Help! Fire! Fire!")

"That is *Madame!*" said Rosal in horror. "The farm is on fire!"

"Go!" said Hagar quickly. Rosal took off, followed by Chavé.

Hagar paused only to tip the kettles over, leaving the laundry inside and douse the fire before running into the *vardo* and getting the bag that contained her herbal remedies. There might be burns to dress. She then followed Rosal at a run.

But it was not the farm. It was the cottage of *Trois Chiminées,* completely engulfed in flames as Hagar arrived, having passed the farm and seen that everything was fine there.

Joisaine and Rosal, with a number of women and older

children from the nearby village had formed a bucket line with water from the garden pool, but it was a losing battle. The house was old and the timbers dry. As Hagar arrived the roof fell in, sending a tower of flame and sparks into the sky, causing the would-be rescuers to scream and retreat from the conflagration. Black smoke hung as a pall every where, making it difficult to see.

Hagar nearly stumbled over *Madame* Brehaut, crouched in the road with a man's head and torso, face down, pillowed in her lap.

"Thank *le bon Dieu!*" said *Madame* when she looked up and saw Hagar. "Have you your simples, *Madam* ? This man is grievously hurt!"

"Was he burned?" Hagar asked, kneeling down beside Madame Brehaut.

"Whipped," said *Madame,* pulling aside what remained of his shirt to reveal a striped and bloody back.

John was muttering, his big hands clenching and unclenching. "Damn Frenchies! Damn Froggies!" he said hoarsely. "Didn't tell them nothing! They had nothing from John Grant! Nothing!"

"It was the French," said *Madame* Brehaut. "They were looking for the Professor, who, *M'sieur* Jean says, by some miracle has escaped from his prison. The Colonel had him whipped." She looked up at Hagar, anger in her face. "They tied him to the porch railing, *Madame*, and then fired the house! If Joisaine had not come to care for the pony he would have burned to death! She cut him down just in time!"

"Where's my Master?"John moaned, turning his head from side to side. "What have they done to him?"

Hagar pulled several bottles and clean cloths from her bag and uncorked one, soaking the cloth in it. This she squeezed out over John's back. He gasped as the cool liquid struck his wounds. He looked up into Hagar's face and shouted "One of them filthy Egyptians! Get her away from me! She'll poison me with her hell-born brews!" He tried to rise to his feet and failed miserably, falling down across *Madame* Brehaut's lap, breathing heavily.

"Stop this foolishness!" *Madame* said severely, as if John were a small child in need of chastisement. "*Madame* Buckland is a skilled herbalist and healer! She is here to help you, you stupid man! Now lie still or I shall call the other women to come and sit on you so that you cannot move!"

John subsided at the fierceness in her voice but he kept muttering beneath his breath, flinching as Hagar gently saw to his wounds and anointed the burns he had received as well, fortunately not as bad as the whip marks on his back. When she was finished his back was bandaged and beginning to feel better. His face and forearms shone with Hagar's burn ointment.

Joisaine, followed by Rosal, came up to them. "It is no use, *Maman*," she said sadly. "The fire had taken too strong a hold on the house. We could not save it."

Léonie Voisin, a woman form the village of St. Cécile, came up and said, in anger and despair, "*Bon jour*, Marie! A fine thing this is when the French beat us half to death and fire our homes! As it is they are starving us to death. Are we now to live in the streets? They are in the village at this moment, tearing things apart. I had best get back to my house before they destroy it too!"

"Thank you for coming and trying to help," said *Madame* Brehaut.

Madame Voisin laughed without mirth. "We shall all of us be getting plenty of practice in the days to come, Marie! Mark my words!" She left, hurrying towards the village.

"Joisaine," said *Madame*, "Go at once to the farm and bring back the farm wagon. *M'sieur* Jean will have to be stretched out flat to be transported. We shall take him in for now, but only if he minds his manners!" she added darkly. She was not about to put up with his nonsense.

Joisaine took off, bareback, her now necessary skirts bunched around her thighs, on the pony Diogenes. He would have to find a refuge at *Les Huit Lapins* as well.

The three women remaining exchanged a look full of meaning. What was going to happen next? Had the French run mad? Were they all to end up burned out, living hand to hand? Only *le bon Dieu* knew and he was telling no one. It was terrible to think that all of this was being done in the name of God.

39
The Pagan Spring

Blériot was waiting for them outside the main building, pacing up and down, tearing at his mane of hair so he looked even more demented than was usual.

"You're late!" he screamed as David drew the cabriolet to a halt in front of him. A soldier ran forward and took Thierry's harness near the bit. The private looked harassed. Blériot had more than likely been on a rampage.

David's pocket watch chimed half after six in its silvery tones as he and Felix climbed out of the cabriolet. They were precisely on time but David forbore mentioning this to Blériot. He had learned enough about the little man in the time he had known him to know that not even hard facts made any difference to him, once he had an idea in his head.

Blériot grabbed Felix's arm and dragged him off, complaining loudly about the stupid men working on the baskets who could not seem to get anything right, and it was up to the *Gitan* to correct them. "For," came Blériot shrill voice as he led Felix away "it is no doubt your fault. You probably translated my directions incorrectly!"

David shook his head. He felt very sorry for Lovel, having to put up with Blériot all day. At least he was free to work on his tax records by himself. He actually did not mind coming out here. He found that he enjoyed Lovel's company. This morning David had told him of what he knew of the Professor's escape and they had speculated upon Fournier's and the Inquisition's probable reaction.

And here at least, he was free of Fournier and Girard and had a window in the room he was allowed to use. It was awkward dragging the tax records back and forth but the work was proceeding quicker now. Uninterrupted, he had been able to concentrate on the forms and was actually becoming used to it.

He picked up his bundle of papers, and slung a well-filled luncheon bag over his shoulder. Majorlaine as usual had packed enough for two. He followed another soldier who stood outside the door and would escort him to the room he worked in, all to maintain Blériot's ridiculous secrecy.

David did not see Lovel again until nearly one o'clock. By that time he was beginning to wonder if Blériot was ever going to allow his translator to eat a nuncheon. At eleven David had been unable to stand it any longer and had eaten one of Majorlaine's flaky pastries filled with plum jam. It had been a long time since breakfast. He felt guilty doing so, for his new friend hadn't that option.

When Lovel at last came, looking both glum and angry, David had the meal laid out and said "Don't say anything, just eat! You look as if you need it."

Felix did not argue with him but sat down and dug into Majorlaine's thick chicken and vegetable sandwiches, pickles, plum pastries and *Gâche Melée*, an apple pudding, a Guernsey speciality that was best served warm, with cream, but was still delicious cold. There were two stone bottles of herbal tea as well.

For a while there was no sound save that of two young healthy appetites being satisfied.

"Pray thank your mother for me," Felix said at last. "She is a wonderful cook. Everything was delicious!"

"I'll tell her. She is glad to provide us with a good meal. I can imagine what Blériot would give us, if he even remembered to do so!" David said and added with a sigh, "What I would not give for a cup of coffee! It would be perfect with these pastries! I am beginning to forget what it tastes like. It has been so long since any was available here. Fournier has a cup whenever he wants it and sometimes the smell of it, drifting down the corridors at Government House makes me want to go in and strangle him and take it from him!"

Felix smiled somewhat sardonically. "Strangling Fournier would be doing us all a favor and strangling Blériot would certainly make me happy. That man is impossible!"

David looked at him in sympathy.

"Late on Saturday afternoon a shipment arrived from France and today he was attempting to teach the men the way he wanted it installed. He is not a patient teacher and having to translate his contradictory instructions to men who don't speak French, with him fretting and fuming to have everything done yesterday is nearly insupportable! If the men do not immediately comprehend what he wants he begins screaming at them and then it is my fault for not translating properly. He also will not wait for me to finish my translation. He shouts at the men as if yelling will make them understand French," said Felix bitterly. "He wants them to work faster than is humanly possible, as if they were automatons. These are men who have been ill, who have been prisoners for a long while and he expects them to work fourteen and sixteen hours a day on two meals a day and about four hours sleep! All the while doing tasks that are unfamiliar."

"He's insane," said David shortly. "Whatever is this latest shipment?"

"Asbestos sheets," said Felix.

"Asbestos?" David repeated blankly. Whatever could Blériot be doing with asbestos?

"Stretch your legs out, one at a time, and flex them," said the Elfin Healer Galen.

With some trepidation, Aurelius obeyed slowly. It had been a long time since he had been able to stretch without pain.

But to his amazement there was not the slightest pain. He stretched and flexed each leg, the joints and muscles feeling as if they were young again. All Galen had done was rub some nice-smelling blue salve into his legs but what a difference it had made!

"Does this mean I can walk again?" Aurelius asked hopefully.

Galen smiled. Like Robin Goodfellow, he was almost impossibly handsome, with golden, shoulder-length hair and green eyes, which seemed to be a common colour amongst

Elves. A silver circlet, with a moonstone in the middle held his hair away from his face and allowed his pointed ears to show.

"Most assuredly," he said. "But do not overtax yourself at first. There is much to see and do here in Faerie and many of our human guests try to see too much at one time. Conserve your strength, for time is not the same as in the World Above and there is all the time that you need."

"I'll see to it that he does not overdo," said Pyewacket.

"I really cannot thank you enough," Aurelius said. "It is completely astonishing! I cannot imagine a doctor at home doing such a thing."

"Many of your Wizard Healers know nearly as much as do we Elves, but we are a very old race and have ancient knowledge not as yet known to humans," said Galen. "but, from what I have been told, your home had no Wizard Healers by the time you were stricken."

Aurelius nodded in agreement and then suddenly thought of young Lovel and asked "I have a young friend who has lost his memory. He was injured in a fall from some rocks at the shore. Could you help him?"

Galen pursed his lips and looked thoughtful . At last he said "I doubt that I can. The Elfin and the human body are much the same, save for the fact that we are immortal and age much more slowly. But our minds; there is a great difference between our minds and the human. The human brain is a very delicate mechanism. Elves do not suffer from mental illnesses, not unless they are part human, which, although a rare occurrence, does happen. Witness Robin! I would likely do more evil than good, were I to attempt to meddle with a human brain, particularly one so grievously injured."

Aurelius was disappointed, as much as for the sake of his own curiosity as for Lovel's well-being and cure.

Galen left shortly after, advising Aurelius as to exercise and again, not to over-use his newly healed limbs.

It was a wonder to Aurelius, to be able to dress by himself and walk about the room. Even his hands, he noted, were improved, as he easily tied his cravat. Someone had cleaned and returned his clothing while he was sleeping and it looked better than it had in a great while, almost new.

"A friend of yours has no memory?" Pyewacket inquired while watching Aurelius dress. "That must be tragic. I cannot imagine losing all my memories!"

"Yes, it distresses him a great deal. He is a young Gypsy, but very well-educated. Indeed, he knows Latin and Greek and many a modern language as well. He cannot remember how or why he was so well-taught. We, David and I, suspect that he was educated to be a teacher. I have no idea, nor does Lovel, why he has not been practicing his profession but I suspect he fell in love and succumbed to the freedom that Gypsies prize so much. He is not long married. His wife is a pretty little thing, I suppose, but she is almost certainly unlettered."

"My Wizard is a scholar as well," said Pyewacket. "He took a double first at Oxford in classics and Wizardry. He is *Magus Magistra*." he added proudly

Aurelius turned to smile at him. "I'm a Cambridge Fellow. You cannot expect me to be impressed by a degree from Oxford!" He shrugged himself into his coat as he spoke, marveling at the ease of doing so. It was if he had shed twenty years. No aches or pains and his body obeyed him immediately, not protesting as it had for the last few years.

And now he had a new world to explore. Robin Goodfellow, who he had met earlier, had promised that he might talk to anyone here he chose to, including the Faerie lore-masters; even take notes for a new book! A new book on Faerie lore, straight from the primary source! It was enough to make a scholar faint from joy.

Father Maël had never been comfortable on horseback. In his youth he had ridden the massive Breton draught horses on the family farm, horses of stolid temperament and which did not move much faster than a jog trot, being bred for the plough and the farm wagon. The army horses were lighter, with more speed and less inclined to be so even-tempered. They seemed to know he was a poor rider and even appeared to be of an argumentative nature, wanting their own way.

Nevertheless, Maël requisitioned a horse and rode out in

the direction of the magic he had felt.

This ability to feel magic, this Sniffing it out, Maël considered a gift from God, to help him in the fight against Satan and his followers, the accursed Witches and Wizards. Maël felt that he was blessed above other men to be able to know with certainty when magic was being used and from whence it emanated. It had enabled him to catch practitioners of the evil art and bring them to justice, even those of the pettiest of magics.

All magic, of course, was evil and even sending an old crone who sold love spells to credulous young girls was a triumph, but Maël had always hoped to catch a major magus, to test his skills and the authority of the Church against the blackest of necromancers. Such a mage would be a worthy foe. But he would go down in defeat, as Maël had no doubts about his own skills, nor of the church's authority.

He had taken the precaution of bringing a small folding map of the island and a compass with him. Several times during the ride he stopped the horse and dismounted, tying the animal well, for he showed a distressing tendency to wish to return to his stable.

That 'tingle' pointed him the right direction, to the southwest. According to the map there was a relatively large town, Pleinmont, near the southwestern tip of the island and then a series of bays going up the coast: Rocquaine, Perelle, Vazon, and between Rocquaine and Perelle Bays was a tiny island, Lithou, which was uninhabited. Maël drew in a breath as he saw the name *Le Creux ès Faies* etched on a promontory that jutted out into the ocean. The Faerie Hollow!

Maël did not believe in Faeries. Such were manifestations of superstition, things conjured by Wizards to keep the peasants in fear and awe. Such names were given to the collections of standing stones and caves where Wizards and Witches practiced their unhallowed rites and conducted their naked orgies where Satan was worshipped. The names served to keep the curious away.

But a mage would be attracted to a place where so much evil had been committed and draw upon the vibrations of evil so as to be able to do an extraordinary feat such as free another mage from a cell protected by Cold Iron.

As Maël put away his map and compass and mounted his

horse he thought again of how no trace had been found of how the magus Bretton had disappeared from his cell. The chains hung upon the wall, undamaged, as if they had been but unlocked. Nothing had been disturbed. Only the blanket from the cot was missing and on the dust of the floor were only the tiny prints of rats' paws, nothing of human or cat feet. It was inexplicable how he had escaped and few things had ever made Maël so angry.

He ws going to look like a fool. He had written a letter to both the head of his order and to his Holiness in Rome, telling them of the powerful Wizard he had in his custody and how the magus would soon burn in the Holy fires of an *auto de fé*.

Perhaps he would find both of them here! Perhaps he could retake the prisoner and capture the new mage as well. He was armed with his rosary, crucifix and Holy Water and his knowledge of how to combat the Black Arts, as well as a bar of Cold Iron.

His excitement grew as he drew nearer to the location of the Faerie's Hollow. He put the horse to the gallop, the prickling of his thumbs and limbs growing stronger. When he at last reached the spot his entire body was like a human weathervane, pointing the way by reason of a quivering tremor in his very bones.

Maël tied up the horse and went to trace the magic from its source.

His quest led him down to the edge of the sea, which puzzled him. The magic seemed to have come up out of the ocean. What type of creature could that be? Merpeople could not leave the sea and walk upon land and compared to a human mage they had little magic. Selchies were only magical in that they could obscenely shift between human and animal form, lasciviously naked when clad in human skin.

But there was magic here, definite magic, powerful magic! Maël followed it, its trail as clear to him as if he had been following a readily marked path. His exhilaration mounted as he climbed the knoll, for the tingle was almost painful. He had never felt anything like it, or even approaching it.

He saw the sign announcing the Faerie Hollow and quickened his steps. Any moment now, he thought, any moment...

Only to be brought up short against a blank wall.

His rage and disappointment were one. He could not believe that there could be nothing there! There had to be a way through, a way around!

Maël searched minutely, even crawling on the ground to peer at every crack in the rock face. He stood upon tiptoe, reaching up with his fingertips to feel above him, searching for something. The feeling of the magic was still strong, but where was it coming from?

After going over and over the gray green rock he had to admit defeat. He had even climbed up on top of the cap stones that marked the top, placed,there, no doubt, by the devil himself. But he could not find a way in or behind it either.

Angered beyond anything he had ever known even that he had experienced at this morning's disappearance, he backed away from the Faerie's Hollow and then felt another tingle, a smaller one, an infinitesimal trace of magic.

He followed this one, climbing a rock face, some what hampered by the skirts of his cassock.

And he found the source. Halfway up the rock face was a spring, hidden by ferns, but with a small statue of a male figure with horns upon its brow. A horn cup, hidden in a crevice, was carved with strange letters. From his studies, Maël knew that these were runes. He could not read them, for the Inquisition forbade the reading of runes, believing that runes were so evil that the mere reading of them would instantly pollute anyone who could understand their message.

Maël could not find the magus, but this filthy example of paganism he could and would do something about.

With an almost savage glee he pulled the heathen statue from its resting place and threw it upon the ground, not wanting to touch it any longer than necessary. Grasping the cross he wore about his neck with one hand, he took a rock in the other and, as he muttered a prayer, smashed the statue to pieces with unnecessary ferocity. He trod the cup underfoot as well, grinding it under his heel. He even considered filling the pool with rocks and dirt, but stopped short of doing that. Innocent animals, God's creatures, might drink at this pool and might die of thirst did he destroy their water supply.

When he at last stamped away in the direction of his

horse he left only bits and pieces of stone and horn upon the ground. Nothing was left to tell what they had been.

He had been gone perhaps ten minutes when a strange little breeze sprang up and caressed the litter on the ground. The bits of stone and horn quivered, shaking and rocking as if there were an earthquake. Suddenly they all flew into the air, separating horn from rock. The two materials spun about in two small, distinct whirlwinds. Moments later, where there had been but debris, there once again stood, in their proper places, a rune-carved horn cup and a small statue of the Horned God as they had stood as guardians of the spring for over one thousand years. It was as if they had never been damaged at all.

40
In the Ruins

Fournier had never had such a frustrating day. The entire island had been searched, thoroughly, and there was no sign of the escaped prisoner. It was almost as if he had never existed. There was, as well, no sign of his books. Those forbidden volumes had completely vanished.

On arriving back at St. Peter Port Fournier had to endure another raking down by Father Maël, who was in a vicious temper. Even Narcisse Roux had cornered Fournier and complained of his lack of diligence in returning the prisoner to him for questioning. The torturer was frustrated. First his instruments were at the bottom of the harbor, then there had been little but old men to torture and now, when a real mage was in his grasp, the man had been spirited away. In Rome Roux had imagined a full dungeon from this island of heretics and hours and hours of delightful abuse of prisoners, their screams ringing in his ears.

The Colonel had a further source of frustration. His last stop had been in the parish of St Martin and in the churchyard of St, Martin *de la Belleuse* where, to his dismay, he found that the primitive, ugly statue of the ancient female called *La Gran'mère du Chimquière* still stood. It had been ordered destroyed ages ago.

After the day he had endured it had been a great pleasure for Fournier to take the parish commander, Lieutenant Bastien Duval, to task over his negligence.

"But, *mon colonel*," that hapless young man had stammered. "Every day I send out men with pick axes, with chisels, and they destroy it! And every morning there it is again!"

"Nonsense!" snapped Fournier. "Do not try my patience, Duval! Such a thing is not possible! You have not indicated this in your reports!"

The Lieutenant flushed. "I had thought it best not to write a report of the destruction of this pagan object until it was actually destroyed, sir," he admitted.

"Have a priest oversee the destruction," Fournier commanded. "Holy water must be sprinkled on the stones and no doubt a priest will know other tricks." He turned a hard eye on the lieutenant. "If you cannot effect the simple removal of a statue, Duval, you will make me wonder if you are fit for this command I entrusted to you!"

With a sudden deep suspicion Fournier and his troops all then circled back to Castel, to the church of St. Marie du Castro and found that the statue there had yet to be destroyed as well. Lt. Martel had the same excuse as Duval. Fournier was beside himself. Was no one competent?

Maël had been incensed about that as well. On his ride out to the coast he had noticed menhirs and dolmans as well as what was known as a cromlech: a circle, cut in the turf, raised with a ditch about it, and circled by a ring of white stones. These were all relics of a pagan past and must be razed. Fournier was not performing his mandate. These remains of the past should be long gone. The second French occupation had been on Guernsey near a month. How long did it take to remove some stones?

Maël's temper had been exacerbated by the fact that he was saddle sore and had parted company from his horse on the way back from the southwest coast. It had taken time to catch the reluctant horse and remount. To have the vexations of the mage's escape, the magical trail ending so abruptly, and then to have Fournier fail in his duty; both to find the escaped prisoner and not to have succeeded in ridding them of these heathen barrows and monuments – Maël's heart was pounding so hard that he could hear it beating in his ears and he shook with rage.

After a screaming argument with Fournier, who was just as frustrated and enraged, Maël went to the room in the castle that had been made into a chapel. There he genuflected to the altar and knelt before it, bowing his head in prayer with his hands covering his face. Slowly he felt himself calming, his heart beat and breathing easing.

He prayed for guidance. It had occurred to him that God was testing him by throwing all of theses difficulties in his path. Why, he could not understand. He was doing God's work and doing it well. He was cleansing the earth of magic and of paganism.Surely God would smile upon this, not put up obstacles in the way?

His entire life had been dedicated to the lofty goals of the Inquisition. He had been true to the vows he had sworn, those of poverty, chastity and obedience. He had never sought rank or glory. Why now was he being punished?

Maël remained in front of the altar a long time.

Fournier had an earthier approach to containing and abating his rage. He sent Girard out to find him a whore, one of those who still plied her trade along the waterfront. He also requisitioned several bottles of brandy and, after a strenuous workout with the woman, in which she was bruised rather badly, he became extremely drunk.

Earlier in the afternoon two seals, heads just above the surface of a choppy sea, had watched the priest search for the entrance to the Faeries' Hollow.

"What is he looking for?" Elspeth asked Grizel in Animal Speech.

"He's a Witch-Sniffer, a priest. He wants to find your Wizard friend and his dragon. He can smell the magic," Grizel explained. "He's an extreme danger to both of them."

"Why don't we shape-shift and when he sees two naked women, panting to mate with him, we can entice him into the water and drown him!" Elspeth suggested.

"Elspeth!" said Grizel, shocked. "It's not our way to drown humans, even evil ones. And besides priests are sworn to celibacy. Most of the priests of the Inquisition have wills of iron and would not be tempted by us."

"Celibacy?" said Elspeth in disbelief. "You mean they don't mate, ever?"

Grizel nodded, her eyes fixed on the priest as he clambered over the rock.

"I'll tell you what," Elspeth said, "that's why they are so evil. Going without mating is not good. It makes males want to fight and females ache. If I don't mate at least once a day I feel like fighting myself. I get so irritable. Mating four or five times a day is even better!"

"Elspeth," said Grizel dryly "ever since I've known you it's been closer to ten or twelve times a day for you!"

Elspeth giggled. "Hamish has a friend, Grizel. He's a huge bull and very virile. I could introduce you. Have you mated at all since the last time you saw your human?"

"No," said Grizel shortly. "And I don't want to meet any bulls, thank you very much."

"That's not healthy. We Selchies are not made like that."

"I'm willing to wait until I can be with David," Grizel stated. "And don't forget, Elspeth, I'm only half a Selchie. I'm not like you."

"But you used to mate with anyone who offered!" Elspeth protested.

"It's different now," Grizel interrupted her. She wanted to leave this subject behind, for her own feelings were inexplicable to her and she could not begin to explain them to Elspeth. Accordingly she said "We'd best be quiet. He'll hear us."

Elspeth, grumbling almost inaudibly, nevertheless subsided.

Grizel wondered at herself. Why was it different now? Why did she prefer to wait until she could lie with David? Why was it so much better with him than with any one else, even though she had to remain in human form when they were together?

When her seal nature had first manifested itself, when she had become an adolescent, the freedom of the sea and the Selchie life had intoxicated her. She had sent most of her time in the sea and the first male who had approached her had not been turned away. She had reveled in the experience and wanted to repeat it, often. She had been almost as eager as Elspeth for mating.

From the very first time she had met David on the cliffs above Fermain Bay she had thought of coupling with him.

And seducing him had not lessened the desire she felt for him. The more times they were together the more she thought about him. She had thought that a few sessions of lovemaking would cure her of the strong attraction she felt. Even now she could hardly wait to see him again. Why? She had never felt like this about a male before.They were momentary partners, satisfying a transient desire.

But she wanted to be with David, even when they were not making love. She worried about him and wondered what he was doing when they were apart from one another. She could not explain these feelings in the least. The thought of being with anyone else, even a virile bull, was distasteful, when but a few weeks ago she would have been glad to meet and mate with a Selchie such as that.

"He's leaving," said Elspeth,"Let's go!" She was eager to show her friend the dragon.

Grizel put out a restraining flipper. "No, wait, we must be certain that he is gone. We cannot take a chance of him seeing us change. He might have weapons that could ensnare us. And as much as even you like mating, Elspeth, I cannot think that you would like being raped by the Inquisition after torture"

Sound carried out over the water and the two Selchies heard Maël scramble up the rock face and a little later, make an inordinate amount of noise.

"Whatever is he doing?" Elspeth exclaimed when the pounding and breaking noises came to them.

Grizel did not know either but she recognized, a little while later, the sound of a horse's iron-shod hooves clattering away. To be on the safe side, she made Elspeth wait ten more minutes before they swam to the shore, changed, and walked up the hill to the Faerie Hollow.

Elspeth had been as good as her word. She had plundered a shipwreck and found, in a galley, several cooper pots,a teakettle, a tea-pot, utensils and plates and cups. She had brought more fish as well and Richard was able to make a semblance of fish stew in one of the copper kettles. It would have been vastly improved by vegetables and herbs but at least it was nourishing and would keep them full and help Pascoe heal.

Pascoe had passed a somewhat restless night. He had complained of some pain and Richard had spread more of the numbing salve around the broken bone.

Richard was worried. He wished that Pascoe could somehow see a draconic veterinarian who was also a Wizard or at the very least a Wizard Healer. Even someone who was used only to mending broken human bones would be better than nothing.

Pascoe, with his keen hearing, had heard someone scrabbling about outside the cave. Richard had arranged a signal with Elspeth, in order that he might open the enchanted door and let her in, but this was not it. It sounded as if someone was trying to force a way in.

In spite of the fact that there was very little likelihood of anyone hearing them Richard and Pascoe sat quietly. Richard, worried about the Inquisition, did not dare send out a seeking to identify who or what was at their front door.

Finally Pascoe said, "Whoever he is, he's gone." They both relaxed.

Half an hour later by Richard's watch, Elspeth's signal came at the wall.

With his wand, Richard opened the door into the cavern and admitted not one but two beautiful naked young women.

"This is my friend Grizel Sarchet," said Elspeth. "She's the one I told you about, the one who's mating with a human. Grizel, this is Richard and his dragon Pascoe. I've offered, but Richard doesn't want to mate with me."

"That's more information than is necessary, Elspeth," said Grizel. "I apologize for my friend and my state of undress," she said to Richard. "When I am going to spend most of the day in the sea or in Faerie I don't bother taking a gown with me. I hope you are not offended. I am half human and understand how humans feel about nudity. And Elspeth thinks about little beside mating," she said with a look at her friend.

"That's because mating is the best thing there is!" said Elspeth cheerfully. "If I could mate all day and all night I would! But the males get tired before I do!"

379

"I'm not offended at all," said Richard, smiling at Elspeth's eagerness. "At my age, my dear, and having spent much time with both Faeries and the Sea-Folk, I am not easily shocked. May I offer you ladies some seaweed tea?"

Grizel accepted graciously. Elspeth took her hand and, tugging at her, said "Come and meet the dragon. He's perfectly lovely!"

Grizel, like her friend, had never seen a dragon this close. No dragons had actually lived on Guernsey. They were only seen flying over or at the Dragon Port.

He was beautiful close up. Even in the mage lights in the cave his scales were tipped with shining copper. He was also friendly, even given that he was hurting. Grizel could see it in his eyes.

"I know of an Elfin Healer," she said impulsively, turning to Richard. "I could go to Faerie and ask him if he would see to Pascoe."

"An Elfin Healer!" said Pascoe in delight. "Richard, an Elfin Healer could have me flying in a week!"

"I had hoped that this would prove an entrance to Faerie," said Richard, pouring seaweed tea into three mugs and a basin for Pascoe. It was not the tastiest of drinks but it was hot and contained many healthful minerals from the sea.

Grizel took a mug from Richard with a murmured thank you. "It became far too well known that this was a gathering place for the Faerie Host of Guernsey and many people came to spy upon them in their dances and revels. The door was closed when my grandfather was a boy. I recall my father telling me abut it." She took a sip of her tea and said "Did you know that a priest was sniffing about your door a little while ago?"

Richard and Pascoe exchanged glances. "We knew someone was out there," Richard said. "but not that it was a priest."

"And one of the Inquisition, no less," said Grizel. "He wore their symbol. I've seen it too many time in St. Peter Port to mistake that black cross on a bed of flames for aught else."

"Grizel lives a good deal with humans," said Elspeth. "I couldn't do that."

"They don't mate often enough for your taste," Grizel

finished for her. Elspeth's single mindedness sometimes annoyed her. There was more to life than sensual pleasure.

"I also don't like wearing clothing. It's stupid," said Elspeth. "I only end in taking it on and off and on and off to mate or to go into the sea. It's a waste of time!" She giggled again. "I'll tell you what. I'm going to Prince Madoc's palace this afternoon," she told Richard "and I will tell him you are here." With Grizel's eye on her Elspeth forbore to mention that she was going there for a romantic *rendezvous* with two Selchies who served the Sea Prince.

"Madoc can get word back to Greymalkin in Devon," said Pascoe. "He must be worried sick about us!"

"And I will go and see the Elfin Healer. Perhaps I can even arrange to open this door into Faerie," said Grizel.

Blériot did not let Felix and David leave until after seven o'clock that night.

David had finished all the tax records he had brought with him by six and had eaten the last crumbs of the food. He was aware of the time going past. They were engaged to dine with Robin in Faerie that evening. David longed to see Grizel, for she would be there and he hoped to spend several hours with her in their bed of moss after dinner.

Last night he had dreamed of her. She was with him at the old farm in Torteval parish. The dream had not been erotic: she was in the kitchen with his mother, walking the land with him, and at the end, telling him that she was with child and that he would soon be a father.

When he awoke he wondered how his mother would feel about a grandchild who was one-quarter seal, or a daughter-in-law who had no self-consciousness about being naked in front of a large group of people and spent more than half her time in the sea in the form of a seal.

It could never work. Not only were they too different and could not live in each other's world, but David suddenly realized that he could never take away her freedom. All he could do was to enjoy the relationship while it lasted, for it was said that Selchies were notoriously fickle and seldom stayed true to one mate. That was the way it had to be, no matter how much heartache he would have to suffer later.

When Lovel came at last he looked as if he had the devil of a headache and Blériot's shrill voice followed him as he came into the room where David waited.

"Tomorrow I want those machines up and running! The men are very slow and stupid and it is up to you, *Gitan*, to make certain that they do not make any errors! You'd best be here on time tomorrow. Six AM sharp!"

"I'm ready to go," David said quickly, picking up the food bag.

Felix took the bundle of tax records. "I was ready to go hours ago," he said shortly.

They were quiet until they had gone through the gate, the guards checking their papers yet again.

When they had left the old Dragon Port behind, Felix, with a frown between his brows, said "Whatever they are paying me it is not enough. I don't think that there is that much money in all the world!"

David laughed sourly. "You will probably be paid what I have been paid since the first French occupation: nothing! We are a conquered people. We are fortunate to be allowed to live. It is too bad for us if we expect pay for what they want us to do."

"But you are the Bailiff of Guernsey!" said Felix, sounding surprised.

"I became the Bailiff by a sort of process of elimination. I was but a junior *Douizaine* in my home parish of Torteval and that only because my father had died unexpectedly and, as were facing invasion by the French for the first time. I was asked to serve in his place until another could be appointed," David explained. "One by one officials in higher positions than mine left the Island or were conscripted into the French army. Some were shot by the French. In the end I was the only one left as I was too crippled to be taken into the army. So I am the Bailiff by default."

"So all the money we will have coming in," said Felix almost to himself, "is what Rosal can earn at the farm. And *Madame* is woefully short of cash,"

David understood this all too well thinking of his own shrinking coffers. They had a tenant at the Torteval farm who could not pay the rent as he had no market for his parsnips and other vegetables. The French paid but little when they bothered to pay at all, far below what the *Guernaise* would have received for the same goods shipped to the Six Nations where Guernsey parsnips were much favored. He and Majorlaine had been forced to dip into their capital, for there were no returns coming in from the investments his father had made in the Six Nations. Interest was accruing but they had no way to tap into it. Money was tight and a constant source of worry.

Each lost in his own thoughts, they spoke but little on the way back to the Professor's, having to hurry in order to beat the curfew.

They smelled the smoke before they saw it.

Thierry snorted and threw up his head and David said "What the devil? Have they been burning the hay ricks again?" This was a favorite pastime of the French patrols.

As Thierry trotted around a corner, still snorting, it suddenly came into view: a smoldering, smoking ruin where once the cottage of *Trois Chiminées* had stood!

Felix gave an inarticulate cry and jumped from the cabriolet before David could even pull up.

"Good God!" said David blankly and halted the cabriolet. Thank God the Professor was safe in Faerie! But where was John? And what had happened here?

Stiffly, he took his cane after wrapping the reins around the whip socket, climbed awkwardly from the carriage.

Felix was looking at the ruins. "It looks like nothing is left. I hope that Grant got out in time!"

"They'll know at the farm; we'll go there. Come on." David urged.

"Look!" Felix pointed to where a sudden glint shone amidst the ashes and debris, amazing in the dim light of evening. He picked his way through the rubble and bent over, a few moments later emerging with a brass bond box, completely undamaged by the fire. "What's this?"

David recognized it at once. "That was a gift from my father. It's been magiced against fire and theft and any kind of damage. It was to keep the Professor's few bits and pieces in, some miniatures and the antiquities they found. Good job finding it. I'm certain that the Professor will be glad to have those things."

The strangest feeling ran over Felix, as if the box was calling to him. He put his fingers on the ornate, chased lock and a violet light flared and the box flew open.

"What did you do?" David demanded.

"I don't know," Felix said, bemused. He looked down into the box and saw a heavy necklace-like object. It was as if someone had melted and curved a solid gold ingot. He took it in his hand and held it up so that David could see it. Even in the deepening dusk and the faint light of the stars it shone with an unearthly glow.

"What is that?" David asked, amazed. He had never seen this before and had thought he was familiar with every piece his father and the Professor had excavated.

"It's a torque, a torque of power," Felix answered.

And how he knew that he could not even begin to guess.

41
On the
Home Front

When by Sunday noon-time Richard and Pascoe failed to return from their trip to Portsmouth, Greymalkin began to grow worried. He had not been too concerned when they had not come back Saturday night as the Admiral was an old friend and they might have got to talking and reminiscing and failed to notice the passage of time.

But by Sunday evening, when there was no sign of them Greymalkin was worried enough to scry Portsmouth. When the Admiral's secretary reported that Richard and Pascoe had departed for home Saturday afternoon, the familiar grew frantic. He scryed Portsmouth again and spoke personally to the Admiral,who was equally concerned and promised to send up two courier dragons and their riders to search the area.

Greymalkin also talked Pearson into going down to the dock and blowing the Triton shell horn for Madoc. The valet was also growing perturbed and it did not take much persuasion on the cat's part.

Madoc was at once anxious and promised to search for them as well. The weather had been excellent lately with not even a heavy fog rolling into the Channel. It had been ideal flying weather with no thunderstorms. There was not much that could bring down an adult dragon. Even the guns of a French frigate lacked the range to reach a dragon. And the Channel Fleet of the Six Nations was doing an admirable job of keeping French ships away from the shores of England.

Before Madoc swam away to notify the Sea-Folk that Richard and his dragon were missing he looked at Greymalkin and the valet with a frown on his face. "I don't like this at all," he said. "First Felix disappears, then Richard and Pascoe are forced to battle a genie and now they have gone missing as well. It seems deliberate to me. They have an enemy."

"Reginald!" said Greymalkin bitterly. "Pascoe and I have discussed this!"

"But surely Mr, Reginald would never –" began Pearson, shocked.

Greymalkin turned on him abruptly and hissed "Do you know the full extent of Reginald's debts, Pearson? I do ! Ask Mr. Gilchrist, the steward! If Reginald keeps on at this rate the estate will be grossly encumbered! Richard is a wealthy man but even so this extravagant expenditure cannot go on forever. And Reginald thinks himself entitled to every penny! What better way to ensure he continues to be able to waste the ready than by making himself the Earl of Belmaray? It is my belief that they caused Felix's and Pyewacket's disappearance. Reginald was no doubt hoping that if Felix were gone he would be made heir and given a much larger share of the Belmaray fortune! Now they've decided to rid themselves of Richard as well! Reginald is no doubt hoping that the Inquisition will take care of Felix for him!" Greymalkin came to an abrupt halt. his gray fur was standing on end, his tail twice its normal size and his ears were flat against his head, his eyes almost shooting sparks.

"I think you've the right of it, Greymalkin," the Sea Prince said. He was riding the surface of the water, and leaning on the dock. His grim look deepened. "I am certain when we do find Richard and Pascoe that some magic will have been involved. But how can we stop this? I am confined to the sea and can do little against magic on land."

"And I haven't any magic at all," said Pearson sadly.

"Neither have I," said Greymalkin. "Which is why I am going to go and see Suzy Chafee"

"Suzy Chafee?" repeated Pearson blankly. "The barmaid at the Green Man?" His tone seems to say "what good could she do?"

"She's also a Witch, Pearson. The Druids are too far away up on Hayne Down at Bowerman's Nose. Without Pascoe I could not get there in a timely fashion. They would help, but if this is deliberate, that Persian will be watching us. I can have no excuse, nor can anyone for calling the carriage to go to Manaton and from there to Hayne Down. But it is well known that I have an – err – amatory connection to the cat at the Green Man, Jenny, who also happens to be Suzy's familiar. Jenny just had a litter of kittens and I'm their father. What could be more natural than me going to visit them?" Greymalkin said. "The only other Wizard in the area is Mr. Harbottle in Torbay and he is well over one hundred years old and only *Magus Majori,* at any rate. But Suzy can convene the Coven with thirteen Witches in the Circle and who knows how many more? They should be a match for any Persian sorcerer!"

Far out to sea, in a deep trench, lay the blue Djinn. He had dragged himself there when, still burning with dragon fire, he had fallen into the sea. Like a wounded animal, he had wanted to crawl away and hide.

The water was colder in the trench, more soothing to his injuries and save for some curious fish, he was left alone. The Sea-Folk did not come here often as it was a barren place, almost void of life.

The Djinn, being a creature of magic, knew enough to shut down all of his facilities, to barely exist in order to use all his energies to heal. He was vaguely aware of being called by his new master but there was little he could do about it. Healing was all he could concentrate upon. He could breathe underwater as easily as he could breathe air and he needed nothing else in the way of nourishment. No creature who remained shut in a lamp or a bottle for centuries needed food or drink. Air and air alone sustained him, as Djinns were born of the desert wind. He would have preferred a hot, dry wind to the sea but it was perhaps better this way. The cold water was more soothing to the type of injury he had sustained.

Slowly he healed, floating at the bottom of the deep trench. He neither thought nor cursed the persons who had done this to him. He merely existed as, very slowly, the dragon fire went out and his non-human body, made of wind and spirit and magic, began to restore itself.

Finally he began to be aware of his surroundings, stirring sluggishly at first, slipping back into his state of suspended animation again and again.

But each period of consciousness lasted longer and longer. It was still comfortable and desirable to return to his peaceful rest where his body could recover and improve. Each time he woke, he felt his strength returning until one morning he awoke and realized that he was cured. He was fully set to rights.

And the next morning, when his Master called again he answered the call. "I hear and obey, O my Master!" he said, and shot up from the trench into the air at tremendous speed.

The Green Man did not open for business until eleven in the morning when the first customers of the day would arrive for the 'shepherd's nuncheon' consisting of thick slices of bread, with melted cheese with a pickle and, if they were fortunate, one of the landlord's famous apple tarts, covered in clotted cream for a dessert, all washed down with 'scrumpy' or farm cider, made from windfall apples.

Customers who had more blunt to lay out could chose a grilled chop with tomatoes, a thick wedge of steak and kidney pie, soup, or a bountiful stew served with fresh bread.

Of course, all of this bounty required preparation so Greymalkin was certain that Suzy, and by extension, Jenny, would be at the inn already, for Suzy's duties were in the kitchen as well as at the bar later in the day.

It was a little over two miles to the village of Belmaray from the Great House and Greymalkin shortened this distance by going cross country at a ground-eating lope. He had made certain to tell the head groom, Bob Oakes, that he was going to visit Jenny and the kittens in case anyone, meaning certain Persian magicians, noted his absence. If Bob thought it a little odd that the Earl's familiar should be taking off when the Earl was seriously overdue from his trip, he said naught about it.

It seemed odd to go by the dragon pen, close by the stables, and not to see Pascoe there, but Greymalkin tried not to think about it. His imagination was overactive as it was and yester eve he had dreamt of all sorts of horrors as to what had happened to Richard and Pascoe.

The village lay in a deep, steep combe, lush with vegetation now, at nearly Midsummer's day. The steep streets were cobbled and the white-washed house and shops were of softly rounded cob with thatched roofs and old, mullioned windows, open on a fine day to a breeze from the not too distant sea. There were flowers everywhere. Almost every building had flower boxes and over it all hung and air of happy prosperity. Richard was an excellent landlord. Most of the buildings in Belmaray village belonged to the estate and most of the tenants were well-pleased and it showed in their care of the properties.

The inn, the Green Man, lay halfway up a steep hill, and featured a carved and painted sign of a rather ferocious green male face, with foliage of oak leaves emerging from head, beard and mustache. The Green Man, sometimes known as Jack i' the Green, or Green George, was an ancient symbol, found carved in many churches and cathedrals, particularly those poised on a ley line or near a Holy Well. He was sometimes identified with the Horned God or with Herne the Hunter but animals knew him to be the spirit of the woodlands and so they taught their Witches and Wizards. Any place in which his image appeared was under his protection.

The Inn was not yet open since the village clock had not as yet struck nine, but already the kitchen was busy and redolent of good smells. Greymalkin sniffed appreciatively as he went around to the back and slipped in the door which stood open to let some of the cooking heat out into the cooler air.

Greymalkin was greeted by name by most of the inn staff. When he inquired after Jenny he was told that she and the kittens were in the tap. He went there at once, for even though he had business with Suzy Jenny would never forgive him if he were to not visit her and his offspring first.

The Inn was quite old, with low ceilings and dark beams, made that way by centuries of smoke from the fireplace and pipes being smoked. Heavy furniture, good sturdy tables and settles by the big, walk-in hearth, provided an inviting room for customers. Rows of gleaming pewter mugs hung behind the shining bar and copper vessels, filled with wildflowers stood on a spacious mantle-piece. Above the mantle was another, ancient carving of the Green Man. The flowers in season, were an offering to him. At this time of day the tap was scrubbed clean and quiet.

Jenny lay in a basket on the hearth, nursing the four kittens, who were now a little over three weeks of age. Unlike a non-familiar cat, familiars tended to have smaller litters and also were far more choosy about a mate. They could also ask their Witches and Wizards for contraceptive spells to prevent too much breeding.

Jenny looked up as Greymalkin approached. She had been purring as she fed the kittens but she left off and said "Grey, I think I've placed three of them already! There's been a steady stream of young Witches and Wizards coming from as far away as Plymouth and Exeter! Three of them seem to have made their choice."

"Our kittens are special!" said Greymalkin in satisfaction. All would be familiars. He came closer and looked down on them with pride.

There were two boys and two girls. One of the little males was black and white, one gray like Greymalkin himself, while one of the girls was a brown tabby like Jenny and the littlest, a girl, was another gray tabby.

One by one the kittens finished nursing and made for their father. At this age they were beginning to play with each other and their mother and even play fighting with one another. Their eyes had been open since they were ten days old and in two more weeks their senses of sight, hearing, taste, smell and touch would be fully developed. By twelve weeks old they would have all the grace and agility of an adult cat. But they would continue to grow and develop for nearly a year. At eight weeks they would go to their new young Witch or Wizard and would learn to speak human language, and read, within a short time, and become useful to their magical partner.

Right now they were endearing little balls of fluff with squeaky mews for voices. They had only just mastered walking and their tails, large in proportion to the rest of their bodies, were stiffly erect to help with balance. Their paw placement was still deliberate, even a bit awkward, but they were eager to explore.

Indulgently, Greymalkin let them crawl under and around him, even licking the milk off their chins. They would get plenty of attention here in the inn. Jenny kept them here in the tap so that people would pick them up and pet and socialize them. Unless a person was a dyed-in-the-wool cat-hater or a curmudgeon, not picking up and cuddling the irresistible kittens was nearly impossible.

After giving his full attention to his progeny for a few moments Greymalkin at last said "Jenny, I need to speak to Suzy privately. It's rather important. Is there a meeting of the Coven soon?"

Of course," said Jenny looking surprised. "The moon is but one day past full and we are nigh onto Midsummer day. Almost every night there will be a ceremony for drawing down moon power for the crops." In her voice was surprise and a little rebuke. Greymalkin ought to know this as well as did she.

"I should have remembered that," he said ruefully as a kitten tried to get up on his back and fell backwards with a squeal. "I've been rather preoccupied lately and not giving enough attention to the calendar." By this he meant the lunar calendar.

Jenny nodded, for he had told her of everything that had happened from Felix and Pyewacket's disappearance to the blue Djinn that had threatened them. "Has this something to do with your Wizard's going missing?" she asked. "Although I don't know how something as big as a dragon can go missing!"

Greymalkin looked startled. "You know about that?"

"Everybody in the village knows about it," she said a little dryly. "People here think a lot of your Richard and of Felix too and they've been much upset since all these troubles began. Nobody wants Reginald to be the new Earl." She stood up and stretched. "If you will look after the kittens I shall go and fetch Suzy from the kitchen. You can be as private as you like in here until the customers start coming."

Greymalkin stretched his length out on the floor and allowed the kittens to jump on him, which they did with enthusiasm.

In a few moments Jenny was back with Suzy, her Witch.

Suzy was a buxom young woman of two and twenty, with brown hair curling in a natural riot all over her head. She had large hazel eyes and freckles across her nose. She had been baking, for she was rubbing her hands free of flour on a towel and her rolled up sleeves and apron were sprinkled with flour as well.

"What's this all about, then?" she asked, after greeting Greymalkin.

Jenny took over the kitten-minding while Pyewacket begin to explain what had happened and the conclusions he had reached.

Suzy's normally good-natured face darkened as he spoke. When he was done she said "So this bloody foreigner thinks he can come in here and bring his foreign magics with him, does he? And interfere with our family?" Like most of the villagers, Suzy thought of the Jourdaines as 'her' family. "Mayhap he's never come up against an English Witch, never mind an entire Coven of 'em! Never you mind, Greymalkin, we'll soon clip his wings for him! The rest of my Coven will be just as angry as I am! And I ain't afraid of Mr. Reginald. He's a damned poor excuse for a Wizard, if you was to ask me! We'll put them both to the right-about, we will!"

42
The Altar of the
Sheel-Na-Gig

Monday Evening, late

Reginald could not believe what Bahram was telling him.

"You did what? "he stammered, rising to his feet and swaying a little. He was forced to cling to the back of a chair. For once his imbalance was not from drink but from countless hours spent with the insatiable *houri*. She had worn him out, her appetite surpassing even his. Reginald's eyes were sunk deep in his head and his hands trembled like an old man's. He had finally had to ask Bahram to take her away, something that he had never thought could happen to him as, since his early youth, he had a voracious appetite for carnal pleasure. But he had finally met his match.

"I have eliminated the last obstacle to you becoming the lord of Belmaray," said Bahram smoothly. "Your grandfather will not be returning from his journey. By now he and the dragon are either dead or in the hands of the Inquisition. It is only a matter of time before the priests find your cousin as well and they will both die. You will inherit everything."

Reginald stared at him if he could not quite fathom what he was saying. "What, what did you do?" he said, horrified. He still retained enough grasp on morality to shrink, again, from murder.

Bahram looked at him in exasperation. "Do you want to be wealthy or not?" he demanded.

"Well, yes, but –" he gave a shudder. "Didn't think that we would have to kill everybody!" he burst out. "That's four murders!"

"Four?" Bahram queried, raising an eyebrow. "Did you commit some murders without me, Reynard?"

"Learned it in school. Dragons and familiars ain't considered animals since they can think and talk. It's like

393

killing a human being: a capital crime!" He gulped and put a hand up to his throat as if he could already feel the hangman's noose. "I'll swing!" he said hoarsely. "It's the Nubbing Cheat for me!"

"Nonsense!" said Bahram bracingly. "Who will ever know?"

"They found Felix, didn't they?" Reginald retorted with a flash of spirit.

"You need a drink." Bahram said. Normally he was against Reginald drinking but at the moment his dupe needed the false courage that imbibing would bring. The Persian walked to the drawing room table where the crystal decanters of liquor were kept and poured out a large dram of whiskey for Reginald. It was about all the liquor or wine left in the house.

"You should lose no time in claiming your birthright," said Bahram, handing him over the glass. "How does one go about these things in England?" In Persia, one made a public declaration and lost no time in killing one's rivals, a practice not frowned upon there as it was in this benighted country.

"Go and see old Jerningham. He's the family shyster," answered Reginald. "He's like to come to cuffs with me over this, though. He ain't never fancied me above half. Like as not he'll give me a rake-down and sconce the reckoning. Keep the money all tied up. Called me a perfect block once."

"I congratulate Mr. Jerningham on his perspicacity," said Bahram. He would be very glad to get rid of Reginald. As a conspirator and fellow criminal he left a lot to be desired.

"Your man-at-law will probably desire you to name an heir to your property," Bahram continued.

"Don't have to do that," Reginald said, looking longingly at the bottle Bahram had replaced on the table. He had downed the glass in one gulp. "Mean to say, all the property's entailed. Goes along with the title. Most of the money's entailed too, part of the property."

Bahram frowned. "What does this mean, entailed?"

Reginald licked his lips. "Ain't no lawyer, but think it means the estate is tied up so that it can't be broken up or any of it sold, right down to the paintings and gew-gaws in the house, even the jewelry. M' grandfather once bored me to flinders by yammering on about how the Earl is only a steward for those who come after him and how everything had to be kept all right and tight for people who ain't even born yet. Devilish lot of claptrap if you was to ask me. Of course my dear cuz, toad-eater that he was, agreed with all this hokum. Can't even sell a damned snuff box if I was to need the money, nor a foot of the lands."

Bahram looked thunderous. He had not expected this. "Even though you were the holder of the title you could not sell or dispose of, say, a valuable art work?"

Reginald shook his head. "Not unless I wanted to see the inside of a gaol cell," he said. "There's stiffish penalties for selling entailed goods. Devilish difficult to break an entail, too."

"But who will inherit all of this after you if you cannot leave it where you please?" Bahram demanded.

"M' cousin Babbington. Lives near Tunbridge Wells. Don't remember how we're connected, but he's in line for the title after me."

"But should he predecease you?" The Persian wanted to know.

"Oh, I've a lot more cousins," Reginald said.

"If there were none left? " Bahram persisted.

"Then everything would go to the Crown and there'd be no more Earldom," said Reginald. "There's a term for that, what is it?" He thought for a moment, wishing he had another drink to help the thinking process.

Bahram was considerably incensed. He had thought to become Reginald's heir. There were too many laws in this country, ridiculous, stupid laws that interfered with one's plans.

Reginald had been wistfully contemplating his empty glass and now glanced up to where French doors looked out over a garden, which was lit by permanent mage lights.

A what he saw there he goggled, his eyes growing large and he began to stammer. "Ali! L-l-look!" he pointed at the door, the glass falling on the carpet from suddenly nerveless fingers.

Bahram turned impatiently, wondering if Reginald was suffering from hallucinations after but a single glass of whisky.

But there, looking in, was a huge blue face, a large hand

raised to tap on the glass.

When he saw Bahram looking at him, the Djinn made an obeisance and said in his booming voice "I have come at last, O my master, and am ready to do your bidding. I regret to tell you that I failed in my last execution of your orders but I beg that you will let me fulfill your desires again. This time I will not fail, for I now know my enemy."

Reginald said weakly "That's your creature? What the hell is it?"

"A Djinn," said Bahram shortly. "A slave of the lamp."

"A lamp? Like Aladdin?" Reginald said. "Can anyone rub this lamp and get three wishes? Why don't we just ask it for mountains of the rhino and ready, heh?"

"Fool of an infidel!" said the Djinn in contempt, crossing his arms across chest. "Do you not know that there are many different types of Djinns with many different skills? I am a Djinn of pain and death! I do not grant *wishes*!" he added, saying the word wishes as if it were an obscenity. "There are but few treasure Djinns in all of the world, O stupid one!"

He then went on "My master, even now there is someone listening at the door, and on these ill-formed hills females attempt to raise magic. As if a woman could have much magic!" he added in scorn.

Bahram walked to the door of the drawing room and jerked it open abruptly. Swann, caught off balance with his ear to the door, fell forward in to the room.

Bahram grabbed his arm in a tight, painful grasp, jerking the butler to his feet. "Do you think to spy upon us?" he demanded.

With immense dignity Swann pulled away from him and straightened his waistcoat and smoothed his hair. "I was instructed by Mr Horrocks and his lordship to keep a weather eye upon you," he replied. "After all, it is his lordship who pays my wages."

"Well,if that don't beat the Dutch!" Reginald said, affronted. "I've a mind to darken your daylights for you!" He raised his clenched threateningly towards Swann's face. "When I'm master here you and Old Horrocks will be out on your rumps without a character! You're both in bad loaf with me!"

Swann gave him the sort of icy, almost pitying look only

the very best butlers could give to those they considered inferior. "You will never be master here," he said "It shall never be allowed."

"What do those women do out on the hills?" said Bahram suddenly.

"Naught that needs concern you," said Swann witheringly.

Bahram made a gesture and Swann found himself two feet above the floor with what felt like an iron fist tightening about his throat. He gasped and choked, trying futilely to pull nothing tangible away from his neck before he strangled to death.

The Persian let him drop. "Now," he said, "do you tell him what I wish to know or do I repeat the process, or perhaps give you to the Djinn to pull apart?"

Swann, half prone on the floor, massaging his throat, shot him a look of pure venom. "They raise power to take care of you!" he said hoarsely. "Damned bloody foreigner! Greymalkin will never let Master Reginald step into his lordship's shoes!"

Bahram laughed. "Am I supposed to be afraid of a pack of women and a cat?" he demanded. "When I have not only my considerable powers but a Djinn at my command?"

"His lordship had little trouble defeating that thing before!" said Swann defiantly.

"He was a man, not a weak woman," said Bahram. "Reynard, get a pistol and take this one and the other servants to the wine cellar. Lock them in there. I shall go and rid ourselves of these females and the cat who dares to challenge me."

By long tradition the local Witches met at a small stone Circle known as the Nine Sisters that was composed of nine standing stones at the top of a nearby tor. It was a high, secure location and afforded spectacular views of the surrounding countryside.

The Circle itself was on undoubted antiquity, its origins long forgotten. But Witches had danced here as long as anyone could remember and in old records of the area mention was made again and again of the Witches' Dancing Floor.

The stones, kept in good repair and tended by the Witches over the centuries, stood on average eight foot high and rectangular in shape, in a perfect Circle about a soft swathe of green turf. In the center stood an alter, very old and weather-worn, carved with images of a female, legs wide apart displaying her genitals, her chin supported in her hands and grinning. This was an image that was found on a few churches in Britain, and very few other places. Those dated from the twelfth century. But this image, or Sheel-Na-Gig, on the altar in the Circle of stones was far older and nearly worn away in places. She was believed to be a symbol of a Celtic goddess of fertility and destruction.

Much later, although no one knew exactly when, images of the moon in its various stages had been added to the altar, for the moon was extremely important to the rituals of the Witches. They called down its goodness and power through dancing and rites, absorbed the energy through their flesh and sent it, strengthened by other energies they had previously gathered through crystals and other stones into the earth to make the fields fertile, to grow crops and to fatten the animals by making the grass lush.

Since the month was June but not yet the Summer Solstice, the altar was still decorated with the flowers of the last sabbat: Beltane or May Eve, ivy, roses and marigolds.

Candles of green would be lit at the beginning of the rituals and a feast of woodruff wine, clover tea, scones with clotted cream, as well as hearty prawn, beef, chicken and cucumber sandwiches would be eaten before the Ritual and the dancing began, as magic needed fuel.

One by one the Witches arrived, all clad for the moment in long green belted gowns, adorned with embroidery on the yoke and sleeve ends and down the front panel of the same flowers that adorned the altar. Some carried embroidered bags as well of differing sizes. They all wore their hair unbound, held off their brows by silver fillets, that bore a the shape of the crescent mon turned horns upward. Above this, high on the back of their heads they wore wreaths of ivy.

Each Witch (there were twenty-five of them, some who came a long ways away and of all ages from eight to eighty) bowed to the altar and then shed her robe, pulling it over her head and then adding it to a pile behind the feast table. Most of them were accompanied by their familiars, cats, hedgehogs, ferrets and owls for the most part, although Witches had an especial affinity for cats.

All the Witches were sky-clad, bodies gleaming with the seasonal anointing oil of lily of the valley. Earlier in the day before leaving home, each Witch had taken a purifying bath before anointing with the proper oil and donning her robe.

Greymalkin arrived with Suzy in good time. Jenny would not be able to attend as the kittens could not be left alone at this stage, being ripe for mischief.

Greymalkin licked his chops as the good odors of clotted cream, chicken and prawns floated towards him. Being a Wizard's familiar, he had only been an observer at Witches' rituals, never a participant and he hoped that the familiars would be granted a share as they were when Wizards convened.

Suzy looked down at him and laughed as she saw that tongue pass over his lips and said "Don't you be worrying! You'll get your share." She untied the belt at her waist as she spoke and slipped her robe off, adding it to the pile. Each robe was embroidered differently, according to its owner's fancy, so there was no difficulty in telling which robe belonged to whom.

Much like a Wizard's gathering, the feast came first, with general, non-Coven conversation, much like a moonlit, ladies-only garden party, save that the ladies all wore nothing except their wreaths and circlets. The Witches' bodies began absorbing the moonlight as soon as they were within the Circle of stones so it was important to have as much exposure as possible.

Suzy made certain that Greymalkin had a plate of prawns and chicken and a bowl of the lovely Devon cream that was so thick and rich.

One of the chief topics of conversation was the disappearance of Richard and Pascoe. All were worried. Greymalkin was gratified to see how many of the ladies were very upset by this circumstance.

All the Witches were not 'ladies'. They came from all walks of life, from a Viscountess to a shepherd's wife. Here they were all equal, sisters in magic.

Lavinia Carstairs, the oldest Witch, was also Coven Mistress and wore a moonstone in the midst of the crescent moon on her brow as benefited her status. When everyone had eaten their fill, she called the Coven to order and went to the altar. With a tiny flame on her forefinger, she lit the candles.

Thirteen of the Witches formed the inner Circle of the altar. It was considered an honor to be chosen for this duty, the primary dance to invoke the goodness of the moon.

About the altar two members of the inner Circle were busily drawing with their wands, fetched from a special pocket in the robes, a Circle that glowed with and caught the moonlight. About this was inscribed then many names of the moon and her goddesses: Diana, Cybele, Artemis...the two Witches were careful to stay inside the Circle they were drawing. A large secondary circle was drawn around this Circle and in this, the other twelve Witches who were not in the primary dance knelt, sinking back on their heels. They too, would dance later.

With the other familiars, Greymalkin sat in the inner Circle. Usually Wizards only attended the Witches' dances by invitation, or on the Great Sabbats and celebrations of the year: Imbolc or Candlemas in February; the Vernal Equinox; Beltane - May Eve; Summer Solstice or Litha; Lammas in August; Mabon, which was the Autumn Equinox; Samhain on All Hallow's Eve, and Yule, the Winter Solstice. Greymalkin had never seen a Witches' Sabbat from the very beginning, although he supposed that this, a minor working for the earth's fertility, was an Esbat

He watched and listened as the chant and the dance began. Several of the women in the outer circle played ethereal pipes and one had a small lap harp, another softly struck a drum, not like the strong rhythms used both by Wizards and Druids. It was more unearthly in tone. Once in a while a familiar would prompt a young Witch who seemed to forget the chant or the hand and body movements that accompanied it.

The moonlight seemed to become stronger and stronger and gradually the surrounding vistas disappeared behind a blue-white haze, almost like fog. The bare bodies glowed as the chant rose in volume and the beat grew stronger, Witches whirling and leaping in the intoxication of music and moonlight. The women in the outer Circle rose and danced as well, all, even the oldest, were lithe and graceful.

After a long while, one by one, the dancers halted, sinking to the earth. The haze sank into the earth with them. From here, Greymalkin knew, the goodness and power of the moonlight would go deep into the earth, to be used by the plants of the fields, the fruited trees and the grasses eaten by the cattle and other domestic animals. These important moon rituals were the chief reason that the Six Nations had such agricultural riches and the finest grain and meats in the world.

Greymalkin had heard of non-magicals persons who thought that the sky-clad dances were nothing but depraved orgies. Certainly no magical person thought so. The Witches and their families were proud of their contribution to the bounty of the Six Nations and saw nothing in the least lascivious about dancing naked beneath the moon.

After over an hour of dancing and chanting all were sharp-set and a second round of feasting, this of the lighter candied violets, cakes, fried honey rolls and sweet dessert scones with clotted cream were eaten. Robes would not be resumed until the Coven was dismissed, for moon bathing was healthy and beautifying to the skin.

When the second feast was finished, Suzy asked for everyone's attention, and with Greymalkin's help, told them about Reginald and the Persian. Before the two had even finished telling their tale angry murmurs began filling the air.

"Barbara!" Lavinia spoke sharply to one of the other Witches who had danced in the inner Circle." You are the crystal keeper. Be so good as to set them up and we shall set up a crystal scry to find the Earl and his dragon. Is everyone willing to stay late and do this?" It was already well past midnight.

There were murmurs and nods of assent from everyone.

"Richard tried using a pendulum when Felix disappeared but it would not work. It was as if he had disappeared off the face of the earth," Greymalkin offered.

"One Wizard using a pendulum is not the same as twenty-five Witches linking crystal. Things can be seen in crystal which cannot be seen in a scry bowl or found by a pendulum," Lavinia said. "And I know what you are going to say, that a Wizard Augur's crystal ball is notoriously inaccurate," she said as Greymalkin opened his mouth to speak.

"Men have no business tampering with crystal," said a tall, red-headed Witch.

Barbara was busy laying out a line of crystals, large ones on sticks which went into the earth and seemed to march on a straight line from the altar to where the moon still hung in the sky. One the altar itself she removed the garnet that had adorned it as seasonal stone and placed a huge crystal cut and faceted so that the top was a flat surface, highly polished.

Then Barbara took up from a bag beneath the table a baton with a head of fleece and, starting at the furthest crystal from the altar, struck each one softly.

So sensitive were the crystals that each resonated, the pure note hanging in the air, each one blending with the one after and before to form a beautifully harmonious chord. The moonlight followed each note and poured through every crystal, one by one under the musical notes and the light both flooded the large crystal on the altar.

The Witches had all resumed their kneeling postures on the ground, including the thirteen of the inner Circle, who knelt close to the altar. They began chanting in an ancient language, softly and melodically, in perfect harmony with the crystal notes still hanging in the air.

The big crystal hummed and throbbed and burst into a blue white light.

"Now," said Lavinia in satisfaction, "we shall see what we can see!"

43
The Wrath of the Pixies

The crystal thrummed and emitted a loud note. Lavinia looked into it and began to say "Here –" and then gave a great gasp at what she saw there. "Wands at the ready!" she shouted and whirled to face the other Witches. "We are under attack! It will be here in a very few minutes!"

Each Witch called her wand. They flew from the pile of robes into waiting hands. Barbara and two helpers moved the crystals on their rods quickly, standing them between the stones. The familiars streamed towards the altar, Greymalkin joining them. Lavinia cast a protective dome over the animals. No matter what attacked, they, and the ancient altar would be safe.

The Witches began another chant. This one was different than the drawing down of the moon; it was in a minor key, low and dark. Greymalkin felt his fur stand on end as power began to stir and leaped around the circle, from stone to crystal. It crackled in the air and Greymalkin noticed that the fur and feathers on the other animals and birds was electrified as well.

Quickly the visible power leaped until it encircled the standing stones, a glowing blue-white ring that played over the oiled bodies of the Witches, giving them an otherworldly glow.

And outside the stone circle something else was happening. Greymalkin at first thought it was a flock of tiny green birds, arcing upwards from the ground. He also began to hear bells ringing wildly that seemed to be coming from underground.

Whatever it was rose in a solid stream of many bodies and went at an astonishing rate around the circle, so fast it was a green blur. Then several forms broke loose from the mass and rose into the air, only to dive straight down at the

Witches, who seemed completely unperturbed by this phenomenon. They had risen to their feet in the chant, arms stretched up to the moon.

The green things stopped in the air in front of Lavinia and Greymalkin could see that they were not birds at all, but small, green people. Some of them wore green clothing, others were naked, but they all had green skin. All were red-headed with small, pale, wedge-like faces set with elongated dark eyes and turned-up noses. Their mops of hair stuck out beneath tall green hats, rather like stiffened night caps. Their bodies were thin, with abnormally long feet and hands and extremely long, pointed ears stuck through the edges of their caps. In spite of the fact that they were flying they had no wings.

"Pixies!" thought Greymalkin in wonder. He had read about them but he had never seen one. They lived underground and were well known for mischief making such as leading travelers astray, much like the Will o' the Wisps, and stealing horses, riding them to exhaustion and returning them to their stables with knotted manes and tails, sweated and wild-eyed. Pixies were peculiar to the West Country, particularly on Dartmoor here in Devon and in neighboring Somerset and Cornwall. It was said that they lived in the ground beneath a Circle of stones and now Greymalkin had proof of this.

Lavinia looked at the lead little green wingless creature. It was impossible for Greymalkin to tell its sex. Some creatures of Faerie were androgynous and the familiar could not tell even by its voice, for it was shrill and piping. "We be here!" it announced to Lavinia.

"Thank you for coming at our call," she said and curtseyed to the creature, as if she wore a stately gown instead of nothing at all.

"What comes?" asked another Pixie.

"That!" Lavinia pointed to the sky to the south where a giant blue figure was even now streaking towards them.

"Not him again!" was Greymalkin's first thought. *"I thought Richard and Pascoe killed him!"*

A furious buzzing arose from the horde of pixies, as if a swarm of bees had gone mad. "Dang furriner!" several little voices yelled in a strong Devonian accent. "Dang'n vor for a

404

liddle vule! Doan 'e know this be pixie country an' 'e bain't velcome?"

Greymalkin found it rather amusing that the pixies referred to the blue giant, many times their size, as a 'little fool'.

The familiar could not imagine what the tiny pixies could do to the great blue Djinn for none of them were much larger that a human hand of average size, in spite of the fact that there must be hundreds of them.

Then the lead pixie grinned at Lavinia and showed sharp, pointed teeth. He held up his hands, which now ended in sharp talons, as did the toes on his feet. He looked suddenly far more dangerous.

The Djinn, traveling fast towards the Circle of Stones, had little save contempt for the group of women there assembled. He saw the power but thought nothing of it. It was only women's magic, a poor, pathetic thing compared to the power he and his Master shared. Even as the chant continued and a cone of power began to rise, towering into the night sky like an inverted top spinning rapidly, the Djinn disregarded it. Only in the edge of his vision did he notice the green swarm rising at him.

Below him, Bahram galloped on a horse taken from Richard's stable. The horse was Devon-born and knew all too well that there were Pixies about and he began to fight with his rider, wanting to get away from the creatures who were no friend to horses. Bahram was a skilled horseman but even so it took all his strength and ability to force the horse to keep heading towards the stones.

No more than did the Djinn did Bahram give much attention to the tiny green creatures. He shot a bolt of red magic at them and they screamed, scattering. That took care of them, or so he thought.

The screams were not of pain but of rage.The pixies, in a precision of flight that would cite admiration in a dragon, re-grouped and split evenly in two groups of furiously flying green blurs. One group went after Bahram, the other after the Djinn.

When they were almost upon Bahram the horse went mad and reared up, flailing out with his front hooves, screaming in fear. When this show of defiance did not stop the pixies and Bahram kept urging him forward the horse threw himself over backwards in an attempt to rid himself of his rider who hadn't the sense to get away from the pixies.

A split second before the horse fell on his back Bahram threw himself sideways and avoided being crushed under the weight of the horse. He heard the saddle-tree crack. That could have been his back.

Snorting wildly, the horse got to its feet, saddle broken and askew, reins dangling. But before it could run to the safety of its stable, magiced against Pixie incursions, the pixies had it and with glee, twenty or thirty of them clung to the shattered saddle and to the reins. They began to drive the horse into a circle, where it galloped as many of the pixies maliciously knotted its mane and tail as the poor beast was ridden to a lather.

The balance of the group attacked Bahram, biting, scratching and clawing at him, their shrill voices creating a horrid din in his ears. They flew at his face and at his hands, some managing to crawl inside his clothes. biting and ripping his skin. There was no defense against them and his magics fell short of their target for the pixies were blindingly fast and each burst of defensive magic seemed to make them angrier.

"To me!" Bahram called to the Djinn."Defend your master!"

But the Djinn had problems of its own. He too, was under attack by a troop of pixies. They should have not been able to hurt him as much as they did, but the pain was exquiste. His torso, under the vest, was bare and he soon had a multitude of voracious, sharp-toothed pixies tormenting him. He bellowed and swatted at them, but they only attacked the fiercer, their humming, so like that of bees, swelling as they did so. He tried to put his hands over his ears but there were too many of them, clawing at his face and biting his tender ears. Crazed by the pain and the noise he attempted to get away from them, quite failing to notice that they were driving him towards the cone of power, now towering in the sky, signing its own song, as underneath it the Witches still chanted.

The torment became much worse as the Pixies used finger nails and toes and the Djinn, oblivious to everything else, allowed them to push him exactly where they wanted him.

He meet the cone of power with a boom like thunder and screamed in rage and agony. At Lavinia's command the Witches lifted their wands and poured additional magic into the cone.

With a last despairing cry the Djinn exploded, blue remains dissolved by the tremendous power of the cone and the wands. The pixies laughed in delight. "Serves thou right, tha girt stupid vule of a furriner! This be pixie land!" one called out in derision.

And at the Dower House,in the room at the top of the stairs, the brass lamp that had been the Djinn's home for centuries, fell into dust. He was well and truly dead.

The pixies had turned Bahram so that he might see the destruction of his slave.

Bahram could no longer fight the pixies. Blood ran down his hands and into his eyes.They had bitten him and dug at his flesh, even pulling handfuls of hair out of his head after ripping off his turban. His clothes, and his nerves,were in tatters.

The cone of power collapsed in on itself, harmlessly fading into the ground as the Witches ceased chanting. At a gesture from Lavinia the two Circles were broken and the Witches grabbed their robes, slipping into them as they ran forward to where the pixie horde held Bahram. Lavinia released the dome over the familiars and the animals and birds ran and flew towards the spot as well.

The horse had been ridden to exhaustion in a circle, leaving a round pattern on the springy turf. This was a *gallitrap* or Faerie Ring.

Greymalkin was the first to arrive at the Persian sorcerer's feet. "Are you responsible for Richard and Pascoe's disappearance?" he demanded. "Did you and Reginald attempt to murder Felix?"

"What hast tha done to our good Earl Richard an' Master Felix?" cried Pigwiggin, the leader of the pixies, his clawed fingers inches from Bahram's eyes. He was outraged that a foreigner had dared to use his un-English magics in the pixie's West Country and to harm their very own people.

The Persian said "You can prove nothing. In spite of the

beating he had undergone his voice was still cold and full of contempt.

"Many people in the village here saw that Djinn and it is known that Richard dueled with it," said Greymalkin."And as a familiar my testimony is admissible in court. I saw it attempt to murder Richard and all here could see its evil intent tonight! And it answers to you, Persian! It's obvious as well that you were coming here to harm our Witches."

"He caught cold at that!" said Suzy in satisfaction.

"Throw him on the ground," Greymalkin ordered.

The pixies obeyed, relishing the opportunity to push him over and jump upon Bahram. Although each pixie was tiny and weighed less than nothing, a large group of them was more than enough to keep down even a large, strong man.

Greymalkin sat down near Bahram's face and lifted a paw. He extended his claws and took a swipe at the man's nose.

Bahram' head jerked back too late. Three deep red and bleeding scratches appeared on his nose.

"Now," said the familiar in a deceptively pleasant voice, "suppose you tell me everything, and I do mean *everything*, including Reginald's part in all of this. Or I might very well lose control over my paw and relieve you of an eyeball or your nose!"

Bahram stared defiantly at the cat. Greymalkin, fast as only a cat could attack, sprang forward with a yowl and laid one the sorcerer's cheek with a white-mittened paw, perilously close to the eye.

Bahram flinched violently and began to talk rapidly "It was Reynard's idea, all of it. He wanted more money for his women and gambling. I, too, needed money and I agreed to help him for a sum he was to pay me."

With only a little more urging from Greymalkin the entire tale was told: how Felix had been caught unawares, dozing in the sun and struck from behind by Reginald, fed the syrup of forgetfulness and tossed overboard to drown and how Pyewacket had been thrown overboard in a sack. They heard about the Djinn and the waterspout raised by the Ahriman that sent Richard and Pascoe to Guernsey.

If dagger-looks could have killed, Bahram would l have been long dead before the narrative had even ended. Witches and pixies both were furious.

"Suzy," said Lavinia, "go to the village and awaken the constable."

"NO!" said Pigwiggin loudly. "No, he be ours to bring justice on! Toss un!"

The pixies threw Bahram in the middle of the *gallitrap*.

"By our laws, tha hast crosst th' line. A criminal confessed outtn his own mouth hangs him do he put but one foot in th' gallitrap! But we be merciful, us pixies," said Pigwiggin.

"Eh, now, zur," he continued, hovering close in front of Bahram's face. "I do be giving tha a fine choice. We cast tha in th' peaty bog yonder and shouldst tha make tha way outtn it, why, tha is free to go. A rare fine bargain that be for sure!"

Bahram, furious, sat up and said "I will send you all to Gehenna! I will make no bargains with you!" He raised his hands in a menacing gesture.

The pixies went into paroxysms of high, piercing giggles. "You be ourn noaw," said Pigwiggin. "Tha magics doan work in yon *gallitrap,* furriner!"

This was true as Bahram found. When he reached for his power there was naught there. He could do nothing as the pixies swarmed around him again lifting him in spite of his struggles and curses in Persian, into the air and carrying him away.

"I didn't know there was a bog in the area," Greymalkin said to Suzy. "I thought they were all on the moor." He meant Dartmoor.

"There usually are not," said Suzy dryly.

A long wail was heard and a resounding splash. Then came a horrible burbling cry and a sound of some tremendous suction.

Pigwiggin, alone, returned and said "Poor furriner! Never learned tha doan struggle in the peaty bog! All mucky he were afore him drowned! Swallowed up nice, he were!" On his face was a particularly malicious grin.

"That's that then," said Greymalkin in satisfaction. "Now onto bearding Reginald in his den and turn him over to the law!"

But when they reached the Dower House it was to find Reginald, a broken man, tied to a chair in the drawing room, and the servants, all armed with weapons of fireplace pokers, shovels brooms and mops, standing guard over him while the local constable took a statement.

Reginald had been unable to resist drinking down the last of the whiskey for some Dutch courage and in his fuddled sate had been easily overcome by the servants as he had not thought to relieve the housekeeper of her keys. The servants did not stay locked in the cellar for very long. Bow Street had been scryed and were on their way by dragon-back from London.

With Bahram dead and Reginald about to go to gaol, Richard, Pascoe and Felix were safe from any more efforts against their lives, Greymalkin thought in satisfaction as, an hour later, he watched a Bow Street runner put a chastened, weeping and cuffed Reginald on an immense black dragon for transport to Newgate prison.

But they were still in incredible danger there on Guernsey. How could they ever be rescued from that situation with the French in control of the island and the clear and present danger of the Inquisition?

44
Monday Evening

It was nearing nine and close to curfew when David arrived back at the cottage he shared with his mother near St. Peter Port. After leaving Lovel he had driven as fast as he had dared in the gathering dusk so that he would not be still out on the road after nine. All notion of going to Faerie to sup with Robin and the Professor was forgotten. He wanted but a small meal and his bed. The day had been a long one. Even the thought of joining Grizel in their mossy bed barely tempted him.

Majorlaine greeted his arrival with relief, running forward from the kitchen door when she saw him coming from the stable and throwing her arms around him. "I thought the Inquisition had taken you!" she cried, tears running down her face. "They have been here twice today and tore the house and barn apart! What are they searching for, David? They would not answer my questions and ordered me to keep quiet!"

"The Professor escaped from Castle Cornet late last night, *Maman*, and they think he is hiding somewhere on the island," said David.

"Is he still here?" Majorlaine asked quickly.

"He is well and safe, where they will never find him," said David as they continued to walk towards the house. "That is all I shall tell you. It's best you do not know."

"And Suie, the cat? Is he safe as well?" Majorlaine swatted to know.

"He is with the Professor." It was with a sense of comfort that Davis saw the open door to the kitchen, light streaming from it on to the cobbles of the yard. It was a welcoming sight.

"David, there is a young woman here to see you!" said Majorlaine, her voice growing suddenly sharp. "She seems quite anxious to talk to you. She comes from Sark and claims to be Hughes Sarchet's daughter! I do not remember Hughes ever mentioning a child! His wife died when they had been married but a short time."

Grizel, here? David's steps quickened as much as he could manage. "Where is she?" he said. What had brought her here?

Majorlaine knew him too well. There was an elation, an eagerness in his voice that had not been there five minutes earlier.

There was something strange about this young woman. She claimed to be from Sark but how had she come here when the French did not allow travel between the islands? How had she met David? And, more importantly, what was she to David?

"She has been having tea with me in the kitchen," Majorlaine said and then gave a little gasp as David's face was revealed in the light coming from the door. He looked like a man going to meet his lover.

Grizel had been sitting at the kitchen table and stood up quickly, putting down a tea-cup as David entered the room.

For a moment he confronted a stranger. She was not in her old blue gown with the heavy bronze hair streaming down her back, but in a neat sprig muslin dress with a pale pink Spencer jacket and a frill about her throat. Her hair was swept up off her neck and face and a pink capote, a fabric cap, lay on the table. Fingerless lace mitts on her hands covered the webs between her fingers and she even wore dainty pink slippers.

David had completely forgotten that his mother was watching his every move. The sight of Grizel was like a tonic. "Grizel, you look beautiful!" he said, limping forward and taking her hand in his free one. "To what do I owe this visit? It is a welcome one!"

"I was concerned when you did not come to see the Professor tonight," she said and leaning forward she said in a very low voice. "And I wanted you in our bed."

David felt his face grow hot, for her voice was full of a promise of shared passion. He was glad that his back was towards his mother. Pray God she did not see and realize why he grew so discomfited. "I was detained by that madman out at the Dragon Port," he said. "He kept Lovel and me until nearly eight.I had to hurry to get back here in time before curfew was rung."

Grizel studied him with a slight frown. "You look exhausted!" she said."Damn that man! Is your leg bothering you? Sit down and get off it. Your mother has made some lovely tea and there is more than likely some left."

Majorlaine gasped in shock. Not only had the young lady said 'damn' but she spoke easily to David of his injured leg and what was more, he was not growling at her for this, but allowing her to guide him to a chair and fetch a footstool from the fireside! They bore the appearance of long acquaintances of some intimacy.

The young woman poured David a cup of Majorlaine's rose-hip tea as outside the bells in the church at St. Peter Port began to ring curfew.

"You will have to spend the night here, *Mam'selle* Sarchet," said Majorlaine reluctantly, joining them at the table."You will be arrested if you go out of doors now. And however did you get here from Sark?" she added curiously as Grizel poured her a second cp of tea as well.

Grizel exchanged a look with David, almost as if she were asking him a question and it was answered. "I swam here," she said at last.

"You swam all the way from Sark?" Majorlaine gasped. "Such a thing is not possible! It is miles and miles!"

"It is not too far for a seal, *Madame*," said Grizel. "For you see, I am half a Selchie."

Majorlaine gasped and let her teacup drop with a clatter into the saucer. All her life she had heard of Selchies, had even thought she had seen them basking in the sun on rocks off the coast. But she had never met one. She had thought that there would be something of the animal about them when they were in human form, a coarseness. But this self - possessed young woman whom David appeared to know so well, looked very human indeed. In fact, she was beautiful in very human terms.

And Majorlaine realized with a jolt as she looked at the two of them, so in accord with one another, that her son, for whom she had prayed daily to fall in love, was at last in that state.

But he was in love with a seal, something not even fully human.

Rosal was extremely worried as the hours went by and Felix did not come. She had worked all day at the farm and come home with a fistful of coins and a basket full of produce. She had given the food to Hagar and put the coins in the hiding place and then went first to the bed in the woods and refreshed the grasses and flower petals. She then went to the pool and washed the sweat from her body, eager to be ready for him when he came home. Once they had eaten they would go into the woods and begin making love. She was now as anxious for Felix's embraces as she had dreaded Sylvester's. Their wedding night had been wonderful and she wanted to repeat it.

As darkness drew in, though, she was worried. All day long there had been French troops on the roads. *Les Huit Lapins* had been visited twice and the soldiers had searched the barns and house both times, even tearing down the hay-ricks and removing the animals from their stalls, poking the straw bedding with bayonets. Hagar had reported that they had visited the *vardo* and again torn everything out of it, not finding the hidden monies and the fortune-telling paraphernalia because between the inside floor and the outside wagon bottom was, their officer had said, 'too shallow'. Too shallow for what they had not informed her. They had gone through the woods as well, with bayonets, pushing them into shrubs and turf.

Whatever had happened was bad and Rosal was afraid that they would blame her Rom for it. The *Gajé* always blamed the Romany. They had already beaten him once. Even now, perhaps he was lying beside the road, unconscious...her active imagination painted many pictures, all of which ended with him dead or dying.

When he came at last she flew to his side and flung her arms about his neck, Chavé beside her, his tail wagging furiously. "I was so worried!" she cried.

Felix did not repulse her as Sylvester would have done

but instead gathered her against him and buried his face in her hair, holding her as if he would never let her go. All day long her image had lived in his mind's eye, as a refuge to which he could go. "Rosal," he said, his voice muffled in her hair. "I have thought about you all day!" Even though his head was throbbing he could think of nothing but being alone with her and taking her into his arms.

She was extremely gratified to hear this.

"Before you two begin removing each other's clothing," came Hagar's dry voice, "the supper is ready and will soon spoil if it is not eaten. Time enough for that when you are fed and have had your tea."

They broke apart, a little guiltily, and Felix stooped to pat Chavé. "He kept me very late tonight. There was much work," he said as they joined Hagar at the fireside.

Hagar saw the shadow of pain in his face and said nothing but fetched her headache remedy. She spilled the herbs into a chipped cup and poured hot water over them and as he smelled their fragrance Felix said gratefully, "Thank you, Hagar. That is just what I need. That man I am working for would try the patience of a saint!" He wished that he could tell them of what he was doing but Fournier had made it clear that he could not discuss the goings-on at the Dragon Port with 'outsiders' or he and anyone he had told would be punished, severely. It was bad enough that he was going to have to tell them that there would be no money coming for all of this work. But he would put off doing that as long as possible. Instead he asked about the shocking fire at *Trois Chiminées* and was incensed to learn that it had been the French who burned it.

"I am glad that Grant escaped and that you were there to doctor him Hagar," Felix said as he took bites of a tasty vegetable stew, mopped up with flat bread. after the details of the fire had been related to him.

Hagar sniffed. "That one is a stupid *Giorgio*. He would rather be in pain than bear my touch! A filthy Egyptian with her hell-born brews, he called me. I wonder that you could bear to be in the house of such a man."

"The Professor is nothing like Grant," Felix said. "I had hoped that we would be able to visit the Professor this evening," he said, "but it is now too late and I am tired. I have to be there even earlier tomorrow."

"It is a wonder to me that he does not have you sleep there!" said Hagar.

"Fournier would never allow that and he told Blériot so."

"Whatever are they doing out there?" Rosal asked curiously.

Felix looked at her apologetically. "I can't tell you that," he said. "It has to be kept secret. Sir David is not allowed to tell his family either. I don't like keeping secrets from you."

"The French and their secrets!" said Hagar scornfully. "People will talk. They should know that and sooner or later everyone will know what they are attempting to hide."

Particularly once the balloons are being flown, Felix thought. There would be no possibility that the large balloons, with their brilliant flight bags of red, white and blue that were even now being sewn, could be hidden. Unless, as David had joked, Blériot's brilliant invention was an invisibility device.

The first flight would not be far in the future. Blériot was driving the men hard to complete one particular balloon and it was to contain some sort of mechanism, Felix thought. even though he himself was not familiar with mechanics. Nothing of what Blériot was directing the men to assemble seemed in the least familiar to him. It was a hodge-podge of gears and levers. But as he told David on their homewards journey today, it was to fit in the peculiar cavity in the basket, which today had been lined with asbestos. Their best guess was that it was some sort of weapon, although Felix had seen nothing resembling a gun barrel or other weapon of destruction. Blériot had already said that he and he alone would add 'the finishing touches' to the project. The prototype would be finished and tested before any others were made and the test done by Blériot himself. The little man was jealous of anyone else having his knowledge. Most of the plans and the design, he had boasted, were all in his head, where they were safe. He had destroyed those he had shown to the First Consul.

Felix could not tell his family of another matter,of the torque he and David had found in the ruins of *Trois Chiminées*. To tell the truth, he was afraid of the thing. So much power hummed throughout it that he had not wanted to hold it, but had dropped it back into the magiced box.

It was readily apparent that they had to somehow hide it but there was no safe place to place it on the island where a Witch-Sniffer could not ferret it out. Neither one of them dared keep it.

Reluctantly, Felix told David about his encounter with the dryad and the flower Faerie in the woods and of their offer to help. David said it was the perfect solution: give the box to Flowerlet and Daphne and the Faeries could convey it to the Professor.

Felix had done this on the way back from the burned-out cottage and found the two Faerie beings happy to oblige. For himself, he was more than glad to get rid of the torque. It gave him a very odd feeling. David was extremely curious about it and was determined to ask the Professor about it the next time they met, but Felix only wanted to be shut of it. Of course, David had not held it in his hands.

Now as his headache receded, Felix resolutely put all thoughts of torques and balloons and Blériot to the back of his mind. *Madame* had sent a strawberry cake, with cream, home with Rosal and after this delectable treat was finished, he would go with Rosal into the woods and, after loving her, would sleep with her in his arms, all pain and unanswerable questions put aside for the space of a night.

By Monday evening Richard was pleased with Pascoe's progress. The dragon's temperature, although still elevated, had not climbed and he had only once complained of pain. He still had to hold the wing outstretched, but a rock rolled under the wing helped relieved the strain of this and he was as comfortable as could be expected. His appetite was good, although he had expressed a wistful longing for a haunch of beef rather than the endless fish. Richard had a good supply of calcium tablets and was carefully monitoring Pascoe's calcium level, which was counted by a simple spell.

Since Pascoe was asleep a good amount of the time Richard's biggest problem was boredom. Elspeth came once a day but stayed only a short while. It was the height of the

Selchie mating season and that was first and foremost on her mind. If she was very fortunate she would end with pup from all this mating but it was unlikely. Many female Selchies never pupped, in spite of the constant mating. It seemed to Richard that this overwhelming urge to mate was linked to the low birth rate amongst the Selchies. Their sex drive, like most of the magical creatures, had to be great to maximize the chance of pregnancy. From the age of fourteen to about thirty-five or so, a female Selchie thought of little else besides mating. Grizel Sarchet, being but half Selchie, would not be quite as eager for a male embrace. This morning Elspeth had talked in wonder of how Grizel actually prefered to wait for her human lover, and she did not mate with him every day! Elspeth found this unbelievable.

Richard smiled as he thought of Elspeth. He found it amusing that she never ceased to offer to sleep with him. He wished instead that she offered to bring him some books of any type or a news-sheet, even one printed in French. While Pascoe was sleeping, and he slept a great deal as it was the best thing for healing, the hours were long as Richard had not thought to take a book with him on the short trip to Portsmouth. On any overnight stay he always had a volume of some sort, usually a novel or a history. Richard also missed Greymalkin. He and his familiar had many interesting conversations, for the cat was as well-read as his Wizard. Were Pascoe awake they could have amused themselves with word games and conundrums, for dragons liked nothing better than a challenging puzzle.

Richard was dozing and the fire was dying back when an eerie phosphorescent light filled the cave. Richard came to his full senses at once and in the low light of the fire he could see Pascoe's eyes open. They gleamed in the firelight like a cat's. Both of them knew what this meant. They were to have visitors who were not of this world.

The rock face in the back of the cave, where the door into Faerie would have been in the days before the Faeries themselves had sealed it, split open, silently, allowing a glimpse of very old trees, a breath of flowers on the air and, far off, high sweet voices mingled with silvery bells.

An Elf in green stepped into the cave and bowed. "I am Galen," he said. "I have been sent to help the injured dragon and to bid you both come to Faerie, to the realm of Robin Goodfellow. Be ye welcome!" he added with a courtly bow.

45
In Faerie

Before they used the door into Faerie Galen looked at Pascoe's damaged phalange. The Elfin healer said that Richard had done a fine job in splinting the broken wing, but nevertheless he made a slight adjustment and then, with his Healing magics, knit the bone.

Pascoe sighed in relief as he felt the wing mend and all the other scrapes, slight tears and bruises he had suffered were cured as well. "When can I fly again?" he asked Galen eagerly.

The Healer smiled as he removed the splint, now no longer needed. "Do not be too impatient, my friend. A se'enight will see you in the air again, but not before."

Pascoe looked crestfallen at the prohibition. A week would take forever to go by to one who was accustomed to daily flights. But at least the week would be spent in Faerie where he would be outrageously spoilt, as Faerie creatures adored dragons.

With Pascoe's wing mended there was no reason to delay leaving the cave and going into Faerie. Galen told Richard that he might leave Pascoe's tack behind. He would send someone to fetch it and the Faerie saddlers would treat it for the damage it had suffered in the salt water immersion. Galen would also make it possible for Elspeth to be contacted as Richard hated to repay her help by leaving her unsure of what had happened to them.

Richard had been a Faerie friend since his early youth and had spent a good deal of time in the realm, but each time he entered the Faerie world he was struck anew by its beauty and peace. Everywhere one looked was a vista of natural beauty. The Faeries, particularly the Elves, loved trees and most of their houses were built high in the trees or inside one. Flowers of all seasons were everywhere and the temperature was always that of a perfect summer's day, with a light, sweet-scented breeze. There was rarely any snow, and never rainstorms or thunder and lightning in Faerie, the lack of which only added to the sense of timelessness. Once in a while a soft rain fell, which was odd, because as far as Richard could determine, Faerie lay underground. But a sun rose and set in a sky that boasted the same blue colour and clouds as in the world above, although they never blocked the sun; a moon appeared at night in a field of stars, and the seasons changed, although winter lasted a very short time.

Galen politely inquired at which court Richard had been made a Faerie friend, for a gold star shone on his forehead, as it did on Pascoe's.

"In my own West Country," Richard answered, "those of my house have long been welcome at the court of Queen Mab."

"You are the second person who has newly come to this realm bearing the sign of Faerie favor," Galen remarked.

"Richard!" said Pascoe eagerly as he walked behind the Elf and the Earl. Already, the very few Faerie children were peeping at him from behind the safety of leaves.

Richard had the same thought. " My grandson is missing somewhere on this island," he said. "He is a Wizard and a Faerie friend also."

Galen shook his head. "The other Faerie friend I have been told of is a young Gypsy."

"A Gypsy!" said Richard in astonishment, for it was almost a law that a Faerie friend was a highly qualified Witch or Wizard. Gypsies had little real magic. They had some concealment spells and some few of the women had healing talents or a true gift for fortune telling and the second sight, but Richard had never heard of a Wizard Gypsy.

"I shall introduce you to him when he is amongst us again but human affairs keep him busy. The Professor, a human scholar taking refuge from the French, to whom I shall also introduce you, is quite fond of the Gypsy lad and thinks highly of him," said Galen.

He showed Richard to a comfortable house in the lower branches of a tree. The walls were but light curtains and the roof made of leaves, but Richard was quite used to this and noted with approval the soft cushions on the bed, usually filled with thistledown, and low, inviting furniture. He was even happier when Galen showed him a bathing room and told him that fresh clothing would be brought to him.

Outside the house was a deep, warm, sand wallow for Pascoe, into which the dragon settled with a sigh of contentment. It had been difficult for both of them, sleeping on only a pile of grasses.

Galen indicated that food would be forthcoming and they parted, Richard to bathe and Pascoe to dream of beef, while Galen returned to his patients.

Aurelius had little idea of how long he had really been in Faerie. They told him that time was far different here and he believed it, for his appetite and his perception of the passing of time had altered. Sometimes it seemed as but as hour had gone by, yet he would look up to see the unearthly sun setting, not realizing how much time had passed as he read a scroll, made notes or talked to a Faerie lore-master. The internal clock which had always served him so well and told him when it was time to wake, time to eat, and time to sleep had failed. Food was always available. It seemed to him that he had but to *think* he was hungry, and the charming Elf maid who had been assigned to see to his needs appeared with a laden tray of delicious food. Her name was Alodie, and she was an excellent source of information about Faerie, always glad to answer any questions. However, he had been rather out of countenance when she had shown up several times not wearing a stitch of clothing.

Pyewacket had been amused by Aurelius' embarrassment. "Faerie creatures are very casual about nudity. Many of them never wear clothes at all, for example, the Flower Faeries," said the cat, "and even the Elves, who look so much like humans, consider clothing optional.Their religion requires that they worship as their Gods made them. I can tell her that it makes you uneasy. She would not wish to make you in the least uncomfortable or distressed for to do so would break their laws of hospitality."

"I expected some lascivious behavior," confessed Aurelius, "for I have read of such. And artists do portray the Faerie world as being unclothed..." His voice trailed off as he shook his head. "But I am an old bachelor and have never become accustomed to nubile young females of any race completely unclad in my presence."

Pyewacket chuckled and promised to speak to Alodie. Thereafter she was always demurely clad when she delivered meals or cleaned Aurelius' room.

In spite of some shocks (the amount of easy lovemaking that went on was also unsettling to Aurelius) he was finding his sojourn in Faerie fascinating. He already had a sheaf of notes and gathered more information each day. All he met were most cooperative. Many of the Faerie folk he met were eager for a new book, one of truths, to be written about them. Many of the volumes that had been written, they claimed, were full of misinformation, penned by non-magicals who had never even been to Faerie, but had relied on folk tales and outright lies. Those of Faerie of the Selighe court, never stole children, for one example. They took human children only when the child was being abused and, when the child was grown, gave the child the choice of remaining in Faerie or rejoining the world. Aurelius met some human children who had been horribly treated in the World Above and were more than glad to come to Faerie, where they were treasured, for none in Faerie had many children at all, which was a sadness in all of the Faerie world.

And his health had continued to improve. Each day he had a session with Galen and he was feeling completely rejuvenated. He could walk any distance now, and write for a long time. He no longer need the spectacles he had used for reading, which was fortunate for they had been left behind when he was arrested.

He still wondered what had happened to John however, and wished that his young friends could come and visit. Somehow, Aurelius could not see John here in Faerie. There would be too much of which the manservant would disapprove and there would be little for him to do. Grizel Sarchet had come to visit him and Pyewacket, decently dressed in a worn blue gown, and explained that David and Lovel were being kept for long hours each day by the strange man at the Dragon Port.

But all in all, it was a relief and a joy to be here, away from the danger of the French, health returning and an enthralling research and writing project.

Fournier awoke Monday morning with a hideous hangover and a strange, completely naked woman in his bed. He rid himself of the woman by summoning Girard and ordering him to take her away but the headache and nausea was not so easy to dismiss.

The headache was not improved by an order from Father Maël to report to his office at once and Fournier's head was pounding violently by the time the Witch-Sniffer had raked him over the coals for his troops' failure to find the escaped prisoner the day before. The priest spoke sarcastically about the ineptitude of Fournier and his men and how they had no doubt overlooked something. "Wizards are wily!" the priest declared. "The troops will go out again today. I myself will accompany you in my carriage and each troop will take a Witch-Sniffer with them. It is thought that Wizards can turn themselves into inanimate objects and fly through the air on broomsticks. This last fact is well established here in Guernsey, for it has been reported to me that many house bear a Witch's chair, on the roof at the base of the chimney."

Fournier had seen the stone shelves projecting from the chimneys out over the roofs of many house. He had thought this a convenience for the chimney sweeps' ladders. Now, unwisely, he said "Is that what that is for?" wishing that his head did not feel as if it would fall off at any moment.

"Don't be so stupid, Fournier!" snapped Father Maël. He was in no good humor. He was a mass of stiffness from the horseback ride and still writhed when he thought of the struggle with the stone door and the sign of paganism he had destroyed. "Those are resting places for the Witches who fly to their unholy Sabbats on broomsticks! No doubt the few good Catholics who lived here were afraid of the Witches' invading their homes if a place was not provided for them to rest."

He turned to his desk and unlocked a drawer, pulling out

an ornate box. He opened it to show Fournier a bundle of crucifixes on chains. "I shall issue these to the men. They are blessed by his Holiness himself. If your men find a tree or rock where it should not be they can confront it with this and command it to change in the name of *le bon Dieu* and the Holy Roman church. Wizards shrink from the true cross! The so-called Celtic cross of the Irish heretics is a perversion! The Wizard will have to change back to his true form or risk destruction!"

A tree or rock where it shouldn't be? Fournier blinked, wondering if the pain in his head was affecting his hearing. Surely the priest did not mean that they were to look at trees and rocks? Who could remember where trees and rocks were, unless a tree had been felled or a large boulder had been rolled away from its place?

But that was exactly what Maël meant. Every inch of the island was to be scrutinized by a Witch-Sniffer and properly armed soldiers. The slightest tinge of magic was to be traced to its source. They were going to find that Wizard!

John Grant was in a bad skin as well. His back was excruciating and each movement pulled at the deep stripes. And the burns, light though they were, for Joisaine had cut him down in time, were a torment as well. He could only lay up on the bed on his stomach, a most uncomfortable position.

He lay in one of the upstairs rooms at *Les Huit Lapins*. *Madame* had put him near the window, where he could get a cool breeze and look out upon the farm.

He spent most of the day after his flogging that morning dozing on and off. Each awakening was painful and he cursed fluently as he tried to move and could not without a gasp of agony.

He cursed everything from the French to the whip that had marred his back. But most of all he cursed the Gypsy. Everything had gone wrong from the moment that piece of trash had stepped into the house. It was all his fault, all of it! Somehow, John promised himself, he would pay that thieving Egyptian back. He was just not certain how.

He was not mollified at all when, mid-day, *Madame* told him that word had come that the Professor was safe. Instead this put him into a fret. How was his master to get on without the services of his manservant? Had the place he had been taken a Bath chair for him? Who was getting his meals and taking care of his things?

Madame did not tell him where his Master was, only that he was safe. She had the news of his safety from Rosal, who, of course, had heard it from Felix. *Madame* Brehaut was wise enough not to tell John where she had the news. And even Rosal did not know exactly where the Professor was or how to get there.

John was further enraged, when, with a nuncheon tray, *Madame* brought him his one remaining jacket. It still smelled faintly of smoke, even though *Madame* had burned pastilles in the coal shovel beneath it as it hung out in the breezy porch. To John's fury, a large "P" had been stitched to the left breast of the jacket.

"What's that doing there?" he demanded in surly, belligerent tones.

"It is a necessity," said Marie Brehaut calmly. With a husband and three sons she was well-used to men and their ill-tempers when they were sick or hurt. "Tomorrow you must go to the assembly at the church and they will look for this mark. You do not wish for another whipping, do you?"

"You ain't wearing no mark!" he said in an accusatory tone.

"I am both French and a Catholic, *M'sieur* Jean. All others must wear their marks. Even those of French descent who are Protestants must wear a P as do you."

John hated it when she pronounced his name *Zhawn*. He had seen the way it was spelled and he had not believed that the French called men Jean. Why, that was a woman's name! Just another example of their depravity.

He would not let her help him eat, but dismissed her without expressing any gratitude for the meal or for taking him in. Nor had he offered any grateful phrases to Hagar, still convinced she was trying to poison him.

The soup and bread was good but he could eat very little of it. It was nearly impossible to eat in this position and it seemed to choke him. Swallowing was difficult.

As he pushed the tray away sudden tears filled his eyes. Why had they ever left Cambridge? They had been happy there. The Master had his colleagues and his books and students. He himself had friends, other servants who one could meet at one of the many pubs and jaw with, or play a game of darts, all of them good English servants who didn't chatter away nine to the dozen in French! John even had a staff, a house maid and a boot and knife boy, to lord it over.

And he had never, not even once, seen a damned Gypsy in Cambridge!

Outside, he heard a woman laugh. Raising himself slightly on his elbows, a painful process, he saw below him the Gypsy girl walking with Joisaine, each carrying baskets of something; early peas, mayhap.

His eyes narrowed as he stared at her and a look of cunning came over his face. The Gypsy's woman! She was a fetching little piece! The Gypsy appeared to dote upon her. He probably would not care to lose her.

John began to laugh silently as he realized what he could do to avenge himself on the Gypsy, the author of all his miseries.

46
Looking For Magic in All the Wrong Places

Tuesday morning again was bright and sun-filled. It was with extreme reluctance that Felix left Rosal and the bed of bracken to face another day with Blériot. He wished that he really were a Wizard as people kept insisting he was. Perhaps there was some spell to completely negate Blériot. To do so would be a service to humanity.

He met David even earlier than the day before as Blériot had wanted them there by six.

David was yawning loudly. In spite of feeling too tired at first he had ended in going to Faerie with Grizel the previous evening. After his mother was asleep Grizel had come to his room and taken him to their usual trysting place where they had spent hours making love. His fatigue had not struck until he returned to the World Above and time had once gain run in its proper course. However, he would not have traded that time with her even for a good night's sleep.

Even the soldiers at the various check points seemed heavy-eyed. They had been pressed into the search yesterday and now a rumor was flying about that there was to be another search today.

"I am glad the Professor is safe," David said in a low voice when they were well away from the parish boundary, that of Forest, the last they would have to cross before the final point of examination at the old Dragon Point itself. "But I am very worried about French reprisals. I don't think they will stop searching until they find something."

Felix agreed. "Fournier is like a terrier and those priests of the Inquisition have been denied the pleasure of torturing a man they consider a real Wizard. It will make them eager to find someome."

David gave him a glance as the cabriolet bowled along. "We'd better do our best to keep you away from the

428

Inquisition," he remarked. "According to what the Professor told me before he was arrested a trained Witch-Sniffer could "smell" the magic on you."

"Even if I can't perform any magic?" Felix inquired.

David frowned." I don't know. I now wish I had studied more about the Inquisition and their methods but there seemed little possibility of ever coming in contact with them."

"And if I ever knew, I have forgotten," Felix said, rather sadly.

"Not forgotten, can't remember," David said. "One day it will all come back," he added confidently.

Felix wished that he himself were as certain as David. Every time he tried to remember he failed, the pain in his head just as bad, as if not worse,than it had been immediately after his injury. The head injury had healed and that gave him no more trouble. The pain seemed to be from inside his brain. He had flashes of recognition and trying to track those down was agonizing. He had to very shortly give up on any effort in that direction. Very often he woke with a throbbing head, for fragments of dreams tormented him. Even here at the Dragon Port there were things that seemed as if he ought to know and ended in the inevitable head pain when he attempted to follow the thread of recollection.

Only being with Rosal gave him any peace. All day long he now clung to the thought of going home to her and the quiet of the woods and the bed of bracken. Only that kept him sane. The rest of his life had too many frustrations, too many unanswered questions for any comfort to be had. He was in a fair way to falling very deeply in love with her, wanting to be with her even when they were not in bed. He now not only wanted her but needed her as well.

They both fell silent, each young man thinking of the woman he loved. David still did not know what to do about Grizel. Last night had proved to him that he would do anything, even forgo much needed sleep to be with her. The amount of time they spent together had not lessened his passion for her.

But he had seen Majorlaine's face when Grizel had confessed to being a Selchie. And he was fairly certain that his mother, a canny soul, had guessed the nature of their relationship. She knew all the old songs about the Selchies;

about their passionate love of sexual congress, their faithlessness, their need to be free, how they prefered nudity. She had been polite enough to Grizel last night and at the breakfast table this morning but she was glad to see the back of the Selchie when Grizel left. If Majorlaine had even guessed that David had actually been with her when his mother thought him sleeping celibate in his bed it would have meant an argument. David was nearly thirty but his mother could still make him feel like a small boy when she disapproved. Majorlaine was an exceedingly moral woman. She thought that a sexual union outside of marriage was wrong and more than likely especially if the union were with a half-human creature from the sea.

Grizel had told him last night that she was sleeping with him and him alone. What did she mean by that? Was she nursing feelings of love, not just lust for him? If there were only time just to talk, not these snatched moments when passion overwhelmed them!

The Dragon Port was bustling with activity when they arrived and soldiers seemed to be everywhere. Blériot, almost frothing at the mouth with rage, gave them no greeting at all but began screaming at once, tearing at his hair. Today, however his first target was David "You're the Governor here!" he screamed. "Make them stop! They're ruining everything! Putting their filthy hands all over my materials and demanding to be let into my office and the workrooms! No one goes in there save me and my workers! You, *Gitan*," he added, turning to Felix, "Tell them to stop in whatever tongue it is that they speak. They don't seem to speak French!"

The little man became almost incoherent when David had to tell him that as the Bailiff under French rule he had no real power and that the soldiers were but doing their duty, searching for an escaped prisoner.

"I don't care if it was a still-living Louis Capet himself who made good his escape!" The inventor shrilled, referring to the late guillotined French King. "They have no right at all to disturb my work! The First Consul gave *me* the right to everything as I want it! And I do not want these soldiers mucking about!" Bleariest shrieked, jumping up and down in rage and ripping savagely at his maltreated hair.

Felix thought *"Here we go again!"* He had heard far more about the rights granted Blériot by the First Consul than he had ever wished to do.

Things went from bad to worse. The soldiers, who were indeed searching for Aurelius under Fournier's orders, broke down the door to the office when Blériot refused to give them the key and searched it thoroughly, tapping the walls and lifting floorboards. They completely disturbed Blériot's paper-work which was in a form of controlled chaos, comprehensible only to the inventor himself. They dragged everything in the various workrooms out of doors and searched every inch of the dormitories as well. They looked auspiciously at any of the prisoners who in the least resembled the description of Aurelius. One middle-aged man, haggard from illness and long captivity, who had very light, almost white, blonde hair, was even whipped to try and make him confess to being the escaped prisoner. The soldiers only released him when it was found, even under torture, that he could not be made to speak English.

Girard was in charge of the search and he brusquely ordered David and Felix to a room where he promptly locked them in. The room had already been thoroughly scoured.

They could still hear Blériot screaming until a few minutes later when Girard gave an order and they heard another door slam and the little man's shrill screeches were instantly muffled.

"The French do have some compassion!" David said in satisfaction. "Imagine being shut up with him all day!"

Girard had left them the bag that Majorlaine had again packed with foodstuffs and since there were two chairs and a dusty table in the room, David suggested thta they have a mid-morning repast. Breakfast had been a long time ago and there were damson plum tarts to eat.

That day, Tuesday, the 7th of June, lived for a long time in *Guernaise* memory as a day when the French went mad and all sorts of horrors and even some amusement were visited upon the island. At the required assembly that

431

morning many indignities were suffered by the hapless islanders. Any one suspected of being the prisoner was questioned brutally. Even old women were partially stripped, with no regard for their years or modesty, to prove that they were indeed female and not the missing prisoner in disguise. Old men even remotely answering the description were subject to beatings and torture. And the *Guernaise* were treated to the spectacle of French soldiers and priests leveling crucifixes at trees, rocks and shrubs, commanding them to change.

The *Guernaise* knew far more about Wizards than did the French and could not help but laugh at the notion that a Wizard could change himself into a rock or a tree.

Every dolman and barrow was entered and searched both by soldiers and a Witch-Sniffer. and crews set to tearing them apart. A priest oversaw the demolition of the two ancient female statues and Fournier himself directed the destruction, with charges of gunpowder, of the *L'Autel de Déhus,* the Goblin's Barrow, at Paradis in remote Vale Parish in the northernmost part of the island. He also ordered many ancient trees cut down, particularly the oaks, for they were used in the pagan worships of Druids.

Maël, in spite of his aches from unaccustomed horseback riding, followed Fournier about all day. In the afternoon he watched as an entire troop of soldiers searched for an entrance to the Faerie's Hollow. The traces of magic were fading.They were not as strong as they had been. Maël felt at once that whoever or whatever had done magic here was gone and even should they be able to enter the Faerie cave the magus would have departed. But of course, they were unable to enter, despite the best efforts of priest and soldier and gunpowder.

Maël was further enraged when he discovered the pagan statue of the Horned God and the cup inscribed in runes to be returned. Of course, he attributed this to a human agency. Some local heretic, a heathen who looked out for this ungodly idol, had replaced it. The thing was crude, as pagan idols so often were and easily carved by an artist of little skill. He took satisfaction in destroying it once again and directed two soldiers to grind it to powder.

But at the end of the long day of search, torture and

eradication they were no closer to finding the prisoner, for no trees or racks had proved to be mages in disguise nor had any of the beatings and threatening yielded any sort of clue about where the missing Wizard had been hidden. It was as if he were no longer in Guernsey at all but had somehow vanished into the ether.

Aurelius now awoke each morning with a sense of purpose. His returned health had stimulated his mind and already he had a outline for a book on Faerie lore and had notes for several chapters.

Tuesday morning he sat at the spacious desk provided him by his Faerie hosts and looked with satisfaction around the room. His beloved books had been sent to his room and put into a massive book shelf. He had been more than pleased to discover that all the books damaged by the French had been skillfully mended, repaired so beautifully that he could detect no sign that they had ever been mangled and defaced. Even the books that had been purchased second-hand looked as if they were brand new.

"I have everything I need to begin," he said to Pyewacket, who was curled up with his paws tucked under him on a corner of the desk. They had become great friends. It no longer seemed odd to talk to a cat and receive a reply.

"I am only sorry that I cannot write, for I could serve as your amanuensis," said Pyewacket. "However I can read and can check facts for you if needs be."

"Thank you, Pyewacket. I shall no doubt avail myself of your services. I do wish young Lovel could be here," said Aurelius. "He not only knows the subject, but can translate some of the more obscure texts and writes a fine, clear hand."

By now Pyewacket had heard the complete story about the young Gypsy, and Aurelius was aware that Pyewacket was searching for his Wizard. It was a common bond. They were both missing someone of whom they were more than fond. Aurelius had the advantage for he knew where the Gypsy lad was. Circumstance prevented Lovel from visiting, however. Grizel Sarchet had visited yesterday and told him of the long hours at the Dragon Port.

The sheer curtain that served as a wall lifted and Galen appeared. Elves seemed to make no noise when they walked .

"Professor, there is someone here I would l like for you to meet." and he stepped into the room, closely followed by a human man. "This is –" Galen began but did not finish, for with a glad cry of "Richard!" Pyewacket sprang off the desk and launched himself at the man.

Richard caught the cat in mid-air and exclaimed in pleasure at seeing him alive and well. Pyewacket began to purr, very loudly as Richard fondled his head, ears and chin.

"Is Felix with you?" asked Pyewacket eagerly, looking about as if his Wizard would be appearing at any moment.

"I hoped he would be with you," said Richard ruefully.

Pyewacket's purring abruptly ceased. "No," he said sadly, "he is still missing." He recollected his manners and said "Richard, I should like you to meet a new friend, Professor Aurelius Bretton, late of Cambridge. Professor, this is my Wizard's grandfather, Richard Jourdaine, the Earl of Belmaray."

The two men shook hands, Richard balancing Pyewacket on his shoulder. The cat seemed to want to stay with Richard, seemingly to be closer to Felix by being with his relative.

"Belmaray?" said Aurelius thoughtfully. "Your library, my lord, is famous even in Cambridge. Is it true it runs to ten thousand volumes?"

"Ten thousand, two hundred and twenty-three to be precise," said Richard. "We are quite proud of our collection."

He began to list off several of the choicer items until Pyewacket interrupted with barely concealed impatience. "But whatever are you doing here, Richard? Did you come to search for my Wizard? Where is Greymalkin?"

Aurelius offered the Elf and the Earl seats and listened with interest. It was as exciting as a tale from *The Arabian Nights* as Richard recounted what had happened since he last saw Pyewacket. Then Pyewacket told his tale.

"It was Reginald and that Persian mage that threw me overboard to die! I was stuffed in a sack and nearly drowned!" the cat concluded indignantly.

Richard looked troubled. "Greymalkin and Pascoe insist that Reginald and his friend had evil intent all along. I hate to think –"

Pyewacket snorted. "Well, you should listen to them! It's my belief they threw my Wizard overboard! You know yourself that he would have never let anyone hurt me. They must have taken him by surprise, for in a magical duel they would have had no chance against a *Magus Magistra!*"

Aurelius had listened carefully to every word said and now he remarked, "How very interesting it is that both young men, my Gypsy and your missing Wizard, share the Christian name of Felix. It is not a common name perhaps, but –"

Pyewacket and Richard looked at each other, struck by a wild surmise. Pyewacket said slowly, "You never mentioned that your Gypsy was called Felix. You always call him Lovel."

"At Cambridge, you must know, we are accustomed to call the students by their surnames," said Aurelius. "And you usually say 'my Wizard' when you speak of him. The similarity in names just now struck me."

"It couldn't be!" said the cat.

"Perhaps it is!" said Richard a wild hope in his expression . "We must meet this Gypsy at once!"

47
The Torque

"It cannot be so," Aurelius protested. "It is but a coincidence. Lovel looks a proper Gypsy, although he can pass as a gentleman. He wears a gold earring and moreover, has been on Guernsey since Michaelmas. He is married as well, to a Gypsy girl. They live with her aunt in a caravan in the wood belonging to my former neighbor, *Madame* Brehaut. And you," he said, turning to Pyewacket, "have described your Wizard as outgoing and cheerful. Lovel is quiet, even withdrawn at times, not prone to whistling and singing at his tasks as you have indicated. And he has, as well, a streak of white in his hair, here," he touched the crown of his head and drew his fingers forward to the front. "The same Christian names are but a concomitance. Judging by what I have been told the only similarity is in the name." His voice was vehement, surprising even himself in its force.

Pyewacket's furry face, so expressive, had grown longer with each sentence. "It would seem you are right," he said sadly. "I thought perhaps he had disguised himself, to keep away from the sight of the Inquisition." the familiar sighed painfully.

"I thought so too, for one wild moment," said Richard, stroking the disappointed cat. "But since the Inquisition is infamous for maltreating the Romanies it would scarce be a judicious disguise."

Aurelius was surprised at himself. His heart was beating fast and his hands were trembling. He had actually been terrified when the Earl and the cat had thought that his Gypsy was the missing Wizard. He did not want to lose the young man's company. He had even indulged dreams of a far more pleasant winter, of long evenings and good talk in front of the fire, of research and scholarly exchanges with a fine mind. In a short time he had become exceedingly fond of

Lovel, and had looked forward to a long relationship, even to the point of offering him and his wife a home. He now realized that he did not want his scholar to be another's grandson, to be taken back to Devon and never to be seen by Aurelius again. But he was certain that the Gypsy and the missing Wizard were not the same person, concentrating only on the differences and ignoring the similarities. He was certain that when Lovel finally came to Faerie and the Earl and the cat met him, that he would prove to be just what Aurelius thought him, a Gypsy, a highly educated Gypsy, but only that.

But Aurelius did enjoy the visit that followed after Galen's departure — the Earl, in spite of having attended Oxford, proved to be a true man of letters, no mere collector of books who valued them but as an investment. They were able to discuss many of the books in Aurelius' library and the Earl was even able to give Aurelius a list of volumes he might find useful for the current project and where they might be available when the French at last left the island.

While Richard conversed with Aurelius and Pyewacket fell into a morose silence, a small Faerie arrived with several others. They were holding a box between them that Aurelius recognized at once.

"Whatever is this doing here?" he exclaimed.

"The mage asked me to deliver this to you," explained the apple blossom Faerie Flowerlet.

"Thank you," said Aurelius,although he had no idea what she meant, and took it from her. He knew nothing of any mage. He could not understand why the box had been sent to him, unless John and Lovel thought that the French might take it. But he could not remember ever showing the box or where it was secured to Lovel, although he had certainly intended to do so. John knew where it was kept, of course, but he could not imagine Lovel and John working together. Flowerlet, when questioned, proved to know nothing of the circumstances or the actual identity of the mage in question. It was a mystery that would be solved only when he saw his young friend or John again, which he hoped would be soon.

Since he and his guest had fallen into a discussion of the antiquities on Guernsey, particularly the barrow graves, he decided that he might show Richard his unearthed treasures (for they had quickly progressed to Christian name terms being contemporaries in age and like-minded scholars). Aurelius flipped open the lid of the box and almost dropped it as a blinding greenish light burst forth and a strange humming filled the air.

"What in the name of –?" he began.

At the first sight of that light Richard had drawn his wand from its pocket and now said tersely "Pray put the box upon the ground.It may be dangerous!"

Aurelius obeyed with alacrity. He watched as Richard drew a complicated set of passes over the box with his wand that resulted in a violet box of pulsating light forming itself over it.

"This is a containment spell," Richard explained. "From the feel of it, whatever is in that box is very old magic indeed and sometimes old magic can act in unexpected ways. In a containment field I can examine it and determine if it is something of which to be extremely wary."

He then pointed the wand at Aurelius's treasure box and commanded *"Tollere."*

The contents of the box rose into the air, and hung there, floating in a lazy circle, several miniatures, a silver snuff box, spear heads and arrow tips of very old provenance and an object of shining gold that was the source of the magical energy.

Richard drew in his breath sharply when he saw what it was. "A torque — a Celtic torque of power!" he said. "And someone has awakened it. Where had you that?" he asked Aurelius in some excitement.

"I told you of my friend, Nazaire Dieudonné. This was the last thing he found before his death. Indeed, he died the very next day after he brought it to me, of a sudden stroke. By then I was no longer able to accompany him on his treasure hunts. This was found up in Vale, in what the locals call the Goblin's Barrow."

"That is not Goblin's work!" said Pyewacket, his tail lashing.

"No, it is definitely Celtic, about the first century before Christ, I would guess, done in *La Tène* style. Look at the exquisite foliage designs!" said Richard in appreciation. "What a beautiful thing!"

It was indeed. It was a collar of pure gold, hollow, and would have fastened about the throat of some high-ranking Celt. A hinge connected the half hoops at the back, while a more elaborate fastening was worn in the front.

"To whom is it dedicated?" Pyewacket said. "I don't think it is Taranis, Richard, like the one found in Avebury."

"Taranis?" Aurelius inquired. The name sounded familiar.

"The ruler of the skies, particularly of the thunder and lightning," Richard said. "Remember your Roman poets, Professor? In the epic poem about the Roman civil wars his brief mention of the Gaulish Gods: *'Cruel Teutates, satisfied by bloody sacrifice / Horrible Esus with his barbaric altars / And Taranis, more brutal than Scythian Diana..'*. The Romans thought that all those sacrificed to Taranis were burned alive in wicker cages. Supposedly, someone yielding the torque of Taranis can call down thunder and lightning."

"Is that true?" Aurelius, remembering now where he had read the name of Taranis in the poetry of the first century, Spanish-born poet, Lucan.

"Taranis is considered a Dark God," said Richard. "We are sworn to the Light. To meddle with Taranis is to meddle in the Dark." He was bending close to the violet box, studying the torque closely. "There are other figures in amongst the florals," he said "But I cannot quite make them out." He leveled his wand at the torque and said *"Amplificatio,"* and the torque was suddenly twice its size and the figures were easy to see.

In amongst the twining leaves and vines were, from right to left, figures of hounds in full cry, followed by men on running horses. The final figure held a horn to his lips. So well done were the figures that one could almost hear the baying of the hounds and the shouts of the men, with the horn crying out over all.

"By Bastet's whiskers!" exclaimed Pyewacket, blinking. "Richard, it isn't –?"

"Yes, Pye, this torque summons the Wild Hunt. And unless we are able find the magus who awoke it and he is very powerful, *Magistra* class, we are in for a very bad time," said Richard grimly.

It was nearing one o'clock in the afternoon before the soldiers left the Dragon Port, releasing both David and Felix and Blériot at long last.

Blériot had not calmed at all during his incarceration. When let out of his temporary prison he began screaming abuse at Girard, demanding to see Fournier to vent his spleen and make complaint. He threatened that a letter outlining all the indignities he had suffered and how the troops had impeded his progress with their stupidity would be on the next boat to France, directed to the First Consul.

Everything must needs be restored to order, he demanded and was further enraged to the point of gibbering when Girard said firmly that putting things back was not in his orders and he and his men were to join the Colonel and the Senior Witch-Sniffer to make their report. Restoring order was Blériot's affair.

It took all the afternoon and into the evening. David helped as much as he could as well.

It was again almost eight o'clock before Felix and David were finally released. Blériot had a screeching fit when the young officer in charge said that, no, the two *Guernaise* could not spend the evening there in order to work longer. The Colonel's instructions were explicit. They were to return to their parishes. The pass that Fournier had issued only allowed them to be abroad during the day. The officer, Lieutenant Paul Petit, was adamant — he knew to whom he had to answer.The First Consul was far away in Paris and Fournier was here. It was all over the island : the punishment Fournier had ordered for the hapless Pascal Mercier, the guard at Castle Cornet, who had been whipped until near death.

Blériot continued to scream, running out after them as they headed towards David's cabriolet. "It will take weeks, weeks I tell you, to make up for this loss of time! The First Consul expects this invasion to have taken place by the date of the anniversary of the Fall of the Bastille! That is but a mere five weeks away!" he shrieked.

Petit was then guilty of an error in judgment. He was

tired, hungry and completely sick of Blériot and his tantrums. He said now in tones of contempt, "If you think, *M'sieur,* that we will conquer England with balloons, you are sadly mistaken! The Montgolfiers' experiments proved that balloons can never be of any use save as an entertainment."

Blériot turned on him like a rabid wolf. "The Montgolfiers! I *spit* upon them! They have not my genius!" And spit he did, narrowly missing Petit's shining boots. Then a further outraged expression came over his features. "Who told you? Who told you what I am doing? You have been snooping about, don't deny it! I shall have your head!" He leaped at Petit as if to strangle him.

It was at this moment, when Blériot's attention was elsewhere that Felix and David chose to leave, a soldier having brought Thierry and the cabriolet up. Other soldiers began to rush up, to save their officer from being assaulted by the maddened Blériot. The two *Guernaise* were able to slip away in the ensuing melee.

"What a day!" said David as he set Thierry trotting towards the gate. "He's a mad-man! It gives me a very poor opinion of Napoleon Bonaparte, that he could entrust the invasion of England to someone who is clearly a lunatic! At least we can be certain that England is more than likely safe from invasion."

Felix did not agree at once and David shot him a look of inquiry. "You don't actually think that he could succeed?"

"It's just something that one of the German engineers said to me," said Felix slowly. "He remarked that the machinery they were building was a great deal like the engines he had read of, engines that could propel and steer a boat, although these are considerably smaller."

"I read an article in *the Gentleman's Magazine* about a steam tug, the *Charlotte Dundas,* that was tried in Scotland, in the Forth and Clyde canal only last year during the peace. It was said, also, that the Americans are experimenting with steam," David said.

"What if he has discovered a way to guide a balloon where he wants it to go with engines, whether steam or something else?" Felix said, looking worried. "What if he can attach rockets or swivel guns to the balloons and make them go where he wants them to go and kill people by dropping weapons upon their homes? "

"But can a balloon carry the weight of a steam engine?" David inquired, wrinkling his brow. He knew so little about the mechanics of either invention.

"The engineer, Schmidt, said not. He called what they are building here 'toys'. All the same, I am worried. I don't know if even all of the dragons in the Six Nations could combat a fleet of well armed, steam-powered and well-steered balloons," Felix confessed.

"I'll talk to the Professor and Robin tonight and see what they think," David offered. "Do you go with me to Faerie tonight?"

Felix shook his head and rubbed his forehead. "No, I've the devil of a headache. All I want is one of Hagar's headache cures and my bed. Pray give the Professor my regards."

"And what are we to do with this, pray tell?" inquired Robin Goodfellow, looking at the torque. "It's a curse, hanging over us!"

Richard had, with careful magic, removed the torque to its own opaque violet receptacle that now hung in the air above Aurelius's box where his other treasures had been allowed to gently subside.

"Only the mage who woke it can put it back to sleep," said Pyewacket, sounding depressed. "Anything could set it off and bring down the Wild Hunt on us."

"And only the mage who woke it can hope to control the Wild Hunt," added Richard grimly. "The Hunt *can* be controlled. It has been used before now to defend or protect England, once one can make the huntsmen understand that it is England they defend. The Huntsmen will help but they will listen to no one but the one who woke them once they have made covenant with him."

"I have read something of the Wild Hunt," said Aurelius "but I am not quite certain of what it is capable."

"Death and destruction," said Robin, all of his customary good humor fled from his face. "My father has an uneasy truce with the leader of the Wild Hunt, Gwyn ap Nudd. It is he who really leads the Hunt, although he is known by many names. He is King of the Underworld, the World Below ours. It is he who was known as Pluto to the Romans. The Wild Hunt brings with it the tempest and the demon wind, looking for the souls of un-baptized children and of the damned. Those who look upon the Hunt are sometimes struck dead. The Wild Hunt could not be bound by Merlin as were the Unselighe creatures, for Gwyn ap Nudd is, many say, a God."

"It has been nearly three hundred years since the Wild Hunt rode the sky," said Richard. "They would probably torment mankind far more often were it not that time in any of the kingdoms of Faerie, whether Dark or Light is far different that the time we know in the World Above. There, three hundred years is but the blink of an eye. But now, awakened, they stir and will not be contained."

"Good God!" said Aurelius, completely appalled.

48
The Coming Storm

On Wednesday morning the sky was sullen and leaden looking with heavy air, almost stifling. Thunder growled far away in the distance towards the English coast and in that same direction ominous black clouds boiled low on the horizon.

"It looks as if we are in for another bad storm," David remarked as he halted the cabriolet at the end of the lane that lead to *Les Huit Lapins* farm, so that Felix could swing up into the carriage.

"Is the weather usually so bad this time of year?" Felix settled himself into the seat. To David, his friend looked tired and pale and rubbed again and again at his forehead as if he still had a headache.

"No," David answered and clucked to Thierry to step out and turned the cabriolet handily in the narrow lane. "July is usually the sunniest month but June can be quite fair as well. September can be stormy in the Channel, particularly at the time of the equinox."

"Mabon storms," said Felix absently and then suddenly bent forward and grabbed at his head as if to keep it from exploding. "Oh, God!" he groaned, "If this headache would only go away!"

David pulled up the cabriolet and looked at him in concern. "You're in no fit case to put up with that madman today. You should be laid down upon your bed! Perhaps the weather is worsening your headache. My mother often suffers from the headache when a storm is coming, especially a storm with heavy winds. I'm taking you back to the farm. You're not going out there today."

"What will Fournier say?" Felix did not raise his head but continued to support it in his hands as it were too heavy to hold up.

David bit back an impulse to say "Who cares?" instead saying "People *do* become ill. And working in close proximity to Blériot is enough to make anyone sick! I thought he would take off in an apoplexy yesterday! Do go home and get into bed. Leave me to deal with Fournier."

"Thank you," said Felix gratefully. His head was very bad and the thought of laying down in the comfortable bed in the *vardo* was much more appealing than another day of Blériot's ranting and impossible demands. He had gone to sleep last night with a headache, able only to hold Rosal in his arms, as much as he had wished to make love to her. Even Hagar's sovereign headache remedy had not worked its usual magic. Now this coming bad weather seemed to be aggravating the pain.

David did not say anything else as he tooled the cabriolet through the woods and down to the clearing where the *vardo* stood. Felix was thankful for this. The torment in his head was increasing by the moment. It seemed to be linked somehow to the rising wind that was now beginning to toss the tree branches about and talking would only make it worse.

They found Hagar and Rosal hitching the pony to the *vardo*. "What is it?" Rosal cried in alarm as the cabriolet came to a halt in front of the fire Hagar was dousing with water. Rosal ran up to the side of the carriage and peered anxiously at Felix.

"A bad headache," David answered as he wound the reins around the whip socket. Thierry and Kälo greeted one another with sharp whinnies and Chavé followed Rosal to the carriage, whining anxiously.

"Oh, I'm glad you brought him home!" cried Rosal. "*Madame* says that the storm will be very bad and she sent word for us to come to the farm and put the *vardo* in the barn until it passes. We were just about to leave." She reached up to Felix as she spoke and tried to support him as he almost fell from the carriage.

David came around the carriage to help and ended in helping the two women get Felix into the *vardo* and into the bed, for he was in such torment that he could do little to help them. A huge gust of wind snapped the canvas walls of the *vardo* and the whole caravan quivered.

"It's the best thing that you go to the farm," said David. "Listen to the trees! It is almost as if they are crying out in protest" The branches outdoors creaked and groaned. "In this wind there will be many limbs down."

Hagar came forward and looked down at Felix, who was now lying back with an arm across his forehead, eyes closed and his lips pressed tightly together. Rosal had thrown a quilt over him and was tucking it around him, her face distressed.

"I do not understand it," Hagar said in a low voice, as if she was speaking to herself. "The dose I gave him last night should have cured the headache."

"He looks as ill as when he first was injured," said Rosal worriedly. "Can you make the remedy stronger, Hagar?"

"Yes, but not by much," Hagar answered. "I shall not give it to him until we reach the farm. He was difficult enough to get into the *vardo* while still conscious." She looked up at David. "Thank you for bringing him home and for your help," she said. "You had best get to your own home, for this will be a very powerful storm. I can feel it in my bones" She did not add that she had seen it in the cards last night as well.

"I should be able to get there before it breaks," David said confidently. "It is coming from the west and I go east."

Thierry was quivering with nerves when David approached the cabriolet. The gelding had crowded close to Kälo and the horse and pony were touching noses as if for mutual comfort.

David looked up at the sky, visible in patches between the now wildly tossing branches. Towards the ocean, to the west, it was nearly black and huge clouds rolled. The smell of the sea was very strong and between bursts of wind David could hear the waves crashing on the rock-bound shore. It was getting much worse, very rapidly.

He had scarcely given a very nervous Thierry orders to step out when he heard the *vardo* creak and come after him. They followed him to the end of the lane and then turned off to the farm.

Once free of the woods, out on the road that went through St Cécile, David dropped his hands and let Thierry run. A great mass of black was roiling up behind them and even over the wind David thought, in some confusion, that he heard a horn blowing.

Father Maël sat at his desk, hands clasped tightly together on the blotter in front of him, a frown between his eyes. He had just now returned to the office after a night spent in the chapel in front of the altar.

Why had everything gone so wrong? Had God abandoned him? The escaped Wizard was nowhere to be found. Every inch of land, every house, building, barrow and cave on the entire island had been searched at least twice. There was no way, or so the Witch-Sniffer thought, in which he could have been taken off by boat. Naval patrols constantly searched the waters here at irregular intervals so that no one could learn a pattern of when they would be checking. Almost all of the boats except the few fishing vessels tied in the harbor here had been confiscated. And the prisoner was elderly and crippled! Where could such a man have gone? None of the tortures and the whippings of the *Guernaise* had yielded any information.

So deep in his own thoughts was the priest that he looked up, startled, when a loud bang came at his window that looked out over the harbor, just as the dim light was cut off by a pair of shutters being closed. A bar outside thumped into place.

The door to his office opened abruptly and Roux peered in. "Excuse me, Father," said the torturer, his round face apprehensive "But there is a very bad storm coming and we are doing all we can to minimize the damage it will do. All the doors and windows are being shuttered and everything that can be moved inside is being moved. It came up so suddenly!" Roux did not like storms and sweat shone on his face. "I was up early of course for matins and lauds and by the time the mass was finished, the clear sky had clouded over and the wind had risen. Now it is as black as pitch out! The sea is covered in white foam!" He had scarcely finished speaking when a huge *boom* shook the castle. Roux flinched.

"Are we being fired upon?" Maël was on his feet at once.

"No, it is the wind or the sea, or both!" said Roux, his face taking on a greenish pallor. He was frightened half to death and wished that he were somewhere inland, away from the sea. Switzerland would be a good place.

Maël looked at him in contempt "It is only weather, Roux, weather which comes from God."

"You have not seen this weather, Father. It comes not from God but from the Devil himself!" Roux crossed himself reverently and took the beads of his rosary in his hand for comfort.

"Why do you not go and torture someone, Roux?" Maël suggested sarcastically. "The screams will drown out the wind."

Roux brightened visibly. "This is true! Thank you, Father! The soldiers brought in a young woman last night. She spit at them and was most uncooperative when questioned. She has an excellent figure! I shall order her stripped and tied up at once!" he said eagerly and bustled off, calling for the guard.

More wind slammed into the castle, making even the ancient stone edifice shudder.

Maël frowned. Surely summer was not the season for these wild storms? He left the office, noticing the frenzied activity of the preparations as he headed towards the stairs that led to the roof.

He could feel the force of the wind even before he stepped out on the roof. He was forced to cling to the door frame and flatten himself against the wall or the wind would have taken him.

And when he saw the towering mass of black cloud that was rapidly advancing from the west he could not blame Roux for thinking it was Devil driven.

It was enormous, mounting high in the sky, the clouds churning as if coming to a furious boil. The wind was strong and sharp and whistled by his ears. Below the castle waves dashed against the rocks, white foam leaping high into the air. The tide was running abnormally high, pushed by an offshore wind. There was as well rain mixed in with the wind, not steadily as yet, but enough to sting the face.

There was a sharp smell to the air, a strange sulfurous tang. Maël took a deep breath and bent over, coughing as he realized what it had to be. Brimstone!

As he continued to cough he was suddenly convinced that he heard mocking laughter.

"It is very bad in the World Above," said Amaryllis, the lily Faerie, a look of worry on her red and gold face. "Many of my flowers will be destroyed."

"Why, what is happening?" asked Pascoe. The dragon was laying upon a bank of wild thyme, its pleasant scent rising from beneath him. Sprays of wild roses and eglantine arched over him, their odors mingling with the thyme. All about him in the air hung dozens of Faeries of every colour. Some of them had even left their flowers to come and see him. The busy hum of their wings made a descant to the Elfin voices and silver bells in the distance.

"The Wild Hunt has been awakened," said Amaryllis in accents of horror.

All of the other Faeries shrieked in dismay and rose in a shining cloud of agitation.

"What!" Pascoe sat up from his languid posture and steam trickled from his nostrils.

"Robin even now speaks of it to your Wizard," Amaryllis informed him. "They must try to find the mage who awoke them."

"But they are only awake. Not about to get loose, are they?" Pascoe demanded.

"No, for Robin has the torque, not the foolish mage who brought the torque to life. But they will try to break the bonds that hold them in Annwn," the flower Faerie said. "And in the World Above comes the tempest of their anger."

Pascoe shivered. He had read of the Wild Hunt and the terror and death it could bring.

Richard had wanted to go with Robin when the Hobgoblin had gone into the World Above to look for both the mage and the reason why the box had been brought to Aurelius. But Robin had thought it too dangerous. The flower

449

Faeries had reported that the Inquisition was everywhere searching for Aurelius and Witch-Sniffers abounded. Robin could disappear easily, even make himself invisible which Richard could not as the spells for both dematerialization and invisibility had been lost to Wizards when Merlin had disappeared.

It seemed a long time to both Richard and Aurelius, keeping company with each other, until Robin returned. Aurelius had told them of how Lovel had cast a Mage light, wondering if his young friend was the cause of the torque's awakening, but Robin did not think so. "A mage light is not a sign of power," said the hobgoblin.

Richard agreed. "It is the very first thing a young Wizard learns to make. A raw beginner, even a person with only a touch of magic, can make a Mage light. Some never progress much beyond that point. If you had even a touch of magic, Aurelius, I could probably teach you to make a Mage light. Gypsies have but little natural magic."

Nevertheless, Robin promised to find Lovel and satisfy Aurelius's curiosity as to why and by whose hand the box had been sent. He also promised to look in on John.

When he returned at last his face was set in a frown, "Grave tidings," he said. "Your home has been burned to the ground, Professor. Your manservant is missing, and the caravan you told me of where your Gypsy friend dwelt is missing as well. I could not stay long in the area for the Inquisition has planted stakes of Cold Iron all about your former home. The flower Faeries have fled. And the storm raised by the anger of the Wild Hunt grows strong." His frown deepened. "I must go and speak to my father and ask his advice. It may be that the power of Oberon can contain the Wild Hunt, but I know that not for certain."

The Bright Court of Oberon, although the Elfin King traveled freely all over the British Isles, was in England, in the Cotswolds, in an Elfhame known as the Hollow Hills.

Aurelius had sunk into a chair, stunned by Robin's news. "Burned to the ground!" he echoed. "John and Lovel both missing? Dear God, what has happened?"

"We shall l find out, never fear," promised Robin. "But now I *must* speak to my father. Pray excuse me, gentlemen." With a short but still graceful bow he was gone in a burst of green light.

Aurelius looked stunned. Richard walked to a table where a tray of liquid refreshment stood. He found what he was looking for; a wine made of the fruit of the elder tree. It was a potent restorative. He poured a glass and took it to Aurelius, insisting that the Professor drink it down.

It served to steady his nerves but his hands still shook as he looked up at Richard. "What is happening?" he asked almost plaintively. "The world as I knew it has fallen into ruins! What ill news will my next visitor bring?"

49
The Day of
the Storm

For years afterwards, the storm of June 8th, 1803 was the yardstick by which all others were measured. From the very beginning there was something terrifying and supernatural about it.

Even the occupying French forces gave way before its fury. The guard houses which were small, flimsy structures at the parish boundaries, were closed and no patrols went out. Soldiers who usually were on sentinel watch on the roofs of various forts were spared this duty. Everything that could be closed and tied down against the storm was. And no one in their right mind ventured out of doors.

David arrived home as the wind was beginning to shriek and send debris flying through the air. He could see his mother struggling with the shutters that many people on the island had installed some years ago when worried about French invasion.

Majorlaine turned as she heard the sound of Thierry's hooves on the cobbles of the stable yard. "Oh, thank *le bon Dieu!*" she cried as she saw David. "I prayed that you would come home and not stay out on the road! Quickly! Stable Thierry and help me with the shutters."

David drove the cabriolet into the barn and as quickly as he could took Thierry from between the shafts and put him into his stall. The gelding was shivering and wild-eyed. David hoped that the familiar surroundings would calm him. The other animals, two goats and their cow, and some dozen chickens were stirring uneasily. The barn, like their cottage, was of stone and in good repair. The animals should be safe.

After struggling to shut and bolt the shutters, (it needed both of them to do so against the rising wind) David sent his mother into the house and went back out to the barn and made certain that the animals had plenty of water and food. He got back into the kitchen just as the heavens opened and rain began pouring down. Thunder crashed, louder than the noise made when the *Acadie* had blown up in the harbor, followed immediately by brilliant lightning that arced across the sky from cloud to cloud. He shut the arched door firmly against the tempest and limped towards the fire.

The closing of the shutters had made the interior of the house quite dark and Majorlaine was bustling about lighting candles and oil lamps. "Sit down," she urged her son. "You look tired. We'll have some tea and some bread and cheese. I've a *cassoulet* on the hob and there is an Ormer casserole for today's dinner. I am so glad you came home, David! I was so worried. And I did not like to be alone. Listen to that wind! In all my days I have never heard anything like it!"

The stone house, even with its thick walls, shuddered under the impact of the wind. "It's almost as if there is someone out there, screaming," said Majorlaine, filling a kettle from a sink spigot that lead from a gravity-fed tank on the roof.

"This storm came up very suddenly," said David. His coat was damp. He removed it and hung it in front of the fire. He took the filled kettle from his mother and hung it on the pot hook that hung from the lug pole across the fireplace. Hanging on an old-fashioned adjustable pot trammel simmered the *cassoulet*, redolent of chicken, sausage, white beans, tomatoes and herbs.

"We miss the weather Augurs such as Hughes Sarchet," said Majorlaine, slicing bread. "Hughes would have warned us long since about this storm and we could have better prepared for it. I am worried about what it will do to my kitchen garden and my herbs," she added.

David was worried about that as well. The crops in the fields and the fruit trees were vulnerable and the first cutting of hay should have been soon. This was going to cause a great deal of hardship and he expected to hear from distraught islanders facing ruin in the face of the unseasonable weather.

For one brief moment he wondered if the Faeries had gone beyond the line in trying to rid themselves of the French presence. Had they caused this strange, unnatural weather?

But no, the more he saw of Robin the better he liked and trusted the hobgoblin. What was more, *Grizel* liked and trusted him, and David trusted Grizel completely.

The kettle boiled and Majorlaine made the tea, calling David to the table. Outside the tile roof began to sound as if shot were being dropped upon it. "Damn!" said David. "Hail! That will be even more damaging." He felt very depressed as yet more problems were piling up, and all of them seemingly insurmountable. Every day he thought things couldn't get any worse, and yet they always did.

Majorlaine began pouring tea and said, not looking at him, but concentrating on the teapot, "David, we have to talk about that seal-woman."

David's heart sank. He had hoped that this conversation would not happen. Whatever his mother thought, he knew he could not give up seeing Grizel, or loving her.

Marie Brehaut had to help Rosal and Hagar get Felix into the kitchen. The wind was blowing so that Joisaine had to stand in front of the door to keep it from slamming shut. Thunder rattled the windows of the house. When she was no longer needed to hold the door Joisaine went to Kälo and led the pony and the *vardo* into the barn. There were extra stalls now and she made the pony comfortable in one of them, leaving the *vardo* under cover in the big stone barn. Earlier she had brought in the animals that usually stayed outside: the chickens and sheep, and the one pig left to them had been driven into his covered sty.

She emerged from the barn into a nightmare of a howling gale and pouring rain. In minutes she was drenched to the skin and struggled with the barn door which the wind seemed to want to tear from her grasp. She felt someone's strength added to hers and looked up to see Hagar pushing with her. She, too, was soaked.

They had to hang onto one another to get back to the

house, for the wind was incredible. Joisaine felt as if it would lift her off her feet and carry her away.

They found *Madame* putting Felix to bed in the now mostly unused 'green bed' or *lit d'fouaille*, which stood in a corner of the big room that served as kitchen, dining and living space. The family now slept in the upstairs, a later addition to the earlier house. *Madame* had found this built- in bed useful when the children were ill. She had been able to keep the sick child near her as she cooked, baked and did laundry. Now it would serve a useful purpose for her afflicted guest.

"*Vite, vite!*" said *Madame,* pausing in tucking a quilt about Felix. Rosal was timidly stroking his forehead with a pad soaked in lavender water. *Madame* looked at the two drenched women. "Above stairs with you and change at once! Wash your feet first. There is hot water on the hob. Your feet are covered in mud! Joisaine, show our guest where the towels are, if you please."

She then turned her attention back to Felix. "When did this come on?" she asked Rosal, a frown between her brows. She had never seen anyone so sick from a headache. He was as pale as death and seemed almost unconscious.

"He came home yesterday with a bad headache," Rosal said. "He still has headaches, ever since the fall. But he still had it this morning and it must have become worse, for Sir David brought him back to our *vardo* and said my Rom was too sick to go to the place he is working. Hagar's herbs aren't working. She says that she will give him a stronger dose now."

Felix, hovering on the brink of unconsciousness, was only dimly aware of the two women. They seemed very far away. His head seemed to be pounding to the rhythm of thundering hooves, of men shouting and the baying of hounds.

"The dogs," he murmured.

"What is that?" *Madame* said sharply and bent closer.

"The dogs," he said again, faintly.

"Something about a dog," she said to Rosal. "Perhaps he is worried that your dog is safe. Men do prize their dogs!"

"Chavé is here," Rosal said, calling the coally over. He was a very subdued dog at the moment, who had his tail between his legs and whined as he slunk over to Rosal. At her command he put his front paws up on the bed and nosed at Felix. "See? Chavé is here!" she said.

Something was struggling to come to the fore of his memory, something important. There was so much pain. Every blast of wind that made the ancient stone house tremble gave rise to more swift, fiery jabs of agony. Why couldn't he remember what was so important?

Joisaine, followed by Hagar, came back downstairs. "It is terrible up there, Maman!" she exclaimed. "The wind sounds as if it is trying to strip the tiles from the roof and it shrieks so! It almost sounds as if there are voices in the wind!" She shivered. "Oh, how I wish it would end!"

Hagar went to the closed stove, where a kettle steamed. She had brought in her herb bag and left it on the settle. Now she took out a packet of herbs and dumped it into a cup taken from the dresser that held plates, tureens, serving bowls and the common mugs used every day.

A strong herbal fragrance wafted out into the room as Hagar poured hot water over the plant material in the mug. When she replaced the kettle on the back of the stove she lifted her head sharply. "I hear dogs baying," she said. "Listen!"

The sound was far away, but quite clear.

"I think I hear a horn too!" said Joisaine. "Who could be out in such weather? Are they hunting? I shall go and take a look!"

As from a great distance Felix heard Joisaine's intent and he suddenly realized what it was that he was struggling to acknowledge. "No!" he shouted, trying to sit up, his eyes opened wide. "No! You mustn't look out, none of you! "he grabbed at Rosal's hand, which was on his brow. "Promise me! Promise me !" he said wildly. "None of you will look out!"

He was so agitated that Rosal said at once that she would not look out, no matter what. It was not until the others promised as well that he relaxed and let himself fall back down on the pillows, his eyes closed and breathing heavily.

"Felix," asked Rosal quietly, "why can't we look out? It's just bad weather."

"No, it's not just bad weather! I can't explain why I know you should not look out. But something terrible will happen if you do."

"Something terrible?" asked Joisaine, coming closer.

"Such as what?"

"Your death," he said shortly and closing his eyes, turned his face to the wall.

"Richard," said Pyewacket thoughtfully "you don't think that it was Felix that summoned the Wild Hunt, do you?"

Richard was looking at a scroll with Aurelius. It was quite ancient and had it not been under a preservation spell it would have crumbled to dust long since.

Outside Aurelius' 'room' lay Pascoe. One of the gossamer 'walls' had been raised so that Pascoe could talk to the occupants.

Now the dragon answered before Richard could, "Certainly not, Pyewacket! Felix knows better than that and even if he were desperate enough to do such a crack-brained thing he would have known that he needed the torque to control them. He would have not let go of it!" The dragon looked affronted. "After all, Felix is *Magus Magistra*! He is well aware of these things!"

"Hear me out." said Pyewacket "I know that he knows what he is doing; I *am* his familiar! But suppose he were desperate enough to call up the Wild Hunt to rid the island of the French, for instance? And supposed in the middle of the ritual he was interrupted by the Inquisition. What better place to send the torque for safe-keeping than to its rightful owner? He could show up here at any moment!" the cat said excitedly, his tail lashing.

"That won't wash," said Richard kindly. "Felix is unacquainted with Aurelius. How would he know where to send it? And how could he have got his hands upon the torque in the first place? It has been locked away in Aurelius' house for years. And no *Magus Magistra* worth his salt would do something as rash as to begin a calling and them not complete it. That is why there is such a powerful storm raging in the World Above. The Wild Hunt is angered. They cannot get through completely. They are caught between that world and theirs and the storm is the manifestation of their anger. We could only hear echoes of the hooves and hounds if we're up Above. "

"But torques and their like call to Wizards and Witches," said Pyewacket stubbornly. "That's how the torque in Avebury was found. Perhaps it called to him and he did a Summoning charm!"

"In which case he would have followed the proper protocols and contained it!" said Richard sharply. He felt sorry for the familiar but his scenarios were becoming increasingly ingenious. He was becoming desperate to find his Wizard. Richard thought of Greymalkin with a pang. He missed his own familiar and knew that Grey would be worried to death and more than likely fretting. He hoped that Elspeth had indeed told Madoc and the Prince had dispatched some one to Devon before this storm broke. A storm like this one kept most of the Sea-Folk at the bottom of the sea, safe in their palaces of coral and crystal. Some few were on duty, watching for distressed ships and would attempt to save as many of the humans abroad as was possible. Contrary to what the Inquisition preached the Sea-Folk did not call up storms to drown sailors.

"The Wild Hunt is not actually abroad then?" inquired Aurelius with interest.

Richard shook his head. "No. Whoever used the torque only started the calling. It needs to be completed."

"Who would call such a monstrous host?" said Aurelius, looking grave. "I would think it injudicious to say the least!"

"They have been called several times before," said Richard "The last time was in the days of the Armada. Sir Francis Drake was a mighty Wizard and called upon them to defend Britain. They helped bring down the tempest that sank the Armada, along with the cones of power raised by Wizards and Witches. The Hunt was allowed to take the souls of many a Spanish sailor as payment. Their usual function is to collect the souls of the damned and the un-baptized, but they also take any unwary person who chances to look upon them."

"That is why everyone must be so careful to have their children baptized right away," said Pascoe. "There are very few damned souls in the Six Nations nowadays. I think that must account for why we see so little of the Wild Hunt in these modern times."

"Perhpas not, but I surely think that the Inquisition, with its many cruelties, would rank high in the legions of the damned," said Aurelius.

"There are Wild Hunts on the Continent," said Richard. "In France , for one, it is known as *L'Armée Furieuse*, led by *Le Grande Vaneur de Fontainebleau*. And I daresay they drag a fair amount of Inquisitors down to hell, deservedly so."

"It isn't always death to see them," said Pascoe. "They were used to be seen far up in the sky, almost silently passing, foretelling some cataclysmic event such as war, natural disaster, or even a political or economic catastrophe. It is said that *L'Armée Furieuse* appeared riding the storm before the outbreak of the French revolution and here in England before the Norman Invasion."

"Fascinating!" murmured Aurelius. "I have read but little of this phenomenon." His fingers itched for a pencil to make notes. He was learning so much here, so much more than he had ever imagined existed.

A green light began to grow near Pascoe and the dragon surveyed it with interest as Robin Goodfellow manifested his corporeal presence.

The Hobgoblin looked tired. His air of being about to laugh at any moment had vanished. "I have been to see my father Oberon," he announced. "He was well aware of the ill will of the Wild Hunt. He spoke to Gwyn ap Nudd but Gwyn insists the storm must sound blow itself out. The Hunt is incensed.The calling must either be reversed or completed. Gwyn can only hold the undead Host so long. They give us twenty-four hours to do so or they *will* ride. And the sands began running through Gwyn's hourglass even as my father left Annwn."

50
Revelations of Love

John heard the rising wind and the shutters banging as he lay in bed upstairs at *Les Huit Lapins*. A while ago *Madame* had come up and closed and locked the interior shutter, explaining that a very bad storm was coming. He also heard, a little later, female voices in the hall and the sound of cupboards opening.

Still later, in which time rain had begun to lash at the windows, *Madame* came upstairs again and stood, frowning down at John for a moment. "I think it best, *M'sieur* Jean," she said at last "that you go below stairs. In this wind I worry about tiles being ripped from the roof and perhaps a leak forming. Joisaine has made up the couch for you. It will be easier for us to tend to you as well. I have here the dressing gown of my husband and I shall help you on with it and help you downstairs as well."

As John levered himself up on his elbows she said "I must warn you that I have the Romanies below, sheltering here from the storm. I want none of your nonsense. You will mind your tongue or I shall personally remove the bandages and pour salt in your wounds and take pleasure in doing so!"

John looked at her, surprised. She sounded so fierce, as if she would actually do such a terrible thing. He met her eyes and saw that she meant what she said.

He grunted. "It's no skin off my nose if you want to be robbed blind, letting Egyptian trash into your house," he said. "Just don't ask me to do the pretty to them."

"That is too much to expect," she said dryly. "If you will refrain from calling them names and acting as if you were polluted by being in the same room with them, it will be sufficient," she returned.

John was actually glad to be offered the opportunity to go below stairs, for the noise of the storm was increasing every moment and the old house creaked and groaned with every blast of wind, trembling on its foundation. John felt as if he were high in a tree, insecure and in danger of falling. As he struggled to get into the dressing gown (he also wore a nightshirt that had belonged to Eudes Brehaut and some of that gentleman's stockings as everything of his own had been destroyed in the fire) hail began to strike the roof, making an ungodly din. Indeed, he could scarcely hear anything over it and did not think it would be pleasant to lay here and listen to that for any length of time. As long as those damned Gypsies did not intrude themselves upon his notice he could put up with them, particularly when he thought of the fire in the kitchen and a nice hot cup of tea.

It was an exertion that left him shaking and covered in sweat, to don the dressing gown and a pair of leather slippers and go below stairs, leaning heavily on *Madame's* arm. Fortunately, she was a strong woman and made no complaint. By the time they reached the kitchen and the couch, drawn invitingly near the fire by Joisaine, John was trembling in every limb and in pain from his back. He sank down gratefully on the couch, getting back into the most comfortable position which was on his stomach. He scarcely even noticed the Gypsies, only dimly aware that there were more people in the room that just *Madame* and her daughter.

It was quieter down here, although he could still feel the shudders of the house and hear the wind scream.

Rosal had curled up beside Felix on the spacious *lit d'fouaille*. She had stooped sponging his brow for it seemed to do little good. She was trying to be as quiet and as still as possible. Looking at him one would have thought him asleep, save for the tale-tell line between his eyebrows and his tightened lips. He lay on his side, turned to the wall, with his head deep in the pillows as if the pillows could absorb the pain. The bed lay in a dark alcove, sheltered from the light of the fire and that of the oil lamp that swung from the ceiling.

But nothing could diminish the noise outside. It terrified Rosal. She had lived through some bad storms but nothing like this and she could see from the other faces in the room that it was unique to them as well. She could not but help think that somehow her Rom's headache was tied to the storm.It seemed to worsen as the storm intensified. Some persons, she knew, were very weather sensitive, but he had not suffered like this on the last bad storm they had. Or had he? She suddenly remembered that he had spent that night at the Professor's house.

She also wished that John was not now in the kitchen. She did not like or trust him. When they had met at the Professor's to discuss helping him escape from gaol, she had felt John's contemptuous eyes upon her and heard every disparaging thing he said. What kind of trouble would he make now? She wished that *Madame* Brehaut had not taken him in.

"Rosal," came Felix's voice in a thin thread of whisper. Without opening his eyes he extended a hand to her, groping.

She took his hand at once and pressed her cheek against it. "I'm here," she whispered.

"Don't leave me," he said, so quietly she had to bend closer to hear

"I will never leave you," she promised, still in a low voice. "You're my Rom and – " she hesitated and then said quickly the words she had never said to anyone but her lost child and to the dog and pony "I love you."

And it was true, she realized. She *did* love him and her happiness was now all tied up with him, a man, not a baby.

"I love you," he said on a sigh and slipped into sleep.

She did not let go his hand, but kept a grasp upon it, even as it relaxed in her grip. She was so lost in the wonder of her realization that she did not see John's eyes, glaring at her from across the room, spite and calculation written in their hooded glance.

"Whoever he is, he's in some pain right about now," said Richard gloomily, over a cup of tea.

"The Wizard who called up the hunt, you mean?" said Pascoe. A dragon-sized cup of tea stood in front of him. Aurelius had been fascinated by the neat, quiet and polite way the dragon used his tongue to sip up the tea.

Richard nodded as the others at the table, Robin,

462

Aurelius, Pyewacket and Galen, looked at him in interest.

"There are few worse things one can do to oneself than leave a spell incomplete, especially one such as this calling. Once you've released the energies involved in spell-casting they must be completed to be properly controlled. An uncompleted spell can rebound and cause the Wizard significant pain."

"Symptoms?" asked Galen with interest. Elfin magic was inherent, not learned, although a Wizard or Witch in the World Above had to be born with a predilection toward magic. Magic had to be awakened in a child and properly guided and taught for that child to come to his or her full magical potential. Elves were born with the ancient knowledge and used no wands and very few spells. Galen found the differences fascinating.

"The most vulnerable part of the body suffers," Richard explained. "In some it might be the stomach, or the joints, or a violent headache, whatever part of the mage's body is the weakest. We all have a weak point."

"Then all we have to do is look for someone who is ill?" said Pyewacket eagerly.

Richard shook his head. "I wish it were that easy, Pye," he answered.

"And I wish time were not hurtling by," added Robin. "I cannot even send out any Faeries to look for a mage until the storm Above passes. They would be dashed to their deaths, trying to fly in such wind and rain. It is far too dangerous in the World Above for anyone, even with magic, to be abroad."

"Even a dragon could not fly in such wind, not to mention the lightning," said Pascoe.

"Did Gwyn ap Nudd indicate how long we could expect to be plagued by this storm?" Richard asked Robin.

"At the very least four hours, perhaps as long as twelve," said Robin, looking depressed. "And Gwyn has chosen to count the time in human terms, not those of Faerie."

"Twelve hours!" Aurelius echoed, looking appalled. "But surely that will cut the time for the search very close indeed!"

Richard sighed. "And when you consider that we must not only find this mage but get him to complete the calling, or call it off in that time, it will be a damned close-run thing."

The conversation with his mother about Grizel had not gone well, to David's dismay. He had really not expected it to do so. Majorlaine was stern in her beliefs and they did not include countenancing her only son's *liaison* with a half-seal.

She had gone right to the heart of the matter. "You have obviously an intimate relationship with that seal-woman," she said, fixing her eyes on his face. "How long has this been going on? And do not tell me," she raised her hand as David began to protest "that you are of age, that it is none of my business with whom you share a bed! It *is* my business! What if there is a child? My grandchild, my grandchild who would be part seal! And how can you hope to make a good marriage, a marriage with someone entirely human if you are involved with a creature from the sea? They are sirens, David! They enchant men and make them blind to human women! I want a daughter-in-law whom I can welcome to the family, who will give you human babies, not a naked hussy who is like to turn into a seal and swim off with a herd of her own kind, indiscriminately giving herself to male seals and human men alike! You know the songs and tales as well as I. She will not remain faithful to you. Faithfulness is not in their nature. They are pleasure seekers, these seal-women. Sooner or later she will go back to the sea! And any children will feel the call of the sea as well. You know this! Even now she is probably sleeping with another seal or even another man. The longer you are with her the harder it will be to break away from her. I do not wish to see you die of a broken heart when she throws you over, as she no doubt will! I ask you again, how long has this been going on?"

"Since the last week in May," he admitted. He could see by her face that she was determined to have this information no matter how he denied her.

Majorlaine's face cleared of its frown. "Then it has not been a very long time. You can easily break away from her before she has her claws into you and you are lovesick!" she said eagerly. "David, you must break it off, don't you see that?" as her son said nothing but stared into his tea cup, a heavy frown on his features.

A pain ripped through his body as David thought of never seeing Grizel again, of never loving her, of spending no more hours in their mossy bed together. He thought of everything he loved about her; not just her beautiful body and her delight and skill in lovemaking but her sense of fun, her quick mind, her frankness, her passionate sense of right and wrong, her truthfulness and the matter-of-fact way she had accepted his physical hurts and limitations. She made him feel happy on so many levels and she was now rapidly becoming his repose and peace. He could not give her up. When she was done with him the pain would be even worse than when his *fiancée* had been killed. But ending it would be her choice. He could not do it. He wanted her on any terms, as long as was possible.

"I am sorry, *Maman*, but I cannot break it off," he now said quietly. "I love her too much. If there were any way in which I might marry her I would. I know it is impossible. But I will not and cannot curb her freedom. I cannot see her as farmer's wife, content to live at Torteval with us. I know that I will be hurt badly when she leaves me but I cannot give her up and you cannot ask me to do so. All of your arguments are true and if I was wise I should listen to you. But I fear I am not wise." He looked at her, a rueful smile twisting his lips. "I have been happy with her for the first time since Ghislaine was killed. Please, *Maman*, do not begrudge me that! When she is done with me I promise you that I will do my best to forget her and look about me for a human wife and give you those grandchildren you want. But until that time I want to be with Grizel, even if there is no future in it."

In the parlor, behind a door set ajar, unseen by either of them, stood Grizel, naked and still wet. She had come straight here from Faerie by way of Madoc's palace, unaffected by the storm in the mortal world. Since Robin had given her, for as a magical creature she was privileged, the Word she needed to open a portal into Faerie, she had gone easily between the two worlds. The Faeries had opened a portal for her use into David's bedroom and she had arrived only minutes earlier.

In spite of the fury of the tempest out of doors she had, with the acute hearing of an animal, heard most of the conversation between David and his mother as she came down the stairs and went into the parlor which opened into the kitchen.

She looked down at herself as Majorlaine described her as a "naked hussy" and wondered again why humans, females in particular, were so upset about nudity. One came into the world naked after all and taking a gown about with her at all times was both a nuisance and impractical. She much prefered being like this. It was far easier to shape-shift if one did not have to disrobe first for the garments would be destroyed in the shift. Wearing her 'church clothes' when she had called upon David earlier had been a concession to his mother's sensibilities.

She held her breath and leaned against the wall, feeling a bit shaky as she listened to Majorlaine's arguments and waited for David to speak.

When he said he would not give her up she was so relieved that she felt light-headed. The thought of never seeing him again was insupportable. And then she realized what else he had said. He said that she made him happy! He said that he loved her!

Was that why she no longer wanted anyone else? Why she thought about him constantly and wanted to be with him even when they were not making love? Was she in love with him as well?

She remembered the talks she had had with her mother before Mother had died, killed by a harpoon from a French fishing vessel. Mother had said that she never regretted giving up her freedom to be with Grizel's father and him alone. He sent her to the sea quite often as he knew how much a Selchie needed to be in the sea. Brenna Cameron had been happy with Hughes Sarchet and faithful to him, even though, as her daughter had been later, she had been with both seals and other Selchies before they met. Brenna had hoped for the same love for her daughter. And now it seemed, it had come at last, when Grizel had nearly given up hope. She was nearing thirty, after all. But she did love David! That was why she was so unhappy when they were parted.

Grizel took a deep breath and tossed her still damp hair back over her shoulders. She would not hide herself. She was proud to be a Selchie. It was what she was and David's mother had best get used to the fact.

She opened the door and stepped into the room. "If that was a proposal, David, I accept," she said, looking straight into his eyes. "I would be proud and honored to marry you and give you children,which by the way would only be one quarter seal. They may be just good swimmers and not Selchies at all," she added, looking then at Majorlaine.

"Grizel!" David gasped, hauling himself to his feet with the aid of the edge of the table "What do you mean?" he stammered.

Majorlaine gasped and turned her head away from the shameful sight of a naked woman in her kitchen.

"Isn't it obvious? I mean I love you and I want to spend the rest of my life with you!" she said. Men were so dense!

"Excuse my appearance, Lady Dieudonné," she said "but I have come almost straight from the sea and when David and I marry you will have to get used to the sight of my bare skin, as I do not intend to begin hauling a waterproof bag of clothing with me wherever I go. It is just not practical. I am as God made me and He finds no fault in it, so neither should you. And I am completely capable of remaining faithful to David. Since I met him I have neither had nor wanted anyone else. My mother was completely faithful to my father until the day she died. You should not believe every old song and legend you hear," she added.

David stood rather shakily, joy filling every inch of his being. "Grizel!" he said."Grizel!" and stumbling across the room with his cane unnoticed on the floor, took her in his arms. "Dear God, but I love you! When will you marry me?"

She let him kiss her hungrily for a moment and said "We can plan the wedding later, David. I came here to take you to Faerie. Robin wants to talk to you and it's rather important."

He nodded. "Will you be all right, *Maman*? You will not even notice I am gone, for time runs differently in Faerie."

Majorlaine looked dazed. First of all a naked Selchie in her kitchen, proposing to her son and now David spoke casually of visiting a mythical place! Whatever was going on? She could only nod, watching how tightly David held the seal-woman and the look of sheer happiness on his face.

Grizel left David's embrace and bent to the floor to picked up his cane where it had fallen. "I pledge to you, Lady Dieudonné, that I will be a good wife to David and a good

467

mother to his children, your grandchildren. You will never have cause to complain of me for any reason," she said earnestly.

Majorlaine said, in a rather constricted voice. "Pray come to supper tonight. If you are to marry David we need to become acquainted." It was one of the bravest things she had ever said, for everything in her wanted to reject the Selchie woman. But one look at David's face...

"Thank you for that," said Grizel. "I shall accept and come decently clothed," she added with a smile at Majorlaine's still largely averted face. "Come, David! We must go. There is a portal into Faerie above stairs."

She drew David after her and Majorlaine heard them go up the stairs, leaving her alone with only the ticking of the long case clock from the parlor and the sound of the wind and rain battering the house. It all seemed as if it might be some fantastic dream, save for the small, wet footprints of bare feet on the flagged stone kitchen floor.

David was pleased to see the Professor in such good health and to see that Pyewacket had been reunited with at least part of his family. He was also pleased to meet Richard and his dragon. Like the Selchies, he had never seen a dragon in person.

Robin wasted no time in acquainting David with all of the facts of the case. "So I thought, that as Bailiff of Guernsey and knowing just about all of the islanders, you might have some idea who the mage was that awakened the torque."

"By awakening would you mean perhaps a coloured light and making it glow?" David asked.

Richard exchange a significant look with Robin. "Exactly!" he said, leaning forward and looking at David with interest. "Did you see such a thing?"

David nodded. "I did indeed. It was Lovel who opened your box magically, Professor, with a violet light, and made the torque begin to glow when he took it in his hands. He even said it was a torque of power. I had no idea what it was. When I questioned him he said he had no idea how he knew that."

"Lovel!" echoed Aurelius, surprised. "But from what you said," he turned to Richard "it would take a powerful mage –"

"It would indeed," said Richard looking both grim and hopeful. "I think we need to locate this young Lovel immediately and bring him here."

51
Return to Devon

"But we do not know where Lovel might be," said Aurelius. "Robin said his caravan had disappeared."

"They've gone to take shelter from the storm at *Les Huit Lapins* farm," said David. "I saw them go there myself." He told them how he had returned Lovel to his family when it had become apparent that his headache was unbearable.

"That makes it certain," announced Richard. "It was your young Gypsy," he said to Aurelius "that awakened the torque. The headache he suffers from is the uncompleted magic affecting him."

"Might I go to the farm through Faerie and fetch him here?" David offered.

Richard shook his head. "He would be little good to us, or to himself until the storm passes. It would only increase his pain to bring him here. We have little choice but to wait and, at any rate, since the calling is mortal magic the ceremony to conclude it must be done in the World Above, preferably in a sacred place such as a stone Circle."

"The French have just finished destroying all of the Circles and barrows and whatever else they could find," said David glumly, exchanging a glance with Grizel.

Robin laughed out loud, the first time in days that he sounded his merry self. "I think that the French will be in for a great surprise when they do go and survey their handiwork! They will not find things as they left them!"

David grinned suddenly. "I heard about the repeated repair of *La Gran'mère*! Fournier has nearly had an apoplexy over it! I can just see his face when he finds out. Oh, it is such a good joke!" "

"Are there preparations to make before hand?" Aurelius inquired.

"Yes," Richard said and turned to Robin. "I shall need a

very great favor, Robin. I need rather urgently to visit my library and my Tower. Is it possible for me to travel through Faerie to Devon?"

"Of course," said Robin graciously. "As a Faerie friend you are entitled. I shall take you there myself, immediately."

Stealthily, over a steaming cup of tea, John watched the two Gypsies in the built-in bed. Madame had served it to him in something she called a pap boat, used for invalids. It was certainly easier to drink from for someone laying upon his stomach. It was in the shape of a fanciful dolphin, and had a closed top. The dolphin's mouth was the spout from which John drank and he held it by the tail to lift it to his mouth.

He could see how much that damn Gypsy thought of his little piece of tail. He held tight to her hand as she curled beside him. That was the best way to strike at him, through her. John did not want to involve the Inquisition again. That had proved one of the worst mistakes he had ever made. Even now no one would tell him where the Professor was; even Sir David had only said, "He is safe and where the Inquisition cannot find him. It's best that you do not know in case you are questioned."

When John had protested that it was his right to know and did they not trust him, Sir David had looked right at him and said in the coldest tones John had ever heard from him, "We do not, in fact, trust you, John, and you brought that upon yourself. All I will tell you is that he is indeed safe."

John was positive that the damned Gypsy knew where the Professor was, from the way he and Sir David had talked on Monday morning. He actually knew from the way they had NOT talked, carefully avoiding the subject of the Professor, which had seemed very odd to John. It made him angry beyond measure that the Egyptian knew and he, the Professor's trusted manservant for more years than he cared to count, was treated as if he meant to hurt and endanger his master.

He wasn't sure yet exactly what he could do, to hurt that stinking Gypsy as much as he himself had been hurt. But he *would* come up with a plan.

Everything that had happned was all his fault. John was glad even now to see the Gypsy suffering with a bad headache. If John had his way he would be suffering a lot worse. If the Gypsy had never come to their home things would still be going on as they always had. They'd be safe and snug in the cottage and the Professor would not now be a fugitive. *Madame* had told him that there were even posters hung up, offering a reward for the Professor or for information leading to his capture.

He watched and studied the Gypsies, mulling over plans in his mind.

In spite of the fact that John took care not be seen staring directly at them Rosal still felt his inimical glare upon her and Felix. She could feel his hatred coming off him as if it were a creeping miasma.

Hagar also noticed the spiteful, speculative glances accorded Rosa and her Rom. No more than did Rosal did she trust the manservant. If he could do them a harm, he would.

She was not going to let it happen if she could help it. She owed Rosal her life and Felix had never been anything but kind and helpful to her, even though she was no kin of either of them. She rather liked being thought of as Rosal's aunt. It gave her a feeling of belonging to them, as she was really a member of a small *cumpania*. The feeling of separateness that she had endued for love had disappeared. She was no longer an outcast (for the Romany had declared her *mahrime)* and the *Giorgios* had not welcomed her either. She would read the cards again tonight. Perhaps they would give her a clue as to what that man was planning behind that evil face of his.

Greymalkin was dozing in Richard's favorite chair in the library at Belmaray. The last several days had been exhausting. There were all sorts of loose ends to tie up. Greymalkin,as well as most of the Witches and familiars in the Coven, had been questioned by both the local sheriff and the magistrate, as well as Bow Street, as to the manner of Bahram's demise and Reginald's confession to attempted murder. There was some question as to whether or not Richard and Pascoe were still alive. If they were not, Reginald would be charged with being an accessory to murder and would more than likely dance at Tyburn tree. If convicted of attempted murder he might be so fortunate as to only be dampened, relieved of his magic, and sent to Van Dieman's land in the Antipodes, where he would live the rest of his life in exile.

It was the least that Reginald deserved, thought the familiar. Look at the pain and grief he had caused everyone! And that Bahram! The Persian sorcerer had proved to have a lengthy criminal record, both in his own country and in several others. It had turned out that Bow Street had been warned about him and indeed had strongly cautioned him about trying any of his tricks here when first he came to the Six Nations. They had found, with the help of the forensic Wizards from Bow street, Bahram's grimoire above stairs in his attic workshop. Bow Street had taken it for examination although they would need an interpreter or a Translation Table to read the Persian script.

It had all turned out well. The menace to his family was gone, but Greymalkin could have rested easier if he only knew that all of them, — Richard, Felix and Pascoe, were safe.

And now to top it off, though, they were having yet another storm. The Weather Augurs said that but the fringe of the storm touched upon Devon. The bulk of it, and a bad one it was, was over the Channel Islands. Greymalkin supposed this was why he had not heard from Madoc, although he had coaxed Pearson again to blow the Triton horn. For the Sea-Folk were all busy during a great storm, trying to prevent loss of life in the shipping channels. Many of them spent the time in the great palaces under the sea when the waves and the surface of the ocean were storm-tossed. But many of the Mermen, personally led by Madoc, volunteered to patrol the affected areas and save as many of those in sinking ships as could be managed. But there were many more humans at peril in any tempest than there were Sea-Folk to save them.

Greymalkin said a prayer to Bastet that Felix on Guernsey was out of harm's way and that wherever Richard and Pascoe were, they, too, were safe.

Half asleep, he was taken by surprise when a green light began to glow in front of the fireplace. He sat up abruptly, and sprang to his feet, his ears flattened against his head, eyes dilated, whiskers bristling and his tail thumping on the chair seat. His fur stood on end and his back arched as he planted his feet firmly on the chair, prepared to unsheathe his claws and attack. He let out a long hiss, his teeth bared threateningly. Was this some other creature of Bahram's ?

But the green mist turned into a door and through it stepped Richard, followed by a strange young man who smelled, to Greymalkin's sensitive nose, of Faerie.

Greymalkin gave a cry of joy and sprang towards his Wizard. Richard caught him in mid-air and held Greymalkin close to his face so that the familiar could rub his face possessively against Richard's cheek and fill the room with a rumbling purr of contentment.

"Where did you come from?" Grey demanded when the first excesses of greeting had passed. "Is Pascoe all right?"

"I'll explain as we go. I've a good deal to gather up in a short time, Grey, and have to go back almost immediately," Richard said, putting his familiar back on the chair, in spite of clinging claws that told him Greymalkin wanted to stay close to him. "By the way, Greymalkin, this gentleman is Robin Goodfellow. Would you be so good as to show him where we keep the volumes on Callings and the materials lists? I have to get up to the Tower and gather some necessities. Where is Reginald? Has he been behaving himself?"

Greymalkin glanced at a case clock. "By now he is more than likely cooling his heels in a cell in Newgate," he said.

Richard stared at him for a moment and then said dryly, "Well, I can see that you've a great deal to tell me as well!"

Robin gathered up several books that Greymalkin showed him on the subject of Callings and then followed the familiar to a small circular stair behind a bookcase, cleverly hidden. This lead up to Richard's Tower.

"A fine library," said Robin as they traversed the narrow, winding stair.

"We're proud of it," said Greymalkin. "Richard is considered to have the finest arcane library outside of the colleges of Merlin and of Dee. What is this all about, Hobgoblin?" he asked curiously.

Robin smiled. "Ah, you recognize me," he said.

Greymalkin snorted. "Show me a cat, even a non-magical one, who does not recognize a Hob when he meets one and I'll show you a dead cat!"

They reached the top landing where a huge arched door barred the entrance to Richard's Wizard's tower. The door was of Devon oak, and strapped and studded with nails of a silver alloy, magiced to be as strong as Cold Iron.

Greymalkin touched a paw to the massive door and it swung open easily.

Richard had hurriedly thrown up several mage lights and was now seen packing a case with what he felt he would need for the coming ceremony.

"Grey," he said. "I need you to come back with me. I've found Pyewacket but we need to prompt a young Wizard who is, from what I have been told, both ill-trained and suffering from a head injury. I'll have to walk him through a Calling ceremony and could use both you and Pyewacket to help with prompts and props."

"Of course," said his familiar. "I'll just tell Horrocks where I am going. There have been more than enough mysterious disappearances around here lately! But what kind of calling, Richard?"

"He began to call the Wild Hunt," said Richard, folding two robes of deep sapphire blue and putting them inside a small corded trunk. The Gypsy would more than likely not have robes of his own, nor a wand. One would have to be made on the spot.

"Bastet's whiskers!" gasped Greymalkin, looking shocked. "The Wild Hunt! Was he mad?"

"Just unaware, I think," Richard answered. He turned to the hobgoblin. "Robin, if you and Grey could look in the book the large blue one, *Materia Magicus,* and see what else we need for a Calling ceremony, anointing oils and such, and make certain I am packing two of everything?"

Robin nodded and flipped through the top volume until he found the correct page and began to read it out to the cat, who hopped up on the table top and checked the contents of the bag as Richard continued to pull items from drawers and shelves. As he worked he began to tell Greymalkin all that had happened since he and Pascoe had left for Portsmouth, interspersed with Grey's tales of what had gone on here at home.

Twelve hours later the storm finally abated. It was early evening before the heavy rain, intermingled with hail, stopped falling. Then the wind died back. As it was not yet Midsummer's day, at six in the evening the sky was still light and a watery sun made its appearance as the clouds began to disperse.

When a thin finger of sunlight appeared through a crack in a shutter Joisaine exclaimed with pleasure and threw the shutter in the dining room open. "It has stopped!" she said happily. "But, oh, I can see tiles from the roof and branches all over the yard!"

"That will not be all the damage, I am certain," said her mother, frowning. "We will need to go and look over the fields, Joisaine, to see what remains to us and what can be salvaged."

Rosal was glad to see that as the fury of the storm lessened, so had the pain lines on Felix's face. As it quieted he fell into a natural sleep. When Joisaine opened the shutters he stirred and woke, looking up into her anxious face.

He smiled up at her. "My good angel," he said sleepily. "I am always waking and finding you bending over me, to take care of me."

"You're better?" she said anxiously.

"I still have the headache, but it is not even half as bad as it was," he said, and with her help, sat up. He felt as if he had been ill for quite a long time, as he had been just after his accident. He also felt as tired as if he had been digging ditches all day.

Felix felt someone's eyes on him and looked up to see John glaring at him.

"Hello, Grant," he said, trying to be as pleasant as he could, which was difficult in light of the malevolence he saw in John's features and knowing that this man had tried to give him to the Inquisition for burning. "I trust you are doing better now?"

"And how should I be doing after being half-way flogged to death, you bloody –" John snarled.

"*M'sieur* Jean!" said *Madame* sharply."I have warned you!"

Before she could say any more a thunderous knocking came at the door.

"Pray God this is not the French!" *Madame* declared as she bustled towards the door."They will probably try to blame this storm on us!"

52
Preparations

A trifle hesitantly, fearing the worst, *Madame* opened the door.

But to her immense relief it was not the French, but Sir David Dieudonné, whom she knew slightly. Behind him was a young woman she did not know. Sir David wore a look of anxiety.

"To what do I owe this honor; the Bailiff of Guernsey calling upon me?" she asked.

"*Bon jour, Madame*," said David with a courteous bow. "I am seeking Mr. Lovel. Is he here?"

When *Madame* said "the Bailiff of Guernsey", Felix sat up, assuming that David had come to take him to the Dragon Port. Blériot, he knew, would be enraged that they had not come this day and Fournier would no doubt support any of the little man's dictums. Felix's stomach twisted in a knot as he thought of dealing with Blériot demands while he was still feeling so fragile.

Rosal frowned and said "You're never going out there tonight!" showing that she had reached the same conclusion. "You've been sick all day! They can't expect it!"

Madame invited David and the young woman, whom he introduced as his *fiancée*, Grizel Sarchet, into the room.

"I have to go, Rosal," said Felix in an under voice to her as all the others' attention was on the Bailiff and his lady. "If I don't obey them they will take out their anger on you and Hagar. I don't want to see either of you whipped or given to Fournier's troops."

She looked stubborn but made no demur when Felix got out of the bed, a bit gingerly, and went across the room to greet David. He offered his congratulations as well on the news of the engagement. "Are we to go out to the Dragon Port tonight?" he asked.

David did not look particularly happy for a newly engaged man. "No," he said abruptly. "Look here, do you remember the torque we found in the ruins of the Professor's cottage? It seems you have inadvertently awoken it and called down the Wild Hunt on us. This storm was a manifestation of their anger at being partially called."

Hagar gasped. Of all of the people in the room she knew the most about the wild Hunt, for her mother, the *cumpania's* wise woman, had told her stories of it.

"But I never meant —" Felix said, distressed.

"No, of course not," David agreed. "But as it has been explained to me, since you awoke it, you must be the one to send it back where it belongs."

"I don't even know how I awoke it!" Felix protested, "much less how to send it back!"

"We have a Wizard who will guide you," said Grizel, speaking for the first time. "He is in Faerie, where we need to go as soon as possible. There is no time to explain any more. Suffice it to say that the Hunt must be contained," she said as the faces about her looked puzzled and questions seemed about to be asked. She was conscious of the time allotment ticking away. The Wizard had said that there was a good deal of preparatory work to do.

Rosal looked worried. "What shall I do?" she asked fearfully.

"There is nothing you can do in Faerie," said Grizel. "This rests strictly upon the shoulders of the Wizards."

Felix took his wife by the shoulders, "Stay here with *Madame*," he urged "There is a great deal to do here and our *vardo* needs to return to the woods as well. You'll be safe here and I won't have to worry about you."

"But I'll have to worry about *you!*" she said in a low voice.

He took her in his arms and kissed her. "Wait for me," he whispered. "When we are returned to the woods we shall find a dry place for a bed."

She nodded and then watched as he left with Sir David and Grizel Sarchet. She did not want him to go. Only a little while ago he had been too ill to open his eyes and now they were again dragging him off to do something she did not comprehend.

Now that she had found him, why could they not be just

left in peace? Rosal thought longingly of a different life; when the French would not be here: of a simple life of their work, and quiet evenings, of country pleasures, and now this new joy of love. If only they could have the life she envisioned, of time spent together, of hard work followed by good sleep and making love, and children, of dancing and telling fortunes, and music and laughter. Why did it all have to be so very complicated with mysterious people such as this *M'sieur* Blériot and the French ruining everything and now trips to Faerie!

Robin and Richard had found a place for the Calling: the Cromlech near the Faeries' Hollow where Richard and Pascoe had sheltered. Richard had cast an illusion of emptiness about it about it, an illusion that tapped into the ley lines to sustain it. "Unfortunately," he said, as he, Robin and the two cats surveyed it, "any Witch-Sniffer with any skill whatsoever is going to sniff out this magic within two hours, perhaps a little more. The more power expended, the stronger the scent. But there is nothing I can do about that. I hope to be through this in an hour or less and that depends on how much coaxing this young man needs."

The Cromlech was a perfect Circle excised in the springy turf. About it was a ditch nearly two foot wide, cut deeply, in which not even a weed grew. Nothing ever grew there. A few feet from this was a ring of large white stones. "It really is perfect in its way," Richard murmured.

He had already taken a ritual bath of purification, and anointed himself with an oil blended of sandalwood and vanilla. This he explained to an interested Robin, was to aid in greater concentration, increase psychic ability and actually boost the magic. It would help the Gypsy lad who did not know what he was doing, to focus on the task at hand.

Over his properly anointed body he wore the robe of sapphire blue silk which represented the sky and therefore the Light. He tied about his waist of a cord of gold, for the sun, since he was also a Druid.

Robin was endlessly fascinated by human magic. Unlike that of the Faerie folk it involved spells, rituals and charms, among other things that the Fair Folk did not need, for their magic was as natural as was breathing. He asked many questions as Richard prepared the site.

Richard had asked David and Grizel to make certain that young Lovel bathed and was anointed properly and clad in the robe before they brought him to the Cromlech. Everything would be ready when they arrived.

Outside the inner Circle of the Cromlech, sat the two familiars, crouched in front of a book, going over the wording of the rituals and the hand gestures and wand movements that would accompany it. A primary function of a familiar was to be close at hand, often with a grimoire open to the relevant page, ready to prompt a Wizard's memory, should occasion demand, in a long or complicated spell.

Richard busied himself with a stone he had placed, with Robin's assistance, in the middle of the Cromlech. It was a very large stone, waist high and roughly square in shape. With a tap of his wand Richard made it squarer still and told Robin that a square altar represented the air, the element of the Wild Hunt.

The top of the stone was flattened and Richard threw a blue cloth, matching his robe, over it, drawn from the bag,his Wizard's casket, that sat at his feet. On this altar top he began to set out the trappings needed.

A stone, standing for the earth, faced north. A bowl of water, symbolizing that element faced the west, while an orange candle, fire, looked south and lastly, a copper dragon scale embodied the air to the east.

"Pascoe wanted to be here," Richard said to Robin "but as he still cannot fly and we may have to end this suddenly I thought it best that he remain in Faerie. However, since a dragon is as much a creature of the air as any bird, a dragon scale makes an excellent representation of the element of air. This is Pascoe's contribution to the spell of Return."

Richard then lifted a carefully wrapped bundle from his casket. The silk slid off to reveal a glowing moonstone.

"A thing of beauty," said Robin in admiration,"and pulsating with power, if I am not mistaken."

Richard grimaced. "This will be as a beacon to any Witch-Sniffer," he admitted, "but it cannot be helped. I have used a look-away spell, but it cannot be sustained for a long time. I can only hope that we are done before the French are upon us."

"Do what must needs be done. I have sent my people out to waylay, entrap and confound any who dare come near. We will not be disturbed by any mortal," said Robin confidently.

Richard set the moonstone in the middle of the elemental symbols; this epitomized a fifth element, that of the spirit.

Around these representations he then set a circle of candles of alternating blue and white: blue for calming and soothing, white for peace. These, and the orange candle, Richard lit with a wave of his hand. In spite of a stiff breeze off the sea, where the surf still pounded the shore, the candles burned clear and straight. When Richard was satisfied that they would burn true he doused them. They would be lit again at the proper time .

At one side of the altar he set a bowl of salt and on the other a bowl of incense which, when lit, would smell of frankincense, roses and bluebells. This scent was meant for appeasement.

Next, a bejeweled chalice was set out on the altar top, which was becoming crowded. Beside it went a decanter of the proper ritual wine.

"How did the Gypsy awaken the torque without all of this preparation?" Robin asked curiously. "According to Sir David's account he merely picked it up."

"The magic of the torque is a different type of magic," said Richard, as he continued to place items on the crowded altar top. "A simpler, older magic, that depends on the harnessing and propitiation of gods and elementals. But it is far more dangerous, for gods and elementals, unlike the ley lines we use today, are creatures of passions and sometimes they cannot be controlled. Gods and elementals are easy to arouse but not as easy to keep in their places. They inhabit such old pieces as the torque and send out a call to any magical person who might hear it. A properly trained Wizard would have recognized that call for what it was and contained the torque as I did before his touch could awaken it. That is why these things have been buried. But many times they are so potent that they work their way up out of the earth, even into human hands, then ready to call on a mage, come awake from his touch and wreak havoc. Most of them are Dark magic."

"You place materials to honor each element," said Robin "is that not the same as an elemental?"

"No, an element is just that,an element of earth, air, fire, water; but an elemental is a creature of the element. Some claim that they were created from nature in long ago magical rites and some claim that they are of the Dark, on the same level as demons. What is known that they are soulless and have no moral compass. They worship no God and live in the moment, existing only by instinct and what pleases them at the time. The elementals are the goblins, of earth, sylphs of air, nereids and nymphs of water, and salamanders of fire. Save for salamanders they bear a certain resemblance to humanity. In ancient times mages also created an elemental to do certain tasks, which was all it could do, and the mage had to impart some of his own consciousness to the elemental. It was a dangerous matter to do magic in that fashion. The elemental could turn on the mage. But they can be contained by the use of binding rituals such as this one we do now. And lesser Gods, such a Gwyn ap Nudd, can be bound by the invocation of certain Words of the Light, but the power raised must be contained properly."

Robin shook his head. "I'm not certain that I under-stand."

Richard laughed. "Human magic is not something that can be explained in five minutes." He took up his wand as he spoke and commanded the torque, still suspended in the violet box, to rise out of the casket. It would remain floating in the air until Richard manipulated it about the Gypsy's neck.

He looked about him. Everything was just about ready. The anointing oil and violet ribbons lay upon the altar. That part of the candle lighting, the 'dressing' of the candles, would have to be done by the young man.

Soon the moon would rise. This Working had to be done as soon as possible. Richard was not certain that it would 'take' immediately. Sometimes spells took time to Work. This was not something he had ever done, for he had only read about it. Indeed, he could not recall ever hearing that anyone had done any sort of Calling in recent years. The book from which he had obtained his information was a copy of one over three hundred years old. To add to this was the strain of having to 'walk' someone through a complicated ceremony with a lot to remember. Thank goodness the cats were here to help.

Outside the ring of white stones the air shimmered and turned the green of Faerie. An arched door appeared and through it stepped David and Grizel followed by –

"Felix!" Richard cried joyfully.

Pyewacket gave a great meow of happiness and galloped for the young man in the blue robe, launching himself into the air as he drew near.

Felix automatically caught him but he stared at both Richard and Pyewacket, now in his arms and said blankly."Who are you people?"

53
The Appeasement

"Felix!" Pyewacket exclaimed in joy which quickly turned to puzzlement as he realized his Wizard was not greeting him with equal fervor. Felix's arms were stiff and his Wizard was looking at him as if he had never before seen him. "Felix! What's wrong?" the familiar faltered.

Richard, a look of deep concern on his face, came forward from his place beside the altar just as Aurelius came through the green door behind Felix.

"What is the matter, Felix ?" asked Richard, disquiet on his features and in his voice. Where was the look of happiness, the wide smile and relief that should have been on his grandson's face at this reunion with his grandfather and his familiar? There was a blankness about his gaze, a lack of recognition that twisted like a knife in Richard's heart and would in Pyewacket's as well.

You appear to know me, sir," said Felix to Richard, "but I do not know you."

"He's your grandfather!" cried Pyewacket, his tail lashing violently. "I'm your familiar! How can you claim not to know us?"

"He has no memory of anything past several weeks ago," said Aurelius sadly. His own heart was heavy. He had lost his young friend as surely as the sun rose in the east. His Gypsy *was* the Earl's missing grandson. All his dreams of companionship, of shared scholarship, of something approaching a family: all were gone.

"And that is because that black magician Bahram gave him a syrup of forgetfulness before he and Reginald pitched him over the side of the *Star of the Sea* to drown!" put in Greymalkin.

Felix, to Pyewacket's chagrin, was not holding him in the loving, comforting way he usually did. Indeed, his Wizard felt stiff and awkward, and Pyewacket did not like the way he looked, as if he had been recently ill. And there was that strange white streak in his hair! Whatever was going on? Was what Greymalkin said true? Was Felix under a spell?

"My grandfather?" said Felix, stammering a little in his confusion. "But how can it be?" He put Pyewacket down on the green turf and took a step towards Richard.

As glad as he was to see Felix and know that he was alive (although whether he was *well* was a moot point). And as much as he himself wanted answers, Richard realized that proceeding with the ceremony was the most important thing at the moment. They were running out of time.

"We will have to talk later," he said abruptly. "The moon is rising and it is time to begin."

Felix looked as if he wanted to protest this decision but made no further demur when Robin said gently, "Personal concerns must be laid aside for now. This work is too important, for everyone on the islands."

Richard looked at the others; David, Grizel, Aurelius and Robin. "You may stay if you wish, but stay inside the Circle of stones, for your own protection. I am hoping to appease Gwyn ap Nudd without him appearing to us but I cannot guarantee that. Stay inside the outer Circle. His wrath cannot harm you there. But do not, whatever you do, step inside the Inner Circle once we have begun, even you, Robin," he said with a half smile.

The Hobgoblin nodded.

"Pyewacket," Richard said to the still agitated familiar. "Please come here with the book and be ready with Greymalkin to prompt us if needs be."

Pyewacket, his black fur looking plastered to his body, tail drooping and an expression of anguish on his be-whiskered face, did not look as if he would be able to prompt a simple candle lighting ceremony. But he took his place by Greymalkin beside the altar. He cast an anguished glance at Felix, which his Wizard did not see as his attention was fixed on Richard.

He had to ask. "Even if you have forgotten both me and your familiar," Richard inquired of his grandson "do you remember any of your magic?"

Felix shook his head. He was still trying to cope with the

fact of suddenly having gained a relative and a familiar, moreover, a relative who was a Wizard.

Richard sighed. That would be too easy, of course. "Then I shall have to guide you," he said. "Pray go and stand by the altar, my boy, while I draw our Working Circles."

Ordinarily, when they were Working together, he and Felix would share the tasks of preparations. Richard had always been pleased at how well they had Worked in tandem and proud of Felix's skill. It was going to hurt to see him, once again, as he had been when but a child of eight, a rank beginner with little or no esoteric knowledge. Richard had been one of Felix's earliest teachers but right now he would have much prefered his grandson with all of his wits about him, and his usual cheerful expression.

As Richard took out his wand he saw, out of the corner of his eye, Felix go automatically to the proper place. His body remembered, even if his mind did not .

As he took a deep breath and grounded and shielded himself, Richard thought of what Greymalkin had told him, of how Bahram had given Felix a very potent potion and of how Reginald had struck his cousin down in a fit of greed. If Bahram was not already dead Richard would have gladly killed him. To steal someone's memory away was a terrible thing. But Richard dragged his thoughts back to the matter at hand. Magic required full concentration.

He began to inscribe the magical working Outer Circle, turning widdershins from north around the compass. As he did so, violet light leaped from his wand to go between the rocks. At each cardinal point he inscribed, in the air, the sigil of each ruling angel: Uriel of the North, Gabriel of the West, Michael of the South, and Raphael of the East. Each of these great angels also ruled the element that sat on the altar, facing in the correct direction.

To the watchers, it was an eerie sight. The violet light, coming from no source but the wand, hung in the air. The letters in the Celestial script that Richard had traced in the air also hung there, glowing. They became conscious of some-thing else. just behind the sigils: four Presences that were felt and not entirely seen but exuded only goodness and peace. It was a new experience for all of them as David, Grizel and Aurelius had never watched magicians at work and Robin's magical tradition was far different.

Richard then repeated the same pattern on the Inner Circle surrounding the green turf of the Cromlech. But to this he added a pentagram, a six-pointed star. "This is a symbol of the divine source from which all life in created," he told the watchers. "When broken down it contains all the other alchemical symbols for all four elements. This, like the Outer circle, will protect us from the Wild Hunt."

He then stepped up to the altar where Felix stood.

"Are you really my grandfather?" Felix asked searchingly, in a low voice, looking at Richard as if staring at him would recall him to mind.

"Yes, I am," Richard said briefly. "There will be time to answer all of your questions later as I've many for you as well. But now we have to Work. You will need to follow my directions precisely, as quickly as possible. Our familiars" he looked down quickly at the cats "will prompt us if we forget. Will you promise to do just as I tell you?"

Felix murmured his assent. Already he was aware of a strange feeling coursing through his veins. It was rather dizzying.

Richard tapped Felix lightly with his wand, grounding and shielding him as the younger man could not do it for himself.

At once, the dizzy, disconnected feeling stopped and Felix was immediately conscious of a feeling of connectedness with the earth. Power pulsed under his feet and began to flow into him.

Richard handed him a wand. "This is a temporary wand, given freely by an oak tree. Put it in your belt for now; you will need it later."

"Now we must, quickly, anoint and dress the candles."

Felix nodded. He could not remember at all this man who claimed to be related to him. And nothing of what they were doing seemed familiar.

Richard pulled a candle towards himself. "Since this is a calling we are sending energy outwards, therefore the candle is anointed with a drop of essential oil and then wiped out from the middle to the ends."

How it hurt to see Felix, who had been such a quick, instinctive Wizard, look as if he was lost in a foreign country!

His movements were awkward and uncertain.

But then, suddenly, with no prompting, he picked up a length of violet ribbon, began to wind it widdershins about the candle, ending it and tying it off some few inches below the top.

"Good!" said Richard. "You remembered!"

" I can do things," said Felix, without looking up from his task "if I do not think about how I know it."

Richard was pleased with this. Perhaps this would not be as difficult as he had feared. "When the candles are dressed, we'll light them with our wands, starting with the blue candle at the north and go widdershins from there. I'll light the blue; you light the white ones."

Felix nodded gain, biting his lip. He was not certain how he would light a candle with magic but the trick was not to think about it. Thinking led to pain, which led to becoming incapacitated.

To his relief, a spark appeared at the end of his wand and lit the wick. In a few moments all of the candles were burning steadily, even the orange one symbolizing fire.

Then Richard stuck his wand in his belt and took a pinch of salt form the bowl, signifying that Felix was to do the same. "Try and repeat this with me," he said " Lord of Life, this offering I make."

Felix did so, as they both cast the salt into the wind.

Then they drank a draught from the ritual cup which was mugwort and cinquefoil added to rose petal liqueur for protection and awareness. Then poured out a libation in front of the altar, saying in turn "Great Lady, I salute thee."

Finally Richard lit the incense of vanilla and sandalwood, coaxing the scent outwards with his wand.

"Now," said Richard, a trifle grimly "for the torque."

It had reposed behind the altar, hanging in the air in its containment box. It glowed even brighter as it responded to the magic it felt.

With his wand, not touching it with his hands, Richard manipulated the torque out from the containment box and levitated it so that hung in front of Felix. "I am afraid, my boy," he said "that you are going to have to wear this thing."

Felix did not like even the idea of this since he had disliked and feared the torque since he had first touched it.

The thought of actually wearing it was repugnant. But he had promised to obey all of the elder Wizard's orders, so, without a word, he put his head back and felt the thing slide about his throat and clasp itself about his neck.

It was much lighter than he thought it would be and was not uncomfortable but it was so full of a singing power that for a moment he felt weak-kneed.

Richard handed him a censor that smelled of lavender. "Cast this in the directions of the compass, starting with north and then to west and so on," said Richard. "Say *'Pax'* in a loud, firm voice as you do so."

"Peace?" said Felix.

"Exactly," said Richard. "This is a ritual of appeasement, to bring a peaceful end to your inadvertent calling."

Felix obeyed as best he could, felling that being firm at this moment was quite beyond him.

This was then repeated with a censor of violet. The sweet smells mingled and blended on a suddenly rising wind.

Then Richard had Felix face to the north, with his arms raised, wand in his left hand. Richard withdrew a silver bell from his casket on the ground and instructed Felix to hold this aloft in his right hand.

"You must have a clear purpose in your mind, which in this case is to send the Wild Hunt back to Annwn where they belong. Face each direction, beginning with the north and after repeating the verse I shall give you and then ring the bell three times, loudly and firmly."

Felix nodded, listening intently as Richard repeated the verse he was to say.

"It is not great poetry, but it accomplishes what it needs to," said Richard.

"We'll prompt you, if needs be," came Greymalkin's voice from near their feet. "Don't worry if you can't completely remember it."

Felix was grateful for their presence. There was something comforting about a cat.

He took a deep breath and facing the North repeated the simple verse:

When thrice rings the silver bell,
Peace, be still.
Lightning, thunder, wind and rain,

Peace, be still.
Hound to kennel, huntsman home,
Peace, be still.
Nag to stable, hark to my bell,
Peace, be still.

He then rang the bell three times, a few seconds between each ring.

Felix needed prompting twice on the next three repeats, each time Pyewacket quickly supplied the missing portion of the verse.

And as the bell rang, it became deeper and deeper in tone until it sounded as would an immense church bell, tolling, rather than ringing.

And something else happened as the incantation was repeated. Wind began to blow, in gusts, sharp and cold from the west.

Richard had worried about this and said sharply "The rest of you, down on the ground! Now!" David and Grizel fell to the ground, his arm going protectively around her. Aurelius, his intellectual curiosity aroused, had to be pulled down by Robin.

For in the west clouds were rapidly forming, swelling to enormous size in towering, anvil shape, thunderheads, born from nothing. They were black and angry clouds, boiling in the sky and began to flicker with lightning as they drew nearer, until it seemed they were directly overhead.

In the very midst of the clouds, where it was blackest and darkest, a form began to appear, that of an enormous black horse of mighty mien with red eyes flaming, and a rider cloaked in black. At its huge feathered hooves, hounds, dark as night, with dead eyes, milled, giving tongue that echoed over the countryside in eerie fashion.

It was Gwyn ap Nudd himself.

54
A Proposition
From Annwn

Very little could be seen of the horse's rider save for pale, rather skeletal hands. The tall, deep hood of the black cloak he wore obscured his features. The cloak was fastened at his throat with a Celtic brooch of a red dragon.

The horse did not stand easily as a well-mannered hunter should, but sidled and half-reared, snorting. Was it only the imagination of the watchers or did thin streams of flame shoot out of those nostrils?

The hounds ran back and forth between his legs, looking as if they were in imminent danger of being trampled beneath those mighty, restless hooves. All of the hounds were as black as the horse and rider, with curiously blank, staring eyes. They now and then gave tongue until the rider lashed at them with a whip such as used by the whipper-ins in the hunting field, but with far more violence than a hunt servant would ever use.

Several of the midnight hounds yelped and slunk away, sterns dragging.

The dark rider, with hand of iron, superb seat and heels armed with wicked spurs brought the restive horse under control. From beneath the hood a voice like thunder said " I take it ill, Wizards, that we are first called and then sent back to Annwn with no chance to hunt."

In spite of the wind Richard stood firm, having anchored himself to the Cromlech with the help of the ley lines that pulsated so strongly beneath this sacred spot. Felix clung to the altar, the torque gleaming at his throat, his face lifted to the sight of the Lord of the Underworld. Richard was pleased to note that his grandson showed no sign of fear at the sight the spectral being; rather, he wore a look of curiosity, as if he wanted to understand what it was he saw. The others, even the Hobgoblin, lay flat on the turf, as if trying to shrink into it so as not to be noticed by the fearsome specter in the clouds.

"You can scarce expect us to welcome you and your huntsmen, Gwyn Ap Nudd," said Richard daringly. "And you were not called deliberately, but accidentally. We play no games with you." He knew that beings such as Gwyn, who had once been Celtic gods, much preferred plain speaking to any roundaboutation.

"But nonetheless we wish to hunt," boomed Gwyn. "We grow bored with the lack of sport afforded us. I have a proposal to lay before you, Wizards; one that shall serve both our purposes." He paused expectantly.

"Go on," said Richard.

Gwyn gave a short sharp laugh. "What, you do not reject my idea out of hand, Wizard?"

"To do so would be foolish until I know what it is you propose," Richard answered.

"Five days from now, the Hunt shall visit these islands again," said Gwyn. "Our purpose will be to take the damned, those false priests of the Inquisition. And in doing so, we shall rid the islands of the French which have plagued you for so long. This is *British* soil and it has been so for centuries and it shall remain so as long as the Wild Hunt exists! The French have no right to be here. Drake asked us to repel the invaders. So has the torque wielder." He nodded at Felix.

"And will you keep the same covenant with us that you made with Drake?" Richard demanded.

Gwyn inclined his head. "So I promise. And I shall sign a pact as I did with Drake on leaf of gold in my life's blood. Can you provide such a document, Wizard?"

"I can," said Richard and bent to his casket.

Gold was often needed in rituals and every Wizard carried sheets of gold leaf and a gold ingot or two. Richard bespelled the gold leaf to form a flat sheet and then asked Pyewacket to open the Book of Callings, for there was a reproduction of the exact covenant Drake had signed with Gwyn all those centuries ago. The Wild Hunt had abided by this pact to the letter.

This, with the aid of his wand, Richard copied onto the gold leaf, thinking rightly that the archaic language would please the Lord of the Underworld.

He then took the document to Felix, along with a black-handled silver knife and a long quill of red, its feathers tipped with gold, from his casket. "You must sign this," he said to Felix, "as you are the one who originally called the Hunt."

Felix looked at him in some trepidation and swallowed hard, the only sign of any nervousness "What must I do?" he asked.

"It must be signed in your blood," said Richard. "I shall nick your finger with this ritual *athame* and take in this quill, freely given by a living phoenix, a drop of blood for your signature."

Felix allowed him to prick his finger with the very tip of the *athame,* which was needle sharp, and watched as Richard deftly caught the single drop of blood in the sharpened point of the quill.

"He must sign with his full name and rank," called Gwyn.

Felix looked worried at this. "But I don't know –" he began.

"But I do," said Richard soothingly. "Your full name is Felix Alexander Cedric Jourdaine and your worldly rank is Viscount Hightor, while your magical rankings are those of *Magus Magistra* and Master Druid."

Felix looked taken aback at all of this, but obediently signed all of it to the place indicated, with Richard prompting him when he faltered.

Below his signature appeared that of Gwyn ap Nudd, Lord of Annwn and of the Plant Annwn, (the subterranean Faeries), Master of the Wild Hunt and Celtic god of battles and the dead, this last claim inscribed in very ancient Celtic runes. The letters gleamed bright red before fading, indicating, that though put on the gold sheet magically, they were indeed blood.

"The Hobgoblin shall keep this document in Faerie," Gwyn ordered, nodding at Robin. "Five days hence, at the hour of dawn, from this very place, the hunt begins. I hope that you are a good rider!" he said to Felix, the suspicion of a rather nasty laugh in his loud voice.

"A good rider?" said Pyewacket faintly as the figures in the sky above disappeared and the clouds began to fold in upon themselves. "Richard, he doesn't mean –?"

"Yes, " said Richard grimly. "I am very much afraid that

494

Felix will have to ride with the Wild Hunt."

Father Maël had gone to bed that evening in the worst of moods. Not a trace of any mage whatsoever had been found. He was also convinced that the storm of that Wednesday had been devil-wrought. There had been no signs that it was coming; it was just suddenly there, wreaking its havoc over all the Channel. People were talking of strange sounds that had been heard during the course of the storm, those of hunting horns, dogs in full cry and even galloping hooves.

It was all peasant superstition! he thought savagely as once again he tried to find a comfortable position in his bed and tried to stop thinking about the missing mage so that he could fall asleep. Last night sheer exhaustion had carried him off, but tonight, perhaps due to the weather, and the fall from the horse, every bone in his body ached and he was unable to relax sufficiently to slide into sleep. His mind went round and round in circles.

More and more he was becoming convinced that God was either testing or punishing him. He could not imagine what transgressions he had committed against God, unless the Almighty was displeased with his progress in ridding these islands of heretics and mages. But Maël did not see how he could have done that any faster. Now the pagan barrows and idols were destroyed, everyone was attending church, those living in sin had been united in Holy matrimony, all of the irreligious nonsense of dancing and wanton dress had been suppressed... no, it had to be some sort of test.

But of what? His dedication to the task? His faith? God worked in mysterious ways, Maël well knew, but this way seemed more mysterious than most.

He was still awake at moonrise, hot and uncomfortable, his blankets and sheet tangled about him, for he had done little save toss and turn. He had a headache and was just considering rising from his bed to read some improving work and have a cup of herbal tea (willow bark tea was a sovereign remedy for headache) when he felt that 'tingle' invade his body.

Someone was working magic! He sat bolt upright in bed and reached for the bell-rope that would summon Roux. He would not wait! This time he would go right out after the magician and catch him in the act.

He had to ring twice more, as Roux, having both tortured and sexually assaulted the young girl brought in by the soldiers, was deep in a contented sleep. She had screamed loudly and had been satisfying in all other ways as well, having a ripe, luscious body. He looked forward to more torture and rape when he woke.

When at last Roux stumbled into Maël's room, his superior was nearly dressed. "Get my carriage," he snapped as Roux, disheveled and yawning loudly, inquired what the priest wanted.

"Your carriage?" Roux said in surprise "But, Father! The time!" he looked out the window into darkness.

"I have sniffed out a magician, Roux, and this time we are going to catch him!" said Maël, his eyes gleaming in a manner that made him resemble some beast of prey. "Get out the carriage and be certain to bring a compass! You will have another to play your games with tomorrow!"

It was nearing dawn before the ceremony was truly ended, for removal of the Circles and taking down the altar was as important as setting them up. Once the Circles were down the others could join them and David and Grizel helped pack up the casket, for Felix was sunk deep in fatigue, huddled on the turf, his head hanging and looking completely exhausted. Pyewacket crouched near him.

David was burning with questions, but Richard and Robin were deep in conversation about the coming ride and he hesitated to interrupt them. Grizel, too, was silent, following Greymalkin's instructions as the familiar divided his attention between directing the helpers and listening to his Wizard and the Hobgoblin. Aurelius seemed lost in contemplation. His were sad thoughts, if one could judge by his face, and he stood to one side, not speaking or looking at anyone.

At last, when the casket was packed and his intense

speech with Robin done, Richard said "And now I shall take Felix back to Faerie. We've much to talk about."

But David shook his head. "Excuse me, my lord, but we are both of us due out at the Dragon Port today. If we do not show, Fournier will again tear apart this island and punish anyone he can find. I am sorry, but I am afraid that your talk must wait for the evening."

"But he is in no fit shape to do aught else than seek his bed!" cried Pyewacket angrily. "Even the questions will have to wait!"

Felix raised his head. "No, Sir David is right. I must go to the Dragon Port," he said tiredly. "I cannot let others be punished because of me. Fournier will not hesitate to do so."

"Then take a draught of this cordial," said Robin and withdrew a silver bottle of Elfin workmanship from the breast of the old fashioned jerkin he wore. "It will revive you and give you strength for the day. We can answer all questions this evening, even should you be kept late there. I shall come and fetch you myself."

Felix looked doubtful. He was tired right down to his bones and his head ached from the information he had received this night, but a swallow of the delicious elixir sent new life surging into him, making him feel as he could even deal with Blériot's tantrums that day. He was able to stand and went to Richard. "I want answers to my questions as well as you do, sir," he said earnestly. "I have been in the dark too long."

"Till tonight then, my boy," said Richard, love and concern in his face.

David was consulting his pocket watch. "We must hurry," he said. "We are due at the Dragon Port at six and I still have to fetch my carriage and a nuncheon for us and you will have to change, as well."

Robin laughed. "Grizel, will you be so good as to show them the short way to do all of that?"

Reluctantly, Richard only wrung Felix's hand, saying "Until this evening then," when what he wanted was to fold his arms around his grandson, relive his mind of all its anxiety and see the confusion in his eyes disappear.

Felix looked searchingly at Richard, but only nodded and murmured something about talking to Rosal before stepping after David and Grizel into a green door that appeared over the Cromlech. Grizel knew her way about Faerie very well now and could show Felix and David where they had to go. Aurelius stayed behind.

"Who is Rosal?" inquired Greymalkin, who with the keen hearing of a cat had heard this low-voiced remark.

"Rosal is his wife," said Aurelius, coming to stand with Richard and Robin and the two cats, wondering why they did not know this.

"His wife?" yelped Pyewacket. "But Felix is not married! At least he wasn't on the nineteenth of May when he was thrown from his yacht to die!"

Aurelius stared at the cat in confusion. This did not tally with what he knew of young Lovel's story.

And with a sudden jolt Aurelius realized that the young man was no longer Lovel, nor even a Gypsy! Indeed, had not the Earl referred to him as the Viscount Hightor? How did it come about then that the heir to an Earldom had married a Gypsy girl?

Aurelius' new youth seemed to have deserted him, for he felt suddenly every one of his years. This night had been both fraught with disappointment and overwhelming events and had only raised more questions, questions that would have to wait to be answered for hours yet. And from the looks on the faces of the Earl and the two cats he himself was going to be asked some questions very shortly.

Roux was grumbling beneath his breath. It was dark out with a cold wind and he wished to be back in his warm bed. The moon was still near the full but fitful streamers of clouds chased across its pale surface and blocked what little light it gave, not enough light, in Roux's estimation, to see to drive a horse and carriage along bad roads at a brisk trot.

Maël had ordered out the chaise, a two-wheeled vehicle pulled by one horse. It had a folding leather hood that Maël wanted down so that he could see better and seated two comfortably. In spite of the cantilevered springs Roux felt every bump on the road, for the violent rain yesterday had washed the road into puddles and gullies and the horse seemed to be choosing to trot through every surface hole and hillock that filled the road. Like his superior, Roux was no horseman and the headstrong animal had not wanted to be turned out of his comfortable loose box before breakfast to go splashing through the mud in the dark. The two lamps that burned on the dashboard did little to light the road ahead and when the moon was out, it cast deep shadows from the trees that very often overhung the road. There was a wind that sighed in the trees and Roux shivered. It was a night for goblins and ghosts and things that went bump in the night and Roux did not want to be out in it. Father Maël, now bent over a compass with a small lantern in his hand, would laugh scornfully if Roux expressed his fears. "Superstition!" he would say.

Roux was more right than he realized. They were being watched by several pairs of small eyes from various places along the road.

One was a Flower Faerie, the yellow of a primrose with delicate golden wings and a slim gold body. Her eyes were bright as amber. "Are those the people Robin told us to watch for?" she whispered to her companion.

He was a different sort altogether, thick of body, with heavy features and long, pointed ears. Unlike her, he was clothed in somewhat ragged garments. He was a Hob, like Robin, but of another kind, for he was all of Faerie, with nothing human about him. As he was a hearth Hob, ashes smeared his brown face and hands and he smelt of smoke, the smoke of good, well-seasoned wood.

"Oh, aye," he whispered back. "but we'll not be needing to do aught to them, for they are heading straight for *her*, don't you see?"

The little flower Faerie shivered. "Oh, yes," she breathed. "I own, I was fair afrighted when *she* came!"

"'Tis not for you she comes, but for them," the Hob grinned rather malevolently. "We've only to sit and watch," he added as the chaise headed towards a small bridge spanning a stream. He chuckled, a sound that carried on the wind, causing the horse to flick his ears uneasily and snort.

He knew that something was wrong, even if the human fools he drew in the chaise did not and he stopped short, refusing to step one foot on the bridge, for something wicked was about and the air reeked of blood. He would go no further.

55
The Little Washer at the Ford

"Why are we stopped, Roux?" Maël demanded irritably, looking up from his compass and a map he had balanced perilously on his lap. It was difficult to hold the lantern, the compass and the map all at once. It was beginning to look as if the magic was coming from much the same direction as the first time.

"The horse won't go!" said Roux, equally irritated, slapping the reins up and down against the animal's rump, which accomplished nothing but angering the horse. He laid back his ears with a snort and looked as if he might start kicking at any minute.

"Perhaps there is something wrong with the bridge." Maël sighed in exasperation and put aside his implements. He had heard of horses somehow 'knowing' that a structure was unsafe. No doubt God transmitted such information to animals through the medium of guardian angels, to save the lives of the righteous. After yesterday's violent storm and heavy rainfall there could have been some structural damage to the bridge. "I shall go and have a look at the bridge," he said and climbed down from the chaise, still holding the lantern.

The stream, which Maël remembered as usually placid and shallow, was high and foaming with white water as it furiously passed over the many rocks in its bed.

He walked out onto the bridge. It seemed firm beneath his feet and did not creak or sway. He even tried jumping up and down in various places, feeling foolish as he did so.

But nothing shifted or groaned. It seemed completely solid.

Then, over the noise of the water he heard a strange sound, a sound that he had not heard since his early youth: the sound of wet laundry being slapped on rocks. And as he stood there, he heard a woman crooning in a wordless melody.

Suddenly all the clouds passed away from the face of the moon and the area was flooded with light. Looking upstream, Maël saw a woman, crouched at the edge of the water, washing linens.

Whatever was she doing out here, washing at night, and out here in defiance of the curfew? Was she mad?

She was a small woman, clad in green, with a cap on her head. She kept humming as she scrubbed at the linen which seemed to have some terrible rusty stains on it.

"My good woman," Maël called out. "Have you no idea what time it is? You are out long past curfew! Go now, and I shall not report you."

She raised her head, looked at him and laughed. It was not an evil laugh, rather a small chuckle, but nonetheless Maël felt a chill run down his spine. There was something about her...

She spoke at last and said in accented English that Maël had difficulty making out "Dinna ye ken what ye're seeing laddie-buck? I am the *bean-nighe* and 'tis washin' out yer shrouds I am. Yours and that fine fat auld mannikin wi' th' puir wee horse." She laughed again and Maël felt chilled to the bone. As she squeezed the linens between her brown fingers he saw a red liquid run of them and cascade into the water, where it rushed towards him on the foam. It was as red as blood.

What was a *ban-neeyeh?* "See here, my good woman," Maël began but she laughed again, cutting him off and suddenly stood up on the rocks, her green skirts kilted up around her hips, allowing him to see her feet and lower limbs clearly. The night seemed infinitely brighter.

And to his horror he saw that she had webbed feet that were bright red in colour.

"And fain would I be lookin' to my soul, my bonnie, if I 'twere ye, which thanks all the powers that be I am not!" she said to Mael and then putting back her head, announced to the sky. "I'll be turnnin' hame, now, me laird Gwyn, for I've done yer bidding and 'tis hamesick for the Hielands I am!"

To Maël's complete horror she disappeared, winking out as if she were a candle snuffed by a giant hand.

Beneath his feet, below the bridge, the stream ran red.

"*Sancta Maria!*" came Roux's trembling voice from behind him. The torturer had left the chaise when he heard voices. "What was that? Why is that water red?"

Maël turned to face his torturer. "A manifestation of the Prince of Darkness! Probably conjured by the mage we seek. He tried to terrorize us with illusions and threats of death!"

Roux, with chattering teeth, looking down at the blood-drenched stream, wanted to tell Maël that it was working as he was completely terrorized. He did not know how Maël could be so nonchalant about something so supernatural. He did not comprehend that Maël was just as frightened as he was but had a firmer hold on his emotions and was certain that, as one of God's chosen, he could not be harmed by magic or the paranormal. Roux had heard enough to realize that the non-human woman had said that he and Maël were going to die. And from the way she said it, it was not going to be an easy death.

He gulped audibly, wishing that he were still back in his bed, dreaming of torture. He wished he had never come out here with Maël.

"Come along, Roux," came Mael's harsh voice. The priest wore a heavy frown. "I will not allow this mage to scare us from our duty! I am going to find and capture that mage!"

But when they reached the area to which Maël's Witch-Sniffing abilities led him, the mage was gone. The smell and feel of magic was heavy in the air, and as Mael had suspected, it was near *Les Creux ès Faies* at the Circle in the turf called a Cromlech.

And the Witch-Sniffer's fury knew no bounds when he saw that the Cromlech, which he had last seen hacked to bits, its ditch filled with rubble and the white stones dug up and rolled away, now appeared as if it had never been touched, bearing the same appearance it had borne for centuries past before Fournier's men had destroyed it.

In spite of Grizel's knowledge of the Faerie 'short cuts' which could have brought them instantly to the Dragon Port, David erred on the side of caution and had her take Felix back to the farm of *Les Huit Lapins*, and he drove out from St. Peter Port Parish as was usual to collect him. They had to go through all of Fournier's border crossings, be noted in the log and have their papers approved as usual. Fournier and his men were looking for anything unusual, and suddenly showing up at the Dragon Port with no record of having ever passed the borders would certainly qualify as unusual. David felt that now was not the time to have Fournier cast his eye, or the Inquisition's, upon them and have Felix or himself put into gaol as magicians.

Felix was silent for a long time as David was occupied in negotiating the mess the roads were in after the rain. Once or twice the cabriolet became stuck in the mire and there were limbs across the road that needs must be removed before they could proceed. It made David heartsick to see how much damage had been done to trees, houses, barns and crops in the fields. He would no doubt begin receiving mail and calls from desperate people as soon as he was back in his office at Government House, or even at home, for he would not have the heart to turn any one away, even should they call at midnight.

After they had removed the third tree limb that impeded their progress near a field of flattened barley Felix said in a voice full of self-loathing, "I am responsible for all of this. I called down that, that, *thing* upon us."

"It wasn't your fault," David said reasonably. "How were you to know that touching it would do anything? Your grandfather said that it calls to Wizards as it wants to be released."

"Sir David, do you think he really is my grandfather?" Felix interrupted.

"Yes, I think that there can be no doubt of that," David said. "And I do think it is time you dropped the "Sir', for we are friends, are we not? And at any rate," David added with a short laugh, "from what I overheard, you outrank me!"

504

Felix remembered the string of ranks he had had to inscribe in his own blood on that golden sheet. How could he be a Viscount and the other titles the old man, his grandfather, had listed? It made no sense! What was he doing living in a *vardo* with Rosal and doing farm labor and being treated as a Gypsy by everyone? Why did Rosal know none of this, not even the fact that he was a Wizard?

"What does this mean, *Magus Magistra*?" he asked David. "Do you know? The literal translation is Master Mage."

"I am no expert but there used to be a fair amount of Wizards and Witches on the island and one can't help but absorb some knowledge of the rankings," David answered "Congratulations used to be published in the journals when someone achieved a higher rank. There are four ranks: *Magus Novitiate*, a beginner; *Magus Minorus*, the next step up; *Magus Majori*, which is the rank of the majority of Wizards, and then the top of the trees rank, *Magus Magistra*, which, I gather, relatively few achieve."

"But how could I not know such a thing? How could Rosal not know?" Felix demanded, rubbing his forehead where a headache was beginning. Was this another of the things he hadn't liked about himself? Had he deceived Rosal? Had there been some falling out with his grandfather, so much so that he had left his home and come here to put the past behind him, including the fact that he had a title and was a Wizard?

"I am certain that all of your questions will be answered tonight," said David, seeing the unhappy, pained look his friend wore. "Try not to dwell on it. You'll end with a headache and you'll need all your wits about you to deal with Blériot today. He's bound to be on his high ropes since no work was done yesterday! He'll have pulled out fully half of his hair out by the time we reach the Dragon Port!"

If anything, David was far off the mark. Blériot was beyond enraged. One of the prisoners, seeing the little man rant and rave, had remarked that if Blériot was a dog he'd have been destroyed as mad.

He was pacing up and down in front of his office building, impatient for the arrival of David and Felix, agitated, screaming abuse at anyone who came near him, and leaving behind his pacing a trail of tufts of hair.

Yesterday, in spite of the weather and its threat, he had attempted to pull the unfortunate Johann von Weber from his sick bed. He was stopped by the army doctor, who placed von Weber under armed guards with orders to shoot anyone who did not have permission to come near him, especially Blériot. As there was little love lost between Blériot and all of the soldiers stationed at the Dragon Port, this was not an idle threat. Anyone of them would have positively enjoyed blasting a hole through Blériot. Everyone had suffered the sharp edge of his tongue.

Due to the bad road conditions David and Felix were late. Blériot gave them a tongue lashing as a soldier took charge of Thierry and the cabriolet, screaming in rage as to why they had not showed their faces yesterday and then had the temerity to drag in here this morning late!

Suddenly David had had enough. "Oh, be quiet!" he said. "Even someone as stupid as you must have noticed that we had incredibly bad weather yesterday and that as a result the roads are in horrible condition! You're fortunate that we are here at all! And if you cannot keep quiet about it, I swear that I will call back my horse and carriage and we shall leave! And I do not give a damn how many letters you write to the First Consul!" he added as Blériot began to gobble like an enraged cock-turkey.

Felix hid a smile as Blériot stared at David. No one had ever dared correct him before. The little man's chest swelled as he began to speak, but what he was wont to say was lost forever. A soldier ran up saying "*M'sieur*, the German wants to see you!"

"Which German?" said Blériot crossly, giving David a glance of pure loathing.

"The engineer, *M'sieur* Schmidt!" panted the soldier, who had run all the way. Schmidt had conveyed to him by a series of pantomime that he wanted to see Blériot. His charade of Blériot had been hilarious.

Blériot decided to deal with David later, "Come, *Gitan*,"

he said abruptly. "I   will need you to translate what this Schmidt has to say."

The building that housed the German engineers was filled with a curious, low-pitched humming. The Germans, five of them, were crowded about a low table, talking amongst themselves.

"What is going on?" shrilled Blériot.

At the sound of his voice the Germans stepped back from the table so that he could see.

On the table sat a miniature machine, its gears whirling and its motor humming. At one end of it was inserted a large crystal.

"Aha!" cried Blériot and hurried forward to caress the machine with a possessive hand. "My genius has borne fruit!" he crooned, looking like a fond mother with an exceptionally clever child.

Felix felt a strange jolt as he looked at the crystal in the machine. He was getting rather tired of the feeling that he ought to be recognizing these things, for the crystal sang to him. He had no doubt that no one else heard its song. It was more magic, he was certain of that. But what did it mean?

Blériot did not bother congratulating Schmidt for completing the building of the machine with only his contrary, confusing instructions to go by. "Soon, soon!" he said, looking off into a future that only he could see. "I shall conquer England and all shall bow before my greatness! And this machine," he fondled it again, seeming to delight in the pulsating vibrations that went up his arm and into his thin body, "this is the key to my plan!"

56
Crystal Power

After a long and wearing night, for doing magic was hard work, Richard was more than ready to seek his bed when they returned to Faerie. But he could see that both Pyewacket and Aurelius wanted to speak to him. Only pausing to take a brief, cool bath to get rid of the anointing oil, he had a cup of tea, wishing fleetingly that regular tea were not anathema to the Elves, for a herbal brew did not wake him as well as did a good, strong cup of China.

They met in Aurelius' room, which had become their usual gathering place. It was easier there for Pascoe to participate fully in the conversation.

It was hard to decide which looked the more miserable, Aurelius or Pyewacket. Even Pascoe looked perturbed for he had obviously had an earful from Pyewacket. His face was inserted into the room, between the pulled aside gauze curtains.

All eyes, even Greymalkin's, turned to Richard as he entered and he was right in assuming that they had all been discussing Felix while he was bathing.

"Richard!" Pyewacket burst out at once. "There is something very wrong here! Aurelius said that he was told, by Felix himself, that he was in Guernsey since Michaelmas and married the Gypsy girl then! My Wizard only came to Guernsey for the very first time in mid-May and he did not meet her then. I should have known, for I was with him every minute. Not once did he go off on his own! Indeed, we were only in the harbor here for one day. The *Star of the Sea* was well provisioned and we had no need to go ashore for supplies. We had intended to remain longer in Guernsey but when Reginald and his horrid friend showed up we did not wish to remain in their company any longer than we had to. Felix wanted to get them back to England and out of our hair as soon as was possible. Reginald was pockets to let as usual and showed signs of wanting to stay on the yacht as a sort of floating hotel. We could not have borne that!" he added, his plumy tail lashing. "Felix would not make up a story such as that!"

"Do not forget, Pye," said Richard gently, "that Reginald's horrid friend as you call him, gave Felix a forgetfulness potion. Bahram could have inserted false memories in his mind as well, for he was a most accomplished black sorcerer by all accounts. They did not want him to be found, or remember who he was if he survived the push into the sea."

"Reginald is a fool," remarked Pascoe. "He should have known that Felix would have an underwater breathing spell on himself. Why, I have never known him to go out on one of his boats without one, even when the boat is moored!"

Greymalkin snorted. "Reginald had no sense left! He was nearly always completely foxed, mostly on cheap Blue Ruin, and gin can stew a man's brains! Reginald subsisted on a liquid diet nine-tenths of the time. To a sot such as he was, any plan, no matter how ill-conceived, would seem brilliant. And his friend, although a necromancer, for I do not hesitate to call him so, seemed to understand little about English magic or even our inheritance laws. He confessed that he had though to be made Reginald's heir!"

Aurelius had remained quiet while this discussion was going on. His sense of disappointment and loss was still crushing. He had so hoped that his Gypsy was not the Earl's grandson.

But now he would return to Devon with his new-found grandparent, once Pascoe was able to fly again. Richard felt that even in the safety of Faerie, it was a mistake to stay in Guernsey much longer and he wished his grandson to see a Wizard Healer as soon as was possible and see what could be done about the restoration of his memory. It was hoped that Bahram's grimoire, now in the hands of Bow Street, would yield the formula and spell for the forgetfulness potion. It could then be reversed by a Potions Master and administered by a Wizard Healer. Richard refused to think about what might happen if the spell could not be reversed.

"But why did he claim to be married, and to a Gypsy no less?" Pyewacket continued. "I don't understand that part at all! Was it a subterfuge to keep his identity hidden from the French?"

"He didn't know who he was, Pyewacket," said Pascoe. "Why would he need to hide something he had no knowledge of?"

"Perhaps he just needed some sort of identity. The Inquisition might have tossed him in gaol if he could not account for himself. They have done so on far flimsier pretexts. And perhpas she went along with it for reasons of her own," said Aurelius, sounding tired.

Richard looked at him in sympathy. Aurelius's dismay had been all too readily apparent when Felix's true identity was revealed. "All this guessing is fruitless," he said. "We shall have our answers, or most of them, tonight when Robin brings him here. Right now I am for my bed and a few hours sleep before whatever this evening brings."

Blériot drove the men unmercifully that day. Both the basket and the balloon sack must be made ready within the next five days. Tests had to be conducted, for everything must be perfect by the fourteenth of July.

He was less than pleased when a defect was discovered in one of the silk panels that would cause it to rip if inflated. That would have to be completely replaced. The basket needed more work as well. Several strange wires and heavy lines protruded from the bottom and sides of the wicker-work, which ran to the compartment, asbestos lined, where the small engine would sit.

Under the pretext of explaining things to Schmidt, Felix was able to have small snatches of conversation with the German engineer. Schmidt was a shrewd as he could hold together. Although his role in the army was of a engineer who worked on bridges and fortifications, he had always been interested in the new machines being developed in these modern times. He had studied Dutch journals on the subject, for the Dutch were keenly interested in anything that might improve their trading empire.

"It's some sort of propulsion device," he confided to Felix

as Blériot danced around them, screaming, as two of the other engineers lowered the machine into the space in the basket. "That crystal appears to drive it, which, I confess, mystifies me. All engines I have ever heard of run upon steam, not a chunk of rock. But run this one undoubtedly does!" he scratched his head as he spoke, wondering. "If it were steam-powered he could never carry enough wood or coal to even get the basket off the ground."

Hans Schmidt was a Bavarian, of almost forty-five, with dark blonde hair and a large walrus mustache. He was short and stocky and had a genius for building or repairing almost anything from watches to bridges. It was thanks to him that this project had gone so well, for he had an instinctive feel for machinery. Without Hans Schmidt Blériot would probably be still trying to explain, in his contradictory fashion, how the complex machine was to be built. But Blériot would never give Schmidt the credit he so richly deserved.

"Crystals hold energy," Felix said absently. "They gather it from the moonlight."

Schmidt looked at him as if he was mad. "Moonlight?" he said, looking dubious. "I don't understand that any more than I understand how a crystal can make an engine work! There are two little bumps in there that the crystal rests on, which is linked into the engine with a mass of wires. The bumps are marked with plus and minus signs and he made a big fuss over which way the crystal was inserted. I tell you, friend, yesterday was hell around here without your translations! He kept getting louder and louder and even threw things at us when we did not understand. Bauer has a little French, very little, but it does not run to technical terms. It's more the "is this the way to the tavern?" variety. At one point I thought this crazy man was going to strike poor Bauer when he did not immediately comprehend. He has no patience at all, that miserable little son of a bitch! We can only hope that the engine explodes in his face when he takes it aloft. A spark that ignites the balloon would be acceptable as well!" Schmidt sounded bitter. How interesting this project would have been if Blériot had regarded him as colleague and allowed him to learn the secret of what was being built! Instead he and the others were treated as mindless drones, fit only to take orders. All the prisoners of war thought as little

511

of Blériot as did his own countrymen.

"What are you two talking about?" Blériot suddenly appeared at Felix's elbow, his eyes wild behind his spectacles and every hair on his head standing on end.

"I was explaining to *Herr* Schmidt how careful the men must be in placing the machine, *M'sieur*." said Felix quickly.

"Then why was he doing all the talking?" Blériot shrilled. "You don't fool me, *Gitan,* you're trying to steal my idea and enlisting the aid of this German! But you'll neither of you never be able to understand what I have done here! Only another genius such as myself – and there are none – can even begin to comprehend the incredible complexities, never mind the sheer brilliance of the very notion!" He paused a moment, breathing rapidly, and then said "Did that Fournier set you to it? I well know that he wants the credit for my idea and he thinks to get a Marshal's baton out of this! Well, he'll catch cold at that! Mine is the genius, mine will be the glory! It is I upon whom the First Consol will heap honors, not Fournier. And you can tell him that for me!" He glared at both of them, as if daring them to challenge his statement.

Schmidt, of course, since this tirade had been in French, understood none of this and Felix, who wished he had *not* understood it, had no wish to get into a wrangle with Blériot. It was not as yet noon and there was far too much of the day to get through to waste his energy on an argument he could not win. Blériot was incapable of listening to reason. Once a notion was in his head, there it stayed, no matter how stupid or illogical it might be.

After leaving David and Felix safely at their homes Grizel went back to *Les Huit Lapins*. Felix had arrived there, and left again, so early that only Joisaine, who always did the first milking, was up and about. Grizel had promised to let Rosal know what was happening.

Grizel found the whole mystery surrounding David's new friend and his identity rather intriguing. How had an English Viscount come to marry a Gypsy girl and be living in poverty in a caravan? It was a union as strange as hers and David's would seem to the outside world. And what had happened to his memory? His grandfather was obviously moneyed for one did not carry about sheets of gold and jewels in a casket and keep a dragon unless there was wealth involved. And just as obviously, the Earl cared very deeply for his grandson. Grizel had seen the hurt and disappointment, swiftly suppressed, on Richard's face when Felix had looked at him as if he had never seen him before.

When she called in at the farm she found them just finishing breakfast after having first seen to the animals and surveyed the damage to the farm. A little later in the day, when it had dried out somewhat, Hagar would return the *vardo* to the woods.

"Where is he?" were the first words out of Rosal's mouth as Grizel entered the kitchen. She got up from the table, almost turning over her chair.

Grizel glanced around the kitchen. David had warned her to be careful what she said around John. But he was nowhere in sight.

"Gone to the Dragon Port," Grizel reassured her. "There were some matters to be taken care of, but all went well. And you'll be happy to learn that your Felix has found his grandfather! You'll meet him tonight. Won't it be wonderful to have someone who can supply those missing memories? Had you any idea at all that you were marrying a Viscount?" Grizel laughed as *Madame* and Joisaine exclaimed in surprise.

Rosal, stared at Grizel, her eyes growing wide, and the blood leaving her face. A great roaring sounded in her ears. This could not be happening!

She did not even hear the noise Hagar caused, when rigid with shock, she dropped the teapot she had been about to pour, sending pieces of *Madame's* everyday brown pottery all over the table top. Caught! They were caught, just as the cards had foretold.

Rosal did not think of punishment. She only thought that she would now be alone again, for he would certainly leave her when he knew the truth. And how was she to go on without him? They had been so happy...

513

Upstairs, John forced himself to rise from his bed. His legs shook and he almost fainted when he first set feet to the floor.

He sat on the edge of the bed until his senses steadied. He could not keep to his bed like a fine lady. He had to be up and about,for the plan of his revenge against that damned Gypsy had to take place as soon as he could manage it. He hungered for it. Matters would be set straight if there were no more Gypsy in the picture. He would bend all his energies to getting well and strong.

The next time he stood it was easier.

57
The Lie Revealed

David did very little work on the tax records that day. They were almost finished and with luck he would be able to lay the entire report on Fournier's desk on Monday morning. Instead, he spent most of his time staring out the window and thinking of Grizel.

In between the first visit to Faerie and the ritual they had attended at moonrise there had been time to have their dinner with Majorlaine. Both of the women he loved had been making every effort to accept one another. Majorlaine was stiff and uneasy at first. David was certain that she had been expecting Grizel to show up naked and eat her meal that way.

But Grizel had been attractively and decently dressed in a green muslin dinner gown and slippers that she had obtained in Faerie. And she had worked hard to make herself acceptable to David's mother, admiring both her cooking and the examples of her needlework in the house, and deferring to her at every opportunity.

Majorlaine seemed astonished to learn that Grizel could sew, embroider, and cook and could even speak knowledgeably of these things. David saw her staring, several times, at the webbing between Grizel's fingers. The webs were small and not obtrusive and David himself had long ago ceased to regard them, any more than Grizel noticed his infirmities. But to his mother's eyes they were an enormity.

By the time the evening had ended, Grizel having stayed precisely the right length of time, not too long and not too little, Majorlaine seemed a bit more at ease, but David knew it would take more than one visit for his mother to become used to the fact that her only son was going to marry a Selchie and that her grandchildren would be not quite human. Grizel, it must be admitted, was not what she had wanted as a daughter-in-law. Ghislaine, David's dead *fiancée*, had been loved by Majorlaine and would have been welcomed as a true daughter. Majorlaine had watched her grow up, for the Renoufs owned the neighboring farm in Torteval parish and Ghislaine and David had been playmates in childhood.

But Ghislaine was gone and David had a new love, one that would make him extremely happy. He was not about to give her up, even if his mother never truly approved.

Because of the oddity of time in Faerie, they had a chance to visit their bed of moss and David, as satisfied as he was from that encounter, could hardly wait for the time when they could legally share a bed in his own home.

And if the Wild Hunt, as Gwyn ap Nudd had claimed, could truly rid the island of the French, in only a little while they might be able to wed and have the right to be together always without the fear of the Inquisition and the French Occupation hanging over them. Life could return to normal. This lead to such happy thoughts that David scarcely noticed time passing that day at the Dragon Port.

Hagar insisted that Rosal accompany her when she took the *vardo* back to the camping site. They had both spent the morning helping *Madame* and Joisaine save what could be rescued of the crops and dragging the many branches and debris from the yard and environs. Tiles, which would have to be replaced, were neatly stacked.

It was not until after a nuncheon that Kälo could be harnessed to the caravan and they could return to the camp site in the woods.

They had scarcely left *Madame's* yard, squelching slowly through the mud, when Hagar said, "You know what this means, don't you? His people will tell him the truth and it's prison for us!"

Rosal was driving, Chavé seated up on the driver's bench between her and Hagar. The dog was the only one in a happy mood.

"And he'll leave me," she said in a low voice.

"*Leave* you!" Hagar said scathingly. "That's the least of your troubles, you foolish girl! The Selchie said he is a

Viscount and I know what that means, for Henry, my lover, had friends with titles! He's not just a gentleman but *nobility*. Quality, as the Giorgios call it. They're as Gods compared to us! We're lower than the clods beneath their feet! And they won't hold with him having wed a Romany! We'll hang for sure! They won't be content for him to leave you. No, they'll want to be rid of you! And they'll want to make certain that it never comes to light that he shared a bed with a Gypsy, much less married her! They'll be afraid that you'll hang on his sleeve and demand money not to sell the story to the journals or even insist on your place as his wife. They'd never recover from the shame of that!" She spoke bitterly, for she knew all too well what Rosal's fate would be. "Or mayhap they'll have their lawyer make the marriage go away! And then, even should he keep you as his mistress, he'll grow tired of you one day and throw you into the street without a penny in your pocket. And any children will go with you or else they'll turn on you too and call you Gypsy trash! Believe me, Rosal, no one knows better than I what will happen to you! Any way you look at it you – we – are in deep trouble."

Rosal looked at her, her face whitening and her eyes huge with the fear she was beginning to feel. When she had first heard the news all her thought was of losing him, not what his family might do to her and Hagar.

Now she shivered. The picture Hagar painted was very ugly. She had first hand evidence in Hagar how carelessly a *Gajo* could dispose of a woman he no longer wanted. Even though Felix had said he loved her, would he still feel that way when he found out how she had lied to him about nearly everything? Except for one thing; the fact that she now truly loved him.

The *Gajé* did not feel the same as did the Romany about lying, she had learned from Hagar. Among the Romany, one lied if it was more to one's advantage, or to keep the secrets of their race from outsiders, and to let the *Gajé* hear what they wished to hear. But Hagar had told her that the *Gajé* placed a high premium upon truth and honesty, not that they did not lie too, Hagar had said cynically. But they expected the truth from others, no matter how false they themselves might be.

She had lied for her advantage, to gain herself a Rom, a

517

protector, and a young man who could give her a child, especially the child. But that was no longer as important as it had been. Somehow, *he* had become the most important thing in her life.

"We should try and get away from here," said Hagar, interrupting her bleak thoughts. "Before he comes back with someone who can arrest us and throw us into gaol! For I lied to him just as much as you did. Those nobs, they don't forgive easy, or forget! We've a fair amount of *parné* 'neath the floorboards. Mayhap we can get some fisherman in the north to take us to England. We'll disappear. I've people in England, people who won't know that I was *mahrime* here." This was not likely, but Hagar would say anything to get Rosal to flee with her. All the older woman could see was a prison cell and a noose ahead of them and she was frightened almost to the point of hysteria. She had been too scared even to read the Tarot this morning for she was fearful of what it would tell her.

"No," said Rosal, in spite of the fact that her insides were turning to jelly and her hands beginning to shake. "No, I won't run away. I have to try and explain to Felix why I did what I did. And how would we get past the French, Hagar? We can't get off the island."

"I won't stay to be put into prison and have my neck stretched!" Hagar flashed, her voice shrill with fear. "Don't be stupid, Rosal! Come with me! I'll find a way to get us off this cursed island!"

"When we make camp again I shall give you one half the *parné* and you may do whatever you wish. But I am staying. I have to stay. I owe him that," said Rosal. Already in her mind's eye she was seeing his face and the scorn in his eyes.

"He is a *Giorgio* and you owe him nothing, for that is all we are to the likes of them. Nothing and less than nothing!" spat Hagar.

But Rosal would not listen to her. When the *vardo* arrived at its usual place in the woods, which were now sodden with rain, the campsite littered with broken limbs and leaves, Rosal halted the pony and went into the back of the caravan. There she pulled up the floorboard and withdrew the bag of coins. These she scrupulously divided in half, as nearly as she could, putting in Hagar's pile the small excess that would not let it be divided exactly in one half. She also took Hagar's crystal ball and her deck of cards from beneath the floor and tied them up in a kerchief. Hagar's other belongings she stuffed rather haphazardly into a satchel. The crystal ball and cards went in on top of these.

Hagar was already on the ground when she slid off the driver's seat. the older woman snatched at the little jingling sack that Rosal held out to her.

"I owe you my life, Rosal," said Hagar, stuffing the money bag down the front of her blouse and snatching the satchel from her hand. "But I will not stay to see your ruin and mine. If he lets you live and casts you off come to the field by the river we Romany know as the Nile, outside London. You'll have a place in my tent. Look for the *patrins* to lead you." A *patrin,* meaning leaf, was a bunch of twigs tied with red rags, a branch broken in a particular way, or a notched bone, all aids to direction that only the Romany could read.

Rosal nodded for she could not speak. She felt bereft at Hagar's leaving. They had had only each other for a long time. In her heart she could not blame Hagar for going for whatever happened it was bound to be bad. She wrapped her arms around Hagar, an embrace that was eagerly returned.

There was a Romany saying: "*Sako peskero charo dikkhel,*" meaning "Everyone sees only his own dish." And Felix would be, she was very much afraid, more caring of his own pain at her deceit, his own dish as it were.

And if she were honest with herself, she admitted as she watched Hagar fade away, almost invisibly into the wood, he would be justified in thinking so. She would try to explain. She had to try, but she was very much afraid that she could predict the outcome even without *dukkering*.

Unmindful of the wet and muddy ground Rosal sank down and covered her face with her hands. Chavé, whimpering anxiously, pawed at her, his loving eyes fixed upon her. She reached out and pulled him to her, burying her face in his coat. He whined and tried to lick her face. He could tell that something was wrong. But there was no comfort to be had from him, no comfort anywhere. She was headed down the *lungo drom*, the long road, with no particular place to go and no turning back. Her teeth began to chatter in spite of the warmth of the sun and the heat from the dog's body.

Robin was waiting for them in the lane that led to the farm of *Les Huit Lapins*. He was seated on a half sunken stile and with him was Grizel.

David's heart leaped when he saw her. She was clad in a deep pink gown that left her arms largely bare and had a deep square neckline. She was beautiful.

"I've come to take you directly to Faerie," Robin announced. looking at Felix. "Your grandfather is most anxious to see you."

"But, Rosal —" Felix began.

"Don't worry," Grizel assured him. "I went to see her this morning and told her the good news and she was overcome with pleasure for you." Or so it had seemed to her when Rosal had managed a tremulous smile that morning. "I went to fetch her this afternoon to come with us and she said she was feeling a little under the weather and would prefer to wait for you." She did not tell him that Rosal had pleaded 'female troubles', with which Grizel had sympathized, for before her seal nature had manifested itself she had suffered cruelly from cramps. Thank goodness being a Selchie took care of that annoyance! And Rosal *had* looked poorly.

"You'll see her tonight, after you see your grandfather and we'll make certain it is not late," Robin promised.

"And I'm here to take you through Faerie to shorten the time between the parish boundaries, David, so that we can be on hand as well." said Grizel.

"You don't mind us being there when you talk to your Grandfather Felix?" David inquired.

"No, I shall be glad to have you there," Felix assured him. Indeed, he would be very glad, for as new a friend as was David, he was one of the few familiar faces Felix knew. The others, even though they claimed to know him, were complete strangers.

He was absurdly nervous. All day long, when not having to concentrate on the orders Blériot was barking, possible scenarios of why he had left his home had gone through his head and none of them to his credit. He kept remembering, however, that there had been no look of censure in his grandfather's face, only concern and what had looked like love. But how and why?

The unalterable fact remained that he had told Rosal a pack of lies. Before his memory was damaged he'd not told her of any relatives, or the fact that he was titled and not a Gypsy and fed her a string of untruths about a school. And yet she was happy for him! This, and what else he had thought he had discovered about himself, made him feel sick. Why did all of these people feel such concern and friendship for someone so unworthy who was a liar and what else besides? How could Rosal love him? Not even once did he think that she might be the one at fault. He loved her, therefore he trusted her. He was afraid of what other unpalatable truths about himself would be revealed tonight.

In Faerie, Pyewacket and Richard waited impatiently for Felix to arrive. Pyewacket was the far more fretful. The day seemed endless to the familiar; he even accused Robin of slowing down time, a piece of rudeness for which Richard made him apologize. Greymalkin and Pascoe were anxious as well for the hours to pass. Aurelius, on the other hand, was far less eager, for everything that he had heard had only driven another nail in the coffin of his hopes and dreams. Galen was present as well. The Elfin Healer was fascinated by the memory loss.

At last they came, Robin and Felix, David and Grizel, and again Pyewacket ran forward to jump up in his Wizard's arms. "Hold me properly," he ordered and snuggled his head against Felix's neck. "Ah, that's it!" he sighed and began to purr as Felix's arms, of their own volition, came around him, one hand supporting his bottom and the other spread over the familiar's back. "I shall stay in your lap when you sit down," Pyewacket announced. "See, Grizel,I found him!" he said, looking with a superior smirk at the Selchie. He knew that she had doubted he would ever be reunited with Felix.

"Let's all sit and have some wine," suggested Grey-malkin.

"Hello, Felix," came Pascoe's deep voice. "I am glad to see you well. We have all been very worried about you."

Felix looked a trifle confused at being addressed by a dragon, but he bowed slightly in Pascoe's direction before taking a seat at a long, low table with the others, Pyewacket settling himself comfortably in his lap. Richard served everyone with a glass of amber wine from an impossibly beautiful Elfin made crystal decanter. He had asked Galen to provide this wine on purpose. Richard knew its properties as of old. It was called *methryn* and was a relaxant. This could not but help be an ordeal for his grandson and he himself felt the need of a calmative.

"Why don't you tell us what you remember, my boy?" he suggested to Felix "and we shall fill in the gaps for you."

With frequent sips of the wine, which was incredibly delicious and warming, Felix told them the entire story from the very beginning when he had awoken upon the beach. Some of this was even new to Aurelius and David and they all hung upon his lips.

He spared himself nothing. At the end of his recital Pyewacket, who had been growing extremely restive, burst out, "What a bag of moonshine! There is little or nothing correct in that statement and as for you being at fault in any way, by Bastet's whickers, that is naught but tripe! Here are the facts!" And before anyone could gainsay him, he began telling Felix of that last trip on the *Star of the Sea* and of Reginald's and Bahram's murderous plot.

At first Felix looked confused at what he was hearing for it bore no resemblance to the truth as he knew it. He looked at his grandfather, at the other familiar and the dragon and they all agreed with Pyewacket's version. His fingers tightened in Pyewacket's long fur as he began to put together in his mind what he was hearing and what he had been told. It was obvious that one version was a falsehood.

"And I don't know who this Rosal is," Pyewacket finished angrily, "but when you went over the side, Felix, you were not married, nor involved with anyone!"

The truth broke over Felix like water from a burst dam. She had lied to him! She had claimed him as her husband when he was no such thing. She had let him marry her in a Church, knowing that he was little more than a stranger to her. She had let him assume that he was a lazy layabout and a cad. It was she who was the liar! Had she also lied when she said she loved him?

A choking rage rose in him and for a moment he felt as if his blood was boiling. He felt used and betrayed. He had given her his love and she had paid him back in false coin. For one hideous moment he thought that if she had been present he would have strangled her.

"She tried to steal my life from me," he said angrily. "Little wonder she had not come tonight! She knew what I would find out, that she was naught to me!"

David was shocked. "She seemed to genuinely care for you," he began.

Felix cut him off, with a bitter laugh. "Nothing she said was genuine! I have been manipulated like a marionette on a string! Used for her purposes!" He put Pyewacket from his lap and stood abruptly. "I'll have the truth out of her," he said, looking at Richard. "I want to know why she did this to me. I'm going to see her and demand the truth."

"Not in this frame of mind. You should wait until your emotions are under better control," said Richard in a deliberately soothing voice. "You are far and away too angry at the moment. And there is another matter. You may be legally married to her. I shall have to consult our solicitor."

"What!" Felix sat down abruptly, all the anger draining out of him to be replaced by despair. He wanted to confront her to make her admit what she had done and then never see her again. But if they were legally married... would they be tied, miserably, to one another for life? To be married to a woman he could not trust, forever?

The hurt and pain were profound. Felix felt a deep breach of faith, of trust, on all levels. Anger was beginning to be on equal footing with pain.

Richard gave him another glass of wine. "Drink this and then I shall go with you to see her. We'll have the truth with no bark on it from her. Perhaps there is some rational explanation."

Pyewacket snorted. *What kind of explanation could there possibly be?* the look on his furry face said in derision.

And Felix could only agree with him.

58
Confrontation

At Richard's insistence, they remained a further half hour in Faerie, until Felix had a chance to steady himself, and bring his anger under control.

Richard, watching his grandson's set, stony face, was extremely perturbed. What sort of complications would this 'marriage' make for them?

In England it was difficult to rid oneself of an unwanted spouse. Divorce was expensive and required an Act of Parliament. In Wales, Ireland and Scotland it was easier, but Felix was a legal resident of England and must obey its law. Divorces granted in the other three nations were not consider binding or legal in England. The grounds for divorce were slight. Most were granted for adultery on the part of the female. Perhaps an annulment might be in order since she had deceived him. Or perhaps they might use the fact that Felix had not been married under his true name and he was not a Roman Catholic. But such speculation was worthless as it would require a solicitor's knowledge.

And what a scandal it would make! Parading it through the House of Lords and of Commons would guarantee that the scandal sheets would hear of it!

After hearing how she had lied to and manipulated his grandson, Richard was expecting a scheming jade of a woman, perhaps common and coarse in looks. He had felt that Felix had no doubt married her from a sense of obligation and from the manipulation she had used on a man not in his proper senses. It was an infamous thing to have done.

Robin took them through Faerie to the lane that led down into the woods and they tramped it in silence, Felix looking grim and still, Richard could tell, angry, for his fists were clenched and his eyes very hard and bright.

It was not yet dark, for the long twilight had yet to fade.

Everywhere the westering sun cast long shadows, and made the green leaves and grass glow as if drenched in gold. It was calm and peaceful, a scene of bucolic bliss, despite the many signs of damage from yesterday's wind and rain. The precipitation had left a freshly washed scent in the air. A light breeze stirred the leaves.

Felix could not help but think as they walked along that if he had not learned the truth he would now be coming home to Rosal, to a tidy little supper, and then either into the *vardo* or a bed in the woods, to be alone together and an evening of pleasuring one another.

But never again. She had befuddled and betrayed him. He could trust her no more. She was not what he had thought her to be. Given the way that he felt now, all of the love and the passion he had felt could very easily turn to hatred. For what was love without trust and respect?

Before knowing all of the facts, earlier today he had worried that *he* had deceived her, for everything she told him of his past she had claimed that he had told her first. When he first found out that he had a grandfather he had wondered why Rosal did not know about it. It had seemed inconceivable to him that he could marry a woman and leave out such important facts as that he had a living grandfather, a cousin, and perhaps more relatives as well, and that he came from a titled family, was not a Gypsy and the he was magical. If these were not true lies they were at least sins of omission.

But once he knew that he had not known her the length of time she had claimed, all became clear. He had come to her with no memory from the beginning and had never been able to tell her anything about himself. He could understand, in some fashion, that she had had to make up some tale when she found him and decided to claim him as her husband.

But she had, as well, let him believe that he was a bone idle layabout and was used to taking his pleasure without thinking of her. It seemed iniquitous. And he now thought angrily, as mad at himself as he was at her, that he had been unbelievably gullible. He had been so eager to give himself some sort of identity that he accepted everything she told him, or let him believe, as absolute truth, without question.

In part of this at least he wronged her. In her culture the females did most of the work, leaving the men to please themselves as to whether they worked or not, many of them choosing not to do so. And her only memories of the marriage bed were of Sylvester, a monster of selfishness. Naturally she assumed all men were like that.

They had left the familiars behind for Pyewacket had talked wildly of scratching Rosal's eyes out. He was as angry as his Wizard. Richard thought that this meeting might prove ugly enough without trying to control an enraged familiar.

"How could I have been so stupid!" Felix said suddenly as they walked under the trees. "I believed everything she told me. I spent most of today, since I had no idea of the true story, feeling guilty; that I had been the one that deceived her! But when the cat told me that I did not even come here until the nineteenth of last month... and she let me think ill of myself on other occasions as well."

Feeling a little embarrassed at discussing things of such intimacy, he told Richard a bare outline of what had passed between them. He was feeling more comfortable with the older man every minute but he was not certain that he could place any reliance on his feelings of liking and trust any more. Only look how easily Rosal had tampered with his emotions and taken ruthless advantage of his vulnerability. He did believe what he had been told by this man, because of the dragon agreeing with it. Somehow he knew that dragons would not, could not, lie. But again he had no idea how he knew this.

"You were desperate to know who you were. I can only imagine how frightening it must have been to be without self-knowledge," said Richard gently. "I think almost anyone would have clung to any identity as a life-line. However, that does not forgive or even explain what she did."

"Will I ever have my memory back?" Felix demanded.

"According to Greymalkin, the Persian sorcerer left behind a grimoire. If the potion he used on you is in there, a counter-potion can be prepared and your memory restored. A Wizard Healer should be able to advise us," Richard told him.

He could understand why Felix had taken the blame

upon himself at first. He had always done so, ever since the death of his parents.

They had gone on holiday, on their dragon, to the Lake District and Felix had been left with a good friend of his mother's, who had children that were of an age to be his playmates.

But then Felix had become ill. When his parents were notified they insisted on returning to Devon in bad weather and their dragon had been struck by lightning. Both of them, and the dragon, had died in the explosion of dragon gasses. Felix, eight at the time, had blamed himself. As far as he was concerned it was his fault. If he had not been ill they would have not tried to come home in thunder weather.

It had taken Richard both time and patience to make his grandson see that it was the way things had happened and it was no one's fault, least of all the fault of an eight year old boy. But Richard had seen over the years how, deep in his heart, Felix still blamed himself. If there was one thing Richard would have changed about Felix it would have been this tendency to assign fault to himself.

But perhaps, Richard thought hopefully, if his former recollections were restored, all this might attain the status of an evil dream.

Rosal had taken a long while to recover from the dull despair she had felt. Kälo's whinnies had at last roused her from her painful reflections. The pony could not see why he had to stand there in harness when he could smell both water and grass close by.

Working mechanically, she unharnessed him and staked him out. She put blocks under the wheels of the caravan and started a fire, which smoked and burned in a sullen, fitful manner as most of the wood was soaking wet.

She had no appetite at all. She did make some tea and fed Chavé. Her stomach was too tightly clenched and if she ate she would be sick.

He would come, she was certain of it. She would try and explain to him, but what had seemed to her such a sound, logical plan now seemed more like a lie and a cheat. Hagar had been right. She had not thought it through. She had never really worried over the possible consequences, or imagined falling in love.

She did not know how long she sat by the fire as the sun passed overhead and began to decline. She sipped but little at the tea she had made. It grew cold in the cup but she did not even notice, concerned only with waiting.

There was no conceivable way in which he could not realize that she had lied to him. If Felix had been like Sylvester he would have beaten her and if they had been in a *cumpania*, the rest of the clan would have thought him justified in doing so.

At last, just when she thought she could bear the waiting no longer, she heard someone coming. The cup she held slipped from her fingers, fell to the ground and shattered. She barely noticed it.

Chavé started up, tail wagging as he smelled a familiar scent but then began to bark as he also identified someone he did not know.

Rosal reached out and grabbed his collar as two men stepped inio the clearing.

Rosal scarcely noticed the older man with Felix. Her eyes were fixed painful intensity upon Felix's face. He was angry, she could see that clearly. His brow was thunderous and his eyes were cold.

She shivered and came to her feet. Not even the fire and the warm evening could make her warm.

Richard was surprised. She was not at all what he had pictured. She was small and slight, little more than a child, he thought. Her eyes were enormous in a thin, very pretty face. Her dusky hair was neatly braided under a cap and she wore a plain round gown such as might have been worn by the wife or daughter of one of his tenant farmers. Save for her dark, sloe eyes and gold skin she looked little like a Gypsy.

"Rosal –" Felix's voice was low and full of ire and it sounded as if he was holding his temper in check with difficulty. "I have found you out. This gentleman is my grandfather and he tells me that I had never even been to Guernsey before the nineteenth of May of this year. So I ask you, how could I have met and married you well before last

Christmas as you informed me?"

She swallowed visibly and put a hand to her throat as if she felt she were choking.

"I'm waiting!" he said. "What possible reason could you have for feeding me such a farrago of nonsense?"

"I needed a Rom," she got out. "Hagar and I were alone. And," she added in a sudden burst of candor. "I wanted another baby."

"And that is enough reason to deceive me, to let me be in ignorance of my true identity?" he said.

"I didn't know who you were! I only knew you were called Felix because I heard the man on the boat call you so!" she retorted. "I thought you were his servant when he came and told you he wanted breakfast. I saved your life! If the French had found you they'd have given you to the Inquisition!" She was suddenly angry herself. She *had* saved his life after all. "Would you have been happier if I had left you on the beach to die? Or let the French find you? You seemed so needful to know who you were. That's all you kept asking. You wanted to know all about yourself. We took care of you, Hagar and me. She healed you. I fed you and took care of you just as a proper Romi, a wife, would!"

"But you let me marry you in church, knowing full well I was not and had never been your husband!" he went on, his voice shaking slightly.

"I didn't *make* you marry me! You wanted to!" she flashed.

"Because I thought we were already married Gypsy fashion!" he shouted. "Why did you tell me we were married? Why did you not just tell me I was a stranger you had found on the beach?"

"I wanted a proper Rom, my own man, and a child!" she returned. "I am *mahrime,* an outcast, because of taking Hagar in. No Romany man would ever have me. In some *cumpanias* I would have been stoned. You were the only chance left to me! You're a man; you can't understand how much a woman wants a child! And it seemed to me that you were sent to me by fate. I saw all the signs, in the cards and in the stars and you were my way, the only way it seemed to me, to have another child." She was doing what she had thought she would not, losing her temper. She was growing as angry as he

529

was. From the look on his face he was not listening to her reasons, and not even trying to understand her side of it all.

"Did you think I would never remember, never know that everything you told me was a lie?" he demanded.

"I thought if I made you happy..." Her emotions shifted abruptly and she was plunged back into despair. Her voice broke and she turned away so he could not see the sudden tears in her eyes, wrapping her arms tightly about herself. She had loved him so.

He seemed to suffer the same dashing to the ground from the heights of anger, for his voice was flat and tired when he said. "So what are we to do now? We cannot go on like this. I can't trust you, Rosal. And one needs to be able to trust one's marriage partner. I would never know if you were lying to me or not."

She refused to answer him, stubbornly keeping her back to him so he could not see that tears were now slowly tracing their way down her face, She could taste the salt in them. Turned away from him she could not see that he too, no longer looked so furious, but, rather, lost and yearning, remembering all of a sudden how much he had loved her and how it was to take her into his arms and kiss those red lips.

Richard judged it was time to speak up. As far as he could see no one would come out on top of this argument. They could spend all night going back and forth without accomplishing anything save more ill and hurt feelings. And they were both closer to misery than to anger now.

In spite of the fact that she had indeed beguiled Felix Richard found himself feeling almost sorry for her. "It will be a matter for the attorneys now," he said. "We shall see to it that you want for nothing," he added to Rosal. He reached into his breast pocket and pulled out a well-filled purse. This he put down quietly beside the fire so that she would find it later. He felt that she might refuse it, perhaps even throwing it in their faces. But she could use the money, and family pride, as it did with Reginald's mother, would not allow him to neglect any duty. They certainly owed something to her, even though she and Felix had been married so briefly. although perhaps illegally. But she *had* saved his life. Richard would see to it that there was a decent sized settlement when the marriage ended.

"Come, Felix," he said to his grandson. "No more can be accomplished here. No doubt you, both of you, could use some time alone."

Felix let himself be led away, saying nothing to Rosal, for she would not look at him, acting as if he had already left the campsite. She did not move at all as they walked away.

Chavé followed Felix a little way, confused as to why he was leaving. But less than a quarter of the way up the lane he turned and raced back to Rosal. She, after all was his first love. He found her on the ground, sobbing bitterly, and tried to comfort her as best he could.

"Can we not return to our home, wherever it is?" Felix,with his head down as if he was carefully watching his steps, asked in a dull voice as they traversed the lane "Suddenly, I can no longer bear this place. I want to get away."

"I am afraid not, my boy," said Richard quietly. "In order to placate the French you must continue your duties with them. And in four day's time you must ride with the Wild Hunt. Do you not obey the terms of the Covenant the Hunt will wreak destruction on this land and you will forfeit your life."

59
The Meet

The next four days passed both slowly and quickly; slowly, in misery, for both Felix and Rosal, and quickly, even in Faerie, waiting for the Wild Hunt to ride again.

Felix went about his tasks at the Dragon Port mechanically. Von Weber was still on the sick list as his complaint had proved to be bronchial and it was taking him some little time to recover from it as he had been in such poor condition before taking ill.

Blériot was driving them all hard. He was even more impatient and had several screaming fits when, first of all his machine did not fit into the asbestos-lined cavity as well as he had expected and the balloon itself had to be re-sewn several times. He blamed this on the workmanship, not on a bale of inferior silk as should have been the case.

One group of men he now had working on wooden items that resembled fish fins. There was also a thing that resembled a child's pin- wheel. These would be attached to the basket in some fashion, and again, Blériot was quite secretive about this. He would take care of that his own self, he declared, when Schmidt, through Felix, inquired as to what they were.

When alone with David, driving back and forth to the Dragon Port, Felix refused to speak of his own concerns, not mentioning Rosal at all. He instead inquired about David and Grizel's wedding plans. This in spite of David giving him every opportunity to talk. The hurt was too deep, even though he had come to think of David as a good friend.

Pyewacket noticed a sad change in his Wizard. He had always been light-hearted, even merry, and loved to talk over what he had been studying and reading. Now he was quiet and sad, subject to frequent headaches, especially after returning to Faerie from the Dragon Port. Most nights he retired to bed, quite early, after only picking at his food.

Pyewacket was quite upset by this and demanded mournfully of Richard two days before the Hunt was to ride, if Felix would always be like this, would he never return to his old self?

"He's gone through a great deal, Pye," Richard remonstrated with the familiar. "You cannot expect him to be just the same. He's got both physical pain and raw emotions to be sorted out. When he regains his memory and this is well behind him, perhaps he will return to his old self. But life, you must know, has a way of changing us. No one remains static, that would be unconscionable, for that would mean that one learned nothing from their life journey."

Pyewacket looked up at him, his eyes looking huge and sad. "I thought that if we were just together again... but he does not really seem to want me near him!" His voice was almost a howl of misery. "His own familiar! He always confided in me!"

"You're a stranger to him yet," said Pascoe, who had been listening to this conversation with interest. They were all outside in the sand wallow, near Richard's tree house, Richard, the dragon and the two familiars. Felix had gone up to bed a short while ago. Richard suspected, however, that his grandson did not sleep, but just lay awake in the dark, for he did not look well-rested in the morning.

"Don't forget, Pyewacket, he has no memories of any of us. We're all unknowns as far as he is concerned," said Greymalkin patiently. He felt sorry for Pyewacket, for not only had his Wizard forgotten him and changed almost out of recognition, but Pyewacket himself had suffered a near drowning, having to live in hiding, been tossed in gaol and been threatened with the Inquisition. He had not had an easy time of it lately, but at least he knew who his friends were. "Just be patient. He'll want you again, particularly once he recovers his memories of you and you'll be back on the old footing, you'll see."

Pyewacket had to be content with this, although it nearly broke his heart.

Rosal found it difficult to go about her life as was usual. She cared little for anything at all, moving about her tasks in a dazed fashion. All she could see was his face, full of anger and scorn.

No word of love had passed between them at that last meeting. When she had seen how angry he was, she had not attempted to protest her love, her very real love. Felix would not have believed her.

She had gone to the farm the first day after their confrontation but *Madame* had sent her home. "It's my belief you are sickening for something," said Marie Brehaut looking at Rosal's pale, miserable face and her lack of appetite. "Go home and crawl into bed and have *Madame* Buckland brew you a posset."

Rosal had not been able to admit to even these kind friends that she was now alone. She let them think that Hagar still shared the *vardo*, that Felix still came home to her each evening.

She gladly went back to the caravan in the woods and crawled into the bed in the *vardo*, huddled there in a state of numb misery, rising only to feed Chavé and the pony and eating but little herself. She existed mainly on soup made from herbs and tea. She tried her best not to think at all, only seeking to sleep, dreamlessly where she could forget her pain.

On Sunday the 12th of June, Felix did not attend church for he was at the Dragon Port, Blériot having obtained a dispensation so that his translator could be out there, helping supervise the final touches to the balloon. Blériot figured upon a month of trials for his invention and there was a small group of Fournier's officers to train before the invasion of England officially began by the date of the fall of the Bastille, July 14th. A month would be barely enough. Not that Blériot wanted any help, but he could not man all of the balloons by himself. However, he would make it clear to them that he and he alone was the supreme authority and his would be all the credit.

He had already set his workers to turning out more

balloons as quickly as was possible. He reasoned that having built the first one they ought to be able to build the others, and the machines, in no time flat. He justified the Sunday work by assuming that the needs of France came before even the needs of the church.

Rosal had dragged herself from bed Sunday morning when she heard the church bells begin to ring to call everyone to Mass. She half hoped to see Felix at church. Perhaps time had softened his attitude and she could once more try to explain. And maybe this time she would tell him she loved him and that her love was no lie. She freely admitted to herself that she wanted him back on any terms.

But she ws doomed to disappointment for he was not there. Her other worry, that Hagar would be missed, did not come to pass. No one noticed as the priests were much occupied with Fournier's continued search for mages and, from the pulpit, Father Meurice delivered a thundering condemnation of magic and all who would not do their duty and turn over any mage to the Inquisition.

She went back to the *vardo* after a short conversation with Marie Brehaut, who recommended Rosal return to her bed and see the army doctor if she continued to feel as badly as she looked.

Rosal returned home and went back to bed, shedding her clothing carelessly and crawling under the quilt with Chavé beside her, his furry body pressed close to hers. She could not seem to get warm and lay there almost in a stupor, pain, even greater than that she had felt when Cinerella died, gripping her. At least then she had her hatred of Sylvester to cling to, to give her a reason to go on. But now there was only pain and grief and regret and an overwhelming sense that she had lost something infinitely precious.

Up until that Monday, they had been enjoying a stretch

of fine weather since Wednesday's storm and the island was somewhat recovering from the damage. As he had thought, David had many worries and complaints of the islanders to deal with, most of which had been written once it was discovered that he was no longer at Government House during the day. Since travel was constrained, only those from his own parish were free to call on him at home, in the evening.

There was little he could do. He pinned all his hopes on Gwyn ap Nudd, hoping that the Wild Hunt would indeed chase the French away. Then he might apply to the Six Nations for help.

During the night of the 12th and into the early morning hours of the 13th the weather's aspect changed entirely as the starry sky gave way to a vast canopy of thick, dark clouds. Just before dawn it had begun to rain fitfully and Felix and his party, waiting at the Cromlech for Gwyn ap Nudd to appear, were soon damp. Richard did not dare cast a rain shied and draw more attention to the Cromlech as a source of magic. He had been informed of Maël's search for the magic he had sniffed out.

The Elves had provided Felix with riding dress of breeches, boots and a shirt, open at the neck, all in black, as that was Gwyn's colour.

With them waited Robin, the familiars, and, at his own insistence, Pascoe. No one spoke as they waited for dawn. It would be a sullen, gray dawn, for there was not a single gap in the thick layer of clouds.

Felix was clenching and unclenching his fists as they waited, his face set and strained looking.

Richard could not blame him, for no one could fail to be nervous at the thought of riding one of Gwyn's Hell-steeds through the sky. Even Sir Francis Drake, the last to do so, had no doubt suffered worry over such an undertaking.

Richard put a hand on Felix's shoulder. His grandson felt as tense and as stiff as a plank. "Don't worry, my boy," he said in what he hoped were reassuring tones. "You're a fine rider. I had no hesitation in taking you with me to the finest hunts in Britain. Assheton-Smith himself, the master of the Quorn, said you were a bruising rider and pluck to the backbone!" Too late he realized that these references would mean naught to Felix's damaged memory. But Richard himself was highly nervous about what ws to come.

"And you need not worry about falling," said Pascoe. "Galen has said that I may fly now and I shall be right behind you, to catch you should you part company with your horse."

Richard looked at him astonished. "How can you stay aloft during a ride of the Wild Hunt?" he demanded. "What about the lightning? Do not be foolish, Pascoe! "

"I shall stay well behind, them, Richard," said the dragon easily. "The wind and lightning they generate is carried ahead and around them. But I cannot take the chance that Felix might fall from the back of that Hell-steed. Those horses do not appear to have amiable temperaments. I can dart in and catch him. I am far faster than any horse, even a horse from Annwn," he added confidently.

Felix turned to look at him. "Thank you," he said gratefully. Last night he had dreamed over and over again, of falling from from a great height. He had been reading about dragons and magic since coming to live in Faerie and he had read of how intensively dragons trained to catch falling persons. To know that someone would be watching over him was a great comfort.

Pyewacket crouched miserably at Felix's feet. He had wanted to go, to ride on the crupper, but Richard had forbidden it. Felix would have enough to do, he said sternly, to watch out for himself, much less worry over Pyewacket.

Greymalkin looked at him in sympathy. If it had been Richard going, he would have wished to accompany him. But he knew, for he was a sensible cat, that the very idea was foolish.

"Hark!" said Robin, bringing up his head sharply and turning to the West. "I hear the horn!"

Even as he spoke a horn rang out in a quickly delivered double note. This was the 'moving out' signal.

Above them the clouds grew blacker still and, as they had when Gwyn appeared to them, began to boil. Lightning flickered and thunder rolled ominously in the distance. Felix, listening intently, was not certain if it were thunder or the sound of many hooves.

In the blink of an eye the hunt was upon them, hounds in front, eager to find quarry, contained by black cloaked whippers-in with long thonged hunting whips.

Gwyn was in the front of his field, astride the same hell born steed he had ridden before. But this time he held the reins of an equally fierce coal-black horse. As Gwyn saw the group beneath him on the Cromlech he laughed aloud and called down,"Wizard, you must needs leave the protection of your Cromlech to mount, for my horses will not step one hoof in such place!"

Reluctantly, Felix left the protection of the Cromlech and walked outside the ring of white stones as well. Richard followed him. "Stay here," Richard directed the familiars. "Those hounds could dispose of you in one bite." Greymalkin and Pyewacket both hissed, ears laid flat and fur extended.

At full tilt, Gwyn ap Nudd galloped down the sky, as if he was riding down a steep hill, pulling the rider-less horse behind him. He stopped in front of Richard and Felix. "Here is your mount, Wizard," he said tauntingly. "I think he is up to your weight! You'll find a black cloak on the cantle of the saddle. Put it on and draw the hood up over your head."

Felix obeyed. The sight of the animal he was expected to ride filled him with trepidation. It was a stallion, black of course, and huge in size, with a heavy neck and forequarters, and his hindquarters bunched with muscle. He had a wicked, rolling eye and tossed his head repeatedly as far as he could, for a running martingale, suitable or a horse who would more than likely be jumping, held his head down. He wore a saddle that on so a broad back appeared minuscule. The tack was all of black leather.

"I'll give you a leg up," said Richard "He must be eighteen hands high!" The horse's back was over both their heads.

Gwyn watched with a sardonic smile as Felix mounted, which was not an easy task, for the horse snorted and sidled. "I chose this animal carefully, Wizard. He has a mouth of silk, even though he is somewhat headstrong. But he is a sweet go-er and a flying leaper. There are no fences up here, but clouds are our barriers and the field enjoys a good run," said Gwyn and added with one of his mirthless laughs, "His name is Beelzebub!"

Felix sat deep in the saddle and took up the reins. Richard, acting as groom, had held the reins near the bit and now let go the animals' head. Felix was glad to see that the horse wore a Pelham bridle, with two sets of reins. The curb chain beneath his chin on the bottom rein would exert more control.

The horse was extremely powerful and Felix was very conscious of this. It was rather like riding a volcano, one that was in the process of erupting.

Gwyn turned his horse and began to ascend to the sky. With little urging from Felix, Beelzebub followed.

To Felix's surprise it was like topping a very steep hill. Automatically, he leaned over the great black horse's withers, to make the climb easier for him. There was a feeling of something solid beneath the horse's hooves that he had not expected. It was the same when they reached the pack of hounds and the rest of the field. The cloud they stood upon seemed as solid as the earth so far beneath. Felix did *not* look down.

There were some twenty couple of hounds. This meant forty hounds all together. How many riders Felix was not as certain for it hurt the eye to look directly upon them, even though they all wore black hoods, with their faces deep in shadows.

The huntsman blew the moving off signal yet again, and the field moved out at a brisk canter, unlike an earthly hunting field which would begin the meet with a trot or even a walk.

The massive huntsman, his horn as black as everything else in the field, blew light, doubled notes that meant 'drawing' which was a signal to the hounds to look for quarry.

Richard, watching from below, was interested to note that the Wild Hunt was using the modern hunting calls and protocols. In this, they kept up with the times.

Felix seemed to be handling his huge mount well at the moment. Richard suddenly wished that he had thought to go with Pascoe, but the dragon was not wearing his saddle and he would refuse to take Richard aloft without it. At any rate, the copper dragon had already spiraled up into the air, following the field at a discreet distance. He was flying easily, Richard noticed with relief.

A strong wind had sprung up and moved the clouds

above towards the east, where St. Peter Port lay. The hounds were drawing the area and suddenly one gave tongue. One after another the other hounds honored him until they were in full cry. A series of short, rapid staccato notes sounded. This was doubling, and served to encourage the hounds to give chase.

Richard heard Gwyn call out in his deep voice "Hoick, Hoick! Chevy! Hark Forward! Hark forward! Tantivy!"

The horn blew three notes. This signaled tantivy, rapidly, and the field moved away at a full gallop, leaping over a cloud bank, six feet high at the very least, in a stream of black, horses and hounds all clearing it easily.

Richard strained to see what was happening. He had already lost sight of Felix. Obviously his grandson had survived that first formidable jump, for Pascoe still glided behind the field. Richard had no doubts that Pascoe would see and rescue Felix if he was tossed from that great black beast.

Richard wondered, apropos of nothing, what scent the damned gave off to the hounds. For these Cwn Annwn were not hunting fox, but human souls. And it seemed as if they had drawn the line on one or more already.

In the distance, the hounds gave tongue again, their cry sounding like wild lamentations. Some said they wept for the souls of the damned, destined for eternal fire. Seeing those dead eyes in their faces, Richard doubted that they ever felt pity enough to weep. Anyone hearing that sound was more than like to die of sheer terror.

60
The Wild Ride

As dawn broke over the Dragon Port Blériot had the men open the roof of the tallest shed. He then dismissed them brusquely, to be alone with his finished creation and to savor the sense of completion and satisfaction he felt.

Last night, quite late, he had filled the red, white and blue bag, in alternating multiple gored panels, with the hot air necessary to let it rise upwards, as hot air was lighter than cold air. Blériot had invented an ingenious system of valves that could easily control the air from the two burners that filled the envelope, the body,of the balloon. The machine was in place, waiting for the crystal to be inserted

Blériot had gone without sleep the evening before in order to privately install the last parts of his design. A wheel, like a ship's wheel, was now connected through the basket walls to the wooden fish fins, one on each side of the basket. The wheel was also attached to the outsized pinwheel which now was at the rear. He could stand behind the wheel from a vantage point and see everything below.

He had also attached several swivel guns to the edge of the basket and a bucket full of hollow metallic canisters, which were filled with gunpowder, was upon the floor. These had long fuses which could be lit before they were dropped from the air. He ws not quite happy with this arrangement. He was working on a design that would allow him to pull a rope and drop them, but this would have to do for now.

On the whole, he was well-pleased with his efforts. It would take the British completely by surprise: a balloon that could not only be directed as to where its aeronaut wished it to go but dropped death from the skies. There could be no defense against it! He discounted Wizards and dragons since he had read that Wizards did not fight the enemies of Britain and dragons did not kill. Had he read more than one book, and that written by someone with only second or third hand knowledge, he might have realized what an error he was making, but one of his greatest faults was impatience.

He stood, a little after dawn, looking up at the balloon as it strained against its tethering ropes, waiting to fly free. It was a thing of beauty, a weapon of war, invincible in Blériot's eyes. In the weeks to come there would be an entire fleet of these formidable machines and he would be their Admiral. He rather liked the sound of that. Admiral Blériot!

Today, in spite of the promise of ill weather, he was going to test her out. The very last thing he had done was to have one of the prisoners who seemed to have a flair for such things, paint a sign with the name he had chosen for her. He himself had attached it to the side of the basket. *Le Conquérant,* the Conqueror, it read.

When he took her up, a *Tricoleur* flag would fly from one of the lines that held the silk envelope to the basket, so that there could be no doubt that this weapon was of France.

The sky looked dark and threatening through the opening in the roof. But this did not matter for this balloon did not depend upon the wind for her motion. Blériot had the crystals.

He had stumbled upon them quite by accident. He had hired an ancient *château,* somewhat in ruins, for a laboratory, far away from prying eyes. He was conducting experiments with the new phenomenon of electricity, to see if it had any practical uses. In a hiding place, exposed by a caved-in floor, he had found a cache of crystals. He had been intrigued by them at once. And, when handling them he had felt the same sensation that the use of electricity gave him, he was struck by his brilliant idea. Why could the energy he felt in them not be harnessed?

Many months later he had found a way to use them and that had led to this idea, the finest manifestation of his genius. Instead of steam, which necessitated carrying a tremendous weight of wood or coal, the crystal energized the machine. The machine was much smaller than a steam engine as well. He was overjoyed at how much power a small crystal generated. He felt no curiosity at how the crystals had become to be in the old *château,* for it was enough that they were there. In his conceit, he thought that they were meant

542

for him to find them. It never occurred to him that they were a product of Witchcraft, left there almost a millennia ago by a Witch who had been forced to flee the wrath of the Church when magic was first proscribed in France. If he had known this, he would still have felt himself justified in using them, even though the use of such materials was forbidden. All he could see was the fame and fortune he would enjoy and the final recognition of his brilliance. Everyone who had ever laughed at his sometimes far-fetched (or so they always said) notions would be shown as the morons they were.

He crossed the room to the rope ladder that hung from the basket and began to climb it. Soon he would be air-bourne! He had rigged all the ropes so that he could cast off by himself. He wanted to share this moment of triumph with no one.

Father Maël, feeling more than a little disgruntled, had risen early for Matins and Lauds and then had ordered a simple breakfast of coffee and *croissants* brought to his office. He stood in the window, munching a buttery *croissant* and sipping at his coffee, staring morosely out at the harbor. It was a gray and dark day, he noted, thinking that the weather was just as vile as was the rest of this hot-bed of heresy.

He was at a loss as to what to do next. There was no sign anywhere of the escaped mage. And what is more, reports had begun arriving that claimed that the barrows, and dolmens and shrines and statues of the pagan religions had reappeared. No one could say how this had happned. Area commanders were now admitting that the work which had begun on the new fortifications, even on the much anticipated brothels, was not proceeding apace as they had previously reported. There were many instances of work destroyed in the night, of tools and materials gone missing, even of explosions; all, when investigated, were impossible to track down. And now, the English prisoners of war, brought from French battlefields, were beginning to disappear as well. There was no trace of them to be found, just like the mage.

Whatever was going on, it had to be the work of a very powerful mage, or even a group of them. Or perhaps Satan himself in collusion with his underlings. How could one priest, or even two or three, fight the Devil himself?

For the first time in his career Maël felt overwhelmed and abandoned by God. Never had things gone so wrong. Despite the long hours he spent praying for help and guidance he felt no closer to receiving any of either commodity. Unless things changed radically his monthly reports to the Holy Father in Rome and to the head of his Order would had to be filled with admissions of failure.

The door to his office burst open, unheralded by any knock. Roux, his face white and sweating, ran in, panting. "Father Maël!" he burst out. "Have you seen the weather? It is another Hell-born storm such as we suffered less than a week ago! The men are saying it is Witch weather and we shall soon see Witches mounted on their broomsticks, flying aloft and flying down to snatch them as sacrifices for their unholy rites!" That Roux also believed this was obvious.

Mael turned to him, with a look of disgust on his face. "That was a windstorm, with heavy rain, Roux, and naught else!" he said in reprimand. "I read all the foolishness in the reports of horns sounding, dogs baying and it is all superstitious nonsense!"

"Perhpas it is *L'Armée Furieuse!*" said Roux in inspiration. "Perhaps because these islands were once French they still ride in the sky here!"

"Do not be more ridiculous than you can help!" the Witch-Sniffer snapped. He was furious that someone like Roux could so readily believe all of this peasant idiocy. Roux was supposedly an educated man.

"My own father, God rest his soul, saw *le Grand Vaneur,* the Great Huntsman himself and scarcely a seven-night later the Bastille fell!" Roux insisted stubbornly. "My father was a good, sober, Christian man, not given to flights of fancy!"

"Even good, sober, Christian men can see visions after a lengthy visit to the wine shop!" retorted Maël. "To judge by your behavior, Roux, your late father liked his wine a little too much!"

"Come up upon the roof with me!" Roux challenged. "You will see that this is unnatural!"

"If I can show you that this is naught but God's weather will you cease to plague me about this and make no more mention of such old wives' tales?" said Maël.

Roux nodded in agreement. "But you shall see, Father, with your own eyes!" he promised and held open the door for his superior to precede him into the hall.

Very quickly the ride with the Wild Hunt had become a test of endurance for Felix. Even though he could not say with certainty that he had never ridden such a horse, he thought it more than likely that he had not done so. The animal was strong and willful and once the horn blew Tantivy, Felix found it a tremendous effort to hold him in check. The manners of the Hunting Field held that a guest never passed the Master of the Hounds, or over-ran the hounds and he would be fortunate indeed if this did not happen. He could only imagine what Gwyn ap Nudd would have to say to such a breach of etiquette.

The jumps that they took at a full gallop were huge, and terrifyingly solid for clouds. Felix had talked a bit about hunting with his grandfather and had been given a quick lesson in what was done and not done at a Meet and he had learned that one did not go out of one's way to soar over large jumps for to do so would be the actions of a thruster, which was very bad form indeed. It was very stupid as well to put oneself and one's mount at such unnecessary risk. Some riders at human hunts did not jump at all, going miles out of their way to find a gate.

But he was not certain that he could hold this horse or even stay on. The jumps were becoming higher and wider and the wind fiercer. The hounds giving tongue was increasing in volume and the other riders were shouting at the top of their voices, mostly hunting calls, and urging their mounts on.

One of the cardinal rules of hunting was "get over the ground as light as you can" but this was very heavy going indeed.

He could only imagine the effect that seeing this Field and its master overhead would have on people. Those that lived through it, that is.

A ferocious gust of wind swept the hood from Felix's

head. He dared not let go one hand on the reins to replace it. He needed every bit of his strength to hold the horse as even the curb chain was having but little effect on Beelzebub's willfulness.

Off to his left, Felix could see, fortunately still in front of him, Gwyn ap Nudd, sitting easily in the saddle, cloak streaming out behind him. Felix was uncertain as to whether the wind was being created by the weather or if the passage of horse and hound through the sky made it. Whatever did cause it, the wind was nearly gale force.

Gwyn lifted his arm, and with a hunting crop in his emaciated pale hand, pointed to a place below them. "There!" he cried exultantly "There, my boys, is our quarry! And soon the hounds will have run them to earth!"

The horn blew 'gone away'. This was a series of quick, pulsating notes and the hounds again gave tongue, their cries louder and more excited. This was the 'music' of the hounds and many gentlemen hunters found it the finest music in the world, stirring the blood as it did in both horse and man, anticipating a good run. But in these hounds of Hell it was bloodcurdling.

Now the banks of clouds came closer together and it seemed as if Beelzebub had scarcely landed before he took off again, clever as a cat, shifting his feet for these in-and-out jumps.

Felix marveled at the fact that he was still mounted. He did not know how he was managing it. Even some of the other members of the Field had come to grief. Several rider-less horses, reins streaming in the wind, had galloped by Beelzebub.

The Hell-Steed seemed to know his business. Felix wisely dropped his hands and let the reins slide through his fingers, keeping but the lightest contact with the horse's mouth. Felix concentrated on keeping his seat, and being with the horse as the powerful muscles bunched beneath him, readying for the jump.

Ahead of the balance of the field several riders had parted company with their mounts. The huntsman, a bold rider, and Gwyn went on past. There was no stopping to inquire after the health of the fallen rider. Of course, being demonic, it was very unlikely that they could be injured.

After all of the hounds had cleared the jump Gwyn and the huntsman sailed over and promptly disappeared from sight. This could only mean one thing, which was confirmed by the sound of the pack. After going over an almost impossibly high cloud that easily equaled a five-barred gate, there was a sharp drop on the other side.

"Trust your horse," a voice said in Felix's mind.

He did so, and tightened his knees, giving over the impetus to Beelzebub.

The great horse soared over the solid cloud, dropping lightly on the sharply sloping opposite side. Felix, steadied for the jolt and downward rush, only slightly lurched as Beelzebub kept up his headlong, heart-stopping pace down a black bank of cloud.

At the bottom of the slope was a sharp right turn and then another jump. Smoothly, the black horse lifted off and cleared it effortlessly. A flying leaper indeed!

On the other side of this cloud hedge Felix could again see the pack, going steadily downhill towards the ground. And he could at last see the covert they had drawn scent from: the town of St. Peter Port and Castle Cornet, the headquarters of the Inquisition.

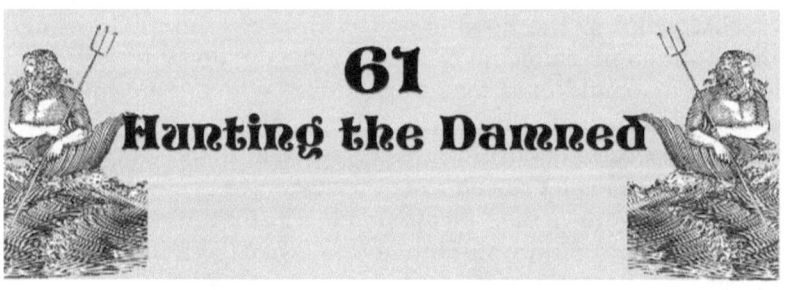

61
Hunting the Damned

Once again Maël stepped out onto the roof of the Castle, seeing as before a black, rolling sky and feeling a wind that tugged at his cassock as if it wanted to carry him off.

But there was one huge difference between this time and the last. The sky was filled with the sound of hounds in full cry, the thunder of galloping hooves and cries of "Hoick! Hoick!" from inhuman throats. And this time Maël could not insist that it was the sound of wind. or of thunder, for it was all too apparent that it truly was the cry of hounds and the beat of hooves.

Beside him, Roux screamed, as the clouds parted and they could see the ghastly hunters streaming down from a break in the clouds, saw the midnight hounds with their flat, dead eyes, saw the immense hooves of the ebony Hell-Steeds churning up bits of cloud as if it were turf they galloped over. Roux tried to turn and run back into the Castle but he could not move. It was if his shoes had been nailed to the roof.

Mael leaned forward, his hands gripping the thick edge of the machicolation of the top of the wall he stood behind. "It is not possible!" he muttered to himself. Oddly enough, he was not terrified as was Roux, rather, he was angered, for his long-held beliefs that apparitions such as this were but a superstition or at the most an illusion cast by a talented mage, were being shattered. He sniffed no human magic that could account for this. His mind seized on the one thing that explained it. It was the work of Satan himself! His right hand crept to the cross that swung at his throat and he grasped it firmly.

The hunt came to a halt some ten feet in the sky above the castle. Below them, in the street, Maël could hear screaming and crying, the sound of people running and Girard yelling at horror-struck men, intent only on escaping, to return to their posts.

The hounds milled about in the sky, under the restive feet of the horses, the whipper-ins controlling them with difficulty as the scent of the prey was strong.

Mael held the cross aloft. "Begone, you cursed fiends of Hell!" he shouted. "I command you, creatures of darkness, to return to Hell form whence you came!"

A figure on a horse somewhat larger than the others gave a low mocking laugh and rode a little ways forward. "Do you think, human, that your cross has the least effect on me or my Hunters? I was a god in these Celtic lands long before the White Christ came to these shores!" He threw back his head and the hood fell back.

Roux whimpered and tried to hide his face in his hands.

The countenance revealed was completely inhuman: a long, narrow face, with hard black eyes under thin, soaring brows. It was a beautiful, but terrible face, the skin dark and glowing with an unearthly shine. Black hair, as black as the horse he rode, fell to his shoulders from a widow's peak on his high forehead. And from that hair sprouted antlers, not a headdress of any sort, but springing from his skull. They resembled the antlers of a deer, a six point stag, and gleamed with polished horn and tracery of gold. About his neck he wore a heavy torque made of golden chains. Otherwise his torso was bare and gleamed with oil.

'It is the task of myself and my hunters," Gwyn said "to gather the souls of the damned, amongst others. And in order to add pleasure and a bit of good sport, we hunt them."

"What have you to do with us?" Maël demanded. "We are men of God! Doing God's work for the Holy Inquisition!"

Gwyn laughed again, an ugly, mocking sound. Behind him, on the sidling Beelzebub, Felix shivered. Before the Hunt had come to stand he had pulled the hood well up over his head again.

"God's work?" Gwyn demanded. "Is it God's work to torture, to rape, to extract confessions from innocent persons who will confess to anything in order to stop the pain of the lash or the rack or the *bastinado*? And is it God's work to enjoy this? And all because they believe in a different form of worship than do you! Gods care little as to the forms of worship as the worship itself is what matters and the

549

sincerity in the heart of the worshipper, the obedience to the word of the God. The laws of your Inquisition are man-made, not made by God."

"And therefore such as you are doubly damned. You flout the laws of the God and the law of humanity," he pronounced.

Mael's lips opened on a hot retort but he suddenly found that he ws unable to utter little beyond a harsh croak. Dropping the cross, his hands flew to his throat.

"And now for some sport!" cried the huntsman, and lifted the horn to his lips where he sounded 'away', a thrilling series of quick doubled notes that pulsated in the ear.

Mael and Roux found themselves on the ground, outside the city, with no idea how they got there. The sky was full of hounds and horses and the Huntsman cracked his incredibly long whip at them. "Run!" he cried. "Run for your lives!"

Roux, with a yell of sheer terror took to his heels at once, but Maël at first stood his ground. He would not give into the hell-born imps!

But one of the *Cwn Annwn* leaped straight at him, its jaws opened wide, snarling and growling, obviously intent on ripping out his throat. He ducked its leap and ran after Roux, with no idea of where he was going or how he was going to escape.

Gwyn was holding in his horse who wished to bound after the horses and hounds now streaming in a river of black after the two hapless Frenchmen. He stood in his stirrups and said in excellent French in a voice like thunder, "Frenchmen! You will leave this island in two days time, or we will be back! We will hunt down, kill and take with us to the Underworld everyone of you who remains behind! So declare I, Gwyn ap Nudd, Lord of Annwn!"

His horse reared and squealed, fighting the hand on the bridle. A strong westerly wind sent Gwyn's cloak snapping out behind him. His entire figure simmered with an eerie glow against the black clouds and the phenomenon known as St Elmo's fire danced up and down his antlers, making him look even more demonic to the frightened soldiers on the ground. Panicking, the soldiers tossed down their arms and began to run towards the harbor, where the ships were anchored, ships that could take them from this accursed place.

Beelzebub had remained behind with Gwyn and his mount. He too was eager to join the chase but some compulsion made him remain behind, although he snorted and half-reared, giving Felix a thoroughly uncomfortable ride.

"Come, Wizard!" Gwyn shouted to Felix as the wind rose in a screaming fury and rain began to lash down in long lances. Lightning spat from a cloud almost too close for Felix's comfort. "We must be in at the kill!"

He had but to lean forward and his mount, called Lucifer (Gwyn though it a great joke to name his Hell-Steeds from the Christian devil's many names) took off at a great rate of speed after the field.

Beelzebub, followed, flat out, the bit between his teeth.

Felix gave up all attempts at guiding him or maintaining any control. He concentrated instead on staying on, crouching low over the animal's neck, for the rush of wind was now so strong that had he sat up in the saddle, the force of it would have swept him from the Hell-Steed's back.

Beelzebub seemed determined to keep pace with Lucifer, who was now moving so quickly that he was passing most of the members of the Field. Ahead, Felix could hear the now excited cries of the hounds, giving tongue as they chased down the quarry.

In at the kill. As much as Felix hated the Inquisition he did not wish to see someone killed in any manner. But amongst the articles in the covenant he signed had been one forbidding him to interfere with the Wild Hunt in any manner. Protesting the death of the Inquisitors would be construed as interference. Richard had carefully explained to him that he must not violate the terms of the covenant for, to do so would be to put themselves and the *Guernaise* in extreme danger.

But even so, the thought of seeing Mael and Roux die, as much as they might deserve it for their persecution of the innocent, was a chilling one and made him feel more than a little sick.

Pascoe had flown both behind and above the Hunt. They seemed to carry the wind along with them and it streamed out in a broad band behind them. But flying a thousand feet or so above them kept Pascoe out of the damaging effect and away from the lightning they carried with them. His ultra-keen dragon-sight, far superior to that of a hawk or an eagle, would see if Felix took a tumble and nothing could dive faster than a dragon. He was very confident that he could catch Felix if it became necessary.

How wonderful it felt to be in the air again! It was unnatural for a dragon not to fly. It was what they were made for.

There was no strain or weakness in the healed phalange. Pascoe reflected on how fortunate they were to have found an Elfin Healer. Without Galen's skills he might have been much longer recuperating from the broken bone. But now they could go home when this Wild Hunt was over and get Felix to a Wizard Healer and have his memory restored. It had hurt the dragon badly enough when Felix had looked at him, a dragon he had known since childhood, with no recognition. Pascoe could only imagine how dreadful it had been for Pyewacket and Richard.

He took another close look at the Hunt. Felix was holding his own nicely, Pascoe thought. He had seen Felix on horseback many times and he had always though the young man at home to a peg on any blood cattle he chanced to throw a leg over.

Pascoe watched as the Hunt plunged towards the ground and confronted the Inquisitors. He made lazy circles overhead as the two began to run from the Hunt.

Pascoe grimaced. As little as did Felix did he relish seeing the death of these two. They were evil, it was true, but the copper dragon much disliked seeing anyone harmed.

The Hunt was now only a foot or so above the ground, although going at an incredible rate of speed, the hounds baying in close pursuit. The two humans could have no chance of escape, but Pascoe knew from his reading that the Wild Hunt would tease them, let them imagine that they *might* escape and all for the sake of a better run.

Up here Pascoe had a bird's eye view of the entire island. He became conscious of several thumping booms, and stretched his long neck to look westward, where the sound seemed to be coming from.

He saw one of the strangest things he had ever seen: a basket, hanging from a bag of red, white and blue silk. Smoke hung in the air near it and rose from the ground beneath it.

A hot air balloon! Pascoe had never seen one up close. He had read of them in the journals, for watching balloon ascensions was a popular pastime amongst the *haut ton* in London and other fashionable gathering places.

Most dragons had no good opinion of balloons as they could see no need for them. Dragons were available in all of the Six Nations for transport and for hauling air freight. The dragons were happy to be able to provide these services. Dragons liked to work and earn their own way and enjoyed being with people.

The whole premise of a balloon was silly for the things could not be steered and were at the whim of the winds. Nor did they look out for their passengers as a dragon did. A dragon could read a map and plot a course as well, independent of his or her rider. All the rider needed to do was tell the dragon where he wished to go.

As far as Pascoe could see a balloon required constant attention. It was a struggle to keep it in the air and to get it to earth again. It was not dependable. It was more than likely just a fad, with no practical application.

But as Pascoe watched this balloon it did a strange thing. It reversed direction. In spite of the fact that the wind was westerly the balloon was suddenly heading steadily against the wind!

He could see a figure leaning over the basket, catching sight of the Wild Hunt. The man hefted something that had a fire on one end and dropped it over the Hunt.

It exploded amidst the horses and riders, sending them tumbling in all directions. There was little real damage for the riders and horses were immortal and could not be hurt.

But there was one among them who could be not just hurt but killed: Felix. And he, Pascoe, would not let that happen.

With a mighty thrust of his wings and a roll to the side, Pascoe switched direction, and, looking grim and determined, headed for the balloon. Part of his job was to protect his family and he had never neglected that duty yet. He would teach this crazed balloonist a sharp lesson.

62
The End of the Meet

Pascoe back-winged just shy of the balloon and said loudly "Stop that at once, you idiot! Have you any idea at whom you are throwing those ridiculous bombs? That is Gwyn ap Nudd and the Wild Hunt! He'll not stand for it! He'd as soon kill you as look at you!" He spoke in English, without thinking.

Blériot, who had been hanging over the side of the basket, an expression of utter glee on his face, whirled around, startled by the sound of a voice coming from the air.

His expression changed to one of consternation than changed back to one of relish as he took in the sight of the copper dragon. "Oh. this is indeed a fortunate happenstance!" he said in French. "A dragon, appearing out of nowhere! Now I shall be able to see how my brilliant invention destroys these reptiles of the air!" He sprang towards the swivel gun and aimed it at Pascoe. "Don't gibber at me!" he called out in his shrill voice." I don't understand dragon talk!"

"You mean you don't understand the King's English!" Pascoe returned, this time in French. "What do you think you are doing?" He easily ducked as the swivel gun emitted a shot at him.

Blériot was no marksman, as his acquaintanceship with guns was slight. He thought one had but to point and press the trigger. He had no idea of aim, or the skill it took to properly site a gun, particularly one mounted on an unstable platform such as a balloon. "Stand still!" he shrieked at Pascoe. "How can I kill you if you keep moving about like that?"

Pascoe looked at him in disbelief. This man was a complete fool!

The dragon handily dodged three more shots, for Blériot was becoming frustrated and his aim was wild. He screamed imprecations at Pascoe as Pascoe darted about in the air. Within a few moments Pascoe could judge the range of the shot and none even came near him.

Below them, the Wild Hunt had passed on in pursuit of its quarry. After stealing a glance to see if Felix was in any danger, Pascoe gave his attention back to the madman in the balloon

Then Blériot began throwing bombs at him. These missed as well but fell to the earth where they began doing fearful damage to fields and even, to Pascoe's horror, a house. People, screaming, ran out of it, barely ahead of a fire that burst through the roof.

Pascoe felt anger pour through him, a rage that stimulated his dragon gasses and opened his internal chambers so that he was prepared, much as his ancestors, a millennia ago, had prepared for battle. Once again he felt as he had the day the Blue Djinn had threatened Richard and his home. It was a dragon's duty to protect and defend humans but *this* person was evil, hurtling his instruments of destruction at the earth below, irregardless of whom he hurt. There was even a child amongst the people that had come from that house! Like all dragons, Pascoe adored children. He let out a fearful bellow that sent the balloon hurtling backwards and Blériot fell to the floor of the basket.

The wheel that guided the balloon spun madly and for a few dizzying moments the balloon went in a circle much like a child's top.

"NO!" yelled Blériot and hauled himself to his feet with difficulty, grabbing the wheel. With all of his might he pulled it hard to the right, wheeling away from Pascoe and steadying the balloon. He had designed the mechanism to be easy to steer and it was fortunate that he had done so, for he had little real strength in his thin body.

He quickly pulled levers, one to stop the pinwheel at the stern from propelling it forward and another to fix the wheel, so that he could fire the swivel gun again at Pascoe.

The dragon shot straight up in the air, rapidly, in a maneuver that would only be used in a fight, for normally he would spiral upwards.

"Hah!" cried Blériot in triumph. "Coward! You can't run from me fast enough!" He jumped up and down in delight, shaking his fist at Pascoe's retreating form. He had been certain that dragons would be terrified of his war machine and this proved it!

He congratulated himself too soon. When he was high enough Pascoe turned and dove, so quickly that Blériot had little time to react.

The great copper dragon plummeted towards the balloon, dropping like a raptor on prey. Blériot tried to get out of his way but could not get the balloon moving quickly enough.

With a snarl of rage Pascoe tore past the basket, and extending one three-toed claw, grabbed the swivel gun and wrenched it from its perch. In an incredible display of his command over the air, Pascoe leveled off abruptly under the balloon and with a contemptuous flick of his talons threw the swivel gun to the ground.

Three more times Pascoe thrust hard up into the air, hurtling downwards from over a mile up, at tremendous speed, and each time tore off one of the four swivel guns that Blériot had mounted, one on each side of the basket.

Desperately, Blériot tried to out-maneuver him. As well as the balloon could now move it had neither the speed or the capability of a dragon in the air. Pascoe was fast and agile; although no longer young he kept himself fit, and to his joy, the Elf-healed phalange showed no signs of strain or pain. Pascoe could roll and back and twist in the air, which the balloon could not. It was confined to up and down and straight forward or a slight curve of movement. And so great was Pascoe's accuracy that he tore away only the gun and its fitting, doing minimal damage the sides of the basket.

With one last dive Pascoe ripped off the pinwheel arrangement that gave the basket its impetus.

Blériot was now frothing at the mouth, resembling even further the mad dog one of the prisoners had termed him. He picked up a bomb, lighting the fuse with shaking hands from a spill he lit from the brazier that kept the gasses heated. This he threw at Pascoe with as hard as he could, with a screamed curse.

It missed, going much too slowly to even touch a dragon.

But it fell on a building beneath them that Pascoe recognized as a school.

It was empty, for when the mothers of the children in

this parish (they were now over Castel) had seen the terrible sights in the sky that morning they had kept the children home.

What if there *had* been children in that building? They would have been killed! Pascoe literally saw red, a heated vision of the balloon and its evil little aeronaut was in his vision and his gas cavities filled to capacity as he took a deep breath, opened his maw wide and let out a wall of fierce flame.

He never intended what happened. The ferocity of the flame surprised even him. It was both wider and deeper than he thought it would be. He only meant to frighten and intimidate the man into stopping menacing the countryside.

The basket, dried and varnished willow withes, went up like a torch and faster than anyone might have imagined, the flames leaped to the silk and met the volatile, highly flammable gas that was inside the balloon and it erupted in a ball of flame.

The last thing that Pascoe heard was Blériot's shrieks of agony as he died.

And since Blériot had been so stupidly secretive and so jealous of sharing his knowledge, with him died the idea of both crystal energy to move machinery and the design for a self-propelled balloon.

Like a cat with a mouse, the Wild Hunt let Mael and Roux think that they had escaped, only to catch up with them time and again.

Roux was terrified, panting and sobbing as he ran, holding onto his side where a pain like a hot iron stabbed him. He fell frequently and got up only when Maël yanked him to his feet.

If Maël was scared he did not show it outwardly. He was almost preternaturally cold and contemptuous of Roux's wailing and crying. He said nothing to Roux, though, beyond a terse, in his restored voice, "Get up!" each time the torturer fell.

Both the pack of hounds and the horses with their riders

were nearly upon the ground, only a foot or so above the earth. Felix had no more fear of falling to his death. His entire attention was on the huntsman and his horn and the unnecessary cruelty of the chase. He knew that both the Senior Witch-Sniffer and the torturer were evil and no doubt deserved punishment, but he could not see why Gwyn ap Nudd was drawing out the inevitable. Surely, to judge by Gwyn's use of the phrase 'the kill' the justice meted out to these two was to be painful and permanent and then to be damned for all eternity on top of that! Why prolong it?

The members of the field, from what their eager posture indicated, were almost as hungry as the hounds for blood. Their cries filled the air and they urged their horses forward to a reckless pace.

The huntsman blew 'gone away'. The fox, or in this case, the men, had left their covert, a copse they had taken refuge in to catch their breath. The hounds gave tongue again and took off after the men at the thrilling notes of the horn, doubled, that gave both a sense of urgency to the hounds and a signal to the field that it was time to take off at a gallop in pursuit of the hounds. As the field moved out, headlong, into their fastest pace, the huntsman again blew Tantivy and all about Felix the air was filled with the excited cries of the riders.

Beelzebub kept well up just behind Gwyn's Lucifer, seeming to understand that his place was to follow the Master of Hounds. This was well, for Felix had lost all control of him. The Hell Steed had a powerful neck and jaws and he had taken the bit between his teeth. Even the curb chain seemed to have no effect on him. He went neck or nothing over the ground.

To be in at the kill, and, Felix suspected, to make the fences they were taking more thrilling the field was now on the ground. It seemed to Felix that they went deliberately out of their way to jump over the highest, most difficult places, high banks covered in furze, tall fences, streams, anything and everything that a horse could, or couldn't if he were not a Hell-Steed, jump.

It was all done at top speed, reckless sped, with the ground rushing by under the great hooves. No one seemed to have ever heard of the sage advice 'ride fast at water and slow at timber' for each obstacle was approached at break-neck pace and leaped at the highest point.

How he managed to stay on and not take a toss, a toss that might have very well broken his neck, Felix could never afterwards say. He just held on with grim determination, knees and legs gripping the Hell-Steed's sides, feet, heels down, his weight in his heels. Contrary to the accepted mode of riding, he did not lean backwards as the jump was cleared, but let the horse's motion thrust him up almost over his neck, waiting for the gathering of his muscles for the jump to begin rather than anticipating it and thus getting ahead of the horse. Perhaps this was wrong, but it seemed to be working.

Ahead of the field, as they came down over the last barrier, a huge board fence out lining a pasture for cows, Felix could see Mael and Roux running ahead of them, both beginning to lag badly. How long had this been going on? The sun was beginning to hang lower in the sky.

By some strange, invisible communication the Huntsman was keeping the hounds somewhat in check, behind the two men. Even though he continued to blow 'gone away', which served to encourage the hounds, they had not yet caught them.

Roux was floundering, at the end of his endurance, when Gwyn suddenly gestured to the Huntsman and he raised the horn to his lips and blew a strange call, long and wavering and sending a chill down Felix's spine. It was eerie, unearthly and had the effect of slowing the entire field. The horses and hounds slowed of their own accord and in a few moments had surrounded both Roux and Maël in a huge circle.

Gwyn pushed through the hounds, who were still making music, and lashed at them with his whip, quieting them. Beelzebub followed Lucifer, completely disregarding Felix's wishes.

"Well, priests, you have given us good sport!" observed Gwyn, staring down at them.

The rest of the riders gave a ragged cheer, obviously in a pleased mood.

"But the time has come to end it. I am for Annwn, which shall be your new home as well," Gwyn ap Nudd observed. He had not restored his hood to his head and his antlers gleamed in the light. He ran the thongs of the whip through his skeletal hand.

Roux, sobbing, fell to his knees. "Please, my lord, I beg you, whatever it is I am guilty of, I will repent! Only let me live!" He looked up at Gwyn, his face blanched, his eyes full of terror. He spoke with difficulty, for he was breathing as a broken bellows.

"He can do nothing to us," said Maël sternly. "We are protected by God." He did not kneel, but his hand firmly grasped the cross at his throat and he stared straight into Gwyn's face with no outwards sign of fear.

"Enough of this!" Gwyn said as Roux's sobbing filled the void of air left suddenly silent. He gave a signal and with hideous growls, the hounds leapt.

Until the moment they began to tear at his flesh, Maël still thought that God would save him.

Felix closed his eyes against the horror of this sight and wished he could close his ears to the sounds of Roux's screams. He felt darkness sweep over him as the hounds began their bloody work. He almost fell from the saddle but felt a hand at his elbow and Gwyn's voice in his ear. "You have acquitted yourself well so far, Wizard! But if you fall to the ground now even I cannot control the hounds and they will tear you limb from limb as they are tearing the damned. And you, Wizard, are not damned. I am afraid that I should have to sustain a visit from someone I would rather not deal with if I allowed harm to come to you."

He bent down and took Beelzebub's bridle near to the bit and led the horse out of the excited melee that surrounded the hound's grisly work.

When they were well away he said "Your part of the bargain has been fulfilled, Wizard. I am pleased. You have bottom and are a bruising rider as well. I shall leave you here where you will be safe from my hounds. We shall continue to harrow the French. Even now, they are boarding their ships. But we shall make quite certain that they leave. If you ever wish to ride with us again –"

"Thank you, my lord, but no. I shall ride but on the ground from here on in," said Felix faintly as he slid, more falling off than properly dismounting, from the saddle.

Gwyn laughed. As Felix, opening his eyes, looked up, Gwyn saluted him with his hunting crop and then, standing in his stirrups, boomed "Huntsman!"

A long wavering, tremolo note from the horn, rather sad sounding, pierced the air. It was a signal to the hounds, congratulating them for a job well done, but to the field it meant the end of the meet.

Then another long and mournful wail, extravagantly flourished sounded. This was blowing for home and first the hounds and then the horse began to stream up into the air. As Felix watched he could see two formless black shapes on the cruppers of the Whippers-in, all that was left of Maël and Roux: their black, damned souls.

Abruptly, Felix's legs lost all of their strength and he found himself on his knees on the ground. He was wretchedly sick, for he could still smell the blood in the air, and he dared not even look in the direction of the kill, for fear of what he would see. He was very glad that he had been unable to eat much breakfast that morning.

A few minutes later, Pascoe found him there and the copper dragon at once flamed the remains with such a hot fire that they turned to ash almost immediately.

He then nuzzled Felix in sympathy, and Felix, grateful for his touch, put his arms up around the dragons' neck. Pascoe was equally glad to have the comfort of a member of his own family, for reaction had set in for him too. He had never before killed a human being and everything in him was aghast at what he had done.

Ten minutes later Richard and Robin arrived to take them back to Faerie.

63
The Bluebell Wood

Matters had gone very ill for Colonel Fournier that morning. He had been awakened at an early hour, scarcely even light, by an urgent pigeon message from Lieutenant Petit out at the Dragon Port.

Blériot had run mad, it said. The inventor had informed Petit that he had dismissed the translator and his escort and even as Petit was writing the message to his superior, the man was setting about taking the balloon up his own self. He had locked everyone out of the balloon shed, after having the prisoners open the overhead door, and would admit no one, even though the tests were supposed to be conducted under the supervision of the army. Fournier swore a blue streak, crushing this message in his hand and throwing it at the wall in a rage.

Then to make matters worse, the weather was again appalling, the sky filled with dark clouds as Fournier rode out to the Dragon Port to see if he could stop the inventor's disobedience. The Colonel was yawning loudly for he had been up late the evening before, playing cards.

The inventor was always threatening to inform the First Consul of this or that. Fournier himself would have plenty to write to the First Consul about for his orders had clearly stated that the trials were to be held under the aegis of the army. Careful notes were to be made and sent to Paris. The old farms on the west side of the island, between Perelle and an Rocquaine bays, had been emptied of people, just to serve as targets. The inventor had not proved at all cooperative. He seemed bent on taking *la gloire* for himself, not sharing it with Fournier. It must never be said that the British Isles were conquered by an insignificant little madman. No, that honor belonged to Arnaud Fournier!

Fournier's horse, a normally sensible, steady animal

named Florentin, a well-trained calvary mount, was nervous. He shied at nothing, his ears flicking back and forth and wanted to go faster than the controlled canter Fournier had set him to do.

Thunder rolled in the distance and lightning flashed but Fournier could not understand Flornetin's distress. Florentin had been his mount in battle, including the battles of Marengo and Hohenlinden, and the horse had been as steady as rock in the midst of cannon fire and gunshot. A little thunder should not disconcert him, even though it looked as if they were in for another truly bad storm.

Fournier had scoffed at those of his men and the priests who had insisted that the previous ill weather had been Satan's weather. He had threatened to put on report those men who had told tales of baying dogs and a horn cry coming from the sky. They had more than likely been drunk, he had told Girard. At Girard's protest that some of the priests had heard these sounds as well, Fournier had declared that they were a pack of superstitious old women. After all, what was religion but superstition? Fournier had firmly embraced the ideals of the Revolution, particularly those that had banished the priests and the Inquisition from France. It should have stayed so. The Inquisition was a useful tool for keeping the lower orders subjugated but Fournier found having to spend most of Sunday in church and giving lip service to religious precepts quite irksome.

It was a bad storm; that was all.

His trip to the Dragon Port accomplished naught. Blériot was gone by the time he arrived. Petit, who had a team of men trying to break down the stoutly constructed door, admitted that he could not have stopped him.

Looking at the door, built to Blériot's specifications, Fournier could not help but think that the inventor had this in his mind all along. He was stealing Fournier's thunder, damn him!

No sight could be seen of the balloon. Petit's men had seen it rise, very fast, and saw it head north, against the prevailing westerly, which was blowing quite strongly and smelling of the rain to come. It also bore on its strong currents a sulphuric stench that made one cough and want too have a handkerchief over one's face.

"At least we know that part of the experiment works," said Fournier sourly to Petit as they stood outside the balloon storage shed where the men had given up battering the door.

"I was amazed at how well it moved against the wind," Petit admitted. He had seen balloon ascensions in Paris and knew the fragile craft to be at the mercy of the element of air.

"He is no doubt heading for the target sight," said Fournier, frowning. "I shall follow on horseback and watch. I shall be able to send a report to Paris, even though it should have been written from the basket of the balloon, rather than on the ground. Damn that arrogant little bastard!"

"It will be a formidable weapon, *mon Colonel,* for it is fast as well," said Petit, motioning to a nearby corporal standing stiffly at attention in the presence of the Colonel.

"Bring up the Colonel's horse," he ordered, and the corporal, saluting, took off at a run.

It was as they stood there, waiting for Florentin, that they heard the hounds, followed by the horn of Gwyn ap Nudd's Huntsman.

At the first eerie howl Petit blanched and crossed himself. "Mother of God!" he exclaimed. "What is that? It is the wrong time of year for the English foxhunting." Petit, being of a scholarly turn of mind, had studied the British Isles extensively when preparing for this posting.

"Feral dogs, no doubt, and a bugle from one of our forts, distorted by this wind," said Fournier tersely.

Petit looked at him doubtfully. His grandfather, who lived in Lorraine, had a pack of stag hounds, and even they did not sound like that. And the other sound – that was a hunting horn, not a bugle. But he did not say anything as he did not want another tongue-lashing from the Colonel over something that he could not have prevented, short of locking Blériot in his rooms. He had been given no authority to do that.

Florentin arrived with a sweating coat and wildly rolling eyes. The private who served as one of the grooms, had trouble holding him for he was half-rearing and plunging.

"What have you been doing to my horse?" Fournier demanded angrily. "He has not been cooled out at all!"

"Excuse me, sir," the private panted. "But I cooled him myself. All the horses have been like this ever since that hell horn sounded and they heard those dogs. They're all fretted up, trying to kick down their stalls and neighing their heads off!"

Florentin stood up his hind legs and let out a screaming sort of noise. Only with the greatest difficulty did the private retain his hold on the reins.

When Florentin came back down to earth Petit, taking a look at the horse said, "Perhaps, Colonel, you should not attempt – "

"Are you trying to tell me what to do, Petit?" Fournier spat out."I have been a horseman longer than you have been alive. I am well able to handle him."

Petit flushed in humiliation, "No, of course not, sir, but I am concerned."

"Be so good as to shut your mouth!" Fournier said shortly. "Go to his head, fool!" he yelled at the private.

Never had Florentin, so well trained, such an exemplary example of a calvary horse, behaved so badly. It was well that Fournier was indeed, as he claimed, a master horseman. He had trained at the *École de Cavalerie* at Saumur, before the Revolution, where his father and his grandfather, also Cavalrymen, had trained.

Florentin tried to prevent his rider mounting by going in a tight circle. Fournier put a stop to this by shortening the left rein so that Florentin's head was almost against the saddle.If he had kept turning he would have fallen over.

All the same, it was a challenge to mount. Once in the saddle Fournier felt the hump in his mount's back that meant he was going to buck. So his rider heavily applied his aids and made the horse trot out. A few miles of this fast trot and Florentin would be as level-headed as he was normally. Fournier made a mental note to have Sergeant Poulin, in charge of the stables in St. Peter Port, on the carpet before him. Obviously, Florentin was not getting enough exercise. Fournier somewhat regretted the circumstance that kept him behind a desk instead of on horseback, but this opportunity to advance his career had been too good to pass up. One did not say no to the First Consul .

It was a strange ride from the beginning. The uncanny weather, the sounds in the air, the smell and Florentin's behavior, all combined to make even Fournier a trifle uneasy. The roads were deserted as well, not a soul stirring. Fournier was not too surprised at this for it was a Monday, not an assembly day after all, but where were the people toiling in the fields, or about other business? Children should be on their way to school as well, After a short time off to help with spring planting the brats should be at their desks again until nearly July.

Lost in these and other thoughts Fournier did not notice that the land was subtly changing about him. The houses along the sides of the road had disappeared. He was in a thick wood, with ancient, enormous trees, lit only by the strange light from above, a dark light, for the sunshine was dissolved in the dark mass of billowing cloud. Above his head, a wind made the treetops creak and groan, their leaves rustling madly. It almost sounded as if there were voices in the wind.

There was something very strange about this wood. There were bluebells blooming all over the ground. Fournier was not one to notice flowers but even he wondered at this. Did bluebells not bloom earlier in the year? And where the hell was he? This was not the road to the target area!

Florentin stopped abruptly, snorting, and gave out a long whinny. Suddenly, out of nowhere, a cloaked and hooded figure appeared on the path in front of Fournier, on a path that had grown increasingly narrow between the overhanging branches of huge oak and beech trees.

Standing in his stirrups, Fournier shouted "Are you insane, to step out in front of a horse like that? Remove yourself from my path!"

The figure said nothing, but flung up a hand with impossibly long slender fingers, and Florentin went mad.

He wrenched the bit from Fournier's control, put down his head and began to buck, squealing madly as he jumped into the sky and then hit the earth with neck-snapping force.

In spite of all his experience, Fournier had never ridden a horse that twisted and plunged so badly. It ws as if he had clapped a saddle on an unbroken horse, caught in the wild. First he lost his stirrups and then his seat, falling off with an ignominious thump. He hit the ground with such force that he momentarily lost consciousness. As he slid into blackness he heard the noise of dozens and dozens of tiny bells ringing.

When he came to his senses he was propped up against the bottom of an oak tree. Standing about him in a circle were about a dozen young women who looked as if they had stepped off a Grecian vase painting, a look that the current fashion sought to emulate but had not quite succeeded in doing.

They were all slender and tall, with lovely figures and all were beautiful, clad in simple variations of a Greek *chiton* or the girded *peplos* that Fournier had seen in Greek statues. Some wore it off the shoulder, some had one breast bare, and one or two wore nothing at all save a ribbon in their hair or a band of gold rising to a point in the middle. This was the *stephane* that held back a crown of curls. They had hair of gold, of black and brown and even red, and eyes of differing colours, but all had one thing in common: their skin was slightly green.

Fournier raised his hand to his head and closed his eyes. He was still unconscious, that was what was happening. This was a dream. There could be no other explanation.

"Tree-killer!" the young women began to hiss in low voices. "Killer and despoiler who wantonly murdered our sisters! Tree-killer! Tree-killer! Tree-killer!"

"Silence, sisters," came a new voice, and the young women parted to let the hooded figure that had so spooked Florentin glided into their midst.

She, for the voice was definitely feminine, came to stand in front of Fournier. She threw back her hood. Her face, although older than that of the others, was nonetheless the loveliest Fournier had ever seen, but still faintly green.

"It was you, was it not, who commanded the destruction of the sacred grove at the place men call *Le Creux ès Faies*?" she said sternly. "You did not wield the axe yourself but you made the men cut down those venerable oaks, oaks that have existed for thousands of years! They were revered as objects of worship by the Druids, amongst others. And it was you who ordered the destruction of many other shrines and scared places as well."

"They were objects of pagan superstition," said Fournier defensively, wishing that he felt well enough to stand and get out of here. There was something menacing about these young women, as beautiful as they were. At any other time he would have made advances to one or more of them, particularly the naked ones.

"Do you not know that when an oak is cut down, without permission, without proper rites and blessing, that the hamadryad that dwells with in it dies as well, in extreme pain?" she said, her face set in lines of anger.

"*Madame*, do not tell me nursery tales of Faeries and tree nymphs!" said Fournier in scorn. "Nursery tales to frighten naughty children!"

"What do you think that we are, fool?" she said as if disgusted by his stupidity. "We are dryads of willow, ash, beech, and elder amongst others. I am Athene, hamadryad of the elder oak, the oldest tree of this land, and fortunately spared from your axe. By long tradition I am leader of these, my sister dryads. Tree-killer you have been judged and tree-killer you shall die."

"Die?" echoed Fournier blankly.

"You heard the bluebells ring, did you not?" she said. "That was your death knell, mortal. In parts of our British lands they are known as Dead-man's Bells, and to be in a bluebell wood when they ring is to be in danger, in a place of enchantments, and the place of one's death."

She raised her hands over her head and clapped once.

The air was filled with hundreds of shimmering blue shapes, flying through the air, tiny voices shrieking gleefully. They each held a brown object which they threw at Fournier.These proved to be acorns, and they provided a painful bombardment.

Swearing, he threw his hands up about his face and leaned backwards into the trunk of the tree as if to make himself smaller.

To his horror he felt something begin to close around him.

"*Merde!*" he screamed, struggling. He looked down and

saw roots growing over his feet and bark beginning to creep about his body. "No! This can't be happening!" he said hysterically.

"No one shall ever know what happened to you, mortal. You shall be forgotten, your grave unmarked," said Athene in satisfaction while the other dryads shouted "Death to the tree-killer!"

It was the last thing Fournier heard as the bark closed over his face and he slowly smothered to death.

It was not until many, many years later, when the oak had died a natural death, that his bones were discovered after a gale had uprooted the dead tree. There was much speculation as to how a skeleton had come to be inside a tree trunk, but no one ever advanced a reasonable explanation.

64
The Abduction

David had been immensely grateful that Blériot had dismissed Felix on that Sunday. Going out to the Dragon Port every day was becoming a burden and when David had suggested to Fournier that Felix be allowed to go out there by himself, if it were still necessary, Fournier had given him a brusque no. The Bailiff was responsible for the *Gitan's* conduct. Gypsies were not to be trusted. The *Gitan* would shirk his work. Only constant scrutiny would keep him at his task and David was to be held accountable.

So on that Monday, David slept late, a late hour for a farmer that is, until after six. His mother too, lay in bed longer than her usual habit, in spite of the nasty weather out of doors. And, still sleepy, they were both startled when a thunderous pounding came at the door while they sat at breakfast.

It was a panting, disheveled, slightly damp Aristide Boileau, their only tenant, who worked the small farm attached to their even smaller estate here in St. Peter Port. The farm supplied David and Majorlaine with vegetables and fruit. Boileau was a man of nearly sixty, somewhat crippled with arthritis and had been rejected by the French army as unfit for service.

"I have run all the way, Sir David!" he exclaimed, as Majorlaine insisted he come into the kitchen and be seated at the table. She poured him out a cup of herbal tea.

"Drink that before you speak," Majorlaine insisted.

Boileau took only a gulp and said excitedly "The French are leaving! They are running to the harbor!"

"*Mon Dieu!*" Majorlaine gasped. Putting a hand to her breast, where her heart had began to beat wildly, she sank into a chair and stared at Boileau in disbelief.

"The sky is full of horses and hounds of blackness!" said

Boleau. "It is as my grandsire told: *Le Armée Furieuse!* And the Master of the Hunt ordered the French to leave the island, else they will be killed and taken to Hell! And they are obeying!"

David too, was excited. Gwyn ap Nudd had done as he promised! They would be free of the French!

His first thought was that now he and Grizel could be married, but immediately he chided himself for his selfishness, for this was a great day for *all* the islands! Free at last!

Gwyn ap Nudd had given the French two days to leave, but, full of terror, they managed it in less than a day. Everything was abandoned in the chaos of their flight. Fournier, Maël and Roux were nowhere to be found and the Junior Witch-Sniffers and the assistant torturers disappeared as well. Girard tried to institute some order from the hysterical flight but soon had to give it up as a bad job, for no one paid the least attention to his orders. It was the same on every French occupied Channel island.

The overcrowded ships sailed from St. Peter Port and other ports on a course to France, harried by some of Gwyn's cohorts. They had scarcely cleared the harbor when they were caught by the Channel Fleet of the Six Nations.

Having discarded many of their guns and powder at the bottom of the harbor in order to crowd more men onto each ship, they had little defense and spent the balance of the war as prisoners in Dartmoor and various other prisons.

John had spent all his time since the first bad storm driving himself hard, to conquer the weakness that he still felt at times. He ate every scrap of food *Madame* brought him to build up his strength.

He had a sense of time running out. He had to do something to get his revenge on that damned Gypsy and return to the Professor's service before it was too late, before the Gypsy was even more in the Professor's good graces and John's master discovered that he had no further need for his old servant.

He would demand two things. That the Gypsy never see the Professor again and that he, John, was to be taken to where his master was now, so that he might go back into the Professor's service. Things would then be as they were before the bloody Gypsy had come along. The cottage could be rebuilt or, even better, he could perhaps persuade the Professor to return to Cambridge.

And the best way to get at that Gypsy was through his woman.

John, from his upstairs window, watched carefully as to the woman's comings and goings. To his disappointment, after the storm, she had disappeared. He was now well enough to come downstairs and take his meals at the kitchen table. He listened carefully to Joisaine and *Madame's* talk for an explanation of where she could be. They spoke in English, for *Madame* said it was rude to speak their own language in front of *M'sieur* Jean, who spoke it so poorly.

He soon found out that the Gypsy woman was ill, and that *Madame* had told her to stay in bed until she was well again.

"Perhaps she is *enceinte*," said Joisaine, as she cleaned the table of dishes on Sunday evening. "Would that not be lovely, *Maman*? A little *bébé*!"

The French word she used sounded enough like *baby* that John understood what she meant. 'Lovely' was not a word he would use to describe the Gypsy woman perhaps being with child. Again, John felt sick at the thought of the Gypsies breeding. The Professor would be certain to take them in if he knew the woman was carrying a child. The Professor's tender heart would be appalled at the thought of them spending the winter in a caravan. John forgot that the Professor had no home to offer them. John had not been thinking clearly for a long while.

It had to be soon. He had to be well enough to do what had to be done. Already *Madame* had spoken to him about making other arrangements for his keep as soon as he was entirely well. No more than Joisaine did she enjoy John's glowering, sullen presence in their home. She could not have him at the farm permanently. But she had done her duty by him.

Yes, it had to be soon. John had seen the Gypsy slut at church, without her so-called husband, and she did look green in the gills.

He soon found out that the Gypsy was still spending all of his time out at the Dragon Port so he would not be around to thwart any plans John made. The old woman John discounted, as, even injured, he was strong enough to subdue her. She looked both old and ill much of the time.

He chose Monday as the day for his plan, and having made up his mind to do the deed, slept the sleep of the just the night before.

John awoke early on Monday morning, resolved to take care of the Gypsies this very day. He was not disconcerted by the ill weather blowing up outside. He heard the horns and the baying of hounds and gave it no thought. That had naught to do with him and soon the Wild Hunt was gone past Castel, streaming towards St. Peter Port, leaving only the storm of wind and rain in their wake.

It was necessary to deceive *Madame*. Fully dressed, he lay under the blankets when she came upstairs to secure the shutters and declined her invitation to join them in the kitchen as they were in for another day of wind and rain.

Gruffly, he said that he had a headache and so would prefer to sleep it off. *Madame* accepted his excuse and returned downstairs. Rosal and her family, she said conversationally, in case John was staying above stairs to avoid the Gypsies, had chosen to stay in the *vardo* as well. Pray to *le bon Dieu* that this storm was not the equal of the last!

When he was certain that she had gone down the stairs and into the kitchen, John, stealthily, holding his boots in one hand, crept into the hall and stood listening for a while. He was glad to feel his back much improved in all ways. He had scarcely a twinge from the old injury or the new. He refused to give Hagar's healing herbs their due, however.

From the sound of the voices, now gibble-gabbling in French, he could tell that *Madame* and her daughter were both in the kitchen.

He had become familiar with the house over the course of his stay and there was a little-used door on one side of the house, far from the kitchen. It was locked only with a drop bar and John, whilst *Madame* and Joisaine were hard at work out of doors, had oiled the hinges and the lifting mechanism so that it opened silently. It was far enough from the kitchen that he could steal out, undetected.

This he did, pausing only to put on his boots and shut the little door firmly behind him. He set off for the woods in which the *vardo* lay, taking care to keep well away from the kitchen windows and utterly disregarding the tempest and the strange sounds and smells in the air. He had other, more important business.

Rosal, since Felix had confronted her, had existed in a state of numb despair, alternating with bouts of crying. Now she was crying less, for her tears came less easily now, but the despair had not abated.

She scarcely noticed the bad weather out of doors and had been surprised when Joisaine had arrived, just after dawn, with an invitation to spend the hours of the storm at the farm.

Joisaine was surprised that she did not wish to go to the farm, but accepted Rosal's excuses. The girl had assumed that Hagar was perhaps still in bed in the *vardo* and also thought that Rosal's husband must have gone to his employment, for she did not inquire after either of them. She did leave a crock of soup that Madame had made for Rosal's health.

Rosal had trouble with both of her animals that morning. Kälo broke his halter after rearing and whinnying in terror and ran off into the woods. Chavé did not run away but he howled so mournfully and whimpered so that Rosal was forced to push him outside in the rain. She could still hear him howling from shelter under the high body of the *vardo,* but at least the sound was further away from her distressed nerves.

She pulled the quilts up around her ears and a pillow over her head. What was wrong with them today? It was what she did not need at the moment. She felt as if she could not cope with one more thing.

She never heard the baying of the Cwn Annwn, or the Huntsman's horn. She fell into a half waking doze, worn out from an excess of emotion and lack of sleep.

The first intimation that something was wrong came when rough hands pulled the blankets from her body and hands grabbed at her, pinning her wrists together and a large weight settled on her legs.

Rosal screamed in terror and fought. Her first thought was that whoever it was meant rape. She called for Chavé but no furry friend came to her rescue. Her struggles were ineffectual as the man who had gripped her wrists so tightly laughed at her. He was big, and stronger than her, for she was weak from not eating and lack of sleep... She recognized the Professor's manservant with horror. He was her enemy!

"I've taken care of the dog," John said, giving her a shake when she kept struggling. "Bashed his head in, I did, and I'll do the same to you if you ain't quiet!" He shook her again, so hard that her head flopped back and forth on her neck.

Glancing quickly about John saw several of Rosal's brightly coloured scarves hanging from a peg on the wall of the *vardo*. It was easy to keep her confined, for she was small and slender and one of John's big hands easily encompassed both her wrists held together. She could do nothing to repel him in spite of her squirming and attempts to kick at him.

But when she would not stop struggling and cursing him between screams, he lost his temper completely and struck her an open-handed blow across the face so violent that it made her eyes roll up in her head. She fell backwards, unconscious.

John was grateful for this as he was now to the point where he cared little how he treated her. She was the means to an end and was only Egyptian trash at that. She scarcely deserved any consideration or kindness from him.

Her being insensible made it easier for him to tie her wrists and then her ankles together with her own scarves. For

575

good measure he tied a gag about that nasty mouth of hers as well.

He left a note on the bed, written on an end-paper he had torn from one of *Madame's* few books. Writing that note had been the most difficult part of this entire plan.

He tossed Rosal's limp body up over his shoulder, wincing as pain lanced across his barely healed back. Never mind, the pain would be worth it when everything was set to rights once more. Fortunately, she was a light weight.

He left the door to the *vardo* open behind him. The note, weighed down by a platter from the cupboard, fluttered in the wind. The paper was folded over once and, on the top, in an ill-formed, uphill scrawl it read "lovil". And inside was a list of John's directions, laboriously penned.

After supper at *Les Huit Lapins* farm that evening, *Madame* was uneasy. The storm, now blown out, dying in a lovely peaceful sunset, had been a bad one again. Marie Brehaut and her daughter, like most of the people on the island, had remained indoors, away from what was happening in the sky. They had heard the booming voice ordering the French to go and later had heard as well, a tremendous explosion. Neighbors had already come by to report having seen a huge fireball in the sky. One boy had even claimed to see a dragon! One thing was certain: the French had fled and there was much elation and relief.

But *Madame* was uneasy about Rosal and her family and sent Joisaine to check on her. The storm had been fierce and *Madame* now regretted that she had not insisted that Rosal and Hagar join them as before.

Joisaine knew that there was something wrong straight away. Chavé did not run to greet her as he usually did when she came to the *vardo*. As she entered the clearing she saw further evidence of wrongness. There was no fire. Ever since she had known the Gypsies a fire, except in heavy rain, always burned at their camp site.

Drawing closer Joisaine saw that the tripod which held up the kettle had been overturned, the contents of the kettle spilled out on the ground. And tossed in the fire pit was a log, with blood on one end.

Terrified, Joisaine took in the other signs. The door to the *vardo* swung open. There was no sign of Kälo or Chavé or of anyone.

"Rosal!" Joisaine called, her voice shrill with anxiety. "Rosal!"

A whimper answered her.

"Chavé!" Joisaine exclaimed and ran to the source the sound came from, under the *vardo*.

The girl crawled under the caravan and found the dog. He feebly wagged his tail but did not sit up as she approached and fell to her knees beside him. The mere movement of his tail seemed to exhaust him.

The white fur on his face and ruff was dark with spilled blood. He had been hit on the head, Joisaine realized. Blood still trickled sluggishly from a deep cut.

Who would do such a thing? And where was Rosal that she was not able to care for the dog that she loved so well?

Chavé needed care and Joisaine had a very bad feeling about what had happed to Rosal and Hagar. She carefully touched Chavé's nose very gently. "Good dog," she whispered. "I shall go and fetch my *Maman* and some of the neighbors. We will tend you and find out what has happened to your people."

Within a half an hour she was back, with *Madame* and several neighbors. The *vardo* was searched, the signs of violence noted and the note found. Chavé was loaded onto a gate to be carried to the farm where he would be tended by old Yves Fouquet, who was as good as any trained veterinarian, everyone claimed.

Madame, unaware that Felix and Hagar were no longer living with Rosal, sent Jacques Bretagne, thirteen year old grandson of a neighbor, on the fastest horse in the area to tell Sir David Dieudonné of what had happened, and to see if he knew where Felix was working so that he might be fetched home to help find his missing family. Everyone agreed that it was indeed fortunate that the French had departed so precipitously, as there was now no barrier to Jacques riding cross country at a desperate gallop, with no check points to pass through and no permission need to go to St. Peter Port.

577

All the neighbors were horrified that such violence had taken place so near to their homes. Who could have done such a thing? And why?

But *Madame* had a good idea who and why. She had found John missing when she went to tell him of retreat of the French. And she was very afraid of what he would do to Rosal and her aunt, given his blind hatred of the Gypsies.

65
The Rescue

The   streets of St. Peter Port were full of cheering
throngs. It was not perhaps as noisy as it would have been
were there men and boys to add to the sound and congestion,
but the older folks, women and young children were overjoyed
at the departure of the French and had brought out long
hidden *Guernaise* flags and those of the Six Nations. These
were waving enthusiastically in the light of many torches. A
rag-tag   band was playing, both *God Save the King* and
Sarnia Cherie as well as *Rule Britannia* in deference to the
British man o' war, *H.M.S. Pegasus,* a ship of the line of 100
guns, that was now anchored in the harbor, flying an
Admiral's pennant.

Somewhere had been unearthed a box of fireworks and
these now burst over the harbor, their sparkle and colour
reflected in the nearly empty harbor waters, for besides the
Pegasus, there were only a few fishing vessels remaining at
their moorings. But the harbor was full of leaping dolphins
and Sea-Folk blowing conch shells.

David and his guests stood in the windows of his office in
Government House looking out over the harbor. *His* office
once   more,   all   signs   of   Fournier's   occupation   hastily
banished. With him was Grizel and Majorlaine, and also
Aurelius, Richard and Felix, the familiars and Richard's old
friend, Admiral Breckinridge. Robin had declined an
invitation. Faerie, unlike the Sea-Folk, only revealed itself to
a select few.

"A most satisfactory conclusion," said Admiral Roger
Breckinridge. He was a bluff and hearty man with a loud
shipboard voice, his face tanned and leathered by years at
sea, his hair, worn naval fashion in an old style queue, now
pure white. "I think that you will have no more trouble with
these Frenchies, Sir David."

"Not with the King's promise of troops and the Royal Navy guarding us," said David gratefully. On his desk lay a red Dispatch Box from Whitehall, outlining the disposition of troops that were meant to fortify the islands. Plans were already underway to restore the Dragon Post and begin shipping much needed supplies to the beleaguered islands.

"Now if our men could be restored to us," said Majorlaine wistfully.

"The Royal Navy can do little about that, ma'am," said the Admiral with regret. "I am very much afraid that once the Corsican has his hands on them he won't let go of any men he has in his grasp, not when he seems to be bent on conquering the world. You may very well have to wait until our war with France ends before they are returned to you."

"*If t*hey all can come back," said Majorlaine in a low voice.

A gasp arose from outside as amidst the fireworks there suddenly appeared a large copper-coloured dragon.

Richard chuckled. "Dragons adore fireworks, especially Pascoe. He knows how dramatically the colours glint off his scales!"

As he spoke, Richard stole a sidelong glance at Felix, who had been very quiet since the Wild Hunt had ended. Pascoe, too, had been uncharacteristically silent, but the dragon was now trying to raise his spirits by flying amidst the sparkle of the fireworks. Felix had not even wished to come to the celebration, but Richard did not wish to leave him alone to brood. The sooner Richard could get his grandson home to Devon and in the hands of a Wizard Healer, the better; too much had happened to him as of late, not the least this loss of memory.

The Admiral, who stood near Richard, saw his glance and said, sipping a glass of a fine sherry he had brought from the *Pegasus*, "Your grandson is much changed from the last time we met. Has he ever thought of becoming a Naval Wind Wizard? There's nothing like a sojourn in the service."

"Even though his element is air, Roger, Felix has little talent as a Wind Wizard. That's a talent has to be born in one," said Richard. His friend thought that joining the Navy was the cure for everything from a broken heart to ill health.

"Pity," said the Admiral. "I've often thought it a damned

shame that the services are closed to Wizards, save Wind Wizards and Augurs."

"We're sworn not to harm, save in defense of our own lives and that of family or against black magicians," Richard explained yet again. This was an old argument.

"What about the defense of one's country, eh?" the Admiral demanded.

The door to David's office burst open. A small, slight boy with a thatch of brown hair stood there panting. He looked agitated, eyes big in his face "Please, *Messieurs!*" he said breathlessly. "I have a most important message for Sir David Dieudonné!" he looked about the room with painful intensity, not certain that he knew which gentleman was the Bailiff.

"I am Dieudonné," said that gentleman, stepping forward.

"Oh, sir, *Madame* Brehaut told me to tell you that *M'sieur* Jean Grant has gone mad and has stolen away the Gypsy girl and that you would know where her husband is!"

"What!" Felix, who had been staring unseeingly at the firework lit harbor put down his un-tasted sherry abruptly on David's desk. "I am her husband, boy! When did this happen?" His voice was sharp with anxiety.

"*Madame* was not certain, *M'sieur*," answered Jacques, turning to face Felix. "*Mam'selle* Joisaine found her gone, and the dog hurt. *Madame* has a note for you that we found in the caravan. *Madame* thinks you should come at once!"

"Might I borrow your horse, David?" Felix asked quickly.

"Why ride a horse when much quicker transport is at hand?" said Richard. "Pascoe is wearing a brand new four seat saddle, a gift from Robin, and he can have us there in minutes." He stepped to the window and raising his fingers to his lips, let out a piercing whistle which, augmented by magic, was audible to Pascoe even over the noise of crowd, music and fireworks. The dragon wheeled towards the shore and obedient to Richard's hand signals, landed in the water near the dock.

"I'm coming with you," Aurelius announced. "He's my man-servant after all." What had John done? And why had he done such a thing?

The Admiral reached inside his jacket and brought out a business-like looking pistol. "Here, Richard, take this. If you're dealing with a mad man you might need it."

"Thank you, but I've my wand. Magic is all I'll need," Richard said hastily. There would be no shooting if he had anything to say about it. With guns in the equation, innocent blood could too easily be spilled.

Felix was already halfway out the door and starting down the stairs when Richard and Aurelius and the two familiars followed him.

As the tide was near high Pascoe was floating almost at the level of the dock. "What has happened?" the dragon asked as the party came hurrying up. Overhead more fireworks exploded in the sky, adding a strange and rather lurid light to the scene.

"My man-servant seems to have kidnapped Rosal Lovel," said Aurelius, a little breathless from the pace Felix had set on the way to the dock.

"Kidnapped a young woman!" echoed Pascoe. "Where?"

"Castel," said Felix briefly, dropping into the saddle and beginning to secure the safety harness. His fingers knew how it should be fastened. He was too worried to wonder at his familiarity with this procedure. He all too well remembered the hostility, the outright hatred, John had shown him and Rosal. And that boy said that Chavé had been hurt as well. Had the brave dog been trying to defend Rosal?

Since the Elves had saddled Pascoe Richard felt he could forego the safety check of the harness that was mandatory before a flight in order to take off quickly. He showed Aurelius how to strap himself into the saddle, put the familiars in the travel basket and then settled himself in. "We're ready, Pascoe," he announced.

The copper dragon swam out a little way and then threw himself up into the air in a great shower of water. He spiraled up into the night sky, his night vision excellent as he headed west towards Castel at top speed.

John, in spite of the pain it caused him, pushed Rosal higher up onto his shoulder as he stumbled through the woods towards the site of his old home, *Trois Chiminées*. She was still unconscious from the blow he had dealt her and lolled limply on his shoulder. He was glad of this, for he was certain that else wise she would still be kicking and fighting. He had not imagined that she would struggle and fight so much. He had expected her to be terror stricken and come with him obediently.

In spite of his burden, John soon reached his goal: the shed in which Diogenes the pony had lived. The shed had survived the fire and here John would have the advantage of being on his home ground. It was here that the note directed that damned Gypsy to come if he wanted to see his woman alive again.

Joisaine, a conscientious girl, had come and cleaned the shed after Diogenes had been taken to the stable at *Les Huit Lapins,* so it was onto clean, sweet straw that John dumped Rosal's limp body.

He straightened up slowly, looking at her in satisfaction. He would leave the bindings and the gag in place and then as he looked around the stable (he had come by earlier and lit a lantern) he saw a coil of rope. This he tied about her ankles for good measure and snubbed it to a ring in the wall, half of a set of cross-tie rings that had been used to tie up the pony for grooming.

From his pocket John withdrew a knife, stolen from *Madame's* kitchen. He had not dared to steal her big cooking knife. That would have been missed. This little one would have to do. Fleetingly he wished that he had a gun but he had never handled one and had no idea how to load it. He would have liked to blow a hole through that damned Gypsy.

He had no idea how long it would take the Egyptian to get here. John did not know where he had been this day. But he would find the note when he came back to the caravan and he'd be here as soon as he could, given how he felt about this little slut. And she certainly looked the part, John thought, with her hair all in disarray and her shift, the only garment she wore, torn in the struggle, hanging off her. Since she had been in bed so early in the day John had no doubts but what she had been entertaining some man and him not her husband. He felt no stir of desire as he looked at her for he hated Gypsies too much. To lie with her would make him dirty.

John made himself as comfortable as he could on an overturned bucket and settled down to wait. There was a whetstone in the stable and he began to sharpen the knife to a finer edge than it had ever known.

Pascoe landed in the fore-yard of the farm, where *Madame* normally kept her sheep in the winter. It was a tight squeeze but Pascoe was skilled and experienced.

He caused a sensation amongst the neighbors who were still waiting with *Madame* and Joisaine, eager to see that unfolding drama. Several persons who had been watching old Yves Fouquet doctor Chavé ran outside. Three children cried *"Regardez! C'est un dragon!"*, jumping up and down in excitement.

Pascoe had scarcely folded his wings when Felix vaulted off and ran into the house, followed a slower pace by Richard and Aurelius. A number of people seemed to want to want to ask questions of Richard about Pascoe, but he only said tersely "Ask him yourself" and nodded at Pascoe.

Felix, in spite of his fear for Rosal, went to Chavé and stroked the dog, saying to him in a low voice, "Did you take your hurts trying to defend her?" Chavé whined and licked Felix's hand.

"He's a good patient," said Fouquet. "Let me clean him up with not a snarl or snap."

"Take good care of him," Felix said and then turned to *Madame,* waiting at his elbow.

"He left this for you," she said simply and handed him the rather grubby little note.

"Gipsee" it ran
If you wants to see the woman alive you cum to the stabull at 3 chimnees. You must doo as I say or she wil die.
John Grant

After quickly scanning this Felix handed it to Richard. "Please, *Madame*, tell me everything you know," Felix begged.

"It was Joisaine that found it, and Chavé," said Marie

Brehaut. Joisaine stepped up and quickly outlined the circumstances. She was pale and her eyes big with worry. She would never forget the sight of the disturbed caravan or the dog's injuries. Now, like her mother, she was filled with fear for Rosal and Hagar.

"We have seen no sign of Hagar," said *Madame*. "Men are out searching the woods in case he did her a injury and –" it was difficult to say the rest of it "and left her to die out there."

"He's gone mad!" said Aurelius, much distressed. "I would have never suspected behavior of this sort from John! He's been a good and faithful servant for years!"

"He always disliked me," said Felix, "I could never understand why."

"His little brother was stolen by Gypsies, he told David so," said Aurelius. "I should have seen this coming!" he chided himself. "John was so bitter, so unhappy! He must have thought that Felix was taking his place..."

"There will be time enough for reproaches and recriminations later," said Richard grimly. "Right now there is a young woman to rescue. " he withdrew his wand from his inside pocket as he spoke.

"*Madame* Brehaut," said Felix quickly. "This is my grandfather, the Earl of Belmaray."

Madame dropped a curtsey and realized why Felix looked so different. He was dressed, like his grandfather in Elfin made clothing cut in fashionable style and fitted as if made by the finest tailor in London. If she had ever seen Felix dressed like this, she thought, she would never have mistaken him for a Gypsy.

"We shall go to this stable," Richard announced. "And please, let no one follow us or I shall throw up a preventive barrier. This man Grant is obviously crazed. We don't know what he will do and I cannot worry about protecting on-lookers." A few of the old men had looked as if they were eager to follow Felix and see the rest of the story to its end.

"I am coming along," said Aurelius firmly. "He might listen to me."

"Very well," agreed Richard . Once again Felix was ahead of them, out the door and heading towards the lane.

By the time Felix reached the shed outside the burned ruins of Aurelius's cottage, he was running, his heart pounding fast.

The moon had risen. Felix was not even certain how late it was. The moonlight made ghastly shadows amongst the remains of the cottage, with only one of the chimneys and the one wall, leaning drunkenly, still standing. There was a small illumination coming from under the door of the shed and through the only window which was normally covered with an old burlap feed sack.

"Grant!" Felix called. "Grant! I'm here! Let her go! Your quarrel is with me!"

The door flew open and there was John with Rosal held tightly against him, in one arm. She was gagged and tied at the wrists and ankles with her own brightly coloured scarves. In the other hand John had a knife, held to her throat.

"That's Mr. Grant to you, you dirty Gypsy!" he snarled. "Never knew your place, did you? Well, you're going to learn it tonight! I knew your bit of skirt would fetch you. If you don't want to see her choke on her own blood, you've got to give me your word, not that the word of a stinking tinker is worth its salt, to leave here and leave me and the Professor alone! We don't need you and we don't want you!"

"Let her go, please!" said Felix, his voice shaking."I'll promise anything you like. Only let her go!" He did not like the way Rosal's head hung down and how limp she seemed. What had he done to her already? Her shift hung half-off, almost down to her waist. Had he violated her as well?

With relief, he heard Richard and the Professor arrive behind him.

"Dear God!" Aurelius murmured, taking in the moonlit scene before him. "John, it's Professor Bretton!" he said, raising his voice. "Let her go, John! This will resolve nothing! You might be liable to criminal charges!"

"Professor!" John said almost happily. "They wouldn't tell me where you were! I knew you could not get on without me! I want you to tell this damned Gypsy to go away and leave us alone! We don't need him."

Richard too, was studying the scene before him, noting how John held the slender girl, how the knife pressed against her throat.

He raised his wand and said *"Exarmare!"*

Several things happened all at once. The knife flew out of John's hand, spinning wildly and embedded itself in the nearby trunk of a tree. Rosal and John fell apart, she to fall to the grass and John to slam against the side of the shed. He landed hard upon his barely healed back and with a groan, fell to his knees and then to the ground,

Felix ran forward and gathered Rosal up into his arms. He pulled up the remains of her shift over her bosom and tore the gag and ties from her mouth and limbs.

Aurelius made his way to John.

The manservant had curled up into a ball, and was sobbing. "All his fault! All his fault! We were so happy! I just want everything to be the way it was! All his fault!"

Aurelius was aghast. "He's completely mad!" he said as Richard came up behind him. "I don't know what to do..." his voice trailed off. "I suppose he belongs in a madhouse, but those places are horrible! I can't do that to John!"

Richard put a sympathetic hand on his shoulder. "I know a Wizard Healer," he said "who specializes in the treatment of the insane. His hospital is humane and well-run and he's had some great successes in treating those who other doctors have declared incurable. I shall contact him for you. Neither Felix nor I will prosecute him for this night's work."

"I blame myself. John was never happy here on Guernsey. He missed his home and his friends and felt isolated because he had little French and would not learn more. If I had not been so selfish I might have noticed, but I was happy here, at least until the French came," Aurelius said.

"We can't know what is in another's mind, Aurelius," said Richard. "This might have been coming on for years. Perhaps events suddenly conspired to turn him mad. It is hardly your fault. I will help you see that he is well cared for."

With this Aurelius had to be content. It was to be a long time before he ceased to blame himself.

When Rosal first awoke her heart leaped with joy, for Felix was leaning over her, a look of concern and worry on his face. "You came back!" she said happily and started to reach up to him.

He drew away slightly. "I was worried about you. We did not know what Grant had done to you. Rosal, he didn't –?"

Her arms fell back and she sat up, feeling a sudden *frisson* of cold inside. She saw that she was not in the *vardo* as she thought, but in the 'green bed' in *Madame's* kitchen in what was probably one of *Madame's* night gowns, for it was far and away too large.

What had happened came rushing back. "No. He hit me, that's all." she answered, discerning his meaning. "Did you get me away from him?" she asked hopefully. Surely he loved her if he had come after her to save her!

"No, you have my grandfather to thank for that," Felix answered. Part of him wanted to take her in his arms and never let her go, but another part whispered that he could not trust her for she had lied to him more than once.

He stood up and looked down at her. "Rosal, tonight has proved that I still have feelings for you but I think that we'd best spend some time apart. I have to get my memory back and find out if what I feel for you is real love, the love we can make a marriage from, or whether I myself, with your help, deluded myself into thinking I was in love. Do you understand that? And I am not even certain that we are legally married! That's why I am going to Devon with my grandfather tomorrow."

She did not understand, not really. All she knew was that she loved him and wanted him to stay with her. She looked back up at him, tears beginning to fill her eyes.

"You shall want for nothing," he said. "I've asked David to keep an eye on you. If there is anything you ever need, just let him know and he will get word to me."

She wanted nothing save him. But, right now, he did not want her.

There was little more to be done. Rosal had to explain that Hagar had run off, nearly a week ago and John had not attacked her. *Madame* allowed a heavily bandaged Chavé to climb into the bed with Rosal. John was taken onto *Pegasus* and placed in the brig. He would be conveyed to Portsmouth, where Richard would meet him, with his Healer friend, from there to be conveyed to the Surrey Hospital for the Insane.

It was quite late when all of these arrangements were made and Pascoe finally took off back to St. Peter Port where David and Grizel had said that they would wait for word of what had happened, no matter how late.

After seeing to Rosal's comfort, *Madame* and Joisaine went to bed, exhausted.

But Rosal lay a wake a long time, crying so quietly that no even the slightest of sobs escaped her lips. He had not even kissed her good-bye, only said 'goodbye'. Would she ever see him again? Would he decide when he retrieved his memories that he did not love her, never had loved her and never wished to see her again? At this dismal thought she cried even harder, while Chavé licked away her tears in sympathy.

66
At the Time
of the New Moon

The next morning, before they left for Devon, Felix spoke to his grandfather about how badly he felt about Aurelius's house burning down. "It is my fault," he said earnestly, "for had I not made a mage light and John had not behaved as he did, the cottage would still be standing. Do I have any money of my own that I could give him to rebuild it?"

"You have a handsome fortune of your own," said Richard, pleased by this thoughtfulness, a sure sign that his grandson had not changed as much as Pyewacket sometimes feared he had. "But as it happens, the matter is all taken care of. I arranged with Aurelius, on behalf of the British Museum, to purchase the torque from him. I am on the board of governors and am empowered to make purchases. The torque is worth a very good sum, enough to rebuild any number of cottages, even though he insisted on giving half to David Dieudonné as it was his father who found it. But it will leave the Professor with a nice nest egg. I shall be reimbursed by the Museum. This torque is something they will wish to add to their Special Collection of magical items. Too, there it will be properly contained, a danger to no one at the Museum. "But," he added, watching the change of expression of Felix's face carefully "if you wish to contribute some funds to the care of John Grant –."

"Yes, I do!" Felix said eagerly. "If it were not for me, perhaps he would still be sane. I feel so guilty about that"

"You are feeling guilty about far too many things," Richard thought. But time enough to deal with that when they were at home again. He only said "I shall have our man of business sit down with you when we reach home and go over the disposition of your fortune."

"I should like that," said Felix "for I wish to make good

provision for Rosal." He looked over Richard's shoulder and said in a carefully neutral voice." I should not like for her to want for anything."

"And that is as it should be," said Richard approvingly.

Felix looked so relieved at this that Richard realized that his grandson had thought he might not approve. Richard also realized, and this hurt, that to Felix, he was still a stranger, not a familiar, loved grandparent, someone whose reactions he would know without consultation as he had before.

And Pascoe, as well, was feeling remorse for having killed a human being. Not harming a human was a law that was deeply imbedded in a dragon's consciousness. Richard had explained to the dragon that he had done his country a great service. He had prevented the invasion of England by the French. Admiral Breckinridge said Pascoe deserved a medal and intended to speak to the proper authorities in the government about it.

Pyewacket too, was still depressed that he and Felix were no longer on the same footing, although Felix was beginning to turn to the cat more and more. Time would take care of that but on the whole it was a far from cheerful group that would leave Guernsey for Weymouth where they would have tea and then continue to Devon. Richard would scry Belmaray from Weymouth and announce their coming. Horrocks and the entire staff would be quite put out if they were given no warning in order that they might organize some sort of celebration.

But most of all, Richard wanted to contact Sir Jermyn Sloane, a top of the trees Wizard Healer, about Felix's loss of memory and what could be done to restore it.

David and Felix agreed to write to one another. Not only did Felix wish for David to keep an eye on Rosal, but the two young men had conceived a genuine liking for one another. Aurelius agreed to keep in touch with the two Jourdaines as well.

It was a straight flight of about seventy-five statute miles north to Weymouth from Guernsey. At moderate speed of between thirty-five and fifty miles per hour a dragon such as Pascoe could do this easily in about an hour and a half. They could have returned home to Devon through Faerie, but Pascoe had really wished to fly and make absolutely certain that his phalange was completely healed.

After the two storms they had suffered it was a beautiful day and an excellent day for flying. Weymouth was reached with no incident. There was a large Dragon Port available and they were all able to have a pleasant tea at a tea-room that catered to Wizards and Witches and their familiars, as well as dragons.

Felix could eat very little. He was becoming nervous about this return to a home he did not remember. If he hoped that the sight of Belmaray would somehow miraculously restore his memory, he said nothing about it to any of the others.

Richard knew better than to hope for that for a potion had been used to steal his memory, a counter-potion and, more than likely, a ritual of some sort, would be needed to return it.

But Belmaray awoke no response in Felix's memory. It was a beautiful property but so large! The *vardo* which he had shared with Rosal could be dropped in the front hall and lost. Ten such *vardos* would have not filled the entrance hall.

Even stranger was the deference shown to him by the servants, always bowing and addressing him as 'my lord' when he was used to being treated as if he were beneath contempt. Richard was now insistent that Felix use the heir's title. Felix had not wanted to do so earlier as, to him, Viscount Hightor was his father's title and he felt strange being called so. Richard wanted to make it very plain to everyone that Felix indeed was indeed his heir. Perhaps Reginald had some how that idea that his cousin, not being called by the title, was not the proper heir.

Again, the only place Felix felt truly at home was in the library, which was filled with books between whose covers were familiar facts and writings that he had not forgotten.

The library became his refuge, that and David's frequent letters, which had often addenda from Grizel, who seemed to be making it her business to watch out for Rosal.

It was with regret that Felix turned down an invitation to their wedding, for that week he was to have a consultation with Sir Jermyn Sloane and hopefully begin his treatment.

Since their arrival back at Belmaray letters and scrys had flown back and forth between London and Devon. Sir Jermyn had let them know that he would have to study the matter, for he would need both the services of a Potions Master and the *Hakim*, or doctor, on the staff of the Persian Embassy. Bahram's grimoire had been translated and fortunately, the potion he had used was fully inscribed. Richard wrote to the Wizard Healer all the particulars of the case and Felix noted his part as well.

It was not until mid-July that Sir Jermyn felt that he was ready to make a beginning on a course of treatment.

Monday, July 18th, was a hot and sultry day. Heat shimmered over the fields of ripening wheat and barley and over the mounds of newly cut and stacked hay. Not a breeze stirred the leaves of the trees in the park around Belmaray. Far off in the distance thunder growled. There had been a thunder storm that morning in the early hours but it had done little to cool the close air. Now the sky was a heavy, brassy blue, the threat of thunder far out to sea.

Felix sat out of doors, in shirtsleeves, with his familiar and Pascoe in the dragon pen. The protective canvas walls of the dragon pen were rolled up to catch any breeze and it was topped by an American lightning rod to ensure Pascoe's safety. Every few moments the dragon lifted his wings and fanned a little air over them.

"I like the warmth," complained Pyewacket, for like all cats he was a warmth seeker, "but this is too hot! It makes me wish that I could pant like a dog!" It was too hot even to sit in Felix's lap, although he had been invited. Their relationship had improved markedly. Pyewacket still found his Wizard sadly changed, but Felix now always wanted Pyewacket close at hand.

"Are you nervous?" Pascoe asked Felix kindly. The dragon now wore spiraled bands of gold, with sapphires, on his horns, which had been awarded by a grateful government in recognition of his prevention of Invasion. This had done a great deal to reconcile him to having had killed a human being, no matter how inadvertently. And little matter what a miserable excuse for a human being Blériot had been.

It no longer seemed odd to Felix to have conversations with a dragon and a cat. "Yes," he now admitted. "Grandfather did some reading and it seems more than likely that there will be a Ritual and a potion to drink as well."

"Ugh!" said Pyewacket. "Most potions are nasty!"

"To a cat they are nasty," said Pascoe. "Human potions are made to taste appealingly to human beings. The veterinarian gives us potions when we need them that are magically flavored to appeal to us. Felix would not enjoy a potion that tasted of raw fish or dragon treats, just as you would not enjoy one that tasted of cinnamon or honey."

"I just hope that it works," said Felix in a low voice. "I want to remember so badly! This is my home. I grew up here, Grandfather told me, yet I remember none of it. Every day, I come across something, a person, or a place or an event that I should be able to remember but it is only a blank and to try to remember brings terrible pain."

Pyewacket looked at him in sympathy. More than once he had curled up with Felix on his bed, using his purr to soothe his Wizard into sleep when he had a bad headache, caused, mostly, by trying too hard to remember.

Pascoe raised his head. "I hear wings," he said. "This will be Sir Jermyn, no doubt."

A dot appeared in the sky and rapidly descended until the three of them could see a hippogriffe with a rider.

Most doctors rode hippogriffes rather than dragons as the part horse, part griffin with the head of an eagle, could go places most horses could but could fly as well. Many doctors treated patients in areas where there was no room for dragons. A hippogriffe was not as fast as a dragon, but they had incredible stamina and did not fear lightning any more that a person with the sense to respect its power did.

The hippogriffe landed near the dragon pen and took a few running steps before he stopped.

Felix stood up as the rider dismounted, and then walked towards the 'griffe and his rider. Pyewacket followed him.

Sir Jermyn was a tall, powerfully built man who looked

as if he would be more at home on the deck of a pirate ship than practicing medicine. His countenance was rugged, and his graying dark hair untidy. He looked as if he cared little for the fads of fashion, for his dress was slightly shabby and the pockets bulged with notepads, pencils and medical instruments, a circumstance that would have filled a dandy with horror. He had piercing gray eyes under shaggy brows and he looked as if he could detect a lie or an excuse in a trifle. They were to find that he had little use for many members of the human race and could not abide either the shirking of responsibility or especially, stupidity. This last, he explained, was why he refused to treat any members of the Royal Family.

He opened a basket on the back of the 'griffe's saddle and lifted out a stocky, solidly gray cat without one bit of white, whose coat gleamed with blue highlights in the sun. The cat wore gold-rimmed spectacles over his amber eyes and looked about him with interest.

"Ha!" Sir Jermyn looked up as Felix approached. "I daresay you are my patient, Felix Jourdaine. I am, as you have no doubt guessed, for you do not look at all stupid, Jermyn Sloane."

"Yes sir," Felix answered. "This is my familiar, Pyewacket. And Pascoe, our dragon."

"I'm Bailey," the gray cat announced. He looked up at the hippogriffe. "This is my friend Linnaeus."

Pascoe came out of the dragon pan and said to the hippogriffe politely. "Pray join me in the dragon pen. You can have a good roll in the sand and I shall order some cool drinks and food if you are hungry."

"Thank you," said the 'griffe, bowing his head graciously.

As Sir Jermyn unclipped his medical supplies, contained in two bulging saddle bags, from Linaeus's back, a groom came hurrying out of the stables. "I'll see to your 'griffe, sir!" Bob Oakes said. "I daresay he'd like his saddle off and bit of cold water mist on his feathers on such a hot day."

"Oh, yes, please!" said the hippogriffe. "Then I shall be happy to join you," He bowed his head in Pascoe's direction.

Satisfied that his 'griffe was to be well taken care of, Sir Jermyn swung the heavy saddle bags over his shoulders and allowed Felix and Pyewacket to lead him and Bailey to the house.

On such a hot day the coolest place was the conservatory, a large, ornately domed glass house built by Richard's father in Chinoiserie style. It was filled with plants, shrubs and even small trees and the many windows in the roof could be opened. There were also shades and shutters that could be raised or lowered for the requirements of the many plants. Two fountains provided the cooling noise of falling water.

"Ah, this is something like!" exclaimed Sir Jermyn in pleasure as Horrocks, who had met the party at the door, led him to the room where Richard waited.

"Shall I bring cool drinks, my lord ? Cook has made some very fine lemonade," Horrocks asked as Sir Jermyn took a seat with Richard and Felix at a round, glass-topped table made of wrought iron, painted white. "Unless Sir Jermyn would prefer sherry or something stronger?"

Sir Jermyn shook his head. "No, thank you. I shall be Working magic tonight and must needs have a completely clear head. Lemonade will do the trick."

"Tonight?" Felix echoed, looking a trifle perturbed.

"The ritual the Persian *Hakim* and I came up with must begin on the first night of he new moon. As you are no doubt aware the waxing moon's timing is the beginning of new cycles; its lesson is to invoke knowing and its magic is for health and personal issues which is most auspicious for what we are hoping to achieve."

"I hope you do not mind, my lord" he added , turning to Richard, "but I have taken the liberty of inviting myself to be your guest for the period of the new moon, so I shall be with you until the 26th. I am afraid that this ritual must be repeated every evening. A transport dragon will be arriving later with my trunk."

He then tuned back to Felix. "I am also afraid that you are in for a bad winter, young man. This treatment will be neither comfortable or of short duration. I shall be obliged to repeat it every month until we are satisfied that your memory is largely intact."

"A bad *winter*?" Felix repeated in dismay. "But it is only July!"

"I estimate it will take at least seven months for a complete treatment," said Sir Jermyn. As Felix looked at him, taken aback, the Wizard Healer said "The brain and memory are fragile. It would be completely injudicious to bring back your memory in a rush. Even if you did have amnesia caused by say, a blow to the head, your memory would probably return piecemeal, rather than all at once. And you have suffered both a potion designed for amnesia and a blow to the head. As they say, better sure than sorry. And the amount of the rather unpleasant potion I have to give you, needed for the full return of memory would make you extremely ill. In this case, the cure is almost worse than the illness."

"I want to remember, no matter what it takes," said Felix determinedly.

"Then we start tonight," said Sir Jermyn in satisfaction.

"I have followed your instructions in every particular," put in Richard. "Everything on our end is ready. We are fortunate in having a well-supplied shop for Wizarding supplies in Torquay. I think you will find that we are well prepared."

"Excellent!" said Sir Jermyn as Horrocks appeared with a tray of lemonade.

Sir Jermyn took out a large pocket watch and consulted it. "It is now close on eleven. After thoroughly checking your physical condition I am going to brew you a potion," he said to Felix "that will send you to sleep for several hours. I shall want you to fast the rest of the day as tonight's potion will do best on an empty stomach. We shall begin the ritual at sunset, after you and your grandfather and I have prepared properly."

After drinking the sleeping potion Felix went up to bed, to sleep for several hours. Sir Jermyn had noticed his heavy, shadowed eyes and rightly assumed that he had not been sleeping well. For what was to come he needed to be well rested.

Felix, who had always shared Pearson with his grandfather when necessary, now had a valet of his own who was eagerly studying the many extra matters that one needed to properly valet a Wizard. These included matters such as ritual baths, anointing oils and the proper colours of robes needed for various ceremonies. The valet was a young man who had been promoted from footman as Felix did not want a complete stranger. He had seen Wallace about the house since his return and was used to him.

Wallace was an apt pupil, Pearson reported and when Felix went above stairs after taking the potion, Wallace had the bed and the room ready. Shutters were closed in front of the open window, and everything done to the Healer's instructions complete to the lavender pillow for sleep, psychic balance and to bring emotions under control and an amethyst beneath the pillow for peace, protection and sleep.

Felix did not think he would be able to close his eyes for he was too wrought up and anxious, but he fell immediately into a deep, dreamless sleep after imbibing the potion. He only awoke when he heard the rattle of the curtain rings above the bed and Wallace saying "Excuse me, my lord, but it wants but two hours to sunset and Sir Jermyn has said that it is time for your bath."

Felix sat up abruptly. It was to begin. His trepidation had vanished, now all he could think of was that his memory would return. And then he would know what was needful to do about Rosal and if any future between them was possible or desirable.

Aurelius was quite thankful that he had sold that torque to the British Museum, for not only had he John to take care of now, but he did want to rebuild his cottage. Unfortunately, this meant importing workmen from England, as the work force on the island still consisted but of old men and young boys.

But the British had brought everything from stone masons to carpenters with them when the troops began to arrive and although preference was given to defensive structures, Aurelius was able to contract men who were able to give him several days a week to rebuilding his home. *Trois Chiminées* would rise from the ashes, better than ever, more spacious and convenient.

On an afternoon in mid-July Aurelius had come from Faerie where he was still living, working industriously on his book, to see the progress of the new cottage. It stood in the same place as had the old structure and would boast the same three chimneys. Later, he was to take tea with David, his *fiancée* and mother in St. Peter Port.

The cottage had been framed and the chimneys were rising. Aurelius walked around it, speaking to the masons and studying it all with pride. His library was to be twice the size of the former one. Robin and others in Faerie had gifted him with many more volumes since his sojourn in Faerie had begun and a large package of books had arrived from Richard and Felix as well. Aurelius still grieved in his heart that he would no longer share the cottage with Felix as he had hoped, but the letters exchanged with those in Devon were frequent and Richard had hinted at an invitation for Christmas. The Dragon Post was regular between England and Guernsey now and books and newspapers were readily obtainable. People were even returning now that the French were gone and the British had made a firm commitment to keeping the Channel Islands out of French hands.

As Aurelius stood admiring his new abode and thinking about a new garden (for that had suffered in the fire as well) he heard a soft, hesitant step behind him and turned to see Rosal. She stopped in her tracks and looked at him rather as if she was afraid of being rejected by him. She was still wearing what she called *Gajé* dress, and was wrapped in a voluminous shawl, in spite of the warmth of the day. She looked as if she had not been well recently.

"Mrs. Lovel, or perhaps I had ought to say my lady?" he said for he was not certain how to address her. Richard had written that the solicitors were still wrestling with the legality of the wedding.

"Rosal will do," she said. "Professor, I want to ask you something."

"Do you wish to hear about Felix? I am in regular contact." Aurelius began.

She shook her head. "No, Grizel Sarchet tells me everything that he writes to Sir David." She looked down at the ground, her thin fingers playing with the fringe of the shawl. Aurelius noted that she still wore her wedding ring. "The thing is," she said hesitantly "if he does want me back, if he can forgive me, I want him to be proud of me." She looked up, straight at Aurelius, her look at once pleading and determined. "Professor, will you teach me to read and write?"

67
Ritual and Remembrance

Pyewacket had not accompanied Felix up to bed, for Bailey had indicated that he needed to speak to him.

Three familiars sat on the edge of the fountain, which was a design of a Nereid pouring out a stream of water from a shell. The stonework was cooling and the area was quiet. Greymalkin had asked if he might join the others. They could hear Richard and Sir Jermyn talking in the background, somewhat muffled by the sound of water spilling into the scallop shell that formed the basin of the fountain.

Bailey said to Pyewacket, "You've an important part in this ritual as well, even though your Wizard will not need prompting. As Jermyn explained to me, this potion will overwhelm him with images when it begins to work. Memories will flood his mind and he will need soothing."

"I always soothe him with my purr!" said Pyewacket a little indignantly.

Bailey shook his head. "You'll need a special purr. Jermyn says that it is best that your Wizard remember mostly in dreams so there is a purr we medical familiars know for soothing and special dreams. Wizard Healers call them treatment dreams and they are often used in the treatment of mental agitation or in this case, amnesia. So I am going to teach you the purr and we'd better begin practicing now because it will be needed a very short while after he takes the potion and the ritual begins."

Because of the bond between Wizard or Witch and his or her familiar, the familiar was best able to soothe his or her own Witch or Wizard. Even hedgehogs and ferrets had a peculiar 'hum' that could soothe and send to sleep while an owl possessed an almost hypnotic unblinking stare that eased their human partner into rest.

"Shouldn't I go up now and help Felix sleep?" asked

Pyewacket, looking at Greymalkin as if for guidance.

Bailey smiled. "One of Jermyn's special potions will send him off to restful sleep effortlessly. Now, come, I shall teach you what you must do."

Greymalkin stayed. He was interested always to learn new things as one never knew when something might come in handy.

Wallace had a bath waiting. It was of a tepid temperature, as even with the sun declining the weather was still hot.

Proud of himself, Wallace had put the correct cleansing herbs in a little muslin bag tied with blue string of the proper colour. He, of course, had shown this to his mentor Pearson who had declared everything 'all right and tight'.

The muslin bag contained basil leaves, bay leaves, sprigs of oregano, a sprig of tarragon, some oats and a pinch of sea salt. The herbs had been fresh picked as well, this morning when the dew still lay on them. This was considered a cleansing bath.

Ritual bathing, Pearson explained, not only cleansed the Wizard's body, but washed away psychic dirt as well that from negative energies in the atmosphere, many of which could be created by one's own negative thoughts and emotions. It was important for anyone making magic to be psychically clean and their working area must be that way as well. While bathing, the magician was to visualize all the impurities and negativity being washed away, and tossed out with the bath water.

After the bath Felix would anoint himself with oil of cloves, which cleansed the mind and assisted in past life recall, usually taken to mean one's previous incarnation, but in this case Sir Jermyn hoped that the spicy scent of cloves would aid in Felix remembering the past of *this* lifetime.

With Pearson's approval Wallace lay out a light blue robe that would fit loosely so that it would not restrict the flow of energies around the body. Traditionally, nothing was worn beneath it save the anointing oil and one's own skin. These robes were used for naught save magic working and were kept in a special cupboard. Pearson told Wallace as they chose the robe that, on the next day, he would show the young man how to wash the working robes as they required delicate handling with special cleansers and purified water.

The robe was blue. Blue was soothing and calming; it promoted Truth and inner reflection. Blue would be the colour of the candles in the ritual as well. The colour honored the lunar deities and stood for healing and wisdom.

Once Felix had bathed and anointed himself with oil of cloves, he donned the robe and went to wait by himself, as instructed, in a small room called the meditation room. It was filled with an incense of rosemary 'for remembrance' and little besides a bench and a table for the incense burner. It had but a small clerestory window, filled with hanging crystals. First he took deep breathes as directed by Sir Jermyn, until he felt energized, standing with feet slightly apart, trying to visualize drawing a golden light inside himself with each deep breath. Then he sat quietly, waiting for Sir Jermyn to send for him.

Sir Jermyn was pleased to find that Richard had anticipated his every need, followed the instructions he had sent and had taken the trouble to set up a properly dedicated altar. He had , as well, psychically cleansed the area and had everything they might need in the course of the ritual close to hand.

"It is a pleasure to work with intelligent patients," the Healer said approvingly. "Some of the people who have pledged themselves faithfully to prepare for my visits have nothing done and no supplies ready when I arrive. I can only carry so much on the back of a hippogriffe. And so many rituals are tuned to the moon and to other natural phenomenon that if they are not ready I must needs return the next month, early this next time and do the preparations my own self; simple preparations in many cases that any *Magus Minorus* ought to be able to do."

"I trust that you charge them more for the inconvenience," said Richard dryly.

"You are quite correct! How they squall when they see my bill!" Sir Jermyn grinned at him.

Before they went above stairs to begin their own preparations, the transport dragon having arrived with the Healer's trunk, Sir Jermyn said to Richard, "I must confess to you that this is a gamble. The potion given your grandson was the blackest of black magic, a truly evil thing. Men have gone mad from it. The Persian *Hakim* thinks that the girl of whom you told me, who gave him an identity, might just have saved his reason. The *Hakim* said he saw, once in Persia, a man who slipped over the edge of sanity when no one could tell him who he was or any of his past. Of course, that is the intent of it, to drive a man to madness and death. The counter potion is singularly powerful, for the Potions Master I consulted in London said it must be administered in minute doses as too large a dose can be fatal. That is why this will be such a long, drawn-out affair. Fortunately, his young lordship did not receive a full dose of the original potion, but he was given enough to be exceedingly damaging."

"They expected him to drown," said Richard a little bitterly.

"It's a good thing that Persian was killed by pixies," said Sir Jermyn. "His own government would have had a much less pleasant death than drowning in a bog for him. I believe the Persian ambassador mentioned drawing and quartering. The current Caliph is very against the black arts. What of the other young fellow?"

Richard hesitated and then said shortly. "I have not told Felix as yet but I received a massage from Bow Street yester eve. They found Reginald dead in his cell yesterday morning. Preliminary investigation by the Bow Street Forensic Wizards indicates that his soul was stolen by demon or demons unknown."

Richard could not know it, but Ahriman, summoned by Bahram to call up the waterspout that landed Richard and Pascoe on Guernsey, had collected his fee, the fee promised him by Bahram: Reginald's soul.

"He has enough on his mind now and there is time to tell that later," said Sir Jermyn. "It is time we made our own preparations."

It was nearing sunset when the three familiars and their Wizards went into the walled garden that contained the movable altar used by generations of the Jourdaine family. It was always best to conduct magic out of doors whenever possible and the summer night was perfect. It was clear as twilight fell across the landscape. At the coming of dusk a land breeze had sprung up and was blowing the Aeolian harps and strings of bells Sir Jermyn had placed around the area where the Working Circle would be drawn.

A small cot stood at the foot of the altar where Felix would lay. Candles stood all about it on heavy, tall candle stands. All the candles were properly anointed, wiped middle to ends with oil of cloves and dressed in ribbons that matched the altar cloths.

Sir Jermyn was further pleased to see the altar already adorned in violet, blue and yellow, the colours of an air ritual, with feathers and fans, representing air, on the altar and incense of lavender and sandalwood. There was an offering of lavender sticks as well.

"Open-aired, facing east, perfect!" the Healer said in satisfaction. He had already asked Richard Felix's natal day. It was October 1st so that he was a Libra. Therefore his element *was* air, and his Archangel was Raphael, the healer, which could not have been better. It being a Monday too, was fortunate as the planetary influence was the moon and this strengthened dreaming powers and psychic ones as well.

To Felix, practically everything he saw that night was as if it were brand-new. There were some similarities to the calling of the Wild Hunt ritual. A Circle was drawn with Sir Jermyn's wand, which was of oak (for wisdom, strength and endurance) tipped with an emerald. Green was the Healer's colour and Sir Jermyn's Working robes were always green as well. For this night's work he wore a sash of the proper air colours, an intertwined Celtic knot work of yellow, violet and blue. Richard, over his white Druidical robes, wore a sash of the same colours.

The element of air governed all elements of the mind and

mental activity. Therefore, any ceremony dedicated to mental healing was always an air ceremony. Even though the time of magical correspondence for air was dawn, it had been found, over time, that the rising of the new moon gave the best results in this sort of Healing magic.

The sun was just disappearing below the horizon when the ceremony began. Sir Jermyn drew the Circle, starting in the east, with green light from his wand, briefly honoring each cardinal compass point. Since this was a Healing Circle and not a Calling, the Circle was cast in a deosil, or clockwise direction.

Watching from his position on the cot, Felix again wondered if he would fully regain his memory. At one time, according to his grandfather, he had known and understood all of the magicals symbols and rituals easily. In fact he had a Master of Arts in the subject, or so he had been told. Now it all seemed so strange to him. He still kept hoping that something would seem familiar, that of its own, memory would come back. But Sir Jermyn had explained that a potion had stolen his memory and it could not be brought back without another potion and a great deal of time and trouble. Felix had to resign himself to that.

"Don't worry, "Pyewacket, who lay beside him, whispered. "Sir Jermyn is accounted a Nonesuch amongst healers. He trained at Edinburgh!"

"I am glad you are here with me, Pye," Felix said and put his hand on Pyewacket's head.

Pyewacket was filled with joy and he almost began purring before it was time for him to do so. This was more like his Wizard!

Richard was honored that Sir Jermyn had asked him if he wished to participate. This was a compliment for many times Sir Jermyn actually locked the family out of the Circle with a repulsion spell.

Now Richard and the Healer lit the candles on the altar and the ones that stood about Felix's cot. They went though the parts of the ritual that Felix remembered from the Calling ceremony: the offering, the drink from the ritual cup (in this case a cup of a rosemary infusion, with honey), the salutation to God and Goddess,and the libation. Some things were common to all Workings.

All three cats were inside the Circle and from over the wall, an interested Pascoe watched. Servants crowded the kitchen, as one could see this garden from the windows of that room.

Sir Jermyn stood in front of the altar, facing east, and raised his arms, his wand in his right hand. He began the preliminary incantation, tracing the alchemical sign of air (an upright triangle bisected by a horizontal line) in the air as he spoke. It hung there, in green fire, above the altar.

Air, the element of life and breath,
For to breath is to live.
Air, ruler of the east,
Ruler of the new day,
Of the new moon, the new year,
The element of thought and ideals.
Under your clear skies
Where you govern the mind
Lend me your powers to heal
By the new moon in the east,
Let this man be healed.

The waxing new moon, of course, even on such a clear night, could not be seen. That orb was actually setting at about sunset on this first day of the new moon. And it was so near the sun in the sky that it was not visible because of the sun's glare. It would be two days before it would first be visible, appearing then to have moved away from the sun, a slim crescent in the west, its horns facing away from the sun while the bright side faced towards the sun.

When Sir Jermyn finished the incantation the entire area was suddenly flooded with light, as if a full, not a new moon, shone down. All of this light was concentrated in the person of the Healer.

Working quickly, he took a silver chalice from the Wizard's casket at his feet and mixed pre-measured herbs with *aqua vitae*. He touched his wand to the chalice, the emerald focus stone on the tip now glowing with green fire. He murmured in some strange language. Even Felix, linguist that he was, did not understand what the Healer was saying. They found out afterwards that it was an incantation given him by the Persian *Hakim* The cup began to glow as well and what looked like steam rose from it. A pungent smell also rose.

The three familiars wrinkled their noses as Sir Jermyn advanced on Felix and said "I am afraid that you are going to have to drink this down. The only good part is that there is not a lot of it. It is as palatable as the *Hakim* and I could make it without altering its properties."

Felix eyed it doubtfully. It did not smell or look particularly appetizing, not like the Elixir that Robin had given him after the Calling of the Wild Hunt. After the slightest hesitation he lifted the cup to his lips and drained it in one gulp. There was less than half a tea-cup full in the chalice.

It was very harsh and bitter. "What was it like before you made it palatable?" he gasped when he could speak again. The potion caused his eyes to water and his stomach to roll. It burned the throat going down as well.

"Much, much worse," said the Healer cheerfully. "Try to keep it down, will you? Lay back down and try not to think about it." He looked down at Pyewacket. "A soothing purr would be applicable here, not the dream purr, though, Your regular relaxing purr will do very nicely."

Pyewacket obeyed and Felix lay back, closing his eyes. He had wanted to watch the rest of the ritual but that would have to wait for the world to steady somewhat. That stuff was indeed nasty. But if it brought back his memory...

Richard, the other two familiars and Pascoe watched as Sir Jermyn went on with the balance of the Healing Ritual. A wind from the east had sprung up, making eerie music from the Aeolian harps. "The wind is with us," the Healer murmured. This was always a good sign.

He then took a gold candle from the casket at his feet. It was in a small holder and beside it he lay, in quick succession, a golden quill, a piece of vellum, a lime, a spool of golden thread, a square of orange cloth and his *athame*, or ritual knife, which was of magiced silver with a handle of elder wood.

He assumed again the position before the altar, with arms raised and his wand at the ready. This time he drew a complicated sign in the air, that again, hung there in green as Sir Jermyn began to speak.

Archangel Raphael, healing spirit,
Chief of the Order of Virtues,
Regent of the Sun,
One of the Four Great Presences
Set over all the diseases
And all the wounds of the children of man.
You who healed Abraham and Jacob,
I light this flame to honor your presence
And beg of you to consider my prayer.
Bless these healing objects which lay before me.

As he spoke, he lit the candle with the tip of his wand. The flame sprang up, strong and straight in spite of the freshening east wind.

Richard drew in his breath. The flame told him that there was indeed a presence here, one who gave his approval.

Sir Jermyn held his hands over the objects on the altar and through them ran a strong green light, outlining each of the materials on the altar. Sir Jermyn picked up his glowing *athame* and held it out before him, holding the very tip of the blade. Light danced up and down the blade until it seemed to glow white hot. But it did not burn the Healer's fingers.

Quickly, after laying the still bright athame aside, Sir Jermyn took up the golden quill (it was a phoenix feather, Richard noted) and wrote something on the vellum, which he folded three times. He seemed lost in intense concentration and Richard tried not to do anything that might disturb him, and, looking at Pascoe, put a finger to his lips. The familiars knew better than to interrupt a ritual, unless the Wizard seemed to need prompting.

The dragon nodded, understanding the need for quiet.

Sir Jermyn then cut the lime in half lengthwise with the athame and placed the paper, still folded, inside the two halves. He cut a length of the gold thread and bound the lime with it. The lime in turn went into the square of orange material, securing this with more gold thread.

He then held his hands over the lime, making a silent Healer's invocation, as the green light flowed off his hands and over the fruit.

Much of magic was symbolic. Richard knew that Felix's name was inscribed on the vellum and that the lime symbolized the green of healing magic. Lime was held to be powerful as it fought the sailor's bane, scurvy. The bound lime would then be offered to the ash tree that stood within the magic Circle and the spirit of the tree would help aid in healing. So much magic had been performed here over the centuries that the tree had immense power. This walled garden was now a sacred place and from so much magic a ley line had been created and ran directly from this place to the Nine Sisters up on the moor.

The last of the Ritual was to bury the lime at the foot of the ash and ask for the tree's spirit to help in the healing.

Felix had been unable to open his eyes. The potion had made him feel quite ill but as the Ritual went on he was conscious of a comforting presence and he began to feel better. He also became overwhelmingly sleepy and as Pyewacket, at a nod from Bailey, began to purr, he gave into the compulsion and slid into sleep.

"There!" said Sir Jermyn in satisfaction, as he backed away from the tree and the green light faded. "We've the blessing of air and angel and if that Persian potion works the way it is supposed to, he should awake with some true memories on the morrow. Would you be so good as to help me take down the Circle my lord?"

Richard nodded. The Healer looked very tired. Unlike Felix he had eaten a hearty meal beforehand and would no doubt be glad of the supper Richard had ordered prepared for after the ceremony.

"Have your servants carry him up to bed," Sir Jermyn directed when the Circle was down, indicating Felix. "Let him sleep as long as possible and awaken naturally. Purr as long as you can manage," he added to Pyewacket.

And even now, as two footmen came out, at Richard's call to carry him up to his room, Felix was beginning to remember in dreams.

68
Olwen's Secret

Even with all the many preparations for the wedding Grizel went regularly to see Rosal. She was concerned that the other woman seemed depressed and lethargic since Felix's departure. Grizel could understand that. She knew how she would feel if she were to be separated from David. And, unlike her, Rosal had no idea what was to happen in the future. Grizel, perhaps unfortunately (for it was always easier to side with one person or the other) could understand both sides of the separation; both why Felix felt he had to regain his memory and perhaps his trust in her. And she also understood that perhaps a part of Rosal's present anguish was not just losing a lover, mayhap for all time, but also guilt at having deceived him. It was a bad situation.

Grizel had hoped that Felix would return to Guernsey for the wedding. Perhaps she might have contrived to get him and Rosal together so they could at least talk. But the beginning of his treatment coincided with the week before she and David were to wed. David was disappointed that his friend would not be there but it could not be helped. A handsome wedding gift, a complete tea service from Minton's, had arrived from Richard and Felix, with a letter from Richard conveying their best wishes and that Felix was going to be more than a little ill from the treatment. The Healer expected this, but it was nonetheless bad news.

Two days before the wedding Grizel walked up from the beach towards the woods where the *vardo* stood. She still found it easier to swim around the island than use a horse and carriage. This time however, she carried her waterproof bag with a gown and shoes inside and after shape-shifting at the little harbor of Gull Rocks, put on her dress and slung the bag over her shoulder .

The *vardo* still stood in the woods of *Madame* Brehaut

and Rosal had gone back to work at the farm. What was wrong with Rosal's health was not physical. She said that she liked to work, and wanted to do so but *Madame* was concerned about her and would let her work a scant half-day. At this time of year there was not all that much work as they waited for the harvest.

The last time that Grizel had visited the neighborhood *Madame* had expressed a wish that Hagar would return. No one knew where she was. It was not known if she had been able to flee the island as she had hoped. If anyone had helped her leave they were keeping remarkably mum about it. *Madame* thought that Rosal needed someone with her. The girl refused to come and live at the farm, giving a vague 'perhaps' when *Madame* said that she *must* come for the winter.

After a short walk, Grizel was at the clearing and found Rosal sitting by the fire clad in her *Gajé* clothing and a shawl. Chavé looked up as Grizel approached and gave a short bark, his tail wagging. He liked Grizel very well as she smelled right to him.

Rosal had a book, of all things, in her laps and by her feet lay a slate and a slate pencil.

Rosal looked up quickly, her face clouded, as Chavé barked but her countenance cleared as she saw Grizel. She had come to like the Selchie quite a bit.

"What's all this?" said Grizel as she sat down on the other end of the log.

"I'm learning to read and write. The Professor is teaching me," said Rosal simply. "Please, don't tell anyone. I want it to be a surprise for Felix."

Grizel at once gave her word. "I won't even tell David. That's a marvelous idea, Rosal! How are you doing at it?"

Rosal picked up the slate and showed it to her. There, in somewhat straggling letters, was painstakingly inscribed "Rosal". "It's hard," she confessed. "Things aren't spelled the way they sound at all sometimes. But the Professor is very patient with me. I must seem stupid to him. But I do want to learn so much!"

"That's half the battle, wanting to do something and sticking to it. I was a little older than most children when I first learned to read. After my mother died my father let me run wild and it seemed very hard to me also. Then suddenly it all made sense and I began to read easily. I daresay that will happen for you as well," said Grizel encouragingly.

"I hope so," said Rosal. She reached out and swung the kettle that hung from the tripod over the flames of the low fire. "I'll make us some tea."

Grizel picked up her bag that she had laid by her feet. "And I brought you some Guernsey *Gâche*. My mother-in-law to be showed me how to make it this morning. David loves it. I never made it before as my father did not care for anything with sultanas in it."

They had each eaten a slice of *Gâche* and drunk a cup of tea before Rosal said hesitantly, "*Mam'selle* Sarchet –"

"Rosal, we're friends. It's time you began to call me Grizel! After all, you're coming to the wedding. I won't take any more excuses!"

"Grizel," Rosal's voice was still tentative even though she gave Grizel a slight smile."There's something I need to know besides reading and writing. If Felix still wants me,if it would not be too much trouble, could you teach me how to be a lady, a real *Gajé* lady?"

Sir Jermyn Sloane had not exaggerated when he said that Felix would have a bad winter. The treatments were prolonged and did nothing to ease the almost permanent headache he seemed to have at times. This was caused, Sir Jermyn said severely, by straining to remember.

It was difficult not to try to regain more memory. More came back almost every day, fastest on the nights of the new moon when he took the potion and underwent the ritual, but always at night. He would wake up each time with more and more memory intact.

Aurelius was a faithful correspondent that winter. He had decided against coming to them for Christmas as his cottage was still being built, and he was looking for a publisher for his book, which was almost finished. And Richard had writ him of how Felix was none too well at present.

Aurelius often wrote to Richard about Rosal. He had come to know her well and, with the knack he had always had of drawing out reluctant young persons, he soon found out more about her than she realized.

I have come to understand, he wrote to Richard in late November, *why she deceived Felix as to who he was. She has not had an easy life. Her father sounds a brute and the man he married her to sounds even worse. He was older than her father when they wed, forty-five to her sixteen, and she had no say in the matter. I have confirmed with Madame Brehaut and others that her late husband treated her very badly indeed. He put her out to work while he lazed about, gambling and drinking. It is well-known that he beat her often.*

There is a very ugly story about how her husband, Sylvester Lovel, exposed their sick baby to ill weather so that the child would die. The story was widespread enough that the parish priest was concerned. There might have been an investigation had the French not invaded.

He then told Richard all the circumstances of how Rosal had taken in Hagar and what it had cost her.

I can see why she snatched at the chance to achieve some sort of happiness in her life. She often speaks wistfully of a home, a family. Does Felix ever speak of her?

Richard sighed and put the letter down. He was sitting beside a shielded mage light near Felix's bed, with Greymalkin laying quietly at his feet.

It was the 18th of February and last night had been the final night of the new moon and this was always the time when Felix was most ill. The potion did not agree with him. There was more and more nausea and the rush of memory was almost overwhelming. Pyewacket nearly wore out his purr at these times. Now, Felix had been asleep for some hours. Richard often sat with him on these nights. They both found this comforting.

But every day Felix remembered more. Even Sir Jermyn had been encouraged. He thought that soon they might be able to dispense with the potion all together.

Richard could only be glad for this. More and more he hated seeing Felix undergo the potion drinking and the resulting illness. But it *was* working and Felix was determined to undergo the full course of treatment. He wanted back every memory that had been his before Bahram and Reginald had tried to kill him.

And Felix spoke but rarely of Rosal. That he thought of her quite a bit Richard was certain. Felix was quieter, more introspective, than he was used to be. At times a particular look would fall over his face, often when they were sitting together in the library, each with a book. Richard thought then that he was thinking of her. The look was one of longing, one of wistfulness. Richard knew that look well as he himself had worn it often enough after Olwen died. But Felix, at least, had another chance.

"It's all coming back," said Felix's voice suddenly out of the darkness shrouding the room.

"Go back to sleep!" said Pyewacket, sounding almost indignant. "You're supposed to sleep as much as possible!"

"What is coming back? A special memory?" asked Richard. He folded Aurelius' letter and left it on the table. He moved to a chair at Felix's bedside and threw up a small mage light so that he could see his grandson.

"Magic, my memories of learning and doing magic," Felix said excitedly, pushing himself a little up on the pile of thick pillows. "It has all seemed so strange but now I remember you giving me my first lessons and attending both Eton and Oxford! I think I could work magic on my own now."

"That is wonderful!" said Richard. It had been difficult to see Felix so unsure and unknowing of something that had been as instinctive to him as breathing.

"Perhaps I have remembered all that I need to," Felix said. "Perhaps we can cease the treatments."

Pyewacket looked at him. "You still have a headache," he said accusingly.

"Well, yes," his Wizard admitted.

The familiar snorted. "Then don't talk to me about ending your treatments yet!"

"Were you reading a letter just now, Grandfather?" Felix queried, when at Pyewacket's behest he lay down again. "From the Professor?" He added, "Does he say anything about Rosal?" He tried to hide the eagerness in his voice. Richard gave him a sharp look. There was still a great deal of caring there.

"Yes, I shall read it to you if you like." Before Richard

could rise to fetch the letter Greymalkin jumped to the table top, picked up the letter in his mouth and jumped down again, trotting over to Richard and offering it to him. Richard drew the mage light closer to himself and away from Felix so that the light would not aggravate his headache.

"Thank you, Grey," Richard bent and took the letter from his familiar. "As Aurelius told us earlier she has gone to live with *Madame* Brehaut for the winter –"

"I'm glad of that," Felix interrupted. "I hated to think of her all by herself in the *vardo* for the winter. It's only canvas and hasn't much heat."

He listened in silence as Richard read the rest of the letter. "I hadn't realized how bad her life must have been," Felix said almost in a whisper. "I guessed that her first husband had been a selfish bastard, but not that he was a complete blackguard."

He was quiet a moment and then said suddenly, "Grandfather, would I be an utter fool to take her back and try to make a go of our marriage? I can't seem to stop thinking about her! I was worried that I perhaps was actually in love with someone else whom I could not recall but I have remembered now. There is no one and Rosal is all I can think about."

"I cannot make that decision for you," said Richard. "You are the one who has to forgive and forget. *Can y*ou forgive her?"

"I have given it a great deal of thought," Felix answered. "I think perhaps I can. She saved my life. Sir Jermyn even has told me that she might have saved my sanity by giving me an identity to hold onto. I shall always be grateful for that."

"Gratitude," Richard pointed out "is not love."

Felix shifted on the pillows. "She is in my mind constantly," he said. "It is not just that she is attractive and I enjoy bedding her." He had now remembered that he could say such things to Richard without his grandfather being shocked or moralizing about it, "I admire her. I admire her compassion for her misfits, as Hagar called herself and the dog and pony. My God, what it cost her to take Hagar in! She knew what would happen when she invited Hagar to live with her, but she did it anyway and was shunned not only by her

616

family, but her entire clan for an act of compassion! She has a kind heart and is very brave. As frightened as she was of the French she offered to dance for them so that we might to save the Professor. We seemed to understand one another so well." he sighed and said "What I now worry about is twofold. That we may trust each other again and how will she adapt to all of this?" He waved his hand about the room but Richard knew that 'all of this' referred to Belmaray and the privileged life they led.

"Rosal has never learned the manners people will expect of her if she is to be my wife. Will it make her unhappy to be here, in a place so different from what she is used to? She is not even literate," he finished sadly. "Our life of books will seem so strange and she cannot participate in it."

Richard glanced at the ormolu clock on the mantelpiece. "It is getting late," he announced. "We both need rest. All of your worries are valid, my boy. On the morrow I shall show you something that might have some bearing on your decision, something I thought never would make any difference in your life. But I see now that it has everything to do with it."

He would say no more, only promising that in the morning they would talk further.

Felix had not thought that he would sleep again, wondering about what his grandfather might be speaking of, but he did fall into a restful, deep sleep, and awoke the next day feeling better than he had in a long time. His mind felt extraordinarily clear and sharp. Everything he looked at that morning as Wallace helped him shave and get ready for the day seemed to hold a memory. He could look at the things in his room or at the view out the window and say "I remember that." It was a heady feeling, after living in the dark of uncertainty for so long.

Over Wallace's protests he dressed, rather than wearing a dressing gown as he had for some while, because a good part of every day was spent laying down upon his bed.

Richard was pleased to see Felix looking so well but

would not allow himself, over breakfast, to be teased into revealing his secret.

"I have directed that a fire be laid in both fireplaces in the Long Gallery, my lord, as your lordship desired, and I myself have fetched the items that your lordship wished to be brought down from above stairs," said Horrocks to Richard as he poured more tea for his employer.

"Excellent! Thank you, Horrocks," said Richard approvingly.

"More toast, Thomas," ordered the butler to one of the young footmen. " And perhaps more sausage as well, my lord?" he said to Felix.

Felix nodded. "Every thing tastes extraordinarily well this morning!"

Both Richard and the two familiars looked pleased to see this evidence of returning appetite. Pyewacket, whose appetite had been almost as poor as his Wizard's as of late, said from his high-seated chair "More sausage for me as well, Horrocks, if you please."

The butler bowed. "Very good, sir."

When breakfast was done, at last Richard said, "What I want to show you, Felix, is in the Long Gallery."

This apartment, which took up the entire right end of the old house, was full of family portraits dating back to before the time of Queen Elizabeth. These were so numerous that they had to be displayed in three descending rows upon the walls. Even on the dullest days the Long Gallery was well lit, for its outer wall was composed of a multitude of large windows.

It was a bright, still chill day, even though in the walled gardens crocus were beginning to poke up from the earth and Bob Oakes swore he had heard a thrush. But spring, true spring was still in the future.

Richard led Felix and the two familiars to a familiar portrait at the far end of the gallery. The portraits were arranged by time and the far end held the more recent portraits.

This picture had been pained nearly fifty years earlier by Sir Joshua Reynolds, a Devon man himself. It showed a young Richard, a little younger than Felix was now, and his first wife, Olwen, who had died in childbed only six years after they were wed. They wore the formal silks and satins of the middle of the previous century. Richard, his dark hair tied back,was in full-skirted coat and knee breeches, and Olwen wasin blue silk, her domed, panniered skirt adorned with ribbons and artificial flowers. She was very beautiful, with un-powdered dark, thick hair and dark brown eyes. They had been portrayed by Sir Joshua as if they were in the garden, Olwen sitting upon a rustic seat while Richard stood beside her. She was slight and small, with a tiny waist and an air of fragility. Two cats sat at their feet, one recognizable as Greymalkin. The other was a demure marmalade tabby.

"I see a lot of her in you," said Richard softly to Felix. "I wish that you might have known her."

"I just re-read her Garden Book," Felix offered. "I remembered it just after Christmas and wanted to reacquaint myself with it. I wish I had known her, for the book is not only charming and replete with garden lore, but full of humor and shrewd observations as well."

"She was a lovely woman," said Greymalkin sadly. He had loved her familiar, Arianrhod, very much. But when her Witch died, the lovely cat had just faded away until she too, was dead.

"What I am now going to show you, my boy, is something that only Grey and I know, and I thought never to tell anyone, for such was Olwen's request. But I think that she would want you to know now, considering the circumstances."

In front of one of the fireplaces, now burning fragrant apple wood, was a low Pembroke table and two chairs drawn up near.

A portfolio, such as young ladies used for sketching, lay on the shining surface. It was of considerable age, for the leather edges were cracked and the blue ribbon that kept it tightly closed was faded and frayed.

Inviting Felix to sit down opposite him, Richard picked up the portfolio and untied the ribbon.

Pyewacket was as curious as his Wizard and jumped into Felix's lap so that he might see what lay within the portfolio. Greymalkin had seen the contents far too many times to have any curiosity about it left.

"I have always kept this private and hidden, said Richard. "I promised Olwen I would do so when it was made."

As he spoke he took a sheet of thick paper used for water-colour painting out of the portfolio and handed it to Felix.

"It looks like Rosal!" said Felix when he studied the portrait in his hands.

Indeed, it looked much like Rosal: the same tangle of black hair, the dark eyes, the short bright skirt exposing bare legs and feet and white blouse, the narrow waist girded by a dark cinch. But there was a difference. This young woman looked supremely happy and confident. Whomever had painted the picture had caught her on the verge of laughing for one could see it in the curve of her red lips, in the glance of the dark eyes.

"That was your grandmother when first I met her," said Richard as Felix stared at him in amazement.

"My grandmother was a Gypsy!" he said, astonished. Pyewacket gasped.

"Half a Gypsy," corrected Richard. "Her father was a Welsh shepherd and a very fine Wizard. It was said there was a family connection to Merlin. Indeed, the family name was Emrys, as was his."

"I went on a walking tour of Wales during the Long Vacation from Oxford in my first year there,' " he continued, in a reminiscent tone. "I was high in the Black Mountains, lost, when I chanced upon her. She was washing their clothing in a mountain stream and at the very first sight of her I knew I loved her." He sighed and took the picture from Felix and gazed down upon it.

"It took me a long time to persuade her to marry me. She offered to be my mistress, but I wanted her as my wife, to have beside me always, not hidden away in some tawdry back street." Richard said, looking at the portrait with sadness. How long ago it had been!

"Why would she not consent?" Felix inquired.

"She was certain that she would not fit into my life, that I might become ashamed of her because she was a Gypsy and moreover, like your Rosal, illiterate and ignorant of the ways of the *ton*."

"Illiterate?" echoed Felix. "But she was a Witch, and her the Garden Book —"

"To please me, she learned her letters and her Witchcraft was what we used to call 'natural' magic, taught by word of

620

mouth, mother to daughter. Before she would marry me she arranged to stay with the local minister and his wife, there in Wales, who were gently born and from them she learned all she need to know to conform to what society would expect of the bride of the heir to an Earldom. She did that for me, out of love. And out of love I agreed to a deception. She was afraid of what people would say of me if they found out I had married a Gypsy. So we let everyone think that she was the niece of the Minister Glendyr and his wife, well born, genteel, Welsh folk. She knew all too well what most people thought of Gypsies and she did not want me to be ashamed of her. As if I ever could be so! We did not even tell my parents and they came to love her sincerely. She had a fine mind, my Olwen, and learned quickly. In a year one could not tell that she had not grown up in a house such as this. It is for her sake that I allow the Gypsies to camp upon Belmaray land, when most of the others in this county drive them away and regard them with fear and loathing."

Richard sighed again, and put the portrait that he had been studying down and looked straight at Felix. "I am telling you all of this because if you do love and still want your Rosal, if you have forgiven her, if you truly love and want to please one another you can work together to overcome the differences in circumstances. It may not be easy –"

"Do you know what this means, Felix?" interrupted Pyewacket excitedly. "You're part Gypsy as well!"

Felix looked startled. "So I am!" he said in surprise.

"About an eighth part, I should think," said Greymalkin.

"I want to try again," said Felix suddenly. "I have to at least try. I do still love her. I know now that it was not something I myself, or she, talked me into. I am going to," he said determinedly, "write a letter to Grizel Dieudonné and ask that she read an enclosure to Rosal and ask Rosal to come here, since Sir Jermyn will not let me travel as yet."

"Wait until Sir Jermyn declares you completely cured," said Greymalkin. "You want to be at your best when she comes, not invalidish still. And then perhaps we could go and fetch her with Pascoe!"

"I have a better idea," said Richard. "Aurelius Bretton has found a publisher. He told me so in a postscript to the letter I had yesterday and he will be going up to Town at the end of next month to see about having his book printed. I shall suggest to him that he escort Rosal to us."

"And that will give you time to have fully recovered!" said Pyewacket to his Wizard.

Felix had to agree.As much as he wanted to see Rosal, to take her in his arms, even the emotions of this morning had given him the headache once more, although not as bad as it had been. He wanted to be fit when she came and in order to do so he would strictly obey every command of Sir Jermyn's, including swallowing an entire casket of noxious potions.

69
Spring

Wednesday, 25th of April, 1804

Spring had come fully to Devon. New grass, brilliant green, covered the lawns, growing so quickly that the gardeners could scare keep it scythed. Every tree had burst into leaf and those that blossomed were heavily laden with bloom. Flowers were everywhere in great profusion and the air was sweet and warm.

Felix stood in the open window of his room and inhaled deeply. The air smelled of new growth, freshly turned earth with a tinge of salt air. it was a beautiful day. The sky overhead was the pale blue of spring, with only a few puffy white fair weather clouds floating overhead. In through the window came a chorus of bird song. Felix's room, at the back of the house, looked towards the sea and the water there was bright blue as well. He could see the *Star of the Sea,* from this height, riding at anchor near the dock.

Would Rosal like sailing? Would she like his home? And most importantly, would she feel comfortable here and with him?

"It's nearly ten, my lord," Wallace's voice interrupted his thoughts.

Felix turned and saw Wallace holding up a new dark green jacket. Felix was completely dressed save for his jacket and had nervously discarded cravat after cravat as he had dressed. She was arriving today and he wanted to look his best. Sir Jermyn had been able to banish the white streak in his hair and a fortnight ago he had gone up to Town with Richard and had visited their tailor and a barber. Since they were at home in the country, where Town dress would have appeared ridiculous, Felix chose more casual riding dress with top boots and breeches, but they still fit superbly.

And he now looked, and, more importantly, felt, fit and healthy. The headaches had been banished entirely and there had been no more potions since late February. His appetite had come back and the healthy exercise of riding, walking and working on his yacht had brought back all of his old energy and physical condition.

It had also been extremely gratifying to be able to fully participate in magical rituals again, to known the spells and have magic at his call, to feel the energies of the four elements and the ley lines once more, to be able to look about him and remember people, places, events, all of his past. It was a blessing worth every bit of pain of the past winter.

Wallace helped him shrug in to the coat and Pyewacket said approvingly, "There! You look exceedingly fine. She will be swept away!"

"It's been nearly a year since I saw her, Pye," Felix said nervously, and eased a finger inside a cravat that suddenly seemed too tight. "It was the beginning of June when I returned here and we have not directly communicated since then."

As time went on, it had become awkward, having to send messages to Rosal through the Dieudonnés or Aurelius. Felix had been very unhappy with his letters to her, once he had come to realize that he wanted to try to resume their marriage. The letters he penned seemed very stiff and formal but he was always conscious that someone had to read them to her and he felt constrained about writing what he really felt. And her replies, of course, had to be written by others and consequently, they were short and stiff as well.

"It shouldn't be long now, my lord," said Wallace soothingly. All the servants were aware of what was happening today and had made a special effort. Cook was making a marvelous meal, the house shone with cleaning and bowls of spring flowers were everywhere. An adjoining room, with dressing room and a new water-closet and bath, had been made ready for Rosal, but if Felix had his way she would be sleeping all of the time in his bed, not her own.

Aurelius, who had indeed escorted Rosal, had scryed from London the day before, saying that they would be traveling by post chaise, in easy stages, and arriving sometime before noon today.

Felix had wanted to meet the ferry that had landed them in Weymouth when they first came from Guernsey, but Aurelius had written that Rosal wanted to go to London and purchase some new clothing before coming to Devon. Felix had been disappointed, but he understood that she wanted to look her best, for he felt the same way. New, becoming clothing gave one confidence. She would be nervous enough about coming to a place like Belmaray, which was completely outside her experience, never mind arriving there in *Madame* Brehaut's cast-offs or her Romany dress.

All the same, the waiting was onerous, and Felix decided to go to the dragon pen and ask Pascoe to go up and see if the post chaise was in sight. How he wished that Aurelius had hired a dragon transport and they had flown! It would have been so much faster! But neither Aurelius or Rosal was used to dragon flight and he supposed they were nervous or perhaps had never even thought of hiring a dragon. And like as not, Rosal had no flying suit, which for a female consisted of a split skirt and boots.

With a thank you to Wallace he walked briskly out of the room, followed closely by Pyewacket.

The post chaise, called a Yellow Bounder, due to the fact that it had a yellow body, swept along a road that was neither too dusty or too muddy. Wizards kept English roads in good condition, smoothing out the ruts, sprinkling the dust down and drying the mud with magic.

Inside, Aurelius sat opposite Rosal with his back to the horses. With Rosal sat Joisaine Brehaut, who had come as a chaperone for Rosal and because the Gypsy was nervous and needed the support of another woman. Grizel had wanted to come, but since she had just discovered herself to be *enceinte*, David would not hear of her traveling so early in the pregnancy.

Beside Aurelius sat a well-behaved Chavé, who had spent a good part of the journey hanging his head out the window whenever the passengers had lowered the glass.

Aurelius could not suppress a sigh as he looked at Rosal.

625

He was going to miss her. He had become exceedingly fond of her once she had become his pupil. She was eager to learn and worked harder than any student Aurelius had ever taught.

Somehow, his newly rebuilt cottage no longer pleased him as well as it had. The more spacious rooms, the large library, the Faerie planted garden... as wonderful as it all was, he would be alone there. He could hire servants to replace John but it would not be as he had imagined when he had thought to take Felix and Rosal into his household. He supposed he was a selfish old crock, wanting their company, never mind what was best for them. He almost dreaded going back to Guernsey, with only occasional visitors, both human and Faerie, to look forward to.

Rosal was going to surprise Felix in more ways than one. She looked a proper young lady in modish, well-made clothing in bang-up to the minute style, rather daring as to colour, but one suiting Rosal's dark colouring. She wore a carriage dress of white, banded with poppy coloured braid, and worn with a poppy-coloured short Spencer jacket. Her white straw poke bonnet was adorned with poppies. Beneath this bonnet her hair had been fashionably trimmed and, as was proper, she wore a married woman's cap, a trifle of gauze and lace.

And then there were other 'surprises' she had to reveal to a hopefully pleased husband, among them her new ability to read and write.

Joisaine was excited. She had never been away from Guernsey before and she was interested in everything. She carried a large basket in her lap. It belonged to Rosal but Joisaine had begged to hold it during the journey down from London. It had very special contents.

Rosal, Aurelius noticed, was nervous. Over and over again, she twisted her wedding ring around her finger, blind to the beauty of the passing scenery which Joisaine was enjoying so much.

"I am quite certain that everything will turn out just as you hope, my dear," said Aurelius kindly to Rosal, as once more she turned the ring on her finger and bit her lip.

Rosal looked up at him. She had become fond of him too. Never in her earlier life had she imagined she would become so close to so many *Gajé*, and even try to become one of them, much less fall in love with a *Gajo* and marry him. And to her amazement she had been accepted everywhere as a *Gajo,* in London, at the grand hotel where they had stayed, at the Mantua-maker's and the milliner's shop where she purchased her new clothing, and last night at the inn. No one had found her out, that she was only a Romany in masquerade.

"I hope you are right," she said. Her voice was more cultured. She had a good ear and had set herself to sounding like the Professor and Grizel as much as was possible. Reading was also teaching her more cultivated habits of speech. Reading had also become one of her chief joys. She now understood Felix's passion for books.

"I am certain that I am right," he said, even though he was depressed at the thought of losing her as well. He leaned forward and said earnestly "Don't be intimidated, my dear, either by the size of the house or the servants or the company. We've looked at pictures of the house, you've studied a little of its history and Mistress Grizel and the Dowager Lady Dieudonné have taught you how to go on both in company and with the servants. Just remember what you have been taught. You have been an apt pupil on all fronts. And you will keep learning all of your life."

"I just want him to be proud of me," she said. "I don't want him to ever be ashamed of having married me and making me a lady."

"He's a fool if he thinks that way!" said Joisaine, taking her attention from the basket in her lap. She had alternated between looking out the window and looking in the basket. "He's gaining so much by taking you to wife!" she added, with a grin. She too, wore new clothes, a gift from Rosal, who had spent very little of the generous allowance Felix had paid her every month without fail and therefore, had a good amount to spend in the London shops.

A large shadow passed overhead. Joisaine peered out the window and said "That was a dragon!"

"More than likely Pascoe," said Aurelius, sitting back. "They're waiting for us, no doubt! It shouldn't be long now!"

Rosal's stomach was tied in knots. She had been unable to eat much breakfast. Everyone said she should not feel so nervous, for he had written to say he wanted her back, that they should make a new beginning, that he still loved her.

But she still worried.

The post chaise began to slow. "We are more than likely approaching the house" said Aurelius. He took out a large pocket watch and consulted it. "We have made excellent time. It is just after ten."

Rosal's stomach did a complete flip. She looked down at herself . Would Felix like the way she looked? The *modiste* in London had assured her that the carriage dress as not only *à la mode*, but suited her wonderfully well. Both Aurelius and Joisaine had been loud in their praise. But what matted the most was Felix's opinion. She wanted to see both admiration and approval on his face.

In spite of having studied pictures of the ancient manor of Belmaray Rosal was still awed when the post chaise swept up the graveled carriage way and she saw the noble pile rising in front of her.

Only a bit of the original Norman building remained at the far end, on the opposite end from the gallery. Much of the present house had been constructed in the early 18th century by Richard's grandfather who had been a notable collector of art. The house had been expanded and built to show off the statuary and paintings he had acquired and had been done, including the façade, in Palladian style.

Towers stood at each end. Aurelius had explained to her that these were Wizard's Towers. He had a book with engravings of most of the great houses of England and he had shown her the pictures of Belmaray, so she was familiar with what the house looked like. But a picture could not prepare her for the sheer size of it. It rose three stories, made of the local granite, with a multitude of windows gleaming in the sun. A small stretch of water, bordered by gardens of knot work, stood before the house, reflecting its grandeur. A small dome rose slightly above the columned front and Rosal saw to her dismay, that the sweeping crab-pincer steps that led down from an imposing first floor portico, were crowded with servants. Lady Dieudonné had warned her that they would wish to greet her and would be very curious to see her.

The large ornate door at the top of the stairs opened and Felix, followed by his familiar and his Grandfather and another cat hurried out. Before the post boy could dismount Felix was at the door of the carriage, pulling down the step and opening the door.

"Ladies first, my dear," said Aurelius to Rosal.

"Go ahead," said Joisaine, indicating the basket. "I can take care of this."

But Chavé upset all their plans. With a loud "Woof!" he launched himself from the carriage and ran to Felix, jumping up on him eagerly, glad to see him.

And so it was that their eyes met over the excited dog and she saw all of the look on his face that she had hoped to see. He was happy to see her indeed. A few moments later when Chavé had been placated, she was in his arms, and irregardless of the interested audience, he kissed her.

Aurelius descended from the carriage and turned to help Joisaine out. Richard came forward and offered his hand to the Professor. "I'm glad to see you here at last!" he said.

Joisaine descended slowly and carefully from the carriage. Aurelius turned to help her out, but she bumped the basket against the door and it gave a short cry of protest.

"Oh, let me!" said Rosal, darting forward.

"Another pet. Rosal?" said Felix, teasingly. She could not resist taking animals that no one else wanted. This sounded like a kitten. Belmaray was a large house. There was plenty of room for any amount of Rosal's strays.

Rosal took the basket from Joisaine and carried it over to him. "Not a pet, no," she said and with her free hand swept back the covering blanket. "Your daughter!"

Felix, stunned, could not say anything at all for a moment. There, nestled in amongst fluffy blankets was a tiny child, with dusky curls and as he looked, she yawned and opened her eyes and looked straight at him.

"She was born on the 8th of March," said Rosal a bit nervously. "I named her Emma Marie, but if you don't like it –"

"No, it is a beautiful name," he said, never taking his eyes off the baby. "She's so tiny! Is she healthy?"

Rosal laughed. He did not seem displeased, but reached out to the child and touched her soft curls

. "She's very healthy, the doctor said. He said he'd never seen a more perfect baby!"

Felix looked up at her. "Rosal, why didn't you let me know? I would have come –"

She shook her head. "I wanted you to take me back because you loved and wanted me, not because I was to have your child."

He understood at once. Had he not felt the same way about not being able to be with her until his memory had been restored?

"May I hold her?" he asked.

Rosal nodded and showed him how to hold the child properly. "She's a very good baby," she said proudly.

He was enchanted with her, and proudly showed her off to Richard, the familiars and Pascoe. The servants crowded around as well. Mrs. Grumidge, the housekeeper worried over whom she might appoint as a nursery maid. The house had been cleaned from top to bottom, so the nurseries were clean and ready but a fire would need to be laid and linens put on the crib, but staff was needed.

"You look as if you could use a bit of refreshment," said Richard quietly to Aurelius.

"Yes," said Aurelius thankfully. "I am not used to traveling with a very small child. She was reasonably well-behaved but at that age, there does to be a certain amount of crying. I cannot ascertain how Rosal and Miss Brehaut seemed to know just what the child wanted without her being able to tell them!"

Richard and Greymalkin led the way up the stairs and through the house to the enormous library. A tray had been set out on a low table between two leather-covered chairs.

Aurelius looked about him in awe. Only the library at Cambridge approached the size of this cavernous room. Gold-topped Corinthian columns held up a balcony to enable access to the second level of books, under a barrel vaulted ceiling painted with medallions of classical mythology. There were large windows looking out towards the sea, and even between the windows rose tiers of books.

There were three Adam fireplaces, with Wedgwood friezes depicting the Three Muses. Over the principle fireplace had been inscribed a Francis Bacon quote, "*nam ipsa scientua potestas est*" translated as 'knowledge itself is power', a sentiment with which Aurelius heartily agreed.

He sat down with Richard, accepting a glass of port. "It would take a lifetime to explore such a library," he said appreciatively as Greymalkin jumped up on the arm of Richard's chair.

"That is what I wanted to talk to you about," said Richard. He had noticed the sadness on his friend's face when he looked at Rosal and Felix and in his letters there had been an undertone of the loneliness he would feel when both of them were gone to Devon, only to return perhaps, for fleeting visits. Not that he had complained. Aurelius would never do that.

Aurelius looked at Richard, puzzled as to his meaning.

"My librarian has informed me that he wishes to retire," said Richard slowly, swirling the ruby port about in his glass. "I am well aware that you have just finished building your house once more and are busy with your book, but I wondered if you might possibly consider coming to us as our librarian."

"Good heavens!" Aurelius said in surprise.

"The position is not a sinecure," Richard cautioned. "We often welcome scholars to use the library here as we have many rare volumes. And the library is constantly expanding. Indeed, I have hired an architect to consult on adding a new extension as this area is at about capacity. We would appreciate your ideas on that as well. "

"And there would still be enough time," put in Greymalkin "to continue your writing and research as well. We have access to Faerie here."

"There is a nice suite of rooms available to the librarian, as well, and enough room for all of your books," Richard continued. "Other than being paid a salary, in all other ways you would be a member of the family, taking your meals with us, or not as you chose."

"I don't know what to say!" Aurelius stammered. To be here, in charge of this handsome library, and what was more to have the company of those he had come to care for!

"Say yes!" said Greymalkin. "Pascoe might easily bring all your traps from Guernsey in one flight, even as many books as you have, or we may bring them through Faerie. Just say yes, Professor," he urged.

Aurelius did not have to give it much thought. Instead of lonely evenings he would have congenial company, other scholars to converse with and work he would enjoy. "Yes, he said. "I accept with pleasure."

631

Richard and Greymalkin both looked immensely pleased. "Felix will be very happy to hear this," said Richard. "We had both hoped."

"But," Aurelius, feeling suddenly light-hearted, said "it is only too bad that you are not Cambridge men! My reputation might not survive, working for those who had the dubious taste to attend Oxford!"

They all laughed and settled back to discuss the details.

Joisaine had taken little Emma and gone off to inspect the nursery with the housekeeper. One of the housemaids had been appointed nursery maid and Felix's old nurse, living unhappily in retirement, had been sent for and would more than likely arrive on the morrow, eager to nurture a new generation of Jourdaines.

After introduction to the servants, in which she acquitted herself very well indeed, Felix took Rosal off to the side of the house, where a carefully tended Wilderness surrounded a small belvedere on a bit of lawn. A path from the Wilderness ran down the hill and ended at the dock where the *Star of the Sea* lay.

There were rustic seats in the belvedere and Felix carefully put Rosal in one and said softly, bending towards her. "You look beautiful, Rosal!" He bent and kissed her gently.

Chavé barked, his tail wagging.

"Don't interrupt them!" Pyewacket said to him in Animal Speech.

Chavé looked sideways at him. "I usually chase cats," he returned "but I'm a guest here."

"You're going to be living here now," Pyewacket retorted "and there will be no chasing of cats! I am a familiar, after all. Pascoe would never allow you to chase me, at any rate."

"Pascoe?" queried Chavé, putting his head to one side.

"The dragon," answered Pyewacket.

The coally looked taken aback. "A dragon!" he echoed. He would have to behave himself, that was for certain. He lay down, with a sideways look at the cat.

But Rosal was happy now. That was what mattered. He had been unable to comfort her during the long winter when she cried often. This seemed like a good place. Already he caught the scent of rabbits. And he had little Emma to guard now as well. He was also happy to see Felix once more and know that they would all be together again. Now if Kälo could just be here.

"That is a very attractive bonnet," said Felix, sitting beside Rosal and putting his arm behind her shoulders on the back of the wicker sopha, "but it makes it difficult to kiss you properly and see your face."

She took it off, laying it carefully on the roomy seat beside her. Her hair had been cut short in front and curled naturally about her face. She had been unable to bear its being cut fashionably short all over, *á la* Titus, and so had kept it long in back where it was wound up in a Grecian knot under a filmy little cap.

"I've another surprise for you," she said a little hesitantly.

"As nice a surprise as Emma?" he said.

"I hope that you will think so," she said and said "I've learned to read and write. The Professor taught me. And Grizel Dieudonné and her Mama-in-law have taught me how to behave like a lady. I did it so you will be proud of me."

Felix remembered what his grandfather had said of Olwen: that she had educated herself for love of him. And here was Rosal offering the same gift. "I am proud of you, Rosal, very proud indeed. It must have been a difficult time for you, studying so hard and carrying a child," he said

"It made me happier, because I was so unhappy at being parted from you. I tried to write to you once I knew how but I ended in being too uncertain of what to say."

She turned in the circle of his arm and faced him. "I really do love you," she said earnestly. "I didn't realize just how much until I thought I never would see you again. I was always afraid that you were going to send word that you wanted to be rid of me. And I'm sorrier than I could ever say that I lied to you!" she added passionately, tears suddenly standing in her eyes.

"It doesn't matter any more. I love you and don't want to live without you any more," he said quietly. "We're together now and we're going to make a brand new start, you and I and Emma."

There would be time enough a little later to tell her that the lawyers had decided it best if they quietly remarried.

"And never tell lies ever again," she said, her hand creeping up to his lapel.

It was an invitation to a long, deep and satisfying kiss.

Chavé barked in approval and Pyewacket said in satisfaction. "All's well that ends well!"

Epilogue
10 Years Later

The Island of Guernsey, June, 1814

Each summer had seen Felix and Rosal and their growing family spend some time on Guernsey. They built a house for their summer holidays in a part of the woods that they had purchased from *Madame* Brehaut. And part of the summer holiday was spent, just the two of them, in the *vardo* they still owned, carefree, in Romany dress, in their own private world, while the children stayed with their great grandfather and "Uncle" Aurelius in his cottage of *Trois Chiminées.*

This year was an especially happy occasion. It had been an exciting late winter and spring. In January British forces had reached Toulouse from the Iberian Peninsula, having routed Marshal Soult. On March 10th, Napoleon Bonaparte had been defeated at the battle of Laon. On March 30th, the forces of the Sixth Coalition, consisting of the Six Nations, Austria, Prussia, Russia Sweden, and a confederation of German States had marched into Paris. Napoleon had abdicated on April 6th. May 30th saw the signing of the Treaty of Paris, ending the long war.

And the men of Guernsey and the other Channel Islands had begun to come home.

A grand celebration had been planned for the returning men, although far too many of them would never return, lost on some European battle field or vanished in the snows of Russia in Bonaparte's ill-fated invasion.

Almost as soon as the abdication the men had come trickling back to the Islands. The Army of the Occupation, under Lord Wellington, had made it an especial duty to locate the men of the Channel Islands.

David, no longer Bailiff, a position he had gladly surrendered with the return of the remaining men who had governed the Bailiwick, had been appointed a special agent for Repatriation of Missing *Guernaise* and had made a trip to Paris earlier in the year to help with finding and identifying the homecoming (or deceased) men. His office assisted them in locating family and friends, many of who were still scattered, not wishing to leave the safety of the Six Nations until the war was finally done. The office had expanded into finding homes and jobs for these men as well, as necessary. They also found family members to notify them of the death of their men who had been killed. Grizel headed up a Ladies' Committee that was raising money for grave markers and a monument to those lost during their forced conscription.

Both of them were glad to see their friends from Devon. As happy as the ending of the war had been, they were now dealing with the grief over those who had never returned and it was a relief to talk to people who were not grieving.

"It's been difficult," said Grizel as they sat on the little beach at Gull Rocks, picnicking beneath a brilliant June sky. "So many people hoped for so long that their son or husband or brother would return. I try to go with David, whenever I can, when he has to break bad news to someone, particularly another woman. Two of *Madame* Brehaut's sons did not come back. As far as David could find out Gilles died in Russia on the retreat from Moscow and Gautier was killed at Jena, early in the war. But her husband and Evrard came back, whole of limb."

"There were far too many deaths, deaths that should have never happned were it not for the French Occupation. And there is the problem as well, of those who are returning maimed," David put in. Like the rest of them, he was casually dressed in old clothes and bare feet. Many of the lines of pain he had worn in the past were gone, for he had put himself into Galen's hands and was almost cured of the lameness caused by the leg wounds. He and Grizel swam daily as well.

"Grandfather spoke in the House of Lords about the plight of the returning soldiers and sailors," said Felix and added a little bitterly, "Some of the peers thought it very amusing. Now that they have no more need of the men who defeated Napoleon, they seem to be uncaring of their fate."

"But we're doing what we are able to do," said Rosal proudly. "No soldier or sailor is ever turned away without a good meal and a sack of coins, just as no Romany is ever refused a campsite at Belmaray." She had seen the signs in the woods, left by the Romany, so many times, indicating that Belmaray was a good place.

Further down on the shore played the six children that belonged to the two couples. Emma was the eldest. She now had a brother, Cedric and a young sister, Casilda, which had been the name of Rosal's mother. The Dieudonné children consisted of André, middle child Fleurette and the youngest, a boy called Étienne. They knew each other well, as they had visited back and forth for years.The Dieudonnés had been as many times to Devon as the Jourdaines had been to Guernsey. The friendship had grown and deepened over the years.

Majorlaine watched over the children, while she in turn was watched by Pascoe. Any child straying too far away was apt to be gathered in with a tender talon. Near the edge of the water Richard and Aurelius walked, talking animatedly, occasionally bending over to look at the rock-strewn beach. Last summer they had found some Celtic artifacts on this beach and missed no opportunity to look for others.

A companionable silence fell as they continued to sit near the remains of a bountiful picnic meal. Tonight there was to be a gala ball at Government House. Once such an event would have held naught but terror for Rosal. Now she looked forward to it. Even though she still sometimes wondered at how such a thing had happened to her, she was now secure in her role as Felix's Viscountess.

"So Emma is to be a Witch?" Grizel asked. In addition to Pyewacket , Greymalkin and Chavé on the beach, there was a new familiar: Tibby, a gray and white striped kitten, who had chosen Emma as her Witch during the winter. She was a descendant of Greymalkin's and Jenny's. "Are any of the others magical?"

"It's too early to tell, Grandfather says. They need to be at least eight years old. Cedric is only seven and Cassie is five," answered Rosal. "Emma is ten and we could tell once she was eight that she was going to be magical. Her school

637

teaches magic as well as everything else she needs to know."

"Do you think any of yours will be Selchies?" asked Felix.

David laughed. "If André is not a Selchie I will be surprised! He is the best swimmer I have ever seen who is *not* a Selchie. He could swim rings around me when he was only three! And he is absolutely fearless in the water."

"But he will not be a true Selchie until he attains puberty. That is when a part-Selchie shows the first signs: the webbing between the fingers and toes, breathing underwater and then shape-shifting," said Grizel. "We are not yet certain about Fleurette and Étienne. She swims well but he seems a little nervous of the water. But he is only four and he may grow out of that. We spend a lot of time in the water and he has grown used to seeing me change. We see a fair amount of Elspeth and Hamish, too. They've only the one pup, Angus, who is best friends with André." In spite of her joy in mating, Elspeth had only quickened once and she envied Grizel with her three healthy children and another on the way. Grizel was certain, for this had been confirmed by Galen, that it was her half-human status that made her so fertile. Elspeth was completely a Selchie.

"Felix, does the Professor ever hear anything of his old servant, John?" David inquired. " He was used to go and visit him in Hospital, did he not?"

"Yes," Felix replied on a sigh. "He was a faithful visitor. In spite of the Wizard Healers John never recovered his mind. But he had the best of care and we heard just before we came here that he had quietly died. Aurelius paid for him to be buried in his native village in Essex, where his family was interred and caused a handsome stone to be erected." Felix still felt at least partially responsible for John's mental aberration and could not be swayed otherwise.

"Papa, Papa!" shouted Cedric, running up as fast as his legs could carry him. He looked a great deal as his grandfather Richard had looked at his age with dark brown hair and very blue eyes. "Come and play cricket with us. You too, Uncle David! André has a cricket bat and a ball."

"André's second great love, next to the water is cricket!" said David with a groan. "I play more cricket!" But he rose, easily now, and went with Felix and Cedric to a place down on the beach where André was eagerly clearing a pitch.

The two women began to clear the dishes away into the enormous basket it had been packed in. "Everything tastes so good out of doors," said Rosal.

"That's easy to see for there's next to nothing left here!" said Grizel. "And if I know my brood they'll be wanting more food after running about on the beach all afternoon! Speaking of food, *Belle-mère* and I are going to be baking for Joisaine's wedding tomorrow if you'd care to join us."

Joisaine Brehaut was to marry a young man, Lucien Chantarelle, who had been taken quite young to serve as a drummer boy in the French army, and had miraculously come back whole about a year ago. He had escaped from the army and had returned to Guernsey on a French smuggler.

Rosal consented and the talk fell to Joisaine's wedding and the preparations for it.

Rosal was dimly aware of other people walking down the path that led the beach, the very same path on which she had discovered Felix, nearly eleven years ago now. It was a public beach and boat landing so she did even glance up as she heard the footsteps.

She was therefore surprised when she heard a voice say in surprise."Rosal? Rosal Lovel?"

She looked up from the basket as did Grizel. There was a fashionably clad lady on the arm of an older gentleman, staring in amazement at her. Rosal had no idea who she was at first and then she said, as recognition dawned "Hagar? Hagar!" She leaped to her feet and ran forward to throw her arms about the woman. "Hagar! I thought you were dead!"

Hagar laughed shakily "And I was certain that you were in gaol!"

"He still loved me, Hagar! I am Rosal Jourdaine now," said Rosal eagerly. "And now we live in Devon and have three children. We are visiting our good friends this summer. You remember Grizel .She is now Lady Dieudonné and three of those children you see playing at cricket with our husbands are hers."

"And this is *my* husband," announced Hagar proudly "Henry Utley." She pulled off a lace mitt an showed Rosal her wedding band, flanked by a large diamond.

"But isn't he –?" Rosal began in confusion.

Henry Utley smiled ruefully. He was a little heavy-set,

with blonde thinning hair, but still a good- looking man. " –
the damn fool who left her behind?" he finished. "That was
the stupidest thing I have ever done in my life. I was far and
away too concerned with what others would say and I paid
dearly for it. No sooner than I reached England did I begin
regretting it. And then five years ago, I chanced to go to a
horse fair and found her *dukkering* there. I apologized and
admitted what a fool I had been and this wonderful woman
forgave me. I lost no time in making it permanent this time. I
shall never let her go again!" He put his hand on Hagar's
hand that still lay on his arm.

"And Charles, our son Charles, has come to love me as
well, Rosal! I have a granddaughter now!" said Hagar
happily.

"I am so glad for you!" said Rosal sincerely. "But, Hagar
how did you get off the island?'

Grizel invited them to sit and found a half bottle of wine
in the basket. "Let's drink to old friends," she suggested and
stood up, to wave to Felix and David to join them.

 Hagar told her story of a fisherman who had been
willing, for practically all the money she had, to chance the
French blockade and take her to the Isle of Wight. Listening,
Rosal was filled with happiness as she watched Felix,
followed by a barking Chavé and the children, walked up the
beach towards them.

Eleven years ago she had only wanted a baby, convinced
that only that one thing would make her happy.

Now she had so much more than that, husband, children,
relatives and friends and a home.

She at last had her own *cumpania,* far better than any
she ever could have imagined.

The End

From the pen of

G.M.S. Altman
(continued)

Dippel's Oil

John Calvin Ramsey was a genius, a computer technician extraordinaire who tolerated his mundane public life only because he held loftier aspirations. One day he planned to be the most powerful man on earth, someone with all the money anyone could ever want and the long life to in which to enjoy it. For that reason, John Calvin was on a quest: to find one very special man who he knew held an ancient and monumental secret.

He longed to find this man and spent countless hours pouring over arcane documents, internet sites and tracing history from the 17th century to the present.

He was ready to pledge himself as his most obedient, diligent, loyal, and grateful student.

And then John Calvin was going to kill him.

ISBN: 978-1-888071-17-7 Trade Paperback $14.95 336 pages (also on Kindle)

HELENENTHAL

BOOKS

www.galtman.books.officelive.com

ISABELLA LEAGUE
Adult Fantasy Novels

The Jongleur

The year is 1811 in an England where Wizards and Witches practice their magic and dragons carry the Royal Mail.

It is up to a young English Witch and a French émigré Wizard to thwart the black magic of the Jongleur and his unholy allies of the Unselighe Court before they succeed in ridding Britain of white magic and magicians – and making the British Isles a conquered land.

ISBN: 978-1-888071-16-0 Trade Paperback $21.95 626 pages (also on Kindle)

Land of the Firebird

When Professor of Dracophilology Simon Stillfield is asked to go to far away Russia to help set up a dragon post like that in the British Isles, his first impulse is to refuse. To his knowledge, there are few dragons in Russia besides the feral Ice Dragons of Siberia. But when a disappointment in love makes him long for a change of scene, Simon, his dragon friend Lakota and familiar Janus embark on a strange adventure in a distant, largely unknown land.

When a young boy Simon has befriended is kidnapped by an Ice Dragon, Simon must attempt a rescue, and face Russian Witches, Rusalka, and an evil Necro-mancer who seems bent on killing him — for an unknown reason. It will take all of Simon's resources — magical and otherwise — to confront danger, death — and love.

ISBN: 978-1-888071-18-4 Trade Paperback $16.95 422 pages (also on Kindle)

Dragons' Pearls

The dragons of China, ancient and wise, were angry. Not only had the dragon temples fallen into disuse with no offerings or worship, but no dragon adviser sat by the

Emperor's side in the Forbidden City. And now something more terrible was happening – for both the dragons and for China itself: someone was killing dragons with magic, selling their flesh and bones for profit and stealing their pearls – the fount of all their wisdom and knowledge – even the power to fly – that they wore under their chins.

When one of the great Celestial Dragons came to the scholar of dragons, Dr. Quong Lee, for his help, the elderly man could only think of one person to help him battle this black wickedness – and the dragons – and his country. He needed not only a dragon expert, but a magician – for there were no White magicians left in China.

ISBN: 978-1-888071-19-1 Trade Paperback $16.95 324 pages (also on Kindle)

Murder Moon

When in the autumn of 1844 the blood red moon rose over the Six Nations of the British Isles, the magical population of Witches and Wizards were facing perilous times. For those magical persons of unstable character, or those who suffered from a long stress, were liable to commit mayhem, violence – and murder.

Stuart Delmar, a Forensic Wizard with the Bow Street Police in London, was abruptly ordered back to his former home in Dublin, Ireland. Armed with magic, and the help of his brilliant familiar, the cat Dr. Foster, Stuart begins his search for a clever and vicious murderer.

Time was running out – there were too many suspects, too many alibis and the woman he is coming to love is in danger of going to the gallows for a crime he was certain she had not committed.

ISBN: 978-1-888071-20-7 Trade Paperback $16.95 468 pages (also on Kindle)

Darkest Magic

India 1857

Young Witch Rosamunde DeLacey has married in haste and is repenting in leisure. Now she is on her way out to India with her familiar, the cat Sinéad, to join her soldier husband who is unfortunately non-magical. Escorting her is her cousin, the Wizard Alan Stillfield, his familiar a ferret named Cathal, and dragon, Brendan. Rosamunde has secretly loved Alan all of her life, and it was to escape seeing him married to another that she so hurriedly wed.

Little do they know that they travel to a land seething with rebellion and the worst of necromancy. The northern region of India, where Alan goes to visit a college chum, seems at first to be safer until a devastating illness robs Alan of nearly all of his magic.

Rosamunde, too, has waning powers. When the rebellion finally comes she is at the mercy of an evil slaver, who sells her to become the possession of the black sorceress, the Maharani of Jhaniput and her depraved son, the Maharajah, worshippers of the drinker of blood, Kali, the Black One.

Only Alan, with little magic at his command, can save his cousin. Her rescue will only come if an ancient prophecy is fulfilled, dragon fire can cleanse the land. Until then Alan must endure the pain of seeing his cousin enslaved by Darkest Magic.

ISBN: 1-888071-2-14

EAN-13 978-1888071-2-14 Trade Paperback $19.95 586 pages (also on Kindle)

HELENENTHAL

BOOKS

www.galtman.books.officelive.com

www.ingramcontent.com/pod-product-compliance
Lightning Source LLC
Chambersburg PA
CBHW020453020726
47493CB00001B/8